I0760349

# THE HERO'S EQUINOX

## TJ Young & The Orishas

ANTOINE BANDELE

*Edited By*
FIONA MCLAREN

*Edited By*
CALLAN BROWN

*Illustrated By*
ARTHUR BOWLING

BANDELE
BOOKS

Publisher: Bandele Books
Interior Design: Vellum
Editors: Fiona McLaren, Callan Brown
Illustrator: Arthur Bowling
Cover Design: Mibl Art
Ornamental Break Design: Bolaji Olaloye

ISBN: 978-1-951905-23-1 (Ebook edition)

ISBN: 978-1-951905-45-3 (Paperback edition)

ISBN: 978-1-951905-44-6 (Hardback edition)

First Edition | June 22, 2025

# CONTENTS

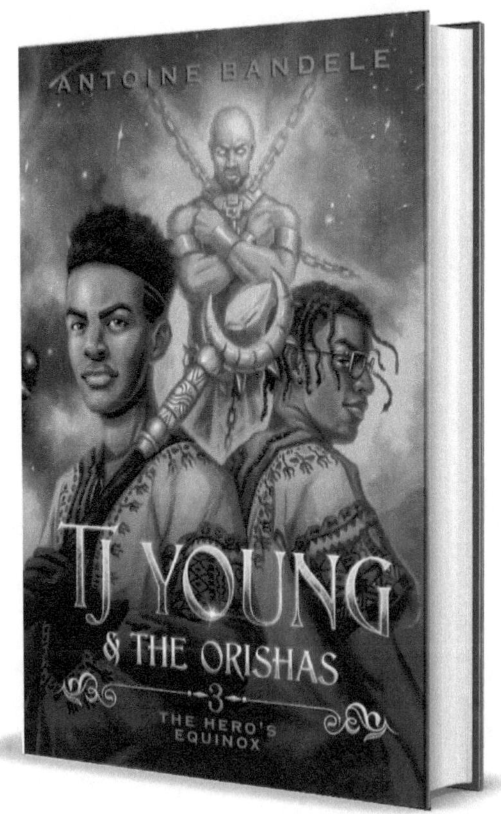


*The Hero's Equinox* is the third book in the *TJ Young & The Orishas* series, a collection of stories based around lore and mythology from West Africa and the African diaspora.

If you enjoy this story and are interested in the rest of TJ's adventures, you can join Antoine Bandele's e-mail alerts list. He'll send you notifications for new book releases, exclusive updates, and behind-the-page content.

Visit this link:
antoinebandele.com/stay-in-touch

And for the complete timeline and reading order visit:
https://www.antoinebandele.com/tj-young-timeline

**Read the free prequel short story to**
***The Hero's Equinox!***

*What happens when the God of Thunder dies?*
*You blame his Orisha comrade, of course.*

Thor of Asgard is dead. And Shango of the Orishas is to blame.

A cosmic war has been waged for countless ages between the deities of Earth and a strange force of shadows known as the God Eaters. Many of Earth's greatest heroes have fallen to this mysterious enemy, but Thor and Shango have stood firm where other champions have failed.
Until now.

Dragged from the warfront, Shango is held in chains by the Court of All, interrogated over how Thor died under an Orisha's watch.

Some deities claim foul play, others are charging Shango with negligence. But they all agree Shango's abilities can no longer be trusted.

Shango is determined to prove his innocence and clear his name. There is no other option. If he fails, he'll spend the rest of his days in the Dungeon of Deities… or worse.

*Delve into this prequel novella to* The Hero's Equinox, *a young adult fantasy based on the West African mythology of the Orishas.*

Visit this link to read the prequel story:
https://www.antoinebandele.com/book-page-an-axe-for-a-hammer

## PRONUNCIATION GUIDE

### Characters

A·de·o·la - ah'day'yo'lah
A·de·ye·mi - ah'day'yea'me
A·yo·de·ji - eye'o'day'gee
Bo·la·we - bow'la'way
Du Bois - do'bwa
E·me·ka - eh'meh'kah
E·ni·o·la - eh'knee'o'lah
I·fe·da·yo - ee'fey'die'yo
Man·uel·a - man'well'ah
Nin·ki Nan·ka - kneen'key nah'kah
Ti·ti·lay·o - tee'tee'lie'yo
To·mo·ri Jo·mi·lo·ju - toe'moe'ree joe'mee'low'jew
Gra·vés - gra'ves
U·mar - oo'mar

### Orishas

Ba·ba·lu A·ye - ba'ba'loo ah'yay
E·shu - eh'shoe
I·be·ji - e'bae'jee
O·ba·ta·la - o'ba'ta'la
O·du·du·wa - o'do'do'wah
O·gi·yan - o'gee'yan
O·gun - o'goon
O·ko - o'ko
O·lo·du·ma·re - o'low'do'ma'ray
O·lo·kun - o'low'koon
O·lo·sa - o'low'sah
O·ri - o'ree
O·run·mi·la - o'rune'mee'lah
O·sain - o'sane
O·sho·si - oh'show'she
O·shun - o'shoon
O·ya - oi'ya
Shan·go - shon'go
Ye·mo·ja - ye'mo'jah

Ye·wa - ye'wah

Terms

A·she - a'shay
A·so o·ke - ah'so o'kay
A·zi·za - ah'zee'zah
Ba·ba·la·wo - ba'ba'la'woah
Da·shi·ki - da'she'key
E·mi - e'mee
E·re I·da·ra·ya - eh'ray e'da'rie'yah
I·fa - ee'fah
Im·pun·du·lu - eem'poon'doo'loo
Ki·shi - key'she
Ma·mi Wa·ta - mah'mee wa'tah
Og·bon - og'bon
O·lo·shi - o'lo'she
Zo·bo - zo'bo

Locations

A·bu·ja - a'boo'jah
I·le-I·fe - e'lay e'fay
La·gos - la'gos
Man·da·wa·ca - man'de'wa'ca
O·yo - oi'yo

*This story is*
*a work of fantasy fiction*
*and not an accurate depiction of*
*the living practice of Ifa*
*and its many branches and followers*
*in the Motherland*
*and the diaspora.*

# 1

# ACT NOW, THINK LATER

BEING THE HERO SUCKED.

When TJ was young, water was a refuge, whether it had been cookouts with his family off sandy beaches or lively water park trips out under the sun. Now? TJ steered clear of water like it had personally wronged him.

In a way, it had.

After all, Olokun, the Orisha of the Deep, was the manifestation of the perilous element. Anytime TJ took a shower or even had a simple drink of water, his mind sprung violently to images of people drowning, screaming, calling his name for respite.

The grief healers said visiting large bodies of water would help his healing process, and that facing his fear would hasten his recovery from it. He lied when he told them he had spent loads of time around water. He just… couldn't face it right now.

Hadn't he faced enough? What did they know, anyway? Had they fought three deities before they were even sixteen? No. Didn't think so!

TJ sighed and threw a skipping rock he had been grasping harder and harder. It skimmed across Oshun's Lake within Ifa Academy in one, two, three arcs before splashing beneath the water's surface, sinking. Vanishing. Like all those skyscrapers did. TJ's heart pounded harder, its drum beat an urging to run away or scream. He swallowed the surge of fear boiling up and kicked at the dirt at his feet.

Okay, so it was true he had gone *near* the lake. He just didn't go all the way to the water, sticking to the safety of the whispering willows. But for some reason that day, the twinkling of the waters, through the curtained branches of the trees, seemed to call to him.

He took slow steps to the water. With each movement forward, a scream assaulted his ears. With each shuffle across the dirt, a creaking of metal shrieked in his mind. Images of his friend Ayo—still in a coma back in the Hospital Tree—flashed in his mind, and his best friend Manny, who he had burdened with his depression.

"C'mon, let's go to Mami Wata's," Manny would ask, and TJ would leave her in silence. "We don't gotta sit by the water."

"There's a *Major League Crossover* tournament in the village," she would say with that Brooklyn husk. "We should go. Take our mind off things."

TJ threw the memories aside. No, he couldn't do it. He couldn't take being at the lake anymore.

All because he played the hero.

But Dad's voice echoed in his ear, calm and steady, a stark contrast to the relentless expectations from Mom.

"Sometimes being brave means facing what scares you the most, son," Dad had said during one of their late-night talks. TJ could still see Dad's encouraging smile under his sharp goatee, the way he believed in TJ without piling on pressure.

Mom's words, however, were like weights, always reminding him of what he should achieve, the hero she expected him to be. All because of what Dayo did before him, what his whole family line had done before him. "We Abimbolas always succeed, Tomori Jomiloju. Keep pushing."

It was Dad's quiet support that nudged him forward now, a gentle push to confront his fears, not out of obligation, but because Dad would be proud of him for trying.

So he sighed again and pressed on. One step. Two steps. Three steps. Four. On the fifth step, he had to close his eyes as his imagination made the waters rise from the lake like a tidal wave. Shutting his eyes didn't help, though. It just opened him more fully to another nightmare. Giant glowing eyes stared at him.

Olokun's eyes.

TJ's heart raced and his breath caught in his throat. *No fear, you wuss!* he thought. *No fear!*

He opened his eyes to find himself just at the lake's shore, with water lapping at his sneakers. He had done it. He'd made it to the water at least. That was better than what he had done over the last few months.

But it wasn't enough. Despite their insistence that he try, his grief healers would have told him not to push himself too hard. Not when he'd made a successful step in the right direction. TJ didn't listen to that advice, though. For there was more to this for him than just overcoming a fear. He wanted to see his sister's face—Dayo's face—once more, see her in the water's reflection like he had seen her before in that hospital mirror and on that tablet screen. Maybe she could help him make sense of his new life as a hero. It was always supposed to be her, anyway.

Until the Keepers killed her.

TJ swallowed deeply and pulled off the leather gloves that covered his hands these days. They hid the deep scarring, a reminder of the impossible levels of Ashe he had to channel to stop Olokun. To the clouded, it would've looked like he had vitiligo.

If only it were that simple.

Twenty-seven and thirty-four. That's how many bones and muscles were in the human hand. And TJ had to know every one of them, from his carpal bones, metacarpal bones, and phalanges, not to mention his extrinsic and intrinsic muscles. Biology had always been one of TJ's least favorite subjects. Now he had to almost be an expert as he constantly used his Ashe to move what were now paralyzed hands. Angry heat swelled in his belly anytime he used Oya's Wind to wrap around his dead fingers and pulled them away for the most basic of tasks—like dipping his hand into Oshun's Lake.

He could still feel sensation though—as if that was any consolation. Once the tips of his fingers sunk into the cool and green waters, the scarring on his arms glowed brightly as they always did when he used Ashe now.

But he wasn't using his Ashe…

TJ pulled his hands away from the waters, but they wouldn't give. His muscles clenched in fear. Was it Olokun taking him under? TJ's throat went dry as the mystical radiance spread out along with the ripples, and a face emerged. A hard face, not soft like his sister's. Then the face spoke with a distorted underwater rasp.

*Tomori Jomiloju?*

"H-How are you doing this?" TJ asked. "I thought communicating with mortals was forbidden?"

*The old rules are dying, young mortal. The Gatekeeper keeps the ways no longer. He hasn't been seen for several moons, in fact. You may see many more Orishas reaching out from now on.*

"Y-you're an Orisha, too?"

The Orisha continued speaking directly to TJ's mind with a deep and deliberate voice. His face almost looked wooden. Strong. *Oh, yes! My apologies. I am Oshosi, Orisha of the Hunt. But for our purpose now, your Orisha of Justice.*

"Orisha of Justice? What's that supposed to mean?"

*You must come with me. The Court of All summons you. They claim you are responsible for the death of the Norse God of Thunder, Thor.*

*Did I just hear that right?* TJ thought as the world around him faded into a dull hum, his vision narrowing to the accusing voice before him. A cold sweat slicked his palms as he pulled them from the water.

Ever since the tidal wave that thrashed the coast of Lagos, Nigeria, there had been a protocol for any sightings of the Orishas. These weren't official protocols. They couldn't be found in some directory of the United Council of Magical Peoples, or within the rulebook of Ifa Academy of Tomorrow's Diviners. It was a pact between two people.

A pact between TJ Young and his former Headmistress—Elder Adeyemi.

That agreement spiked through TJ's mind as he stared blankly at the lake below him. Had this been a few years ago, TJ would never have been able to believe such a circumstance. A few years ago, the most eventful thing to happen to him on a Friday afternoon was being served decent pepperoni pizza at his ordinary school's cafeteria. These days, though, messages from ethereal beings were a dime a dozen.

And he missed those pizzas.

Even so… being told you were the key reason for a Norse God's death was still out of the ordinary.

Even for him.

It just didn't make sense. TJ had never known Thor before. He didn't even know he existed like that. Not for real. So why was he being blamed at all?

TJ peered over both his shoulders at the quiet forest around him and pulled his gloves back on. Most of the other students would've been heading to lunch. He'd been alone, save for the chirping birds and the insects that skitted over the lake.

He peered down at the image of the Orisha in the waters and asked cautiously, "Um… can you say that again? I think you've got the wrong guy. I've never met Thor before." The closest TJ had come to anything related to the Norse pantheon was a few months ago. "I mean… I *did* go to the Frost Realm to get Yemoja's gemstone. And I did melt an ice giant—but that was by accident!"

Maybe that ice giant had housed part of Thor's essence?

*I am sure, mortal,* the Orisha Oshosi thought-spoke. *And your responsibility in Thor's passing is a bit complicated. I shall explain it on the way.*

"Huh? 'Explain it on the way'? What's that mean?"

*As I told you. The Court of All is summoning you.*

TJ didn't have the energy for this. "Um… sorry, but I can't just up and leave. I got finals next week. In fact, I'm supposed to tell someone when an Orisha makes contact with me."

Oshosi flitted his long fingers in annoyance, rippling the water from below. *There is no time for that. And you shall only be gone a few moments in your time. Shango needs you.*

TJ's eyes lit up. "Wait! You've seen Shango? Where? We haven't seen him in months—not since he helped us with Olokun."

*As I said, I will explain everything. But we must go. Immediately. The Court is going to Channel him.* TJ gave him a questioning look. *Kill him, child. You're the only one who can save him.*

"How?"

*And why me? Again,* TJ thought.

*Just by being you,* Ososhi said. *You just have to be honest about what happened the day you met Shango. Now,* he clapped his hands together, making the water splash. *I'm told you've a talent for traveling between realms and empowering Ashe. I can't pull mortals across Planes, even with Eshu not manning the gates, but you are no ordinary mortal, are you?*

TJ dropped his head, staring down at his hands sadly. "No… I'm not."

*But I wish I was.*

*Well then, draw my Ashe and fall through.* The watery image of Oshosi began to swirl like a drain being uncorked.

TJ's insides froze. Not again. Not after Olokun. "I—I can't. Can we use an earth portal? Even fire would be okay."

*Unfortunately, no. Only the Golden Fountain can grant access to the Court of All.* TJ took a step back. *With what you did at Eko Atlantic, you're clearly capable.*

TJ's whole body trembled. It was like he was standing at the door of an airplane, about to plunge a thousand feet. Only that would've been better. Much better.

Oshosi slowed his swirling waters, his eyes narrowing on TJ like a hunter. *Young mortal, I see your fear. The water has wounded you, but do not forget, it is also a source of life.* TJ swallowed. The Orisha was right. Those were the first lessons he received at Camp Olosa. The elements… Olokun… they were both faces of life and death.

*Be the hunter, child,* Oshosi said. *Facing fear is the only way to truly know your strength. Pressure makes diamonds.*

"I don't wanna be a diamond," TJ mumbled, chin quivering. "All due respect, but you really don't get it. That wave... it… it messed me up. I'm not tryna go near no water."

*Change your tone, mortal.* Oshosi's voice went dark. *You may be different from the others in your realm, but an Orisha is still due their respect. But,* his voice softened, *I do understand. You are standing inches from water now, are you not?* TJ stayed quiet at that. *When I was mortal, I once faced a kishi I thought unbeatable. But I learned its ways, its habits. I respected its power and found my own.*

TJ frowned, kicking at the dirt. "I'm not no hunter."

*The fact I could reach out to you here means that you are,* Oshosi countered gently. *A hunter finds the heart of his fear and masters it. The water is your challenge. But you won't face it alone. I'll guide you, step by step.*

TJ gave Oshun's Lake another once over. He had traveled through water portals before. It didn't usually take long. Only a few seconds. But these days, he could barely take a bath. How could he allow himself to be completely engulfed by the element, to submit himself to the horrors he knew would haunt him?

"You for real?" TJ asked. "You think I can do this?"

*I know you can, young diviner,* Oshosi said. *A hunter is wise because he learns. He is brave because he faces the unknown.*

TJ straightened his back, feigning confidence. Oshosi smiled, a glint of pride in his rippling eyes. *Better. Now, together, let's turn that fear into strength. We'll approach the water not as enemies, but as allies.*

TJ took a deep breath, the air filling his lungs with the damp soil around him. "Ashe," he said, as though he were completing a prayer for Oshosi. In a way, it felt like he was. Most other diviners communed with feelings and faith. More often than not, TJ communed in a more literal sense. "I'll trust you. But you really got to help me, please."

*C'mon, TJ,* he thought to himself. *You're not facing this alone. Move your damn feet forward.*

He owed Shango that much. The Orisha saved him and everyone else, now it was time for him to return the favor.

TJ's pulse raced as he inched closer to the swirling whirlpool in the lake, his fingers trembling. Each step came heavier, nightmarish cries and screams echoing in his ears, mingling with the shattering of breaking glass. He hesitated at the water's edge, muscles taut. Gritting his teeth, he summoned a hunter's courage, holding every ounce of it he could. With a deep breath, he plunged his foot into the churning waters, bracing for the unknown.

*Great work,* Oshosi said, *now I'll take it from here.*

A twisting current wrapped around TJ's ankle and he plunged downward, fear seizing him as his gut was left back on the shores of the lake.

## 2

# THE GOD EATERS

TJ PLUNGED INTO THE PORTAL, WATER PRESSING IN ON HIM LIKE a suffocating tunnel. His chest tightened as memories of carefree waterpark rides twisted into nightmares. He used to love the tube rides at those places. Now, with the current tossing him around like laundry in a spin cycle, he was just hoping to make it out in one piece.

It didn't help that, despite traveling through mystical portals over the past year, TJ still hadn't found his "portal legs." He didn't get motion sick exactly, but it was something close to it. Everything in the Ethereal Realms was like that. Almost like real life, just a touch different, a touch... *off*.

To quell the queasiness in his stomach, he stared straight out at the bare feet of Oshosi just ahead of him. Now that TJ had crossed over, Oshosi appeared more like an ordinary man with the unique clothing of an ancient Yoruba hunter-gatherer. Animal hides covered his loins; a quiver of arrows was slung across his back; and a bundle of bunched-up dreadlocks sat atop his head between a green-and-white feather headdress. The only key difference between him and an ordinary man was his size. The rough pair of soles TJ was staring at as the Orisha swam ahead of him was at least three or four times the length of Dad's size thirteen Jordans.

"Orunmila's Stars, mortal," the Orisha said over his shoulder, "could you be any more clumsy? I'm getting seasick just watching you struggle over there."

"My bad! My bad!" TJ tried to steady himself, but his shoulders kept thrashing into the waves on either side of the portal. But it meant taking his foot off the pedal, making his mystical swim more of a doggy paddle than a dolphin's vault.

"Great! Now you're going too slow!"

"Sorry! Sorry!" TJ willed himself to torpedo forward, but the rushing waters around his ears were too much. He couldn't focus on swimming and managing the screams pressing into his ears.

"Oh, my word. Remind me to note this to the Courts. There's no way a mortal of your low skill could possibly be responsible for the demise of Thor. This is very good for your case!"

"Gee, thanks for the confidence."

"Apologies for the bluntness. I'm just... surprised. Shango and Eshu have spoken highly of you."

TJ was used to being criticized for his lack of magical skill. He had started magic school three years later than most of his peers and he was a bit of a slow learner, anyway. But he thought he had made a lot of improvement over the last year at Ifa Academy. But what did everyone expect? He wasn't just a slow learner. All last year he had to worry about the Lagos coast too. He barely knew this Oshosi —outside of his studies—but he wanted to prove he was a mortal well above "low skill."

TJ was always having to prove himself.

"So you're a very unique mortal, I hear." The Orisha's voice sounded different now that TJ was with him in the "flesh." The distortion of the water communication back at the lake had hidden the slight gravel in his voice.

"Yeah," TJ answered, "that's what everyone says. I'm supposed to be this 'in-between'. Not an Orisha, but not a mortal either."

It sounded like Oshosi was sniffing at the air. "Yes, I can agree with that. Very odd. We Orishas don't have demi-gods like the Greeks." He sniffed the air again as they charged headlong through the water tunnel. "I've been trying to place your Ashe. You're certainly a bit off. So, tell me, what's your story? I've only heard a sliver from Shango after he returned, and it'll be a little while until we arrive."

TJ told all that he could remember to Oshosi, everything from the moment he touched his sister at her funeral and acquired the use of Ashe, to how he went to Camp Olosa and mistakenly released Olokun from his chains in the Aqua Realm, to how Oya reached out to his best friend Manny in the streets of New York.

It was nice, distracting himself from the crashing waters at his flanks by talking around the fear threatening to seize him up. Some of the cries that whistled in his mind were toning down to whispers.

"Oh, Oya!" Oshosi interjected. "You'll see her too. She's got herself arrested as well."

"What!?"

"Don't worry. Her charges are less severe. She just might have maimed a deity or two when they were trying to bring Shango in."

*Great.*

Manny was going to be so pissed off when she found out that Oya had been captured as well. She was angry enough a year ago when her aligned Orisha had been trapped in a magical staff.

"That reminds me," TJ said. "I keep hearing this thing about the Great Separation. Eshu mentioned it a few times. Even Elder Adeyemi. One of my counselors at camp told us this story that the Separation happened because old-school diviners were using magic for war instead of peace. And when the Great Monarch tried to take the magic back, They just up and disappeared. Is that... true?"

Oshosi did a little barrel roll through a rough patch in the water tunnel before saying, "Oh yes, I suppose rumors like that do tend to happen when there isn't an explanation. In fact, most Orishas don't know the full story. I've still no clue where Olodumare is or what They're up to. But no, the Separation was not created just because of magical misuse. It was to protect humanity against a greater threat: The God Eaters. The same entities Shango and Thor have been fighting all these ages."

*The God Eaters,* TJ thought. Images of dark spirits and wisps of smoke violently filled his mind, and something tapped at the inside of his chest. The pictures in his head were more than just an overactive imagination, he knew. He knew it because the sensation that swelled in his heart sat right between that oddity he felt anytime he traveled the Planes. Something *almost* familiar—as though he were watching someone else's nightmares.

"I—I feel it. Feel them, I mean... how?"

"They are a primordial darkness. All deities feel them deeply, and," Oshosi gave another peek over his shoulder, "deity-likes. We think the Eaters date back before the creation of all."

TJ rubbed at his chest as he swam near Oshosi's ankle. "I don't like how this feels... it feels... wrong."

"Yes, the Eaters tend to have that effect, even to the Great Pantheons." Oshosi's large head hooked over his shoulder, watching TJ's reaction. "I suppose you'll want to know who they are, eh?"

TJ nodded but wasn't sure he was ready to learn about a group of enemies that put fear in the hearts of even the Great Deities.

"The long and short of it is that they are devourers of magic. Otherlings. Beyonders. Fiends. Even the Athena's and the Sarawati's of us lack the words for them. They're voids. Beyond nothingness. Their singular goal seems to be wiping out all magic from all realities in the same way bed bugs have a singular goal of draining their hosts of blood. You still have those, eh?"

TJ groaned as he thought back to the summer he and his family visited Chicago. They were stretched for cash and had to stay in less-than-savory motels. One of them had a horde of bed bugs that hitched a ride back to Los Angeles with them. Shivering from the memory, TJ replied, "Yeah... we still got 'em."

"Well, the Eaters are like that. Most of them seem to be blind. They react only to the use of magic, just like those little bloodsuckers can almost smell iron in the air."

"Actually, bed bugs don't really 'smell' blood. They're attracted to body heat and the smell of human breath though. Carbon dioxide or something like that." TJ wasn't clear on all the details when he and his family became experts on all things bed bugs. "But yeah, I get you."

Oshosi gave TJ an approving nod, his green-and-white feathered headdress scraping along the water vortex. "You know, seems the Great Separation wasn't all that bad. You mortals still managed to figure out the world even without us feeding you magic like we did in the good ol' days."

"Is that why the Great Separation happened to begin with? To separate the battlefield. To exterminate those things at a safe distance? The um... God Eaters?" It was a strange sound over TJ's lips, and it stirred another tapping at his chest and a stream of mysterious images in his mind.

"Partially. Well, it seems like the most that can be done is to fight them off. How to exterminate them would be a most-needed discovery. The Great Separation was made to protect humanity and all our worshippers. So a few pantheons teamed up and created the End Realm. We Yoruba call it *Ijọba Ipari.*"

TJ nodded, his worries about the water and Olokun almost overshadowed by talks of God Eaters and End Realms. Were they about to approach an apocalyptic landscape? Was it even safe to go to this Court of All where this *war* was taking place?

"Essentially, what we've done between all the great champions of Earth is create a pocket in space and time to 'contain' the threat." Oshosi closed his eyes and smiled proudly. "It was the greatest alliance forged between the pantheons. I was there when we Orishas were called upon. We were so strong back then. So strong. But now... Now we have heroes like Thor falling on the battlefield. And another on trial. Scary business." His tone went dark. "Most troubling indeed."

TJ swallowed deeply as he veered to one side, the liquid vortex taking a sharp bend. "Is that why the Orishas didn't come back to help us with the slave trade? Biafra? SARs? All the rest? Why can't the deities just come back and help the Mortal Realm out just a little bit and then go back to fight the war? Shango did."

"That's the chief reason Shango has been incarcerated," Oshosi said. "Think of it this way: The heroes of the village—the pantheons and other ethereal forces—are manning the gates against a horde of hyenas. And they're the best archers in the whole town. But they have a wall the size of China to defend.

"Now, these guys are perfect shots and they have infinite ammo. But eventually, there's going to be too many hyenas, and they'll get overrun. What would happen if you think even one of those archers loses their position?"

TJ painted the picture in his mind: an image of Shango sneaking away from his post just to let a horde of wild dogs in. "The hyenas would come over that wall of China faster."

"You got it, child. That's why we need you to get Shango off his charges and get him back on that wall."

"Great, no pressure," TJ said, half to himself.

"Ah, you'll be all right, mortal. The Fates say all you have to do is tell your story true. Do that, and everything will work itself out. God Eaters included—with any luck."

TJ couldn't believe he had let himself get caught up in this mess, and he was terrified of what the consequences might be. He bit his lip to near-bleeding. All he could do now was hope that the Great Judges would be lenient and that he wouldn't have to pay too high a price for his and Shango's mistake.

Well, Shango's mistake really.

TJ wasn't the one to pull him away—not directly, at least. But somehow he knew the rules of the divine would be different from his mortal ones.

TJ shook himself. Thinking was bad for him. He did it too much, and his musing always turned to the worst. To avoid such ponderings, he shifted focus back to the conversation. He hadn't explained what happened during his first year at Ifa Academy yet, for one. But when he started to speak again, the vortex gradually transformed from blue to gold. The gilded sheen merged with the sapphire like the stripes of a zebra at first, then overtook it in a wide radiance. It got so bright that TJ had to cover his eyes and look through his fingers. Oshosi broke through a barrier ahead of them and floated like a hovering bee. TJ's entrance was far less graceful. He hadn't realized they were stopping and his forward momentum had him tumbling forward without breaks.

"Ahhh!" TJ shouted as glinting sprinkles of gold dotted the edges of his vision. He was hurtling straight toward an impossibly tall, gilded podium. A woman sat behind it, a giant woman with a white blindfold over her eyes.

TJ's head was going to drive straight into her chest!

"*Afẹfẹ, wá sí mi.*" He tried to summon Oya's Wind to slow himself down but everything was happening too fast.

The woman lifted a single finger.

TJ's forehead pressed into it like it was a pillow and he stopped on a dime. No whiplash. No violent jerk. He just stopped. Frozen in place.

The colossal woman and TJ stared at each other awkwardly. The blindfolded woman's expression was entirely placid—at least her brows and lips seemed as much. TJ, however, must've appeared like a total dork, with a hanging mouth and bulging eyes. His limbs were at awkward angles too, in front of his face, ready to brace for what should've been a much more violent impact.

"Can I assume this is the mortal, TJ Young?" the woman said with a very gentle, very calm voice.

"So sorry, High Judge Themis!" TJ couldn't see but felt the tension of Oshosi's words from behind. "Apologies, Tomori Jomiloju. I should've told you to slow down before we approached."

*High Judge Themis?* TJ thought frantically. The *Greek Goddess of Justice?*

# 3

# THE COURT OF ALL

Embarrassment raced through TJ like scalding water. He had nearly slammed into a Greek Goddess like a freight train! That would've been quite the introduction.

TJ tried to speak, to apologize, but his mouth was frozen in an awkward mid yelp. Whatever spell Themis had him under had ceased all movement in his body.

"What's that?" a godly voice said from the side. "What's the mortal mumbling?"

Themis pressed a very large finger into TJ's forehead, and TJ floated backward from her. As soon as he did, he had control of his mouth again and he spluttered a, "Sorry, sorry, sorry! I didn't mean to come at you like that! I didn't know I'd come out of that portal so fast! I didn't—"

TJ's surroundings stopped his rambling. Where the heck were they? All around them stood grandiose walls of gold columns in the shape of armored statues. High windows let in light that didn't seem like rays from the sun but from... something else. Something heavenly. Divine.

Dripping water from his dashiki and soaked Afro, TJ hovered backward from a large stand that seated seven. Themis was in the middle. At her sides were more giants, some with blue skin and others that didn't look humanoid at all. Behind TJ gathered an audience of even more entities that must've been observing deities, gods, and spirits. It looked just like a courthouse back in the Mortal Realm, only this one seemed more like a circus housed in a golden temple. A fountain the size of a football field sat in the middle of the space. That must've been where TJ had shot out from.

*Didn't Oshosi say something about a Golden Fountain?*

"Esteemed Court of All," Oshosi began, "please welcome Tomori Jomiloju Young of the Mortal Realm. A voice for the case against Shango, the Orisha of the Yoruba, the Hero of Oyo, the defender of the Andromeda front, the savior of—"

"That'll be quite enough, Defender Oshosi," the blue god—who TJ just then noticed was sitting atop a bull—commanded.

TJ—who had still been floating—finally settled on the perfectly unblemished marble floor. Well, unblemished except for the puddle created by TJ's drenched clothing and hair.

"Didn't think I'd see you so soon, mortal." Shango sat serenely just to the side of the Justice Council. But he was far from the Shango TJ was familiar with. The Orisha who had helped him fight Olokun just a few months prior appeared more like a shell of a person than a deified man. Paleness dominated his skin, his bald head; dark circles shadowed his eyes; and it seemed like every chain in the universe was wrapped around his body. "How's that Ayodeji boy? Still a blabber-mouth?"

TJ frowned at that. Ayo hadn't woken up since he got back, just like Adeola hadn't woken right away when she'd returned from the Orisha Planes. The difference was that Adeola crossed over for a single night. Ayo was gone for nearly three months.

"Um..." TJ started, keeping his voice low as Oshosi and the Council spoke. "He's still in a coma."

"A coma?"

"Basically... a forever sleep."

"Forever sleep?" Shango asked, and then, with some condescension, said, "That's death, my child."

"Um..." TJ's eyes darted away from all the others that watched him eerily. "I-I'm not explaining it right. He's alive. Just sleeping."

"I see... Well, thank you for coming, young mortal. Perhaps you can shed light on why Anansi died for you."

"Yes, indeed," Themis interrupted, her tone anxious despite it being monotone.

TJ zipped his head from Shango to Themis, waiting for further clarification. Were all the gods dying like flies? When did Anansi suddenly enter the chat of the dead? Dizziness seized TJ's head momentarily.

"Well..." Oshosi cut in gently. "I wouldn't call it dying exactly, more like his very essence being snared."

"Pause." TJ worked the tips of his fingers into his temple. "I thought it was Thor who died."

"Oh, he did," the blue god sitting on the bull said matter-of-factly. "When Shango returned from the Mortal Realm, he claimed to have found Thor in a tangle with Jörmungandr before the Asgardian fell. Only... there is no evidence of The World Serpent's remains."

"That's because Thor obliterated the beast before you all arrived," Shango said bitterly. Something in his tone told TJ he had repeated this fact several times.

Ignoring Shango, the blue god continued. "Anansi very recently left us just before Oshosi sought you out."

TJ had to settle his mind. Why couldn't Elder Adeyemi or one of his other teachers have a direct hotline to these gods who were always checking for TJ? After last year, all TJ wanted to do was retire from a life of ethereal entanglements to the boring and ordinary life of a teenager. He'd even take on a boring after-school job as a trade. There was a time when he fantasized about being a superhero, saving people and defeating villains. But in real life... that stuff just wasn't it. It sucked, and he wasn't built for it.

Was it too much to ask to only have to worry about which magical university would accept him in a few years, not which deity would die "because of him"?

Oshosi should've given him a warning about Anansi. TJ had studied up on him a bit last term, especially with some of the exchange students who came from Ghana. Anansi's demise didn't make sense though. He wasn't some warrior; he was a trickster like Eshu. Thor dying in the middle of some Great War checked out. TJ even remembered that Jörmungandr was Thor's immortal enemy. Didn't Ayo tell him that one of his friends from Greystone said it was prophesied that Thor would meet his end to the World Serpent? Anansi, who was supposed to be the Lord of Story for the

Akan people, wouldn't be on a battlefield. Was the war so bad that even non-warriors were fighting as well?

Oshosi gave TJ a sheepish wave between two spotlights streaming down from the gilded windows. "A lot of our fellows have perished in these trying times. Which is why we have you here to give us some insight."

*Orunmila's Stars*, TJ thought, *these gods are... desperate.*

"All agreed that the threat we face must be fought," Oshosi said. "Not all agreed on how that should be done. The fates in particular had... objections. To the best of our knowledge they have been pursuing their own solutions in secret all these years. We have not seen or heard from them in several ages. Until now..."

"So, mortal," said another god on the judges' panel, likely of Norse origin considering his great white beard that was braided down to his chest. "Our concerns about Thor's demise are tied to Anansi. From your best recollection, has the Spider communed with you recently?"

TJ shook his head. "No, I don't think so."

"Not even as a whisper in your dreams? No messages Anansi may have passed on?"

TJ shrugged. "I mean... maybe. But dreams are weird. Last night, I was playing basketball with a giant talking panda in a flying teacup. Was that a message from Anansi?"

The courtroom got quiet and scowls were exchanged. A few of the more comical spirits in the audience chuckled. TJ hadn't meant it to be funny; he was just covering up his nerves.

Oshosi stepped in. "Could it be, Esteemed Judges, that this Court is wrong, that what Shango did—going back to the Mortal Realm, that is—was exactly what he should have done, as it was prompted by the Fates, by Anansi and the rest?"

Another blue giant with an elephant head spoke directly into TJ's mind. *The Fates work in mysterious ways. Just your being here could already be altering timelines we are not aware of, young mortal.*

"Be that as it may, Ganesha," another woman, with hair dark as night and gold wings bright as day, added at the high table, "this mortal boy deserves a better answer if we are to be helpful to him, and he to us."

"What answer can we give?" the other blue-skinned god said. "Anansi left us with little and less."

With a respectful annoyance, TJ asked, "Wait. So you all brought me out here and don't even know what for?" What kind of war was this? This Justice Council wasn't just desperate. They were absolutely clueless, grasping for anything. TJ leaned in close to Oshosi, cupping his hands. "I thought I was supposed to get Shango free?"

"That was my hope as well," the Orisha returned. "Are you sure you had no visions of the Spider? Not even a hint of something?"

TJ shook his head. "No, I've never met Thor or Anansi or most of anyone in this room."

"Anansi spoke of you as a literal key," Themis explained evenly. "And from what we've heard from Oya and Shango here, we are most curious about your... abilities. Can you explain to the court what your magic is capable of?"

TJ turned to find Oya among the audience behind him. She looked absolutely regal; her ebony skin contrasted beautifully against her burgundy wraps and gold necklaces and bangles. When they locked eyes, she gave TJ an encouraging nod.

TJ held back a sigh. He'd already had to tell Oshosi, now all these Gods? "Well, it started at my sister's funeral last summer. I didn't really have magic before then. But when I touched her, it all came flooding in. I call my powers a battery pack." Themis scrunched her brow. "Uh... a boosting power. I'm not all that great with my Ashe on my own usually, but I make people around me better. And over the last year, I've discovered other things I can do like... I can sap other diviner's magic and use it for myself or my friends like a loop. When I was getting chased by Eshu in the Sky Realm, I was able to sort of 'turn off' my magic so he couldn't find me and my friends. Oh! And I can basically unlock the space between realms... but that's kinda new."

"It is true," Shango confirmed. "Eshu had my mortal, Ayodeji, and me locked out of Orun—the Orisha Planes. We wouldn't have made it through if not for Tomori Jomiloju."

Another of the judges that TJ actually recognized from his history textbook as the Egyptian god Ma'at fluttered her large eagle wings. "Hold there, young mortal. This might be Anansi's calling. I would like to hear more about this ability. Please explain how you breached the borders of an ethereal space."

"Well, I guess it started with Ol' Sally—she's a giant alligator from the summer camp I went to. She led me and my friends into the Aqua Realm. I thought it was her who got us across, but then I unlocked this old passage at my academy, and then there was the golden chain to the Sky Realm…"

"Have you ever generated a portal of your own accord?" Themis asked. "Without the assistance of this Ol' Sally or a golden chain."

TJ pulled off his gloves to show the white streaks that snaked across his brown skin. "That's how I got these markings. I've only done it once, and only because I was desperate."

A hush fell over the Council as they all gave each other questioning looks. The god with the elephant twitched their ears anxiously. Even the giant bull seemed disturbed by TJ's words, huffing through its wide nostrils.

"The mortal's power is growing," commented the Norse god gravely. "It seems he needed assistance before but can now manifest thresholds on his own. Could you generate a path for yourself now?"

"Um… I don't think so. Last time I did it, my hands froze up." TJ lifted his hands to the court again, letting them flop after he stopped using his passive Ashe. "They stiffened up at first. Now they're technically paralyzed. I use Oya's Wind to get them moving again."

"I can attest to that," Oya said from behind TJ. "Even now, the mortal pulls from my source."

"Thanks, and it's good to see you again, Windweaver," TJ said.

"You as well, boy. How is Manuela?"

"As good as she can be." TJ turned back to the council of judges, pulling his gloves back on. "The healers said I should have been split apart by the Ashe I used. The magic I used to punch through the Aqua Realm, I mean."

"To breach an ethereal realm as a mere mortal, yes," Themis said. "You should have been pulled apart. Your human body cannot contain the magic you apparently demonstrated. Can this be confirmed?" Her chin inclined to Oya at the public benches.

"Yes, Esteemed Judge." Oya stood and curtsied in the Yoruba

style this time, two knees on the ground and her head held low. "I saw the mortal do it. And he got us back from the Orisha Sky Realm to the Mortal Realm as well. He possesses great power," she gave him a side eye, "despite his lack of experience and earthly limitations."

"Um… is that a problem?" TJ swallowed. "Me making portals and all that? 'Cause it sounds like it could be a problem, by how y'all are talkin'."

"That remains to be seen." Themis gestured to a side podium decorated in golden wings that flapped silently. Behind it stood a four-armed man with a white beard, guy-liner, and a golden crown. "Lord Vishvakarman, Great Architect, what do you make of this mortal and his powers?"

Vishvakarman used three of his arms to carve an orb in his hands. An orb looking very much like a planet.

*Does this guy really create planets in his spare time?*

The god's one free hand pulled a hookah from his lips. His voice was reedy and he snorted often. "If left in the wrong hands, the mortal's power could be exploited, I'm sure. Traveling to the End Realm in particular could prove… problematic for our war efforts." The Great Architect leaned forward at his podium, squinting. The red lines painted on his forehead scrunched up as he said, "We should lock him away. I'd like to do some experiments. His power could be used to stitch the fissures we've suffered these past centuries. More and more Eaters find new cracks every day."

TJ's neck drew back sharply. This was escalating quickly. What in the hell did he mean "lock him away."

Oshosi cleared his throat. "Great Architect, this is Shango's trial, not the mortal's. Tomori Jomiloju Young is merely here to give testimony, nothing more. The humans are expecting him back on my Hunter's Word."

A burly man who looked like a younger version of Thor scoffed. "When have we ever cared for deals with humans? If Vishvakarman says we should jail the boy, we should."

"Aye," a red-headed man who looked to be his brother said. They both sat at a table adjacent to Oshosi's. They must've been the prosecution against Shango. Other Asgardians speaking on the late Thor's behalf, perhaps.

*Great...* TJ thought with an internal groan. He set his forehead into his hand and rubbed. When he was done he squinted out one of the tall windows. The starfield beyond the golden columns of armored statues did seem like they were being split apart and restitched, as though some invisible force was playing connect the dots. Was that the painting of the war? The God Eaters ripping through and the War Gods battling them back?

Oshosi lifted from his table, his hands clenched into fists. Though his words were bitter, he kept his tone as neutral as possible. "Need I remind the prosecution and court that the mortal, Tomori Jomiloju Young, is of the Orisha, not a follower of the Hindi or Asgardians? I've seen the experiments the Great Architect has conducted. It could leave the boy with mind rot."

"Mind rot!?" Sick filled TJ's stomach as he blurted the words. "I'm not dangerous. Oshosi was just complaining about my portalling when we were coming here.'" He brushed Oshosi along the ankle, beckoning him to lean down. "I thought you said they wouldn't be impressed with me."

"Well, I didn't factor in your ability to breach realms on your own at the time, child," the Orisha confessed quietly.

"One potential mortal sacrifice could win us a thousand more years of protection," the red-headed man at the adjacent table said. "This could be what Anansi meant when he said the boy is the key. It's a fair trade. After all, isn't that why we're all here? To save Midgar and its magic users from the Eaters?"

"Hey! That ain't fair at all." TJ forced courage into his words. "I was just back at school, minding my own business, and now you're talking about—"

"Esteemed Judges," Oshosi cut in, "Are we creating a new case for the mortal diviner? If so, I formally request my due time to prepare. I cannot defend without notice." He stretched a hand to Shango. "And besides that, the Hero has submitted himself to the End Realm. He made that vow knowingly. Tomori Jomiloju Young has not."

"No, we are not creating a new case." Themis' words cut sharp. "Defender Oshosi, you shall be personally responsible for this TJ Young as we consult on what should be done with him and his most troublesome abilities. Until we summon him again, he will *not* traverse the realms under *any* circumstances. Is this understood?"

Oshosi dipped his head low, his feathered headdress drooping lamely. "Of course, High Judge Themis. We thank you for your Grace."

"It would seem this mortal diviner is not here to clear Shango of his desertion, as you might have hoped," Themis said. "However, the Great Architect is correct. The fissures have grown in too large a number. And Shango has compromised our position. I have one more question before I decide on the Orisha's fate." Shango straightened in his seat, his chains clinking. "Shango of the Orisha, do you, with all honesty in your heart, re-submit yourself to the End Realm until the God Eaters are vanquished? Do you swear, on spirit and soul, *never* to return to the Mortal Realm or put our borders here in jeopardy?"

"I cannot, Esteemed Judges," Shango answered earnestly. "If my people need me again, I will choose them." He turned to Oya. "And I will choose her. Always."

"Then, sadly," Themis began, "This court has no choice but to sentence you to The Channeling."

"No! You cannot do this!" Oya bellowed from the audience. She gave no warning as she stood up straight, a storm flashing behind her without warning. The tattered robes of four dark figures behind her blew back. Skeletal hands rose to cover their shadowed faces as the courtroom darkened.

The Windweaver wasted no time in slicing her storm between the judges' podium and Shango. She manifested air-steps and rushed forward with arcing strides, an outstretched hand flung desperately toward her husband. It was an awesome display of power, but gilded mechanical guards were already lunging from the sides.

They weren't just decoration.

Shango shook violently against his chains as Oshosi pulled TJ away from the tempest's rage. There was nothing that could be done against Shango's chains, and Oshosi must've known Oya's attack was going to be fruitless.

Oya thrashed wind against the guards' faceless helmets but their armor did not budge. Their chests radiated with a bright light that seemed to suppress the Orisha's Ashe. Hot winds quelled to wisps, lashing gales to a gentle ocean breeze. Another pair of mechanical guards bound Oya by the wrist with cuffs that seemed to still her Ashe *completely* as she continued to wail.

A sharp clink of chains pulled TJ's attention to Shango. His expression, dark and unreadable at first, cracked open with rage the moment Oya stumbled under the heavy grip of the guards. He surged forward, only to be yanked back by the enchanted chains biting into his wrists and ankles. Sparks of fire flickered across his skin before extinguishing, swallowed by the magic-suppressing metal.

"Remove the Windweaver as well, please," Themis ordered the guards, who were already tugging Oya away. The Orisha was writhing and struggling like a wild hurricane, making it very difficult for the mechanical-looking guards to do their jobs. TJ would have continued watching, but Themis's calm voice drew back his attention. "Defender Oshosi, please escort your patron safely back from whence he came. The Court of All is now dismissed."

# 4

# FALL OF THE FATE

A LOUD VOICE IN TJ'S HEAD TOLD HIM NOT TO LISTEN TO reason, told him to rush after Oya, to empower her with his own Ashe. This didn't seem fair at all, but—a mortal among gods—what could he do?

He looked down to his hands, flexed them with the remnants of Oya's Wind.

*In this place, you will find strength you do not know in this world,* Ol' Sally had once said to him. And he could feel it right then and there. Somehow, he knew he'd have the strength to help Oya.

TJ battled between bared teeth and an unfocused gaze. How dare they invoke The Channeling on Shango for pledging himself to the mortals who empowered him in the first place? How dare these gods rough up Oya?

TJ flicked a glance back at Shango, who still stood rigid, his fury barely contained. A low rumble rolled from deep in his chest, like distant thunder building on the horizon. Even without his powers, the force of his presence filled the room, heavy as a storm cloud. The Orishas ire stirred in TJ. Had he passively been drawing from Shango's muted Ashe?

"Easy there, little hunter." Oshosi had leaned down close to TJ, a giant hand holding TJ's heaving chest back. "This isn't the time to pounce."

"But—"

"There'll be time to repay the offense against Oya later, young mortal. Trust me." Oshosi's voice had taken on a very different tone. An earnest one. Despite him being as calm as a predator, TJ could feel the tension coiling even in his light touch. This was the Hunter's True Voice. Not the one he used with the courts. And it was dangerous.

And that danger calmed TJ down.

All the deities stood up immediately upon being dismissed.

"Hey!" TJ called out to the judges at the podium. "How's this Court gonna get angry with Shango for leavin' his post when all of you are here slingin' judgment?"

Themis had already turned away, but stopped at TJ's words. For a moment, her blindfold considered the young mortal before turning to Oshosi. "This one has a mouth on him, doesn't he?"

"The mortals have not known our power for quite some time," Oshosi answered. "Respect is hard to come by when that happens. We're working on it, High Judge. Please forgive the young diviner."

TJ chewed on the inside of his lip. It almost sounded like he was being chided by an auntie and uncle.

"But, to answer you, mortal," Themis said as she flipped her white robes over her shoulder. "We are the Justices, not Gods of War. Those you saw here who are part of that band were not with us in the physical sense." She waved a slow hand to the prosecution table where the Thor lookalikes sat. They dissipated into a shower of sparks. A few other deities at the back of the public benches withered away into mists that drifted through the nooks and crannies of the grand room. Others not of the war aspect transformed into dragons or birds to take flight through the tall open windows of gold. Most used the football field-sized central fountain to return to wherever they had come from. The only ones who remained were the golden guards and Shango.

"Oh..." TJ rubbed the back of his neck. "My bad."

Themis cleared her throat knowingly. "Oshosi, as I said, make sure this one does not wander or stray. Transgression will not be tolerated." She did not wait for an answer as she turned, went down a set of steps, and disappeared from view.

"Well." Oshosi placed his giant hands on his waist with a huff, returning to his more affable disposition. "That's not exactly how I saw this going. In fact, that went much worse. Much, much worse."

"What do we do now?" TJ asked, avoiding Shango's eyes, though the Orisha didn't seem to care for TJ as a pair of mechanical-looking guards pulled him away.

"Right now," Oshosi answered, "I'm going to make sure Shango is comfortable in his cell before The Channeling, then I'll see what'll be done with Oya."

"What about me?"

"Like the High Judge said, you need to be back on the Mortal Realm where you belong. I'll drop you off quickly and return here, eh?"

TJ nodded, and heat filled his ears. The trickle of fountain water behind him brought his attention to the thinning queue of gods gathering there. At the head of the line, a colossal stoneman fell through the fountain waters with a *plop*.

"You know how it's done, eh?" Oshosi asked. "Just think of that lake you were by before."

TJ recalled how he got back from the Sky Realm to Ifa Academy last year. During that whole ordeal, he just imagined Oracle Rock, and—with some concerted effort—he was soaring through the air and straight back to the Mortal Realm.

"Yes, I've done it before. But..." His mind flashed to another liquid vortex of nightmare fuel, and his heart hammered.

"Best to do it in one jump, mortal," Oshosi sounded from above. TJ gave the Orisha a sheepish grin, then stared down into the golden fountain in horror. He would've really liked it if his heart would stop pounding on his chest so hard. On the other side, a ghostly image of Emeka emerged. TJ seized up, rubbed his eyes, and looked again. No, it wasn't Emeka that he saw. It was the other deities he had seen ahead of him as they glided through mystical currents of time and space.

"Still thinking of Olokun?" Oshosi asked.

"Nah..." TJ said, "not this time. I mean... all that mess with that Justice Council got me twisted."

"Oh good. Well, go on in. I could also push you if that'll help," Oshosi said plainly.

TJ stiffened. "No, no. I can do it myself!" He jumped up and swung his legs over the side of the fountain. Cool water wrapped around his ankles. The liquid tugged as though it were pulling him down into it by force.

*Oh, damn...* He didn't like that *at all.*

Nightmarish images of Olokun manifested between his legs. The portal must've been connected to the ley lines of the Mortal Realm. And if they were using water, Olokun could see, right?

"On second thought..." TJ started to remove his legs from the fountain pool.

"We don't have time for this. I must attend Shango," Oshosi said. "Be a hunter. Here, I'll help." A great big meaty hand pressed into TJ's back. Before he could remind the Orisha that he did *not* want to be pushed, he was already falling headfirst into the vortex.

Immediately, golden waters rushed around his ears. He somersaulted a few times as vomit bubbled up his throat. It was like getting pushed into the pool by Dad when his swimming instructor said TJ was "ready enough." Just like then, TJ had no clue what was up or down. Was he even going in the correct direction? How could he even tell? Maybe it didn't matter. He wasn't sure where he was going when he and his friends had used the lightning tunnel with Oya last year. Things turned out okay back then. He just *felt* the right direction to go. And the faster he found the direction, the sooner he could be away from the water and somewhere very dry.

TJ whipped his head wildly to each side of the vortex, which had changed from a hue of gold to one of a more ocean blue. That had to be a good sign. At least he wasn't heading back to that courtroom again. Several images even flitted in and out beyond the barrier: A luminous forest, an endless crimson desert with glass spires, and a frozen expanse with mists that seemed to hide threatening shadows. None of those were what he was searching for, so he closed his eyes and summoned his Ashe.

"Right behind you, child," Oshosi said through the countercurrent. "You're doing surprisingly well this time. You see? All you have to do is summon a hunter's courage."

TJ was just good at putting on a face. Even for himself. Inside, he was a mess of jitters and quivers.

TJ pictured being back along the banks of Oshun's Lake. He

imagined the hot lick of the Nigerian dry winds, how the lake smelled of an earthy odor. More than that, he painted a picture of the fairies and birds that soared along its edges.

As the image in his mind took greater shape, a metaphorical hook latched onto his chest and tugged—like a fisher reeling in a catch… and TJ was the prize. Unlike a fish, however, TJ allowed himself to be pulled. He knew it meant his exit.

There was so much to tell everyone when he got back. No wonder the Orishas and so many others were gone. All the pantheons, it seemed. And on top of that, it seemed like they were losing. Ayo was in his coma, so he had never been able to mention anything about God Eaters or a cosmic war. Had he met Themis too?

But what could mere mortals do to help? And more importantly, how was TJ going to get out of being experimented on by that multi-armed god with the snort?

"Wait! Wait!" Oshosi called after him. "Where are you going?"

Just as the pull on his chest seemed to wrap around him fully, TJ opened his eyes. The image before him did *not* look like Oshun's Lake. Instead, it appeared as a strange collection of shapes. Shadows of deep blues and purples. TJ thought he might've seen something like it before. He just wasn't sure when or where. What he did know was that he was clearly going in the wrong direction.

Closing his eyes again, TJ tried to "break" the mystical grip around his chest, but it wouldn't give, and it sent him careening far to the side.

"Stop! Stop!" Oshosi shouted with more panic this time. "I can't reach you like that. Stop veering off!"

*What do you think I'm trying to do!?* TJ thought but didn't say. He was too busy wrestling with the invisible hold on him. TJ had been given simple directions, and they seemed easy enough to follow. But he was screwing even this up, as usual.

At least it was on brand for him.

*Let go!* TJ thought-shouted at the clutch on his chest that simply *wouldn't* give. He couldn't shake it, and soon he was shot straight through the tear in space to all that purple and blue.

Again, TJ was spinning head over heels, though now he lacked the guide of the vortex tunnel to follow. He soared in the middle of space, farther and farther from the whirlpool of water behind. Eventually his spin slowed to a gentle floating. Finding his balance, TJ stared up, and his jaw dropped.

Above and around him were more colossal figures. He thought they'd be just as amorphous as they seemed within the tunnel, but they began to take definitive shapes, some TJ recognized. In all, there were three.

To the left was a silhouette of a half-man, half-spider, his shoulders slumped and zombie-like. Anansi? To the right was another deity he didn't recognize. They had two faces: one on front and one on the back. They too were hunched over like floating corpses.

Wait, were these the Fates?

Yes, they had to be!

The one that wasn't slumped over, front and center, was Orunmila, the Orisha of the Stars. His sister's Orisha—Dayo's Orisha. TJ couldn't be completely sure, since Orunmila was nothing but a shadowy figure, but he held onto a gnarled staff that had been described in several of TJ's classes.

"What are you doing?" TJ questioned. "Why did you pull me out? I have to go back to the Mortal Realm like Themis told me to! Oshosi was just behind me..." TJ turned but there was nothing there. No jet of water racing along the stars from before, no Orisha of the Hunt. Nothing. Just a cold and unwelcoming starscape.

Oh damn... was he stuck here?

TJ turned back to the giant figures. Anansi's skin had no color to it, like it had been vacuumed out. The two-faced deity as well. Neither had any expression. If they had been killed, it was as though it had happened in their sleep.

The central figure that had to be Orunmila looked healthy though, with deep umber skin. But he did not speak, did not answer. He simply stared. Eerily. Blankly. Something about the shadowy figures reminded TJ of when he first felt Ashe. When he had touched Dayo at her funeral, he had been transported to a place of strange shapes and sounds just like this.

Maybe Orunmila was trying to communicate with him, and TJ was just not picking up on it. The judges in the Court of All kept talking about the Fates and what he was meant to do, but what did they want from him? Why weren't they clear with their directions?

TJ thought back to his conversations with Oracle Ruby. She had explained that divination was finicky because of the muddled "translation" of the deities. That the Fates shrouded themselves in mystery for reasons unknown. With them silent even now, with TJ right in front of them, he had to wonder... Were there rules binding them not to reveal what the future told?

TJ was about to speak again when Orunmila leaned his giant head in close. The Orishas's entire head was a tall as TJ's entire height. Orunmila got near enough that TJ could make out the age lines on his forehead, the bags beneath his eyes. Several beaded necklaces of green and yellow hung around his neck. They matched his long green robes and yellow bandana.

His mouth began to move, twitching and straining as though his lips were glued together. It took several moments before he spoke only three words. "Follow the ancestors."

And then, very suddenly, Orunmila changed. First, his eyes went gray and cloudy as he jabbed at his ears in pain. But just as soon as he lifted his hands, they went limp at his side, and it was as if his last words were croaked out painfully.

"Submit... to... Time... for... Monarch's... return..."

Though he was wizened and old-looking already, now his skin was devoid of pigmentation and all life. He was nothing more than an empty husk. The same way Dayo looked in her casket. The same way Anansi and the other deity at his side looked. And through his unique vision, TJ could see a black smoke spill from Orunmila's eyes, nose, and mouth. When the transformation was complete, more shadows joined the first three. Other Fates? TJ couldn't be sure. He tried to cry out to them, to squint and make out who they were. But they paid him no mind, and wrapped their arms around the three now-dead deities. The starfield warped around their forms. First slow and steady, then rapid and shaky until they were all gone.

"Wait!" TJ outstretched a hand to them, but the invisible hook had him again. A sharp sensation cut through TJ's heart. It wasn't painful though, more like he was being shocked back to life. A cacophony of sounds—some that made sense, others that did not—assaulted his ears. "No, wait! Don't take me. What's going on!?"

And then… nothing but silence.

Before TJ could make full sense of what was going on, he flew backward, yanked by the gripping force around his chest. Then he was plunged into the liquid portal once more.

# 5

# LOST TIME

TJ SCREAMED. TJ SCREAMED *LOUDLY*. NOT A SHORT YELP, BUT the kind of yell that slipped out on a roller coaster drop. The problem with that? He let in a lungful of water that raced through his chest. His howls turned into spluttering fits of coughs; he couldn't get the water out fast enough.

Again, he was back to that beach, back to Olokun. Back to the terrible screams, the horrible cries.

"Wait, wait," a Nigerian man's voice said. "Stop moving. Let me help you."

How could the man tell him to wait? TJ was drowning. He was trapped beneath strong waves. But... he wasn't. The water had gone. In its place, mud and grass stuck to his exposed, sweat-soaked neck and forearms.

TJ glanced about, skittishly. No Fates either. Instead of galaxy clouds of sapphire and violet, there was a smattering of ordinary clouds over a sunset sky. Before him and the man, a canopy of trees. The croaking of frogs filled the air and dirt caked the back of his dashiki uniform.

"You came shooting straight out of the lake, my guy," the man said. TJ focused his eyes on him. The man fluttered his hands over TJ and muttered a familiar phrase of Yoruba. "*Omí, wá sí mi. Yọ ara rẹ kuro.*"

The remnants of the water churning painfully through TJ's

chest slithered from his mouth and onto the ground. Its trickle rivered through the dirt and back into a lake.

"Welcome back to Ifa Academy, TJ." The man smiled down on him as he held out a wrinkled hand. "You really are some good luck charm, eh? People were worried about you, but I knew you were all right. Oshosi's my Orisha and he said you'd be all good."

TJ took his hand and let himself be lifted. His head was spinning. "T-thank you…" He searched for a name. He didn't think he'd seen the man before. Maybe he was a new teacher. "Um… sorry, have we met?"

A shadow of a frown crossed the man's lips, which were framed by a graying beard. "Don't trip, man. Not even my mom recognizes me most of the time these days."

TJ tilted his head.

"It's John, remember? I led the juniors through Ebony Towers when Olokun attacked."

TJ's stomach plummeted, a whirlwind of unease roiling within. His brow creased deeply, eyes darting as he tried to anchor himself to the present, to John's familiar yet distant face. A vague sense of recognition tugged at the edges of his memory.

There was no way this guy could be John. John was older than TJ by a couple of years, sure, but not a few *decades*. Alarms blared in TJ's mind as he whipped his head over his shoulders. How long had he been gone?

Heart slamming against his chest, TJ asked, "John, what year is it?"

"Huh?" John asked. "I-it's the same year… what happened to you? Where have you been?"

"What happened to *you*, dude? You're not supposed to be this ol —" TJ caught himself mid-sentence. He wasn't in some wacky time-travel situation. He was just an idiot. John was one of the senior students who had helped create portals for those who needed assistance getting away from Olokun's tidal waves. There were a lot of students like him, those who aged from sixteen or seventeen to forty, fifty, or even sixty. It was a byproduct of a novice using portal travel without the right experience. TJ thought back to his living room when he was being ushered back to Nigeria to explain himself to the UCMP. The officers had warned TJ then about the risks, and John was a prime example.

"Oh, man… my bad, John."

"CDS is a bitch, right?" John slapped his bony, aged hand over TJ's shoulder. CDS stood for Chrono Displacement Syndrome. "Don't look so down, my guy. Hey, at least I don't get carded when I want some palm wine, eh?"

"Yeah, right…" TJ couldn't erase the frown from his face. It was his fault John and so many others were in the condition they were in now. "So… how long have I been gone? Is the school year already over?"

"The term ended two months ago. You came back just in time for the second week of the new term."

TJ's stomach dropped again. "The new term!?"

He had missed all of the summer vacation!

*Only a few minutes my ass, Oshosi!*

"Yeah, man. So what were you doing? Did you find Eshu? Did Olokun try to drown you again? Oshosi said you were on some mission and that you'd be fine but then he went silent." John's youthful fervor didn't quite match the age lines carving under his eyes.

*Oshosi said I was fine?* TJ thought. Was Oshosi caught up in a time warp of some kind as well?

"I gotta talk to the Headmistress," TJ said, ignoring the questions that were still spilling out of John's mouth.

"Oh!" John snapped his fingers. "Yeah, yeah. She'll probably want to see you. Um… I think she's at Oracle Rock. Her and Ruby have been spending a lot of time there trying to figure out what's been going on with you. Do you want me to make you a portal there?"

"No! No!" TJ threw up a hand. "I mean… nah, man. Let's just walk. I think I've had enough of portals for, apparently, a few months."

ᛉ

ON THE WALK TO ORACLE ROCK, JOHN'S STOMACH RUMBLED.

He asked TJ if it was okay if they stopped by the mess hall first, which TJ had no issue with.

"Look who's back among the living!" John announced as he and TJ arrived for the early evening dinner. Like always, orange crystal light painted the pillars of the open-face canopy. The students nearest them lifted their heads from plates of meat pies and soup. A bowl of peaches made TJ's mouth water, and his spirit brightened.

That's right… he hadn't eaten in a while. A *long* while, apparently. But after all the portal travel, he didn't have the biggest appetite.

"Fatima!" John called out. "You owe me thirty for thinking TJ would come back with a lisp!"

"Have 'im say somethin'!" Fatima called back with a London accent from one of the tables in the middle, her hijab framing her heart-shaped face. She would've been an SS3 this year, wouldn't she? She was good with portals so she had kept her youthful face, unlike some of her other friends who sat beside her. Most weren't as old-looking as John, but several had streaks of white going through their fades and side-swept locs.

"I do *not* have a lisp," TJ spoke clearly, though his utterance of "lisp" did sound a bit like one. But it was a hard word to say!

TJ leaned in close to John. "Was no one actually worried about me? I could've died on the other side."

"Nah, after what you did at Eko Atlantic, people are thinking you're an Orisha or something, my guy. You always come back!"

Fatima ambled over and stuffed a fistful of enchanted cowries into John's waiting palm. Then she added, "It also helps that The Third Eye keeps singing your praises on Evo."

"And Oshosi said you'd be fine, so… no need for tears." That last voice sent spikes of excitement through TJ's heart. It wasn't Fatima's or John's. Even before he turned, he could already see the pair of perfect dimples and the big curly hair in his mind's eye.

"Manny!" he called out, but the customary bear hug from his best friend smothered his words. This embrace was different, however. She had given him warm hugs before, but this one was a bit tighter, a bit deeper. And for the first time, she leaned in and kissed him softly on the cheek. Heat filled TJ's ears, and he had half a mind to kiss her back if they weren't in the middle of the mess hall. Instead, he pressed his chin into the top of Manny's head and murmured, "Well, at least someone was worried."

When they parted, Manny still holding onto TJ's waist, he noticed wetness around his friend's eyes before she said, "I might not remember what goes on on the other side, but I remember the feeling of danger. You never really know, you know? And a whole summer is a long time. Ayo was gone even longer, but still..." She rubbed nervously along TJ's back. "It helped that I went to Madame Lucienne's. She communed with Yewa and said your spirit never passed her graveyard so—"

Without thinking, TJ leaned in and kissed her back on the cheek, the rest of the student body be damned. "It's good, Manny. I'm good. For real, for real."

Manny's dimples caved deeply over blushing skin in such a cute way that TJ almost kissed her again. He couldn't help it.

She scrunched up her nose in that cute way she always had before saying, "It also didn't help that I missed you—"

"Always making it weird," TJ finished for her. "I know, I know. I'm working on it."

"Barely."

TJ rolled his eyes. "Fine, barely."

They grinned and giggled at each other simultaneously, Manny's smile coming with a slight overbite.

"It's about time y'all started dating, eh!" Umar said from the far table, a journal and a crossover ball in his hands. Just over his shoulder, where John and the other SS3 students were congregating, TJ spotted curious eyes from Eniola, his ex.

"We are not dating!" TJ and Manny responded in chorus, quickly letting go of each other. Eniola kept looking, however, as though she was considering coming over to give TJ... he didn't know what.

TJ was glad she didn't.

The tension between him and Manny was still something unspoken between the two of them. They both knew they liked one another. Like, like-liked each other. But all of last term, TJ was too depressed to think about being with Manny like that. After that hug and the kisses on the cheek though...

"Hold that thought," Manny said. A jolt ran through TJ's core.

Did she know what he was thinking? "I've gotta go grab some soup… long day. Wait for me here?"

TJ nodded, then sat with Umar, a unique-looking kid, with his lanky body and short limbs. Today he was wearing a Nigerian national crossover jersey of green-and-white that rested at his forearms instead of his biceps.

"So, TJ. Next year. You think Manny can lead Ifa to its first Youth World Series in a decade?"

TJ shrugged. "Oh, is that happening already?"

As TJ sat waiting, several groups of students came up to him to say hello, or to poke him to make sure he was real. After a while, the groups thinned out and TJ noticed a few curious titles on Umar's journal that were writing themselves:

*Umar Adebayo's Dream Journal*

*Eko Atlantic Reconstruction still underway; UCMP says magical support vital*

*UK Branch of the Conservators of Mystical Artifacts, Greystone Academy, and Japanese Enclave report theft.*

*Nigeria overcomes Benin in crossover qualifier 21-13, avoiding relegation, but did Benin try to cheat?*

Interesting… Umar had some very specific dreams. He must've noticed TJ gawking because he laughed and leaned in close to whisper, "I got a little help to smuggle in headlines from *Evocation*. Go ahead, you can look through it. There's a lot you'll need to catch up on, eh?" He pointed to the last headline TJ had read. "Nigeria won because of me. No one believes me, but I know it! My baba took me to the game and I swear my telepathy was strong enough to influence the coach's calls."

Smuggling in headlines from *Evo*? Ayo had done the same to his own dream journal last term. Did that mean Ayo helped him? Did that mean that Ayo was…

"A'ight, I'm back!" Manny said, balancing two bowls of peanut soup in her hand. The rich, nutty aroma drifted into TJ's nose, making his mouth water. Maybe he was hungry after all. The steam from both was thick, but Manny used wind magic to keep it from her face.

"Two bowls?" TJ asked.

"Oh, right!" Manny cringed. "I should have gotten one for you too!"

"Woah, big appetite, Manny!" Umar's crooked smile widened. "Getting ready to try out for Nigeria already? The Greenhorn Invitational is still a few years off, no?"

Manny rolled her eyes. "Not everything is about crossover, Umar."

Umar's face was completely serious. "I beg to differ. Crossover is life."

"And nah, the second bowl isn't for me," Manny said. "I'm takin' it up to Ayo. He's got another session in the Hospital Tree."

"Ayo's awake!?" TJ blurted out.

"Oh, right!" Manny grimaced. "Yeah, he woke up a little after you went missing. Here." She handed him a bowl. "You hungry too? You must be!"

TJ grabbed at his stomach, still queasy from all the portal trips. "Nah, I'm good for now. But I'll hold this for Ayo. C'mon, let's go see him."

TJ and Manny made off for the Hospital Tree as John called after them. "Hey! We still have to go to Oracle Rock!" But neither of them paid him much attention, already lost in the thick of the forest campus, caught up in the kind of conversation close friends always get into after a long period apart. TJ explained all that had happened to him on the other side.

"Lucky!" Manny exclaimed. "I used to love reading about Themis and the Greek Gods as a kid."

TJ shook his head. "Nah, she wasn't all that cool. If anything, I think she wanted to put me in that Channeling *with* Shango."

"Yeah… that part sucks," she said as leaves stirred overhead against the night wind. "Ugh, next time an Orisha wants to take you somewhere, don't forget me!"

"I didn't have a choice! And Oshosi said it wouldn't take long."

Manny had gotten a little taller, or perhaps a bit more toned, TJ couldn't be entirely sure in the low light of the dirt paths. What had she gotten up to? There was a fair bit of time there when she didn't have him *or* Ayo. Maybe that explained why her biceps seemed so defined under her tank-top dashiki. When TJ was freaked out, he wasted away in a corner of his room. When Manny was stressed, working out was her answer.

"Can you believe these fools were placing bets on if you'd come back with brain damage?" Manny said irritably as they passed through the willows.

TJ chuckled. "Yeah… John won one of those bets, apparently. He was… *extra* happy. I mean, not just the bet, the whole time I was talking to him."

"Well, he lost decades of his life. He's making the most of his time, I guess."

TJ seized up as the horror of those tidal waves entered his mind. "Because of me…"

"No." Manny stopped, placing a hand on TJ's arm. "Because of Olokun, because of the UCMP not giving a damn about the clouded. *Not* because of you, TJ. And don't you forget that! You hear me?" She shook his arm a little. "Do you hear me?"

"Yes," TJ said more sharply than he intended.

Manny fixed him with a deep look, her brown eyes searching for the truth in his words. It took a long moment before she let go of his arm. "Okay… how are your nightmares?"

"They still suck."

"Yeah… mine too."

They started walking again, more slowly this time. Fireflies danced around them, creating a mesmerizing light show that illuminated the winding path ahead, leading them deeper into the heart of the academy's mystical grounds. Their shoulders were practically magnetized with how tightly they walked together.

TJ and Manny had already been close, but the ordeal at Eko Atlantic was a whole other thing that brought them even closer. Near-death experiences and tidal waves the size of skyscrapers tended to do that sort of thing by themselves, but the way Manny had helped TJ after it all… he didn't deserve her.

A charged silence fell between them. The fireflies continued their dance through the air, casting a soft, flickering light on the path. But Manny's stride slowed, her expression turning pensive, almost troubled.

"Manny, what's up?" TJ asked.

She hesitated, biting her lip. For a long moment, she just walked beside him in silence, her gaze fixed on the rippled surface of the river they crossed. Then, with a deep breath, she finally spoke.

"Okay, I think we're far enough away now," she said, her voice barely above a whisper. She reached into her pocket with deliberate slowness, drawing out a small, ordinary-looking hand mirror. Her hands trembled slightly as she held it up, the reflective surface catching the glow of the fireflies. "The Keepers have been contacting me."

TJ's stomach bottomed out. "What!? You're lying."

"I'm not."

"Through that?" TJ's voice cracked, a sharp edge of fear slicing through his calm. The mention of the Keepers sent a wave of cold dread through him. Those radicals, with their callous methods and relentless pursuit of returning the Orishas to full power on Earth, posed a real danger. And now they had a direct line to Manny?

"Through any mirror," Manny said. "It's actually really annoying. I had to enchant every reflection at my parents' all summer to stop them."

The Keepers were always up to something, and usually not anything good. The next time TJ saw any of them, he swore to himself it would be on sight. They killed his friend Emeka—no, *murdered* him. Not to mention all the damage to Eko Atlantic. And for what?

"What do they want?" TJ asked, his insides still boiling from the mention of the group.

"To break Shango out of that Court of All you were just talking about. They—well, just Bolawe really—has been keeping tabs on me, asking where you are."

"What? How do they know about that already?"

"I'm guessing Oshosi." Manny stuffed the mirror back in her pocket and started walking up the Hospital Tree just at the end of one of the bridges. "The Keepers are experts at communicating with Orishas now. I mean, they've been tryin' to do it for years already with your sister, right?"

"Have you told anyone?"

"Just Elder Adeyemi. Anytime they try to get through to me, I tell her right away. She's got her own plans, I'm sure she'll explain."

"What did they want? What did they ask you?"

"Oh, you know. Same ol' same ol'. Mostly just asking about you and where you were." Manny stopped halfway up the Hospital Tree at one of the tree-house balconies. An oak door stood before them. The crack at the bottom flickered with what must've been more crystal light.

"All right, we're at Ayo's room," Manny said. "A few things before we see him. He's not exactly the Ayo you remember. I mean, he is, but… something happened when he got back."

A sharp pain pricked at TJ. The way Manny had stopped to warn him made him uneasy. Ayo had been in a coma for months, but even Adeola, who had also crossed over and had a hard time waking up, was okay in the end.

"His memory is gone, right?" TJ asked. They already knew that would happen. Not even Manny remembered the times they went to the Orisha Planes.

"Not just that…" A shadow fell over Manny's face. "You'll know it when you see him, just… don't make a big thing about it. He's sensitive about it right now."

"What do you mean? What's wrong with Ayo?"

# 6

# VIP, NO REGULAR

Manny led TJ into Ayo's Hospital Tree room. As soon as she swung in the oak door, a wave of familiarity washed over TJ. He had been there a fair few times now, particularly since the traumatic experience of the Eko Atlantic Drowning. The Hospital Tree had always been a place of solace and recovery for him.

Nestled within the expansive boughs of an ancient tree, its interior had been crafted with care to offer a soothing atmosphere. The natural wooden walls, radiating with warm amber light from the embedded crystals, exuded a sense of calm and safety. Soft moss covered parts of the floor, releasing a gentle, earthy fragrance with each step. Delicate vines adorned with small, luminescent flowers intertwined gracefully along the ceiling.

The healers had designed this space to heal not just the body but also the soul.

However, as TJ stepped into the room assigned to Ayo, he was struck by the stark contrast to the rest of the Hospital Tree. Gone was the tranquil, cozy ambiance. Instead, Ayo had transformed his room into something resembling a rich kid's haven.

The room was sleek and modern, with high-tech gadgets and luxurious furnishings. The walls were lined with state-of-the-art screens displaying various magical and mundane channels. A floating sound system emitted soft, ambient music, the notes twirling magically in the air.

In one corner of the room stood a lavish gaming setup, complete with the latest edition of *Major League Crossover*. Ayo's bed was just as opulent, draped in fine satin that shimmered with a subtle enchantment, adjusting temperature and comfort automatically. Shelves were filled with an array of magical artifacts and expensive collectibles.

TJ paused in the doorway, hands stuffed deep into his pockets, and gave a slow shake of his head. Then, he saw Ayo, who looked healthy enough and who was clearly moving around with ease, head bobbing to the music, though his face was turned away.

TJ's brow furrowed; why had Manny warned him? Was something wrong with Ayo's face? He was still the shortest of the group, and pudgy as ever. He looked like the same old Ayo from what he could tell. What was the big deal?

"Nah, no way they let you bring all this stuff into your room," TJ said with a huge laugh.

Ayo turned and his face lit up with a bright, welcoming smile as he saw TJ, and he moved toward him in a smooth, confident stride. In a single motion, he brought TJ in with a dap and one-armed hug. TJ laughed and held the hug a little longer than usual. He knew Ayo would wake up again, just like their classmates seemed to know TJ would come back, but it was nice having his friend in full health and looking chipper as ever. Ayo wasn't exactly a hugger but he held on longer too. Longer than TJ would have expected. Even so… Ayo was the first to break away.

TJ took in his friend's face again. Nope, there wasn't anything wrong there. He still had his long braids that fell over his face, complete with designer glasses that sat atop his wide nose. The only difference in his appearance was an "N"-shaped tattoo under his left eye. But that had been there before TJ had gone, had been there when Ayo came back from the other side.

No, there wasn't anything different about Ayo's face, but as his friend opened his mouth to speak, no sound came out. Instead, Ayo began to communicate using Yoruba sign language.

"You know me, man," Ayo signed. He thumbed over his shoulder to the stereo that belted the Afrobeat lyric:

*VIP. No regular.*

Despite Ayo's words being unvoiced, TJ could imagine his

friend's cocky words in his head perfectly. Then he frowned deeply. He remembered Emeka, who had taught him and Ayo the basics of Yoruba sign language only last year. The memory of the boy—murdered at the hands of the Keepers—hit him anew with a wave of sadness. Shaking off the memory, TJ focused and started signing back with one hand as best he could, asking with a point to Ayo, "What happen to voice?"

His response was met with a sharp smack across the back of the head from Manny. TJ seized up and rubbed at the spot where she hit him. That was going to leave a bump. But she *did* warn him.

"Ugh, what am I going to do with you, TJ?" She rolled her eyes. "Give Ayo his soup before I sock you."

"Oh, right!" TJ said and handed Ayo the soup they had brought him.

"Technically Ayo can speak," Manny narrowed her eyes at their friend, "and he's *supposed* to—like the healers told him to do if he ever wants to get his voice back. But Ayo has a bit of a... stutter."

Judging by the way that Ayo saw himself out of the conversation to tend to his bowl of soup, TJ could tell it was a sore spot for him. Talking was sort of his thing. He got into plenty of trouble off the back of his mouth. And for him to not be able to speak properly must've been a hard blow.

The revelation was a poignant reminder of the lasting effects their magical adventures could have—even on someone as sharp as Ayo. Magic was nothing to play with. Divine magic especially. Ayo's voice, John's advanced age, and TJ's own ruined hands were evidence enough. The room, with all its opulence and magical grandeur, suddenly felt like a façade masking a deeper struggle within Ayo.

"That's okay," TJ joked, "we were getting sick of hearing you run your mouth, anyway."

Ayo gestured at TJ in a way that would have gotten him a detention, but TJ just laughed, glad to have him back, vocally or not.

"So," Ayo signed, "what happen to you all time?"

"Huh?" TJ questioned.

"Uh, I think he meant," Manny started to sign for Ayo, "'what's been going on with you all this time.'" She had clearly improved on her signing since TJ had been gone—for Ayo's benefit.

"Me mistake," Ayo signed. "Need bigger good signing." TJ believed it. For one, Ayo would never say "my mistake" instead of "my bad" if he was still speaking vocally.

"Half school bet *you* return stutter," Ayo continued to sign. "You gone long, same me. Me say everyone no worry. Tell this girl all the time." Ayo thumbed to Manny, who blushed.

"Shoot, I wish I had a stutter compared to what I went through," TJ started before getting another smack from Manny. But TJ figured it was okay since Ayo had brought it up first! After rubbing life back into his arm, he went on to explain what went down at the Court of All.

"Man, man, man, man, man," Ayo signed, getting a laugh from TJ and Manny at his attempt to draw out the signing motion, "you no catch break, eh?"

"None of us do," Manny said from her seated position on the edge of Ayo's satin sheets, digging into her own soup.

"So, TJ," Ayo began, pausing between his bowl of soup and signing, "Manny and me think and want you fill story gap. We no memory what we do in," he paused for a second, clearly struggling with the more complex signing combination, "crazy different world. But... you do."

Manny crossed her legs atop Ayo's bed. "Ayo only remembers us going up the golden chain, and then the next thing he knew, he's wakin' up in this place." She swirled a finger around the room. "Well, you know, before he decked it out with all his stuff."

"Stop side talk," Ayo cut in. "Don't like tone. Me understand. Maybe me too much do it. But me almost live in Hospital Tree because many healers make me do. Anyway," Ayo set his soup bowl down and took a step closer to TJ, "Sounds like me wake when you leave, TJ. Maybe me wake when Shango channeled? Me think me make big problem with Shango. And me no believe me see Thor, but explains this," he lifted his hand to show a copper ring around his index finger, "and this." This time, he pointed to the tattoo under his left eye. "See, same?"

"Oh, woah!" TJ exclaimed. "That's the same symbol. What does it mean?"

TJ squinted between the symbols carved into the ring and the design under Ayo's eye. Both were shaped like an "N" or more like an arch—now that TJ took a closer look. TJ was already familiar with the unexplained tattoo, but he had never noticed the ring before. Ayo always had designer everything, whether it was earrings, rings, glasses, or even his belts. So TJ never paid it much mind.

"We think they're runes," Manny explained, wiping some soup from her mouth. "We hit up one of Ayo's friends at Greystone Academy. They said it translates to 'Uruz', which means 'bull and storms.'"

"Big ring for lightning power." After signing, Ayo lifted his finger to spark it with a bolt of lightning. As magic pulsated from his nail, so too did a light emit from Ayo's eye tattoo, not unlike TJ's uncovered hands when he did magic these days. "At least that is guess of me and Manny," Ayo signed. "Thor give me ring, me think. No had ring in," he paused again, trying to think of a sign, before gesturing out the window into the sky, "crazy different world."

"We really need to get the sign for realm on lock." TJ laughed. "So, you think Thor marked you or something?"

Ayo shrugged then signed, "Me no know. You tell me. Shango speak it?"

TJ shook his head. "Nah, he didn't. I mean, he didn't really have time to with the trial and everything. Maybe Oshosi knows more about that stuff."

"That shouldn't be too much trouble," Manny said as she finished her soup. "Elder Adeyemi has been in regular contact with Oshosi. She'll give us answers." As she slurped up her last spoonful she edged her eyes to Ayo's end table. Then she groaned. "Ayooo! Are you *still* messin' around with this?"

"What?" TJ asked curiously as Manny lifted a piece of paper.

"Give back!" Ayo signed. He bolted from his corner of the room and tried to snatch the paper from Manny's hand.

"TJ, catch!" Manny threw the paper in the air and TJ could see the stream of magical wind she used to make it spiral around Ayo's head, just out of reach. Then she eddied its path straight out to TJ, who caught the paper in his hand. On its crumpled sheet, the paper read itself out loud in a Nigerian timbre:

*Level 1 Telepathy: Surface Thought Skimming*

*At this novice stage, the telepath can occasionally catch fragments of thoughts, like overhearing pieces of a distant conversation. It's inconsistent and often limited to strong emotions or thoughts, but keep at it and you'll master the craft in no time, troubled diviner! Just remember to—*

TJ didn't hear the rest because Ayo had snatched the paper away from him, a deep-purple blush coloring his ears.

"I don't get it," TJ said. "What's the big deal? Telepathy is a good skill to learn for what you got going on, no?"

"It's one of the most difficult forms of magic," Manny explained. "Takes years to learn even the basics. And Ayo is trying to take shortcuts." Manny lifted the book from where the page was ripped out. The title read *Clairvoyance for Cretins*, along with a subtitle that said *Master the Art in 30 Days*. It was written by a name TJ was familiar with: Olu Olowokandi. Mom had warned TJ about that guy, said he was always looking for "shortcuts and fake initiations."

*Ah, I was wondering where that library book had run off to*, a gentle voice said from Ayo's window, though it felt like the source came directly from TJ's own mind. They all turned to find a monstrous reptilian head with a neck spotted in a giraffe's coat. TJ's breath caught in his throat.

"Oh, I forgot to mention," Manny said from behind. "Meet our new Headmistress."

*Hello, Tomori Jomiloju Young,* the monster thought-spoke, its dinosaur snout unmoving. *You may address me as Headmistress Ninki Nanka of the Wolof if you're feeling long-winded, or you may simply call me Headmistress.*

## 7

# RISING CREATURES, WANING MAGIC

*They're up here,* Ninki Nanka said, turning her head back out to the forest behind her. TJ was trying his best to keep his heart at a steady pace. What was this thing with its long-spotted neck and dinosaur face?

"We'll be right up!" came a very distant voice from below.

Ninki Nanka moved her head back into the room, sighing. *Oh, Oshosi has a lot to answer for. Tomori Jomiloju, I understand you'd want to see your old friends right away, but you should have come to my office first.*

"Sorry, Headmistress." TJ bowed deeply. The Headmistress' sure cadence seemed to soothe and command at the same time. It almost felt normal, somehow, that TJ was talking to a giant mythical giraffe-creature, despite the goose pimples pressing against his gloves. But where was Elder Adeyemi or even Omo of Fon, who had been the acting headmistress?

TJ hadn't expected Elder Adeyemi to be permanently replaced. A part of him felt a bit sad at the news. It was true she had technically endangered TJ and his friends, but not without cause. It was that or doom tens of thousands of people to death on the coast. Besides, TJ was at fault for not telling Elder Adeyemi the whole truth last year. Even with all the dangers he and his friends were put through, there were so many more who lost their lives for all the trouble…

*And your friend is right, young one.* Ninki Nanka nodded between

Manny and Ayo. *The writings of Mr. Olowokandi will not bring you closer to a mastery of telepathy, Mr. Oyelowo. But since I see you have an interest, I will place you in the appropriate specialist classes this term. You'll see some familiar faces in the sessions, in fact.*

"Yes, Headteacher." Ayo signed and bowed just as deeply, and TJ wondered if he had meant to sign "Headmistress" instead. Had Ayo already had a run-in or two with their new academy leader?

TJ couldn't help but stare. He had a kishi and an aziza as teachers last term, but they didn't quite compare to Ninki Nanka.

Manny nudged him on the elbow and murmured, "Cut it out."

"Where did she come from?" TJ murmured in her ear.

Manny murmured back. "Apparently, Ninki Nanka was Headmistress way back when."

"When? When the Flintstones discovered shoes?"

*I was in retirement, yes. Though not so far back as the stone age, Mr. Young.* The voice rumbled gently in TJ's head, carrying amusement. *I was around when your 'Elder Adeyemi' was a student. I laid dormant, deep in Oshun's Lake not too far from here for a number of years. But the school called on me, and I answered. With magic stirring up in the world as it once did in times past, I thought it might be best for we primordials to take a place at the helm once more.* She rested her chin on the window casually as a black hawk swooped down one of the coiling horns protruding from her scaly head.

TJ barely had time to process that bombshell of a statement when chaos erupted behind him. A flurry of people raced into Ayo's room. Before TJ knew it, he was smothered in the embrace of several arms. Someone was kissing his cheeks non-stop. Another was squeezing around his leg. And someone else was screaming in his ears that he was alive.

Who were these people?

By the time TJ was given enough space to breathe a little, he realized that he had been dog-piled by his family. *All* of his family, it seemed. It wasn't just Mom with her palm-tree-high locs, or Dad with his strong arms, or even his brother, Tunde, with his bright eyes and sun-baked dreads. It was also cousins he hadn't seen in ages, one of which was magnetized to his hip. And his grandparents, family friends. People he hadn't seen since Dayo's funeral a year ago. TJ didn't know how it was possible. It was like the room was expanding to accommodate all the people within. No, the room was *literally* expanding... The large branch that made up the hospital room was growing further out from the main body of the tree to accommodate his *whole* family.

He was gone all summer, after all...

"Two months!? Two whole months!? Thank the Orishas we didn't have another Dayo."

"Divination Today did a good job hushing everything up, eh?"

"I told you TJ was alive!"

Somewhere through the masses, TJ made out Ayo signing desperately as one of his speakers was knocked over on its shelf by a stray aunt. "Slow. Stop. No break!"

A few of TJ's cousins knocked over some of Ayo's collectibles, and whoever was wrapped around TJ's leg kept pushing into Manny, who scuffed up Ayo's satin sheets with her dirty Nikes.

Mom took TJ's cheeks between her long hands. "Oh, honey bunny, we thought we'd never see you again."

"Oh, c'mon, Mom!" Tunde chimed in, rolling his eyes. He wore an Ifa Academy dashiki uniform and TJ nearly forgot that this would be his first year at the school. "If an Orisha like Oshosi said TJ was all right, then he'd be all right, right?" He lowered his voice in TJ's ear. "I wasn't worried one bit." Then, in a louder voice, he said, "So who did you have an adventure with this time? Did Olokun make up with you? There's rumors on Evo saying stuff about you and Thor. What's that all about?"

"A'ight, a'ight, settle down, settle down." Dad's meaty hands held Tunde's shoulders to keep him from jumping up and down anymore. "We'll ask him all those questions later. How you doin', son?"

"I'm good!" TJ answered. "Seriously. It felt like I was only gone an hour. Had no idea I'd lose all summer traveling back."

"Yeah." Dad cracked a smile. "Well, you gave a few of us a scare, being away that long." There was a deeper meaning in Dad's words. Tunde was into magical theory, so his response would always have been less dire than their clouded father. "Still, I may barely understand any of this, but I know one thing. You're made of strong stuff. Just like your ol' man. Just like your sister."

"Thanks, Dad," TJ said as Dad ran his hand lovingly through TJ's naps.

*All right, friends and family of Mr. Young,* Ninki Nanka said apparently in all their heads—as it made Dad jump. *We will release him to your warm embraces and wet kisses soon. Now that you know he's safe and sound, I'd like to have a private word with this young man and a few of my cohorts here.*

There were a few complaints from a set of cousins and a few choice words from the grandparents, but they all eventually made their way out and down the Hospital Tree. As TJ's family filed out, Ayo and Manny followed along.

*No, no,* the Headmistress said, *you two stay. You are involved in all of this.*

As Mom and Dad said their final goodbyes, TJ made out a familiar pair of glasses and a head of locs dyed green at the tips just behind them.

Oracle Ruby!

"You see, Headmistress? I told you that 'one quick to sprout would shepherd in the stunted youth'!" she said, clearly speaking about one of her predictions. "John found TJ and brought him back to us."

TJ bowed to her. "Sorry, it—*apparently*—took me so long to get back."

"Don't worry yourself, Mr. Young." Elder Adeyemi rounded the corner, revealing dazzling robes of literal midnight, each streak of light representing a shooting star. "We knew you would be in good health with Oshosi watching over you." She glided into the room, waved her fingers, and the oak door behind her closed on its own.

"Oi, Manny! Gotten into forecasting, have you?" Ruby grinned as she made her way to the bed where Manny sat cross-legged. Next to Manny sat an Ọpọn Ìfà.

"These? Oh, nah, I was just messin' with some Orunmila combos." Manny rolled a few palm nuts between her fingers, her expression shifting slightly. "But… I haven't been getting anything. No patterns. It's weird."

Ruby's eyes brightened with excitement as she leaned over the board. "Let me have a go at it. I swear, I need to get back into this kind of thing—I've spent too much time on my devices lately since

TJ left us." She flicked the nuts into a quick throw. But the moment they landed, Ruby's grin faltered. The nuts sat in an unfamiliar pattern that didn't seem to make any sense to her at all.

Manny gave her a side-eye. "That's not right, is it?"

"No," Ruby muttered, squinting hard at the board. "No, it bloody isn't." She hesitated before brushing a hand across her face. "I should know this set. Should've spotted it right away..."

Elder Adeyemi cleared her throat, sliding her hands into her wide cuffs. "You're not alone in that. I've been noticing... similar signs. And it isn't just you, Ruby."

Ruby gave her a quick glance, but it was TJ who spoke first. "What do you mean?"

"What's up with Ruby's readings?" Manny turned to Ruby. "Why didn't you remember these Orunmila combos?"

"I've a theory on that," Elder Adeyemi offered. "It would seem the influence of the Orishas is waning. I noticed it first with Shango and Oya's magic diminishing. And that includes the Ashe of their chosen children and their descendants—we diviners who use them as a source."

"Me lightning magic no change. Still same," Ayo signed, then snapped his fingers to show a spark of lightning there.

"Correct, and I've two other working theories on that as well. One, and this would be connected to Miss Martinez as well, is that your powers have not yet waned due to your direct interactions with Shango and Oya in the Ethereal Realms. Two, would be that ring you've got around your finger. Your lightning magic is no longer sourced solely from Shango but from those runes etched in your new set of jewelry."

"That still doesn't track for me," TJ added. "If Thor's dead, wouldn't that mean the ring wouldn't work either?"

Oracle Ruby was the one to step in next, brushing aside Ayo's bed canopy. "Each pantheon manages magic differently, love. It would seem the Asgardians lack the direct channel between mortals and deities like our Orishas have. So if one of their gods goes and kicks it—which happens a fair bit with that lot—the mortals they watch over are not so negatively impacted. But for us Yoruba diviners, who often have direct ancestral ties to our Orishas, the loss of that tether can mess us up proper." Ruby rubbed at her head again. "As you can already see with me." She frowned deeply, her voice going dim. "I can't believe it's possible for me to forget Orunmila's combinations entirely. I only saw Shango and Oya in danger."

TJ's chest caved. The rest of them wouldn't know yet. "Elder Adeyemi… before… you said what's happening to Ruby was not unexpected…"

"Indeed I did. Like Shango and Oya, I wondered if Orunmila might be incapacitated or jailed as well. Oshosi hasn't been able to give us information about He Who Knows The Stars."

"No, that's because," TJ said sadly, "Orunmila… Orunmila is gone."

Ninki Nanka's horns seemed to coil tighter into themselves. Elder Adeyemi uncrossed her arms with concern, her lips parting slightly. Manny and Ayo's jaws dropped. But all the color rushed from Oracle Ruby's face as she stuttered a, "W-What?"

TJ did his best to explain what had happened to him.

"It makes sense," Ruby said. "It makes sense now. I just worry for Shango and Oya. If they are taken from us, they'll be nothing but a whisper as Orunmila is to me now."

"But I don't have a ring from Thor," Manny said, "and my wind from Oya still works like normal."

"You see, Headmistress," Elder Adeyemi said. "It is just as I said. The catalyst for this to work is the young ones here. There is no other way forward that I can see."

"Um…" TJ trailed off. "What are you talking about?"

*After hearing from Oshosi around your initial disappearance,* Ninki Nanka explained, *we received word from the Hunter that both Shango and Oya had been jailed by the Court of All. Elder Adeyemi has been building a team of elite diviners and mages to help release them both. Forcibly.*

TJ swallowed hard, his throat dry. The idea of embarking on a mission to free deities from the Court of All was daunting, to say the least. The giant gods were bad enough, but TJ's mind kept flashing back to the mechanical guards that had tackled Oya with almost no effort.

That pressure didn't seem to register for Ayo, however. "Me guess," Ayo signed excitedly, stumbling over the signs. "*We…* special big team?"

*In my professional opinion, you are not,* Ninki Nanka said, and Ayo frowned.

TJ clenched his fists, feeling a knot twist in his gut. *They're pulling magic from the Orishas...*

He glanced at Manny and Ayo, wondering how long it would be before the cracks started to show in them, too. Would the same happen to him eventually? Was it possible that he'd lose touch with Shango and Oya's Ashe?

"So the Court is channeling Oya too..." TJ said, mostly to himself. "They're *actually* doing it..." And for two months, thanks to TJ's lost time.

TJ's insides fell into a pit. He had no issue feeling Oya's Wind, even now as he used it to flex his crippled fingers. But he suspected that was because of his unique qualities as a diviner. But looking at Ruby's face... he didn't want to see that with everyone else too.

"How do we get them back?" TJ asked earnestly. "Whatever you need from me, Elder Adeyemi, I'll do it."

The former headmistress didn't smile, but her eyes certainly brightened in their subtle way. Even the falling stars on her robes seemed to shine in approval. It made TJ warm inside. He'd always loved that pride from her.

*Not so fast, Mr. Young.* The current and more monstrous headmistress stuck her head farther into the room, forcing the black hawk on her horn to duck. *I do not dispute Simisola's theories on the early signs of waning magic you diviners are experiencing, but I do* not *agree that three teenagers should be leading the charge into a heavily fortified dungeon for deities.* She made her slow turn to Elder Adeyemi. *Your agents at the UCMP shall handle this. That or one of our great Orishas.*

"Oh, do not misunderstand me," Adeyemi said. "We will need the Orishas as well. I've plans in motion to mend bridges with Yemoja and Olokun, and Oshosi has been in search of Eshu for assistance."

"What!?" TJ exclaimed. "We're gonna work with the Orishas who were tryna drown us four months ago?"

"Six months," Ayodeji signed, but TJ ignored him.

"And you said Eshu wasn't really Eshu," Manny added. "That he was under some sort of spell, right?"

"This is a very serious ordeal, Mr. Young." Adeyemi spoke

calmly. "We will need our most powerful allies to stand a chance against this Court of All Oshosi has been giving us signs about."

"Allies!?" TJ flustered, his mind fighting his gut on how to properly slap sense into the room.

*That will be all.* Ninki Nanka came in with a finality that not even Elder Adeyemi challenged. *We shall discuss this another time. We've made Mr. Young's family wait long enough as it is. I can already hear their minds getting restless. The boy should have a reunion with his kinfolk before whatever lies ahead of him. I'm sure you can agree to that, Simisola.*

Elder Adeyemi dropped into a half curtsy. "Very well. Ruby, if you'll join me. There are still a few things I'd like to go over."

"Of course, Elder." Ruby left Manny's side and headed for the exit, but not before taking TJ into a hug of her own. Her large body was warm against TJ's. There was love behind the embrace. TJ made sure to hold her just as tight.

"I'm so sorry about Orunmila," he told her.

She broke away with a subtle frown, but she took his hand in her own in an oddly formal way for her. "Follow the ancestors," she whispered in his ear. "If that means anything to you, have a gander at what I've dropped in your pocket, yeah?"

Had she already known what happened to Orunmila? TJ was about to ask his next question out loud, but Ruby's sharp eyes stayed his tongue. The harsh look on Ruby's face disappeared as soon as it appeared before she gave him a sad smile and said, "Always good seeing you, TJ. Don't be a stranger to Oracle Rock this term, eh? Though… not sure how the Rock will be used this term…"

TJ nodded back slowly. Perhaps too slowly. But no one seemed to notice, particularly the mythical headmistress. And in almost the same instance Oracle Ruby and Elder Adeyemi walked over the threshold back out onto the balcony, the subtle prick of a piece of paper poked into TJ's jean pocket.

Before Adeyemi was out of sight, the Elder gave him a small salute, then tapped at where a pocket would have been within her long robes.

# 8

# PARCHMENT WITH A PINPRICK

MANNY AND AYO SAID THEIR GOODBYES AS TJ WAS WHISKED away by his family, led off school grounds with UCMP protection. The sun was completely gone now, hidden below the horizon by the time TJ was led off school grounds for a celebration. TJ had forgotten to ask, but his brother let him know that it was a Friday evening, the second in the school term.

He fished out his phone. He hadn't checked it since his return. The screen lit up with a flurry of missed notifications.

MOM

Honey bunny, we're so excited to see you! Oshosi says you're doing just fine.

AYO

👋 Hope ur ok. Lots 2 discuss. Stay strong bro.

UNKNOWN

Yo TJ! U back for real? We gotta catch up man!

UNKNOWN

Hello, this is Sarah from Divination Today. We'd love to interview you about your mysterious disappearance and return. Please call back at your earliest convenience.

DAD

Hope you're doing okay son. I don't know who to pray to, but I'm thinking of you.

UNKNOWN

Is it true you're back? It's Dele. Would love to do a follow-up for my last story on you. Remember? It was called 'TJ Young, The Unsung Hero'. HMU at your earliest.

TJ's thumb hovered over the messages, unsure where to start. The reporters' text made his stomach churn. He hadn't even begun to process everything himself, let alone consider explaining it to the public.

Twilight cast a dark hue over the bustling streets of New Ile-Ife, one of the few hidden magical hubs around Nigeria and the former Yorubaland. Magical lanterns of orange and blue crystals lit the unpaved roads, illuminating the way for the late-night merchants haggling prices on potions and enchanted kola nuts.

Several oracle shops had clearance signs.

TJ wondered how much divinerkind knew of what happened to Orunmila. His answer came by way of a *Divination Today* headline he read from an elder holding a newspaper:

*Oracles Accuracy Down 90%, Orunmila Unhappy?*

His family, relieved and overjoyed, decided to celebrate his safe return with a visit to Jollof & Jubilee, a fancy restaurant tucked away behind an unassuming alley of the village.

The establishment was renowned for its blend of traditional Nigerian flavors and modern culinary twists. The significance of Jollof & Jubilee went beyond its culinary delights, however; it was here that TJ, known for his heroism in saving Eko Atlantic, was offered free meals. In fact, most everywhere in the village offered him free food, items, or whatever else he might've wanted—though he usually insisted on paying.

But the restaurant also held memories of his past relationship with the owner's daughter, who fondly remembered TJ as "the nicest boy Eniola had ever been with." Clearly, Eniola had not told

Mrs. Afolabi how neglectful TJ had been in their relationship, resulting in her forcing a breakup.

Upon their arrival, the restaurant staff greeted TJ with a hero's welcome. Mrs. Afolabi, who shared in her daughter's long neck and model-esque smile, beamed with pride. She led TJ and his family to a prime table, declaring, "Tonight, the Hero of Eko Atlantic dines on the house!"

"The hero of Eko Atlantic" was not a title TJ had become accustomed to. It made him uncomfortable. He didn't feel like a hero at all. But now he was getting a taste of what his sister went through during her heyday.

"Oh, Yejide," Mrs. Afolabi murmured into Mom's ear as they were being seated. "You must be so proud. Ifedayo's heroism courses through her brother as well."

Mom thanked the woman, a little bashful but prideful all the same.

TJ squirmed. Dayo had always garnered heroic title after heroic title after she graduated from Ifa Academy. To the point she was deemed the Hero of Nigeria by most. Mom never hid how honored she was to be the mother of one of the most talented diviners in an age. And now, with TJ's exploits, she was ending up with two.

The atmosphere in Jollof & Jubilee was electric, filled with the sounds of lively music, laughter, and the tantalizing aromas of Nigerian cuisine: spices of alligator pepper, yaji, and paprika perfuming the air.

As the evening unfolded, TJ found himself engulfed in waves of affection. Relatives took turns embracing him, each hug and kiss a symbol of their relief. His cousins bombarded him with questions about his adventures in hushed, excited tones. To think just a little over a year ago, they didn't even let him play crossover with them.

TJ's mind was only half present though. Hidden away in his pocket was the note from Oracle Ruby and Elder Adeyemi, its secrets tugging at his attention amidst the revelry.

Despite his best efforts to stay engaged, the note's presence was a constant distraction. The weight of its unknown message made it difficult for TJ to fully immerse himself in the joy of the moment.

Eventually, he excused himself, which earned a complaint from Mom.

"Let him have a minute to himself, Yejide," Dad said. "We've got all those magic police watching this place."

"Thanks, Dad," TJ said before stepping out into the quiet of New Ile-Ife's enchanted night. It was true. TJ spotted at least a half dozen officers lining the alleyway leading to the restaurant. Probably on Adeyemi's orders.

TJ leaned against the rough mud wall of the alley, the sounds of celebration fading behind him as he fished the crumpled note from his pocket. Just as he was about to unfold it, a voice cut through the quiet.

"TJ Young! Hero of Eko Atlantic! Can I get a quick quote for Eshu's Messenger Press?"

TJ's head snapped up to see a young woman hurrying toward him, floating notepad at her side. Her eyes gleamed with excitement, a press badge swinging wildly from her neck as she dodged puddles. "I'm Adanna from EMP. We'd love to hear about your recent disappearance and miraculous return. Our readers are dying to know—"

Before TJ could respond, two figures materialized from the shadows. They wore casual clothes, but their rigid postures and alert eyes betrayed their true nature.

"Ma'am," one of the undercover UCMP officers said firmly, positioning his wide frame between TJ and the reporter. "This area is off-limits to press."

"But I just need a quick statement!" Adanna protested, trying to peer around the officer's broad shoulders. "Mr. Young, can you tell us where you've been all this time?"

The second officer gently but insistently began guiding the reporter away. "We're going to have to ask you to leave, Miss. No interviews at this time."

Adanna was escorted down the alley, her protests receding into the night. Her floating notepad had stayed behind, like it was waiting for TJ to answer. A third officer peeled away from the shadows and set it on fire. Charred paper drifted through the air with the scent of ash.

A mix of guilt and relief careened through TJ. As much as he appreciated the protection, part of him wondered if he should have said something. Anything to quell the wild rumors that must've been circulating about his absence.

Or maybe he should leave all that to Elder Adeyemi...

Beneath the starlit sky, TJ finally allowed himself to focus on the note. With a deep breath, he reached into his pocket and pulled out the folded paper that had troubled him throughout the celebrations. What were its contents? And why was it given to him with such secrecy?

The note felt very similar to one he received earlier that year from Bolawe and the Keepers when they had told him to stop his actions against Olokun and his tidal wave. Just like that note, the piece of paper in his hand unfurled on its own, revealing a lifelike sketch. Only this time, it wasn't Bolawe's face, but Elder Adeyemi's. She wore a small, flat smile before saying, "*Tomorrow morning, just as the sun clears the horizon, meet me at the Abimbola Family Compound. Bring no one else, save Miss Martinez and Mr. Oyelowo. Make very sure you're not followed, particularly by Headmistress Ninki Nanka. Follow the ancestors.*"

Just like the note from Bolawe, this one ripped itself up, its pieces drifting off into the evening winds. A grim sense of foreboding entered TJ's heart. What was he about to get himself into?

# 9

# ANCESTRAL WHISPERS

LATER THAT NIGHT, WHEN TJ'S FAMILY BROUGHT HIM BACK TO the campus grounds, Mom told him she'd be staying at Grandma's house in New Ile-Ife to keep close to TJ this year. And she expected TJ to visit her every weekend, without fail. TJ responded with a silent groan, but gave Mom a kiss and hug.

The moment TJ hit his pillow in his new dorm room, he drifted into sleep, but rest was elusive. In his dreams, he stood amidst a mystical starfield, surrounded by swirling gas clouds that shimmered with otherworldly hues. Orunmila appeared before him, his figure ethereal against the cosmic backdrop. Over and over, Orunmila repeated the phrase, "*Follow the ancestors,*" his voice echoing like a mantra. Images weaved in and out of the gas clouds—faces and symbols TJ couldn't quite grasp but felt deeply connected to.

*Ah, so that's what happened*, an echoing voice rang out in his head.

Two bright orbs flared among the stars, and a familiar bald head of an albino hue materialized as well. Was that… Obatala?

*Yes, it is I, the Dreamweaver. Hello, young one. We have much work to do yet.*

Abruptly, TJ woke up, the remnants of the dream lingering in his mind. The room was dark, but he still had Obatala's eyes plastered in his head. Could he not escape the responsibilities of his waking world, even in his dreams? Or was it just his subconscious playing games with him?

TJ blinked the grogginess from his eyes as he took in his surroundings. Nestled in the roots of an ancient tree, the room was meant for the Senior Secondary School male students. A sharp contrast to his cave-like dormitory from the previous year with the juniors. The walls were alive with the gentle pulse of the tree, and the air was rich with the scent of earth and wood. His bed, carved directly from the root, had a natural, comforting curve that followed the shape of his body.

Beside him, his roommates, including Ayo, slept soundly, their gentle breathing almost a rhythmic lullaby. Ayo was *supposed* to still be in the Hospital Tree, but he requested to bunk near TJ.

TJ carefully extracted himself from his bedding, trying not to disturb the tranquility of the early morning. His gaze fell on the journal Dayo had given him through her best friend, Adeola, back at Camp Olosa. Rubbing the grit from his eyes, TJ flipped through the pages filled with magical theory, personal notes, and cryptic symbols. But some of the details were dim.

*"Imọlẹ Orunmila, wá sí mi,"* TJ spoke the spell phrase, and the scars on his forearm pulsed faintly. He pulled his cover over his head, then removed his gloves from his hand to light the pages more clearly. At least Orunmila's Glow was still working for him. Did it work for Ruby as well? Or would the talent have been lost?

In the dim light, TJ traced the designs that mirrored the images from his dream. They pointed toward something called "the forgotten path," an apparent reference to the ancestral plane. At least… that's what he thought. He still wasn't great with his Yoruba or the iconography of Ifa.

TJ's brow furrowed as he stumbled upon notes Dayo made about TJ himself—about his lack of magic and his unique place in the Abimbola family line on their mother's side. Something about a… curse. Or something about reincarnation? Again, he couldn't be sure with his shoddy translations. But how had he missed it before? He'd been through the journal several times, and now that he had the strange dream, it was as though new information was revealing itself. The connection was unclear, but the implication was that Dayo had been on the cusp of an important discovery. Something that dealt with TJ directly. So she was thinking about him for those three years after all.

That made TJ feel a bit better.

Aware of the time, TJ nudged Ayo awake. It took a few moments, but his friend forced his lids open. When it looked like his eyes were in focus, TJ lifted his glowing hands to his face and said softly, "We need to go meet Elder Adeyemi in the village. It's important. She said we can't be followed."

Ayo, seemingly understanding the gravity of the request or overly eager for another adventure with Orishas, shook the sleep from his face immediately and got ready quietly.

Together, they stepped out into the pre-dawn light of Ifa Academy's forest. The leaves underfoot stirred with energy as they used air-stepping, allowing them to move swiftly and silently through the treetops. Their destination was Manny's dorm, high in the canopy, where the female Junior Secondary School students were housed.

Once they reached the girl's window, TJ shot a concentrated wind blast through Manny's unruly morning hair. Just enough to wake her but not disturb the other girls. Manny's annoyance at being woken early was expressed through grunts and groans. She met them at the window carved out of her tree-top dorm. Her thick hair was wild and flat on one side where she had slept on it, and sleep was caked under her eyes.

TJ still thought she was the prettiest girl he'd ever seen.

"Elder Adeyemi wants to meet with us," TJ explained in a hushed tone as he balanced on a tree branch. "She said to make sure we're not followed. So we should go before everyone wakes, especially the Headmistress."

Manny's face changed as quickly as Ayo's had. With a resigned sigh, she said, "Give me five minutes. Maybe ten. Sade is a light sleeper."

Ayo pinched his nose, before signing with another, "No forget deodorant. You stink, girl. God. Damn."

Manny retorted with a curse that nearly woke the girl nearest her bed, but whoever it was was snoring again in no time.

After *fifteen* minutes, Manny joined them, and the trio began their descent from the treetops. The surrounding forest was waking up, the first rays of the sun piercing through the foliage, casting a magical glow on their path.

As they moved through the forest, the usual sounds of wildlife subdued. There was a sense of anticipation in the air, a feeling that something substantial was about to unfold. TJ knew they all had the same question on their mind: What could Elder Adeyemi want with them? Somehow, they all knew to leave their questions unvoiced until they were off campus. Once they crossed through the guardian statues of Ifa Academy, through the underground entrance chamber, and out into the village of New Ile-Ife, they were met with more UCMP officials.

"Mr. Young," one of them said. "We'll keep our distance today, but we'll be watching you from afar."

"Uh, yeah… thanks," TJ said as he and his friends pulled away out of earshot.

"Do you think Adeyemi is gonna have us cross over to the Court of All today?" Manny asked as the morning wind lifted the two roughly wound dutch braids she had her hair in.

"Doubt it," TJ said. "I have a feeling even Oshosi doesn't have front-door privileges to that place." He shrugged, keeping his voice low as they passed into the village center, where the giant mural of his sister sat behind the Oduduwa statue head. There weren't a lot of people out considering it was early Saturday morning. But TJ wanted to be careful.

"Wait," Manny said. "Don't look—but look. Who's that following us?"

TJ and Ayo looked.

"Ugh, you two!" Manny groaned.

Mirroring their pace were two additional men wearing ordinary robes. When TJ, Manny, and Ayo stopped, they stopped. When the group of friends walked, they walked. When TJ caught a glimpse of their UCMP badges, he let out a sigh. "That's just Adeyemi's people. Remember those two guards I had last year? Looks like I'll have more. Looks like they're trying to keep their distance this time around." Something that was a relief to TJ.

"Oh, right, right," Manny said. "Damn, so if you don't think we'll cross over, then what? Maybe they got word from Oshosi?"

"What about hand mirror?" Ayo signed toward Manny. "Maybe Keepers send new message."

"C'mon, Ayo," Manny said. "You gotta at least try to train your voice. At least a few minutes a day."

"I-I-I d-d-don't w-w-want—" Ayo started to say out loud, but TJ put a hand to his friend's shoulder.

"It's okay, man. Go at your own pace."

Manny groaned. "Nah, don't let him get away with it. It's going to be hard, but he can do it." But she let it go, pulling out her hand mirror. "Oh, shit. The Keepers *did* leave a message! Look!" She twisted her mirror to them. The glass was fogged up with a message that simply read:

*Follow the ancestors...*

"THERE IT IS," AYO SIGNED.

A tremble swept through TJ. If one of the Keepers was at his family's ancestral homestead, it wasn't going to be pretty. For them. His hand tried to curl into a fist but stayed stiff. That only made him angrier. Flashes of Emeka's lifeless body struck his mind like a battering ram. He almost forgot himself until he heard Manny's voice.

"Yo, Teej, you a'ight?" she asked. She and Ayo were giving him worried looks.

"Yeah, I'm fine," TJ bit out. "We're almost there. Just another right past The Walking Stick."

Just ahead of TJ's ancestral compound was the space held for another family close to his own: the Yemisi-Ojo compound. As they passed by, TJ couldn't help but compare it to the old apartment complexes and motels back in Los Angeles. The traditional Yoruba complex had a small courtyard in the middle, surrounded by housing that sheltered extended families. The mud-wall homes with bamboo thatch, nestled side by side, housed members of the same extended family, creating a close-knit community. The compound was mostly quiet, with only a few early risers moving about.

As they moved closer, TJ spotted Titi, Ayo's on-again, off-again girlfriend-not-girlfriend, but more importantly, Emeka's twin sister. TJ jabbed Ayo on the arm, whispering, "I said to make sure we weren't followed."

Ayo looked taken aback, signing back defensively, "Me no think she follow." Then he spoke. "I mean. I d-d-didn't think she f-f-follow us."

Manny interjected, sucking her teeth, "You idiots, she didn't follow us. Listen. She's crying."

TJ and Ayo paused their bickering and refocused. Titi was indeed kneeling and praying before the entrance of one of the homes, surrounded by offerings and flowers. A single picture of her twin brother Emeka rested among the tributes.

Guilt poured into TJ. He felt bad for even thinking she might be following them.

He signaled for his friends to hang back, eyeing the UCMP officials that shadowed them a building down, and the ones in plain clothes farther down. He hadn't seen Titi since he had returned and hadn't visited Emeka's memorial, which he knew he should have the previous night. Carefully, TJ approached her, but a crunch of a branch underfoot caught Titi's attention.

"Sorry, I didn't want to disturb you," TJ said softly.

Titi wiped her tears away. "It's okay. I was about to leave, anyway. I try to come early so I can... do this alone." She swallowed. "Good to see you again. Well, I saw you at the mess hall but you looked busy. I knew Oshosi would keep you safe. Do you... want to sit?"

TJ nodded and sat next to her. She still sobbed, though more quietly than before. TJ could barely imagine the pain of losing a twin; losing Dayo was hard enough. He considered putting an arm around Titi to console her, but he didn't really know her like that. So he just remained still.

After a moment of shared silence, Titi asked, "How did you deal with Dayo's death? The pain... it feels like Emeka just died yesterday. Over and over."

TJ took a moment before answering. Truthfully, he still wasn't over Dayo's death. It still hurt. But he remembered something, and said, "Well, my mom always said... energy never really dies..."

"It's only transferred," Titi finished his thought. "Yeah, *ìyá* says the same thing."

"Right. And sometimes... I feel Dayo's spirit within me. I see her too. Before you and Emeka came to the hospital a few months back, when I visited your cousin, Adeola, I swear I saw her in the mirror, but..." He trailed off, not wanting to sound delusional.

"It's okay. I see Emeka too. All the time." Titi placed a comforting hand on his knee.

TJ didn't think what they experienced was the same, but he knew that wasn't the right thing to say. Instead, he let his eyes fall on one of the offerings at Emeka's memorial—a doll of Obatala, the Dreamweaver.

There was that Orisha again. Was it a sign that TJ actually saw him last night?

The doll was a pretty good rendition of the Obatala TJ met last year—the one who might've infiltrated his dreams last night. It had the same bald head, a clean-shaven face, and a gentle expression of the wise and long-lived Orisha.

Titi explained she had been trying to recall memories with Emeka by touching the doll, using the magic she inherited from her Orisha, Oshosi.

"Do you know what Psychometry is?"

"I think so..." TJ said. "We learned a bit about it last year, right? That day I was in that elective with you. It's the ability to read memories from objects, yeah?"

"Yes," Titi confirmed. "Do you know the principles behind it?"

"Not really. I'm not great at school, in case you hadn't noticed from all of last year."

Titi cracked her first smile, her tears nearly cleared away from her cheeks. "Don't worry, even among Oshosi's divine children, maybe thirty percent know the ability at all, and only ten percent go on to become proficient." She went on to explain the magical principles involved, relating it to Oshosi, who used Psychometry to track animals during his hunts.

TJ lifted a hand. "Is it okay if I..."

"Use that special Ashe of yours to use my ability? Go right ahead." She adjusted her glasses. "Where was I? Oh, yes. The residual energy theory..."

TJ hadn't spoken to Titi much, and he was surprised with how technical she was when speaking. Listening to her was like being in a classroom and TJ wanted for a more casual explanation. But he listened. As he did so, he subtly sapped a bit of her magic, boosting his ability from her own. Touching the doll, using Titi's energy, he got a flash memory. But he didn't see Emeka. He didn't see anything really. Instead, he heard a pair of familiar voices. It was Dayo and Adeola. Had they used this doll before?

*Deola,* Dayo was saying in his head, *you don't understand what you're saying. Opening the ancestral path through Obatala isn't just about reconnecting with the Orishas. There's a reason it's been sealed for generations.*

*But, Dayo,* this voice belonged to Adeola, *we can't keep living in the dark, separated from our heritage, our roots. The Orishas are part of who we are. We need to bridge that gap.*

*I get it. I do. But it's not just about us. There's something else, something beyond our understanding, lurking behind that portal. If we open it, we risk unleashing something we can't control.*

*You keep sayin' that, but you never explain yourself.*

*Because I don't* know *what I'm seeing.* Dayo's voice was angrier now, frustrated. *Orunmila's stars are so faint right now…*

*You can't hide this from the other Keepers for long. When they find out, they'll—*

The memory cut off abruptly.

Titi must've noticed the change in TJ's expression because she asked, with some excitement, "No way! You got it that fast? I hadn't even explained calibration and focus! What did you see?"

"Uh… I'm not sure," TJ lied. "I think I saw… Emeka playing… *Major League Crossover.*"

Titi sucked her teeth. "Maaan, not even Shango could pull him away from that game if he tried." She closed her eyes and smiled, still touching the doll. "You're right. I can almost hear his laughter." She opened her eyes again and nudged her head into TJ's shoulder. "Thanks, TJ. That was a nice memory. It helps to think about the joy he had in his life… when he had it."

"No, um… thank you," TJ said, genuinely grateful, but feeling a bit wrong for not being completely honest about what he had heard. To stave off the unease in his gut, he thanked Titi for the talk and told her not to be a stranger at school.

"Hah, of course," she said, then joked. "Maybe when Ayo and I make up this time—"

"You guys are broken up again!?"

"I'm sure he told you we don't like labels, but yeah, we're not 'technically' an item at the moment. But we always find each other again. And when that happens, we should do a double date with you and Manny."

"Manny and I are *not* dating."

"Yet." Titi gave him knowing eyes. "Two-thirds of all friendships turn into romantic ones. Even more so between best friends." Heat flared in TJ's ears. "Okay, okay, enough teasing. I see them waiting for you at the entrance. Don't keep them staring and gawking."

TJ gave Titi a goodbye hug and, with a final glance at Emeka's memorial, felt a renewed sense of purpose. The mysteries of the ancestral path and the voices he heard in his vision lingered in his mind. He told Manny and Ayo what had just happened as they continued their journey to the Abimbola family compound.

"What do you think your sister was talkin' about?" Manny asked.

TJ thought he finally understood what his sister was so afraid of, what the "uncontrollable source" behind the veil actually was. It could only be one thing.

The God Eaters.

# 10

# TOMORI JOMILOJU

"THE GOD EATERS?" MANNY MURMURED LOUDLY AS THEY LEFT the Yemisi-Ojo courtyard for TJ's family compound, their guard tracking from behind.

"It's so obvious." TJ facepalmed, the effort taxing since he had to use Oya's Wind to do it. It didn't help that he was already drained from the object-reading Titi taught him. "That's why Themis and all those other court deities were trippin' on me breaking a border between the Mortal Realm and the Aqua Realm. I bet this ancestral path is unmarked or something, a way the Keepers originally planned to hit up the Orishas before I came along and leaked them the cheat codes."

"That may be why they also mess with—" Ayo stopped signing and sighed in frustration, holding his hand up to his face as though halving it to represent a reflection.

Manny laughed as she guessed at Ayo's improvised sign. "Mirror realm?"

Ayo nodded. "Mirror Realm is old magic. Not from Orishas, not... fire-water-ground-wind."

"Elemental?" TJ asked.

Ayo nodded again, scowling. "Keepers try hard break through." TJ had to hand it to him, Ayo was getting better with the stand-in signs.

"I don't think the God Eaters are getting through that Court of

All, though," TJ said. "Not with what I saw. All those powerful gods up there just have to be too much. But maybe they're scoping out some backdoor, like this ancestral path or whatever."

"Maybe," Manny said, stopping at the central well. "So, where are we supposed to go, anyway?"

When they had passed through the entrance to TJ's family compound, the UCMP officials shadowing them stopped to guard the entrance. TJ noted the space looked almost identical to the Yemisi-Ojo one, with the central courtyard and the surrounding mud-wall homes with thatched roofing. The only difference was that a water well used by the surrounding community homes anchored this courtyard.

TJ looked around. There was an eerie stillness about them. The usually bustling courtyard—a lively hub of children's laughter and elders chatting on porches—was now ghostly quiet. The silence, punctured only by the songs of birds, left a sense of foreboding. Early morning light cast long, stark shadows across the traditional Yoruba mud-wall homes. TJ got the queasy feeling they were being watched.

Manny gulped when TJ caught her eye.

"Do you remember everything Adeyemi said?" she asked. "Did she say anything else about what we s'posed to do when we get here?"

TJ shook his head, eyeing a black hawk perched on a roof nearby. "Nah, she just said to show up."

"Maybe someone follow us," Ayo signed. "And she not come here until we alone."

TJ gave the black hawk another glance. Was it a shape-shifter? He had met one last term. The bird seemed to be staring at them with a bit *too* much awareness. TJ wished he knew some telepathy so he could secretly say as much to his friends. It sucked that Ayo hadn't learned any yet. Even a talent for animal speech would be helpful at the moment. As TJ considered going back and asking the guards, a whisper sounded beneath his foot.

*"Tomori Jomiloju, down here,"* the familiar voice said. *"By the well!"*

"Did y'all hear that?" TJ asked. Manny and Ayo just shrugged, but TJ searched near the edge of the well, anyway. He found a puddle pooling in a clump of moss climbing up the mud well. Within the liquid, Oshosi's sharp features were revealed.

*"Only you and some of your primordial creatures can hear me in the Mortal Realm, remember?"* He waved with a calloused hand. *"Come down the well. Simisola Adeyemi awaits you."*

Ayo signed, "Bruh, you talk to that small water?"

"Yeah," TJ said, "it's Oshosi again." He turned to the Orisha. "What's going on? What happened after I got yanked out of that portal? You kept telling people here I was fine! I lost two months!"

*"Details, details,"* Oshosi said, waving the notion away. *"Come on down and we'll talk it out. But you'll need a ritual, talking like this is draining my Ashe."*

"What's he saying?" Manny asked.

"He's telling us to drop down the well."

Manny quirked an eyebrow. "Come again?"

"Oh, c'mon," TJ jeered. "We let a giant alligator drown us at camp, and we climbed an endless golden chain to the heavens. This is nothing."

"You go first, then," Ayo signed.

"Our fearless leader," Manny added.

TJ scoffed. "Oh gee, if only I had friends who were aligned with the bravest Orishas." Ayo and Manny crossed their arms expectantly. "Fine," TJ said—but without the confidence he was looking for. He swung his legs over the lip of the well, taking a moment before he jumped. There would likely be water down below. A series of creepy cries were already echoing up to him. More reminders of Eko Atlantic. When would he ever get a break?

"Come on, TJ," he mumbled to himself. "Be the hunter."

"Well, c'mon," Manny egged him on. "Before someone sees us. Adeyemi said not to be followed. And this should be nothing. You're the one who broke the plane between the Mortal Realm and—"

"Okay, okay, okay." TJ waved them away. "I'm going, I'm going." But he didn't jump as he should have. Instead, he gave another look to the roof. The black hawk wasn't there anymore. Maybe it was just a bird after all. And it meant he couldn't use the excuse that they were indeed being followed.

The dark, gaping hole of the well called to TJ with its cold breath. He couldn't see the bottom, and that was probably the point.

He tried to convince himself that he could always slow his fall with some air-stepping if worse came to worst, but doing it and thinking it were two very different things. Before too much fear could seep its way into his heart, he scooted his butt off the edge and took the plunge.

"Ahhh!" he screamed.

The terrible sensation of his stomach leaving his body punched him in the gut—and he was glad he hadn't had breakfast yet. But just as soon as his stomach took the leap, it settled again, and it felt like TJ was floating in the middle of a kiddie pool. Only... there was no water.

*Thank the Orishas.*

"Are you okay?" Manny's voice echoed down to him.

He was about to say he was more than okay and for her to take the jump too, but his voice seemed to reverberate against an invisible ceiling above as he spoke.

"Teee Jaaay!" Manny called down again. "Oh, wait, Ayo's pointin' at something. Is that Oshosi tellin' us to jump too? The puddle you was talkin' to is vibrating."

It was like the voices could go only one way, and he was still slowly descending. But it seemed like Oshosi had gotten the message across somehow, because the rush of Manny's body coming down sounded above, along with her own scream of, "Ahhh!"

"Can you hear me now?" TJ asked.

"Yes!" she answered. "What is this?"

"Well-transport, I guess." It was still pitch black. A moment later, a third set of screams came and Ayo was right above them.

"Oh!" TJ said, a little surprised as his feet met the ground. "I found the bottom. Don't worry, you float down really slow."

"Do you see anything around you?" Manny asked.

"Nothing," TJ answered, squinting against the dark. But something materialized a few yards ahead of him: a purple flame on a torch. "Wait, no! I see something. Someone's coming."

"E-E-Elder Ade-y-y-yemi?" Ayo asked in a stutter from farther above.

"I-I can't tell." TJ rubbed his eyes, trying to make out who was holding the torch. When the figure was fifty yards away, TJ could finally discern two pointed ears and the distinct flapping of wings. It wasn't until the figure was twenty yards away that TJ knew who it was.

"Welcome, Tomori Jomiloju," said Teacher Omo of Fon in her tiny yet rough fae voice, "to Operation Stormbreak."

TEACHER OMO OF FON, WITH HER POINTED EARS AND RHYTHMIC wingbeats, guided TJ, Manny, and Ayo through the underground labyrinth. The deeper they ventured, the more the air thrummed with a palpable magic. It was still dark except for the purple light from Teacher Omo's torch, but colorful, mystical wisps filled TJ's vision. Soon, it wasn't just his unique perception that lit the way. There was more, much more.

Fungi clinging to the walls emitted a gentle bioluminescent glow, casting an otherworldly light on their path. TJ's eyes widened with awe. He turned to Manny and Ayo to see faces identical to what his own must've looked like. Then the space opened up to reveal more.

The heart of the underground domain was a sprawling command center, bustling with activity. Diviners, deep in concentration, were stationed at desks crafted from what appeared to be living wood. The surfaces of these desks undulated gently, as if breathing, displaying a kaleidoscope of magical data and topographical layouts in the wood itself. TJ couldn't help but notice most of those layouts appeared very similar to the Court of All, down to the Olympic pool-sized central fountain and the mechanical statue guards on the outskirts. Despite the curious eyes of TJ, Manny, and Ayo, none of the diviners stopped to look up at their new guests—too engrossed in their work. One diviner threw kola nuts atop an Ọpọn Ìfà, whispering prayers. To TJ's Ashe Vision, there was no evidence of any response at all, and TJ frowned. Another diviner mixed a concoction of potions that bubbled over the vials she desperately tried to cork. And a man nearly as large as a bull peered into a crystal ball filled with mysterious smoke.

"This is a hidden UCMP facility," Teacher Omo of Fon explained, her ebony skin glowing under the dim desk lamps they passed. "Unplotted on any map. Mundane and mystical both. All of these agents are dedicated to this operation on a need-to-know basis."

It was like being in a spy movie, and TJ couldn't help but be filled with a sense of importance. Maybe Manny was right. Elder Adeyemi might have already figured out a way to the Court of All and she was rushing them along before Ninki Nanka caught wind.

Among this hive of activity, a curious pull forced TJ toward one desk in particular. It was more ornate than the others, with familiar carvings—like the ones that littered Grandma's home. TJ drifted closer to the desk to find a family photo embedded in the uplifted wood. The desk even twisted to TJ with a creak, giving him a better look. It was a photo of a group of people. His family. His mother's family: the Abimbolas, frozen in a moment of unguarded joy in the New Ile-Ife courtyard.

*Is this... Grandma's desk? Is she a UCMP officer too?*

"Oh my god," Manny nearly squealed, holding her fists near her mouth. "TJ is that li'l you?"

Out of the corner of TJ's eye, Ayo signed, "Damn, and me think you have a bad hairline at camp. This many more bad."

Ignoring them, TJ reached out to touch the photograph. He wasn't looking at the younger version of himself, who was cut half off from the frame, or his mother or his father, who were smiling broadly. The photo was taken so long ago that even Tunde wasn't there. No. His eyes were only for his sister Dayo. In the photo, she was still a pre-teen, still a couple of years before her time at Ifa Academy. With a single finger, TJ brushed against Dayo's cheek, and his body jolted.

The sensation was immediate and disorienting, plunging him into yet another memory, but it wasn't his. He was looking through Dayo's eyes. As though he were in the world of the photo itself. The younger TJ from the memory looked back at him, his Afro more unruly than he ever remembered it being, his own smile infectious. He never felt this before, never felt what Dayo did so intimately. She had always said she loved TJ, that she cared for him dearly. But to actively feel it in that moment was overwhelming.

Auntie Erika stood in the middle of the New Ile-Ife courtyard. She set up a camera on a precarious tripod likely held up by Oya's Wind or Ogun's Earth, then set a ten-second timer. As she shuffled back to the family, the TJ in the vision left Dayo's side. TJ—in Dayo's body—felt himself frown. Where was he running off to? Her expression changed when she realized TJ was pulling Grandma up from a bench she was struggling to get up from. How had she missed that? Why was it only TJ who noticed?

The camera flashed, and neither the vision-TJ nor Grandma made it into the photo.

*This boy—he's the best of us. So pure, so… innocent.*

No, not the boy… *him*.

It was like TJ was within Dayo's mind and out of it at the same time.

He had to tell himself—no, Dayo had to tell *TJ*. The boy had to know how special he was. TJ could feel Dayo about to say something, her eyes stinging with tears of affection. But before the words could form, he was pulled abruptly back to reality.

"Tomori Jomiloju, there you are!" came Grandma's voice. "So sorry I couldn't make it to the festivities last night. I was helping with a favor for Adeyemi."

There were tears welling in TJ's eyes. He wiped them away before Grandma, Omo of Fon, or his friends could see. Then he stroked the ground before Grandma in respect, saying, "*Ẹ kú arọ, ìyá àgbà.*"

"Oooh!" she said with surprise in her voice. Her thick cheeks pressed into her beady, twinkling eyes. She had to tip-toe to cup TJ's face in her palms. In Yoruba, she said, "*Your Yoruba is much better now, child. I'm proud.*"

"Eh," Teacher Omo squinted a little. "His intonations still need a fair bit of work."

"Yeah… my grandma says that all the time." TJ let the photo slip from his fingers. It landed softly toward the ground but the desk caught it with a branch.

Grandma nodded toward the frame. "Oh yes, such a lovely day that was. We ended up taking another photo, but you trying to pull me in was always my favorite." She pinched his cheeks. "It was your first time to New Ile-Ife. Do you remember?"

Grandma had no idea how much he *actually* remembered. But he wasn't ready to confess that. He still felt half on the brink of tears. "No," he said, a bit choked up. "I don't remember."

"No, you were so young. I didn't think you would. It was a memorial for your second great-great-grandfather's passing day, my mother's father. Do you want to guess his name?"

A rushing sensation flushed through TJ's chest. He did know the name. How could he not? "Tomori Jomiloju?"

"That's right." Grandma smiled and her eyes disappeared as she did so. "*Bàbá-àgbà* Tomori Jomiloju. Lived to be 165. Would have made the clouded record books if he hadn't lived exclusively in a diviner village his whole life. All those cursed were supposed to be blessed with long life, at least—if they grew to be old, of course. But, oh, he was so like you, that man. Kind. Curious. And most notably… clouded." She whispered the last word and elbowed TJ. "There's always at least one in our family line. Well, until you broke the curse."

"Curse?" Manny asked, taking another peek at the photo and cheesing at the younger TJ again.

"Curse you say?" Omo of Fon also hovered closer to the photo. "Did the Abimbolas used to have diviner enemies that I'm not aware of? The Keepers didn't exist back then, did they?"

Grandma shrugged. "No one really knows. We can't trace back that far. But most of the family agrees that *àtúnwáyé* was more likely at play."

That word sounded familiar to TJ, but he didn't remember the meaning. It was Ayo who explained it, of course, as he signed, "Àtúnwáyé. Born again in family line. One thing to next. One bad thing from past family can move to now family."

Grandma looked to TJ and Manny for assistance. Manny was the one to help translate for Ayo.

"Right you are, young man," Grandma said. "The Abimbola's have always had one—only *one*—member of our extended family *without* magic. And that remained true for generations until my grandchild came along and showed the Orishas otherwise." She gave TJ a proud rubbing of his back. "Ah, but no more of that. We shouldn't keep Simisola waiting. Come. She's in the meeting hall."

# 11

# OPERATION STORMBREAK

TJ, Manny, and Ayo stood with open jaws, swallowed by the vast circular room. The centerpiece was a massive table, its surface alive with glowing mist impressions of the Court of All.

*How did they manage that?* TJ thought, then he realized that Oshosi must have helped there.

Like the private desks outside the room, the stone seemed alive, and the command center resonated with a gentle, rhythmic sound of cascading water from an elegant waterfall at the back. Orange and blue crystals lit the craggy walls containing it all. The group occupying the space appeared tightly wound and stressed, their rigid shoulders and stiff backs giving it away.

At the center of it all was Elder Adeyemi. Gone were her usual dazzling robes, replaced today by the colors of a UCMP official—navy with gold trim—woven in an exquisite aṣọ òkè

design. It was a stark reminder of the seriousness of their mission. TJ had only seen her in the garb a handful of times before. He definitely preferred the twinkling robes of floating lilies or whimsical starfields of shooting stars.

Around the Elder sat several individuals, a mix of familiar and unfamiliar faces. Among those unknown to TJ was a UCMP official whose attire resembled that of a Viking warlord, signaling his Norwegian roots. Like Adeyemi, his outfit was homogenized under navy and gold colors—though his thick tunic was sleeveless.

Colorful runic tattoos covered his arms. He and the Elder conversed in low, urgent tones as they turned their eyes up to the trio and Teacher Omo of Fon, who led them.

TJ's gaze then shifted to the group of people he recognized. His mother, with her distinct palm-tree high locs, sat beside Ayo's father, who was the spitting image of Ayo, except for his balding head.

*Grandma* and *Mom are here?* TJ thought.

Maybe Adeyemi had learned her lesson from last year and was involving his family sooner rather than later. That was probably why Ayo's dad was there, too.

Oracle Ruby sat just to the other side of Elder Adeyemi. Her green-dyed locs were tucked away into a navy-and-gold headwrap. Then there was a woman who could easily be mistaken for an older, lighter-skinned version of Manny, her deep dimples prominent even with her serious demeanor. But her long, straight black hair stood in contrast to Manny's curls. And instead of a symbol of the Orishas or the Asgardians, she wore a silver necklace with a crucified Jesus.

"Manny, who's that?"

"That's my Tia Teresa," she mumbled back. "Remember my cousin who died? Jessica?"

"A little bit..." TJ admitted. He didn't remember the name, but he did remember how she looked very much like Manny. Her apparition had shown itself in that submarine when they encountered Yewa in the Aqua Realm.

"Well," Manny said, "that's Jessie's mother."

"I thought you said she was a diviner under Santería? Didn't she give you those Oya earrings you like?"

"She *used* to be. And, yeah, she did. Long story."

A flurry of questions raced through TJ's mind. The things the former headmistress usually had them do were dangerous enough. TJ didn't know how he felt about involving their families.

"What is Elder Adeyemi getting us into?" TJ whispered, his voice barely audible over the hum of conversations and the gentle rush of the waterfall.

Before they could ponder further, Elder Adeyemi stood up, her gaze sweeping across the room, commanding immediate attention. "Welcome, everyone. We have much to discuss and even more to prepare for. Operation Stormbreak is not just about rescuing

Shango and Oya; it's about preserving the very essence of our magic and heritage. And we'll need to work directly with the Orishas to achieve this. Which reminds me..." Her eyes fell on TJ. "Mr. Young, if you would, could you join me for a moment, please?"

TJ nodded smartly and stepped forward. His sneakers scuffed along the rocky surface until he reached Adeyemi. He couldn't see from where he was before, but behind her was a collection of items: Roasted peanuts, trail mix, jerky, jars of milk stirred with honey, manacles, traps, and several bows and arrows.

"What's this?" TJ asked.

"An offering to Oshosi," the Elder explained. "You seem able to communicate with him and others freely. But we wish to speak to him more directly as well. If you would," she gestured a hand toward the open space at the center of the offering circle, "I would like to start the ritual. Just like our lessons from last term. You remember them, yes?"

TJ nodded. How could he forget?

"It will be like with Eshu last year," Adeyemi went on. "However, we'll only have Oshosi for a little while before he's pulled back to the other side by The Great Separation set by the Great Monarch." She turned to the whole of the group. "I will start the prayer. Everyone, follow along."

The Nordic guy took a step away from the group and bowed his dirty-blond hair respectfully. TJ made his way to the middle of the offering circle. Once he stood at its center, the scent of earth and wood filled his nose, and the caress of a gentle breeze brushed along his skin. The strong pull of the Hunter tugged deep within his heart. Adeyemi began her chant, and everyone else followed along:

*Great Oshosi, whose arrow can pierce the sky*
*Whose steps, though light, make earth tremble*
*Whose shadow strikes the uninitiated*
*and shines light upon the initiated*

Energy surged through TJ, and as he learned all last term, he funneled the group's prayers through his own Ashe and pushed it back out to call out to the spirit of Oshosi. But the amount of energy didn't quite add up. TJ searched the room. The man who looked like a Viking merely observed like before. That made sense; his power was with the Asgardians. But Manny's aunt wasn't chanting at all. Instead, she clutched her cross and pinched her lips.

*I pray to you for great protection against my foes and against ill fate*
*Protect me as you have protected all who pray to you with pure heart and good intentions*

TJ tried to make up for the missing link, summoning strength to the point where he stopped using Oya's Wind and allowed his arms to go stiff.

*Protect me as I protect those who are weaker than I*
*I will serve the Light if you do this now*
*Ashe*

"Ashe," the rest of the group repeated, and a wood-scented breeze rushed through the cavern space. The waterfall bent and rippled, and Oshosi emerged—his face sharp and timeless, with eyes that gleamed like the edge of a freshly sharpened blade. His expression shifted with unsettling ease, one moment calm as morning mist, the next brimming with the quiet intensity of a hunter locking onto prey.

TJ took a little jump back, suppressing a yelp.

"What is it?" Elder Adeyemi asked.

*It is The Pathfinder, The Silent Hunter, Protector of Justice*, Oshosi thought-spoke in TJ's mind.

The voice must have sounded in Mom's mind as well, for she stood from her seat, then prostrated—though she did it in the wrong direction. Same with Elder Adeyemi and Oracle Ruby, who curtsied but not toward Oshosi directly. The only one who bowed in the right direction was Ayo's dad, but that probably wasn't intentional.

"What?" TJ canted his head. "You don't see Oshosi in the waterfall?"

"Oh, is that where he's showing up for you?" Manny said, adjusting her curtsey from the table and toward the waterfall at the back of the command center.

*Looks like the boy is the only one who can,* Oshosi said, *which makes sense, considering what I witnessed at the Court of All.*

"What?" TJ asked. "I thought Orishas were communing with mortals this whole time."

"Yes, love," Oracle Ruby said, "But through candlelights and wind through the trees. Not direct voices. Not like this."

Tears welled in Elder Adeyemi's eyes as she asked, "It is an honor, Great Oshosi. Have you made progress with the Courts and their judges?"

Though TJ was the only one to see it, Oshosi frowned. *These past two mortal moons since Tomori Jomiloju's… disappearance, I have tried every diplomatic path I know. Themis and the Court of All refuse to release Shango and Oya, and thus, The Channeling continues. They won't have long. Less than a mortal year at most. So we'll need to take them back by force. We should move during Shango's Equinox, The Hero's Equinox, near the third moon of the new year. He'll be most powerful then.*

"Come again?" Mom asked as she returned to her seat. "Disappearance? I was under the impression Oshosi was watching over my child this whole time."

*That was deliberate,* Oshosi answered. *When you mortals hear of such cosmic events, you tend to think the worst and… what's the phrase you use these days… freak out?"* Mom made a fist over her end of the desk, and Oshosi added, *I knew the boy hadn't passed if that's the worry. The Fates have been showing themselves more often lately. And after Shango's trial, I suspected they had something to do with young Tomori Jomiloju. What's more, I consulted Yewa at her graveyards when I could not find the boy in the Mortal Realm. And she confirmed she had not seen him. It is my understanding that the young mortal here, Manuela, confirmed the same, in her own way…*

Manny blushed. "Yeah…" She seemed to be avoiding the eye contact of her tia at the end of the table, who was giving her a bombastic side-eye—there was probably a story there.

*So all is well.* Oshosi smiled, clearly thinking that would quell all the tension in the room. It didn't. Still, Elder Adeyemi pressed on.

"Be that as it may," she began, "we have other business to attend to. Children, if you would, could you please take a seat next to your family members?" TJ, Manny, and Ayo obeyed. Once they were seated, Elder Adeyemi stood up to say, "Everyone, welcome to New

Ile-Ife. This operation is under the jurisdiction of the United Council of Magical Peoples, but it will not be officially on the record for reasons that will soon become clear. It is why our team is so small. Those outside this room have limited information to avoid potential leaks. All those within, however... will be subjected to the tongue-tied trance." Manny and Ayo gulped. They both had intimate knowledge of that curse.

Elder Adeyemi lifted a hand to the other UCMP officials. "Let me introduce to you one of my closest colleagues, who is joining us from across the globe. Tore Stadheim of Greystone Academy. What we are about to propose to you today is highly dangerous but of the utmost importance. Agent Stadheim, if you would..."

Elder Adeyemi sat as the Viking dude stood up. "Hello, my friends," he said with a much more casual voice than TJ had expected. "I wanted to be a part of this when my enclave received confirmation that the prophecy around Thor's death had been set to stone. I'm devastated to hear that your deities of the storm have been compromised. And from the reports, it would seem like this Channeling is sapping from your divine children as well." He cleared his throat. "Our magic as rune casters works a bit differently. There isn't the same sort of worship loop as there is with your pantheon. With my guidance, I hope to help young Ayodeji with the lightning rune that was given to him by Thor."

"I thought that's why *I* was here," Ayo's father cut in sharply. "It will be me who will shepherd through this storm. We are trueborns of Shango. Our line is a direct one to the Great Hero himself."

*Oh, right...* TJ remembered how stern Ayo's father had been when they were all in a meeting similar to this at the New Ile-Ife embassy. At that time, they were discussing the Olokun attack on Eko Atlantic.

This Tore Stadheim didn't seem phased, however, as he answered, "Your role in this mission will be vital, yes, Mr. Oyelowo. But that ring around your child's finger has little connection to Shango or any Orisha. As you say, you are a trueborn, so your knowledge of how to work the ring—or the 'Uruz' rune, more aptly —would be quite limited. Do you not agree?"

Ayo's hands had been resting on the table. But as soon as the topic of his ring came up, he hid them beneath it.

Mr. Oyelowo looked near to a scowl. "Perhaps that's the reason our magic of the storms is waning to begin with. Because we are not paying enough homage to our great ancestors, and instead, casting them off for other pantheons and their trinkets, which we have no business interacting with."

"Unfortunately, that's not quite it," Oracle Ruby chimed in. "It is The Channeling. We may be able to counter some of its impact—buy us some more time with some extra worship. But it won't be enough."

Mr. Oyelowo groaned; TJ didn't think he was buying it.

"Let us return to our primary objective," Elder Adeyemi began, her voice calm yet firm. "Our plan of attack must be precise and well-informed. This map," she gestured to the detailed layout before them, "shows only what Oshosi has seen, from the so-called judgment room to the halls leading to Shango and Oya's cells."

At her cue, Oshosi's image shimmered within the waterfall at the back of the room, his features sharp and focused. *Indeed,* he confirmed, his voice echoing in TJ's—and TJ assumed—everyone else's minds. *I've traversed these halls as far as I am able, mapping the path from the judgment room to where our Orishas are being held. However, beyond that, much remains unknown, though I have my theories of what we'll encounter.* He paused for a moment, allowing the gravity of his words to sink in. *The Court of All is not designed to kill—but to trap. Deities, by their nature, find it challenging to harm each other, so the most they can do is hinder an escape. It's easier to confine and drain their powers. This jailbreak will not be simple.*

The map, with its limited scope, suddenly seemed even more daunting to TJ. In the past, he had only been able to evade the Orishas or make deals—never defeat one. If the other gods were anything like the deities of *his* pantheon, he wasn't sure what he could do to help.

*This task has a few layers to it,* Oshosi explained as the table display transformed. The first image was a familiar one. A place TJ had visited not long ago: The Sky Realm. It was littered with floating islands holding up several fortresses. *First, we'll need to figure out how to reverse The Channeling via TJ. I've no access to their cells anymore, so we'll need to recruit Obatala and dreamwalk.*

"Dreamwalking?" Mom asked, still answering an inch in the

wrong direction from where Oshosi's face was. "That's advanced magic. University levels, no?"

Elder Adeyemi nodded. "And your son may have the raw ability to acquire it naturally."

TJ chewed the inside of his mouth, eyes dipping to the table of offerings. It was probably true, especially if he would be boosting or siphoning from the Dreamweaver himself. He'd done a good job learning Psychometry from Titi not a half hour ago.

*There's just one issue with dreamwalking,* Oshosi went on. *Most deities do not dream...*

"Oh! I can help there." Agent Stadheim lifted a finger with a smirk. "While it is true the likes of Themis or Yamaraja do not dream—at least not to a point we could exploit—the Asgardians do. So it is my proposal that we infiltrate the mind of Forseti to gather intelligence."

Grandma hunched over the table slowly, interlacing her wrinkled fingers. "Surely Forseti has defenses to ward off such infiltrations?"

*He does,* Oshosi said, *Morpheus of the Greeks is his personal guard. But Morpheus is stretched thin, warding off the God Eaters from dominating the mind of all the dreamers in the End Realm.*

"Wait." Manny lifted in her seat, orange and blue light from the wall crystals mixing over her face. "TJ, you told us Eshu was saying something like that. That his mind was corrupted when he attacked us in the Sky Realm and off the coast."

*Yes,* Oshosi said, *we suspect that was the Eaters playing their tricks. But we can't be sure. There's still so little we know about how they work.*

"This is great and everything," TJ said, "but how are we supposed to get back to the Court of All in the first place?" He looked up to Oshosi. "That golden fountain we came through?"

*No,* Oshosi confessed. *The fountain is too well guarded. We'll need a backdoor instead. Though the fountain will serve as an eventual exit.*

"Does a divine place like this even have a backdoor?" Mr. Oyelowo asked.

"I wonder then if..." Grandma spoke up for the second time. Everyone turned to her. "Perhaps we'll have to use the ancestral paths." She gave TJ a knowing look. Is that why she was part of this mission? Is that why she told him about his second great-grandfather and all that stuff about their ancestors? It had to be. TJ had no idea Grandma was so keyed into their ancestral line. Her expertise was in stafflore. But he supposed it made sense. She was, after all, the closest one to the ancestors at this point in her life.

"Follow the ancestors," Elder Adeyemi and Oracle Ruby said simultaneously.

"Wait," TJ said, "so when Orunmila told me that, y'all heard that too?"

"Atop Oracle Rock, yes," Ruby said.

"We spent many nights there when you were gone," Elder Adeyemi added. "Listening for everything. Anything. And that message sounded the loudest."

Grandma nodded. "We couldn't be sure through our Ọpọ́n Ifa readings with Oshosi. But we could guess through Ruby's algorithms. And it got me thinking. Apparently—as the story goes, correct me if I'm wrong, Great Hunter—Ayo birthed himself from Shango's chest when he was in the Sky Realm. Is that right, young man?"

Ayo shrugged and signed, "Me no know. I no remember thing from other side. Just feeling. But feels right, yes."

The discussion made TJ perk up for once. His dream and the message from Orunmila said as much. "So Orunmila was telling me to go through the ancestral path?" he asked. "And my sister has all these notes about it in her journal. Whatever Ayo did must've gotten him on that same route."

Oshosi's smile grew so wide that more flecks of water were cast from the waterfall, spattering over the manacles and traps on the offering table. *Whew. Glad we have something to go on. Because I had nothing. We are on the right track, then, and Orunmila's sacrifice will not be in vain. Clearly, this will be our backdoor to Shango and Oya.*

"So…" Manny started to say, "we'll just have to be 'birthed' through each of our Orishas to get directly into their cells? And TJ can boost them, get them back to full strength and we make a plan to bust them out? Wouldn't this Court of All sense that?"

*In theory, they shouldn't. The ancestral path has been largely neglected since the start of The Great Separation.* Oshosi nodded, misting more water that landed on Mr. Oyelowo's bald head. *It should be unaccounted for as far as the Court of All is concerned. We Orishas didn't give up all our secrets, after all. I happen to know for a fact that the Celtic gods chose not to bind themselves to the End Realm at all, nor most of the Mesoamerican spirits. And don't get me started on the Abrahamic deities and all the secrets they still hold close to their chests."*

TJ noticed Manny's aunt clutching at the cross on her neck.

"Still, it won't be as simple as just using the ancestral path," Oracle Ruby said. "With Shango and Oya's magic waning, and..." she frowned deeply, "... with Orunmila gone. We can't rely solely on what worked for Ayo in the Sky Realm. We'll need a boost to ensure this 'backdoor' will work."

TJ figured that was his cue. "And by boost, you mean me, right?"

Ruby gave him a so-so head gesture. "Partially, yes. But more importantly, we'll need to tap into the full ancestral tree of both Ayo and Manny, specifically their secondary associations with Yemoja and Ogun."

Mr. Oyelowo bristled. "My family is pure! Ogun has never been a part of our lineage! We claim only Shango, and he to us."

Ruby politely disagreed. "My oracle readings of Ayodeji last term suggest otherwise. No one diviner is ever so 'pure,' despite what our fellows might believe."

Before an argument could erupt, Manny interjected, her voice tinged with uncertainty. "What about my connection to Yemoja? She and Olokun almost flooded Eko Atlantic. No way they're coming through for us."

The room fell silent, the gravity of Manny's concerns hanging heavy in the air. Oshosi spoke up. *As we said, this won't be easy.* His voice became distorted and faded. *Looks like the ritual is wearing off. I trust you all can take it the rest of the way. I'll inform the Courts of TJ's whereabouts, his meeting with the Fates, and how he will stay put in the Mortal Realm. Until next time, my children.* And so he was gone, nothing more than an ordinary waterfall now.

Elder Adeyemi rose to her feet once more. "Oshosi is right. This mission is fraught with risks, and..." She took a beat. It seemed like her lips were struggling to form words, to let her say what she was about to say. "And... what I am about to propose will not sit well with many of you. But know that I exhausted all other options before I fostered this... relationship." She waved a hand toward the waterfall at the back of the room, where Oshosi's face had been. The water rippled and parted, revealing a figure stepping through the cascading veil.

The collective gasp was audible as the one responsible for the drowning of Eko Atlantic, for murdering Emeka, for taking Dayo away from TJ, stepped into the room: Olugbala. Mr. Bolawe.

# 12

# THE ENEMY OF MY ENEMY

BOLAWE HAD AN UNASSUMING FACE, MARRED BY POCKMARKED skin, and an unkempt Afro that gave him a disheveled appearance. He was dressed simply in a white dashiki, his expression neutral, betraying nothing of his intentions.

TJ hated *everything* about him.

Before Bolawe could even utter a greeting, TJ was on his feet, propelled by a surge of anger. His mind was a blur of motion, his body acting on instinct. He lunged toward Bolawe, magic coursing through his veins. Strong and ferocious. TJ's first strike of magic was like a thunderbolt riding a tornado, unleashed with a raw power he hadn't known he possessed.

Then it made sense.

To his side, Manny and Ayo were also on their feet, their own magic braiding with his. Wind howled. Lightning sparked. Pure Ashe swirled around them all, a storm of elemental fury that amplified TJ's attack. Together, they unleashed a three-pronged assault, a vortex of wind and lightning that struck Bolawe squarely in the chest.

The impact was colossal. Bolawe exploded into a thousand pieces, scattering like shards of glass. TJ stood there, breathless, his heart racing. Shock rippled through him as adrenaline quickly leaked out of his fingertips. They had just obliterated a man with a single blow.

*He* had just murdered someone. On sight.

Conflicting emotions warred within TJ—the triumph of strength mixed with a dawning horror of destruction. It was scary… having that power. His teachers had mentioned that Obatala at one time had been even more destructive than Shango or Olokun, but he had sworn off of it. As unabated power coursed through TJ's ruined arms, he could understand where Obatala was coming from.

Before the true impact of what they had done could fully sink in, the pieces of TJ's former mentor began to coalesce. Bolawe reformed in front of them, whole and unharmed, frowning at the trio.

"*And this is why it's important to teach the ethics of Ashe use to our young,*" Bolawe said in an odd tone in Elder Adeyemi's direction. "*Impressive display of magic, children. Not even Elder Adeyemi would've been able to stop you with that speed. I knew you'd find your true Ashe one day, Mr. Young.*"

"Reflexes of true warriors, you three," Omo of Fon said bitterly.

TJ's heart still raced as he stared at Bolawe, reformed and unharmed. He barely had time to process what had just happened when Mom's voice cut through the tension, making him flinch. "Tomori Jomiloju Young!"

TJ turned to see her, Mr. Oyelowo, and Tia Teresa approaching, their faces etched with hard lines and pinched scowls.

"What were you thinking?" Mom demanded, her eyes flashing. She got her hands around TJ's shoulders, shaking them. "Attacking someone without provocation? Is this how I raised you?"

TJ wanted to say yes. If anything, he was following her lead when she attacked that UCMP official last year. But he knew better than to talk back now.

Mr. Oyelowo's deep voice rumbled with disapproval as he addressed his son. "Ayodeji, I expected more honor from you. This reckless behavior is unacceptable."

TJ exchanged angry glances with Manny and Ayo. No way they were taking this lying down. Not after everything. His jaw tightened. If the adults wanted them to act sorry, they'd have to wait a long time.

"Unprovoked?" TJ barked. "You can't be serious, Mom. That's Bolawe. Or did we all forget he's the reason Dayo's dead?"

Manny folded her arms, stepping closer to TJ. "Yeah, last time I checked, we weren't exactly cool with mass murderers." She shot a glare at her aunt. "Unprovoked? Please. We saw him, and we did what anyone with sense would do."

Tia Teresa's lips pressed into a thin line. "That's not how we solve things."

Manny gave a harsh laugh. "Solve? You think we were trying to *solve* anything?" She jabbed a finger at Bolawe, still standing there whole, looking bored. "We were making sure he didn't solve *us* first."

Ayo snorted, then signed, "You think you can play by rules with people like him? Baba, wake up. He kill us if we give him chance."

TJ stepped forward, his eyes blazing. "What were we supposed to do, *Mom*? Offer him tea? Ask if he's found inner peace? We had one shot, and we took it."

His mom's mouth tightened, her hands on her hips. "You didn't *think*, Tomori Jomiloju."

"We thought enough! You want us to stand here, act polite, and hope the guy who *killed our family* plays nice?" The words hung heavy between them. TJ saw it—just for a second—that flicker of pain in her eyes. Mom knew. She just didn't want to admit it.

Meanwhile, Bolawe stood there, untouched, like none of it mattered. Like nothing they did ever would.

And that? That made TJ want to blast him all over again.

His mom stared him down, and TJ could feel the scolding coming before she even opened her mouth. He hated this part—the way they were supposed to act like they'd done something wrong when *Bolawe* was the monster in the room.

Manny sighed first, slow and heavy, like it physically hurt to say the words. "Fine. Sorry," she muttered, kicking at the ground. "Next time we'll... I don't know..."

Ayo huffed through his nose, shooting a sideways glance at his dad before signing, "Yeah... we just react. Sorry."

As TJ muttered his apology, a knot of defiance tightened in his chest. He couldn't bring himself to feel truly sorry. Bolawe's presence here, after everything he'd done, felt like a slap in the face. The man had caused so much pain, so much destruction. He needed to answer for his crimes, not stand here nonchalantly as if nothing had happened.

How in the world had he survived that attack, anyway?

TJ squinted, taking a closer look. His heart wasn't sure how it should beat. Fast or slow? Suspended in a moment. Bolawe's skin had an odd quality to it, the edges refracting light like a mirror.

Then it dawned on TJ.

Bolawe wasn't physically there. Not really. The shards that pieced him back together were the fine lines of a reflection. Glass. Mirrors. TJ couldn't have seen it before. Not with his rage, nor from his distance. But now that he only stood a few inches from Bolawe, he could see it: The imperfections around the man's face. It was like a thousand crystals were reflecting his body. He was somewhere else, projecting himself into the room from wherever he was. The man before them was more an advanced hologram than flesh and blood.

TJ gave Manny a sidelong glance. Did she realize the same thing? TJ's eyes drifted down to her jeans, where light caught the glint of the mirror in her pocket.

Bolawe's smile broadened, clearly noticing TJ's realization. *"That's right. I remain in the Mirror Realm. Your Ashe is strong, but you can't harm me through this projection. You see, Simisola, I knew I couldn't be there in person."*

TJ caught the smallest hint of a scowl under Elder Adeyemi's usually placid face before she turned it into a forced smile. "So it seems, Olufemi." There was a silent heat to her tone. Had she proposed Bolawe be there in person as a ploy to arrest him, to trap him? Only for him to decline, knowing better. What could he possibly have in his possession to be allowed access to their team? He didn't have magic like TJ did. He didn't even have combative skills like Elder Adeyemi. All he had were his despicable followers.

They didn't need them, or him!

"I'm gonna mess you up for what you did to Emeka," TJ said, so low and so cold he almost didn't recognize his own voice. His fists clenched without him even thinking about Oya's Wind, electricity buzzing behind his tight curl.

"TJ!" Mom scolded from behind.

*"Simmer down now, boy,"* Bolawe said, nodding to TJ's arms. *"You have a glowing tell these days, I see."*

TJ glanced down at the gloves covering most of his forearms. It was true, some of the scars on his arm were glowing. He adjusted his gloves to cover them up.

*"Yes, let's not start this alliance with more reckless uses of Ashe,"* Bolawe said.

TJ seethed. Of course, it made sense for the Keepers to get involved. They had always wanted the Orishas to return with full force, as their spirits had in times past. And even the other diviners who respected The Great Separation wouldn't want Shango and Oya becoming mystical dust. Their goals were aligned. For now.

And TJ didn't have to like it one bit.

Bolawe's expression changed then—the same look TJ had become familiar with when he saw the man as a nurturing mentor. *"I'm truly sorry for what happened to that young man."* Bolawe swallowed. *"But I would do it again if it meant bringing back Olokun."*

"You *fucking* asshole!" Manny snarled at TJ's side, her overbite accentuating the expression. Her aunt still had her arm around her, and she held Manny back with a single hand. TJ's Ashe vision revealed an angelic, golden wall holding Manny back. It was strange and made his insides churn, like looking at the arcane magic of those British conservators last year.

"We can't let him get away with it!" Manny shouted. "We can't!"

Elder Adeyemi's face broke for a moment, another quick change that TJ nearly missed had he not been watching for the reaction. A hint of watery eyes. "Manuela. Children. These outbursts have to stop. Too much is at stake right now, as much as I understand how you're feeling."

A deep sickness infected every part of TJ. He hated the feeling. His nostrils wouldn't stop flaring, and he didn't think he could clench his jaw harder if he tried.

"Ruby, if you could continue," Elder Adeyemi said.

"Of course, Elder." Oracle Ruby nodded, though she seemed a bit shaken by the emotional fervor in the room. "The reason we'll need Olugbala and the Keepers' assistance lies with Ayo and Manny's secondary alignments, which will be crucial for traversing the ancestral path. And that 'launch point,' we believe, has to come by way of the Frost Realm."

*The Frost Realm?* TJ recalled his harrowing experience there, where he battled an Asgardian ice giant—a jötunn, Elder Adeyemi had called it. Goosebumps raised on his arm at the memory. A phantom and icy chill ran along the back of his neck.

"Wait," TJ said, "didn't I melt that place?"

Mr. Stadheim sat up a little straighter, his bushy brown eyebrows quirking upward. "You did what, child?" His tone wasn't accusatory, surprisingly. It was... curious.

"By accident! I swear. Long story." TJ's words didn't seem to quell Mr. Stadheim's hiked brows. "What doesn't make sense is those British conservators took what was left of it back to their archive or museum or whatever."

*"And the Keepers took it back."* Bolawe stepped forward, his Mirror Realm form crunching as he walked. *"Yemoja had a hand in creating that space. The claim is hers.* Ours. *Not just the Keepers. All diviners."* He turned to Mr. Stadheim. *"Whatever Asgardian she was working with holds claim to the realm as well. So my cohorts and I set the balance right."* He lifted his hand to reveal a tiny vial. A sliver of blue liquid sloshed around at the bottom.

"You Keepers are crafty, aren't you?" Mr. Oyelowo hummed under his lips, and TJ wasn't a fan of how complimentary the words sounded.

*"We Keepers are resourceful,"* Bolawe said. *"So, let's talk terms. In exchange for this* vital *component, we, the Keepers of The Old Way, request access to the archives of the United Council of Magical Peoples, specifically their records on The Great Separation and the bindings of the Orishas. Additionally, we need assurance of non-interference in our upcoming negotiations with the Court of All and a pledge to support our bid to reintegrate the Orishas into modern diviner practices."*

TJ struggled to process the enormity of what Bolawe was asking for. The Keepers, known for their radical and often violent methods, were seeking access to sensitive information that could potentially give them an edge in their personal war. TJ couldn't shake off a sense of dread.

It would be Eko Atlantic all over again. But probably worse.

Much worse.

"No," TJ said flatly, speaking for the adults before they could answer. "Like hell we'll give you any of those things, *òlòṣí*." Years of keeping a clean mouth in front of Mom went straight out of the window. And it was the first time TJ swore in Yoruba. Not to mention the thick accent behind his words. They felt powerful. "Of course we wouldn't agree to that. You're crazy if you think—"

Elder Adeyemi held up a hand, her eyes locking onto Bolawe's projection with an intensity that TJ recognized as dangerous. Now Bolawe was *really* going to hear it.

"Olufemi, your demands are steep. Access to the UCMP archives is not something we grant lightly, especially to those who have a history of misusing such knowledge."

TJ nodded as though watching a debate on television. Elder Adeyemi was right to be cautious. Giving the Keepers access to those archives was like handing them a loaded gun.

Bolawe's smile didn't falter. *"And yet, without the Frost Realm, your operation*—our *operation—is doomed to fail. The risks you face are far greater without my assistance."*

Elder Adeyemi's gaze didn't waver. "We need guarantees, Olufemi. Assurance that this information won't be used to further any radical agendas. We also require oversight during your negotiations with the Court of All."

*"Oversight? By whom? Your council members? They would only hinder our progress."*

"Then we'll appoint neutral parties," Elder Adeyemi countered swiftly. "Representatives from multiple magical communities who have no direct stake in the Keepers' goals."

TJ couldn't help but think that was a fair compromise. He glanced at Manny and Ayo, noting their equally tense expressions.

Bolawe seemed to consider this for a moment before nodding slowly. *"Very well. Neutral oversight can be arranged, provided it doesn't impede our plans."*

Elder Adeyemi pressed on, her tone steely. "As for the rest… that's a more… delicate matter."

TJ's stomach twisted in disapproval. There had to be another way than siding with the Keepers, in any capacity.

*"You need our help just as much as we need yours,"* Bolawe said calmly.

*"We can't waste time dancing around this issue. Our objectives align more than you realize."*

Elder Adeyemi's silence spoke volumes as she weighed her options. TJ wanted to shout at her to refuse, but he understood the stakes well enough to wait to see what the Elder would counter with next.

"All right," Elder Adeyemi finally said, her voice heavy with reluctant resolve. "I'll campaign that the United Council will support your bid—but only under strict guidelines and review processes established by the UCMP."

TJ's heart sank slightly. That was still giving the Keepers too much.

Bolawe's smile widened triumphantly. *"Agreed."*

"Then the terms are set, Olufemi," Elder Adeyemi said, her words slicing through TJ's previous protest as if it were mere air. TJ wanted to clench his fists at his sides again, but magical fatigue had set in. Instead, his hands just shook erratically.

Elder Adeyemi watched him with an almost resigned demeanor, allowing TJ's quiet anger to run its course. After a moment that felt like a brief eternity, she spoke. "Mr. Young, I know this is hard to accept. But our options are limited. We must prioritize Shango and Oya's safety above all else. It's a bitter pill, but we have to swallow it—dry as it might be."

TJ's jaw tightened, his teeth grinding together as he fought to keep his anger in check. Bolawe, undisturbed by the tension, continued outlining the plan. *"Once we reform the Frost Realm, using the drops we have left, and under Yemoja's guidance—with Mr. Stadheim's assistance, I hope—we can use it as a launch point to the ancestral plane. We will remain undetected by this Court of All."*

TJ crossed his arms tightly across his chest.

*"Then,"* Bolawe continued, *"Ayodeji and Manuela will channel through Ogun and Yemoja here on our side, to connect with Shango and Oya there in the End Realm. And you, Tomori Jomiloju, you will be the conduit, boosting this connection via the use of a constructed staff."*

*Staff? What did he mean by that?* The only staff TJ ever used was Dayo's, and that one had been destroyed when he crossed the planes at Eko Atlantic. Were they going to get him a new one?

TJ's brow furrowed, his mind racing with possibilities, with "what ifs". Could there be another way? A path they hadn't seen? A path where they weren't allied with the Keepers. Bolawe just told them the whole plan. All they had to do was steal the Frost Realm waters back from them. But deep down, he knew if Elder Adeyemi hadn't found an alternative, it was unlikely he could, no matter how much time he put into the Library Tree at the academy. Besides, time wasn't on their side. The Hero's Equinox was only half a year away. A sense of helplessness washed over TJ, mingled with frustration. The Keepers, with all their questionable motives, held the resources they needed.

And there was nothing TJ could do about it.

"And because of this ancestral path," Tia Teresa brought up. "I assume that's why we are here." She gestured between Mom and Mr. Oyelowo. It was the first time TJ had properly listened to her voice. It sounded almost like that old actress Rosie Perez. Where Manny's voice husked, her aunt's voice rasped. They shared in the New York accent, though.

"That's correct," Elder Adeyemi answered.

"You should all attend your family histories as well," Mr. Stadheim added as he scratched his dark blond beard. "You might meet a disgruntled grandmother or two along the way in this place."

Grandma coughed, excusing herself. TJ's thoughts drifted to the possibility of encountering his sister Dayo on this ancestral path. The idea brought an easy lightness to his chest. Feeling her essence—and occasionally seeing her in mirrors—had been comforting, but the prospect of meeting her spirit, as tangible as meeting an Orisha, stirred a deep joy in his heart. Yet his reverie was interrupted as Tore Stadheim outlined the next phase of the plan.

"That's why we—the other UCMP officials outside these doors and myself—can't journey to the End Realm," he explained. "Only those with a direct connection can traverse this path. Ayo's bond with Shango and Manny's with Oya make them essential. Particularly the fact that they have crossed over twice before. The issue then is that this mission's success hinges on a trio of teenagers, which is, no offense, less than ideal."

"They'll be ready," Grandma said, giving each teenager a confident nod. A familiar pride had entered her voice.

"I think that's enough for now," Elder Adeyemi concluded. "The plan may seem daunting, but if we take each step one at a time, I'm confident we shall prevail. Thank you for your time, everyone. Take your rest. Work starts this coming Monday."

After a short while, the room began to empty. TJ, Manny, and Ayo exchanged pointed glares with Bolawe, maddogging him like he repped another gang. In a way, he did. The rude staring was not returned, however, as Bolawe's Mirror Realm form dissolved, making the staredown very one-sided.

Just as TJ was about to leave, Elder Adeyemi pulled him aside. "I'm sorry to put you in that position, Mr. Young. I should have warned you about Bolawe beforehand." She rubbed at the age spots near her temple.

TJ frowned, but nodded. "It's okay."

"However, please know I have a plan for the Keepers," she said. "They are temporary allies, but once Shango and Oya are free, they will face justice. Things are in motion. They will answer for Eko Atlantic; they will answer for Emeka."

An easiness TJ had not felt since the start of the meeting washed over him. So there *was* a larger strategy at play. TJ gave Elder Adeyemi a small smile, and she returned it with a wink.

"See you on Monday?" he asked.

"Oh, no," she said. "Work starts with *you* on Monday, but not with me."

TJ canted his head. What had the Elder meant by that?

# 13

# R&R

Before leaving the command center, TJ wrote a list to keep everything straight in his head:

*1. Gotta figure out how to reverse this channeling thing by dreamwalking with Obatala and Oshosi.*

*2. Open up the ancestral path from Yemoja to Oya through the Frost Realm for Manny.*

*3. Unlock ancestral path from Ogun to Shango using Ayo's Norse ring.*

*4. Complete my staff to sustain the ancestral path ritual to the Court of All jail cell.*

*5. Save Shango and Oya on The Hero's Equinox.*

He looked over the list a second time. Something felt missing. So he wrote:

*6. Don't die.*

Back topside, the afternoon sun hung high in the sky, a blazing orb that bathed the New Ile-Ife village in a warm, golden glow. It was the kind of day that, under normal circumstances, would have filled TJ with a sense of joy. But today, the sun's cheerful rays seemed to mock his inner turmoil. He stood a few feet from the well that led them down to the secret UCMP command center, along with Mom, Grandma, Manny, and Ayo. As he stood there, the enormity of Operation Stormbreak pressed heavily on his mind, eclipsing any warmth the sun could offer.

He had just gotten over—no, just *started* to get over all that happened at Eko Atlantic. He could barely process that nightmare, even now, yet here he was being thrust into another one that even a well-adjusted adult would have trouble handling.

"Well, you get back to Ifa Academy like Elder Adeyemi says, honey bunny." Mom pinched TJ's cheek, her face scrunched up with her usual mix of pride and concern. Did she feel the same as TJ, or would she expect him to rise to the occasion? Again. "You have everything you need, right?"

TJ wanted to say more of what was on his mind, but instead, he simply nodded. "Yes, Mom," and then subtly pushed her hand from his cheek. He didn't want to unload on her. She'd just freak out, or worse, try to help in her overly protective way.

"And say hello to Staffmaster Bamidele," Grandma added. "We're old friends. For all this to work, we'll need to make sure you're fully attuned with a staff built by your own hands. Very, very important." Her forehead wrinkles sunk into her brow. "Do you understand?"

"*Bẹ́ẹ̀ni, iyá àgbà*." TJ nodded affirmatively, realizing then that's what Elder Adeyemi meant by "his work starting on Monday."

"Like Grandma told you, we'll be just here in the homestead." Mom thumbed to the courtyard. "Whenever you need anything. *Anything*. Come to us."

She was giving him an opening, but TJ decided not to take it. He knew it wouldn't result in anything. He was uniquely designed for this specific job. There was no real way out of it. Coping with it was the only thing he needed to worry about.

"No wahala, Mrs. Young," Ayo signed, the Yoruba phrase easier to produce in YSL—go figure. "We watch back for TJ."

Mom and Grandma looked to TJ and Manny for a translation, which they offered.

"*Ah!*" Grandma said in Yoruba. "*Thank you very much, young man.*

*It was good seeing your father out of that office of his for once, especially after all he's been through."*

Ayo frowned. What had Grandma meant by that? It felt like something more than just Mr. Oyelowo losing his son for a few months. Had he gone through some other turmoil recently?

Ayo signed back, "It is very rare, yes."

After a pair of embarrassing kisses from Mom and a nice long hug from Grandma, they all went their separate ways. The comforting presence of Manny and Ayo by TJ's side was a small solace as they prepared to head back to Ifa Academy, but even their familiar camaraderie couldn't fully lift the cloud that hung over TJ.

"How are you guys feeling?" TJ asked as their feet found the main road back to the academy. There was more bustle now as village folk mingled among colorful market stalls, enchantments sparkling in the air. The rhythmic beats of drums echoed through the bustling streets. "I mean," TJ went on, "we've been through so much already. Sometimes I wish we could just, you know, be students. I mean, look what happened to you, Ayo."

"No, man, me big excited. We save Shango? Big cool." Ayo gestured, but clearly his distinct voice was not coming through with his less-than-perfect signing. TJ pressed his lips into an awkward, thin line. He was surprised Ayo himself wasn't more shaken up. But maybe how Manny's toned arms told of her coping mechanism, feigned enthusiasm was Ayo's. Or perhaps Ayo hadn't grown a healthy enough concern for what was going on because he only had the feeling—not the memories—of what happened on the other side. Manny remembered it being dangerous, at least. Ayo's takeaway was much different, apparently. Or he was in denial.

"And, you know," Ayo's signing gestures grew more serious and less exaggerated, "Maybe this show my dad… Maybe he see… see me… that me good like others in family."

TJ wasn't very familiar with Mr. Oyelowo. He'd only seen him twice, both in meeting rooms where they sat across from each other. From what little he gathered, TJ assumed Ayo's relationship with his father was strained. To what extent, he wasn't sure. Ayo refused to talk about it much, even to TJ and Manny.

TJ nodded toward Ayo. "Hey, what about your mom? Maybe

she can get your dad's head on straight. My brother pits my parents against each other all the time."

Ayo's frown stretched down farther as he shook his head. "No, she no can do nothing."

TJ twisted his face into a small scowl, but he let it go. To say Ayo wasn't a trueborn of Shango seemed off the mark. If Mr. Oyelowo had seen what Ayo was capable of in the Sky Realm, seen his ability to craft his own lightning portal, he would've changed his tune.

As they passed by Anansi's Arcade full of Ifa students, Manny perked up. Apparently, it was a newer spot, only opening a few months ago when a few Akan people immigrated from their village to New Ile-Ife. The entrance was shaped around Anansi's large mouth like a carnival show. He wore a tophat with spider webs and his large eyes followed each person who walked in. A little girl hid behind her mother's leg as they entered.

"In fact," Manny peeled to the right, pulling TJ and Ayo by their wrists, "what we need to do is get our minds off this. TJ's right. We need to be kids. The Orishas might not need time off, but *we* do. Plus," she nodded to a large table with *Major League Crossover* on it, "I gotta whoop y'all's asses on this game a few times to settle my nerves."

"Pfft, y-y-you wish," Ayo responded automatically, forgetting to sign. He looked around the arcade wildly, clearly hoping that no one heard him. But most of the students had their noses pressed deeply in their own games.

Manny gave Ayo a stormy look. "You're on, big head."

Manny and Ayo raced into the arcade, bobbing and weaving between the game stations and the teens lining up for their turns. The arcade was a maze of enchantment, draped in the delicate threads of Anansi's spiderweb. The entire space seemed woven together by silken strands that stretched from wall to wall. The very walls held several carved images of Anansi, watching and smiling at all the patrons that passed through, just like the large one outside. For a moment, TJ wondered if these animated Anansi were anything like the dead one he saw. Some of their beaming grins flashed to frowns, and TJ had to rub his eyes.

*No, TJ, stop it. No thinking of dead gods. Think of the here and now.*

Opening his eyes, he focused instead on a group of JS2 students huddled around a game called *Baobab Spirits.* Players took turns placing seeds into carved hollows. Each move released a trapped spirit, granting fleeting magical abilities—time-slowing or teleportation—that could turn the tide of the game.

"Aha!" one boy with wild curls shouted. "I got you now."

"Nu uh, watch this!" another student with cornrows replied, summoning a hidden seed that eliminated half of her opponent's board.

TJ smiled. The game reminded him of an extreme version of *Mancala* that he played with his grandmother on Dad's side—Mom called the game *Ayo Ayo,* though.

In the corner of the arcade, a group of elders gathered around the *Djembe Drums of Destiny,* their wrinkled hands moving with surprising speed and precision. They pounded their hands on a set of drums. As they played, the surrounding air twinkled, elemental spirits appearing in response to their flawless rhythms.

"Baba! Are they real spirits?" a wide-eyed child asked.

"Oh no, those are just echoes."

The elders smiled, their eyes flashing with youthful excitement, as fire sparked and water swirled to the beat of their drums. The final rhythm called forth a powerful Spirit of Harmony, casting a radiant light over their triumphant faces.

TJ slid past them and found Manny and Ayo near the back, where the *Major League Crossover* tables were stationed. The setup was a marvel. TJ was used to playing on sets that were the size of a chessboard. But the ones in the arcade were like a giant foosball table, but alive. Miniature players, no taller than a few inches, zipped across the field, air-stepping and hurling mini earthballs. Tiny spectators cheered from the stands, their high-pitched voices rising in excitement. It was clearly the most popular game, with half the space filled with enormous playtables and teenagers pushing into each other shoulder to shoulder.

It took all of five minutes for Ayo to lose his first game to Manny.

"All right, y'all, prepare to get schooled," TJ said with a grin, rubbing his hands together.

"Yeah, yeah, you're about to see a master at work," Manny shot back, flashing a confident smile.

TJ chuckled, positioning his hands on the controls. The moment the game started, TJ dove in with competitive fervor. His lead attacker wove through the field, tiny playball in hand, darting between Manny's defenders. The audience erupted into cheers as TJ executed a perfect pass to his roamer, who air-stepped over Manny's defender and hurled the playball into the totem. A tiny explosion of confetti burst over the field as TJ celebrated.

"That's how it's done!" TJ exclaimed.

"Nu uh, silly," Manny said. "Did you forget that was the playball, not the scoreball?"

"You still need crossover," Ayo signed. "Other side. Move. Other side. Go go." But it was too late. One of Manny's defenders stopped TJ's attacker with an earthball and took possession of the scoreball. It wasn't long after that when Manny reset the playball and went on to score on TJ again, and again, and again, making TJ's winning moves a distant memory. Ayo facepalmed.

Hours passed in a blur of laughter and friendly trash talk. The arcade hummed with energy, and even more people gathered to watch and join in. Umar showed up a little while later with his crossover friends. But they left when Ayo beat them three times in a row. Even Tunde showed up with half the juniors in the school—popular as ever—but they left when they realized Manny couldn't be beaten. TJ didn't mind though. He could lose to Ayo and Manny all day. Especially Manny. She, like always, was on fire, scoring crossovers with precision, and TJ always liked the way her forehead creased when she concentrated, the way her overbite came over her lips just before she scored. She played the game just like she did on a real crossover field.

Before they knew it, the sun dipped below the horizon, casting the arcade in a deep shade of amber from the wide opening of the entrance. Outside, the crystal lights flickered on, but inside, the game continued, the field lighting up with every magical play. The pressure of TJ's real-life challenges faded with each crossover, replaced by the simple joy of competition.

But eventually, even the endless magic of Anansi's Arcade had to wind down. A loud, jovial voice echoed through the space. "A'ight, kiddos, it's closing time!" The owner, an older man with a fila cap littered with spiderwebs, approached, wiping his hands on a cloth. His accent sounded Caribbean. "I know y'all are having fun, but the arcade needs its rest too."

"Awww, c'mon, j-j-just one more g-g-game?" Ayo pleaded, his hands still on the controls.

"You've said that the last three games," the owner replied with a chuckle, gently prying Ayo's hands from the table.

With exaggerated sighs, they all stepped back, as the tiny players on the field slowed down, waving at the mini audience as they disappeared into their tiny locker rooms. The arcade quieted, the once bustling energy simmering down to a dull hush.

"P-P-Please, c-c-can I p-p-play some m-m-more, s-s-sir," mocked a voice from behind, near the entrance. Two guys and a girl. The guys looked familiar, the girl not so much. TJ squinted. One of the boys was taller than the other, dark-skinned. The shorter of the two had a lighter brown complexion closer to TJ's, but TJ still couldn't remember who they were. It wasn't until the boys did an elaborate handshake and dap that resulted in floating leaves around their arms and fire projected from their mouths like dragons that TJ recognized them.

"Holy shit!" TJ whispered. "Is that Jimoh and LaVont? From Camp Olosa?"

"Yes." Ayo nodded. "Baba say they get accepted back. Me no believe him."

TJ and Manny threw rude gestures their way, but they were already strutting off. When they turned to Ayo, he was frowning.

"Ah, don't listen to those *assholes*," Manny said, placing a hand on her friend's back.

TJ looked over his shoulder again. "I didn't even know they were back this year."

LaVont and Jimoh swaggered away, their jeers trailing behind them like an obnoxious echo. TJ hated the way they walked, each step oozing arrogance—as if they owned the village. It wasn't just their attitudes, but the way they talked down to others, always looking for someone to belittle. They were the epitome of everything TJ used to hate about Ayo, back when Ayo was still a bully, back before he knew there was more to him.

TJ glanced at his friend, who stood there with his shoulders hunched, his earlier excitement deflated by the mockery. Ayo's stutter was something he couldn't control, at least not yet, but that didn't stop jerks like LaVont and Jimoh from using it against him. It wasn't fair, and it made TJ's body shake.

Manny stepped closer to Ayo, her hand still on his shoulder. "Hey, don't let those idiots get to you. They don't matter."

"Yeah," TJ chimed in, "They're just trying to make themselves feel big by puttin' you down. It doesn't mean anything. They didn't even say it to your face 'cause they know you'd mess 'em up in a straight duel."

Ayo's frown didn't disappear, but it softened a bit. He signed, "They... always... do this."

"Yeah, and they always will because they got certified small d—" Manny stopped herself as the owner passed by again. "Sorry, sir! We're leaving right now, sir!" She pulled her friends toward the entrance as she said, "You know what energy I'm talkin' about. Just remember your stutter don't define you, Ayo. You're better than them."

TJ nodded, trying to catch Ayo's eyes. "I mean, c'mon, man, you're one of the last people to hang out with *the* Thor. And I know you don't remember how you crafted that lightning portal in the Sky Realm. But that shit was amazing."

"Mad dope," Manny agreed, even though she wouldn't have remembered either.

"None of them could do something like that," TJ added.

Ayo's expression wavered, a small flicker of pride in his eyes. "T-T-Thanks, you guys."

"Anytime," Manny said, letting his shoulder go and punching it instead. "Now, let's get out of here. I'm starving after that Grade-A butt-whooping I just gave you both."

TJ smiled as they made their way out of the arcade, the warmth of their camaraderie making the lingering shadows of LaVont and Jimoh's mockery fade. TJ glanced back at the darkening arcade. The giant Anansi closed his eyes, as though to go to sleep, and his mouth began to shut with the doors.

For a few precious hours, TJ had been able to escape into the game, into the simple pleasure of playing—or mostly getting his butt handed to him—with his friends. The pressure of the real world would return soon enough, but for now, as they walked out into the cool night, TJ felt lighter, his heart lifted by the playful competition and the bond he shared with Manny and Ayo.

Manny was absolutely right. They needed that.

So, out of the blue, as they passed by Mami Wata's, TJ gave her a big hug, then gave Ayo a one-armed embrace, somehow skipping all the while.

"What was that for?" Manny asked. Ayo's slanted brow asked the same question.

TJ shrugged. "Just 'cause."

BACK AT THE ACADEMY, TJ, MANNY, AND AYO GRABBED BOWLS full of puff puffs and steamy mugs of tea from the mess hall. Then they found themselves a patch of grass near the whispering willows, where they could crack jokes and watch the herons skid across branches for a place to sleep. TJ lounged along a tree as Ayo pulled out his crossover board to rematch Manny. TJ almost felt like a dog being treated to his favorite things before being put to sleep. The difference was that the dog had no idea what would come at the end of the day; TJ knew exactly what was coming for him.

The sweet munching of puff puffs, and the crisp evening air on TJ's face, helped to keep those thoughts away though. The laughter around the whispering willows was a soothing balm after their intense game at the arcade. But suddenly, the peaceful atmosphere shattered as pounding feet sounded all around. All of them headed for Oshun's Lake. Through the hanging willows, TJ could make out the figures of other students. Curious murmurs rippled through the crowd, and TJ exchanged a glance with Manny and Ayo.

"Let's go see what's up," Manny said, already on her feet.

They followed the growing crowd toward the lake, where large groups of students had already gathered, their faces illuminated by the soft glow of swarming fireflies. Voices hushed as all eyes turned to the water. It shimmered under the moonlight, the surface glistening with a radiance that seemed to pulse in time with the faint whispers of Ashe in the air.

The water rippled. Slow at first, then with a steady rise, as if something massive stirred beneath. A deep, resonant hum echoed from the depths, sending a shiver through the crowd. The lake surged upward, and from its glimmering depths, the head of Ninki Nanka emerged.

Her giraffe neck, long and elegant, rose gracefully from the water, glistening with droplets that caught the light. Delicate, spiraling horns crowned her head, and her shimmering scales reflected shades of emerald and gold, glowing faintly as though they had captured the essence of the lake itself. She moved with fluid ease, her neck arching high above the surface as she glided in slow, deliberate circles. The lake shimmered, shifting like liquid silk, until the entire surface transformed—undulating and alive, it morphed into a massive, living canvas. It flattened into a glass-like screen.

"What's going on?" TJ asked, spotting Umar in the crowd.

Umar shrugged, his eyes fixed on the water. "There's supposed to be some big announcement from the UCMP on *Divination Today* right now."

TJ's stomach twisted. He couldn't shake the feeling that something bad was coming, especially after that meeting. The crowd hushed as Elder Adeyemi's face appeared on the watery screen, her expression serious and forlorn. Superimposed over her UCMP uniform was her name and position as she said, *"Greetings, Divinerkind. I am here tonight to confess something I had hoped dearly not to be true, but it must be said honestly: It is with great sorrow that I bring news that Orunmila, He Who Knows the Stars, has passed from our higher planes and will no longer guide we Ashe-users in the way of divination…"*

Gasps echoed through the crowd. Some students clutched each other in disbelief, while others stood frozen, unable to process the news. TJ's eyes darted to Oracle Ruby near the shoreline. She was looking like a standing corpse. A few teachers patted her on the shoulder. Teacher Ikenna rubbed her back, his hyena head cooing through his locs.

"That's why I can't predict anything half a damn," John said, rubbing his gray beard.

"But… Orishas can't die, can they?" Fatima held her head in her hand. "Who could kill them?"

Titi stepped up to TJ, her head constantly shaking. "Energy doesn't die; it's only transferred, right, TJ?"

TJ couldn't answer her. He had seen what happened to Orunmila, and deep down, he feared it was more permanent than anyone realized. Adeyemi continued speaking, her tone somber as she alluded to needing the help of all diviner hubs worshiping the Orishas for a great undertaking. Though she didn't mention Shango or Oya, TJ suspected she was referring to their rescue mission.

*"I know this news will come as a great shock to most. None more than those who were claimed by Orunmila as his divine children."* It almost looked like the Elder's eyes fell on Oracle Ruby. *"But know that we need all anointed hands in these trying times. I fear that Orunmila may not be the last. I will be touring all magical hubs that hold any number of diviners, from the coasts of Nigeria and Benin—to our brothers and sisters in the diaspora. In the coming weeks, I will share more information as it becomes relevant. Just know that the United Council is fully backing our efforts."*

As the announcement ended, Adeyemi took questions. TJ felt eyes turning toward him, a pair, then four, and more, their gazes heavy with expectation and curiosity. The weight of their stares was unbearable. When it came to the Orishas, he was the one who was supposed to have all the answers.

"I need to get out of here," TJ muttered to Manny and Ayo, who nodded in understanding.

He raced back to his dorm, his pulse pounding. After everything he had done, everything his sister did, everyone would be on his case. Everyone would have their questions. But TJ couldn't deal with it right now. He needed time to think.

Once inside his dorm, TJ dove under his covers, pulling them tightly around him. The world outside could wait. For now, he needed the safety of darkness and the escape of sleep.

Thankfully, he was too tired to let the stresses of the Court of All and Adeyemi's announcement pile on. The last thing he remembered was falling headfirst into a dream. It wasn't until a little while later that he regretted not staying up a few more hours. Because what awaited him was *not* what he expected.

# 14

# WHAT DREAMS MAY COME

As consciousness slipped from TJ's grasp, he found himself drifting through a familiar dreamscape. At first, the scenes were mundane—laughing with Manny and Ayo by the willows, air-stepping to class with a stack of books threatening to topple from his arms. But gradually, the dream shifted, taking on an other-worldly quality that made the hairs on the back of TJ's neck stand up.

The academy grounds warped and twisted, hallways stretching endlessly before abruptly shrinking into tiny doorways. TJ floated through walls that dissolved like mist, only to find himself in peculiar spaces—underwater classrooms where fish swam between desks, or upside-down libraries with humanoid books checking out books.

As TJ navigated the surreal landscape, the dream continued to morph. One moment he was falling through clouds made of cotton candy, the next he was sprinting across a room of scales where acid-green liquid bubbled far below. The transitions were jarring, leaving TJ disoriented and unsure of what was real.

Suddenly, the chaotic dreamscape stilled into a flat glass wall, a wall TJ was familiar with. It was like seeing out the eyes of a fly or a kaleidoscope without the rainbow fragments. Within the fractures, two figures materialized before him: Oshosi and Obatala. Oshosi's feather-capped head emerged first, followed by his sharp wood-like features, a bright grin plastered on his face. Obatala, in contrast, came into view with a bald, pale head and an expression of perfect stoicism. Their giant forms, like always, were imposing.

"It worked!" Oshosi pumped the air behind the glass. "We got through to you. I wasn't sure if it would be possible, given your unique nature of being mortal but not..."

TJ blinked, trying to process the situation. "We really startin' the dreamwalking *already*? I just wanna crash after this crazy-long day. Adeyemi just told everyone Orunmila is gone, and everyone's finna have eyes on me."

"Did she really? Interesting. You mortals tend not to take information like that very well."

"She's doing it because she believes it will help her campaign the mortals around funneling prayers to your Operation Stormbreak, young mortal," Obatala said, pushing the glass inward with a single finger like a door at the mall. "At least, that's what her dreams tell me. I've been keeping an eye on hers with great interest."

He gestured for TJ to come inside. TJ started forward. Hold on! He wasn't walking, but *floating*, just like he had when he was in the Sky Realm. A tiny human among giant deities.

"Wait!" TJ said, not pushing through the threshold given to him. "I can't pass over. Themis and the Court of All will know."

"No, they won't." Oshosi smiled again. "That's the beauty of our own efforts here today. Come on in, we'll explain everything."

TJ canted his head and swallowed hard, but he went forward, floating into the space he had been in only half a year ago: Obatala's dream room. It was an endless hall of refracted glass that had no ceiling or floor from what TJ could tell. It was just one long tube. Each window looked into the mind of mortal dreams. And it seemed these Orishas had hijacked TJ's own.

"You see," Obatala gestured all around, "you are not truly in the Sky Realm. Think of it like astral projection or ghostwalking."

"In other words, the perfect loophole to our deal with the Court." Oshosi's expression grew serious. "Though don't go telling that to Themis. She would be most displeased with us playing fast and loose. But listen, we need your help to infiltrate Forseti's mind right away. Daydreams at first—they're fast and sporadic, making it harder to detect us, but also harder to decipher."

"Detect us? You mean what you mentioned about Morpheus being Forseti's personal guard?"

"Exactly," Obatala said, floating down at eye level with TJ. "Dreams play a significant role for the Asgardians. For some, it's what makes them more human than gods in certain divine circles. But their dreams often serve as a means of prophecy or divine communication. For example, Baldr dreamed of his own death, which set off a chain of events leading to Ragnarök, the end of their world."

"And it's my working theory," Oshosi added, "that after the appearance of the Fates, Forseti has been inducing dreams in hopes of communicating with them. But it opens himself up to God Eater influence."

"Like… Eshu?" TJ asked.

"Possibly, yes."

"Don't worry too much about the Gatekeeper," Obatala said. "Ever since you released me from his staff, I've been monitoring and shielding his mind as best I can. Though he doesn't know it. And I'd like to keep it that way, please."

TJ nodded, happy to know nothing else would happen where Eshu was concerned. At least for now.

"By the way, young mortal, I never thanked you properly for that ordeal with Eshu."

TJ threw his hands up nonchalantly. "Of course. Any time for an Orisha."

A long and eerie tone thrummed from above, and Oshosi cut in. "We don't have a lot of time to explain. Forseti might be falling into a daydream any moment now. He is charged with hosting The Channeling of Shango and Oya this moon. So, in his meditative state, he may slip momentarily."

A familiar knot of anxiety formed in TJ's stomach. "How do we get in and out of Forseti's mind?"

"That's where a hunter's touch will be needed," Oshosi said. "We can't enter or leave until the subject's consciousness shifts. It's when their veil is weakest. In fact, that's how we're entering your mind now. You've not fully fallen asleep quite yet. But with someone with a powerful mind like Forseti, we need to start with daydreams, then naps, and finally to full slumbers. The reward is information on how to reverse engineer The Channeling. If we don't figure that out, this entire mission falls apart."

"In addition, should Morpheus detect us," Obatala added, "we could be trapped in the Dream World or face the wrath of the Court of All. We aren't breaking any accords with the Court, but there is some ethical etiquette between deities that we are more than bending with this plan."

Despite his reassuring tone, Obatala's words did little to ease TJ's concerns.

"But first," Oshosi said, "we need to establish a connection."

TJ swallowed hard again. "And… how do we do that?"

Obatala's eyes gleamed once more. "Tell us, young mortal. What do you know of the art of Psychometry?"

"Um, I only sort of kind of learned about it." TJ's mind went to his meeting with Titi, and the vision he saw from the past. "I mean, we learned about it in school, but I didn't actually use it until my friend showed me today, before I slept. I heard my sister—saw her too. Actually, I sort of *was* her."

Oshosi and Obatala gave each other profound looks.

"What? Is that good? Bad?"

"For our purposes, mostly good," Oshosi said. "Let's begin."

TJ's eyes widened as Oshosi produced a thin, silvery chain that seemed to shimmer with an odd luster. Depending on how the light from the dream room caught it, it looked more like a golden ribbon or rope.

"This is *Gleipnir,*" Oshosi explained, holding it up. "Forseti used it on Shango during his trial."

TJ leaned in, fascinated. In Oshosi's hands, it looked like an ordinary thing, but as he floated closer, its individual links were as large as a basketball hoop. "What does it do?"

"It's said to be unbreakable. Made from impossible things like the sound of a cat's footfall and the roots of a mountain. Arcane magic. Not something we Orishas, who favor the elements, deal with most of the time. This chain can bind even the mightiest of beings. So Shango never had a chance."

Now that TJ had a better look at it, he did recognize it as one of the many chains the Court of All had wrapped around Shango's body. But that left one question…

"Wait," TJ said, just before touching it. "How did you get that? I thought you were banned from the Court."

Oshosi's lips curled into a mischievous smile. "Let's just say before I was iced out, I did a bit of light ... *borrowing* from the Court's stores."

Obatala shot Oshosi a disapproving look. "A dishonest approach, my old friend."

"A hunter must adapt." Oshosi shrugged, unrepentant.

Obatala closed his eyes and shook his bald head. "You and Eshu are too alike these days."

"You'll be happy to know that Oya and Shango share in your sentiments. Nonetheless, the Trickster has his merits. *Sometimes*."

Obatala sighed and turned to TJ. "Now, young one, let us teach you about Psychometry. Every object has a memory—an imprint left by those who have interacted with it." TJ already knew that thanks to Titi but he wasn't about to interrupt an Orisha.

"Right," Oshosi chimed in. "The key is not just to observe, but to track those memories—like a hunter follows a trail."

TJ nodded. He had an easy enough time following the paths with Titi. If he was going to be helped along by two Orishas, it would be much easier. Only now he would be dealing with a god on the other end. With Titi, he just got a glimpse of his sister and family.

"By combining our powers," Obatala continued, "you'll be uniquely able to use both observation and tracking. You're perfectly suited for this role, young one."

"Okay," TJ said, as a nasty bit of anxiety bubbled up in his chest. "So, what do I do first? And, uh, this thing doesn't come with a 'how to avoid being cursed' manual, does it?"

"Heh, no," Oshosi said. "An Asgardian or another rune warrior would have to activate its properties. For us, we just need to get a reading off it."

TJ floated in the ethereal dreamscape, wishing he had solid ground to gather his bearings and settle his mind. The walls of glass surrounding them pulsed with the countless dreams of mortals. And at the moment, a collection of nightmares cascaded over the many reflections. Obatala and Oshosi flanked him as well, their presence a touch intimidating as their images superimposed over a sequence of ghosts and shadows.

Oshosi held out Gleipnir, its silvery length coiling in his palm. "Here. Take it. Erm—a piece of it, at least."

As TJ grasped the chain, he was surprised by its weight. It felt impossibly light for something so robust-looking. It didn't feel like it carried the burden of countless destinies within its strands.

"Now, focus," Obatala instructed, his voice soft but firm. "Feel the energy within Gleipnir. Let it guide you."

TJ closed his eyes, concentrating on the cool metal against his skin. At first, there was nothing but the weight in his hands. Then, slowly, a tingling sensation crept up his arms.

*That's it,* Oshosi encouraged, now in TJ's mind. *Follow the trail, like a leopard tracking its prey.*

Images flickered behind TJ's eyelids: A giant wolf roaring to the heavens; a grand council chamber with towering golden pillars; Forseti's face, serene and discerning, floating before him.

*Good,* Obatala said. *Hold to that picture.*

TJ forced his mind to stare back at Forseti's wizened face, his graying blond beard, the loose hairs that came over his eyes. It was like Forseti was examining TJ. Did he already know his mind was being infiltrated? Or was TJ seeing a memory from the past?

*Now, let's combine our energies,* Obatala thought-spoke. *Young mortal, use your boosting abilities to amplify our skills.*

No, they hadn't gotten into Forseti's mind yet. That made sense. They had just started, after all. Was TJ himself the chain being held and looked over?

TJ nodded, sweat beading on his forehead as he concentrated on syncing his Ashe with the Orishas'. Then Oshosi's hunter instincts merged with his own, sharpening his focus. It was just like Oshosi said before. It was like being a lion or a tiger sitting and waiting for its meal. Patient despite being so powerful.

*Hunting isn't about how accurately you can shoot an arrow or throw a spear,* Oshosi said in his mind. *It's not about how strong or fast you are, or how sharp your blade is. Don't get me wrong—those things matter. But even more important is patience. Most of a hunt is waiting, watching for the right moment.*

As TJ locked in, truly understanding the role of the hunter in this moment, Obatala's dreamweaving abilities wrapped around him like a comforting blanket, allowing him to slip deeper into the recesses of Forseti's mind.

The visions became clearer, more intense. TJ saw Shango, bound in gleaming chains, his proud face etched with defiance, contorted in pain. Oya's anguished expression flashed before him, her eyes filled with rage and sorrow. Then, a simple runic pattern appeared, its single line seeming to pulse with hidden meaning along a wintery landscape. For some reason, the symbol felt important. But it looked like an ordinary letter "I." What could be so special about that?

Suddenly, the connection broke, and TJ gasped, floating backward and away from the chain. Oshosi steadied him with a firm hand the size of TJ's entire back.

"Well done, young one," Obatala said with a gentle smile.

TJ blinked again, his mind reeling. "Did... did I do it right?"

Oshosi grinned. "You did better than we could have hoped for a first try. That wasn't Forseti's mind directly… just the chain. But now we know we can use Psychometry as a snare, then transition to Obatala's more nuanced ways to finish things off in the subconscious. Those glimpses you saw? They're exactly what we need to start unraveling The Channeling."

Obatala floated down, even with TJ once more. "What *are* you, boy?" He seemed almost to sniff TJ. "This power you possess… I felt it before, of course. But… it's somehow familiar."

"I've been waiting for years for one of you to tell me, honestly." TJ rubbed at his eyes, adjusting his vision to the shimmering dreamscape around him. The glass walls pulsed with disconcerting light, almost ultraviolet. He could almost hear the whispers of sleeping minds, their deep thoughts echoing in the ethereal realm.

"Tomori Jomiloju," Obatala said, "before we proceed, there's something crucial we must discuss."

TJ turned to face the Orisha, still not used to how large he and the rest of his fellows could be. "What is it?"

"When we dive into Forseti's mind properly, you will need an anchor, young one. Something to tether you to the Waking World."

"An anchor?"

"Yes. When we enter Forseti's mind more fully, it will be easy to lose yourself in the dreamscape. The anchor ensures you can return safely and remember what you've learned from within."

"It must be something or someone with a strong emotional bond to you," Oshosi added.

TJ's mind worked through his options. His thoughts immediately went to Manny. Their friendship had grown so much, their connection deep and layered. But as he opened his mouth to suggest it, he noticed the Orishas exchange doubtful glances even before the words came out.

"What about… Manny?" TJ asked, his voice hesitant.

Oshosi's expression softened, a subtle sigh escaping his lips. "Um… teen infatuation might not be strong enough to hold you. We need something more... substantial."

A pang of disappointment slipped into TJ's heart. He understood their concern. But with Manny… everything always felt right… too right. It was never difficult to feel close to her. Or maybe, like Dad said about all of TJ's crushes, it was just puppy love. So TJ forced his thoughts to drift to Dayo. Before he even knew Manny existed, Dayo had been his number one. But as soon as her image formed in his mind, a twinge of uncertainty plucked at him. A usually comforting brush came along his neck where Dayo would often hold him. But now that touch felt foreign. She had changed so much since she left for Ifa all those years ago. Not to mention the reveal that she had been a Keeper. Did he even know who she was anymore?

Despite the Orishas' doubts, TJ couldn't shake the feeling that Manny was the right choice. Their bond might've been new-*ish*, but it felt genuine and strong. And they had been through the Aqua Realm, Sky Realm, and Eko Atlantic together. She never wavered then or now, and TJ doubted she'd waver in the future.

"I want to use Manny. I get that you're worried, but this isn't just some fling or crush. She's my best friend, and I've got mad trust for her. And… well… a lot of love."

Neither Oshosi nor Obatala betrayed anything with their faces, but TJ knew they were suppressing a pair of eye rolls. He didn't care, though. He knew he was right about this.

Obatala studied TJ's face, his ancient eyes seeming to peer into the depths of the young man's soul. After a moment, he nodded.

"Very well. We don't have time to waste, and your conviction is clear. We'll proceed with the young Manuela as your anchor."

"Obatala…" Oshosi groaned.

"It's only a daydream. And in the young mortal's own heart, the bond is true."

Oshosi scratched the edge of his eyebrow. "If Obatala thinks the girl will work, then we'll go along with it."

"Great," TJ said. "Now let's go again." He closed his eyes, focusing on Gleipnir's cool touch against his skin. As he synced his Ashe with the Orishas', a strange tingling sensation coursed through his body.

*Forseti's mind is slipping again in three… two… one…* Obatala's voice echoed softly in his mind once more. *Remember, ground yourself with thoughts of your anchor.*

TJ nodded, picturing Manny's warm smile and infectious laugh, the way she punched him on the arm, the way she hugged him tight, the way she stared at him for no good reason. As he did, his consciousness began to slip away, drifting into a familiar dreamscape. Flashes of everyday scenes with Manny and Ayo sprang forth: laughing in the mess hall, studying atop the Library Tree. But these images quickly warped, twisting into surreal versions of themselves.

The academy grounds stretched and contorted, dirt paths bending at impossible angles. TJ found himself in spaces that defied logic—rooms within rooms, bridges leading to nowhere.

*Good, now let go of your own memories,* Obatala's voice reminded him. *Focus only on Forseti.*

TJ pushed forward, determined. The twisted forest paths changed into wintery valleys and then to endless starfields. Suddenly, Shango's face appeared before him, eyes filled with fire. TJ reached out, but his body seized up, refusing to move.

"Obatala!" TJ called out. Oddly, he yawned despite fear leaking into his voice. "Um… I can't move!"

*Stop!* Obatala's voice was tinged with fear, the first time his cool demeanor had broken. *Come back now. It's Morpheus—he must sense you!*

TJ's mind reeled. The fear that poured into him only made the stasis worse. "But I thought daydreams were supposed to be easy!"

Oshosi's voice cut through the chaos. *Don't fight the fear, Tomori. Ride it. Hide within it. You have to wait until Forseti slips back into consciousness again. That's your path out.*

Swallowing hard, TJ forced himself to relax, letting the fear wash over him. It was terrifying, but he clung to Oshosi's words like a life raft, using the fear to propel himself back. He could feel it, just barely feel Forseti returning to a waking state again. Maybe it was Morpheus himself who was doing it, not realizing he was giving TJ an out.

*Almost there,* Obatala thought-spoke. *The veil will lift soon.*

Just at the edge of his vision, TJ felt more than saw a sliver opening. Just before he broke free, a figure with tattered robes and ghoulish skin hovered down into the scene with Shango, like a demon coming down on its prey. Then TJ was back in Obatala's dream room, gasping for air.

"I... I saw something," TJ panted. "A figure with torn robes... and skin like a... like a corpse. But blue."

Obatala and Oshosi exchanged worried glances. "That was Morpheus," Obatala said grimly. "We're lucky you got out when you did."

Oshosi nodded, his headdress nearly brushing at the top of TJ's head. "Let's hope he mistakes your presence for that of a God Eater. They often attack Forseti's mind, as he is one of the few dreamers on the High Council."

"Only time will tell," Obatala added, his bald head dipping low. "That'll be enough for today, young mortal. You did great work. This is very promising. Now... back to the Waking World with you before I get a knock at my door from a certain Greek god."

Obatala's eyes bloomed white and before TJ knew it, he was pushed out of the dream room and back into the recesses of his own mind.

# 15

# OUT OF THE FOG

TJ'S EYES FLUTTERED OPEN, HIS MIND FOGGY WITH THE remnants of a dream he couldn't quite grasp. But as consciousness seeped in, a tightness seized his body. His arms weighed like lead weights, refusing to budge no matter how hard he willed them to move. His breath came in short, sharp gasps. The hammering of his heart against his chest was painful.

*What's happening?*

He hadn't used his Ashe before sleeping, so he shouldn't have been drained. Why weren't his arms responding to Oya's Wind? The darkness of the dorm room, carved within the great tree bark, pressed in around him.

A rustling came from across the room. Ayo's face appeared, illuminated by the soft glow of bioluminescent fungi dotting the walls, the arch-shaped tattoo glowing under his eye. Through the curtain of his box braids, sharp lines of concern caved into his forehead.

"Help," TJ said, keeping his voice low. "I can't move, man. I can't move nothin'."

With deft movements, Ayo's hands flew through a series of signs. "Use my Ashe. Wind of Oya. Me help."

TJ nodded, grateful for his friend's quick thinking. He focused, drawing on Ayo's offered Ashe and channeling Oya's Wind through his stiff limbs. Slowly, painfully, his fingers twitched, then flexed. Relief washed over him as mobility returned to his arms.

"T-Thanks," TJ whispered, flexing his fingers experimentally, the subtle current of Oya's Wind weaving around them.

Ayo nodded, but concern still lingered in his eyes as he stuttered, "W-W-What was that a-a-all about?"

"No idea…"

As the fear subsided, TJ furrowed his brow. Why had he been unable to move? The question nagged at him even as he dressed and made his way to the mess hall for breakfast.

The cacophony of student chatter filled the air as TJ entered the open canopy, which housed an aroma of yams and egg stew. He spotted Manny across the way, sitting with her crossover team. When she saw him too, she dismissed herself to their usual table far away from the rest of the student body. Before sitting, TJ faced a barrage of questions from what felt like every student at the academy.

"What's going on with Orunmila?"

"Is it true he's really gone?"

"You can save him, can't you, TJ?"

"Give breathing room. Back off, back off." Ayo had to shield TJ from the hordes of students, signing with one finger—the universal signal for "go away."

"That means back the hell up," Manny said, coming in to help. "If you got questions, take it up with the Headmistress or Elder Adeyemi."

"But Adeyemi barely comes to Ifa anymore."

"Not our problem." Manny took TJ's hand and shouldered through the crowd. "Back off and leave him be."

The moment her palm came around his wrist, it was like TJ was hit with a thunderbolt, and suddenly, everything came rushing back: The dream world. Obatala and Oshosi. The shifting landscapes of Forseti's mind. The terrifying encounter with Morpheus. It all flooded his memory in vivid detail.

TJ shot up. His legs wobbled like wet noodles as he stumbled to a collection of rocks *outside* and *away* from the mess hall, his mind reeling from the recollection. He'd been there, in Forseti's dreams, guided by the Orishas. And somehow, in the process, the guardian of dreams himself had nearly caught him. And Manny… her touch… she was… what had the Orishas called it?

"My anchor…" TJ murmured as Ayo shooed away another group of SS2 students that were approaching.

"What's that?" Manny asked, plopping down on a rock with her tray of egg stew.

TJ explained everything that had happened to him in his dreams. As he did, Manny absently traced patterns on the rock beneath her—particularly at the point where TJ's anchor was brought up. Ayo's hands, usually so expressive, lay still in his lap, his eyes wide and attentive.

When TJ finished, a heavy silence hung between them. Manny was the first to break it. "So... I'm your… anchor?"

TJ nodded, heat rising to his cheeks. "Yeah…"

"Damn. Not me for heavy heavy boat thing?" Ayo said, but quickly laughed it off. "No wahala. Me joke, me joke." Then his signing grew more serious. "Danger. Big danger. Dream God trap you easy. Be careful."

"Yeah," TJ agreed, a shiver running down his spine at the memory. "It was close."

Manny leaned forward, her bright brown eyes searching TJ's face. "You okay, TJ? *Really* okay? I know this kind of thing can... you know…"

TJ knew what she meant. His past anxiety attacks weren't exactly a secret among his closest friends. Ayo hadn't seen them firsthand yet, but he was sure Manny told him. He took a deep breath, assessing himself. "I'm... okay. Shaken up, but okay. It's a lot to process, you know?"

"That why you wake bad?" Ayo signed. "Use too much Ashe in dream? I help. When you wake. I help. Every time."

TJ managed a small smile. "I'm good, guys. Thanks. I just... I hope this first week back at Ifa is a bit more normal, you know? After everything that's happened, I could use some routine."

Manny reached out, squeezing his hand. "We've got your back, TJ. Whatever comes next. Lean on us. Promise me."

TJ gulped and got lost in Manny's brown eyes. "Promise."

TJ FOUND HIS MEMORIES OF THE FOLLOWING WEEKS TO BE disjointed. The barrage of events had been so overwhelming that his mind could not take in any more information. The recollections he did retain were deeply disturbing. Among the most nightmarish were the haunting visions of a perishing Shango and Oya mocking him in his nightmares.

*"You are inadequate,"* Shango would say.

*"You're worthless,"* Oya would chime in.

There were more dream sessions with Obatala and Oshosi, but they took things much slower now to avoid Morpheus. There was one session where they were nearly caught, but TJ had to pretend to be a part of the dream by acting like a memory instead of an invasive force.

"There's been another complication," Oshosi had said to end one of their successful sessions. "Forseti caught wind of what Orunmila told you about following the ancestors."

"What? How?"

"His dreams. He seems to be communing, or at least attempting to commune with the Fates... and well..."

"... He caught on to Orunmila's message somehow," Obatala added.

"Okay, so what does that mean for us?"

"It means you must be more cautious when crafting routes on the ancestral paths," Oshosi said. "After The Great Separation, the ancestral bridges were severed along with all others. Many of the Norse ancestors were shunted directly to Valhalla for the Great War —and other paths of the Honorable Dead, where the Asgardians could find them. Now, after hearing Orunmila's message, Forseti believes there's something worth investigating there. So he has dispatched his best ravens to ensure those paths remain closed, as they should be."

Tension came to TJ's shoulders at the mention of ravens. Would they discover the reconnected ancestral path he and his group were planning to recreate? He could only hope they wouldn't stray there.

"Don't concern yourself too much with this news," Obatala said. "Just exercise caution, is all."

On the upside, back in the Waking World, the students at school asked TJ fewer and fewer questions when they realized he had no good answers for them. Well, that and some of them were starting to provoke the wrath of Manny's wind when they got too close. They soon learned to keep their distance.

The adults, including Elder Adeyemi and the rest of her team, were informed of what happened via Manny and Ayo. Supposedly, they agreed that TJ should focus on his studies before they called on him again. But TJ didn't believe it. For his whole first week back, he stressed about finding some sort of divine message. When he walked the dirt path to Elemental Studies, he half expected a raven in the woods to appear, summoning him to Forseti. On his way to the Healers' Tree to give Ayo company for one of his speech sessions, he couldn't tear his eyes away from the reflections in the river at the three-bridge crossing, expecting to see Themis' face shift into view any moment. Even while he was measuring flame lilies in SS1 Alchemy, he fully expected the scales he used to sap his magic and send him flailing through a portal straight into a jail cell.

TJ texted Dad almost every weekend. It was almost all the same conversation:

DAD

Mom told me they got you on some new mission.
You talk to me if you need anything, you hear?

TJ

yeah dad i will thanks

DAD

If you have trouble sleeping make sure you get a
workout in. It'll knock you right out.

TJ

ofc. will do

And on and on those conversations went.

It wasn't until the second to last Friday of the month that TJ let his paranoia settle down into a minor whisper instead of a shouted voice in his head. Staffcrafting classes only met every few weeks, so he had to wait all that time to get started with his own staff. Elder Adeyemi had tried to get the Staffmaster to catch TJ up ahead of time, but the old man was a traditionalist. He would not rush the process he had been cultivating for decades.

"You know something," TJ said at breakfast. "SS1 levels are low-key easier than JS3. No talk of exams. No pop quizzes."

"No burning fruit trees," Ayo signed after taking a bite of food. Even after only a few weeks, his signing had improved significantly. "I hear Manny is one who flying teacher use for example this year." He didn't actually "sign" Teacher Omo of Fon, but instead flapped his hands with wings, which made TJ chuckle.

Manny, who was in Junior Secondary 3 levels, had her head sunk between a mountain of scrolls and books. It was a cloudy day in the mess hall, but extremely humid. So her typical curl pattern was more frizzy and loose. The look reflected the stress on her face.

"I completely forgot that air feeds flame!" Her voice was muffled under her heap of homework.

"Ayo is saying 'how, that's pretty obvious?'"

"Pressure! That's how. Of course I knew that, but I freaked out. And… I don't know. Ever since what happened with Olokun, my water magic ain't been the same. So I've been avoidin' it. He and Yemoja must not be happy with me."

"Ayo's signing that 'that's what you get for being a child of Oya.'"

Manny shot a gust of air through an open hole in her homework hill. The target: Ayo's bowl of oatmeal. The milky oats splattered all over Ayo's face and designer glasses. TJ laughed as Ayo wiped himself clean with a grumble. TJ did a lot of that since being back a full month now. Laughing. He couldn't tell if it was because Manny and Ayo were trying to make him feel better or because their antics always ended up just being genuinely funny. Whatever the case, he appreciated it all the same.

"Uh oh, what did Ayo say now?" Tunde walked up to their table with a plate full of *ẹwa agoyin*—boiled beans with pepper sauce. A half dozen of his new friends followed behind him. Like Dayo, Tunde was a natural extrovert and popular kid. His sibling's popularity used to bother TJ, but now that he had Manny and Ayo, the old sting had mostly faded.

"Ayo insulted Manny's Orisha," TJ explained, using a gust of Oya's Wind to gesture with his hands. "What are you doing here?"

"Oracle Ruby wanted me to tell you to meet her by the Yemoja statue before you head off to your first staffcrafting class today.

Something about a… stormbreak." Tunde gave TJ knowing eyes through the bangs of his sun-baked locs. He wasn't supposed to know anything about Operation Stormbreak, but that had never stopped his baby brother before. Giving a quick look over his shoulders to his friends, Tunde leaned in close to murmur, "You work with Ruby, don't you? Could you put in a good word for me?"

TJ scrunched up his face. "Put in a good word for? I don't think she's hiring any assistants."

Tunde waved his hands in the air, his locs shaking. "Shhh, shhh. Keep it on the low, bro." He pulled TJ in closer. "Nah, I mean… let her know I'm a cool dude. Mature. Wise beyond my years and all that."

TJ was about to speak loudly again before he stopped himself. "Dude, she's, like, fifteen years older than you."

"Fourteen years, eleven months, and twenty-two days."

TJ groaned. "I'm not even going to ask you how you know that."

"Well, can you? She's got the same exact alignment as me. Ogun *and* Orunmila! We're soulmates!"

TJ pressed his fingers into the side of his head. Tunde was the smartest person he knew, but he forgot that he also was just a twelve-year-old. "Don't get your hopes up, man. Holler at one of your friends over there instead."

"Ugh, you're never any help." Tunde stormed off with his friends.

"What that about?" Ayo signed.

"Come on, Ayo," TJ said. "That's simple. You can say that out loud. Try it." Over the past month, he had taken to parenting Ayo the same way Manny had been. It was true Ayo wasn't putting the effort into getting his speech back, and TJ caught him more than a few times reading those quick guides from Olu Olowokandi at night.

Ayo looked out for any eavesdroppers before giving TJ a pout.

"C'mon, man," TJ pressed. "You can do it. At least once a day with me. Manny has you do it every morning and every night."

"Say a few words, Ayo!" Manny's muffled voice shouted from behind her books.

"W-w-what. W-w-was. T-t-that?" Tears welled in Ayo's eyes. He was trying. He really was. That's all TJ could ask for.

"It's okay, dude. I got it. That's enough for today."

Manny sucked her teeth. "Stop babying him, TJ."

TJ ignored her and answered Ayo's question. "It was just my brother being delusional. Said to meet up with Oracle Ruby later."

Manny dropped her books and cleared away her scrolls with a wind whirl. "No! Hell nah! It hasn't even been a full month yet. They can't be askin' for you again already. That's not—"

"Nah, nah, it's not like that," TJ explained. "I mean, if they needed me for a big job, they'd just snatch me up, right? I think she just wanted to talk before Ayo and I go into our staffcrafting session." Manny gave him a look. "Well, that and Tunde has a crush on her. But no, nothing about going back to the Court of All or anything like that."

Manny didn't believe him and—when the time came—walked him all the way to the Yemoja statue to make sure he stayed put in the Mortal Realm. This was despite the fact she was behind on her Elemental Studies and should've been cramming for her exam later that day.

"No wahala, Manny," Ayo signed. "I have TJ's back. You know this."

She scoffed. "You'd drop into a portal the second anyone said 'jump'—Ruby or whoever."

"Y-y-yeah." Ayo shrugged like there wasn't a difference. "L-l-like I-I-I s-s-said..." He finished the rest by signing. "I have TJ's back."

After a few minutes of bickering between Manny and Ayo, Oracle Ruby shuffled her way out from the forest thicket of the main campus to the guardian statues. She wore her usual green-and-white aṣọ òké robes and a headdress that covered her green-tipped locs. Her usually lively face was different though. Her plump cheeks were still turned up in a smile but the shadows under her eyes were more pronounced.

"Sorry to keep you waiting, loves," she said. "Some bloke keeps dumping a massive bundle of roses outside my hut. And the things have a bloody ever-growing charm on them. Powerful charm, really. But quite annoying."

TJ pinched his eyelids shut. *Tunde…*

"Manuela, what're you doing here?" Ruby asked, brushing a rose petal from her shoulder. "Elemental Studies is halfway across campus, no?"

"Just making sure TJ keeps *both* feet in the Mortal Realm." Manny's eyes narrowed, nearly as sharp as the Oya statue that stood behind her.

Ruby chuckled. "You're a good mate, you are. But TJ won't need your protection today. I'm only going to be catching him up with something Ayo and I have been investigatin'. Sister's promise, yeah?" She flicked up a pinky finger. "I will not be taking TJ away to the Frost Realm or anything mad like that."

Manny scowled, but she linked her own pinky with Ruby's. "I'm holding you to that."

"I'd expect nothing less."

Satisfied, Manny turned to TJ to hug him. Then she whispered in his ear. "Catch up at lunch? I wanna hear how your staffmaking goes."

"Deal," TJ said.

They all watched Manny take off into the trees, where she air-stepped into the highest canopy and zoomed away. She probably only had five minutes left to get to class, but TJ would be willing to bet she'd make the trip in less than three.

"The lunar storm will usher in the cosmic damnation…" Oracle Ruby murmured to herself.

"What's that?" TJ asked.

"Very protective, that one." Ruby perked up, fixing her face from a frown to a smile. "Miss Martinez truly shares equal parts of her Orishas. Oya and Yemoja both. That's a fierce combo, that. Enraged compassion ain't nothin' to muck around with."

"Yeah, she has big big crush on my boy," Ayo signed.

TJ elbowed Ayo. "Shut it."

"Come on, before you two are late as well," Oracle Ruby chuckled, beckoning TJ and Ayo to follow.

# 16

# TANGLED PATHS

Oracle Ruby led the way down a side path to a thicker portion of the campus. The path, once clear, surrendered to a tangle of vibrant green, where thick brush and intertwined vines challenged every step. With each stride, the dense canopy above whispered ancient secrets, the air thick with the scent of wildflowers and the distant call of unseen creatures. This must be a place where nonhumans like Teacher Omo of Fon or Teacher Ikenna or Headmistress Ninki Nanka ventured in their free time.

Oracle Ruby took in a big inhale. "Oh, I've always been keen on the freshness of this part of the grounds. I'd drop by more if it wasn't such a mission to get around." She said that last bit as she stepped carefully over a large vine. "I remember coming through here when I first was making my staff. Times were... simpler then."

"You still foggy with your readings of Shango and Oya?" TJ asked.

"A bit," Ruby said sadly. "More than I'd like, that's for sure, but I'm managing. Keeping more of their offerings around me and all that." She played with the Oya coin hanging from her earring.

"So what did you need me for?" TJ asked after a while.

"Ogun," Ruby said simply, turning mostly to his friend. "Ayo, remember what I told you last year.... How your family has ties to Ogun? Well, that may be our way to your ancestral path—as we have no direct link to Shango right now. But Ogun is one of the few

Orishas who haven't reached out to humanity. I've done several rituals and gotten no answer. But we're not worried in the same way as with some of the others. Ogun's *always* been that way. We just need to do something that'll get his attention. Have you ever heard of his Sacred Cabinet?"

Ayo shook his head. TJ had no clue. He'd interacted with a lot of the Orishas but never got a whiff of Ogun.

"From my research," Ruby continued, "it seems like the last time any diviner made contact was through the cabinet. I'm just having trouble locating it. Anything your father might help us with? He's got some good connections with this type of stuff, right?"

Ayo's frown came hard and fast. "I-I-I'll see..."

Ruby huffed. "Ugh, that man. He needs to get over himself and be okay with Ogun."

Ayo's shoulders fell. TJ and Manny already knew to bring up his father as little as possible. Ruby didn't. To be fair on Ruby, though, finding out more about the cabinet was an idea worth putting a pin in.

As they continued walking through the natural maze, TJ changed the subject. "Has it been hard building your staff, Ayo?"

Ayo pressed his lips together as though saying "um." Then he signed, "We... not build staffs yet. Today first time we pick up materials. Bright rocks. Tree pieces. First month we think... long... long think."

"Meditating?" TJ asked, and Ayo nodded.

"You've noticed that SS1 level classes are a bit different from what you've done before?" Oracle Ruby asked as she cleared away more thick brush with a wave of her hand.

"Yeah, I have," TJ confessed. "They're *way* easier."

"That's 'cause the teachers reckon they gotta keep your noggins open for your crafting sessions. Most of what you've been doing's been all theory and not much hands-on, right?"

TJ nodded. It was true that the classes felt more like discussions of magic rather than demonstrative uses of it. He certainly welcomed the change of pace. It meant making a fool of himself a lot less often.

"That's because," Ruby went on, "your classes this term will all funnel directly back into the creation of your staff. The most powerful tool for us diviners."

"Ritual of… past walking," Ayo tried to add.

"Do you mean rite of passage?" TJ asked, questioning Ayo's signing.

"Y-y-yeah. It-it's li-like a d-d-driver's l-l-license, and…" Ayo stuttered but stopped when Ruby peered over her shoulder curiously. She hadn't given him a bad look, but it still made Ayo red around the ears. Ayo dropped his head, forcing his braids to fall over his glasses.

"That's right," Ruby said, ignoring Ayo's bashfulness. "So, tell me, TJ. Have you noticed a common theme among your classwork this term so far?"

TJ searched through his mind, recalling each session from his new teachers. In SS1 Alchemy, there was a particular focus on attuning to the ingredients they used. Last year, they mostly had to commit common recipes to memory, which meant a lot of rote studying. TJ greatly preferred the action of attunement because it was easy for him to pick out the right choices, as though he could sense the best ingredients instead of remembering them from books.

"Like you said…" TJ began. "Everything ties back to staffcrafting. Teacher Falana said he never saw anyone make better selections than me for my alchemy studies this week."

"Good," Ruby returned. "That's good to hear. What else?"

TJ ducked under a low-hanging car-sized branch before an image came to mind. In SS1 Ecology, he was able to easily enter the minds of several baboons to determine which fruits were their favorite. But it was supposed to be easier to communicate with animals.

"When Teacher Goodall had us working with baboons," TJ said, "I was the only one who knew that the group we were working with preferred mangoes over apples."

"I had a feeling that would be the case," Ruby said, "considering the type of diviner you are."

"What do you mean?"

"Staffcrafting isn't something you'll be wrapping up within a single sesh, not even two. You can't just 'flow' into it. You'll be tooling and retooling, searching—and re-searching—for the entire rest of the term until you build the perfect staff for your specific needs."

"Wait..." TJ put a hand to his head. "I only skimmed the list when I looked before. I thought there were only a handful of steps to building a staff. I thought it would take a month, not *months*."

With Shango and Oya being channeled, TJ needed a staff sooner rather than later. Shango's Equinox was still a little ways away, but he was hoping he could have a few months with his staff to practice before shipping off to the End Realm and the Court of All.

"Remember your grandma look at your sister staff for long time last year?" Ayo signed. "And that staff was already built. It takes even more long to make, bro."

TJ dug into his backpack and pulled out the sheet going over the lesson plan for staffcrafting. It read:

*Stage 1: Self-Discovery**
*Stage 2: Material Gathering**
*Stage 3: Design and Builder's Plan**
*Stage 4: Staffcrafting**
*Stage 5: Infusion Period**
*Stage 6: Martial Training**
*Stage 7: Final Trial**

TJ had assumed the seven stages were separated by a day. But then he realized that each had an asterisk that led to more information at the back of his parchment. Some of the stages were as long as six weeks on their own!

When he looked back up at Ruby and Ayo, his mouth dropped.

"Bet you fifty cowries he no read the small words at bottom of page," Ayo signed to Ruby.

Despite TJ not translating for Ayo, Ruby agreed. "He definitely didn't read the footnotes."

"There's *no way* I'll finish a staff in time," TJ said. "The Hero's Equinox is coming before we're scheduled to finish our staffs this term." He pointed to the "martial training" section, his heart in his throat. "This alone is supposed to take place at the end of March and all through April *next* year."

*And why would you need to rush your staffcrafting, Tomori Jomiloju?* The voice sounded loud in TJ's mind—Ninki Nanka's voice. A shiver ran through the whole of TJ's body. She was really making a bad habit of sneaking up on him. TJ turned to find the Headmistress poking her head through the thick vines. She looked right at home among the dense forest. Appropriately sized. She dwarfed most rooms she skulked through. But this forest matched her perfectly. Even her movements were sure-footed despite what seemed like crowded conditions for TJ and the rest. Today, an orange cat was lounging on her scaly back.

TJ was quite literally speechless, so he was glad when Ruby spoke for him. "Hello there, Headmistress. Were you visiting with Madam Koi Koi and the bush babies?"

*Why yes, I was.* Ninki Nanka smiled. *They grow restless but I have settled them. Your previous headmistress did not frequent this part of the campus enough, it seems.*

"I'm just walking these loves to Bamidele's next session," Ruby said. TJ noted she left out the part about Ogun's Sacred Cabinet. "We're getting TJ up to speed since he missed so much."

Ninki Nanka's reptilian eyes seemed to bore into him as she spoke. Even the orange cat on her back stirred from its nap. *Remember, Tomori Jomiloju, the craft of your staff will reveal more than your skill; it will unveil your very essence. I, and many others, will be watching closely.*

Her words sent a chill through TJ—despite the humid air. He could do without all the attention. It was bad enough he had the UCMP and Elder Adeyemi relying on him. Now he had the eyes of the new mythical headmistress and whoever these "others" were on him too. He knew why he was always being watched. He knew it was because he was unique as a diviner, but it still sucked.

As the Headmistress faded back into the brush, TJ was left with a swelling sense of doubt. What would his staffcrafting reveal about him? Did he really want to bear his inner self to this audience of hidden watchers with agendas unknown?

Ruby gave him a reassuring smile, but it did little to lift TJ's mood. He felt utterly alone as they neared the crafting site, his anxiety growing with each step. He steeled himself, resolving to face whatever was to come. But the impending trials filled him less with determination and more with dread.

## 17

# ENEMY OF THE GOOD

As TJ, Ayo, and Ruby made their way through the dense forest, they encountered more students shuffling their way through the brush. The forest—more a jungle—had grown so thick that the morning sun high above barely broke through. But as they continued, a brilliant golden light split between the trees ahead. And, eventually, they found themselves in a wide clearing bordered by a collection of floating staffs.

TJ and Ayo seemed like the last pair of students to arrive. Most of the others were already gathered around, examining the floating shafts of iron and wood.

"Well, see you later, guys," Oracle Ruby said, pulling a loose leaf from her headdress. "Ayo, please keep an eye out for anything you can find on Ogun's Cabinet. It might not be as simple as looking it up in a library. It's gonna be spiritual. So dig deep."

"Thank you," Ayo signed.

"Yeah, thanks, Ruby," TJ said. "See you around?"

She winked. "Whenever you need me, love."

And with that, Ruby vanished into the thick of the forest. Ayo tapped TJ on the shoulder and pointed to one of the floating staffs. It was made of iron and sparked with lightning. But TJ was more interested in another one made of wood that swirled with purple fire and water, casting steam like a sauna.

"Woah!" TJ said. "Let's check this one out first."

Ayo shook his head, then jutted his chin to a group near the staff TJ was interested in. It was LaVont, Jimoh, and that girl from Anansi's Arcade.

"Damn… I still can't believe they made it out of Camp Olosa." There weren't many people who were taller than TJ, but those guys were two of the few. If it wasn't illegal for a diviner to participate in mundane sports, they'd be first-round-pick centers in the NBA.

"Nah, they no pass Camp Olosa…" Ayo signed. "Parents buy them in."

"What? How?"

"You notice how—" He couldn't find the word to sign, so he said, "P-p-pristine those entrance s-s-statues were?"

"No…" TJ really couldn't remember. He didn't notice stuff like that, but Ayo did.

"Well, t-t-that was their p-p-parents who m-m-made that h-h-happen." Ayo went back to signing. "Me no know if Manny take you to crossover pitch. That made better too. All equipment in Hospital Tree? All new."

"Must be nice…" TJ said, taking a look at their outfits. They wore the same dashiki uniforms as everyone else, with colored stripes down the front to denote their Orisha alignments. However, the sunlight from above glinted off gold chains tucked beneath their collars and silver bracelets wrapped around their wrists. "Who's the girl though? I don't remember her from camp."

"Well…" Ayo signed, but his gestures were less animated than usual. "Her name's Aisha. Back before Ifa, she was my Titi before Titi. Kind of."

"What!?" TJ said. "You were gettin' with girls when you were eleven—or wait, ten!?"

Ayo just gave him a prideful shrug, signing, "What can I say? I a true son of Shango."

"Students! Young diviners! Welcome, welcome!" It was Staffmaster Bamidele. But he did not look the same as the first time TJ had seen him. The last time was at that big international meeting before the Olokun attack. Then, the man wore ordinary robes like any other diviner, but now he looked like a forest-dwelling vagabond. In fact, it seemed as though he was part of the forest itself, adorned with a myriad of accessories—beads, amulets, and charms—draping from his neck, wrists, and ankles. And he was barefoot.

"It is great to see you all here," he said. "I know it's been weeks since we last met but meditation is important, and I hope that process will come to fruition today!"

TJ used Oya's Wind to elbow Ayo. "We were supposed to be meditating *all* this time?"

"Yeah..." Ayo signed. "But you no have to. You TJ."

Bamidele's voice was rustic and aged as he said, "Remember, in the pursuit of mastery, we must remember that..." He lifted a finger, waiting.

The whole class, in unison, said, "Perfection is the enemy of the good."

Bamidele smiled and clapped, his hands creating a dust cloud. "Too right you are, class. Too right you are. Perfection is the enemy of the good." He drifted to a floating staff with vines that seemed to actively be growing out of it. A girl with a large curly Afro like Manny sat nearby. "The essence of staffcrafting is not to create an impeccable weapon, but a tool that resonates with your spirit. Imperfect but true. Wild. Like nature."

Bamidele clapped his hands together again, the sound echoing through the quiet forest clearing. "Now, young diviners, it is time to begin the next stage of your staffcrafting journey. After passing the meditation test, you will move on to gathering materials that resonate with your own magical essence." He gestured to the assortment of staffs floating around them. "Each component of your staff—the type of wood, the core, the adornments—will reflect an aspect of your character and abilities. Harmony between the wielder and the tool is key."

The girl Ayo pointed out before, Aisha, raised her hand. "Teacher Bamidele, why is all this necessary? Can't we just be assigned staffs after meditation?"

Bamidele smiled patiently. "An excellent question. This process teaches you the importance of your harmony. The journey of crafting your staff is as meaningful as the end result. You will likely face trials and tests of character along the way that will bind you to your tool more fiercely than if you bought one from a shop. By the way, please do let your parents know that Oshun crystals are half off this weekend at The Walking Stick." The Staffmaster winked, then looked at them wildly. "Well, don't go on gaping at me. Find a spot and begin. Once I sense the harmony in your heart, I will pair you off to go on your search."

TJ shifted nervously as everyone scrambled to find a place to sit.

"Find a floating staff that speaks to you the most!" Bamidele called out over the *patt-patting* of dozens of students finding their places. "Orisha alignments are the most helpful. Find the element that best suits you. These won't be exact matches, of course, but you should use these existing staffs to sense the elements within each that call to you the most: The wood type in this staff, the crystal type in that, or the element surrounding another. Once you hone in, it'll be much easier for you to find the materials you'll need. Happy hunting!"

Ayo went straight for the iron staff that sparked with lightning. TJ was going to go with the one surrounded by fire and water in a steam cloud, but Aisha had taken a position there already. He eyed the rest of the staffs but none of them seemed right. That had always been the case for him in school. Despite visiting the ethereal realms several times, he still had no clue what his true alignment was.

"Uh, sir! Uh, Staffmaster!" TJ raised his hand shakily. "I don't think any of these will work for me. I, um..." He took steps closer to the man. Umar and some of the other students were starting to listen in. When TJ approached Bamidele, he lowered his voice. "I, uh... don't have an Orisha alignment exactly." He pulled at his dashiki uniform to show the blank gray stripes on it.

"Ah, yes, Tomori Jomiloju, isn't it?" Bamidele asked. "Olu's grandchild. Your sister's staff was very difficult to crack last year before that Olokun business. Strong magic in that one, intense bonds between crystal and wood. I was shocked to hear you destroyed it from overuse. I wouldn't think it possible with that particular instrument. So sorry to hear it."

"No problem," TJ said. "Elder Adeyemi tells me that was an extreme anomaly. But yeah... what should I do? Just find a staff at random?"

Bamidele winced at the last word, as though TJ had slapped

him across the face. "*Never* use that word in these sessions, you hear me? There is never anything '*random*' in the realm of stafflore."

"Uh, sorry, I didn't mean random in a bad way," he backpedaled. "I just meant, uh, nothing here seems to be calling out to me specifically. So, you know, maybe it's just better if I just pick one of the staffs at ran—" He cleared his throat awkwardly. "Maybe I'll just, uh, sit over there for now." TJ gestured to an unremarkable brass staff off to the side that lacked the flashy elemental embellishments of the others. "Wouldn't want to offend you further with my poor word choices."

TJ shuffled over and settled down next to the plain brass staff, closing his eyes to meditate and attune his energy to it. But concentrating proved difficult as Bamidele periodically called out pairs of students who had successfully meditated and attuned their energies, allowing them to move on to the next stage of selecting staff materials.

TJ fidgeted, opening one eye to peek at the other students. Emeka's former girlfriend, Tomi, had Ashe casting off her so easily. Titi was glowing strong as well. Ayo was right. He was TJ. This should have been nothing. He didn't need weeks of meditation when he managed communication with Orishas on the regular.

Still, though… TJ struggled to quiet his mind and connect with the nondescript metal rod. Without any adornments or character, it hardly called to him. He wondered if he even had an affinity worth discovering.

The sound of crystalline chimes rang out as the first students succeeded in attuning their energies. TJ sighed, pinching his eyes again to focus on the silence within.

"Mr. Batiste! Miss Yemisi-Ojo! You've passed!" Bamidele announced. "You'll be paired together. Take this sack and venture forth."

TJ cracked an eye open to see LaVont and Titi rise, accept a sack from Bamidele, and head off into the forest together. Ayo was peeking too, clearly uneasy about his ex-girlfriend wandering off with LaVont. Or wait—were Ayo and Titi even boyfriend-girlfriend right now? TJ could never keep track.

"Eyes closed, Mr. Young, Mr. Oyelowo," Bamidele chided.

TJ quickly squeezed his eyes shut again and tried to refocus. He listened as more pairs were called—

"Jimoh and Aisha!"

"Taiwo and Kehinde!"

"Ade and Tomi!"

With each name, TJ fidgeted more. Even Ayo was called eventually, leaving TJ as the lone student remaining.

Well, not entirely alone.

One other student sat cross-legged before the vine-wrapped staff from earlier. The one with the huge Afro. Though the girl had a huge mane of curly hair like Manny's, her skin was a lighter shade of brown, and her nose was thinner. She must've been mixed. TJ didn't recognize her either.

"Don't worry, you two," Bamidele assured them. "I didn't expect you to pass today's session, seeing as you've just arrived, Miss Innes. And Mr. Young, you started with us late. You'll need to spend a month meditating like the others. These things can't be rushed or skipped."

TJ sighed, both relieved and disappointed. At least he hadn't *completely* failed. With more practice, maybe next time he'd be ready. For now, he'd just have to be patient.

He stood up from the plain brass staff, stretching his stiff legs after the long meditation session. He glanced over at the curly-haired girl who was still sitting cross-legged on the forest floor. She seemed lost in thought as she idly drew spirals in the dirt with a twig.

TJ ambled over, scuffing his feet on purpose to alert her of his approach. "Hey there," he said, giving a small wave.

The girl looked up, seeming a bit startled. Her wide brown eyes took him in curiously. "Oh, hello," she replied in a lilting Scottish accent.

"Oh, shoot… that was *not* how I was expecting you to sound." TJ's ears heated. That sounded bad. "I mean… Um… you another exchange student?" She nodded cautiously. "That's what's up. Did you know that Fiona girl? She was here last year." She shook her head. TJ rubbed the back of his neck. That was bad too, like saying all Scottish people knew each other or something. Maybe he should start over. "I'm TJ." He held out a hand. "Or

'Mr. Young,'" he said in his best impression of the burly Staffmaster.

The girl laughed, breaking the tension at last. Then she said, "Freya. Or," she did her best impression as well, "'Miss Innes.'" Freya shook his hand briefly. Her grip was firmer than he had expected.

An awkward silence hung between them for a moment. TJ racked his brain for something else to say. "So, uh… rough session, huh?" He gestured around the now nearly-empty clearing.

Freya gave a rueful half-smile. "Yeah, seems we're the stragglers."

"Well, hey, at least we're in good company," TJ joked. He sat down beside her, idly plucking blades of grass. "You just transferred here from Scotland?"

"Yeah. I'm only here for a few months, though. I've already got a staff. Just broke it. I only need to attune to new material… then I'm gone. I tried rebuilding back home, but the druids there said I might have to reach out to the second half of my ancestral path."

*Follow the ancestors,* TJ thought. Then he looked at Freya with new eyes as he said, "That's what up. Where in Scotland are you from exactly?"

"From a village called Balloch," Freya said. "Everything here in Nigeria is so new to me still. I've only been here once, when I was a baby. But the weather here, the people, the traditions…"

TJ nodded. "Yeah, it's gotta be really different. I'm originally from Los Angeles, so I had to adjust too when I came here."

They both shared in a smile. It was nice having something you could relate to with someone else. Especially someone new.

Freya resumed drawing spirals in the dirt. "I quite like this forest. Reminds me a bit of home."

"Eh, it's pretty cool," TJ agreed, looking up at the shafts of sunlight filtering through the leaves. "If you like bush babies and giant beasts."

Freya scoffed a little, looking near to an eye roll. TJ hoped he hadn't offended her, but his joke didn't get a response.

"So, what do we gotta do to catch up to the others?"

Freya shrugged. "The Celts believed all life moves in spirals, ever-changing but circling back again." Freya traced her finger along the spiral shape she had etched. "Maybe we need to do that, too. Go with the flow, like a spiral. Instead of trying to force our way through." She drew a line through her shape, breaking the spiral.

TJ considered her words. The notion of life spiraling in cycles made him think about reincarnation and the great wheel that the Orishas moved through. The eternal dance between the realms—mortal and divine—intersecting in rhythmic patterns. The spiral also reminded him of the double helix design Dayo's old staff had.

A spark of inspiration hit him then. During the group summoning of Olokun last year, he had siphoned power from his classmates, channeling their collective magic. He had trouble doing it at first, but when he had his private lessons with Elder Adeyemi, she taught him about ripples in the water. TJ imagined them in his mind's eye, how he could feel them in his chest, how they seemed to spiral. What if he tried something similar here with his classmates when they communed at the beginning of class? He could tune into the Ashe of the other students to boost his own ability. To get a sense of his own affinity, and Freya's.

"I just got an idea," TJ said, turning to Freya excitedly. "In a few more sessions, I think I know a way for us to catch up and pass. I'll show you; it'll be really cool. It's sort of my special thing."

Freya quirked an eyebrow, but before she could respond, Staffmaster Bamidele's voice rang out. "That's all for today, you two! We will reconvene next week. Practice your meditation."

TJ stood up and extended a hand to help Freya to her feet. "See you next session?"

She nodded, looking curiously at him for a moment before gathering her things and heading off into the forest. "See you next time," she put on her impression, "'Mr. Young.'"

# 18

# TOO GOOD TO BE TRUE

THE REST OF SEPTEMBER AT IFA ACADEMY BROUGHT A WELCOME sense of normalcy for TJ. As the rainy season came to an end, the rainfall typical of that first month died down to a steady drizzle. The JSS students ducked between the dense forests to avoid getting too wet, while the SS students conjured "wind-brellas"—as Manny called them—to stay dry. Morning mists dissipated faster over the canopy of leaves transitioning to shades of orange and yellow. The packed dirt paths softened under TJ's feet as he made his way between classes.

He fell into a comfortable routine, no longer the newcomer struggling to keep pace. TJ's skills strengthened daily, particularly in his staffcrafting sessions. Under the patient guidance of Staffmaster Bamidele, TJ took those lessons and practiced techniques using Oshun's Lake. He focused intently, learning to manipulate the water by sending out ripples from his hands. Apparently the gesture would translate to Yemoja's Ripple Flow, one of the activating forms with a staff. The circular movements came easier now, combining with inward spirals just as Freya had described from her Celtic teachings.

Freya quickly became a fast friend, even after TJ had nearly offended her again during their second session.

"So, uh, Freya, this might be weird but I was just curious how old you are exactly?" The words spilled out in a rush before he could overthink it. But outside of staffcrafting sessions, TJ didn't have any classes with Freya. She apparently had SS3-level classes. So he had always been curious. Plus, she didn't have as much baby fat in her cheeks, and she just gave off this overall more mature vibe.

Freya, who had been meditating, opened one eye and gave TJ a look. "Do I look *that* old?"

"Nah! Nah!" TJ said from his own cross-legged position. "I know a guy should never ask a girl her age if she looks over twenty-one—least that's what my mom says—but you definitely don't seem *that* old." He paused, wincing. "Not that you look old at all! Wow, sorry. I talk too much and too fast when I'm making a fool of myself." TJ shook his head and tried again. "I'm about to turn sixteen soon, by the way. How about you? How old are you?"

Freya laughed as she ran her hand through her Afro curls. "I just turned eighteen this year."

"Oh snap! You're an adult-adult! Like, a for real, for real adult."

"Yup." Freya pinched her eyes shut again. "I even get to legally drink now. Unlike you Yankees."

TJ grinned. "Scotland is so awesome."

"It has its perks."

"If you two meditated as much as you talked, you'd be caught up with the rest of class by now," Staffmaster Bamidele said from his own meditation spot. "Close those lips and open your minds."

TJ shut his eyes straight away, but felt relieved he hadn't completely embarrassed himself. Talking to Freya was easy, even when he put his foot in his mouth.

She had taken a keen interest in TJ's progress and always asked what surprise he had in store for their next session. Amused by her enthusiasm, TJ just smiled and kept his secret plan to himself. He aimed to develop a communal ritual that would essentially help him leapfrog a few stages as the rest of the students rushed ahead in their staffcrafting progression. But first, he needed more solitary practice.

Plus, it was difficult garnering the right foundation when he didn't get proper rest. At the end of the day, sleep was never really sleep. His slumber was always filled with a new breakthrough with

Oshosi and Obatala as they delved deeper and deeper into Forseti's mind. And it left TJ's Ashe depleted when he woke.

It didn't help that TJ had spent the last few nights in a row trying to talk to Ayo. He'd found his best friend clutching a photo with his mom. And he did this anytime the topic of his father came up.

"How come I've never met your mom?" TJ would ask. Then Ayo would sink into himself. TJ figured it was a sore topic. He didn't think Ayo ever mentioned his parents getting a divorce. So he wasn't sure what was going on. Being unable to figure out how to get his best friend to open up had been pestering the little sleep TJ did get. Several teachers had already scolded him for nodding off during classes.

Still… the more TJ immersed himself in his studies, the less out of place he felt. His remedial lessons in somatic magic and magical theory finally clicked as he saw their connections to staffcrafting. Ayo tutored him in numerology, while TJ quizzed Manny before her weekly exams. In the afternoons, TJ cheered on Ayo at dueling club matches, then joined the crowds for Manny's weekend games of crossover.

Before he knew it, October had arrived, and on that first Sunday, TJ's family threw him a huge sixteenth birthday party. Streamers bedecked the whole courtyard of the Abimbola family compound. Grandma even got the folks at the drum circle to come as well. Mom and Tunde were there too, though Dad had to stay home to continue paying their mortgage. But TJ got a nice text from him.

DAD

Happy birthday, TJ. I'm proud of the man you're becoming. Keep your head up at that academy.

However, that reprieve ended abruptly near the second half of October while TJ was having lunch with Manny and Ayo. A small folded crane landed on their table, quickly unfolding to reveal a message from Teacher Omo of Fon in elegant script. In coded language, the note conveyed that Yemoja had succeeded in her efforts within the Ice Realm. The time had come to reopen the ancestral path and enact the next phase of their plan.

TJ sighed, staring wistfully at his half-eaten meal. "It was nice while it lasted, wasn't it?"

Manny looked puzzled. "What was?"

"Being a regular kid for a few weeks."

Ayo's eyes glinted with anticipation as his hands fluttered animatedly, his signing was getting better every week. "Well, back to work. I excited to see what Cold Place is all about."

TJ nodded slowly. The gravity of what the mission—of what The Hero's Equinox would bring—weighed heavy on him once more.

# 19

# A FRIGID ALLIANCE

THAT WEEKEND, TJ'S BLOOD RAN COLD AS HE STEPPED INTO THE familiar space of the meeting hall under his family's compound. But the room wasn't cold at all. The round table that stood at the center wasn't casting off a chill. The waterfall that cascaded gently at the back against the rock face wasn't freezing. No, it was something else that made TJ's insides like ice.

The wooden schematics of the Court of All were gone, replaced by detailed images of a harsh, frigid landscape: the Frost Realm. A frigid blue blanketed the room from its center. TJ's gaze fell upon a crevice in the icy terrain, bringing back vivid memories of his terrifying encounter with the ice giant that resided there. A shiver ran up his spine as he recognized the very spot, the very scar where he had battled the towering creature.

TJ glanced around at the others gathered and waiting: His friends Manny and Ayo. Their guardians—Mom, Manny's Tia Teresa, and Ayo's father, Mr. Oyelowo. The wise Elder Adeyemi stood at the head of the table with Tore Stadheim from Norway at her side with a different sleeveless outfit that showed off his tatts. The young Oracle Ruby and Grandma rounded out the adult crew today, ready to guide them on their next mission. And in the corner, the silent specter of Bolawe watched through his Mirror Realm projection. TJ scowled, only half-listening as Elder Adeyemi briefed them. After a while, TJ realized everyone was staring at him mid scowl.

"I'm sorry. What was that?" TJ asked.

"The voice of your sister," Elder Adeyemi repeated. "Miss Martinez and Mr. Oyelowo said you heard Dayo's voice when you tried to connect with Shango recently."

"Oh, right," TJ murmured. It was true. In one of his latest dreams, he thought he heard Dayo. But he always thought he heard her. He didn't think it was worth noting. "Um… it wasn't very clear. Obatala said it could just be my own dreams melting into Foreseti's. But I think what I heard was a 'no' in my head. But that could have been my own subconscious warning me about Morpheus."

"Hmmm," Elder Adeyemi pressed a hand to her chin. "I wonder if this may be the same as when you saw Ifedayo in that mirror in the hospital last year."

Bolawe stroked his pockmarked skin thoughtfully. *"Excuse me?"*

"None of your business," TJ said flatly, not even looking his way.

*"TJ, come now. We may not see eye to eye on many things, but we both want to connect with Ifedayo again. If that's even possible…"*

"I said none of your business."

Bolawe continued, undeterred. *"If you're seeing her in mirrors, perhaps I can find her in the realm I'm in now. It's a very obscure place. Even Yewa says she never saw your sister pass into the ancestral plane. Perhaps —"*

"My son said that is none of your business," Mom cut in sharply. "Do you have a follow-up question, Elder Adeyemi?"

The Elder nodded. "Just the one. TJ, has Dayo shown her face to you since that time in the hospital room last year?"

TJ shook his head. He didn't think the vision he saw of her in the past with that photo would have counted. That was a younger version of her. The one he saw in the mirror last year was more current.

"We can discuss this more later. For now, we'll take this outcry as a warning for your actions in Forseti's mind," Elder Adeyemi concluded. "Now, let's move on to today's mission. Olufemi, if you would."

Bolawe took a few steps forward, his footsteps sounding like crunching glass against the stone ground. *"Yemoja and Eshu await you all on the other side. TJ and his team will have to enter under my supervision—as we pass through the shard portal Yemoja has rebuilt. I'll be watching through the reflections of the Frost Realm to make sure everything goes according to plan. I warn you now, try anything untoward, and you'll be dealing with Yemoja directly. You already saw her bad side at Eko Atlantic earlier this year."*

"What about Obatala and Oshosi?" Grandma asked. "Won't they come to help?"

"They're inside one of Forseti's dreams," TJ explained. "Scouting for me. We're transitioning from naps to full dreams soon. But it means they'll be stuck for as long as Forseti is asleep."

Mr. Oyelowo stepped forward, eyeing the icy projection of the Frost Realm with suspicion. "How exactly was this realm constructed?" he asked, directing his question at Bolawe. "Yemoja works with the ocean, not with ice."

Bolawe smoothed his robe, his glass form crunching as he did so. *"It is a joint magical effort between the Asgardians and Yemoja. The realm is, correct me if I'm wrong, Mr. Stadheim, a fragment of Niflheim."*

"That is my understanding as well," Mr. Stadheim concurred. "I'm under the impression the realm combines Norse ice magic with Yemoja's aquatic abilities to create the unique environment."

Mr. Oyelowo scoffed. "Yemoja working with Norse gods? That is not like her. Why has she turned from the old ways?"

Elder Adeyemi held up a hand. "It would seem at some point in the distant past, Yemoja tried to rebuild this path in search of Olodumare, our Lost Monarch. This collaboration allows us access to the ancestral realm once more. Without it, the path would remain closed. In any case, the 'why' of the Frost Realm matters little against the fact that it serves our current purposes."

That last term sparked an image in TJ's mind. He was back in Camp Olosa, back at the purple camp fire when Bolawe had explained the story of "The Forgotten Tale," the last time the greatest of the Orishas, Olodumare, was still around. It was Dayo who was supposed to be the "promised child" who would uncover the "Unseen Monarch." It was likely the reason she joined up with the Keepers to begin with. And it seemed like Yemoja had been searching as well.

"I don't like it," Mr. Oyelowo declared. "Yemoja's magic has weakened because she has polluted it with foreign magicks. She should keep to her own people and stay true to the old ways. But instead, she's meddling in aspects beyond her." He whipped a hand toward Ayo. "This is the kind of magic that led to—" He stopped himself and the shadow of a frown crossed his face before he hardened it again. "Elder Adeyemi, there are likely other ways. I've been working it out. I just need more time to do this the *right* way. If we don't, I fear for what could happen to those involved. Namely, my boy."

"I've heard your theories before, Mobolaji. None have even come close to bearing fruit and we don't have the same amount of time for research and development like your companies."

"I beg you, Elder."

The former headmistress seemed genuinely troubled, but she simply sighed. The kind of sigh that TJ assumed Ayo's dad had heard several times before.

"We go today," Adeyemi said firmly. "And that is final."

Mr. Oyelowo whipped to Ayo. "We will not be part of this, son. Come, we're leaving."

Ayo's eyes widened, and he stuttered out a protest. "B-b-but, B-B-Baba, I g-g-gotta..." He couldn't get it out, so he started signing.

Mr. Oyelowo cut him off sharply. "Speak properly, boy! I don't understand when you wave your hands around and stutter like that."

Ayo took a deep breath. "B-b-but..." A long pause. A very long pause. TJ never heard him stumble so hard before. It wasn't just his disability. "I... I w-w-want t-t-to h-h-help," he forced out.

Mr. Oyelowo shook his head in disgust. "Listen to yourself blabber. This is why you have become broken, just like Yemoja. It's a sign from Olodumare! Our family serves Shango alone, not these foreign gods, these false deities. We Oyelowos are *trueborns*." He took Ayo firmly by the arm. "We shall take the direct path to Shango. The others can use this... perversion... to reach Oya if they wish."

TJ watched in disbelief as Mr. Oyelowo yanked Ayo by the arm, dragging him toward the exit. Ayo's eyes pleaded for help, but his father's grip was ironclad. Before TJ realized what he was doing, his feet had taken him to the far side of the meeting hall, blocking the exit.

"C'mon, sir." TJ lifted his hands, realizing for the first time that he was a head taller than Mr. Oyelowo. The man seemed to notice this too, and his eyes darkened. "What are we doing here? Ayo's part of the squad."

"Please, Mr. Oyelowo," Grandma said, standing up slowly from her seat. "We need Ayo; Shango needs him."

Elder Adeyemi drew to her full height as well. "Ayo's role is crucial."

Oracle Ruby rubbed at her green-tipped locs. "Without him, we might not succeed."

Mr. Oyelowo scoffed, not loosening his grip on Ayo. "Crucial for what? Today's mission is to connect that girl," he pointed wickedly at Manny, "and Oya through Yemoja. What does that have to do with my son?"

"Hey, chill with the pointing, sir," TJ said defensively.

"And *this girl*," Manny rolled her neck, "knows a whole lot more about what your son is capable of than you do."

Mr. Oyelowo's eyes flared, and he was halfway to a retort before Mr. Stadheim cut in and said, "Back home, we rune warriors have a saying: *Einn er engi maðr*. 'One is no man.' We need to stand united in this."

"I don't care about your foreign sayings. My son and I serve Shango alone. We will find our own way to him. *That* was my promise. Not this. My son is under this cursed stutter of his because we have not obeyed Shango properly." He eyed Ruby. "Just like you're likely cursed for always using that technology. Why should we believe this TJ Young? Maybe this boy was wrong, or mistaken. Most who come back from the other side come back mad. Or are we all forgetting how the Great Xavier Du Bois is nothing but a one-phrase simpleton shuffling along the corridors of Babalu-Aye." His eyes went wild under his glasses, like he was convincing himself or coming to some great revelation. "No! Orunmila didn't wither because of some Fate nonsense. He died because his divine children forsaken him for *algorithms*. Did you ever think of that?"

That seemed to wound Ruby as she made herself small in her chair.

What was wrong with this man? He was unhinged. He wasn't a stupid man, from what TJ knew. And his fierce dedication to Shango was admirable, but why couldn't he see the bigger picture? Why was he so against collaborating with the others? TJ wondered if there was a deeper reason behind Mr. Oyelowo's refusal. Maybe it was fear—fear of the unknown, of losing control, of relying on unfamiliar magicks. Or perhaps it was just pride, an unwavering belief that his way was the only way. Whatever it was, TJ couldn't understand why Mr. Oyelowo would risk everything, including his own son's potential to help, just to stick to his principles.

"We're talking about saving Shango and Oya," Mom added, her voice rising in urgency. "And this isn't just about *one* Orisha; it's about the balance of *all* realms."

Mr. Oyelowo shook his head, resolute. "Balance? You're meddling with forces you don't understand." He tugged Ayo again, but TJ stood his ground.

Usually TJ would cower under such confrontation. He didn't like it, but it all seemed to be forgotten in his act to defend his friend. So he poured some of the Hunter's courage into his next words. "Wh-What are you hiding, sir?" Despite his shaky voice, TJ put a hand to the man's chest. "What's got you scared?"

Mr. Oyelowo drew in close before saying, "If you knew the things I knew, you'd do the same. But you do not know these things, so I can only pray for you."

"Then explain i-i-it," Ayo stuttered with less severity this time.

A sadness brushed across Mr. Oyelowo's face. It almost seemed like he was at the edge of divulging something. Instead, he said, "Step out of my way, young man. My son and I are leaving."

Ayo's eyes met TJ's, a silent apology in their depths. TJ's heart ached for his friend, trapped between duty to his father and the desire to help their mission. Reluctantly, TJ pivoted and allowed Mr. Oyelowo to pass. Ayo cast one last, longing glance back at everyone before he crossed the threshold. TJ even glimpsed a few officers staring from their desks as the father and son passed.

"And we're going to figure out how to get that cursed tattoo from under your eye," Mr. Oyelowo was saying as the large doors shut. Even after the stone slabs closed, Ayo's stuttered yells that started up could be heard on the other side. A flush of second-hand embarrassment ran through TJ. He was glad Mom didn't pull his arm like that anymore. TJ bit his lip. Having Ayo by his side always made him feel better, and Ayo's Ashe via Shango always worked so well with Manny's. It was almost too easy boosting them.

Now, they were a little less.

Elder Adeyemi waited until the sound of Ayo's protests receded farther into the reaches of the underground facility before she said, "Anyone else want to leave? Because this would be the time."

TJ threw up a hand. "We're really going to let that happen."

*"Mr. Oyelowo isn't exactly wrong,"* Bolawe spoke up after having been quiet a while. *"His son isn't strictly needed for this part of the operation. And the ancestral magic tying this all together is important to get right. That means* all *parties need to be fully willing for the Ashe to work true. His hesitancy would actually put today's work in jeopardy."*

"So I ask again," Adeyemi said. "Does anyone else here harbor doubts?"

There was a short silence before Manny's aunt said, "No— Though I do have a question for Mr. Stadheim before we continue."

Elder Adeyemi turned to the Norse emissary, who nodded. "What might your question be?"

"This... fragment of Niflheim. I did my own research on the place. Is it true it's associated with one of your underworlds? I was confused about this. I thought Helheim was the underrealm for your pantheon, not this Niflheim."

Tore Stadheim, with the glow of the ice projection casting shadows over his exposed arms and tattoos, spoke up. "Niflheim, the 'Mist World,' is a realm of ice and cold to the north, part of the creation of the cosmos, where primordial frost gave life its beginning. In contrast, Helheim, ruled by Hel, Loki's daughter, lies beneath Yggdrasil's roots, serving as the final resting place for those who die *outside* of battle."

Tia Teresa nodded. "So, there is no possibility of encountering the dead on our journey?"

"Not from the Norse half, no," Mr. Stadheim answered. "But this place Yemoja has designed—if it is tied to this ancestral path—could see some overlap with the dead, in theory."

TJ took particular notice of Manny's aunt, whose face changed slightly at the news. He couldn't determine if the expression was apprehensive or curious.

"There are risks in using this portal," Elder Adeyemi added. "Your minds may become clouded upon returning. But this realm is less formed than others, so the effects should be minor. However, I need your word of approval before we proceed."

Manny's aunt nodded solemnly. "You have my word."

Mom also agreed. "And mine as well."

"Children?" Adeyemi questioned.

"You have my word," TJ and Manny said together.

Ruby gave an approving smile, throwing her green-tipped locks over her shoulder. "Though establishing a bridge is important, this will be good practice for accessing the portal to the Court of All. Consider it active training. A way to get your 'portal legs,' as TJ likes to call it."

Elder Adeyemi surveyed them all. "Very well. Let us begin."

## 20

# THE BROKEN TREE

TJ SHIFTED UNEASILY AS THE GROUP PREPARED FOR THEIR journey into the Frost Realm. Though he tried to appear calm on the outside, his palms were slick with sweat inside his gloves. The last time he had entered this icy domain, it was on a whim, leaping through the portal on the orders of Elder Adeyemi. Now he had time to think, and thinking was never good for TJ's nerves.

Manny pulled on and zipped up a fluffy parka, then snuggled a beanie over her mass of hair, which poked out at the bottom. As her aunt threw on snow gloves and Mom fussed with the straps on her travel bag, TJ's mind wandered back to his previous trip there: The biting cold, the treacherous cliffs, and most vividly, the towering Frost Giant that had nearly smashed him into a pancake. TJ shuddered, remembering the creature's icy skin and murderous blue glare.

Would they encounter more of the giants on this mission? He hoped not.

His thoughts then turned to Mr. Stadheim's chilling words—that they may even face the dead in the Frost Realm. TJ had seen spirits and deities of all sorts, but never a ghost or specter of any kind. The logic didn't make sense, but that seemed worse to him.

Shaking himself, TJ adjusted his own gear, tightening the straps on his gloves inlaid with sheep wool. This was not the time for his overactive imagination to run wild. He needed to focus, so he stared straight at the waterfall cascading down the stone wall, listening to its flow to steady his breathing.

TJ squared his shoulders as Bolawe's Mirror Realm form lifted the ice shard of the Frost Realm between his fingers. At first, it looked like the shard was stuck with him on his side of the Mirror Realm. But as he raised it and handed it to Elder Adeyemi, it seemed to materialize on their side of reality.

*"Remember,"* Bolawe said darkly, *"Yemoja and Eshu will not hesitate. If I or they detect even a whiff of betrayal, Yemoja will seal off the realm and trap you all inside."*

TJ's stomach knotted. Being trapped in the Frost Realm indefinitely didn't appeal to him. But it was the others he worried for more—Mom, Manny, Manny's aunt. What would happen to them, stuck in the icy wasteland?

Just look at the toll crossing realms had taken on Ayo. The stutter, the memory issues... TJ didn't want to imagine his other loved ones suffering the same fate. Or worse.

"Right now, we share the same goals," Elder Adeyemi said evenly. "Let's focus on the mission at hand. No one here intends to betray anyone."

TJ knew this to be untrue—at least that's what the Elder had told him. Eventually, a betrayal against Bolawe was coming. He just doubted it would happen today when Operation Stormbreak was only now kicking off. How Adeyemi would eventually manage it was another thing altogether. Regardless, for now, the Elder's words seemed to diffuse the tension because Bolawe gave a curt nod.

TJ let out a breath, releasing the tension in his shoulders. "Well then. Should we get started?" He turned to Elder Adeyemi. "May I?"

She passed him the icy shard. Even through his gloves, it was cold to the touch, sending a chill up TJ's dead arm. A portion of the scarring exposed under his glove glowed ice blue. He hardly noticed, however, too focused on the realm, willing it to open for them.

"I'm ready when you are," he told the others.

Mom gazed upon TJ lovingly. This would be the first time she'd see him in action. She smiled and said, "I told you, Tomori Jomiloju, didn't I? 'The crest on the head of the peacock simply won't fit any other bird.'"

"'We are all differently endowed,'" Grandma added. "'Be secure in who you are—'"

"Envy no one," TJ finished for her with steady confidence. A tear nearly crested Mom's eyelid. The words gave TJ the energy he needed. *This* is what he was made for.

"Oh, Yejide!" Grandma cooed. "You told your son that one? That's the one I used to tell you when you were a child, wasn't it?"

Mom smiled bashfully.

"All right, everyone, let's link up," TJ said, holding out the icy shard, using Oya's Wind to help him.

Mom stepped forward first, placing a gentle hand on his shoulder. Her touch filled him with warmth and courage. Manny came next, gripping his other shoulder firmly. Her aunt followed suit, completing their human chain.

Manny caught his eye and gave him a reassuring nod. They could do this. Together, they would brave the Frost Realm and complete their mission. All TJ had to do was take that first step through the portal.

"Now remember," Elder Adeyemi told them. "This transport should only work because of the bonds between you. As you move through this realm and into the next, remember the ancestral and mystical connections that bind you, your blood ties, your kinships."

TJ clutched the shard, channeling his Ashe into it. The exposed scars on his arms glowed blue as icy mist began swirling around them. He felt the power of the realm responding, the portal opening. Different energies cast from each of them, sensations familiar to TJ: The feeling he got whenever he made Mom proud. The feeling he got whenever he told a joke and made Manny laugh. The only feeling he couldn't fully determine was the one coming off Tia Teresa. TJ's connection with her was the weakest, after all. Would she make it through okay?

"H-Here we go," TJ said with hesitation. "On three. One… two…"

On three, he released the magic, straight into one of the cracks of the shard. Bright blue light exploded outward, consuming them.

TJ's stomach lurched as they were pulled forward violently. Mom's grip on his shoulder tightened.

Howling wind and stinging ice enveloped them. He could no longer see the others through the raging blizzard. But he could still feel Mom's hand, Manny's hand. They were still linked.

TJ focused everything on maintaining the connection, on keeping them all together as they hurtled through the void between realms. He was their tether, their guide, and he alone would show them the way safely. But there was something holding them back. That sensation that TJ couldn't discern before.

In his mind's eye, an icy tree of white bark sprang to life. Most of its branches were firm and strong, but one was weak and brittle. At its tip, there seemed to be a face carved in the pale wood. A face oddly familiar. Manny's dimples? No, this face was slightly older—the long hair different from Manny's curly one. Was that Manny's aunt's link?

TJ refocused his energy, funneling less into the strong bonds of Mom and Manny, and trying his best to bridge the gap between himself and Tia Teresa. But TJ just couldn't understand what she was feeling. A touch of panic clung to TJ's chest like barbed wire. He had to understand what that feeling was. He had to keep everyone together. What the hell was it? It was a bond he could only... wait! It was the bond between a mother and her child. He could sense it. It was the same thing he felt between himself and his mom. Just in reverse.

Deep in his mind, TJ flipped the switch, and it was like the floodgates had opened up. The branching tree in his mind mended and reformed. And slowly, *oh so slowly,* the icy gale subsided. The light faded. Forms took shape in the fading mist: Towering cliffs, jagged icicles, sparkling snow.

He gasped. They had arrived in the Frost Realm.

# 21

# FRAGMENTS OF MIST AND DARKNESS

TJ SQUINTED AGAINST THE BLINDING WHITE LANDSCAPE, struggling to gain his bearings as the portal's magic faded behind them. Towering cliffs of blue ice surrounded them on all sides, forming a narrow ravine that stretched endlessly into the distance. The walls seemed to touch the sky, colossal and imposing.

Unlike the last time he'd visited the Frost Realm, the sky was no longer fractured and glitchy-looking. And now that it was fully sealed, it seemed to hold in the impossible cold, forcing TJ to pull his scarf around his neck tighter. His breath came out in icy plumes. It was deathly silent, except for the crunch of snow beneath their boots. Even the howling wind from their passage through the portal had stilled.

"Everyone okay?" TJ asked, turning to check on his companions.

Manny gave him a thumbs up, though her teeth chattered violently. Mom nodded, already wrapping her thickly-woven shawl more tightly around her shoulders. Manny's aunt busied herself zipping up her parka.

"I-I can't believe it," Mom said, staring up, eyes starry. "We're in another realm. I never thought I'd see it."

Satisfied they had weathered the transition, TJ surveyed their surroundings. The snowy valley floor was flat and featureless, with no clear path in sight. He frowned. How were they supposed to know which way to go?

As he pondered their next move, a glint caught his eye. TJ turned and saw a thin slit in the icy cliff face behind them. Peering closer, he realized it was the ice fracture they had come through.

On the other side, a massive dark brown eye gazed in at them. TJ jumped, thinking it was a giant they needed to fight, before recognizing the eye as Elder Adeyemi's. Like the last time he was here, she was watching their progress—though this time from the command center.

Her lips moved, but no sound came through. Squinting, TJ looked to the reflective surfaces near him to find Bolawe, who would be the bridge. Not far away, next to the cliff face, TJ found his image in a sheet of ice.

"Oh!" TJ said tonelessly. "Ask Elder Adeyemi if she can hear us. We made it safely into the Frost Realm."

The brown eye crinkled in an apparent smile. Then it withdrew, replaced by a piercing blue one—Mr. Stadheim's.

*"No, they can't hear you,"* Bolawe's icy blue image said. *"But I can relay... wait. Mr. Stadheim is saying something. Oh, no, it's just Oracle Ruby. She's excited you've made it."*

Despite the dire nature of their quest, TJ allowed himself a small smile. At least someone was enjoying themself. That smile faded, however, as Bolawe's visage suddenly appeared in a different sheet of ice closer to him. TJ tensed, scowling at the man's reflection.

"What's our first move?" TJ asked tersely, already dreading the answer. Clearly, they would be relying on Bolawe's guidance in this realm. He disliked having so little information, forced to follow the Keepers' lead blindly.

Before Bolawe could respond, a melodic voice spoke behind them. "It is wonderful to finally meet you properly, Tomori Jomiloju Young."

TJ whirled around. Standing tall—*impossibly tall*—was the Orisha Yemoja. She was regal in her white robes, dark skin contrasting starkly with the icy landscape. A bone-white crown of seashells sat atop her head. Long, matted locs fell from beneath it. Each lock of hair was wrapped by beads, bells, and coral.

TJ gaped up at the towering form of Yemoja, barely able to comprehend her immense size. Gone was the mermaid-like form he recalled from their past encounter. Now Yemoja stood on two breathtakingly long legs of smooth brown skin that revealed themselves when the icy draft lifted her robes occasionally.

TJ shuddered, remembering the devastation Yemoja had wrought on Lagos, on Eko Atlantic. Thousands had drowned that day when she helped her husband summon a tidal wave against the city. He still didn't fully understand why she had attacked so mercilessly.

"Um, are you sure?" TJ asked. "I mean… it's nice to meet me? I thought you'd hate me for stopping you at Eko Atlantic."

Yemoja gave him a gentle, motherly smile. "I believe the lesson was learned. On both sides, don't you think? You will find that I, unlike Olokun, do not hold a grudge."

TJ turned to Manny, who traded a look of exasperation with him. "Well, I'm not prostrating to you, and I hope you understand why."

"TJ…" Mom chided. "That's Yemoja you're speaking to." Mom dropped down in a full prostration. "We are greatly honored, Mother Ocean."

"I-I'm not curtsying or anything either," Manny started to say, more hesitant than TJ.

Mom didn't have words for Manny, but her look told of the disapproval well enough.

"We respect your power," TJ said. "But you do not have my praise."

"And not mine either," Manny added.

Yemoja stood tall and stock still. It was impossible to know what she was thinking, but she thought for a long while before saying, "It has been several ages since a mortal has stood up to me. Accountability from your kind is not something I'm accustomed to…" She took in a deep breath that seemed to suck in all the cold around them. "You must understand, getting our messages to you mortals has been difficult since The Great Separation. So frustrations grow. Usually, I have a cooler head for these things, but Olokun's influence… was greater."

Besides TJ and Manny, the only other one who did not immediately show respect was Manny's aunt, who looked at Yemoja with a near scowl as she examined the Orisha up and down. TJ hoped Yemoja was tall enough that she couldn't see their facial expressions. Manny had to clear her throat. They weren't showing the praise Yemoja might have wanted, but they weren't giving her death stares either.

*What's her auntie's deal?* TJ thought.

Yemoja's eyes narrowed slightly. "While I am thankful for the due respect..." She angled her head to Mom. "I can understand why you are none too pleased with me after recent... *tidal* events."

"With all due respect, you did try to drown thousands of innocent people," TJ said bluntly, shouting up to be heard. "I can't pretend to understand why."

Yemoja drew herself up taller, somehow. "For centuries, your kind has polluted my oceans with waste and oil. Overfished my waters. Used my seas to transport your very ancestors, my divine children, into bondage." Her voice hardened, and TJ would've sworn he saw Yemoja's eyes watering. The Ashe casting off her was so strong, he could almost feel her heartbreak in his own heart. The empathy she held was astounding. "The corporate greed and neglect of humankind could not go unchecked any further," she finished, unapologetic.

Bolawe's image suddenly appeared in a sheet of ice nearby. "*The Great Mother speaks true. Humanity's transgressions against the natural world must have consequences.*"

TJ frowned. He understood Yemoja's anger, but that didn't justify her actions. "I agree we've screwed things up pretty bad, but... those skyscrapers you attacked had nothing to do with overfishing or oil spills."

"Innocent lives were lost," Manny added, head downcast.

Yemoja tilted her head ponderously, considering TJ and Manny's words. Before she could respond, Mom stepped forward and placed a gentle hand on his shoulder.

"You both make valid points," she said gently. "But debating the rights and wrongs of the past will not help us now. We are united by a common purpose—to save Shango and Oya." She turned her earnest gaze to Yemoja. "I know you care deeply for them. As any Mother of All would. Please, will you help us?"

Yemoja studied Mom silently. After a long moment, her expression softened. "You speak wisdom, mother of Tomori Jomiloju." She turned her giant eyes to TJ. "I can see why Olokun likes you."

"Wait, what?" TJ said, surprised. "Olokun *likes* me."

"Well, amused with you, at least. But never mind that. We shall focus on the task at hand."

Just then, Eshu emerged from behind a nearby snowdrift. His large nose and distinctive floppy hat were unmistakable. His exposed belly through his red-and-black loincloth still wasn't free of that perpetual pudge. His expression reminded TJ so much of how he first knew him... as just another friendly camper named Joshua.

TJ tensed as Eshu emerged, his hands balling into fists, barely noticing how easy the effort was now that he was in the ethereal realm. Before TJ could speak, Eshu held up his hands placatingly. "I know you have no love for me, TJ, my old friend. But I swear by all my sibling Orishas, it was not truly me that day on the shores of Lagos. I should have stopped Olokun and Yemoja when things got too far. I *wanted* to."

TJ's gaze sharpened, unconvinced. "Oh really? You were holding that door to the Aqua Realm pretty good." He ripped off one of his gloves and showed his bleach-white skin to Eshu. "Thanks for forcing me to do this, by the way. I'd be fully paralyzed from the elbow down if it wasn't for my Ashe—or the healers."

Eshu's shoulders drooped, and he stared at TJ's hands for a long while, looking truly defeated and hurt. "It was my spiritual body that did all that, yes. But my spiritual mind was not my own. Some alien energy seized me—a hungry cloud that overtook my senses during that time." He shivered. "I have *never* felt such a void before. Not even the darkest, angriest moments of my existence could compare."

"I guess that's why you don't answer some of our prayers then," Manny's aunt mumbled from behind.

"Tia..." Manny scolded. "Not here. Not right now."

TJ's anger wavered slightly. Eshu did seem different—his usual playful demeanor replaced by that haunted, almost fearful look. Still, TJ remained wary.

"The God Eaters," TJ said flatly. "Was it them? Did they make you attack?"

Eshu shook his head helplessly. "I cannot say for certain. All I know is that in those moments, I was not myself. It was as if another entity possessed me entirely. For what little it is worth, you have my sincere apologies for the harm caused."

Studying him closely, TJ was surprised to find he believed Eshu. The regret in the trickster's voice seemed genuine. With a sigh, TJ unclenched his fists. "I accept your apology," he said finally. "But how can we trust you now? If this dark cloud can seize you again at any moment…"

"A fair concern," Eshu said gravely. He turned his eyes up to Yemoja. Eshu was bigger than a human, but Yemoja dwarfed him several times over. "I've mentioned this concern to the Great Mother as well. Yemoja, I do not know if I should even be here. What if this darkness takes me once more? I could endanger you all."

Yemoja gave him a stern look. "You are the Gatekeeper, Eshu. We will need you to reopen the ancestral passages. You cannot back out now."

Eshu still looked uncertain. Manny was the one to step forward this time. "Maybe this is your chance to make up for what happened… To make up for the damage somehow."

"I think you'll be fine," TJ said, thinking back to his meetings with Obatala and how the Dreamweaver said he was protecting Eshu's mind the same way Morpheus was protecting Forseti's.

With a reluctant sigh, Eshu nodded. "I will try my best."

A twinge of sympathy for the Trickster filtered through TJ. He seemed truly disturbed by whatever had seized control of him.

Glancing sidelong, TJ noticed Bolawe observing silently from the reflection of the icy cliff face. His stoic expression gave no hint of his thoughts. TJ's face twisted into a grimace. Bolawe may have brought them all together, but TJ was growing less and less forgiving of the Keeper. The Orishas operated on different rules, primordial morals. Bolawe was human though, and TJ still blamed him not only for Dayo's death but Emeka's too. And who knew what the Keeper's true motives were for this mission to begin with.

Manny looked around the icy ravine, her brow furrowing. "Where's Olokun, anyway? I'm surprised he didn't try to attack the coast again all year."

Yemoja shook her head, the shells and coral in her hair clinking softly. "Olokun was gravely injured during that day. All the Ashe was funneling through them. It will take many moons before Olokun recovers. It could even take decades for them to recover completely. This is why 'natural' phenomena like that don't happen often in your world. It takes an *extraordinary* amount of Ashe."

TJ rubbed his ear under his beanie's ear flap. "Wait, 'they'? I thought Olokun was supposed to be a 'he.'"

Yemoja smiled gently. "In Yoruba, there are no direct translations for 'he' and 'she'. I sometimes get mixed up in that conversion. What's more, Olokun takes many fluid forms." She flung out one of her giant feet. "As can I take on many forms. But Olokun does not mind how you address them, so long as you show the proper divine respect."

"Can we please stop the yapping already?" Eshu cut in nervously with a bit more of the tone TJ was used to from him. But it seemed the tone was meant less for comedic effect as TJ noticed the Orisha's eyes darting around as if expecting a mental attack. "Let's get these humans through the ancestral path quickly. The entrance is just over that ridge." He pointed to a snowy slope just visible at the end of the ravine.

Drawing in a deep breath, TJ steeled himself. "All right. Let's get this thing going."

Alongside Mom, Manny and her aunt, TJ carefully walked the ice toward the ridge. Toward the ancestral path, and whatever lay beyond.

# 22

# KEEP IT 100

JAGGED CLIFFS OF BLUE ICE TOWERED ABOVE THEM, REFRACTING the pale sunlight into dazzling rainbows across the snow as they continued on. An icy wind whipped through the ravine, biting at any exposed skin. TJ shivered, pulling his coat tighter around himself.

"I must admit," Mom said, matching TJ's pace. "I was quite nervous about how all that would go with Yemoja. But you nailed it, TJ. Speaking so openly and honestly with an Orisha takes great courage. You showed respect and criticism well."

TJ bit his lip as he shuffled over the ice. He didn't feel particularly brave. If anything, he'd been stupidly oblivious, interacting with the Orishas without fully grasping the danger. After all he'd endured, fear didn't *always* come naturally anymore. Sometimes he wished it did.

The group continued onward, the crunching of ice echoing off the azure ravine. Bolawe's projection hovered from ice wall to ice wall, scanning the frosty cliffs like a scout.

"*This way,*" his voice boomed coolly.

Yemoja and Eshu walked silently beside them. Yemoja took great effort to go as slow as possible as not to outpace the mortals. Eshu kept glancing at TJ, as if wanting to speak, but said nothing.

"*I'm seeing a large ice pocket ahead,*" came Bolawe's voice through the reflections. *"It appears to be the most direct route. But use caution in traversing it."*

They reached the cavern entrance, a crooked split in the icy mountainside at least fifty feet high, enough space for Yemoja if she crouched. Bolawe's Mirror Realm projection illuminated the way forward with a pale glow. As TJ stepped inside, his breath caught. Thick icicles hung from the ceiling, refracting Bolawe's light into dazzling displays across the cavern walls. Underfoot, the ground was smooth and slick.

Manny stood in awe of the landscape. She saw the ethereal realms for the *first* time *every* time. TJ took several jabs to the shoulder when she pointed out this landmark or that landmark. Ayo would have loved being here.

*Wonder what he's doing now,* TJ thought. *Probably trying to sneak back into the command center.*

*"Heh, this Stadheim fellow is a riot,"* Bolawe relayed. *"Such a bouncy fellow for his size. He says the ice formations here are extraordinary. Says the magical signatures are definitely runic in nature, no doubt the work of the Asgardians."*

TJ took another moment to examine the space around them. It felt oddly familiar. Through his Ashe Vision, he thought he saw a familiar "I" shape blooming behind the ice walls. Where had he seen that before? It wasn't until he caught sight of Manny's eyes that he remembered. She looked at him with a curious brow and something changed in her expression that made her blush. A look that always gave TJ butterflies. Again, she reinforced that she *was* his anchor. Just being near her made TJ feel centered. And as that anchor solidified, it set his mind straight back to the dream world he visited with Oshosi and Obatala. That "I" shape on the ice surfaces was runic in nature. Again, like before, it felt important. But why?

The group slowly picked their way through the cavern, bracing themselves against the walls when the ground sloped downward. Eshu held out a hand, steadying TJ as he slipped. TJ smiled gratefully.

"I've been meaning to ask," Eshu said quietly. "How are Shango and Oya holding up?"

TJ swallowed, mind flashing back to what the Orisha couple were going through each time he caught glimpses through Forseti.

Just last week he dived deep enough to see some pretty horrible images.

"Not great," TJ said. "They're being totally drained."

"Hmm. And how are they doing it? The Court, I mean. Did you see how the magic works? I know you have a knack for that."

TJ shrugged. "We're still figuring it out. But they were in a sort of… dream state. In their minds, they were fighting an endless war. I guess I could sense that's how The Channeling works. Maybe. We're not sure. It's still just a theory since we're deciphering all these dreams. The Court is basically, like, forcing them to use their best magic to um…"

"Extract the essence of two pure warrior spirits," Eshu said sadly, the cold, blue glacial walls around him making him look more melancholic. "Yes… I expected they'd do something like that. That's a powerful illusion they're working, those òlóṣì."

"You think you can help with that?" TJ asked. "Reverse the illusion? Break up The Channeling?"

Eshu turned to him with a wink. "With you by my side, I think almost anything is possible, kid."

"*We're nearing the exit,*" Bolawe called from a reflection up ahead. "*I can sense the ancestral path just beyond. Wow, would you look at that view? You outdid yourself, Yemoja.*"

They stepped out of the cavern onto a narrow cliff path. Steep slopes dropped away on either side, revealing an endless icy landscape stretching to the horizon. In the distance, colossal mountains shone blue-white in the dim sunlight.

Manny's aunt huffed, glaring up at Bolawe's projection. "Yes, yes, we see it's all very impressive. Now pay attention to guiding us!"

TJ studied her as they continued along the path, single-file. Her lips were pressed in a thin line, eyes darting about warily. The closer they drew to the ancestral path, the more tense she became. TJ fell into step behind Manny.

"What's going on with your aunt?" he whispered. "She buggin' out a little, no?"

Manny shrugged. "No idea. This whole mission has been weird from the start."

TJ blew out cold from his nose, exasperated. If Manny's aunt posed a threat to their goal of saving Shango and Oya, that could spell disaster. But out here, what could she really do?

The path ended abruptly, opening onto a sheer cliff face. Far below, through whirling mist, lay their destination—the ancestral path. Ethereal and glowing faintly purple, it wound through the valley below before disappearing into the mountains.

Yemoja turned to the group. "It is time. The journey ahead will not be easy. But stay strong, stay together, and we will prevail."

Centering himself by taking a deep breath, TJ stepped forward with the others to begin the dangerous descent. He peered over the edge of the cliff, the swirling mists obscuring their destination far below. His stomach dropped at the sheer height. There was no way they could climb down safely without aid.

Yemoja crouched. "Climb onto my back, my mortal children. I will carry you down."

Manny scrambled up first, finding handholds on the Orisha's robes and necklaces. TJ followed, hoisting himself onto Yemoja's broad shoulder. Her skin was smooth and cool, like river stones. Mom followed suit. Manny's aunt came next, clearly hesitant to allow an Orisha to aid her. But under Eshu's stern gaze, she reluctantly climbed onto Yemoja's back.

Once they were settled, Yemoja stood slowly.

"Hold on tight now," she rumbled. TJ wrapped his arms around the hem of her white robes as she turned and began descending the cliff face. Her massive hands and feet easily found holds in the rock.

Last came Eshu, twirling his staff. "No need to carry me, Great Mother. I'll make my own way down." He leapt from the cliff, loincloth flapping behind him. TJ gasped, but Eshu landed lightly on a rocky outcrop twenty feet below. With an impish grin, he hopped to the next perch.

Yemoja continued her careful descent, and TJ marveled at her grace and strength, finding solid holds even on the sheerest parts of the cliff. She murmured softly, more to herself than them. "This place, it calls to me. Niflheim working in concert with the Frost Realm. I feel the spirit of creation here. And of death. Perhaps even Olodumare Themself. Their essence is near, *so very close*."

TJ blinked. "You think Olodumare is here? But why?"

"I am not certain, child. But when I call to Them now, there is only silence. A *deliberate* silence. As though They sleep in the depths of this place. And now, with you, that has been *amplified*."

"I tend to have that effect." TJ shivered. He knew that empty silence all too well. The silence of being between realms, between identities. Neither here nor there. "An in-between," he murmured.

Yemoja nodded sagely. "Indeed. If Olodumare slumbers here, we must find and rouse Them. The Great Monarch could bring harmony between us and the mortal realms again. And defend us against this God Eater threat."

"Us?" TJ questioned.

"Sorry, I meant you. Though, I'm told you've heard this before. That—"

"I am neither Orisha nor mortal. At least not all the way on either side."

"Indeed."

As they climbed down, Bolawe's reflection showed itself again. *"Mr. Stadheim says that's 'a compelling notion.' Yemoja, he's asking who aided you in shaping this realm. He is most curious."*

Yemoja inclined her head thoughtfully. "I crafted this realm alongside Hel, Queen of the Dead in Helheim. My own pantheon offered no answers, so I sought wisdom elsewhere."

At this, Tia Teresa frowned, listening intently. Manny's aunt had done the same, it seemed, seeking solace from Catholic saints when the Orishas had failed her.

They were halfway down the cliff now. TJ spotted Eshu far below, waving his staff to clear away mist and illuminate their path. Bolawe's projection flitted about the ice walls, directing their course.

Manny tapped TJ's shoulder. "Hey, can I ask you something? Away from the others? Before we go on."

TJ nodded. "What's up? Your auntie?"

She played with the zipper on her parka. "No, not that..." She trailed off as Yemoja reached the bottom of the cliff and let them down. Eshu and Bolawe waited nearby on the edge of the glowing ancestral path, along with Mom and Tia Teresa.

"All right, team, let's take five!" Eshu beamed. It was nice to see some of his cavalier sensibilities returned.

Manny pulled TJ aside. She chewed her bottom lip, seeming unsure how to begin.

"What's… going on?" TJ asked. The energy between them had definitely shifted, but he didn't know in what way exactly.

Manny took a deep breath. "My memories have been coming back slowly. It's different from the Orisha Planes. The Frost Realm doesn't wipe things away instantly. And… the reverse seems to be true of memories coming back."

TJ's brow furrowed. "What do you remember?"

"You… can't guess?" TJ blanked. He had a hard time keeping track of what people remembered and didn't. He'd never had that issue. Then it dawned on him like a ton of bricks. But before he could say anything, Manny spoke first. "The Chamber of Candor. Where we confessed our… feelings." She paused, as though waiting for TJ to say something, but he was too shell-shocked to respond like a normal person. "Our feelings for each other."

TJ couldn't get a response out. His mind was stuck on record, playing back Manny's sudden surprise. It was true. They'd bared their souls in that magical place, admitting things they'd never dared speak out loud because… well… it was weird. And they had a rule about *not* making things weird.

Manny punched him. "Why didn't you say anything?"

TJ shrugged the pain away, searching her big brown eyes. "Wasn't sure you'd really believe me."

Manny huffed. "Of course I'd believe you, idiot! And I told you at the hospital I felt something. That I wasn't mad anymore."

"Well… why didn't *you* say anything, then?" TJ countered.

"'Cause it's weird, yo!" Manny threw up her hands. "These feelings, they're mad strong but all over the place. And I always thought that I was…" She bit her last words away. "It almost makes me sick."

"Oh, great. I make you sick."

"Nah, nah, not in a bad way. I can't explain it." She took a breath, gaze softening. "But we should talk about this. Promise me we'll talk later. I know you, TJ, don't just leave it on pause."

"Promise," TJ said quickly, but then his tone turned sad. "But when? Between everything… the Court of All. My staffcrafting. Oshosi. Oya. Shango. This place."

Manny considered his words, her forehead scrunching. She took a beat before she spoke again. "You… don't have any court dates in

December, right? No appointments with any Greek Gods or Hindi deities?"

TJ laughed and shook his head. "If I can help it. No, I shouldn't. Only got The Hero's Equinox locked in on the calendar."

"So..." She rocked on her heels. "Be my date for my quinceañera. It'll be in New York. Near my place. I need a '*chambelán de honor*'—uhm—an escort. And I can't think of anyone else I'd want."

TJ blinked in surprise. "But... you won't remember this conversation."

"So make me remember." She poked him in a challenge. "I've been wanting to ask, anyway. If you do something nice for me, I promise future me will say yes. It'll be like my trigger..."

"... your anchor," TJ said softly to himself.

"... And I'll probably blush if you catch me off guard, so don't make fun."

"No promises. But if you turn purple, I'm taking a picture for the yearbook." He laughed, then took her hand. Somehow, their fingers interlaced automatically. "And... thanks for coming at me like that. It might've been another year before I did anything otherwise," TJ said slowly, eyeing Manny's lips a beat too long. He meant it sincerely, but doubts lurked in his mind. Between school, the Court, and the mission, would he have time for Manny in that way? She deserved more than the little he feared he could give her.

Their conversation was interrupted as Eshu announced break time was over. They had to continue onward, into the unknown. TJ and Manny rejoined the others, thoughts swirling with memories, feelings, and the monumental task ahead. There would be time to unravel it all later. For now, they had a job to do.

# 23

# GLACIAL WALLS

TJ AND THE OTHERS ENTERED A VALLEY FILLED WITH SWIRLING mists of ice particles. It was so thick it was difficult to see even a few feet ahead, their vision almost completely obscured. As they pressed forward, ghostly images appeared on the glassy walls around them —visions of ancestors long passed.

"It worked," Yemoja breathed out, gazing upon her creation. "Hel would have been so proud, wherever she is now. We were able to meld her runes and my Ashe as one."

Eshu looked around, skittish. "Good, let's start this thing so we can create the bridge and get outta dodge. TJ? If you would..." He gestured to his hip. "Go ahead and grab on. My Ashe is for the taking."

TJ hesitated, the cold air gnawing into his skin. He looked at Yemoja, her serene face masking the depths of her power. Then, he turned to Eshu, whose eyes twinkled with a mixture of mischief and anticipation.

"All right," TJ said, his voice trembling more from nerves than the cold. He reached out, placing one hand on Yemoja's ankle and the other on Eshu's hip. Immediately, a surge of Ashe, powerful and vibrant, flowed into him. It was like holding onto a rumbling mountain and a tranquil sea at the same time, a perfect blend of chaos and calm.

"Focus, young mortal," Yemoja instructed calmly. "Feel the connection to the ancestors, let the Ashe guide you."

Closing his eyes, TJ concentrated. He envisioned the icy valley around him, felt the cold beneath his feet, and the energy coursing through him. He began to chant softly, words of ancient Yoruba mixing with the universal magic that tied them all together.

The ground beneath them trembled, and the icy walls shimmered, reflecting the ethereal glow of their combined Ashe. A low hum filled the air, growing louder and more resonant, like the heartbeat of the universe itself. The mists started to part, revealing an endless abyss of black beyond the valley.

"Keep going," Eshu encouraged. "You're doing great! Hah! I had forgotten how *good* you are at this."

As TJ continued the ritual, a starfield emerged from the darkness. Tiny points of light flickered into existence, slowly painting themselves across the void. They glinted and danced, forming constellations and celestial patterns.

In the distance, a bright golden light appeared, growing steadily brighter. It was as if the very essence of divinity was calling out to them, beckoning them forward. TJ squinted, trying to make out what it was. Could it be the Court of All?

Before he could ponder further, a sharp gasp from Mom broke his concentration.

"What is it?" TJ asked, his voice tinged with worry.

Mom gasped again as she saw the face of her own grandmother in the glacial walls—a woman TJ barely recognized from very old photos. She had saggy and wrinkled skin, lips thinned out, and bags under her eyes, but she couldn't look more joyful. Full of life.

Shaking with sobs, Mom rushed to the wall, tenderly stroking the image and speaking softly to her grandmother, as if she were really there. *"Mo gbàdúrà sí ọ ní gbogbo alẹ́,"* Mom was saying in Yoruba, *"A kò gbọ́ ohunkóhun padà. Ṣé o ti wà níbí gbogbo ìgbà yìí?"*

"Mrs. Young, what do you see?" Manny asked, squinting.

"You can't see her, can you?" TJ realized.

*"Agent Stadheim says it sounds like we are in the Valley of the Dead now,"* Bolawe said through a reflective ice sheet. *"Only those with a direct bloodline can see their ancestors here. We're mere feet away from the*

*ancestral path of this area."* Bolawe drew away from the ice sheet he spoke from, as though looking back to someone else in his Mirror Realm. *"He also says he can see the readings of the 'Isa' rune embedded throughout the ravine. The rune for stasis and confinement. The spirits everyone is seeing might be stuck here."*

"Wait... 'Isa' rune..." TJ started to say. "Is it shaped like a letter 'I'?"

Bolawe dipped out of his reflection, then returned. *"Uh... yes. How did you know that?"*

"I've been seeing it in my dreams... Forseti's dreams, really. It shows up all the time. What does that mean?"

Bolawe surveyed TJ for a while before finally and slowly smiling. *"It means the book hasn't been written for you yet, young man. And you keep writing new pages in this unique journey of magic of yours."*

TJ was about to respond when one of the glacial walls revealed another elder. This one TJ knew. His second great-grandfather. The last Tomori Jomiloju in his family line. His image was dominated by a thick white beard, bushy gray eyebrows, and funky red glasses. He wore a headwrap and dashiki of bright yellow. His outfit was vivid, loud. And the expression on his face matched. He beamed widely, as though TJ had just hit a home run at a Little League baseball game. He even clapped in an oddly slow way.

Then he stopped suddenly, pulled at the collar of his shirt and pointed to a spot on his skin.

At first, TJ thought his great-grandfather was just pointing to one of his age spots. Then TJ saw it, mesmerized. It was actually a birthmark. The same one TJ had. A mark that looked like a blotchy turtle.

"What does that mean?" TJ asked, touching his own spot near his collarbone.

His great-grandfather just stared and smiled, pointing all the while. So they had the same birthmark. What was that all about? What had Grandma said about him? That he was the last of the Abimbolas to be cursed without Ashe. That TJ had broken that curse, apparently.

Again, his great-grandfather pulled at his collar. Then TJ did the same, looking down at the mark that had always been there his whole life. It pulsated white. Like the scars on his arm—only more… permanent. It bloomed and retracted like a very slow heartbeat. When did it start doing *that*?

Before TJ could consider it further, Manny's aunt suddenly cried out. TJ turned on his heel to find her running toward the image of a young woman farther down the passage. TJ instantly recognized the girl's face—it was Jessica, Manny's cousin who had died years ago. The same cousin he had encountered in the Aqua Realm. He had never met her in person, though, only as a semi-spirit via Yewa. She looked like she could be Manny's sister, except for the lighter skin, angular jaw, and wavier hair. TJ whipped back to his own glacial wall. There was nothing there anymore. No great-grandfather, but his birthmark still pulsed when he checked it.

Spinning to Yemoja and Eshu just behind them, TJ asked, "Can you see any of them?"

They both shook their heads. "Not yet," Yemoja replied. "We likely won't until the ancestral path is restored."

"Not even me," Eshu said. "It was part of the deal in The Great Separation. There is a buffer, a void, between mortals, your ancestors, and we, the Orishas."

Manny's aunt had collapsed in tears before Jessica's likeness. Manny tried to comfort her, to explain it wasn't really her, but her aunt was inconsolable.

"Help her, young mortal," Yemoja said softly. "The ancestral path will not open in her current state."

TJ approached quietly; Tia Teresa wailed and cried. As TJ's gaze lingered on Manny's aunt, the whispers of his companions faded into the background—Mom's own bawling, Yemoja's gentle whispers, Eshu's encouraging tones. TJ moved closer to the icy wall, and Jessica's smiling face appeared to flicker, her mouth moving soundlessly as if speaking to him.

Without warning, the icy valley vanished. TJ found himself standing in the central square of New Ile-Ife, in front of the building that usually displayed Dayo's towering mural.

Only the Oduduwa statue head was the notable feature, and now the wall was blank, the mural gone. In its place stood a group of protesters, led by a teenage girl who was unmistakably Dayo, though clearly younger. This Dayo appeared to be about seventeen or eighteen, definitely no more than two years older than TJ himself now. She shouted passionately into the crystal of her staff like a megaphone, rallying the crowd in protest against the corrupt Nigerian police organization known as SARS.

That was just like Dayo, fighting to break down the apathy that sometimes settled over the Nigerian magical hub toward their mortal neighbors. In the crowd, Jessica roared the loudest. Her image more saturated than the near black-and-white around her.

The scene shifted, blurring before resolving into a dim alleyway. Somewhere deep in New Ile-Ife? TJ couldn't be sure. He now followed several paces behind as the younger Dayo led Jessica down the narrow passage. At the end, Dayo opened a hidden door, admitting them into a secret meeting already in progress.

Inside were a group of Keepers, including Bolawe, Adeola, and a few others TJ had recognized. TJ instantly keyed in to the Keepers' fearsome enforcer, Bisi, her staff raised menacingly as Jessica entered behind Dayo.

"What are you doing here?" she grimaced in Jessica's direction. Jessica cowered, taking a few steps back. "Are you lost, little lamb?"

Dayo waved Bisi's staff away casually, and Bisi actually backed down. Had Dayo already commanded so much respect? TJ had only met Bisi once, had even been hit by one of her excruciating magical bolts. She was fast, and TJ knew even then that her typical attacks would be much more deadly. Yet here, she instantly curled in at the mere touch of Dayo's simple wave.

"No, Sister Bisi," Dayo said smoothly. "She's just curious. She just wants to join the cause."

Jessica nodded weakly. "I can't sit around and do nothing anymore while this country is in turmoil, while the whole world is in the shit. It's time for the Orishas to come back and bring order back for us all."

Dayo smiled in response, and, strangely, TJ felt himself smiling too, as if he were the one speaking instead of merely watching the memory. "Then you've found your home, Jessica," TJ said through Dayo's voice. And in a truly eerie moment, Dayo looked up directly at TJ, meeting his gaze through the icy barrier between them.

A faint whisper tickled TJ's ear, steadily growing louder, though he couldn't make out the words or who was calling. Was it Manny?

His mom? Eshu? TJ only knew he had to keep watching this vision from the past, discover the secrets he never imagined about his sister and what she was getting up to.

The scene shifted once more, and TJ found himself in a dark, claustrophobic room with corrugated metal walls. Animal pelts and taxidermied heads adorned the walls, gazing down with sightless eyes.

TJ's breath caught in his throat as recognition dawned—this was the Keepers' lair in the Makoko slums, the very place they had conducted their blood ritual against him almost exactly a year ago on his birthday. Only now, the space was empty of the creepy oracle and the scent of blood that had permeated his traumatic memories.

Instead, TJ saw Dayo and Jessica, both a few years older than when he'd seen them in the last memory. The two young women were locked in a heated argument, Jessica's face flushed as she gestured emphatically.

"Innocents have died, Dayo!" she cried. "This has gone too far!"

Dayo quickly moved to cover Jessica's mouth with her hand, casting nervous glances over her shoulder as if afraid they'd be overheard. And in that strange overlapping way, TJ felt himself inhabit Dayo's perspective once more—felt the press of his palm against Jessica's lips as she screamed against his fingers.

"Jessie, you have to calm down," TJ heard himself whisper through Dayo's mouth. "We'll talk, I swear. But you have to stay quiet, or Sister Bisi will hear you. You do *not* want Sister Bisi to hear you."

Jessica's muffled protests slowly softened, and she relaxed slightly under Dayo's grip. When Dayo finally pulled her hand away, tears streaked down Jessica's cheeks.

"We have to stop this, Ifedayo..." she choked out weakly. "I didn't know it would be like this."

Dayo flattened Jessica's unruly hair. "Neither did I, Jess. I'm trying to find an exit strategy. As soon as I do, I'll let you know. But you have to keep a straight face in front of the others. Don't let them see you have doubts. Understood?"

Jessica nodded faintly in response. Then the vision dissolved once more, leaving TJ reeling from these revelations. His chest pounded with a fierce, rapid rhythm. It was one thing to hear that

Dayo was a Keeper. It was a different thing entirely to see what it did to those around her.

TJ blinked as the scene shifted again, transporting him to a cramped studio apartment. Outside the grimy windows, the Brooklyn Bridge was visible through the nighttime haze. The space itself was cluttered with discarded takeout containers, unwashed dishes, and piles of wrinkled clothes. It looked like no one had cleaned in months.

Jessica entered, clutching her staff. Before TJ could react, a shriek pierced the air beside him. Manny's aunt had appeared, staring in anguish at her daughter. But she didn't fit into the scene. She was ghostly and arctic-looking. It was as though she had willed herself *into* the vision.

"No, Jessie! *No, mi amor!* Please don't do this! Please!" she cried, rushing toward Jessica. But just like a spirit, she passed right through her.

TJ watched helplessly as Jessica set a note on the table, then solemnly pressed the crystal tip of her staff to her forehead. She stopped for a moment, as though hearing her mother's cries.

"I'm sorry, Mom," she seemed to say. Did she hear Tia Teresa from the other side? Then her lips moved soundlessly again. This time casting one final spell. A bright light filled the room. When it cleared, Jessica's body went limp, collapsing to the floor.

Manny's aunt screamed, hysterical with grief. TJ stood frozen. Manny had mentioned her cousin taking her own life, but witnessing it was shattering. It was an entirely different thing.

Suddenly, Manny was there, pulling her aunt into a fierce embrace. She too appeared as an icy specter. "*Tia,*" she pleaded in Portuguese, "*you have to let her go. You have to let Jessie go.*"

A cracked mirror near Jessica's slumped body caught TJ's attention. Within it was Bolawe, though he looked faded and foggy. "*TJ, Oracle Ruby says you must get them out. Teresa is blocking the ancestral path we need to free Oya. If she cannot release her hold, we will fail.*"

But TJ couldn't move, could not process what he had just learned, had just bared witness to. The vision was blurring, and he began to panic before realizing it was just his own tears welling in his eyes. That it was Dayo who had led Jessica to this horrific end. If Dayo had never recruited her into the Keepers...

The tears crashed down TJ's cheeks unapologetically. The guilt pressed like a crushing weight. He couldn't separate himself from Dayo in this moment, couldn't divide their pain. It was like he was feeling for Jessica's death twice. But how could he know how Dayo felt? *Really* felt. He knew her grief in his heart *too* intimately. The jokes she shared with Jessica that could never be shared again, the Euro trip they would never go on together, the life Jessica was never going to have…

*Because of me…* Dayo's voice said in his head.

*What?* TJ asked back, but he got no answer. His jaw trembled. That had been different. Was that Dayo actually speaking to him?

"We need you, Tomori Jomiloju," Mom urged, and for the first time, TJ could actually feel her hand on his shoulder. Warm against the cold he only realized then had nearly frozen him in place.

"You have to break through this," Mom said. "You're okay, TJ, I'm here, honey. You're all right. It's not real. I know how hard this is but I need you need to break through, TJ. We need to help Teresa through, sweetheart."

It wasn't working. Mom's voice helped but it didn't get him over the edge.

"TJ, it's Manny. Please push through. Please make it stop for tia. I'm begging you."

There it was again. His anchor. It dropped in his gut like the bottom of a sea. The visions began to fade as TJ forced himself back to the present, back to their critical mission. He had to be strong, had to lead them forward. For the Orishas. For his friends.

His family.

The ancestors.

TJ took a deep breath as the visions continued to recede, steadying himself. Now he understood why Manny's aunt had been so insistent on joining them—her sole motivation was the chance to speak to her dead daughter one last time. And for a moment there, it seemed like she had broken through. Did she know that would happen?

TJ could see the strain manifesting physically now, the magic required to reopen the ancestral path visibly fraying as Jessica's spirit resisted leaving. If they didn't hurry, the delicate spellwork would unravel completely. For the first time, TJ properly took in

Yemoja and Eshu, their faces scrunched as they filtered the ritual through their own strained use of Ashe.

TJ crossed to where Manny still held her weeping aunt. He put his arms around them both, lending his strength, giving them his well of Ashe. "I understand how hard this is," he said gently. "I'd give anything to talk to my sister again, too. But we have to move forward, have to let them go."

"No, I can't let her go, I can't lose her again," Manny's aunt cried, not allowing Jessica's spirit to slip through her fingers. "If I hold on tight enough, she can stay. I can change things. The Saints said so."

"*You cannot, Teresa,*" Bolawe said through the mirror. "*We warned you about this. Nothing can be changed. Look around you, the path is fraying. This is the protection fighting against you. Stay strong.*"

"Shut up! Just shut up!" Manny's aunt yelled, and a golden glow emanated from her hands. The mirror on the table shattered into dozens of pieces. "You just want to save those damn Orishas! You don't care about Jessie. You never cared about her, you murdering *bastard!*"

Manny shook her head, wiping her own tears away before wrapping her aunt in another tight embrace. "Listen to me, Tia. Forget him; forget everyone else. Forget the UCMP, the Orishas, even TJ. Listen to your *sobrinha*. Jessie wouldn't want you to be stuck like this. I went through this too in the Aqua Realm. I got through it. It's possible. I *swear* it's possible. Don't get stuck here. I still need you; our whole family needs you."

Gradually, Manny's aunt lifted her head, looking between the two teens. The icy landscape around them flickered as the vision destabilized.

Then, Mom was there. She gently pried TJ and Manny loose and wrapped her own arms around Tia Teresa's shaking form. She sounded half broken herself as she shushed the weeping mother, murmuring, "I know your pain. I lost a daughter too."

Tia Teresa lifted her head, tears streaming down her face. "How… how do you bear it?"

"One day at a time," Mom said, swallowing hard. "And… and by remembering that our loved ones wouldn't want us to be consumed by sorrow. They'd want us to *live*, to find joy again."

Slowly, the flickering of the icy realm stabilized as Tia Teresa's sobs quieted. As he watched the two women embrace, TJ couldn't help but wonder if he should reveal the truth about Dayo's role in Jessica's death. He had seen everything; they had only come in for that horrible, horrible end.

*All because of me…*

TJ's eyes widened as the familiar voice echoed in his mind. Was that Dayo again? It had to be. It wasn't just his own imagination or his own guilt manifesting.

Finally, Tia Teresa whispered hoarsely, "You're right. It's time. I have to let her go."

With visible effort, she released her grip on Jessica's spirit. The ghostly image vanished as the icy walls returned to sheer rock. The spectral New York faded back into a frozen ravine.

"You did it, Teresa. Well done, girl." Mom gave her a big squeeze. "We're here for you. Remember, one day at a time. And you *call* me when things get hard."

Manny's aunt didn't respond, too exhausted, too haggard, too depleted. But she was able to lift her head with new eyes, eyes that didn't look so dead.

The ancestral path stretched out in front of them, glowing like a runway made of stars. It was surreal, pulsing under TJ's feet as if it had its own heartbeat, calling them forward. He could still feel his own pulse hammering from everything they'd just seen—Jessica, the spirits, the memories that felt too heavy to carry. But now, with the bridge open, he forced himself to breathe easier.

Yemoja and Eshu looked wiped out, but their glowing eyes were steady, sending TJ silent encouragement of a job well done.

They had succeeded.

*One path down,* TJ thought, *one more to go.*

Bolawe flickered in a new sheet of ice. "*The team says well done, everyone. A few bumps, but you handled it beautifully.*" He turned away then looked back. "*Heh, Agent Stadheim says it didn't seem like there was much Asgardian magic here, save for the glacial walls themselves. He's glad he wasn't needed on this one.*"

A harsh caw echoed overhead before TJ could respond. Circling above was a jet black raven, its beady gaze fixed on their group.

Yemoja frowned. "Correct me if I'm wrong, Bolawe. And you

can check this with Agent Stadheim. But I do not believe those kinds of birds frequent frosty planes, do they?"

TJ's eyes widened in recognition. "It's one of Forseti's ravens—they monitor the ancestral paths!" He turned to the others in alarm. "It's going to report we opened the way to the Court. We have to stop it! Now!"

# 24

# FROSTED WINGS

TENSION SEIZED TJ AS THE RAVEN TOOK FLIGHT, ITS CAWS echoing off the icy canyon walls. It was going to cross the ancestral path they had just reconstructed. To warn the Court of All. To warn Forseti. To blow up their entire spot.

"Stay with your aunt," TJ told Manny. "She can't help us fight right now."

Manny nodded, embracing her aunt, slumped and exhausted against the blank glacial wall that had once held the last images of her daughter.

"After it!" Mom cried, leaping into action. "*Wa si mi,*" she said, but nothing happened. She turned to TJ. "A little help, son?"

TJ dove into his Ashe and allowed Mom to draw from him so she could call her staff across realms. In an instant, her iron short-staff snapped into her hand from thin air. She waved her rod in swift motions, drew moisture from the mist around them and launched it toward the retreating raven. But the droplets froze mid-air, falling short. The icy Asgardian environment was hindering her water magic.

Yemoja acted swiftly, melting a nearby icicle into a stream of water that rocketed at the raven. Her more powerful Ashe seemed to slice through the limitations of the cold, or perhaps her time with the Asgardians was helping. Then again, the black bird swerved, narrowly avoiding the attack. Perhaps Yemoja's water magic was indeed a touch slower. TJ gritted his teeth, willing his Ashe to life. He couldn't directly combat the raven—its speed was well above his pay grade—but he could support the others.

TJ's Ashe Vision bloomed in a prism as it often did during combat. And at that moment it seemed to sharpen, looking similar to the paths he sometimes saw with Oshosi. Usually he could see vague ways in which to boost or direct his friends. Now, he knew what paths to follow with more certainty, casting his Ashe over his companions to amplify their powers. Had this been a year ago he'd never be able to do it, but after his training at Ifa Academy, after his personal lessons with Elder Adeyemi, his times in the Orishas Planes, he managed it with only a little strain.

Mom's next strike sizzled through the air, a ribbon of water snapping at the raven's tail feathers. Yemoja sent a humongous crashing wave across the bridge of stars, but the raven flapped higher, evading it.

"*We must stop that messenger, no matter what!*" Bolawe shouted, his projected form gliding alongside them through any reflection he could find. "*On your left, Yemoja!*" he called. "*Through the mist.*" The Orisha whipped a twisting cyclone of water in response, but the raven eluded her once more.

Eshu materialized directly in front of the raven's path, weaving illusory copies of himself to confuse it. The raven faltered. Squawked. Swerved through the mirages. TJ's senses heightened. They were gaining on it!

"*Now, Mrs. Young!*" Bolawe commanded.

Mom spun her staff twice. Blades of ice sliced through the illusions, grazing the raven's wing and sending it into a spiraling descent. But it recovered, beating its wings furiously to regain height.

"*The agents at the command center are saying Forseti's raven has elevated healing abilities,*" Bolawe relayed. "*It might be difficult to harm. We need to halt it instead.*"

TJ gritted his teeth, pushed more Ashe into his companions. He couldn't directly fly or shape water like them, but Oya's Wind allowed him to keep pace using air-steps—there was one benefit to using the Windweaver's Ashe all the time.

Yemoja sent a jet of water screaming after the raven. It crashed against an icy outcrop. The raven swerved behind it. Mom followed up with a slicing arc of water, but it only clipped the raven's tail, sending feathers drifting.

Where Yemoja went big, Mom went small. But their combined efforts still couldn't bring the elusive bird down.

It cawed mockingly, putting on a burst of speed. The galaxy bridge shimmered before it—the way back to the Court of All only a few yards away.

"No!" TJ shouted. He couldn't let the raven warn the Court. Desperately, he funneled more of his Ashe into Yemoja directly, and the Orisha's next strike liquified with power, a roaring geyser that engulfed the bridge in steam and spray.

"Mr. Stadheim, we need help!" TJ said toward Bolawe, hoping he'd relay. "Some kind of magic to lock down the raven."

"*Ah, um…*" Bolawe kept looking between his ice sheets and behind him. "*Let's see here… He's saying… a runic binding spell of frost might do the trick. Yeah… I mean, yes! TJ, he says you'll need to visualize the 'Isa' rune while channeling your energy through hand gestures symbolizing stasis and confinement.*"

TJ winced as Bolawe launched into a lengthy, jargon-filled explanation of the proper forms and pronunciations. There was no time for that! The raven was getting away!

"Tell him cliff notes version, please! We're down to seconds here."

"*Right, right, well, simply put—channel your intent through the 'Isa' rune throughout the ravine, and direct it at your target,*" Bolawe summarized. "*You should be able to use the cavern walls to funnel the magic… theoretically. But, TJ, this is extremely advanced magic. Without proper training—*"

"Never stopped me before," TJ said under his breath. To the others, he called out an order of, "Everyone, funnel your Ashe through me! I need your help."

TJ's Ashe Vision showed him something new. The prism in his mind's eye manifested the straight Isa rune. And as he did, he could see the rune engraved all along the ice walls glowing around them. As they showed themselves, a voice in his mind repeated the phrase, "*Stillness, stasis, self control, identity, and focus…*"

He used those images, those runes, and channeled the others' added power to his own. It was an odd mix of Ashe and runic magic, and it made TJ's stomach queasy. It was like trying to mix water with oil, and his throat filled with sick in the effort to make them bind as one.

But the power was there: Yemoja's cool waters, Mom's fierce strength, and Eshu's wily spirit. Filling him to the brim.

Even the ancestors he had seen and felt seemed to work through him, as though the now opened ancestral path had opened the floodgates to their power. The rune glowed in TJ's mind, thrummed with power.

*With intent, TJ,* the voice in his head said. It had to be an ancestor, or maybe Dayo again. It was too often to be a coincidence. *Stillness, stasis, self control, identity, and focus...*

The raven emerged from the mists right before the galaxy bridge. TJ thrust his palms forward, willing the glowing runes of "Isa" to life, using the entirety of the ice walls. A blast of blue energy shot from his hands, slamming into the raven just as it reached the bridge. Ice blossomed outward, encasing the raven in a frozen block before it could cross over.

TJ stared sharply at the frozen raven, realizing with dismay that it was still moving—albeit very slowly. They had only slowed it down, not fully stopped it. But it was only moving a centimeter every few seconds. That would have to do for now.

TJ staggered, suddenly drained. He'd done it, stopped the messenger, though he wasn't quite sure how. Yemoja caught TJ as he sagged.

"Rest easy, young one," she murmured. "You've saved us all today. I'm proud of you." TJ went to smile but he vomited all over Yemoja's giant hand instead. Yemoja groaned a little. "But you are still very much a mortal."

TJ looked down at his hands, noticing that the scars on his right arm had grown longer, now reaching up to his mid-elbow. Was this going to happen every time he overused his magic? What would happen if he didn't have anymore skin to scar? He used Oya's Wind to make a fist and felt a new numbness in his elbow. Was he technically paralyzed there now too? Did he throw up because he used runic magic? Maybe it was only possible in the first place because they were in the Frost Realm. He was too exhausted to consider the severity of it all.

Yemoja moved closer to examine the frozen bird. She tried using her powers to melt the ice or pry the raven loose to take with them, but neither worked. The ice held fast, impervious even to an Orisha's Ashe.

*"Agent Stadheim is saying he doesn't understand how you did this, TJ,"* Bolawe said from an ice sheet. *"Combining Ashe with that advanced frost spell shouldn't have been technically possible."* Bolawe turned from the reflection and then looked back again. *"Heh, but as Elder Adeyemi is putting it so lovingly, 'you are the impossible, Mr. Young.'"*

"He's not like any other bird!" Mom said as she knelt and cleaned the sick from TJ's mouth with Ashe-generated water.

Eshu trotted up next to them on the ancestral bridge, poking at the iced raven as well. "I've not met him, but I'm pretty sure Forseti will come looking for this one. I mean... I would."

TJ gulped down a morsel of vomit as the implications dawned on him—they were on another time clock now. The moment Forseti noticed his missing raven, the moment he found it here in the realm of his own pantheon... it was over. And that could be at any time. TJ was nowhere near ready. They still had to open Ayo's path, and he still needed to build his staff to work the magic of it all. Not to mention Forseti's dreams and figuring out how The Channeling fully worked.

*But at least there still* is *a mission,* he had to remind himself. Then, to the others, he asked, "What are we going to do now?"

Eshu stroked his non-existent beard with exaggeration. "Do not trouble yourself, young one. I will stand guard over the raven and the bridge until you are ready to continue. After all, I am the Gatekeeper. If any more ravens come, I'll throw an illusion up around this area so they don't see these alterations we've made to the Frost Realm." He waved his wooden staff in the air and it was as though the bridge leading to the galaxy clouds above wasn't there at all. "Safe journeys to you all. Get some rest. You've earned it." Then he addressed Yemoja directly. "Mother Ocean, please take the mortals back safely to their realm. They must ready themselves to reach Shango now. And quickly. Even if no one comes looking," he pointed to the raven, which was definitely pecking at the ice like a woodpecker from within, "this one might get loose eventually."

Yemoja nodded. "We shall withdraw for now and reconvene when the time is right."

She gathered up TJ and Mom, lifting them onto her back once more for the long trek out of the icy valley. On their way out, they scooped up Manny and her aunt. Manny had *so* many questions.

"We heard all that fighting, what happened, yo?"

"Nothing great," TJ said as he took one last look at the frozen raven, vowing they would be back before it could escape and sabotage their plans. The mission would go on—they still had to find a way to reach Shango. With Eshu guarding the bridge for now, they at least had a reprieve to regroup and prepare.

And TJ needed to sleep for about two weeks.

# 25

# THE ONLY ONE WHO CAN

TJ, Mom, and Manny alongside her aunt returned once more to the meeting hall. A deeper chill ran through the cavernous room, deeper than it had been before, and TJ shivered slightly as he glanced around. The glowing projections, normally a source of light, now seemed ominous…

So much had happened. He wasn't sure how to keep it all together. The moment with his second great-grandfather and his birthmark came to mind first. TJ pulled off his scarf and peeked at the space between his chest and collarbone. His birthmark wasn't glowing anymore. Was it something that only bloomed in the ethereal realms?

And what about his sister's voice? There had been times over the past few years where TJ thought he felt Dayo, even heard her. And these more recent occurrences were more immediate… closer.

But TJ couldn't keep that all in mind when images of Jessica taking her own life kept flashing like a slideshow over and over, not to mention that chase through the ravine with the raven. TJ's brain was about to explode, and all he could do was rub his temples to ease the pain.

Elder Adeyemi approached, her face creased. Even the golden trim in her robes seemed to dim. "How was the journey? Are you all… all right?"

Before TJ could respond, Tore Stadheim nodded curtly. "That

sounded like quite an intense experience in the valley. You doing okay, young one?"

TJ raised his hand to salute, to show he was okay. But his arm didn't budge. It was stuck, locked in place as if someone had hit pause on him. His chest tightened, breath catching—*No, not again*. It was just like those times after dreamwalking with Oshosi and Obatala, when his body wouldn't obey, as if something unseen was holding him down. He willed his fingers to twitch, his shoulder to shift—anything—but his body wasn't listening.

As Mom pulled off her parka and scarf, she asked, "TJ, what's wrong?"

"It's nothing," TJ said. He focused, trying to summon Oya's Wind to help him, but the well of Ashe within him felt dry. Using so much power in the Frost Realm had drained him completely.

Bolawe's reflection glinted in his Mirror Realm before he said, *"Perhaps I could offer some assistance—"*

"No one was talking to you," TJ snapped. "I can figure this out myself."

Everyone's eyes were on him, their concern palpable. He hated feeling so helpless, so exposed. Elder Adeyemi stepped forward again, her voice gentle but firm. "Mr. Young, let me help you. Use my Ashe to get your hands moving again."

TJ hesitated, pride warring with practicality. Finally, he nodded, reluctantly accepting her offer. As Elder Adeyemi's Ashe flowed into him, the cool breath of Oya spread around his arms. Slowly, movement returned, and he flexed his fingers experimentally.

"Thank you." TJ managed a nod in return, not quite ready to put words to the messed up events. Oracle Ruby hovered nearby, out of the corner of his eye, her presence oddly reassuring despite the fact that she didn't say a word.

Manny's aunt hadn't said much on the ride back, perched high on Yemoja's shoulders. Her face was a mask of grief, rigid and unreadable, and TJ couldn't blame her—he was still shaken to his core. It was a wonder Tia Teresa had been able to let go of her daughter's spirit at all. If TJ had been that close to Dayo, he wasn't sure he'd have had the strength.

Elder Adeyemi moved to Manny's aunt's side, placing a gentle hand on her elbow in a quiet offer of support. But Tia Teresa jerked away, her expression set as she marched out of the room without a backward glance, ignoring the voices calling after her. She shoved open the double doors, letting a sharp stream of light spill in from the office space beyond. A few UCMP officers looked up, startled, as she strode past them, pulling a device from her pocket and speaking rapidly into it as she disappeared down the hall.

TJ squinted. *What's she saying?*

The woman still seemed consumed by sorrow, but how could that be? The cleansing effect of the Frost Realm should have dulled her memories, just like with the Aqua Realm and Sky Realm. Only TJ should've remembered what went on so sharply…

Wait!

The Frost Realm was not a full ethereal construction, not fully complete. It had taken Manny a little while to get her memories back when they had entered. So the same must've been the case for memories leaving everybody's minds as well. It could be an hour or so before the memories left them.

*Lucky for them,* TJ thought.

In an hour, he'd still remember everything. And he'd give anything to forget that moment with Jessica… because of Dayo… because of the Keepers. TJ's throat went dry, and he tried to swallow to make it go away, but his body wasn't listening to him, still too shocked to move, like waking from a nightmare.

If Manny's aunt retained her traumatic recollection, then that meant…

TJ's gaze snapped to Manny. She should've been devastated, too. Jessica was her cousin. Yet Manny stood still, no discernible expression on her face.

Before TJ could ponder this further, he put a hand on her arm. "You should check on your auntie. Make sure she's okay."

Manny nodded, as though coming out of a stupor. Her eyes softened as she hurried after her aunt. As soon as she was out of sight, a swell of sadness hit TJ, so strongly it almost took his breath away.

It was Dayo's fault…

It always seemed to be her fault…

Dayo had introduced Jessica to the Keepers, and that's what led the poor girl down such a dark path. The sadness sat like an elephant on TJ's chest, doubling in intensity with each beat of his heart. He could almost feel Dayo's anguish too, as if he were still immersed in that awful vision, seeing the world through her eyes.

A hand came to rest on his nape. Mom's hand. TJ hadn't even realized tears were rolling down his cheeks until she pulled him into a fierce hug. "Everything will be okay."

TJ shook his head, anger curling his forehead. "*It's Dayo's fault!* Her and the Keepers! They're the reason Jessica—" He couldn't bring himself to say it. "Manny… her aunt… they don't have her anymore *because of Dayo*!"

Mom's face hardened. "Don't you *dare* speak of your sister that way. Ifedayo did what she thought was right at the time. I knew her, same as you. She would never intentionally hurt someone."

Anger flared in TJ's chest. Hot and raw. He wrenched himself out of his mother's embrace. "Nah, you didn't know her like I do! Every time I learn somethin' new about her, it's worse and worse." He glimpsed Bolawe's somber expression in his Mirror Realm form. "Ask *him* what Dayo was really like. Ask any of them Keepers of his!"

"Tomori Jomiloju Young, enough!" Mom yelled, but he was already storming away. She called after him, but he ignored it, fury pounding through his veins. He needed to get away, be alone with the terrible mix of anguish that shifted inside him.

Before the door slammed behind him, he heard Elder Adeyemi saying, "Give him time. Let the boy collect himself. Emotions are running high right now."

TJ darted through the command center, grateful for the reprieve. He just needed a moment to process it all. He wasn't really sure what he should feel, what he should do with himself. As he moved through the open office, he clenched his fists, leather gloves crunching with the strain. Many of the officers and agents seated at their desks stared as he rushed past, but TJ ignored them all.

Eventually, he found his way back topside, emerging into the village courtyard of his family's compound. Late October's humid heat pressed down on him, doing no favors for his poor mood.

From the porch of Grandma's home, Ayo came running up to him, signing, "Hey, TJ, how go in Cold Place? You gone long time! Something big happen?" He said the next two words out loud. "Eh, eh?" Ayo was bouncing on the balls of his feet, his braids jumping with him as he did.

"Not right now, my guy!" TJ grunted.

Ayo's smile faded. "Shango's Axe… you too, eh? Manny and aunt not look happy when they walk out either."

Just then, a stray orange cat rubbed up against TJ's ankle with an affectionate meow. Without thinking, TJ shooed the cat away, sending it scurrying off with an indignant yowl.

"W-w-what the hell, man?" Ayo chided vocally. "Don't be mean to o-o-orange dude." He shifted to signing. "He keep me not alone here while I wait." Before TJ could respond, Ayo shot off and scooped up the offended feline. He nuzzled his face against the cat's fur. TJ instantly felt bad. He hadn't meant to be mean; he was just *so mad*.

Then a voice sounded in his head. Ayo's voice. *You no bad kitty, are you?* he thought-spoke. *No you're not!*

The cat purred and rubbed up against Ayo's cheek. TJ had half a mind to point out that Ayo was able to communicate telepathically with the cat. That must've been a breakthrough for him—animal minds were easier to communicate with, or maybe it was TJ's connection to Ayo, or TJ being TJ. He couldn't decide. He was too angry. Instead, he rolled his eyes, disgusted at himself for being so annoyed.

TJ caught sight of Manny and her aunt at the edge of the courtyard leading out to the main street of the village. Tia Teresa gestured wildly as she shouted. Manny had her arms crossed, shaking her head emphatically in response to whatever her aunt was saying. Teresa jabbed an accusatory finger toward the sky, as if cursing the heavens, before whirling around and stomping off down the street. With a flash of light, the pavement opened up beneath the enraged woman and she disappeared from view, swallowed by the earth portal.

"Tia, wait!" Manny cried out, rushing to the now solid ground where her aunt had vanished. She pounded her fists against the dirt. "Dammit, come back!"

"Not right now," TJ murmured to Ayo, who was still cradling the orange cat and vying for TJ's attention.

*But Ogun's Cabinet!* Ayo thought-spoke. *I think—*

"Not right now. Just… talk to me later when everything cools off. A'ight?"

Leaving a concerned-looking Ayo behind, TJ walked over to where Manny stood over the spot her aunt had vanished through.

"What happened?" TJ asked gently.

Manny whirled around, eyes flashing. "She's throwing shade on the Orishas." She shook her head bitterly. "I don't care what she thinks right now. I just…" Her voice broke, and she looked away, blinking back her anger.

TJ's gut twisted inside. As much as he wanted to rage about Dayo's part in Jessica's fate, he couldn't stand to see Manny so upset. Pushing his own feelings aside, he placed a tentative hand on her shoulder. "C'mon, let's go back to Ifa, back to our favorite willow."

Manny nodded, breathing slowly and heavily to settle her heaving chest. Together, they walked back through the village, TJ's arm wrapped securely around her shoulders.

When they passed by The Walking Stick, TJ ignored the junior salesman who shouted, "You're making a staff this year, aren't you? Come on into the shop. I'll help you get a pass without any effort! Just don't tell Bamidele!"

TJ's dismissals continued as they passed by a tavern full of adults watching a crossover game in a large water bowl. One of them, who was wearing an *Eshu Messenger Press* cap, came barreling toward TJ with a notepad and pen, asking, "I've been meaning to track you down, Mr. Young. When will you finally give *The Press* an interview for your heroics at Eko Atlantic? Did you learn everything you know from your sister?"

"Shut up!" TJ roared. "Shut up about my sister!" He didn't wait to see the reporter's response. Just before TJ led Manny around the final corner to get to Ifa Academy, he caught sight of a few junior students near the Oduduwa statue head and Dayo's mural. They had a book open on the ground that was trying to explain the principles of Shango's fire.

"We're doing just like you said," the female student said, snapping her fingers.

Her friend, a male student, did the same, only producing sparks instead of flames. "We did the prayer to Shango. Gave an offering and everything. Still... nothing."

"I don't know what to tell you," the book said. "I've been training youngsters like yourselves since I went into publication in 1967. You just aren't cut out for the Ashe, clearly."

"But I'm a child of Shango!" the female student said bitterly.

It was all too much. But TJ couldn't keep dark and dower thoughts in his head when he was meant to cheer Manny up. So he cast them from his mind again as he led Manny through the earth entrance of Ifa, through the underground entrance hall, and up through the Summoning Statues. Once they were back on the familiar paths of the academy, dodging crowing roosters and grunting eloko, a few other students shot them curious glances as they passed, but TJ disregarded them as well. Right now, all that mattered was getting Manny somewhere private before she fully broke down.

Or he did.

By the time the whispering willows came into view, Manny's shoulders shook with barely suppressed sobs. As soon as they stepped under the curtain of vines shielding their favorite tree, TJ requested they be let inside the willow's bark. Perhaps because the willow could sense the sadness casting off Manny, it let them in without hesitation, opening its bark for them to step through.

TJ led them into the bark, which opened up wide and large. The inside was not dark at all, letting in light from holes poking through the top. As soon as its bark closed up behind them, Manny turned and collapsed into TJ's arms. He held her close as gut-wrenching sobs overtook her body.

"Don't trip, Manny, I got you," TJ murmured, gently stroking her hair. "I got you. Just let it out."

They stayed that way for a long time, tucked away from prying eyes. TJ kept whispering words of comfort as Manny released the torrent of grief she'd been holding back from the village and through the campus grounds. The whole walk over, TJ could tell her rage was covering her sorrow. Her face was red and contorted the whole time. And she had been holding on to him so tightly, he nearly lost feeling in his ribs.

TJ knew this pain all too well—the feeling of having an older family member's shadow loom over you, tainting even your happiest memories. But he also knew time could dull the sharp edges of that pain. He and Manny would get through this, together. For now, she just needed to grieve. And he would stay by her side for as long as she needed.

"Now it's my turn to take care of you," he said to her softly.

TJ felt her sadness running through him as though it were his own. And in a way, part of that sadness was his, too. Eventually, Manny pulled back a little and spoke between quiet sobs. "You know… I think I could only cry… with you. I never let anyone see. Not even… my family."

"That's not true," TJ said. "You've cried with me before. Ayo, too, technically…"

Manny gave him a look. "When have I cried in front of you?"

"Aqua Realm. Yewa. It was about Jessica then, too. But…"

"I wouldn't remember," Manny finished with a sigh.

TJ nodded. "And neither would Ayo."

Manny sniffled. "It's weird. Sometimes I feel we have half a relationship. Like I'm missing part of it. Something good. And I can already feel the memories fading from today…"

TJ held Manny close. As her sobs quieted, he gently stroked her hair again, hoping his gloves didn't feel too rough. After a while, Manny pulled back slightly, wiping her eyes. "You know. Jessie was always the perfect one. The cousin we all got compared to. Soon as she'd roll up, my parents would switch it up real quick: Museums, fancy restaurants—like that was our usual vibe instead of the parks and the beans and rice we really lived on." Manny let out a bitter laugh. "It was all for Jessie. We never did that stuff otherwise."

"Trust me, I can relate. I got compared to Dayo all the time."

"Yeah, well, that's kinda what happened between me and my aunt. I could never live up to Jessie. Perfect Jessica." She sighed. "No one really says it in my family. They keep quiet about it."

"Mine's the same. My mom always looked away from me until I got my Ashe going."

"Yeah… I sorta kinda noticed that the first time we got in the car with you—when we were going to Camp Olosa. Sorry about that."

They sat in silence, the weight of their shared experiences

hanging between them. TJ's mind got working once more, trying to think of a way to make Manny happy. There was one thing he knew would bring a smile to her face, but it wasn't the right time. The quinceañera would have to wait. There never seemed to be a good moment to bring it up, to bring *them* up.

Just as he warned her about in the Frost Realm.

In what would only be a few more minutes from now, Manny's memories would all be gone. Manny, seeming to know this, spoke again. "I never told you about that night. You're the only one who knows about Jessie, besides my family. But this next bit… I ain't never told no one before." She hugged her knees close to her chest. "I was… with Jessie before she... I was caught up in my own bull and made it all about me, didn't really hear her out. I should've listened..."

Manny's tears flowed again, though more subtly this time. Was this what she had been holding back this whole time? Why that vision had tore her up so much?

"Why do I keep telling you these things?" she wondered aloud.

TJ tried to lighten the mood. "Oh, I don't know. Maybe because you're madly in love with me."

Manny snorted. "Yeah right…" Then in a different, more serious tone, almost to herself, she said, "Yeah… right."

Without warning, she leaned in and kissed TJ on the cheek. Just as quickly, TJ kissed her cheek back, a little awkwardly. Then they broke apart.

"You really are my anchor," TJ murmured, meaning to say it in his head.

"What?"

TJ sighed lightly. "N-Nothing. Nothing."

That was the second time they'd had an exchange like that. It seemed like it was as far as either of them wanted to take it. And that was okay with TJ. He was just happy to see Manny's sorrow drifting away. And soon… the sorrow would feel like nothing more than a distant memory for her.

It was weird. It was like he and Manny were a perfect balance for one another. Where she was usually closed off and sheltered, she bloomed for TJ like a flower. And when TJ was too deferential and shy, Manny punched him into shape. And each of them made each other more… whole or something.

TJ smiled and inwardly rolled his eyes. *Yeah, something like that…*

TJ stayed with Manny all night as she continued to cry, letting out wave after wave of grief. He remained by her side even when the memories faded and she no longer understood why she was so distraught. And he stayed with her even after Oroma, the junior caretaker, arrived to kick them out and send them back to their dorms.

"Curfew is coming," Oroma scolded. "There had better not be no teenagers kissing in there."

"Looks like we'll have to leave," TJ said, breaking from Manny. When they left the tree, they were met with the scolding eyes of Oroma, whose head sat in her lap as she braided her hair.

"Sorry, we're leaving," TJ said. "No kissing. We promise."

"Mmhm," Oroma said, unconvinced. "Just because you're SS levels now don't mean you grown. And you, young lady, are still a junior. Now get!"

Shooed away, TJ led Manny back to her dorms, but not before saying, "So… the first moment we have a Saturday free, we're going to hangout. I'll cover everything." It was a command, not a request, and it seemed to please Manny by the way she blushed.

"You mean like a da—" Manny stopped herself. "Yeah, that sounds nice."

# 26

# A SECRET REVEALED

DAD

Your mom said she can't remember nothing, but she remembers being impressed with what you did at the academy or whatever you're doing right now. She was proud. Real proud. I am too son. You're really rising to the occasion.

DAD

Don't forget to take those supplements I was telling you about. That Miss Gravés said you diviners neglect physical training. I gotta say... I like that lady.

DAD

Keep your head up, son. I love you.

TJ

love u too. ill check out the shops in the village for that gross stuff you want me to drink.

THE END OF OCTOBER AND THE START OF NOVEMBER BROUGHT the start of the dry season to Nigeria. The skies cleared to a brilliant blue as the rains tapered off, and the humidity dropped to more comfortable levels. For the students at Ifa Academy, it was a welcome respite from the sticky heat and torrential downpours of the first couple months.

Life at Ifa continued swiftly, with several notable events marking the passage of the first term. At November's start, the school held its annual Ancestors' Day ceremony, where students honored their personal ancestral lines as well as the great ancestors turned Orishas of Yoruba tradition. Elders from New Ile-Ife joined them, invited onto campus to share stories and songs from ages past. TJ and Manny gave each other knowing looks during the mid-day celebrations. The memory of the Frost Realm and all that happened with Jessica had leaked completely from Manny's mind, but when she asked TJ for a recap, he was as honest as he could be without being indelicate.

A few days after that, Ninki Nanka held the Grand Yemoja Festival, and TJ wondered if the Headmistress was signaling to TJ that she knew what was going on. The students performed elaborate dances along the riverbanks and presented offerings while paying homage to Yemoja. Ninki Nanka watched the whole thing, her spotted giraffe neck poking out from the river depths. For the duration of the ceremony, her yellow eyes found TJ's more times than he was comfortable counting. Maybe Ninki Nanka thought Yemoja would manifest herself and confess the shenanigans she and TJ had been getting up to. Thankfully, there was no such ethereal reveal within the river, though the spirits of the student body were certainly elevated. And that energy seemed to fuel Manny's failing Ashe with Yemoja's magic. That same day, she passed her water magic exams with flying colors, prompting a broad smile from her the entire afternoon. In fact, all of her water magic was stronger since the Frost Realm.

*Good*, TJ had thought. *Keep that smile wide and big*.

He was thankful Manny was comfortable enough to cry in front of him. Seeing her smile, however, was a whole lot better.

Every day that TJ had been back from the Frost Realm, he had spent at least several minutes staring at the mirror in his dorm, or the reflections around campus to see if he could get Dayo talking to him. But nothing he did, as usual, seemed to help. He chalked it up to him being in the unique situation of the ancestral path. Another part of him didn't believe it. That part of him asked what the common denominator between those two situations, or rather, all the situations where he felt or heard Dayo was. Maybe there was no rhyme or reason to any of it at all. Maybe it was always sporadic. To keep his mind off the Dayo mystery, he laid into his list:

1. *Gotta figure out how to reverse this channeling thing by dreamwalking with Obatala and Oshosi.*
2. ~~*Open up the ancestral path from Yemoja to Oya through the Frost Realm for Manny.*~~
3. *Unlock ancestral path from Ogun to Shango's using Ayo's Norse ring. (And find Ogun's Sacred Cabinet)*
4. *Complete my staff to sustain the ancestral path ritual to the Court of All jail cell.*
5. *Save Shango and Oya on The Hero's Equinox.*
6. *Don't die.*

Throughout early November, Ninki Nanka remained an imposing, larger-than-life presence on campus, whether in the trees during Ere Idaraya classes or skulking near the lake's edge. Rumors circulated among students that she spent much of her time in deep meditation, communing with mystical forces beyond their understanding. TJ often caught her speaking to flowers and trees as though they were old friends. Yet none of the plant life spoke back, not like Monsieur Francois—the talking tree from Camp Olosa.

The few times TJ visited Ruby at Oracle Rock he had to wade through a river of roses to get to her tent.

"Sorry, love!" she would say. "When I find out who's doin' this, I'm going to have words for them."

TJ never had the heart to tell her.

By the time the first week of November ended, TJ found himself in the open forest clearing of Staffmaster Bamidele's class. Floating staffs of every shape, size, and material encircled the space—just like before. Most students sat on the ground, attention focused on notebooks filled with diagrams, Yoruba symbols, and lists of materials. The weeks of gathering wood, crystals, and other items had passed, and they were now immersed in bringing their staff designs to life via blueprints.

In a far corner of the clearing sat TJ and Freya, legs crossed in meditation. Freya had her curly hair pulled and tied back. TJ had taken the new look to mean that she knew today was their day. That would have made him nervous usually, but for once, he was confident in his plans.

He opened his eyes and nudged his friend, murmuring, "You ready for the big reveal?"

Freya opened one eye and smiled. "I've *been* waiting for you to let me in on this surprise. I even asked some of the others about what sorta special magic this 'TJ Young' has." A Nigerian accent had started to slip into her Scottish one.

"Oh yeah? What did they tell you?"

"A lot of things, actually. Like how you're on a first-name basis with a few Orishas—or how you saved Eko Atlantic from total ruin. Why didn't you tell me?"

TJ frowned at that, pain slithering down his chest. He picked at his knee before saying, "I don't like talking about that stuff—if you can believe it. But yeah… that's not too far off the mark."

"All right," Freya said, "so you going to use some Orisha secrets to help us catch up?"

"Something like that…"

Looking around at their classmates, whose staffcrafting was much farther along, he knew they had some catching up to do. Jimoh already had a seven-foot scroll of a beautifully intricate staff. It appeared as though it would be carved from ebony wood and adorned with the copper volcano symbols of his Orisha Aganju.

*Bet his 'dear' father had some artist draw that up for him,* TJ thought bitterly.

Titi's designs were a work of art, with a crystalline orb that swirled with mist and colors. She had even enchanted her scroll to give the ink on it motion—though the line work of her sketch was far less neat than Jimoh's. Ayo's was the only design that was nearly as neat. His parchment depicted a solid iron shaft with cracked lightning designs on the edges.

A pang of jealousy nipped at TJ. There was so much palpable excitement stirring within his classmates who had their head start. He wanted to be on their level, too. He had even started drawing designs of what his own staff could look like. Though, if he was being honest, it looked a whole lot like Dayo's staff.

The only staff he had ever used before.

Keeping one eye shut, TJ used a gust of Oya's Wind to help him grab for his backpack and pull out his parchment with his doodles. Next to it were the broken pieces of his sister's old staff. The wood looked lifeless and as dead as the magic that had withered inside it.

Freya must've noticed TJ because she pulled out the parchment scrolls containing her staff designs, confirming she was ready for whatever TJ had planned. She also showed TJ the broken remains of her previous staff.

"So, how's it work?" she asked. "We pray to an Orisha to catch up? You know, I assist at the Library Tree, and Librarian Bello said just listen to what Bamidele says."

"Nah. If this works, we'll start building our staffs *today*."

Freya's eyes went wide. "Today!? That can't be right. We're not even close. And I don't want a half-arsed staff."

"And you won't get one," TJ said with a grin. "Stick with me, old lady. I'll show you the way."

Freya rolled her eyes. She was only a couple years TJ's senior.

"Mr. Young, Miss Innes," Staffmaster Bamidele grunted, "why all the whispering? You should be meditating and focusing on your staff alignments. Elder Adeyemi keeps pestering me about your progress. I keep telling her *no shortcuts*. Don't make me tell her it's *you* holding everything up."

Some of the other students looked up from their scrolls or notepads, clearly intrigued by the staffmaster's admonishment. LaVont and Jimoh were suppressing laughs. Ayo shot TJ an uneasy glance from where he sat with his partner on a lion-hide blanket. He had been a little sore about being left out of the Frost Realm, but after TJ and Manny took him out to Sweet Tooth Ruth's for his favorite sweets, he came around.

TJ stood up confidently and addressed Staffmaster Bamidele. "Sir," he didn't realize how harshly his heart was pounding until he got up, "Freya and I are ready to move onto the next steps of the staffcrafting process. By the end of today's class, we'll not only be sketching designs… we'll be building our staffs!"

This bold proclamation was too much for LaVont and Jimoh, who burst into loud guffaws. "Pass me some of that stuff you hittin'." LaVont exclaimed between laughs. "Like you're gonna pass up all of us after weeks of lessons!"

"Yeah, yeah," Jimoh chimed in. "How you go'n run that?"

TJ ignored them, thinking to himself, *Laugh it up, jerks. They forget they call me Lucky Charm.*

Staffmaster Bamidele frowned at LaVont and Jimoh. "That's enough, you two. Very well, Mr. Young. Show me what you've got."

TJ nodded and gave Freya a sideways glance. "Here goes nothing."

He blew out a long breath, then settled into a crossed-legged sitting position. TJ considered the ritual of finding an alignment with the floating staffs. But rather than focus on just one staff nearby, he communed with *all* of them. He drew on the collective energy and experiences of his classmates over the past few weeks. He dug gloved fingers into the earth and sensed all the sessions, all the students struggling through their crafting. Just like he had done before with the crowds during the rituals with Olokun all last year, now he could use their past failures and successes to guide his way. Just as he learned with Oshosi and Obatala when they dreamwalked. He could've done it that first week if he had known what he did now after weeks with those two Orishas.

*Think of them all like a ripple in the water,* TJ reminded himself. *Just like Elder Adeyemi taught you.*

TJ's ribcage thrummed with a pulse of Ashe, the ancient energy of his ancestors blending with the echoes of his peers' previous explorations. With each breath, he wove through a tapestry of magic, past and present intertwining. The essence of Yemoja's wave cascaded in his chest, Shango's fire—though weak—lit his heart, Ogun's iron tinged his veins, as Oya's quiet storms fueled his spirit. The elemental symphony swelled until TJ released it and recycled it through his Ashe. Before he knew it, something clicked deep in his soul. And he knew he finally found alignment.

He reached out to Freya's own magical spirit. There was clarity in her Ashe as well. But it was different from his own, more clouded. That must've been the parts of her that reached out to her druid heritage. Still, he was able to coax her magic along the right path as well. He could actively feel her breathing more easily.

Then he opened his eyes.

Staffmaster Bamidele stood and began clapping slowly and deliberately. "Well *done,* Mr. Young. Very well done. You too, Miss Innes. I sense perfect *attunement* within you."

Freya leaned over to TJ and said, "Holy shit, mate, that was incredible. Whatever ya were doin', I felt it right in my chest. You *have* been keepin' secrets, haven't ya?"

TJ smiled in satisfaction, especially when he noticed LaVont and Jimoh scowling, unable to meet his gaze anymore.

"Right then," Bamidele declared, clapping his dusty hands together, "Mr. Young, Miss Innes—into the forest with you both. Go find the materials that call to you now. But," he eyed TJ, "Take. Your. Time. These things cannot and should not be rushed. No need to build your staffs today."

*If only you knew,* TJ thought. After the raven in the Frost Realm, TJ didn't have as much time as before. Not only did he need to catch up with his classmates… he needed to surpass them, too. And for once, he knew he could do it.

## 27

# PLANS & PROMISES

TJ AND FREYA VENTURED INTO THE LUSH FOREST, SEARCHING for materials to craft their staffs. The trees seemed alive. Ashe saturated the area, permeating the very air TJ breathed. Ultraviolet hues flooded his vision, allowing him to see the intricate web of magic blanketing everything. Ancient crystals jutted from boulders, remnants of fallen stars from ages past. Aziza and adze flitted between branches, their iridescent feathers shimmering.

Freya skipped alongside TJ, congratulating him again for getting them to this advanced stage of material gathering. "Okay," she said, still skipping. "You gotta give me the scoop on how you did that. Felt like I was bangin' my head against a brick wall for weeks on end, but today... nothin' at all."

TJ grinned mischievously. "A fellow half-diviner like yourself should know a magician never reveals his tricks." He knelt in a bow, pressing a gloved hand to the earth. "But here's one I learned recently."

The exposed scarring on his arm glowed as he activated Oshosi's charm—Psychometry.

"Oh dang!" Freya said. "You glow too? Why haven't I noticed? My partner, Eilean, glows too. Well, not glows, sparkles... I guess? And, well, not white but blue."

"Oh, cool. Is this Eilean a druid too?"

"No, she's a little different. Most druids like me don't sparkle."

"I see," TJ said. "My glow's not by choice. This happened after my meeting with Olokun. But hang on, let me cook..." Ghostly images flashed before TJ's eyes: The paths taken by other students, the successful materials harvested. The scenario reminded him of his last outing with Oshosi, where they navigated a strange dream from Forseti through a space he called Valhalla. Only now—instead of a grand hall atop a snow-swept mountain—the scene before him was a beautiful and mystical forest.

"Awesome, I know where we have to go," TJ said. "Follow me."

They ventured forth until they reached a river that stretched wide. Very wide. And the current was a bit rougher than TJ was expecting. How deep did it go? As TJ stared at the rushing river, his heart sank. The water churned and frothed, a stark reminder of his traumatic encounter with Olokun.

He dropped his hand near the bank and tried to sense it with his magic. To his Ashe Vision, it didn't seem more than three or four feet deep. But it meant he'd have to venture *into* the water. *Not* his first choice. He peeked over his shoulder to Freya, who was at least a dozen yards behind him.

"What's wrong?" TJ asked.

"Uh, I-I don't do well with water..." Freya stretched her long neck between the trees. "Maybe we can find another way around?" The joy and skip seemed long gone from her.

TJ nodded eagerly, relief washing over him. They spent the next few minutes scouting the riverbank, searching for a narrower crossing or a fallen tree to use as a bridge. But as they explored, it became clear that crossing the river was unavoidable.

"What about... air-stepping?" TJ offered half-heartedly, knowing it was a long shot.

Freya shook her head. "I don't know how to do that yet. I've always leaned more druid, and Oya's Wind hasn't worked so well for me lately."

*That would make sense...* TJ thought to himself.

They stood, gaping at each other, the rushing water taunting them. Freya fidgeted with a coiled strand of her hair. "Maybe we don't need whatever's on the other side? There's plenty of materials here..."

TJ sighed, recognizing the anxiety creeping in her voice—the same that gripped him. And in the face of that feeling of danger, Oshosi entered his mind, his voice too.

"That's just the fear talking," TJ said. "We need to cross."

They exchanged a look of shared dread, but TJ forced a smile. For some reason, it was easier to be brave when someone *else* was scared. TJ recalled when Tunde got on his first roller coaster, one that freaked TJ out as well. But he couldn't show that or his little brother would get scared too. So he acted like it was no big thing. Dayo had done the same for him years prior. And now he would do that for Freya.

"Could we… hold hands while we cross?" Freya asked, rubbing at her elbow. "If that's okay with you. I know that's not everyone's cup of tea. My partner wasn't so happy when I—"

"Nah, nah, that's cool." TJ grabbed for Freya's hand with his gloved one, but he missed and ended up slapping his hand against her wrist awkwardly. "Sorry, Oya's Wind has been on the fritz for me a little lately, too." After finally finding her hand properly, Freya gripped on tighter than TJ expected, but her face remained relatively neutral.

"I'll go first," TJ said. "Just... stay close, okay?"

He stepped into the frigid water, suppressing a shudder. Freya followed, her free hand gripping his arm tightly as well. As they waded deeper, the current tugged at their legs, threatening to sweep them away. Each push sent TJ back to that traumatic night. The push and pull of tidal waves. The cracking of wood. The shattering of glass. Each time this happened, TJ took in a deep breath. The words he spoke to Freya were just as much for him as they were for her. "You're doing great. Just a little farther."

Freya nodded, her jaw set with determination. "One step at a time."

A few moments passed, and before they knew it, their feet met solid ground. Out of the blue, Freya threw her arms around TJ. "Thank you for that. I promise I'm not always this… clingy." She took a step away, relinquishing her hold on TJ.

"You're good, dude. C'mon, let's hurry up and get these materials. Show the rest of the students we're not chumps."

"Lead the way, Lucky Charm!"

TJ wasn't even going to ask how she knew that nickname for him.

Under TJ's guidance, he and Freya gathered everything they needed in a flurry of activity. Freya thrived, locating ideal components she admitted she couldn't have found alone, like a moonstone that was hidden under a forest of moss, or snake skin that was camouflaged between a pair of branches. With TJ, she said, it was like riding a bike with training wheels.

Yet as they progressed, TJ struggled. Despite passing the initial test easily, nothing now seemed to resonate for his staff, despite the bounty of choices surrounding them. He wished he could trade ideas with Ayo, but his friend was way back at the clearing—paired away with another classmate. Ayo always knew what to do. And TJ needed his brain and ideas right now.

TJ persisted, though, yanking yew woods and amethyst crystals, chasing eloko creatures for their sap. But nothing worked, and frustration mounted. After making that claim in front of the other students, he dreaded returning empty-handed. There was one piece in particular that was most troubling. A set of cowries were embedded at the root of a tree. When TJ got a faint reading off them, he sensed the previous student, Aisha, who tried to draw from it. The Ashe within the cowries were all spent, despite them having strong associations with Orunmila.

"What are you sensing off those?" Freya asked.

TJ gathered the shells in his hand and threw them to the ground in anger. "A whole lot of nothing. But not surprising, I guess. These were imbued with Orunmila's Ashe."

Freya stopped gathering and came over to TJ, kneeling, her thick ponytail coming over her shoulder. "He's really gone, then? Librarian Bello doesn't believe it—or doesn't *want* to believe it."

"Yeah... he is."

"Yeah, he's not the only one. We just lost one of our Celtic gods too—Cailleach. You know her?" TJ shook his head, so Freya continued, "She's, like, this ancient winter goddess. Imagine an intense old woman—beyond old, with wild white hair, whipping up storms and shaping mountains. Basically, she's here to remind everyone that nature's fierce and wise, like, the ultimate 'don't mess with me' energy as winter shifts into spring."

"What happened now that she's gone?"

Freya shrugged. "I've not heard much on it yet, so I can't say for sure. But I'm sure nothin' good."

"Great..." TJ dropped his head in sadness. Then he lifted his head, perking up. "I don't know... maybe even the dead can manifest Ashe. Orunmila is gone and I'm still able to see hints of the future, feel some of his power. Granted, with the help of Obatala and Oshosi." And... then again, he was TJ Young after all.

"You're American, right?" Freya asked; TJ nodded, unsure where she was going with this. "And you call yourselves a melting pot over there, yeah? It may not be the same, but try to blend elements and cultural motifs. That's where I think I went wrong with my first staff. It wasn't connected to *both* parts of me. I had to connect both my Celtic *and* Yoruba heritage."

"But everything here is basically all associated with the Orishas." TJ pointed to the broken staff poking out of Freya's backpack. "You have all your Celtic charms already to mix with."

Freya nodded to TJ's own backpack. "What about what you got in there? Maybe worth a shot?"

"Maybe..." TJ said sadly. He still wasn't sure about using Dayo's staff after what had happened in the Frost Realm, what he learned had happened with Jessica. Somehow, that seemed to taint the way he felt about it.

"Remember," said Freya gently, then imitated their instructor, "'perfection is the enemy of good'. Just as Bamidele says. Our staffs need to suit us, and *only* us."

TJ nodded, resolving to continue his search. His gaze drifted to the sunlight streaming through the trees. It glinted off something nestled in the underbrush—a discarded bracelet. A friendship bracelet, one that many of the students exchanged on campus. The gems inlaid in the band were said to bind a pair together. It wouldn't help with his staff, but it sparked an idea in TJ's mind.

"Hey, Freya," he said. "Random question. What do you think would be a good way for me to ask someone to a quinceañera?"

Freya smiled knowingly. "Ah, so that's what this is really about." She pretended to inspect a crystal, giving TJ a sideways glance. "Not just staffcrafting advice you're after, is it? It's that Manuela girl, right?"

"What? No! I mean—yes. But no. Wait—how did you know about Manny?"

"I told you… I did my homework," Freya said. "Well, homework on your magic. But that led to learning about the other parts of you too, I guess."

TJ's cheeks grew warm. Was he *that* obvious?

"But wait… I thought Manuela was Brazilian," Freya said. "Isn't a quinceañera for Spanish-speaking girls?"

"Eh, it's complicated. It's really a Latin American thing overall, but Manny says that she hangs around a lot of Puerto Ricans in Brooklyn, so she basically adopted some of their culture."

"Good to know." Freya examined two more crystals on their path. "Which one should I go for—the green or blue?"

TJ pressed a hand to the ground once more to see the path of the previous students who came across this way. "Neither. They won't hold enough magic for a staff. Titi tried to use the green one and nearly messed up the melding with her wood. And the blue is a complete dud."

Freya shook her head with a smile. "Just like I said, bloody training wheels, you are."

They continued walking and TJ said, "Well, I mean, you've been so nice to me. I figured I could get your take on this Manny stuff, too. Since you're new here and all, it's easier to talk to you about it."

"Funny how that works, right?" Freya skipped again, clearly happy to talk about TJ's girl troubles. "How it's easy to tell things or ask things of people you've barely just met."

TJ paused. "Actually, is it too weird I'm asking you this? We do *barely* know each other, I guess."

Freya shrugged. "I don't mind. But first, tell me more about you and Manuela. I want the *full* story."

TJ hesitated briefly, then decided there was no harm in telling Freya. He described their friendship, his infatuation, the things they got into that brought them closer. Freya called him out on omitting details. "I've heard whispers 'bout you dashin' off to meet Orishas. Some of the others say you were friends with Eshu for a whole summer."

TJ's eyes widened. "Wait, you know about that too?"

"Aye, word travels fast around here, especially when it's about crossin' realms. Spill it, then."

TJ shuffled uncomfortably. "Okay, okay. So, Manny and I, we've sorta been on these... adventures. But it's complicated, y'know?"

"How's that?" Freya leaned on a nearby tree, intrigued.

"Like, we both know there's something more than just friendship, but neither of us is brave enough to make the first move, which is weird because Manny is really forward."

"A girl acting different than her usual around you? Oh yeah, that's a prime example of a crush."

"I'm low-key awkward with that kinda stuff, so… yeah, we're pretty much stuck. It's like we're dancing around each other, always one step outta sync."

Freya laughed. "I feel you there. So, this quinceañera thing, ya really wanna ask her?"

"Yeah, I do. But I want it to be special, something memorable. Any ideas?"

"Okay, well, does she like grand gestures or something more personal?"

TJ thought for a moment. "Manny's not shy, but she's not one for the spotlight. Something in between… I guess?"

"Then make it 'bout the journey you've shared. Maybe recreate a moment from one of your adventures, but with a romantic twist."

TJ stopped. "That might not work because of crossing over and the whole memory loss thing. But thanks! Gives me something to start with."

"Anytime. And hey, don't worry about the whole realm-crossing business. You're not alone in this. I've been a regular traveler to the Otherworld—the realm for the Celtic deities—with Eilean."

"You're lying!" TJ stopped idly searching for staff materials, taking in Freya's expression to make sure she wasn't yanking his chain. "Sick! I thought me and my friends were the only ones."

"Nope. At least not according to the UCMP agent who's apparently been on my case the last year or so—most of it without me knowing. They're right sneaky bawbags, they are. There's all sorts of reports on Evo about all the pantheons acting out. It's not just the Orishas."

"You would get along well with my brother, Tunde. He's much better at keeping up with all that stuff."

"Tunde? No way! He's your brother?"

"Why's that so surprising?"

"Ha! I love that kid. He's got jokes."

"And I don't?"

Freya gave him a stink face with a so-so gesture of her hand. "You could work on your delivery a bit." Then she gave him a light jab. "But you're a great water-wading partner."

TJ kept rubbing the back of his naps nervously as they continued walking through the forest together. Freya was so confident and seemingly self-assured. He envied that about her.

"You must have so much experience with guys. I still have no clue what to do around girls I like."

"I can't tell if you meant that as a 'getting around' slight or an 'I'm old with experience' slight."

"No, no, nothing like that! Ugh… you see… I'm terrible at this stuff."

Freya chuckled. "Yeah, I heard about all that awkwardness with you and Eniola, too."

TJ winced. "Oh gosh, I guess I'll just assume you know about *all* my dirty laundry."

"Well, it helps that I have a lot of classes with the girl," Freya said. "You know, she stares at you a lot at the mess hall—Eniola, I mean."

"Yeah… I've noticed that too."

"Hey, don't beat yourself up about it. Outside the terrible breakup, she has good things to say about you. And that means a lot from an ex. They, you know, tend to say the worst things."

TJ perked up a bit at that. "What about you? Any of these Ifa guys catch your eye? I'm not super popular. Well, I mean socially popular. Any time I go to the village, there's someone from *The Press* or *Divination Today* requesting an interview. But I can still put in a good word. You're super dope."

Freya hesitated, her cheeks reddening slightly. "Well… I wouldn't say I have the *most* experience with guys… And well, right now…" She trailed off, growing quiet. TJ glanced at her. "I'm probably more helpful with your girl troubles because…" she trailed off again. "I'm currently into…" Again, she trailed off, and a shadow fell over her eyes.

"Girls?" TJ finished matter-of-factly. "You're only into girls."

"And boys too!" Freya rushed out. "I mean, like, both are… good?" Freya said softly, picking at the inside of her dashiki uniform.

"Oh!" TJ exclaimed, the pieces clicking into place. "That's what you meant by your 'partner' Eilean! I thought she was, like, some UCMP agent or something. But you meant…"

"My girlfriend, yeah," Freya said, biting her lip.

"That's what's up. That's what's up," TJ said sincerely. "I mean I can't blame you. Girls are sort of the best."

The tension in Freya's forehead relaxed, she stood up a little straighter, and she gave TJ a smile. "Yeah. They sort of are, right? But," she bumped TJ on the shoulder, "guys aren't so bad either. You're a decent one."

"Gee, thanks, granny!"

"Okay, I take it back!"

They both laughed together as they gathered the last of their materials. As they walked back to the clearing with the others, TJ's spirits lifted. He may not have built a staff yet like he wanted to, but he had a plan and an idea for asking Manny to her quince thanks to Freya. For once, things were looking up. And he really needed that right now.

# 28

# FORGING A FUTURE FROM THE PAST

DAD

Sorry, I missed your text, son. Had two basketball camps back to back and my part-time at Big 5. Alright, here is my advise for Manny…

DAD

First date vibes! Just be you. We raised you right. Keep it cool, and remember… girls like it when you're real with them. So put the phone away, listen, and keep her laughing. That goes further than you think. And don't go blowing all your money trying to impress her either! Half the time a chill date's the best way to actually get to know somebody. Proud of you, TJ. Let me know how it goes.

TJ

thank u dad! def using this. gimme a sec, ayo about to hook me up with a cut back at the academy. ill let you know how it goes.

TJ SAT PATIENTLY AS AYO CAREFULLY TRIMMED HIS HAIR IN preparation for TJ's upcoming date with Manny that weekend. The steady snipping of the floating clippers was punctuated by playful banter between the other boys in the shared dorm room. The room, lined with bark walls, was littered with the mess typical of teenage boys: clothes and crossover equipment on the floor, textbooks left open, empty potion bottles strewn about. Umar lounged in a corner with a few other SS1 boys, their eyes glued to a crossover game playing on the bark-embedded TV screen. The vibrant colors of the game cast flickering lights across the room.

"I still no believe I cut hair for you." Ayo signed as he neatly and magically tapered TJ's shaggy sides with a floating set of clippers powered by Oya's Wind. "Old me laugh if someone say I do this. Back when time with Jimoh and LaVont was main thing. Don't know what I see in those idiots."

TJ shrugged, then said, with sarcasm, "Big goons following your every move? That's a schoolyard bully's wet dream, man. Especially a bully of your… *height-challenged* stature."

"Forget you!" Ayo scowled, rubbing the tattoo under his eye. "You know I have hot shaver on side of head right now, eh?"

TJ threw up his hands. "I kid, I kid! You're a much better person without them, dude. Real talk."

"Yeah, well…" Ayo started, a smirk playing across his face before he softly said, "You're a… you know… g-g-good influence and w-w-whatnot."

"Gee thanks, my guy. Can you say that a little louder for our bunkmates?" TJ winked, nodding to the other boys huddled around the TV. Then his ears went hot, forgetting the potential offense in his words. "Not like that. My bad, Ayo, you know what I mean."

"D-d-don't trip," he said sadly, quietly.

"You're making progress with your telepathy though, right? You was talkin' to that cat. I heard you."

"Yeah, that guide I use say start with animals. I surprise you hear it. I try make work with dad. Try talk to fish in tank. But maybe that just a TJ thing, eh?"

TJ gave him a look. "Wait. Not that guide everyone told you to stop using from that scammer, right?" Ayo ignored him. "Right, Ayo?"

"Don't push, TJ." Ayo signed, then changed the subject. "I wish you leave forest with finished staff. LaVont and Jimoh laughing big big. I hate it."

TJ waved his hand dismissively. "They won't be laughing for long. I've got a plan that's going to blow everyone away at the next session. My staff will be done months before everyone else's. For real this time." His mind turned to Oya, to Shango. "It has to be…"

"See. I influence you too. I like to hear voice with bravery." Ayo stroked his non-existent beard in thought. "Hmm, I think shave back. What you think? Afro top and shaved sides start to feel …" He couldn't find the word to sign so he stuttered, "P-P-Played out these d-d-days."

"Whatever you think is best. Go for it."

As Ayo carefully trimmed the back of TJ's head, TJ glanced down at his sister's journal sitting in his lap. Using Oya's Wind, he gingerly flipped through the pages, skimming her familiar handwriting. One entry in particular caught his eye, and he leaned forward excitedly.

Ayo jumped as TJ's sudden movement caused him to cut extra hair. He moved in front of TJ so TJ could see him signing animatedly. "Bruh, watch it!" Ayo sucked his teeth. "Well, you for sure no get a…" He wanted to say the word this time. "F-F-Fohawk now."

"My bad, my bad!" TJ said. "But check this out." He pointed to a passage in Dayo's journal. "I think I know what this says, but I'm not sure." While TJ's spoken Yoruba was pretty decent these days, he still had trouble reading it. "Does that part there say something about ancestral wood?"

Ayo adjusted his glasses and gave the journal a once over. "Oh, shit. Yeah… It say Ifedayo get wood of past family from grandmother's... table of family. I mean… family altar. Say it help her finish make staff. That can work, for sure."

TJ took the journal back enthusiastically. "I think I'm going to start my date with Manny by taking her to see my family's ancestral altar. Not the most romantic thing but… maybe it'll be really special to share that part of my heritage with her?" TJ's voice squeaked a little near the end of his sentence.

Ayo chuckled. "I no know about all that. She might not like."

The click of the magical clippers sounded again as Ayo turned them back on. The buzz blended with the distant cheers from the crossover game. Then he tidied up the edges of TJ's cut. "Just don't let history lesson drag too long. Or Manny might get more interested in old family than in you…"

TJ laughed. "Don't worry, I'll keep the date focused on us. But… do you think that would be lame?"

Ayo threw his hands up. "It be l-l-lame to me but you and M-M-Manny be on that g-g-goofy shit so it might work out for you, man. What I know?" Then he signed, "Just don't be late to Mami Wata eating place later. You my guy, my guy, but that favor I ask for you no come cheap."

ᛉ

TJ WALKED OUT TO THE SUMMONING STONES WITH A JITTERY gait. His heart pounded in his chest, echoing the rhythmic pulsing of the ancient monoliths that surrounded him. He paused at the edge of the glade when he caught his first glimpse of Manny. She leaned casually against the weathered Oya statue, staring up at the dappled sunlight that filtered down through the canopy.

Manny was dressed in her characteristic fit—stylish yet comfortable. Today she wore a graphic tee featuring a cute *Kizazi Moto* print, paired with cuffed jeans and white Chuck's. Her hair was styled into two playful space buns, with two braids framing her face and the rest cascading freely down her back. She looked effortlessly put together, radiating an easy confidence.

As TJ's eyes adjusted to the emerald glow of the forest, the scene before him took on an ethereal beauty. Verdant moss and vines crept over the weathered boulders. Manny seemed like one with the surroundings, her inner light somehow accentuated by the mystical ambiance.

Or maybe it was just his mega crush that was painting the picture.

TJ bit the inside of his cheek, wiping his sweaty head with his gloves as he willed his feet to carry him forward. Why was he so nervous? This was Manny, his closest friend. Yet somehow that made it all the more intimidating. With each step he took, TJ's trepidation grew. She was so effortlessly cool, and he was… well, just TJ.

Manny turned to greet him with a casual "Hey!" only she could say so… cool-like. The familiar husk in her voice sent a flutter through TJ's chest. He couldn't help but notice the subtle sheen from her purple lip balm. It was a small detail, but it made his mouth run dry.

"H-hey, Manny!" TJ stammered, cursing himself for sounding like such a dork. "So, uh, I was thinking... well, before we head out to the village, m-maybe we could make a quick stop at my grandma's place?" TJ rambled, tripping over his words, so he lied. "It's just, she keeps asking about you, s-since we're, you know, friends and all, and I haven't actually introduced you two formally, though I guess you met her a few times when we were dealing with all that deity stuff..."

TJ trailed off when Manny's expression shifted from polite interest to something unreadable. *Oh no, did she think this was weird?* He was being weird, wasn't he? He was making it weird. Was he being too eager by suggesting this detour?

"I mean—we totally don't have to!" TJ backpedaled. "It was just a thought, no pressure at all, I just—"

"TJ," Manny interjected gently. "Visiting your grandma sounds great. I'd love to be introduced for real."

TJ blinked. "Wait, really?"

"It's just... don't you think this is moving a little fast? We're not even dating really..."

TJ's stomach bottomed out. Manny laughed, her eyes crinkling. "Kidding, TJ. Obviously." She punched him on his arm. "And yes, really! I think it's sweet that you want me to meet her more formally. Honestly, I'm kind of honored."

A wave of relief washed over TJ. Of course Manny would be cool with this—she was the chillest, most understanding person he knew. He needed to stop doubting her.

Or he needed to stop doubting himself.

"Awesome, thanks, Manny!" TJ grinned, previous anxieties evaporating into the canopy. "I just know she's gonna love you—if she doesn't already."

Manny smiled back warmly. "Well then, lead the way, yo!" She fell into step beside TJ as they headed out of the forest, already chatting easily about the day's plans. TJ didn't even notice the short trip to his family's compound, or the UCMP officers shadowing them, lost in Manny's dimples and conversation. Before he knew it, they were outside the door of Grandma's home.

TJ paused outside the intricately carved door to Grandma's home, admiring the scenes of daily life depicted in the worn brass. Farmers tilled fields alongside elegant hunters pursuing prey through stylized forests. Women gathered water from wells and harvested yams, their movements flowing like a dance. The images wove together a tapestry of Yoruba history and myth, speaking to generations of knowledge passed down through TJ's lineage.

Beside him, Manny traced her fingers along the metalwork. "This is beautiful."

TJ nodded, pride swelling within him. Just then, the door swung open to reveal Grandma, arms outstretched in welcome. "Tomori Jomiloju, you've finally come to visit me!" She folded him into a warm embrace. When they broke apart, TJ dropped down to tap the ground in front of Grandma in respect. Manny followed suit, though she curtsied instead.

"Well, you know," TJ said, "between journeys through the ancestral path and figuring out how to save two of our Orishas, it's been hard."

Grandma waved the excuses away. "And you've brought Manuela. I'm so pleased to properly meet you, child."

"*So happy to meet you too, Mrs. Abimbola,*" Manny said in Yoruba.

"*Oya's Wind!*" Grandma replied, looking very impressed. "*This one's Yoruba is better than yours, Tomori.*"

Manny lifted one shoulder coyly. "*I'm a girl of many talents.*"

"*Oh, I like this one. Come inside!*"

Grandma led TJ and Manny into the cozy interior of her home, the door swinging shut behind them with a soft click. Despite the modest size of the single-story dwelling, the space felt warm and welcoming. Sunlight streamed in through open windows, mingling with the soft glow emitted by the crystals embedded in the walls.

As TJ's eyes adjusted to the change in light, his gaze roamed over the familiar details that made up a brief part of his childhood: Dark wood furniture polished to a lustrous shine. Colorful textiles draped over plush chairs and sofas. Framed family photos chronicling generations of lineage. It was hard to see some of the original wall, there were so many frames all over. In one corner, a broom swept industriously over the smooth stone floor, propelled by a simple animation spell.

Manny looked around with unconcealed curiosity, taking in every unique accent and flourish. "I love it. It feels so cozy."

Grandma beamed. "Why thank you, child. It's not much, but it's home." She bustled toward the small kitchen area. "Grandpa Wendell and your mom are out on the town right now, watching that dueling match at the bar with Grandpa's friends. You two make yourselves comfortable while I prepare some zobo."

As she busied herself filling a kettle from the faucet magically, TJ noticed again how Grandma seemed to have shrunk over the years. Her frame was slender and fragile now, her movements slow and measured.

Manny nudged his arm. "Check out all your baby photos," she teased, nodding to the collection of frames on the wall. TJ flushed, rubbing his neck self-consciously. Before he could stammer out a reply, Grandma returned, bearing a tray with three steaming mugs, and the rich, tart aroma of hibiscus tea filled the room.

"Thank you, ìyá àgbà," TJ said as he accepted his mug. The familiar taste immediately carried him back to carefree afternoons spent there as a child.

Grandma settled herself comfortably into an oversized armchair. "Now tell me, what brings you two here today?"

TJ took a deep breath before responding. "Well, I was hoping I could take a look at the family altar." He tensed. Would Manny be angry about his small fib? "I've been struggling with my staffcrafting," Manny simply looked curious, not annoyed—a relief for TJ, "and I thought maybe tapping into our ancestral magic could help."

Grandma's expression turned solemn. "I see. And did a certain journal give you this idea?"

TJ nodded, not bothering to feign ignorance. "Dayo mentioned using artifacts from the altar for her staff when she made hers. I was hoping to do the same."

"Hmm." Grandma took a thoughtful sip of tea. "Well, far be it from me to stand in the way of your magical education. The altar is yours to explore." Rising slowly, she beckoned for them to follow her down the hall.

TJ shared an excited glance with Manny. This was the breakthrough he had been waiting for. Finally, a chance to connect with his lineage and inherit his rightful power.

"You coulda told me this is what we were really here for," Manny whispered as they passed into the hall.

TJ whispered back, "Yeah, well..." He was embarrassed, he wanted to say. Instead, he just trailed off awkwardly.

"You're so weird sometimes." Manny laughed. "You know that?"

An embarrassing heat curled through TJ as they entered the altar room, the atmosphere shifting. It was more quiet and filled with a sandalwood incense. Sacred. TJ's eyes were immediately drawn to the central display—a family altar that filled the entire room: Pictures strewn all about. Bowls, crystals, and statuettes stacked high to the ceiling of worn orange paint. And bulbous lights lined the entire space in a warm way. Strung up on a wall was an ancient iron staff etched with symbols of Ogun. Grandma's staff.

Beside him, Manny gasped. "It's incredible..."

Grandma hummed under her lips. "It was Tomori Jomiloju who helped me design that one, believe it or not." Manny quirked an eyebrow. "Not my grandchild, obviously. His second great-grandfather. My clouded grandfather."

"Oh yeah, you mentioned that at the command center," Manny said.

Grandma smiled. "Yes, such a sweet man." She stroked a picture of a man that looked almost like a twin to TJ, again, with those funky red glasses. "Not a lick of Ashe in him, but he was full of such dream-like thoughts." She turned to TJ. "Just like this one here."

TJ shifted uncomfortably as Grandma doted over him. He appreciated her warmth, but it only highlighted the gulf between her pride and his own old feelings of inadequacy when it came to magic. When everyone in the family thought he was clouded, too.

Seeking a distraction, TJ's gaze landed on a cluster of photos hidden away in a dark corner of the room. They all depicted Mom with various men TJ didn't recognize. Their attire and surroundings marked them as members of the Yoruba magical community.

"Who are all these men with my mom?" TJ asked, grateful for the diversion.

Grandma glanced over and chuckled fondly. "Ah, yes, your mother was quite popular back in the day. All the finest young diviners were vying for her affections." She pointed to a handsome man with a mischievous grin. "That's Akin Olatunji, one of the first Keepers. Recruited that Bolawe when he failed at politicking the Nigerian government. Oh, yes. Akin was powerful and young but far too arrogant, even then."

Her finger shifted to indicate a studious looking gentleman in a dashiki. "And this one headed up the Bureau of Magical Heritage Preservation for many years."

Manny leaned in with interest. "Oh wow, I recognize him from history class! Didn't he discover a cure for ash fever?"

"That's right," Grandma confirmed with an approving nod. She went on to identify other influential figures and innovators linked to Mom over the years.

Manny let out an impressed whistle. "Daaang, Mrs. Young. Your mom really ran with an elite crowd back in the day!"

"Yeah, no kidding," TJ murmured. It was strange picturing Mom with the magical world's best and brightest, with men who weren't Dad. She'd always just been Mom—loving, stern, and fiercely devoted to family.

A question surfaced in TJ's mind. "If she was so popular, why'd she end up with my dad? I mean, he didn't even have Ashe and…"

*Mom is Ashe all day,* TJ thought sadly. It had been a touchy subject for him for nearly fourteen years.

Grandma grew thoughtful, perhaps sensing TJ's unease. "You know, your mother and father actually split up several times over the years. Many of these men," she pointed to the forgotten pictures in the corner, "many of them were 'in-between' your parents. But your father, clouded as he was, always took her back. And she him."

"But… why?" TJ asked. If Mom had gotten with one of the diviners, she wouldn't have to worry about having a potentially magic-less kid like TJ was for most of his life. "Wouldn't Mom have wanted to be with another diviner?"

"Mmm, perhaps." Grandma tilted her head. "Pride and tradition have always run strong in my daughter. But the fact is, she chose your father, again and again. Their love persisted. And then we got Ifedayo. And then we got another Tomori Jomiloju." She gave him knowing eyes. "A name I suggested, mind you. The moment I laid eyes on you, I knew you were bàbá àgbà coming anew." She eyed TJ meaningfully. "When you're ready, you should ask your mother about it directly. There are some things that are not my place to explain."

An awkward silence fell. TJ absorbed this new perspective on his parents' past, full of fresh mysteries.

After a moment, Manny spoke up brightly. "So, TJ, see anything around here that's calling out to you for your staff?"

Grateful for the redirect, TJ glanced around the altar room with new eyes. Various relics and artifacts glimmered in the soft light. TJ slowly circled the displays, senses attuned for any latent power or connection. The altar was wide and long. He walked its length twice, thrice. Every time he did, it was his great-grandfather's section that called to him the most. So he stopped and surveyed the items before Tomori Jomiloju's photo.

There were the expected Orisha-related objects—chunks of iron sacred to Ogun, volcanic rock for Aganju, a golden bell for Oshun. But mixed among them were artifacts tied to pantheons from around the world: A brass statue from the Hindu faith; a cauldron charm with Celtic script; a polished obsidian mirror like those used by the Aztecs—even a fossilized vertebrae from some prehistoric creature that looked like a mini Ninki Nanka.

"I never realized Great-Grandpa collected so many things from different cultures," TJ said.

Grandma nodded, her expression fond. "Oh yes, bàbá àgbà was endlessly fascinated by all forms of magic and mysticism. He felt drawn to artifacts from belief systems across the world—almost like he was trying to collect the magic he lacked as a clouded."

*Is that why I feel so connected to Freya and her Celtic magic?* TJ thought, then he said out loud, "I'm like Great-Grandpa, too, I guess—seeking out other sources of power because I don't have a clear alignment. I'm a child of no Orisha. Not Shango, not Oya, not Olokun. Not even Eshu."

"Could be, child." Grandma adjusted one of the pictures. "The desire to explore beyond one's familiar boundaries often runs in our family. Not just you and your great-grandfather. But all those who have had the family curse before you, it would seem."

TJ's mind raced, reflecting on his lessons with Freya and Staffmaster Bamidele. A daring idea took shape. "Is it possible..." he began slowly. "Could I use some of Great-Grandpa's artifacts, maybe some stuff from my Scottish friend, alongside the Orisha relics to craft my staff?"

Manny's eyes widened in surprise, but Grandma simply looked pensive. Like Bamidele, Grandma was once a staffmaster. She and he had spent most of last year re-examining Dayo's staff for reuse.

"Hmm, an unconventional approach," Grandma said. "But magic, yes even Ashe, is about connection, and these objects clearly speak to you. Why do you think Ifa traditionally integrates so well with other faith systems?"

"Like Catholicism?" Manny asked. "Santería is pretty big in Latin America. And it's basically a mix of Catholicism and Ifa, a remix of Saints and Orishas. That's what my aunt practices. Well, before..." She frowned and seemed to shrink into herself.

"Exactly," Grandma pointed an excited finger toward Manny, not noticing how Manny's voice had broken off.

"Someone should tell that to Bamidele and Ayo's dad," TJ said.

"Someone should," Grandma agreed. "Ifa is not so dogmatic. It's meant to be fluid."

*Just like Yemoja said,* TJ thought.

"Though I should warn you, grandchild. Staffmaster Bamidele may raise concerns about muddying your Orisha heritage..."

TJ nodded, thinking of Mr. Oyelowo's similar traditional views. But after a moment's thought, he met his Grandma's eye with resolve. "I understand, but I feel like this... weird fusion-staff is my best chance at succeeding." He gestured to the assortment of mystical objects. "I don't have a single clear alignment. Never have. So I need to embrace a blend, just like Great-Grandpa did."

Manny stepped up and gripped TJ's shoulder supportively. "I say trust your instincts. They've gotten you this far."

TJ smiled at her gratefully. Turning back to the altar, he examined several items glimmering with latent power.

*Trust the process,* he told himself, selecting a few resonant artifacts. *Follow the ancestors.*

Grandma watched TJ gather his materials, her expression unreadable. But as he met her gaze, she gave a small nod. "Follow your heart, child. It will not lead you astray."

# 29

# LINED UP AND BUTTONED-DOWN

THE BRIGHT AFTERNOON SUN SHONE DOWN ON TJ AND MANNY as they left Grandma's house, casting everything in a golden hue. It was a perfect day—clear blue skies without a cloud in sight, a light breeze rustling the leaves, and the air still holding the lingering warmth of the morning. TJ couldn't have asked for better weather for his date with Manny.

As they walked down the garden path back toward the village, TJ glanced down at the bundle of items cradled carefully in his arms, wrapped up in the soft cotton satchel Grandma had given him. He had gathered an odd assortment of artifacts and relics from his second great-grandfather's ancestral altar, guided only by instinct and a vague sense of connection.

Manny must have noticed the slightly bewildered look on his face, because she asked, "So, what'd you end up choosing?"

"To be honest, I have no idea what some of this stuff is. But this piece caught my eye right away." He showed her a small golden crescent, etched with tiny hieroglyphs with stylized sunbeams radiating from its back. "I'm pretty sure it's Egyptian. Probably something to do with Ra considering the sun spikes."

Manny's gaze drifted over the other items bundled in the satchel. "Is that a bunch of rune stones?" She pointed to a shaft of carved wood bearing angular script. "Looks Nordic to me. You could use it for the pommel on your staff, maybe? Mr. Stadheim could help."

"Hey, that's a great idea!"

As they continued through the village, he turned the chunk of wood over in his hands, imagining how he could incorporate it into his staff. All around them, villagers went about their daily business —merchants hawked fresh produce and handmade wares with floating displays, children laughed and played air-stepping games in the dirt paths, and neighbors chatted idly in the shade.

"You know, I was thinking about how I can combine different elements in my staff," TJ said after a few moments of comfortable silence. "I can use the core principles of the Orishas, like the elemental energies of the Summoning Stone in the entrance hall. Maybe they'll be the foundation. Ogun represents the cold dryness of earth, Shango is hot and dry like fire—"

"Oya is hot and wet as the sky, and Yemoja is the cold wetness of water," Manny finished for him, nodding along. "So as long as you match up all the pieces with those basic vibes of the Orishas, you should be able to make it all click, right?"

"That's what I'm hoping for," TJ said, part of his mind going to fear for what Staffmaster Bamidele's response would be. But the instructor was hosting Freya, an exchange student who was a druid, not a diviner. So TJ should be able to mix and match as well, right?

As they reached the edge of New Ile-Ife, TJ carefully placed the relics into his satchel, making sure they were tucked in securely for the rest of the day. He was eager to share his ideas with Freya at their next session. With Manny's insights today, he felt like he had a solid direction for crafting his unique staff.

"Thanks for coming with me this morning," TJ said, turning to Manny with a smile. "It really meant a lot to me to be able to share all that with you."

"Of course, yo, I loved getting to know your grandma better. Now I'm looking forward to seeing what you have planned for the rest of our… date," she finished, her shoulder curling into herself.

TJ's heart leaped at her words, and his walk turned into a halfway skip. Grinning, he said, "Don't worry, I think you'll really like what I've got planned for our… date."

Manny's resulting smile lit up her whole face. As they continued down the path, TJ walked with a new lightness in his step. The sun seemed to shine even brighter than before.

TJ smoothed down the front of his crisp cornflower-blue button-up shirt, admiring the sharp creases ironed into it. The shirt fit slim but not too tight across his lanky frame. He had left the top few buttons undone, just enough to look casual but still neat. Ayo had picked it out for him, along with the fitted khaki chinos and brown leather belt, insisting the preppy look would impress Manny. TJ had to admit, now that his hair was freshly cut and styled into a flawless fade, he felt like a new man.

As he and Manny strolled through the lively streets of New Ile-Ife, TJ kept stealing glances at her. The afternoon light made her glow. She was entirely too cute.

"I'm really feeling your new look today," TJ said. "Those space buns are super dope."

Manny grinned. "Thanks! I was in an experimental mood this morning. Wasn't sure I could pull it off, but I'm glad you approve."

They continued chatting and joking easily as they explored the village's bustling marketplace. Vendors called out to them, offering free samples of succulent grilled meat, vibrant tropical fruits, and chilled refreshing drinks. TJ insisted on treating Manny to whatever caught her eye. At one booth, they shared a bowl of puff puffs sprinkled with brown sugar. TJ laughed as a bit of the powdered sugar clung to Manny's nose.

"What? Do I have something on my face?" Manny asked.

"Just a little sugar." TJ gently wiped it away with his thumb. They both flushed slightly at the contact.

Farther down the row of stalls, TJ challenged Manny to a game of *Major League Crossover* at Anansi's Arcade. "I need my revenge!" he said.

TJ spotted several other students from Ifa there, including LaVont and Jimoh. To avoid them, he slipped over to a game station tucked in the far corner, away from most of the noise and chaos. When he and Manny started playing, Manny trounced him soundly, her reflexes lightning-quick.

"Girl, you are brutal!" TJ said after his fifth failed attempt. "You couldn't let me win not one game? The Oya in you really comes out with this game. Where's the Yemoja energy when I need it?"

"Hey, I warned you." Manny giggled. "I ain't ranked Top Ten for junior crossover players in the West African region for nothin'."

As the afternoon wore on, TJ had the time of his life. Being with Manny just felt easy and natural. Unlike his dates with Eniola last year that sometimes felt forced and uncomfortable, time with Manny was entirely effortless. TJ found himself wishing the day would never end. But the sun had started its descent toward the horizon, casting a red, orange, and purple bloom over the village.

"Come on, one last stop," TJ said, leading Manny toward the dockside restaurant—the Mami Wata Eatery. The exposed wood beams and nautical decor gave it a cozy, romantic ambiance. Strings of lanterns had just been lit, their flickering light reflecting off the gentle rippling water.

They were seated at a table right at the railing overlooking the river. A contented sigh escaped TJ's lips as he soaked in the stunning scenery.

"I always love coming here," Manny said lightly. "It always feels so... magical."

As if on cue, a trio of mami wata emerged from the river below, their luminous tails shimmering iridescent blue and green.

"Li'l twin!" they chorused happily, waving to Manny with a splash.

"Love the space buns today," one of them said.

"And those two braids framing yuh face!" said another. "Real nice touch."

"Perfection!" said the third.

Manny greeted them enthusiastically, her dimples caving a mile. The mami wata always fawned over her hair, which was usually big, curly, and as unruly as theirs. TJ took the opportunity to excuse himself, pretending he needed to use the restroom. In actuality, he snuck outside to place a quick text.

Pulling out his phone, TJ texted:

TJ

hey we just got seated

TJ

ur girl is still coming yea? 8pm?

AYO

um... bad news

TJ's stomach dropped to the soles of his feet. Everything was perfect so far. He was so close to a perfect night. It couldn't be ruined now.

TJ

what?

Ayo's text dots kept appearing and reappearing. Why was he taking so long to create a response? Before leaving, Ayo promised that he could get Naija Siren—one of Manny's favorite diviner singers—to come out and help TJ confess his feelings with a song. A song specifically designed for Manny.

AYO

um... u might want to sit down for this.

TJ

bruh dont play like that. what happened?

AYO

So... naija and her band got a last minute gig. big time client. i think some igbo prince

TJ

lol very funny. tell me ur joking

Again, those dreaded three dots flickered in and out on TJ's screen. TJ hadn't realized he was pacing outside Mami Wata's now.

AYO

not joking. sorry bruh. fr fr. i feel bad. this is on me. maybe i can call up someone else but on such short notice...

TJ sent a silent scream up to the heavens. Taking a few moments to settle down, he replied back to Ayo.

TJ

dont trip, man. ill think of smt

AYO

just do u man, u wont go wrong

It took a while before TJ gathered himself. He couldn't go back into that restaurant without a plan. But he was blanking on what he could do. He even had half a mind to sing the song himself.

*Hell no, I'm completely tone deaf.*

The longer he waited, the more likely Manny would wonder where he went off to. And considering how protective she was, she'd come looking to make sure he wasn't whisked away by Elder Adeyemi or Oshosi, or whoever else. More than a few minutes must've passed by, because when TJ was working through his fifth horrible idea, Manny came out, poking her head out the door.

"Hey, yo, you a'ight?" she asked.

TJ spun on his heel and immediately said, "No!—shit, it's you—I mean yeah. Yeah, everything is going great."

Concern laced her face and she came out. "You're sweatin' something fierce, man. You sure?" She looked down the dirt street both ways. "Was it another reporter? Did you spot a Keeper?"

"No… no nothing like that."

"Was it Obatala? Is he hiding in a puddle?"

"Nah, nah, it's chill."

"What is it, TJ? You know I can tell when you're hiding something."

Without thinking, TJ took her hands into his own, interlacing them. It was usually difficult to move them, but at that moment, he couldn't help them from shaking. "No, no. Manny, listen I—I had this huge thing planned. Naija Siren was supposed to come—"

"Naija Siren!" Manny looked down the street again, this time with more excitement in her movements. "You're lying!"

"No, no, listen. She's not coming. Something about a prince or whatever but… but…" He just stared in her big brown eyes. Ayo was right. He could do this himself. "It's all wrong. It wasn't supposed to be this way, but… Look, Manny. I really *really* like you. Like… so much it hurts sometimes." TJ's heart pounded in his chest. His whole world had narrowed down to just the two of them, standing there outside Mami Wata's. The words tumbled out of him in a rush. "Manny, I—I've been trying to find the right way to tell you this for so long. You're just... you're amazing, you know? Like, the way you always have my back, and how you're so strong and brave. And smart too! You're a total dork, and you don't care that you are."

TJ noticed a few people stopping to watch—some of them students from Ifa. His pulse quickened as murmurs rippled through the crowd. Palms sweating and unable to steady his shaking hands, he gave Manny's a firm squeeze and leaned closer. "Come on, let's get some privacy," he whispered, guiding her back inside the Mami Wata Eatery. They slipped past curious glances and returned to their table by the riverside, lanterns casting a soft glow over their faces.

Settling back into their seats, TJ took a deep breath, his chest still tight with nerves. He looked at Manny and picked up where he'd left off, his voice hushed but no less earnest. "When you laugh, Manny... It's the best sound ever. I could listen to it all day. And your dimples? They're adorable. I mean, you're adorable—beautiful, actually. The way you care about people, the passion you put into everything..." His cheeks burned as he stumbled over his words. "You make me want to be better. Braver. You inspire me, Manny. And I... I really, really like you—I think I already said that. It's confusing, but it feels... big, and important, and... yeah."

He paused, his lungs heaving. Manny's eyes glistened, and he wondered if he'd gone too far, if he'd said too much. The faint sound of conversation from nearby tables faded into the background.

Manny dabbed at her eyes, laughing through her tears. "I hate that you're the only one who can make me cry. And damn, TJ, this feels like some kind of marriage proposal."

TJ rubbed the back of his neck, managing a laugh. "I mean, I can get down on one knee if you want..."

"Don't even joke!" Manny raised her hands, half-laughing, half-serious. The tension lifted slightly as they both chuckled, a wave of relief settling over TJ.

He took another steadying breath. "But for real, Manny... we've been through a lot together. I can't imagine anyone else by my side—well, except maybe Ayo, but you know what I mean. You're different. You've always been different. So... would you let me be your escort to your quince? As... your boyfriend?"

The words hung in the air. For a moment, all TJ could hear was the gentle lapping of the water below. Manny's eyes widened before she hunched over, clutching her stomach.

"Oh no, what's wrong?" TJ's heart dropped.

"I just remembered I'm lactose intolerant," she said, feigning gags.

"But… we didn't eat any dairy."

"Nope. Just allergic to all that cheese you just served." She grinned, her eyes sparkling.

"Shut up!" TJ laughed, giving her a playful nudge.

Manny's expression softened, the teasing giving way to something serious. "Really, though… yes. I'd love for you to be my escort. And… my boyfriend."

Suddenly, a familiar trio of voices erupted from the water below. Three mami wata lounged at the river's edge, their tails shimmering beneath the lantern light. "So cute!" one cooed, clapping her hands.

"Adorable, really," another added, her laughter ringing like wind chimes.

The third said, "Kiss her, kiss her!"

But all TJ could focus on was Manny. They embraced, giddy with excitement. And though TJ desperately wanted to kiss her properly, he settled for a quick peck on the cheek, suddenly feeling shy with so many eyes on them. At first, even Manny's expression changed, but it looked more like a sudden realization.

"Wait… I-I told you that." She lowered her voice. "In the you-know-where. I-I… the quince. I remember. I told you to tell me and… But… H-How?"

TJ shrugged with a smile. "You're my anchor." If his connection to Manny allowed him to do the things he did in Forseti's dreams, maybe it could repair her memory as well.

TJ hadn't imagined the day going so perfectly. As he settled back into his seat—fingers interlaced with Manny without him realizing when they had held hands to begin with—TJ couldn't remember what the ground felt like because he was floating.

ᛉ

TJ COULDN'T STOP SMILING AS HE AND MANNY STROLLED HAND-in-hand back toward Ifa Academy. The crystal lanterns, lighting the village paths, shone softly around them, and laughter and music from the restaurants spilled out into the warm night air. But TJ was barely aware of any of it—his senses were filled only with Manny's presence beside him.

The feeling of her hand in his made his pulse race. Her smooth skin against his own sent a drumline up his arm. He kept glancing down in disbelief, still unable to fully process that he was actually holding his girlfriend's hand. *His* girlfriend.

And her name was *Manny*!

As they reached the edge of the village and started down the earthy path leading to Ifa, TJ was suddenly hyper aware of the sound of the gravel crunching under their feet in the stillness. He worried Manny might be able to hear his pounding heart in the quiet. But she seemed perfectly at ease, humming softly to herself as she swung their hands playfully between them.

All too soon, the glowing lights of the central campus came into view through the trees. TJ walked Manny right up to the towering wide tree that housed her dorm. Vines cascaded down its enormous trunk, and a spiral staircase wound its way up to the door of Manny's treehouse high above.

They stopped and turned to face each other, both suddenly shy. TJ scuffed his shoe against an exposed root.

"So... I had a really great time today," he said.

"Yeah, me too," Manny replied, uncharacteristically soft-spoken. "It was sort of… perfect. No one has ever done something like that for me. Or say all that stuff about me like that."

An awkward beat passed. TJ racked his brain trying to think of something charming or smooth to say, but his mind was blank. He gently reached out toward her, but his hand twitched. Then suddenly it was strong again, and through his Ashe Vision, he could see Manny's use of Oya's Wind assisting him. He smiled down at her and tucked a braid back behind Manny's ear so he could see her face more clearly in the soft light. Her eyes shone, deep pools that he could gaze into forever.

Breath hitching, TJ leaned in slowly. Manny met him halfway. Their lips met, tentatively at first. The kiss was clumsy, uncertain—they bumped noses at one point, giggling nervously. But as they found their rhythm, moving in sync, TJ was overwhelmed by the electricity flowing between them. Manny's lips were so soft, so perfect against his own. He lost himself in the sweetness of the moment.

Nothing could have prepared him for this. His dreams and fantasies about kissing Manny had never captured the true magic of the real thing. The forest around them faded away until it was just the two of them, caught up in the wonder of their *first* kiss. When they did finally break away—a brief eternity later—TJ said, cooly, "Sorry for making it weird."

"I'm glad you did make it weird." Manny smiled that perfectly dimpled smile. TJ was ready to dive in for round two when a chorus of giggles sounded from above. He glanced up to see a few of Manny's dormmates crowded at the railing of their treehouse, watching the scene unfold below.

"Is that TJ Young?"

"Yeah, with Manny."

"Told you it would happen this term."

"Oooh, get it, girl!" Titi catcalled.

Manny pulled back, blushing furiously. "All right, show's over."

The girls continued giggling but retreated into their dorm, granting them privacy once more—well, Titi took another peek before retreating again.

"I should probably head in too," Manny said. "But... thank you again for everything today. It really meant the world to me."

"Of course," TJ replied. He still felt like he was floating. "I'm glad I could make it special for you. You deserve that."

Manny smiled, then leaned in to give him one more lingering peck on the lips. "Night, TJ."

"G'night, Manny." TJ watched her ascend the twisting staircase until she disappeared through the doorway at the top. His heart was full to bursting.

As he slowly made his way back to his own dorm, replaying the day's events in his mind, TJ decided today was easily the happiest he had ever been. And it was just the beginning. He and Manny had so much more ahead of them, so many more firsts. He couldn't wait to experience them all together.

# 30

# A WAKING DREAM

WHEN TJ RETURNED TO HIS DORM, THERE WERE ONLY A FEW other SS boys around, most still out in the village. TJ had hoped Ayo would be there so he could tell him all about his date with Manny, but he must've gone as well. It didn't matter either way, because the moment TJ plopped on his bed, he knocked *all the way* out.

Somewhere between his napping and dreaming state, he found himself back in Obatala's dream room. It had been a few days—maybe a week—since he had last been among the endless chamber of fractured glass. A smile split across his face when Obatala and Oshosi floated before him.

"Hello, young mortal," Obatala said, his pale bald head glistening.

Oshosi saluted, making the green and white feathers of his head-dress flutter. "Greetings, Tomori Jomiloju. What's got you looking so giddy?"

TJ didn't realize how wide his grin had been, and he didn't care. "Manny."

"Oh," Oshosi said knowingly, "I see, I see. That one *really* is your anchor..."

"Like I told you," TJ replied with a look, adjusting to the soft, ethereal glow that permeated Obatala's dream room. "So... what do we have to do today? I haven't seen you in a while. Figured you were held up in Forseti's mind or something."

"We were." Obatala drifted down to head level with TJ. The air shimmered with a pearlescent light, casting everything in a gentle hue. "And we have made a major breakthrough. Today, we'll be slipping into Forseti's active subconscious. Not just his dreams. How did your mission in the Frost Realm go?"

"Mostly good, and a little bad."

"How so?" Oshosi asked.

"We got the ancestral path open, but… we had a run in with one of Forseti's ravens you warned me about. Don't worry!" Oshosi eyebrows had hiked up. "I was able to stop it, but… it was through runic magic. I don't know how I did it. Maybe because Yemoja had already mixed with the magic there or whatever. More than that though… I had seen the runic symbol I used before… in Forseti's dreams. The 'Isa' symbol. It looks like a letter 'I'."

Obatala, like always, took his time to process TJ's words. His serene expression flickered with interest, while Oshosi's sharp gaze narrowed slightly. A flutter of anticipation flapped at TJ's chest as he awaited their response.

"This…" Obatala began slowly. "This isn't entirely surprising. Every time we've dived into Forseti's dreams, have you noticed he attempts to reach out to the Fates? The Norns, as the Asgardians call it. He has been trying to reconnect via his slumber, especially after Thor's demise."

"And it would seem," Oshosi added, "that he may be reading the future without realizing it."

"Which explains me seeing that rune, and then it *actually* happening." TJ pondered on all those images he tried to decipher in Forseti's mind. "But… divination like that… it shouldn't be possible, should it? With Orunmila gone?"

"That is the big question, isn't it?" Obatala said as a chime above sounded.

Whispers danced at the edge of TJ's hearing, just beyond comprehension, like the rustle of silk against silk. The room seemed to pulse with a gentle rhythm, as if breathing in time with the universe itself. He'd ventured to this place several times, and it still made him feel a bit… off.

"Ah," Obatala said, "it seems as though Forseti is waking. It is time."

TJ felt a sudden shift as Obatala and Oshosi's Ashe enveloped him. It was different from their previous dreamwalking sessions—this time, it was as if he were being pulled through a sieve, his consciousness stretching and thinning. The familiar dreamscape dissolved around him, replaced by a kaleidoscope of colors and sensations that made no sense to his mortal mind.

*Focus, young one,* Obatala's voice echoed, seeming to come from everywhere and nowhere at once. *Let our combined Ashe guide you. Let your anchor remind you of reality.*

TJ closed his eyes, concentrating on the dual streams of power flowing through him. As usual, Oshosi's energy was sharp and precise, while Obatala's was cool and expansive. As he surrendered to their guidance, the chaotic swirl of sensations coalesced. It was easier than their previous sessions, easier—TJ assumed—because his bond with Manny was that much stronger.

Everything snapped into focus. TJ gasped as he found himself looking through Forseti's eyes, though the view was hazy, as if peering through a fogged window. The Asgardian's drowsy confusion washed over him as his consciousness slowly returned.

*Remarkable,* Oshosi whispered in his mind. *You've done it, TJ. You're in Forseti's subconscious.*

TJ marveled at the clarity of this new experience. Unlike the abstract symbolism of dreams, Forseti's subconscious thoughts flowed around him like a river of more fully-formed ideas and emotions.

*Remember,* Obatala cautioned, *we are here to observe,* not *interfere. Let Forseti's thoughts guide you, but do not lose yourself in them, and do not attempt to alter them.*

As TJ acclimated to this strange new perspective, a surge of excitement rushed through his body that he knew he needed to stamp down. He needed to be neutral, shapeless, formless... like water.

*Thank you, Dad, for introducing me to Bruce Lee.*

Forseti's world came into focus slowly as the Asgardian moved through his early routine—TJ was now his second pair of eyes. Obatala was right, most of his thoughts surrounded the Fates and a way to break through to them. Forseti did his best to focus his mind on the waking world, but his subconscious kept going back to vague foretellings. When the image of a raven flapping its wings against an ice wall manifested, fear spiked through TJ's heart. Was Forseti aware of what happened in the Frost Realm?

TJ felt Forseti grab for his head in frustration.

*Whatever emotion you're feeling right now, TJ, stop it,* Obatala warned.

*Sorry, sorry!* TJ threw back before going zen again. *Focus, TJ.* His breath hitched, and Forseti's mind wavered—just a little, but enough to set TJ's pulse racing. The pressure in his chest tightened, and for a second, everything spun. *Don't. Freak. Out. Not now.*

He squeezed his eyes shut and latched onto the memory of Manny—her smile when he teased her, the way her hand brushed his at Mami Wata's. *Just think about her.* The tension eased. His breathing slowed. Forseti's thoughts drifted back into their hazy flow, and TJ followed, sliding into the rhythm like slipping into warm water.

But then the memories stuck, pulling at him like sticky tape. A little too good. A little too happy. He swelled with positive emotion—right before Forseti's mind flickered in response, disturbed by the wave.

*You're causing ripples, Tomori,* Obatala warned, low but sharp.

What had Dad said before? That positive emotion could be just as bad as the negative. Some basketball coach used to say something like it: *Never get too high, never get too low. Never think you're the best, never think you're the worst.* TJ clenched his jaw. *C'mon, stay cool. Water, not soda fizz.* He blew out a breath, forcing the joy down into a steady hum—quiet enough not to stir Forseti again, but still there if he needed it.

Forseti shook the foreign sensation away as he arrived at the Court of All, walking among the golden pillars and those armored statues. Eventually, Forseti lumbered through an ethereal weapon room. The vast chamber sparkled with a mystical light, illuminating an array of weapons from various pantheons across the world. Gleaming katanas from Japanese mythology hung beside ornate tridents from Greek legends. Aztec macuahuitls bristled with obsidian blades next to Egyptian khopesh swords.

At the center of the room, atop a raised pedestal, rested Mjölnir —Thor's hammer. The weapon's presence seemed to dominate the space, its power palpable even from a distance. As Forseti approached, TJ noticed two figures already there, the same ones from the Court of All at the prosecution table. Somehow, now, he knew their names: Magni and Modi, Thor's sons.

"Still nothing?" Forseti asked, gesturing toward Mjölnir.

Magni shook his red braids, grunting beneath a grizzly red beard. "She refuses to heed us, cousin. It's as if she no longer recognizes us as Thor's blood. I'm telling you, that bastard of an Orisha has cursed her."

"The dwarves confirmed it," Forseti said, his tone grave. "Mjölnir's allegiance has shifted. She answers Shango's call now. Though as to why, they are less certain."

Modi's fist clenched at his side, his blond hair looking wild. "This is unacceptable. What of The Channeling? Surely, if we drain Shango's essence, Mjölnir will return to Asgardian hands where she belongs."

Forseti sighed, and TJ felt the god's weariness as his own. "It is not that simple, cousins. Shango's mind is formidable. It will be many moons yet before his power is fully drained."

A surge of anger ran through TJ at their words, at their casual discussion of draining Shango.

"Then work faster!" Magni snapped. "Every moment Mjölnir remains beyond our reach is an insult to our people. And you said it yourself. The God Eaters will breach Utenheim soon."

"I told you that's what I *think* may happen. The Norns are fickle and my dreams have made less and less sense of late."

Was it just TJ's anger, or was he sensing the irritation Forseti felt for his cohorts? TJ couldn't be sure. He struggled to contain his emotion, knowing it could betray his presence in Forseti's mind. Instead, he focused on Forseti's own frustration with Thor's sons, using it to mask his feelings. He even used LaVont and Jimoh as stand-ins, imagining their faces on the Norse gods.

"Patience," Forseti admonished, turning to leave the chamber. "Some things cannot be rushed, no matter how much we might wish otherwise."

As Forseti exited, leaving the brothers to stew in their ire, TJ breathed a mental sigh of relief. He settled his mind once more as he followed along with Forseti in his head. It wasn't long before Forseti encountered Thor's empty seat in some great hall. The Asgardian knelt and spoke what TJ assumed was a prayer, which ended when he said, "Forgive me for what I have to do to your old friend. It's the only way to protect Utenheim. I hope you'll understand that."

*No, the best way to protect Ijọba Ipari is by putting Shango back on the front lines,* Oshosi thought bitterly.

A wave of heat hit TJ hard, nearly shocking him out of his mental camouflage. He struggled to contain his empathy, finally managing to blend it with Forseti's more muted sorrow when TJ thought of Dayo.

*Careful, young one,* Obatala's gentle reprimand echoed in TJ's mind. *Your emotions are strong. They must not overpower Forseti's.*

Oshosi chimed in. *That might have been my fault, Obatala. The mortal is feeding off me. Yes, boy, I might feel strong emotions, but I contain them on the surface. Think of the hunt. You must become one with your surroundings. In this case, Forseti's mind is your forest. Adapt to its rhythms, its patterns. Let your thoughts flow with his, not against them. Feel the emotion but cast it quickly. Let it roll.*

TJ nodded mentally, refocusing his efforts. As Forseti's day wore on, he found it easier to maintain the delicate balance between observation and immersion.

Finally, Forseti approached a familiar corridor. One TJ had only been able to barely decipher through dreams. A set of walls with prism surfaces. He and Forseti made their way through the maze. TJ tried not to gawk at the creatures and spirits they passed, like the strange shadow creatures who were trapped in a cube of water, or a pair of living trees who seemed to be playing a game with acorns to pass the time.

Were these other prisoners of the Court of All?

Moving forward, the hall transitioned into a silent, crystalline cave, its jewel-toned cliffs standing as silent sentinels. On his left, a towering Rakshasa from Hindu mythology caught his eye, its fearsome visage marked by sharp fangs and glaring eyes. It clawed at the air, its tiger-like growls echoed through TJ, stirring a primal unease in the pit of his stomach. Again, he needed to match Forseti's nonchalance to keep hidden.

*This is great,* Oshosi said, seeming to keep his voice neutral for TJ's sake. *This is exactly the route we'll need to take after saving Shango and Oya. We're close! So close!*

The third section they entered was awash with deep, pulsating crimsons and soothing pinks, like being inside a lava lamp. On their third right turn, a wraith-like Banshee from Celtic lore, with its pallid, flowing robes and hair, hovered above the ground in its glass cell, its mournful wail stretching long within the confines of its chamber. Its cry forced TJ to cover his ears, and then he remembered his ears weren't his own.

*Huh, what was that?* TJ heard Forseti say to himself. He dug a finger in his ear and continued on without event though.

Finally, they approached Shango and Oya's holding chamber. Just as strange as all the rest with its ever-changing glass-like surface. TJ could see the glowing essence of the Orishas, his Ashe Vision at play. Forseti whispered to the seamless wall, something in a language TJ didn't recognize. After a moment, there was a click that echoed throughout the cosmic hall, and a split opened between the smooth glass wall.

Forseti stepped into the cell. It was an ethereal space like all the rest. Though this one housed two egg-shaped prisms with hard edges. And within the odd structure, Shango and Oya floated in what seemed like a suspended sleep. But their eyes were completely open. Worst, they seemed entirely aware, and they were staring straight at TJ—well, Forseti, really.

How could the Court of All do this? This was completely cruel. The Orishas were clearly suffering through this whole process, looking sickly and drained. A sickness pooled into TJ at the sight of the once powerful deities in such a state. And they had only been there a few months! Before he could get chided by Obatala again, TJ reigned in the emotional outburst that was bubbling. He needed to focus.

His spirit tightened as he watched The Channeling unfold before him. The air crackled with a disconcerting energy that would have made the hairs on his arms stand on end if he technically had his own arms. Shango and Oya's bodies were rigid, their faces contorted in silent agony.

Once radiant with divine might, Shango's muscular form, that had pulsed with the power of thunder, now hung gaunt and ashen. TJ had barely known him, but even in their brief time together in the Court of All, his once bright eyes were striking. Now they were dulled to a faint glimmer beneath furrowed brows.

Oya, the tempest incarnate, who had danced with the winds and commanded the storm that fought off Olokun himself, was now reduced to a mere wisp, her vibrant, colorful burgundy garb faded and her breaths shallow, as if the very gales she had woven were snatched from her lungs.

The sight clawed at TJ's chest—a cruel theft of grandeur. These were *his* Orisha. He couldn't let these other deities get away with this. For most of his life, he hadn't cared much for the Orishas, hadn't felt a part of their tribe. But over the past couple of years, he felt like he was one of them. And seeing two of his own in such a sad state made him want to tear their prism cages down.

*Relax, Teej,* he thought to himself. *This is just recon. Save it for the actual mission. Like Oshosi said, 'there will be a time to repay this offense.'*

TJ dove deeper into the deceptive Ashe he, Oshosi, and Obatala manifested, dove farther into Forseti's mind, The Channeling, and in doing so, he saw what Shango was seeing in that very moment. It was strange. It was like Shango was dreaming of an everlasting battle, shoulder to shoulder with a man whose hair was red-ish blond. Thor? Were they sapping Shango's Ashe by forcing him to use all his might in his dream state? Is that how they were forcing the energy from him, by tricking him into exerting himself?

He touched Oya's egg and saw her battling something against tidal waves, back-to-back with Shango. TJ couldn't be sure, but it seemed like part of The Channeling involved extracting the greatest power of each Orisha: their warrior spirits. No, he couldn't be sure, but it was good information to log away for later.

But as he dove deeper, TJ lost the image and sensation of Forseti's ritual. That everlasting battle Shango was fighting had diminished. Instead, TJ's vision jumped to the present. He could see himself touching the chain that bound the egg prisms. No, *Forseti* was touching the chain, but he hadn't meant to.

*What in Odin's name*? Forseti said in his own head. He lifted his hand in front of his face, flexing it. *No... No... it can't be... the Eaters!? Morpheus! Morpheus! The Eaters are in my mind. They have me!*

*Shit!* TJ thought. *Uh... abort, abort! Obatala, get me out! Oshosi, help*!

*Working on it now*, came Obatala's voice.

*Wait, wait, the boy is close*, Oshosi's voice this time. *Hold him a little longer. We need to know exactly how to reverse The Channeling.*

TJ yawned; Forseti yawned. TJ's emotions became Forseti's emotions. There was no stopping it now.

*The boy just yawned*, Obatala said. *Morpheus must be on the move! We have to pull him out. I have to induce a sleep in Forseti now before it's too late.*

*How long will that take?* But even as the words formed in TJ's mind, something new caught his attention in Forseti's consciousness. The god's fear of infiltration had left his mind vulnerable, exposing a potential way to reverse the ritual. Oshosi was right. Could they ever get this close again?

*Wait*, TJ called out to Obatala. *I think I see how to undo this.*

But his excitement was short-lived. In the shadows of the chamber, a figure stirred. TJ's blood ran cold as Morpheus emerged from the darkness. The dream god's form was a nightmarish blend of tattered robes and blue skin, his cold eyes piercing TJ.

Like a gazelle caught in the sight of a lion, panic gripped TJ as he realized he couldn't move. His consciousness was frozen within Forseti's mind, trapped and exposed. Then TJ thought-spoke, *We need to get me out now, please!*

Oshosi's voice rang out urgently. *That's it! I sense the reverse of The Channeling. We have what we need! Obatala, get him out now!*

But TJ couldn't respond. His thoughts came without voice, silent screams echoing in the void of his mind. Obatala's pleas for a response went unanswered as TJ remained paralyzed.

Morpheus' voice, a haunting whisper that seemed to layer on top of itself, spoke directly to TJ. Not in his mind, but as though the god were mere feet away from TJ. "*Show yourself, you filthy parasite,*" he said darkly.

*TJ, ground yourself*! Oshosi commanded. *Think of your anchor. Think of Manny!*

At the mention of Manny's name, memories flooded TJ's mind: Their kiss, the warmth of her hand in his, the way she made his heart soar. The fear began to loosen its grip, and TJ felt his consciousness stir.

Obatala continued the incantation to induce sleep, darkness creeping at the edges of TJ's vision. But as the world faded, Morpheus reached out, his hand stretching impossibly toward TJ's essence. In that final moment, suspended between Obatala's pull and Morpheus' grasp, TJ's fate hung in the balance. A darkness consumed him, and he wasn't sure what he'd find on the other side.

# 31

# A MIDNIGHT STROLL

"YOU D-D-DOG!" AYO MURMURED UNDER A FAINT LIGHT IN THEIR dorm room.

TJ sprang from his bed, looking wild. He felt cold hands across his shoulder. Pulling the collar of his shirt, he found giant frosted fingerprints across his chest. Where had that come from?

"What is t-t-that?" Ayo stuttered low.

TJ tried touching the ice crystals across his chest, but his hands seized up like always after a dream session with Obatala and Oshosi.

"I got you, I g-g-got you," Ayo said, offering his Ashe. When TJ regained his command over Oya's Wind once more, he stared at his exposed chest again, at the frosted handprint on his chest, a cold dread creeping into his bones. His breath came out in ragged gasps, each one a puff of mist in the dim dorm room. He couldn't remember how it got there, and the more he tried to piece it together, the more his mind slipped away from any coherent explanation. But he knew it had something to do with Oshosi and Obatala. What had they gotten up to in his dreams?

"Has that always been t-t-there?" Ayo asked.

"I... I don't know," TJ said. "Maybe after the Frost Realm? No... that can't be right. I'm not sure..."

Ayo's eyes narrowed, and he suggested they head to the Hospital Tree. TJ nodded, and an odd relief washed over him as the frost began to fade. The chill in his chest lessened until it was almost gone, leaving just a faint memory of cold.

"Look," TJ whispered, "it's disappearing."

Ayo peered closer and sighed. "That's g-g-good."

The dorm room was dark except for the faint glow of moonlight filtering through the bark windows. The other boys lay sprawled in their bunks, their soft snores blending into the quiet. Strewn clothes, half-open trunks, and forgotten books sat untouched, their usual chaos subdued by the hush of the night.

TJ rubbed his chest where the frost had been, trying to shake off the lingering unease. "I had a nightmare. Something horrible... paralyzing." He brushed his hand across his lips. The pressure of Manny's kiss still lingered on his own. And then he remembered. He remembered it all!

TJ took a deep breath and began recounting what he remembered from the dream world. He told Ayo about being with Obatala and Oshosi in their dream room, how they discussed Forseti's slipping consciousness and the dangers of crafting ancestral paths. He recounted losing sight of their ritual and seeing Shango fighting, then realizing TJ had taken control of Forseti's hand.

"And then Morpheus appeared," TJ said, shivering at the memory. "I froze up completely. Oshosi tried to get me to focus on Manny to ground myself, but Morpheus reached for me just as Obatala cast a sleep spell. It was like being sucked into darkness. And then—"

"It looks like Obatala's spell w-w-worked," Ayo stuttered. The giant frost print must've been from Morpheus. "Damn, M-M-Manny really has been your s-s-saving grace, hasn't she?"

TJ scratched his cheek slowly, a warmth spreading through him that had nothing to do with Ashe or magic. "No kidding."

"Can't believe you p-p-pulled that off, m-m-man."

"Manny or the stuff with Forseti?"

"Both. But I mean M-M-Manny. T-T-Told you that goofy shit would w-w-work on her." TJ smiled. When Ayo wanted to get his words out quickly, he often spoke, even seeming to forget his stutter for those brief moments. It also didn't help that it was so dark, so he had little choice. Still, it wasn't lost on TJ how comfortable Ayo was with him, and that always felt nice.

"I know," TJ said. "I was so nervous she might say no or reject me or whatever. But it worked out perfectly!"

The two friends dissolved into laughter, their voices echoing off the bark walls of their dorm.

"Hey, keep it down over there!" Umar groaned from somewhere in the dark across the adjoining room.

"My bad!" TJ called back, lowering his voice to an exaggerated whisper.

He and Ayo tried to stifle their amusement, but it was useless. Soon, there were more disgruntled voices joining in with Umar's.

"All right, all right, Shango's Axe!" Ayo signed, still grinning. "I guess we'll go outside b-b-before we wake the whole dorm. Unless you try s-s-signing."

TJ shook his head. Maybe they could find an animal outside to bridge a telepathic convo. TJ was decent enough at understanding Ayo, but signing himself was a different thing. It was much easier to respond vocally. So they crept out into the quiet nighttime grounds of Ifa Academy, the moonlight bathing the campus in silver light. Crystal lights strung between the bridge walkways and treehouses flickered gently in the breeze. Cicadas and night birds sang in the forest, a soothing nocturnal melody.

TJ took a deep breath of the cool night air, feeling fully alive. He was overflowing with so many emotions—joy, excitement, nervousness, and underlying it all, an exhilarating sense of love whenever he pictured Manny's radiant smile, those impossibly adorable dimples.

"I still can't believe she's my girlfriend now," he confessed to Ayo as they strolled beneath the trees. "After all our time together, I was startin' to think she was seeing me only as a friend."

"Nah, everyone know she like you too; she just be on her weird stuff," Ayo signed, scratching the tattoo under his eye. "You two good together. I meet nobody who match like you two." He stopped, saying out loud, "W-w-well. Except me and T-T-Titi, of course."

TJ laughed through his nose, thankful to have such a supportive friend. "By the way, how are your telepathy lessons going? We didn't get to talk enough about you getting through to that cat."

Ayo looked sheepish. "Oh yeah, about that… I not just read that book. I…" He stopped signing for a bit. "I doing the full course."

"What!?" TJ stopped in front of a grand statue of Obatala with glowing blue eyes. Between the Orisha's hands was a small human body that radiated a faint gleam.

"I know, I know," Ayo signed. "Most scam—but some parts actually work."

"I mean, you got the money. But, dude, don't go blowing it all away."

"No wahala, man. I know what I get myself into. And hey—can't argue with results. Look." Ayo placed two fingers on his temple and scrunched up his face. His gaze had landed on a red-eyed owl who nested in a tree nearby.

*Hey there, Mr. Owl. Really like what you did with your feathers. Who hooked you up with the trim, my guy?*

*Mother feeds!* the owl returned. *Mother feeds!*

Ayo turned to TJ. "Y-y-you get any of t-t-that?"

"I did!" TJ said. "Does it only work if you direct your telepathy toward animals?"

"Y-y-yeah. And it seems like only y-y-you can hear me." Ayo frowned, then started signing again, "Bet money, I going to break record for telepathy good speech."

"Telepathy fluency, you mean?"

"Y-y-yeah." Ayo blushed.

"What's the record right now?"

"Three years."

A sharp sense of shame slithered through TJ. That was a very long time for someone like Ayo, but if anyone could break the record, it would be him. He was top of their class, and back in Camp Olosa he easily would've taken the top spot if an Orisha hadn't been one of their fellow campers. Before TJ could respond with words of encouragement, an ominous shadow fell over them. They both froze. Turning slowly, they came face to face with Headmistress Ninki Nanka looming over them. Even in the dark, her massive form was unmistakable.

*Good evening, gentlemen,* she rumbled in their minds. *Out for a midnight stroll?*

"Uh, y-yes, Headmistress," TJ stammered. "Just… getting some air."

She narrowed her eyes skeptically. *I couldn't help overhearing your conversation just now. So, using a scam course instead of attending lessons, eh, Ayo? Tut tut. Just because it's the weekend doesn't mean you should neglect your studies.*

Ayo's eyes bulged under his designer glasses. "Yes, Headmistress," he signed. "I make sure attend all sessions from now on."

*See that you do.* She nodded. Then glanced between them. *Your session partner, Xavier Du Bois, is making great progress these past few weeks. He does miss you so."*

Mr. Du Bois? Ayo never mentioned that he had classes with their old camp counselor. The last time TJ spoke to the man, he was in Babalu-Aye Medical recovering from a curse that forced him to only say one phrase verbally. Telepathy classes sounded like a perfect solution for him too.

*Well, don't stay up too late, boys,* Ninki Nanka said. *Growing diviners need their rest. Enjoy the weekend.*

With surprising grace for her size, she glided away into the darkness with her crocodile slither, evidently continuing her patrol of the grounds. TJ and Ayo waited with bated breath until she was well out of earshot before exhaling.

Sobering up, Ayo lowered his voice. "Speaking of special abilities. I was o-o-out with your brother a few h-h-hours ago. We t-t-think we know where to find Ogun's Sacred C-C-Cabinet."

TJ leaned in. "I'm listening."

## 32

# KEEP IT ON THE LOW

TJ'S FEET DANGLED OVER THE EDGE OF THE THREE-BRIDGE crossing, the cool water rushing over his toes. The early morning sun cast a golden sheen across the river, painting the grounds in warm hues. The faint buzz of cicadas and the distant murmur of students heading to breakfast peppered the air.

As he finished recounting his latest dreamwalking experience to Manny, TJ swallowed down the last of the *agege* bread.

"Damn, yo. That's wild," she said, leaning back and rubbing her temples. "Morpheus showed up again? And that frost—right on your chest? That's messed up. But... Obatala's spell actually worked?"

TJ's hand instinctively moved to his chest where the frost had been. "Yeah, maybe. I mean... I think so. Honestly, I wouldn't have gotten out of that mess without you. But it's weird... Morpheus gets closer every time. He even *talked* to me this time."

Ayo eyed the both of them, giving both of them a cheeky wide grin. "So," he signed. "How you and you feel as couple now? You two find joy in sweet moon time?"

"You mean honeymoon?" Manny asked.

TJ put an arm around Manny. "It feels..."

"We don't know. It hasn't even been twenty-four hours yet. Ask us again in a month or two."

*A month or two*? TJ thought. *So she thinks we have a real chance?*

Teenage relationships didn't usually last all that long. Just look at Ayo and Titi. But TJ was glad to hear that Manny was thinking in terms of months, not weeks.

A rustling of leaves sounded behind them. They all jumped a little—TJ thinking it was Ninki Nanka again—but it was just Tunde. A hesitant gait replaced his brother's usual swagger; his sunbaked dreadlocks didn't bounce playfully like they usually did as he walked. Something was off. As Tunde set down his tray, the fried plantains' aroma wafted over, but TJ's appetite had vanished.

"Hey, what's good T-T-Tunde," Ayo's enthusiastic greeting hung in the air, unanswered. "Everything good with the c-c-cabinet?"

Ayo had filled TJ and Manny in on Tunde and Ruby's secret project. With Orunmila gone, Ruby couldn't use her usual divination methods to locate Ogun's Sacred Cabinet. Instead, she'd rigged up some high-tech tracking system, and Tunde had been helping her fine-tune it. It was exactly the kind of challenge his tech-savvy little brother would relish—though TJ suspected Tunde just wanted to be around his crush. But now, seeing Tunde's uncharacteristically serious expression, a knot formed in TJ's stomach.

"Yeah... about that..." Tunde said, voice barely above a whisper. He glanced around, making sure no other students were within earshot. "There's somethin' y'all need to hear."

The once peaceful morning at the three-bridge crossing now felt tense and uncertain. The gentle lapping of water against the riverbank seemed to echo the unease growing in TJ's chest.

Tunde took a deep breath before continuing. "So, yesterday, remember how I saw you and Manny at Anansi's? Well, I didn't just leave because Manny kept beating us. I saw Ruby and Mom walk by outside, and I followed them. I was hoping to share some new theories with Ruby and," he went red around the ears, "see if Mom would talk me up like she usually does. You know... so Ruby would hear."

"Awww, so you're the one leaving roses in front of her hut," Manny said, perking up. But TJ's brow furrowed. Tunde wasn't looking happy at all. Did Ruby finally reject him or something?

"What happened, bro?"

Tunde's eyes darted around, making sure they were still alone. "They said somethin' about leavin' us out, like 'we may have to cut them out in the end. Go ahead on our own.'" Tunde's voice dropped lower. "Mom even asked if 'the kids' had caught on yet, and Ruby said we're too busy with our studies. She even commented about how you're lookin' half asleep most days, TJ. Said it was sad how much the dreamwalking is taking out of you." He turned to Manny. "And they were going on about your cousin and what happened to her and..." He trailed off.

A jolt of frustration coursed through TJ. He glanced at Ayo, who sat up straighter, fists clenched on his knees. Manny just stared, eyebrows raised.

"Nah, m-m-man," Ayo stuttered. "That's messed up. Ruby's going o-o-over our heads with your m-m-mom! If they're p-p-plottin' behind our backs, t-t-then we gotta handle shit ourselves. We cut them out b-b-before they d-d-do it to us." In his anger, he seemed to forget about his embarrassment at his speech. He hopped off the railing and started pacing in the open space near the bridge. "I knew somethin' was o-o-off, but this? Nah, we ain't lettin' them leave us b-b-behind."

Manny put her hands together like she was calling a timeout. "Hold on a sec. We just gonna drop Ruby like that? Her tech is the only reason we've been on track with the cabinet at all. If we cut her off, what's the backup plan? We ain't got the same kind of resources she got."

Ayo whirled around to face her, eyes narrowed, signing. "We no need her. Me and Tunde work on path a different way. Look, if they plan moves with no us, we gotta move smart too on our own. We no need to share all things we know. What you say, TJ?"

TJ's gaze remained fixed on the rippling water below. He couldn't believe Mom and the others weren't letting them in on everything after *everything* they had done. He wanted to believe in Ruby, in Mom. Maybe they had their reasons. But Tunde's words gnawed at him.

"I hear you, Ayo." TJ's voice came out low. "For real, I do. But cuttin' people off... that's a big move. What if we're wrong? Shouldn't we ask them what they meant at least?"

"Wait, wait," Tunde said, perking up. "Ain't no rush to decide right now. Let's try to work this out ourselves first. There's a few buddies on the message boards on Evo I want to run some stuff through. If that don't hit, then we can figure out the next move."

Manny flipped her hair over her shoulder. "That I can agree with. Ayo?"

Ayo let out a sigh, followed by a scowl. "Fine."

TJ and Ayo spent the next week asking anyone and everyone at the academy and in New Ile-Ife about the whereabouts of Ogun's Sacred Cabinet. But it was hard to do when they were trying to be discreet, so it didn't get back to Elder Adeyemi or Mom or anyone else.

They started with the faculty and staff at Ifa Academy, figuring someone must know something about such an important cultural artifact.

TJ and Ayo lingered after their Elemental Studies class, exchanging glances as the other students filed out. Teacher Oluwaseyi, a stout man with graying dreadlocks, was organizing his papers at the front of the room. TJ took a deep breath, steadying his nerves before approaching.

"Teacher Oluwaseyi," TJ began, his voice carefully casual, "we were wondering if you could tell us more about some of the ancient artifacts associated with the Orishas."

The professor looked up, his eyebrows raised with interest. "Oh? And what's sparked this curiosity, Mr. Young?"

Ayo chimed in. "We're doing some extra research on Orisha h-h-history. Thought it might help with our s-s-staffcrafting."

TJ nodded, building on Ayo's explanation. "Yeah, we're especially interested in items that might have been used for storing or protecting powerful magic. You know, like special containers or…"

"Or c-c-cabinets," Ayo added, earning a subtle elbow from TJ.

Teacher Oluwaseyi stroked his beard thoughtfully. "Fascinating topic, boys. There are indeed many sacred objects in our lore. The *irukè* of Oya, Shango's double-headed axe... but if you're looking for containers, Ogun's Cabinet comes to mind. Though its exact whereabouts have been lost to time."

TJ's toes curled at the mention of Ogun, but he kept his expression neutral. "R-Really? That's interesting. Do you know if anyone's tried to find it recently?"

The teacher chuckled. "Oh, I'm sure there are always those

seeking such powerful relics. But these things have a way of revealing themselves when the time is right, not when we go hunting for them. The Orishas still work in mysterious ways. Even in these new times."

Ayo opened his mouth, but TJ cut in before he could say something too revealing. "Of course, Teacher. We're just curious about the history. Thanks for your time."

As they turned to leave, Teacher Oluwaseyi called out, "Boys? If you're truly interested in this topic, I'd suggest speaking with Elder Adeyemi. She knows far more about these matters than I do."

TJ scratched at his non-existent beard, forcing a smile. "We'll keep that in mind. Thanks again, Teacher!"

Once outside the classroom, TJ let out a long breath. They'd gotten *some* information, but not nearly enough. And now they had to be even more careful—if word got back to Elder Adeyemi about their questions, their whole plan could unravel.

Even Freya, who worked in the Library Tree for her free periods, came up empty in her search through the records. And nothing from her knowledge of the Celtic practices was any help.

"Sorry, guys," Freya told TJ and Manny as she struggled to put away a flying book that kept just outside her reach. "Nothing in the directory talks about anything like that. Ogun is a very secretive Orisha. Most information on him seems lost to oral tradition."

It was as if the cabinet had simply vanished without a trace.

Not deterred, TJ and Ayo took their search into the village, figuring the locals and shopkeepers might have clues. Most shook their heads or shrugged, but a few whispered of a cabinet sold off long ago to pay debts, its sacred purpose forgotten. Each story contradicted the next, describing the cabinet as big as a house or as small as a shoebox. TJ, Manny, and Ayo followed each thread, no matter how thin, but the tales twisted and turned until they were more knot than lead.

By the week's end, they were no closer to finding the cabinet than when they had started. As they sat with Manny at the three-bridge crossing again, dipping their toes in the cool river during lunch, the group snacked on *suya*—beef skewers—while pondering their next move. TJ and Manny held hands, relishing the chance to be close. Ayo didn't seem to mind until their affection turned into a distraction.

"All right, lovebirds, focus up," he signed, then snapped the couple back to attention. "We need figure out so I get path to Shango."

"Sorry, bro, you're right," TJ said. He and Manny separated slightly, though their hands remained entwined.

"Yeah, our bad," Manny added. "So, where does that leave us? No clues from school or the village?"

TJ shook his head. "Not even from the UCMP or Elder Adeyemi."

"Gotta be somewhere we no look," Ayo signed, jabbing his head after each sentence. Then out loud he said, "S-S-Somewhere where lost is… unlost."

"Like a black market for magical objects?" TJ suggested half-heartedly.

"Or a pawn shop for ancient artifacts?" Manny added with just as much indifference.

Ayo suddenly sat up straight. "I'm an i-i-idiot! T-T-That's it! The Veiled Caravan!"

"The what now?" TJ asked.

"It's a black market c-c-caravan, underground shop for s-s-stolen and illegal magical items," Ayo explained eagerly. "It's the only s-s-shop to never get raided by the UCMP. Or a-a-anyone."

"Hey," Manny started to ask, "isn't that where *Divination Today* thought the Frost Realm fragment was before we got ahold of it?"

"Exactly," Ayo signed. "I read that too. If any place has secret things of Ogun, it is *that* place."

"Great, let's go check it out after school," Manny said, nearly skipping.

"No that simple," Ayo countered. "Place almost impossible to find. It moves all the time, and well… it reveals only to invites. Direct invites."

"And I'm guessing an invite is impossible to get?" TJ asked.

"No exactly," Ayo signed. "I mean… I hear rumors always. I mean…" He spoke mostly to himself then. "H-H-He always brags about it, but I n-n-never believe him…"

"What?" TJ and Manny asked in chorus.

"Jimoh. His family owns one c-c-caravan in the group. His whole family runs in K-K-Keeper group. And the ones who use the caravan the most are…"

"Keepers…" TJ's face fell. "So we'd have to get in good with the Keepers just to get inside." He shook his head firmly. "No way. Not after everything with Dayo and Jessica. I can't work with them, especially not Bolawe."

The group sat silently for a moment, pondering their dilemma. A few gulls skittered across the river ahead of them.

"Well, it no like we know any other Keepers to get us in," Ayo finally signed with resignation. "And we already work with Bolawe. So no more harm, eh?"

Manny suddenly perked up. "No. No, wait! We don't have to use Bolawe. We can use someone who probably hates Bolawe as much as we do."

TJ and Ayo titled their heads at Manny in question.

"Adeola," Manny replied matter-of-factly. "She's in jail, but I bet she'd want to screw over Bolawe and the Keepers however she can. She might even confirm if they have the cabinet to begin with."

TJ and Ayo exchanged surprised looks. It wasn't an ideal option, but it did present an opportunity. Perhaps with Adeola's guidance, they could infiltrate the Veiled Caravan without getting further entangled with the Keepers. It was a start at least; the first real lead in their search. They would need to plan their next steps carefully, but the path forward was clearer than it had been all week.

"Great!" TJ said, feeling lighter already. "So, who's getting us into her jail then?"

# 33

# THE GUILELESS GUIDE

IT QUICKLY BECAME APPARENT THAT TJ WOULD HAVE TO BE THE one to visit Adeola. Alone. After a little research, he, Manny, and Ayo discovered that minors under the age of eighteen weren't allowed to visit the Thornriver Correctional Facility—where Adeola was being held. That is, without *adult* supervision. Manny could have asked her aunt, but since Tia Teresa had never met Adeola before, that was an almost guaranteed "no." And Manny didn't want to bother her clouded parents who would have to travel all the way from New York on short notice. Plus, there was no guarantee they'd allow her to visit a creepy magical prison.

Ayo's dad, on the other hand, was familiar with Adeola in passing, but when Ayo got on a water bowl with him, his father refused.

"*You can go to that Orisha-forsaken place after you stop all that sign language and start speaking again,*" he had said bitterly before ending the call in a splash.

"Gee, Ayo, remind me not to send your dad a Christmas card this year," TJ had said.

"He no mean it," Ayo signed sadly. "He has big stress at work, is all."

So that left TJ to ask Mom whether or not he could visit Adeola. Thankfully, she was still in New Ile-Ife with Grandma, so TJ could ask in person.

During the first week of December, TJ sat at the wooden table in Grandma's cozy home, the savory aroma of jollof rice, goat meat stew, and fried plantains filling the air. Mom and Grandma chatted in a mix of English and Yoruba as TJ eagerly scooped healthy portions of food onto his plate. He savored the spicy tomato flavors of the jollof and the tender goat's meat soaked in a rich peanut sauce. The fried plantains provided a sweet contrast to the hearty mains. He didn't usually eat or savor his food as much as he did then... but that's because he was wracked with nerves.

After the satisfying meal, Grandma gathered the empty plates and bowls, taking them to the kitchen to wash up. With her gone, TJ saw his opening. He took a deep breath to steady his jittering hands. "Mom, can I ask you something?"

Mom turned her attentive gaze to him, her eyes peering over her glasses. "Of course, honey bunny. What is it?"

TJ fidgeted with his hands under the table. "Well, I was hoping I could visit someone...." He held his breath, bracing for the inevitable interrogation. Quickly, he added, "Visit Adeola."

Mom simply tilted her head, her towering updo locs tilting with her. "I see. And when were you hoping to go? And more importantly... why?"

TJ blinked. "Oh, um, you know... I'm feeling a bit guilty. And I was thinking tomorrow—if that's okay?"

Mom hummed under her lips, looking TJ over before she shrugged. "That's fine with me. I've been meaning to stop by since I got settled here, but things have just been so busy. Plus, Adeyemi has me going in an out of Benin and Ghana trying to convince people of this ritual during the Hero's Equinox. How long has Adeola been in there?" She leaned back in her chair and a calendar came floating at her side. "My oh my! Has it been that long already? I sure hope her family has been visiting her. They really gave her too long of a sentence just for being associated with the Keepers. They didn't even charge her with any direct crimes."

TJ exhaled slowly; at least she hadn't pressed for more details. A part of him felt guilty about the half-truth, but he consoled himself that some things were better left unsaid.

"Yeah," he said. "I think she'd like the company."

THE NEXT DAY, TJ AND MOM LEFT GRANDMA'S HOUSE EARLY, just as the sun peeked over the horizon of New Ile-Ife. They walked briskly through the streets of the village, exchanging greetings with the villagers already up and about their morning routines. More than a few thanked TJ for his role in saving Eko Atlantic. TJ was too preoccupied with nerves to fully appreciate their gratitude, but Mom made sure to thank them on his behalf, her beam growing with each new person who approached them.

As they reached the forest at the edge of New Ile-Ife, TJ couldn't help but wonder what awaited him at the mysterious prison. He had heard plenty of rumors about the dangerous creatures that guarded the perimeter with all manner of forbidden magics. Part of him was apprehensive, but his boyish curiosity won out.

Soon, they encountered the shaman guide Mom had called on the day before to set up their appointment. She was an elderly woman with stringy gray hair and mismatched eyes that stared intensely at them. When she smiled in greeting, she revealed a row of missing teeth. TJ didn't stand too close for fear of smelling stank breath.

"*Good morning,*" Mom said politely in Yoruba.

"You the one who ordered a visitation with," the shaman, whose voice was reedy, spoke in Southern American English as she fluttered her fingers to manifest a parchment from thin air, "an Adeola Washington?"

"That's right."

The shaman looked them up and down, then started sniffing them. She reminded TJ of someone from Camp Olosa. Straight out of the swamp. TJ gave Mom a look but she signaled for him to keep steady.

"And you are," the shaman said, looking at her parchment again, "Tomori Jomiloju Young?"

"That's me," TJ gritted as he held his breath. As he expected, the shaman cast a foul odor from her mouth. "We're here to visit the correctional facility."

"Good, good. And you, ma'am. You're his guardian mother, Yejide Young?"

"That's correct." Mom scrunched her nose up in a similar way to TJ.

*Someone needs to teach this woman about personal space.*

The shaman gave a jerky nod and scooped up a handful of dirt, licking it with her tongue. TJ cringed.

"Best hurry," she croaked. "The way will only be open a short while." She walked away and started scooping water from the river, tasting it as well.

TJ furrowed his brow, then leaned toward his mom to murmur, "Why do we need a shaman to get there? Can't we just take a portal?"

Mom shook her head. "Only these guides can lead people to Thornriver safely. The location is protected by powerful magic. Old magic."

"Have you been there before?"

"A few times too many; the wretched place gives me chills."

Why would Mom have visited the place? Maybe one of those guys she had been with. One of them had been a Keeper himself, right?

The shaman clicked her tongue impatiently from a squatted position near the river. Now she was rubbing leaves on her wrinkled cheeks. "Enough lollygaggin'. We're on a schedule. *Wa si mi.*" A gnarled staff snapped into existence and into her hand. She traced a shape in the dirt near the riverbank, set her staff head to the border between earth and river, and a shimmering mud portal opened up. "Step lively now!"

TJ and Mom shared a look before following the odd shaman into the portal's dirty and swirling depths.

When TJ and Mom plunged into the swirling vortex of the shaman's portal, the dirt and debris assaulted them from all sides. TJ could barely open his eyes against the onslaught as he was buffeted this way and that through the muddy passageway.

The ride was far from the smoothest portal transition he had ever experienced. It seemed the shaman had just slapped it together without much care, an afterthought for someone who probably ferried visitors to Thornriver on the regular.

Suddenly, TJ and Mom were ejected from the portal, falling in a heap onto a patch of hard, rocky earth. TJ groaned, his whole body protesting against the rough treatment it had just endured. Mud portals were definitely going on his list of least favorite magical transportation methods.

As TJ got his bearings, he glanced around. Just as he had researched, the forest around Thornriver was filled with bone-white trees that gave the landscape an eerie, ghostly feel. He shivered involuntarily.

"Well, that was quite the rollercoaster," Mom quipped as she curled over with a cough, brushing dirt off her aṣọ òkẹ́ robes.

The shaman clicked her tongue. "Bah, it wasn't so bad. You city folk just ain't used to a little roughin'."

She waved her staff and TJ felt his body lifted and placed upright with an invisible force. At first he thought it was a kind gesture, but suddenly cold metal clamped around his wrists—simple silver bracelets. In an instant, his access to Ashe was cut off. It was like losing one of his senses, the ability to see or taste gone in a flash. Where before he could perceive the tendrils of magic weaving through the air, now there was just a void, a blank space where his extra sense used to be. He didn't like it. It was as though he had suddenly gone blind.

"Some warning would have been nice..." TJ mumbled under his breath, still reeling.

The shaman gave a yellow-toothed grin. "Standard procedure—can't have anyone getting clever ideas about using magic where it don't belong."

Mom sighed softly. "I always dread this part."

TJ couldn't blame her. Already he felt diminished, almost ill without his connection to Ashe. Still, they had no choice but to follow as the shaman led them deeper into the bone forest.

The path was treacherous, full of thorns and jagged rocks that threatened to turn their ankles if they didn't watch their steps. Strange sounds echoed around them—howls and shrieks that raised the hair on the back of TJ's neck.

"Sounds like the kishi are feedin' tonight," the shaman remarked casually. "Must've been one of the women tryna escape this time. Tsk, tsk."

Fear sliced through TJ as he thought back to some of his beast books about kishi. Some of the images were quite graphic, a way to fully represent the danger of the half-man half-hyena shapeshifters. Teacher Ikenna back at the academy was also a kishi, but perfectly tame and kind. TJ assumed the hybrid creatures here were the wild, vicious sort. More screams and wails pierced the air, and TJ forced himself to look ahead, avoiding the ghoulish tokoloshe he spotted swinging through the trees, their sightless gouged eyes trained on the travelers.

"Terrible that they keep that poor girl locked up in a horrible place like this," Mom murmured, shaking her head.

It seemed improbable for anyone to escape from this nightmarish forest prison. That improbability turned into total impossibility as the massive edifice of Thornriver Correctional loomed before them, emerging from the trees. The fortress seemed carved from the giant boulders themselves, vines and moss clinging to its imposing façade.

TJ stared in awe until the shaman jostled him forward. "Welcome to Thornriver Correctional Facility for Disturbed Diviners," she announced, pushing against one of the boulders, which was actually a door. A corridor drenched in darkness lay ahead, whispering ominous tales from its silent void.

TJ was starting to regret coming. He should have given Ayo's dad a second call, or forked up funds to fly Manny's parents out to this dastardly place instead...

# 34

# THORNRIVER CORRECTIONAL FACILITY FOR DISTURBED DIVINERS

TJ GLANCED AROUND UNEASILY AS THE TOOTHLESS SHAMAN LED him and Mom deeper into the dark corridors of Thornriver. The cold stone walls and flickering torchlight made the place feel more like a medieval dungeon than a modern correctional facility. TJ wondered how anyone was expected to rehabilitate in such a bleak and unforgiving environment.

The short trip through the prison was chilling in more ways than one. The temperature seemed to drop with every step, and TJ couldn't suppress a shiver. Strange sounds echoed through the halls—distant screams, rattling chains, and inhuman murmurs.

What made TJ quiver the most were the guards—stern, silent aziza roaming the halls with fluttering dark wings and wickedly sharp spears. Their expressions were devoid of any humor or compassion. TJ thought they put even the hardness of Teacher Omo of Fon to shame. These aziza were true warrior guards, and their watchful gazes followed him as he passed.

After a short while, the shaman passed TJ and Mom off to one of the aziza guards in a small waiting area. TJ surveyed his surroundings, surprised to see the room contained not just humans, but also a handful of giants, dark elves, and a lone vampire lurking in the corner.

TJ found himself staring until the aziza guard snapped him back to attention, her voice sharp. "IDs, now. And declare your relation to the inmate."

She stood before a pit of green fire, which threw harsh shadows over her face, making her look even more severe.

"She's a family friend," TJ answered.

Mom added, "Adeola Washington. We should be on the approved visitation list."

The aziza guard scanned her basin of green fire. She chanted into it. Did the flames somehow hold their verification records? After a moment, the aziza nodded. "Checks out. Hand over all belongings—phones, purses, jewelry, wands, staffs, runes, artifacts, and the like." Reluctantly, they handed over their items. "You'll get them back when you leave," the aziza assured them, though her smile wasn't reassuring at all. In fact, TJ would have preferred if she didn't smile. Her entire row of teeth were spiked with impossibly sharp teeth.

"Only one visitor at a time," she declared. "Who's first?"

TJ raised his hand tentatively.

The aziza fixed him with her piercing gaze. "You—with me. You—" she gestured at Mom, "Stay here. No wandering."

TJ gave Mom a quick hug before following the aziza down another dark corridor, hoping the visit with Adeola would be worth braving this nightmare of a prison.

As TJ glanced back nervously, where Mom's figure receded into the shadow, she smiled nervously and waved. "Don't worry yourself, and don't worry about me. I might just start a book club with that vampire. I hear *Dusk of the Blue Moon* is all the rage in their circles. Or is that just a myth?" She shrugged. "I guess I'll find out."

TJ followed the aziza guard down a long, dark corridor illuminated only by a handful of floating torches. Their flickering orange light threw dancing shadows across the cold stone walls. TJ shuddered. This place felt ancient, filled with a deep, primal magic that set his teeth on edge.

How was Adeola faring after nine long months in this dreadful place? Back in the day, she'd always been so lively and vibrant, her eyes dancing with mischief. Would that light still shine in her gaze? Or had it been extinguished by the bleakness of Thornriver?

TJ couldn't imagine surviving more than a few days locked in these shadowy halls. It seemed far worse than even the cosmic prison of the Court of All. At least there he'd been surrounded by gods in a realm of color and light. Here… there was only darkness and despair closing in from all sides.

The aziza guard halted before a heavy stone door. "Block A-4. We're here," she announced curtly before hauling it open.

Beyond lay a small, bare stone room. At the far end stood a shimmering translucent wall stretching from floor to ceiling. It reminded TJ of a placid upright lake. Peering through the odd barrier, he could just make out a familiar figure.

"You've got fifteen minutes," the aziza snapped. "No more."

With that, she shut the door, leaving TJ alone with the upright lake… and Adeola.

As the door boomed closed, TJ noticed an hourglass embedded in the stone, sand already slipping away to mark his limited time. Turning back to the shimmering wall, TJ moved closer until Adeola's features came into focus. She looked so different—head fully shaved, where before it was only half shaved and side-swept in a fashionable way, face scrubbed free of makeup, where before her lips were usually painted purple, and the stylish clothes replaced by a drab gray smock. Like TJ, magic-suppressing bracelets clasped around her wrists. Only her deep brown eyes were the same.

"Adeola… it's me, TJ," he said softly, his steps forward even softer.

Her voice came through warped and hollow. *"TJ? Is that really you?"*

Striving to maintain a semblance of normalcy, TJ injected as much cheerfulness into his voice as he could muster when they exchanged greetings. Yet, the Adeola he saw before him was a far cry from the vivacious, charismatic young woman he knew. Dayo's extroverted best friend. Her energy seemed to have been siphoned away, leaving behind a shell that held none of her typical vibrancy.

TJ shifted his weight awkwardly from foot to foot, trying to find the right words. The shimmering barrier between them made everything feel surreal and distant.

"So... how's the food here?" TJ asked lamely, immediately regretting the question.

Adeola gruffed out a sound instead of laughing. *"About as good as you'd expect in a magical prison. Lots of mystery meat and soggy vegetables."*

TJ winced. "Right. Sorry, that was a dumb question." An uncomfortable silence stretched between them. "How are you... you know, holding up?"

Adeola shrugged, her movements stiff. *"Oh, you know. Just peachy. Love the decor. Very medieval chic."*

TJ forced a chuckle, but it came out more like a cough. "Yeah, it's... something."

Another pause.

"Made any… friends?" TJ asked.

Adeola's eyes hardened. *"Tons. We have slumber parties every night and braid each other's hair. Oh wait, we can't. No hair."* She ran a hand over her shaved head.

TJ's face grew hot. "I'm sorry, I didn't mean—"

*"It's fine,"* Adeola cut him off, her voice flat. *"My bad. This place stay messin' with your vibe heavy. How's the outside world? Still spinnin'?"*

"Yeah, it's... it's been eventful. Lots of changes at Ifa Academy. You ever hear of Ninki Nanka? She's back as the headmistress."

*"That monster under the lake?"*

"She decided to stop sleeping."

*"Sounds thrilling,"* Adeola said, her tone making it clear she found it anything but.

TJ scrambled for something else to say, acutely aware of the sand trickling away in the hourglass. This wasn't going at all how he'd hoped.

Another beat or two passed before Adeola sighed and said, *"This place… it's evil, TJ. Messed up with corruption."* The shadows in her eyes spoke volumes about the toll it had taken on her. TJ's sadness must've shown on his face, for she softened slightly before saying, *"What you doin' here, kid?"*

TJ explained his quest to find Ogun's Sacred Cabinet and needing the location of the Veiled Caravan. "I didn't want to go interrogating any Keepers, so I thought it was safer to come to you instead."

*"I don't know where the place is anymore. The password and location for it changes all the time. My old access is long gone. Expired."*

TJ sighed. "Well… so much for that."

The hourglass sand beat away as TJ avoided Adeola's strong eye contact. So TJ turned his gaze to the strange wall between them. It reminded him a bit of the barrier between the Frost Realm, the one that showed him all those scenes with Jessica and the Keepers.

"*What's wrong, TJ?*" Adeola asked coldly.

TJ wasn't sure what he should say, how much he should share. But now that he had someone mere feet away that knew Jessica in the flesh, he couldn't help asking. "Jessica. Manny's cousin. Did you know her? Is it… is it true she followed you and Dayo to join the Keepers?"

Adeola's eyes flashed with old pain, then it was almost extinguished in the next moment. "*That girl wasn't strong enough. Never was. She was only ever chasing after Dayo's clout.*"

TJ shifted, troubled by her coldness, so unlike the Adeola he once knew. "That's not a very nice thing to say, Deola. She died. Took her own life because of what you and the Keepers got up to."

"*What's all this about cabinets and caravans?*" Adeola finally asked, ignoring TJ's previous words.

TJ hesitated. "I… can't give you the full details. It's for a mission with the UCMP and Elder Adeyemi that I can't discuss." He paused, then added quietly, "One your old leader, Olugbala, is helping us with, actually."

At the mention of Olugbala, Adeola's eyes sharpened. "*Bolawe, huh? That's news to me. Word 'round here is he's not rollin' with the Keepers no more. Rumor has it there was some kind of falling out.*"

TJ's eyes widened. He had assumed Bolawe was still firmly in charge of the Keepers, just in hiding. "Really? I didn't realize he'd had issues with the Keepers, too."

"*Yeah, and whoever took over doesn't know shit about leading, just ravaging. Bet you can guess who that is.*"

Sharp fangs in the night bloomed in TJ's mind. "Sister Bisi."

"*Sister Bisi.*" Adeola nodded, the words coming out like poison.

TJ spoke under his breath then. "No wonder Bolawe never leaves the… um…"

Adeola fixed TJ with an intense stare. "*Go on, tell me where he is. You owe me that much, after all the times I saved Dayo.*"

TJ sighed deeply. "The… He's.. in the Mirror Realm."

*"So that's where he is..."* Adeola murmured, more to herself than TJ. Her eyes took on a calculating gleam that put TJ on edge. TJ could almost see the gears turning in her mind as she processed his words. Her lips moved soundlessly, as if speaking to someone TJ couldn't see. Her mind was clearly racing. But with what thoughts? And did TJ even want to know?

A disembodied voice announced the end of visiting hours in Block A, but Adeola seemed not to hear it.

"Adeola?" TJ asked uncertainly. "Are you okay?"

*Nine months in this place,* TJ thought. *Nine months. That's all it took.*

"Deola. Can you hear me?"

Adeola rocked a little bit more, snapping back to attention. *"Hmm? Oh, yes. My mind just... wanders sometimes."* She glanced over her shoulder nervously before adding in a hushed tone, *"My old password won't work for the caravan anymore. But I think I know how you can get a current one. It'll be dangerous though."*

TJ grinned, trying to lighten the mood. "Danger is my middle name!"

But his cheeky bravado felt hollow in the gloom of Thornriver. He wasn't sure how much he could trust this version of Adeola. And her talk of danger had him on edge. Still, if she could help him locate Ogun's Sacred Cabinet and the caravan it rested in, it would be worth the risk.

# 35

# A TATTERED CURTAIN

TJ's mind was still reeling from his visit with Adeola as he and Mom stepped through the portal back to the outskirts of New Ile-Ife. The severity in Adeola's voice when she spoke of the Veiled Caravan troubled him—especially when most of her speech had been so understated until then. Now that TJ had the information and knew where they had to go, maybe it was a good time to clue in Mom and the others. He battled with his intuition to be forthright when a flapping of wings beat through the forest around them. Out from the brush came Teacher Omo of Fon.

"Oh, good, your mother said you'd be here, Yejide," she said, tipping her head to Mom. "Urgent news on Operation Stormbreak. Adeyemi summons us right away. There's been a new development."

TJ pinched his eyes shut. Could he ever get a break that lasted more than a week? And judging by Teacher Omo's tone and rushed manner, the news was nothing good. Had Shango and Oya already been fully channeled? TJ snapped his fingers and a small flame manifested itself there. Then he whispered, *"Afẹfẹ, wá sí mi,"* and a collection of loose leaves nearby swirled in a spiral. The Ashe was weaker, for sure, but nowhere near gone. Not yet.

Mind still filled with dark stone walls and the blank eyes of Adeola, TJ had little time to dwell on it before he and Mom were ushered into the emergency meeting. The command center was abuzz with activity, magical projections swirling around the room.

One displayed a detailed map of the Frost Realm, while another outlined the bridge they had constructed to infiltrate the Court of All by way of Yemoja and the ancestral path. These images, of course, were only known to this small group. To any other prying eyes in the Frost Realm, the real image would have been shielded by Eshu's illusion wall.

In attendance that day were Manny—though her auntie wasn't there with her—Ayo, Ayo's dad, Omo of Fon, Elder Adeyemi, and Mirror Bolawe. Straight away, TJ moved toward his friends, filling them in on what had happened in hushed tones. However, he could only give them the most bare bones of recaps before Elder Adeyemi began the meeting. Behind her, near the cascading waterfall, were a collection of items. Last time, it was filled with relics associated with Oshosi: candles, bow and arrows, and fruits. Now, sea shells, plantain chips, and white roses covered the space—offerings to Yemoja.

"Ah, good! Mr. Young!" Elder Adeyemi said, her face brightening under the dim cavern light. "Just in time. We've had a hard time deciphering Yemoja's messages. But if you could stand just here, we might be able to commune with her for a little while." She gestured to the ritual spot just in front of the group.

"What happened?" TJ asked as he took his place within the ritual circle.

"We believe Oshosi has been captured. That, or perhaps Eshu's illusion has been broken. We aren't entirely sure."

TJ exchanged nervous looks between Manny and Ayo, who only gave him slight shrugs. This did not sound good at all. Centering himself between the half circle of seaweed and cowries, TJ sunk into his Ashe as everyone around him prayed to Yemoja. It was easier to find Yemoja's spirit within the waterfall. Hers was very similar to Olokun, who TJ had spent all last year praying to. After a short while, Yemoja's giant face rippled at the waterfall at the back of the stone-walled room.

TJ, out of habit, bowed to Yemoja, despite the previous reservations he had had in the Frost Realm. "Hello, Great Mother. I-Is everything all right on that side?"

Like with Oshosi, only TJ and Omo of Fon could hear the spirit voice of Yemoja, as she said, *I'm afraid our situation grows dire. Eshu's protections are weakening. Quickly. He struggles to maintain the illusion. I've never seen him as strained as he is now. Soon, the Court will pierce his tattered curtain. As we expected, Forseti has become suspicious that his raven has not returned. So the Asgardian has started a search himself. More than that, he confronted Eshu in the Frost Realm. Directly.*

As she spoke, Omo of Fon translated for the rest of the room. Murmurs rippled through the small crowd. TJ's gut tightened. Forseti discovering their plans would jeopardize everything. He still needed to finish his staff, and Ayo still needed to unlock his ancestral path. They weren't ready for this. At least what Adeyemi said about Oshosi didn't seem to be true.

*"The good news is,"* Bolawe said from his Mirror Realm form, *"Eshu was able to obscure the raven's location for now. And the bird is still encased in ice. Though it apparently made quite the fight when Forseti approached. However… the illusion wall is still fading. We must act quickly if we are to save Shango and Oya."*

*Not just Shango and Oya now…* Yemoja said darkly. *Oshosi too.*

"What!?" TJ blurted out.

"What?" Manny asked from the far end of the round table. "What did she say?"

"Yemoja says we have to save Oshosi now too."

"Shango's Axe! But, I thought you just see him in dream," Ayo signed.

"I did." TJ turned his head back to the waterfall. "What happened?"

"More signs we are on the wrong path!" Mr. Oyelowo gruffed out but everyone ignored him.

*Obatala said something about Oshosi taking the fall for you…* Yemoja thought-spoke, *something about an encounter with a… Morpheus.*

TJ closed his eyes as he sighed deeply. "No, no, no. That's not right. He never took the fall. Obatala set some spell on me and got me out of Forseti's subconscious. He—"

*All you would remember was seeing black, child. According to Obatala, Morpheus had his hand around your chest but didn't realize what he was holding onto. So Oshosi stepped in. It was always the plan to have the Hunter sacrificed should you be close to being caught.*

Always the plan? TJ had no clue about that.

*No way they have me on a need-to-know basis only,* TJ thought irritably as sickness pooled in his belly. That was yet another Orisha he was responsible for. Who would be next? Yemoja? Eshu? He couldn't take being the one getting them all in trouble like this.

By the time Omo of Fon caught everyone else up, TJ was trying to find his voice. "S-So… what happens to Oshosi now?"

Yemoja lowered her eyes, and TJ knew what was coming next. *After Shango and Oya,* she started to say, *he is to be channeled as well.* An ache came to TJ's head, and he tried to rub it away with little success. *Obatala says not to fret. You've gotten what you needed. You just have to complete your staffcrafting and your path to Shango via the divine child, Ayodeji.*

"Will I get to speak to Obatala again?"

Yemoja shook her head, casting mist from the waterfall that landed on Omo of Fon's wings. *With Morpheus fully alert, it's too unsafe to tap into dreams now. And Forseti has refortified his mind against future infiltrations.* Yemoja's image flickered. *Good fortune, young mortal. Eshu and I will do everything we can on our side. Be well, and Ashe."*

"Ashe," TJ replied weakly as Yemoja's thought-speech went quiet in his mind.

Standing in front of the cascading waterfall, Elder Adeyemi rubbed her hands together thoughtfully. Shadows played across her face, deepening the creases around her eyes and mouth. "There is good news as well," she said weakly, as though trying to inject energy into the dejected room. "I've successfully persuaded the diviner communities of Benin to help empower our ritual during the Hero's Equinox—thanks to Omo of Fon." The aziza bowed her head respectfully. "It's still not enough, of course, but it will go a long way. Yolanda Gravés is making the rounds in Louisiana as well via Camp Olosa. The community there seems most receptive. I'm hoping to bring the Cubans and Brazilians into the fold with the help of…" She angled her head to where Manny's auntie should have been. "Well, we're still working on that."

Elder Adeyemi cleared her throat. "Mr. Young, how fares the progress with your staff? We'll need it completed sooner than later. I may even suggest skipping other classes to prioritize finalizing it. I'll put in a word with the SS1 staff I still keep in touch with."

"I'm not so sure Headmistress Ninki Nanka would approve," Omo of Fon said. "Nor Staffmaster Bamidele. You know how he gets about tradition."

"Rightly so," Mr. Oyelowo said, cleaning his glasses. "Tradition exists for a reason."

Adeyemi lifted a slow-moving hand. "Let me worry about that, Omo."

TJ straightened up, hoping his voice sounded more confident than he felt. "I'm nearly ready to start crafting next week. I've gathered all the materials I'll need… I think. Just have to make sure I can attune to them properly." He chuckled awkwardly, rubbing his neck. "Hopefully wood shop in middle school comes back to me. I'll try to remember not to 'cut corners.'"

A few smiles broke out at his weak joke. Elder Adeyemi frowned a little. She must've known a quip from TJ meant he was masking insecurity. However, she did not make it known in her tone as she said, "Excellent news, Mr. Young. It's imperative you finish your staff soon. We'll be relying heavily on you and Manny when the time comes to initiate the operation. Especially with Ayo's status still uncertain."

Mr. Oyelowo scoffed, which prompted a hiked eyebrow from Adeyemi. Ayo's dad didn't seem to have anything to share after that.

TJ took another look at the empty seat where Manny's auntie should've been. He hadn't seen her since they had left the Frost Realm. Ayo's standing wasn't the only one that was completely up in the air. It was starting to seem like the mission was falling apart just as it was getting going.

"Where *is* Teresa?" Mom asked the table.

Manny shrugged. "She hasn't talked to me for a minute. She keeps going on about being forsaken by the Orishas."

*"The Orishas have forsaken none of their children,"* Bolawe said, calmly but firmly. *"The Great Separation created a fog. And it's* this woman *who has turned away from worshiping the deities of her ancestors, instead focusing on the adopted one from her conquerors."*

Manny scowled. "Hey, careful how you're talking about *that woman*." Then she made a softer face in Elder Adeyemi's direction. "I'll talk to her. She'll come around. She just needs time to stew."

"And what about Oracle Ruby?" TJ asked. "Why isn't she here?"

Elder Adeyemi sighed through her nose. "She is resting, as she has been most of the time these days. With Orunmila's connection severed, she's been having trouble getting clear readings. The extra strain has taken a heavy toll on her."

"You see, we're going about this all the wrong way." Mr. Oyelowo's words cut through the room like the sharp edge of a blade. His voice had that cold, clipped tone that TJ had come to associate with the man—like he was barely holding back a storm of frustration. TJ's stomach churned at the tension building between the adults. He glanced across the table at Ayo, whose jaw was clenched tight, the muscles working beneath his skin. Manny gave him a slight nudge with her shoulder, but Ayo didn't seem to notice. His hands were knotted into fists, resting stiffly on the table.

"I cannot condone this foolishness," Mr. Oyelowo continued, his eyes flicking to Ayo, then back to Elder Adeyemi. "You put the Orishas and their divine children at risk with every moment you delay."

A flicker of something dark passed through Mr. Oyelowo's eyes as he spoke—something that made TJ's skin prickle. It wasn't just frustration; it was fear, buried deep. And it wasn't just about Ayo. There was something more here, something TJ didn't fully understand yet, but he could feel the weight of it. Mr. Oyelowo wasn't just trying to protect Ayo from danger. He was trying to control him.

"Was it not you who took your son from our last mission, Mobolaji," Mom said. "All I've heard from you since we began is complaints and tirades, but little in the way of solutions. Please, tell us your progress for getting Ayo to connect with Shango."

In answer, Mr. Oyelowo growled long and deep.

"Even a working theory would be nice," Mom added.

Still, nothing from the man but pinched lips.

"Your concerns are valid, Mobalaji," Adeyemi said. "But desperate times call for difficult choices. No one here wishes to proceed without Ayo. We are still working on a solution for his travel through Shango, but we must keep all our options open. Singular alignments, as rare as they are, cannot—"

"My family is that rarity!" Mr. Oyelowo bit out, his voice rising. "For generations, we have been aligned with Shango. I can't believe I let you convince me to come back, Simisola. You've offered nothing that stays singularly with Shango. Do you know what you risk by doing that?" His fists curled on the table, knuckles paling against the dark wood. "I told you we will find our *own* way. The *right* way. But it will be done on *my* terms."

The tension in the room thickened, pressing down on TJ. Ayo's eyes were locked on the table, his hands still twisting the copper ring around his finger. TJ could feel the frustration radiating from his friend—the way his father's words seemed to cage him in, like Ayo was just a piece on the board that Mr. Oyelowo was determined to move at his will.

Elder Adeyemi softened her voice, but there was still a firmness there that TJ admired. "I understand your fears more than you know, Mobalaji. But Ayo is not a boy anymore."

There was a flicker of pain in Mr. Oyelowo's eyes at that, a momentary crack in the armor. He blinked, and it was gone, replaced by that rigid, unyielding mask he always wore. But TJ saw it. He saw the way Mr. Oyelowo's fingers twitched, as if he wanted to reach out and pull Ayo back again, away from all of this.

Manny glanced at Ayo, then back at Mr. Oyelowo. "With all due respect, Mr. Oyelowo, Ayo can speak for himself."

The words hung in the air, sharp and heavy, and for a moment, no one spoke. Mr. Oyelowo's eyes narrowed, but he didn't respond. Instead, he turned his attention back to Elder Adeyemi.

"You think you're protecting him," he said, voice low and bitter. "But I won't allow you to sacrifice him to this madness. I thought Yemoja would have had answers, not more bad news."

TJ couldn't help but think back to what Adeola had told him. The warnings about the Veiled Caravan, the dangers they hadn't even begun to face. And here they were, locked in a battle over who would make the decisions, while time slipped away.

TJ spoke up finally. Again, feeling oddly more confident since he was defending his friend instead of speaking up on his own behalf. "We are giving him the chance to make his own choice. As well as you. This magic only works with your *full* consent. It nearly ripped us apart when Manny's auntie wasn't on board. But, sir, you gotta be straight with us. You gotta tell us what's eating at you. What do you fear will happen if we work through Ogun or Thor to get to Shango?" TJ was met with a long stare, so he turned to his friend instead. "Ayo, you can walk away from this. You've earned that right. But I believe in your strength. I believe you *are* ready."

Finally, Ayo lifted his head, his voice steady but low. "I'm not w-w-walking away."

Mr. Oyelowo's jaw tightened. "You're not ready, Ayodeji. You don't understand the cost of this path."

Ayo's hands stilled over the copper ring on his finger. "Then t-t-teach me. You keep saying you want to p-p-protect me, but you're holding back. You c-c-can't have it both ways."

For a moment, Mr. Oyelowo looked like he could be convinced but then another debate sparked between him and his son, with Adeyemi joining in. At least he wasn't rushing out of the meeting room this time. Perhaps it was a step in the right direction—the fact that he was arguing.

TJ, dejected, fell into his seat and tuned out the back-and-forth as the conversation dragged on, their words buzzing like static in the background. The argument about consent gnawed at him—how fragile their unity really was. Manny's auntie had nearly shattered it before, and now Mr. Oyelowo's stubbornness threatened to do the same. It was becoming painfully clear that trust was as vital to their success as Ashe itself. Yet, how could he demand trust from them when he was still keeping secrets of his own?

His thoughts drifted back to Adeola's warning about the Veiled Caravan.

What might the adults ask of him if he revealed what she had told him? Glancing at his friends, he could tell similar concerns weighed on their minds. Ayo's hands twisted the copper ring on his finger, his eyes distant. Manny chewed her lip, fidgeting with one of her braids.

They all knew the information could prove useful. But was it worth the risk of Bolawe discovering Adeola was feeding them information? She had put her trust in TJ by sharing what she knew. To betray that trust could cost her dearly, especially when she was trapped in that prison with all those criminals—some of them Keepers.

*No, remember,* TJ thought, *Bolawe's not rockin' with the Keepers anymore.*

TJ let out a slow breath through his nose. For now, discretion seemed the wisest course. This wasn't the time or place to disclose what he'd learned. He met his friends' gazes and gave a slight shake of his head. Ayo and Manny nodded almost imperceptibly. They would keep Adeola's warning between themselves, at least until the time was right.

The tense exchange between Mr. Oyelowo and Elder Adeyemi continued, but TJ barely heard it. His thoughts were focused on the trials ahead. On finding Ogun's cabinet, braving the Veiled Caravan, and finishing his staff on time. He looked to his list again.

1. ~~Gotta figure out how to reverse this channeling thing by dreamwalking with Obatala and Oshosi.~~
2. ~~Open up the ancestral path from Yemoja to Oya through the Frost Realm for Manny.~~
3. Unlock ancestral path from Ogun to Shango's using Ayo's Norse ring. (And find Ogun's Sacred Cabinet)
4. Complete my staff to sustain the ancestral path ritual to the Court of All jail cell.
5. Save Shango and Oya on The Hero's Equinox.
6. Don't die.

Failure was not an option. He had to be ready

# 36

# ATTUNEMENT & ACQUAINTANCES

Elder Adeyemi and the strings she could pull never ceased to amaze TJ. The next week, he had all the extra time he needed to attune his staff materials, extra time to figure out how to craft his wood and solder his mystical rod together.

In SS Ere Idaraya training, instead of having to run laps with the rest of the class, Teacher Ige told TJ he would be having private workout sessions. Those sessions turned out to be a whole setup for TJ to train in attuning within a private grove—away from the eyes of the other students. Before Teacher Ige left TJ to run with the other students, he had said, "I don't know what you're up to now, Mr. Young, but I owe Adeyemi quite a lot. You take as much time as you need, Hero of Eko Atlantic."

Then, in SS1 Alchemy, Teacher Payne told the class that they would be taking a field trip to the whispering willow to extract sap from their bark to craft Obatala's Soothing Serum—a potion to battle against nightmares, something TJ sorely needed. Only this was an excuse so that TJ could have the whole classroom to himself so he could brew an elixir for the Orunmila crystal he decided to use. The gem was coated with meteorite fragments he needed to melt away so he could get the most out of the crystal. On occasion, Teacher Payne would poke her head in to see how TJ was doing, saying, "Give Adeyemi a good word for me, eh? I used to help your sister just like this when she got up to her missions. I suppose you can't give me a hint on what you're doing, oh? Is Olokun coming back? Are you trying to get Orunmila to commune with us again?" TJ must've given her a face because she quickly followed up with a, "Sorry, sorry, let me get back out to the rest of the class before they start wondering where I went off to."

And it went like that for most of his classes. It was almost like Adeyemi was still the Headmistress. It seemed like everyone owed a favor to her, or at least had so much admiration for her, Dayo, or TJ himself, that they were more than happy to help.

There was only one small hiccup when Ninka Nanka came slithering up to SS1 Elemental Studies. That day, under a dense canopy, the students had been clustered in groups, each surrounding a collection of metamorphic rocks they were meant to transform into early forms of magma. Yet TJ was working by himself, attempting to use his magma to reform the double-helix design of his sister's old staff. Teacher Dossi of Fon had to flap her aziza wings so fast to cover TJ's workstation with a deft use of plant magic. Thankfully, Ninka Nanka was only passing through instead of making an active investigation of the class.

By the time Friday rolled around, TJ was more than ready in his opinion. But he wasn't the only one with a unique curriculum that week. Ayo had also been on a different trajectory than the other students. Only he was going out of his way to get reacquainted with Jimoh, which meant hanging out less with TJ. To get into the Veiled Caravan, they needed a password. And that password had to come by way of a certain Keeper's son. That said, there was no way Ayo could get in good with Jimoh if he was still hanging around TJ. So they—Ayo and TJ—acted like they were fighting and giving one another the cold shoulder.

TJ had missed hanging out with Ayo but he didn't mind it too much when he had realized it meant more one-on-one time with Manny in the private corners of the Library Tree, or the mess hall, the bridges, the whispering willows, and more...

Usually, TJ and Ayo entered classes at different times, but they had been discussing the dueling exhibition between Nigeria and Mexico and had forgotten to keep up appearances.

"Hey, I thought you guys weren't friends anymore," Umar shouted from the side as he juggled a bundle of amethyst crystals.

"What are you talking about?" TJ snapped, his voice a touch too loud. "I can't stand this guy!"

Ayo's eyes widened, and he quickly schooled his features into a scowl. "Feeling's mutual, j-jerk."

Jimoh, LaVont, and Aisha watched them intently from across the forest clearing. He had to think fast.

"Oh yeah?" TJ growled, grabbing Ayo's shirt collar. "You want to say that again?"

Ayo's hands flew up in a flurry of signs. "You... big... dummy... head."

TJ struggled not to laugh at Ayo's ridiculous insult. Instead, he shoved Ayo away, perhaps a bit too gently. Jimoh threw up a questioning eyebrow. It wasn't working. TJ had to go for the low blow.

"Come on, say it with your chest," he told Ayo. "Or can you n-n-not, get the words o-o-out." TJ felt completely sick with himself. He wanted to mouth an automatic "sorry" but that would ruin it all.

Ayo's face changed from one of feigned anger to one that looked more genuine.

A pocket of the class led by Aisha erupted in laughter, and even Jimoh and LaVont seemed convinced by their performance. TJ and Ayo glared at each other. Ayo looked ready to throw a punch but, thankfully, Staffmaster Bamidele came stomping into the clearing. Ayo settled for a rude gesture instead.

TJ made his way to a concerned looking Freya while Ayo sauntered over to Jimoh and LaVont who introduced themselves with their typical firebreathing dabs.

*Good,* TJ thought. *If they're doing that with Ayo, then he must be getting closer with them already.*

Within the circle of floating staffs, Freya struggled under the weight of her bulging satchel as she made her way into the staffcrafting clearing. Her usually bouncy step was hindered by the sheer volume of supplies she had brought with her. TJ could relate; his own bag was filled to the brim with an eclectic mix of materials he had gathered and attuned to throughout the week.

"Why the hell would you mock Ayo like that, TJ?" Freya glared, chiding him with an accent far more Nigerian than Scottish. It only took a handful of months for the change to leak in. TJ automatically prepared himself for a slap across the shoulder but remembered that Freya didn't do that. That was a Manny thing.

"Nah, nah," TJ said, keeping his voice low. "We're just pretending… long story. I didn't actually mean it."

Freya's long dark hair was tied back in a messy bun, a few stray curls escaping to frame her face. She wore a flowing traditional green tunic, cinched at the waist with a belt adorned with various pouches and trinkets.

*She looks just like a druid,* TJ thought. Her look reminded him of the times he, Manny, and Ayo dressed up for their moonlight ritual at Camp Olosa or the golden chain ritual atop Oracle Rock. The green tunic probably gave her a magical boost. Maybe TJ should've worn an Ogun robe or an Olosa bangle. But it was too late to double back to his dorm now.

"Well," Freya said, still scowling from TJ's poor behavior, "whatever you're doing had better be worth it."

"It is, I swear. It's, um… more Orisha stuff."

"Tickets to the next dueling match."

"Huh?"

Freya dropped her bags and placed her hands on her hips, wincing. "You'll make it up to Ayo by getting him tickets to the next dueling match in the village. You hear me?"

"Oh, right." TJ rubbed the back of his head, feeling like he was being scolded by Mom. "Yeah, I'll do that. Good idea."

The clearing was alive with activity as students bustled about, comparing materials and discussing their progress. The air hummed with the energy of anticipation and a hint of competitive spirit. Staffmaster Bamidele moved among the students, offering guidance and encouragement.

"Well…" Freya said. "Looks like you've been busy."

TJ looked back at all the supplies he had. "Yeah, I think I've got everything I need."

Freya winked. "Not that. I was talkin' about you and Manny. Saw you two cuddled up at Oracle Rock the other day."

"Oh! That… Right…" TJ felt himself get lighter. "Yeah, that's been… pretty great. Thanks to you."

Freya laughed. "But yeah, I see you got as much as I did. Your crystal there has a good glow. It's Orunmila's, yeah?"

TJ nodded, setting his bag down with a thud. "Yeah, it is. It was the hardest one to attune."

"Aye, I noticed. Looks like those associated with Orunmilla are having trouble. I thought everything attributed to him was… you know, a dud."

TJ swallowed hard, ignoring her comment as he said, "Yeah… and I've been working like a dog on this all week. I'm just worried about finishing early, you know? What if we screw it up? Bamidele is always talking about not rushing this thing."

Freya chuckled, her eyes darting around the clearing. "I know what you mean. I didn't want anyone thinking we're a couple of show offs or something. That Jimoh kid gets insanely jealous."

"Exactly! And I don't want Staffmaster Bamidele thinkin' we're rushing through the process. I mean, we've put a lot of thought and effort into this, but still…" TJ trailed off, his brow furrowed.

"I'm sure he'll understand," Freya reassured him with her newly-acquired accent. She code-switched hard and fast, TJ realized. "At the end of the day, he just wants us to make a staff that will work best for us, no matter the timing, right?"

TJ nodded. "You're right. Let's get to work."

As the class progressed, TJ and Freya worked diligently on their staffs, their focus unwavering despite the chatter and activity around them. Time melted away as they immersed themselves in the intricate process of crafting their magical tools.

Freya carefully pieced together her staff, soldering elements together with fire magic. She blended elements of her Celtic heritage with Yoruba designs, incorporating a polished piece of oak carved with Celtic knots as the main body of her staff. At the top, she affixed a fern green crystal, aligned with the energy of Osain, the Orisha of Herbs and Healing. Delicate vines, reminiscent of Celtic spirals, were etched along the length of the staff, intertwining with symbols of the Orishas.

TJ, working alongside Freya, offered guidance when needed. "Make sure the crystal is secure. Then I can boost you while you do your final attunement."

Freya nodded. "The hieroglyphs on your golden crescent are a nice touch. Khonsu and Ra, yeah?"

"I think so." TJ wasn't exactly sure. He just felt a call to them without understanding why. Ifa Academy didn't have a whole lot of classes about the Egyptian gods.

"They'll enhance your water and fire magicks nicely."

TJ smiled, grateful for her keen eye. "And I'm really happy with this." He lifted a cauldron charm. "You recognize it, right?"

Freya's eyes went wide as the glint of the charm flickered in her eye. "Wait... where did you find this? It's... that's associated with the Cailleach. But... that'll never work."

"Your dead god, yeah. But I'm telling you, it's got something special about it. Feels like it could be the missing link to my staff."

"I don't know, TJ. Orunmila crystals are one thing, but Cailleach charms... that's a whole different branch of magic."

TJ laughed. "Don't worry, I'll expect an apology when I prove you wrong."

TJ's staff was coming together beautifully. At the core was the Orunmila crystal, levitating between the golden crescent adorned with sunbeams. The crystal pulsed with a soft but radiant emerald green light, signifying its building attunement to TJ's energy. It surprised TJ how well it worked, especially considering the clouded Ashe of Orunmila over the last few months.

Next, TJ incorporated the centerpiece of Dayo's old staff, the double helix design that he had grown so fond of. It served as a reminder of his sister's legacy and the strength she had passed on to him. The wood, smooth and polished, seemed to hum with her latent power.

At the base of the staff, TJ attached a wooden pommel carved with the complete Futhark—the Runic alphabet. He had learned about its significance during his research. He had picked it up from his great-grandfather's altar because he recognized two of the runes... the one he helped use in the Frost Realm to ice the raven and the one tattooed under Ayo's eye and carved into his brass ring from Thor.

To further personalize his staff, TJ added three more charms from different pantheons: a delicate Slavic protection symbol crafted from gold found its place near the top; a small jade carving of a Japanese kitsune, a fox spirit known for its wisdom and magic, was nestled just below the double helix; and finally, the glinting cauldron inspired by Cailleach from the Celtic pantheon hung from the bottom of his staff, its gentle chime adding a musical element to TJ's magic.

TJ and Freya put the finishing touches on their staffs, their hands moving with practiced precision. They both utilized earth magic to reinforce their staffs, the wood bending to their will.

With a satisfied nod, they let Staffmaster Bamidele review their work.

The old man, who smelled like sandalwood that day, nodded in approval. "This is very good work, you two—"

"Sir, I need help with something!" Umar called out from across the clearing. His staff was smoking, and he was manifesting water to put it out.

"Oh dear, let me check on that," Bamidele said to TJ and Freya. "Do you already know what prayers you're using? Mr. Young, because of your unique qualities, I would suggest prayers to at least four Orishas tied to different elements. Miss Innes, for your Orisha half, I might suggest Osain. You know him, yes?"

"He's my strongest alignment, sir," Freya said, nearly skipping.

"Great! Get to that and I'll return for a final and more thorough look—No, no, no, stop that, Mr. Adebayo, you'll only make the fire worse!"

Bamidele stomped off to help as TJ thought back to how he tried to enter the Summoning Stone last year, how he had to feel the Ashe of all those elemental corners. He knew he could do it.

With a hop in their steps now, TJ and Freya began chanting individual rituals over their creations. TJ's chant, mostly in Yoruba, started with a prayer to the four Orishas tied to the base elements: Yemoja, Oya, Shango, and Ogun. His voice, low and steady, carried the weight of his devotion. He even ended with a direct prayer to Orunmila. Like before, TJ was surprised how well the old prayer worked, despite current circumstances.

*Bless me with your light, Orunmila,*
*And keep me on the path of wisdom, justice, and compassion.*
*May I honor you in my thoughts, words, and deeds,*
*And may your wisdom illuminate my journey through life.*
*Ashe.*

In contrast, Freya mainly directed her prayers to the druids and Celtic gods, which were unfamiliar to TJ. The only recognizable name was Osain, to whom Freya offered a short prayer.

*Grant me insight into the mysteries of the natural world,*
*That I may be a healer and protector of all living things.*
*Osain, I thank you for your endless generosity,*
*And pledge to be a steward of the healing herbs you provide.*
*Ashe.*

As their chants continued, TJ's staff shook in his hands. Ashe coursed from the wood and drove straight through his veins. The power was palpable, boosting both his and Freya's prayers until their final attunements solidified. An overwhelming sense of pride filled TJ, the staff feeling like an extension of himself, as if he had possessed it his entire life. The mixing of pantheons didn't muddle the clarity of his magic, his Ashe; instead, it *enhanced* it, creating a deep and perfect harmony.

Freya turned to him, her eyes sparkling. "I should've fixed my staff months ago. This feels… *right*. Judging by your face, yours is all done as well, eh?"

TJ grinned, though mostly at the end of Freya's sentence. Over the past weeks, her Nigerian accent had absolutely leaked into her Scottish one.

"What spells should we cast first to test the foundation?" TJ asked.

Freya, almost bouncing on her heels, beckoned TJ. "C'mon. We should test these things away from everyone else. Deeper in the forest."

"Right." TJ fell in step with Freya and into the forest. Before the trees hid the rest of the class, TJ snuck a glance at Jimoh and LaVont laughing with Ayo.

*Keep it up, Ayo. I'm about to finish my staff. You get that info we need. We're almost there, friend.*

# 37

# BLOOM & DOUBT

Deep in the forest, Freya scanned their surroundings until she spotted a wilting flower near the base of a bush. With a spiraled movement of her staff, she uttered a spellword in Scottish Gaelic that TJ didn't understand. A bright light bloomed from the tip of her crystal, shining upon the dying flower. Instantly, vibrant, colorful blooms burst forth, covering the entire bush. Freya let out a squeal of a laugh, jumped around, and planted a kiss on her staff before turning to TJ. "You gotta try it! It felt *amazin'!*"

TJ eyed a dying vine along a tree bark. Lifting his staff in front of his face, he closed his eyes, his mind drifting back to his very first session with Bolawe at Camp Olosa. He didn't want to think of Bolawe, but he was the only man he knew associated with Osain. Plus, that particular Orisha's Ashe still hung in the air thanks to the residual magic Freya had just used. TJ's crystal began to glow after he mimicked Freya's spiraled staff movement. The vine radiated with light, but before he could complete the spell, Staffmaster Bamidele came rushing through the forest, shouting, "Mr. Young, stop!"

The Staffmaster air-stepped through the trees. Despite his age, his movements were fluid and graceful, fast and deliberate. Bewilderment etched the man's severe face as he approached TJ and Freya.

"What's wrong, Staffmaster?" TJ asked, eyebrows scrunched together.

Bamidele held up a hand, his voice stern. "Do *not* cast that spell, Mr. Young. It can be dangerous. Just like what happened to Banjoko the Bold." His eyes hovered over TJ's gloves.

"Banjoko the who?" Freya asked.

"Like John Henry," TJ said.

"Who's that?"

TJ sighed. Of course Freya wouldn't know either of them. "Basically, if there is improper magic use, unstable use, or if I use too much of it, I can rip myself apart and die like they did."

"Oh," Freya said at first. Then she stepped forward, her bun tilting with her head lean. "I don't get it. How could TJ's staff possibly be dangerous? Mine is workin' fine."

The Staffmaster sighed, his gaze falling on TJ's staff. "The fault is mine. I did not realize you had brought in materials not well suited to a diviner, Mr. Young. I did say I wanted a final review, but Mr. Adebayo and his fire... no matter. No damage was done, thankfully. You should be thanking Mr. Oladipo, though. I wouldn't have known if it wasn't for him pointing out some of the materials you left behind in the clearing."

*Of course it'd be Jimoh...*

TJ's grip tightened on his staff. "What does that mean?"

"In Ifa, for diviners, the staff must be a pure form of Ashe and Ashe alone. Mixing magicks can lead to unpredictable and hazardous results."

Now TJ's hands quivered over his staff. "But... but I prayed to the Orishas when I did my final attunement. Just like you told me. It seemed to work. That has to mean the Orishas approve, right?"

Bamidele shook his head. "You may have achieved final attunement now, but that does not mean your staff will be functional. The staff could... get sick when you're under distress because of your mixing of magic that could never truly meld under your ancestral circumstances." He pointed to the pommel. "This pommel, for example, are these... Nordic runes?" His voice sounded almost affronted.

"Yes, they are," TJ confirmed, almost defiantly. "I don't understand, Staffmaster. Freya is using Celtic and Yoruba materials. Why can't I?"

Freya nodded in agreement, holding her staff close to her chest as though she, too, would be ridiculed for what she had created.

"Because Miss Innes' direct ancestral line includes a Yoruba mother and Celtic father. She is an exception, not the rule. Because you, Mr. Young, do not have direct ancestries with many of these things attached to your staff."

"But… you know about me. You know I'm different. Maybe I'm an exception too?"

Bamidele's eyes widened as he examined TJ's staff more closely. "Orunmila's Stars, is this piece Japanese!? No, no, no, this staff would most certainly produce unreliable magic. Unless you are telling me your immediate ancestral line includes those from Norway, Japan, and... my, is this headpiece Egyptian too? It's one thing to skip steps like you have, but all of this on top of it, that…"

TJ shook violently in his sneakers. He had worked *really* hard. There was *no* way he did anything wrong. "Look, with all due respect, sir, it can't be a big deal if I attuned. I swear. I swear it on the Orishas. My Ashe feels effortless now with it. My hands don't even feel lifeless anymore."

Bamidele's expression turned grave. "Never swear anything on the Orishas about things you do not understand, boy. This is not the way."

"T-Trust me, I know about the Orishas more than you do." TJ wanted to take it back the moment he said it.

"Excuse you, young man?"

"My bad—I mean—my mistake. I shouldn't have said that. But c'mon, Staffmaster. I mean, yeah, I don't think I have Egyptian ancestry or Norse grandparents, but way down the line, we all come from the same source, don't we? It's not a perfect attunement to the purity of the Orishas but—"

"Perfection is the enemy of the good, right?" Freya added.

The Staffmaster's voice came out firmly. "This. Is. Different. This is fundamentally incorrect. This goes against all of the Orishas' primordial laws. If there is no direct ancestral line, you could be in the middle of a precarious situation and Orunmila's Glow won't heed you, Shango's Fire won't manifest, Yemoja's Waters will be nothing but a sprinkle. I've seen it time and time again, Mr. Young. You must make another."

"But Yemoja is already working with the Asgar—" He stopped himself abruptly, realizing he had nearly revealed a secret Elder Adeyemi specifically said needed to be kept under wraps. Freya seemed to give him a knowing sidelong glance. It was bad enough he told the Staffmaster he knew more about the Orishas—no matter how valid.

Bamidele must've taken TJ's silence as acceptance, though, his expression softening. "I'm so sorry, young man. You have a great talent, that cannot be denied. More raw potential than even your sister. And I know you worked hard. But if you did it once, you can do it again... with the *proper* materials. I believe in you. It's impressive you got this far this fast. You should be proud of that. Do not fret, you are well ahead of schedule as it is. Well ahead."

*But I'm not,* TJ thought. *Shango is dying; Forseti is battering away at Eshu's illusion. I don't have time anymore.*

It didn't seem as though the Staffmaster was very good at consoling. His half-hearted pat on TJ's back was almost too mechanical. But it seemed like he felt he had done the trick since TJ didn't have any more retorts. So he turned to Freya to say, "Miss Innes, I'm so happy to see you reform your staff, and much sooner than either of us expected." He gestured to the bush with its rainbow of crowded flowers. "That is very impressive work, young lady. I'll let the druid enclave know of my approval, but your final trial will be with your own people. Understood?"

Freya nodded, though stilted gratitude entered her voice as she curtsied. "Yes, Staffmaster. Thank you so much for your guidance."

As Bamidele left, Freya turned to TJ, her eyes filled with remorse. "I should really be thankin' you, TJ. And I'm sorry for what the Staffmaster said. I feel a bit responsible—no, *completely* responsible—since, you know, I was the one who told you to mix up different elements like that. I didn't think there was any direct ancestral element to it."

"Neither did I."

TJ stared down at his staff, a mix of sadness and admiration swirling within him. He had poured his heart and soul into crafting this masterpiece, meticulously selecting each element and charm to create a harmonious blend of his heritage and the magical traditions he had encountered. It should have accounted for something that he used items that called to his great-grandfather, right? But how could TJ say anything against a Staffmaster like Bamidele?

ᛉ

AS TJ AND FREYA SLUMPED BACK TO THE CLEARING, THE weight of disappointment hung heavy in the air. Freya tried cracking jokes, but they did nothing to lift TJ's spirit. The once vibrant colors of the forest seemed muted, the chirping of birds a distant echo. TJ went through the motions of cleaning up his materials, his movements slow and mechanical. He listened to Bamidele's final speech, the words washing over him without really sinking in.

When Bamidele dismissed the class, the other students shuffled out, their excited chatter fading into the background. Soon, TJ and Freya were left alone in the clearing, the silence broken only by the rustling of leaves.

"I'm really gonna miss you, TJ," Freya said softly, her eyes warm but sad. "I know we've not known each other for long, but you've been a brilliant friend. I'm so, so sorry about what happened wi' your staff. I still think it's beautiful, and I know how much work you put into it. I hope you keep pushing with it."

TJ managed a small smile, his gaze still fixed on his staff. "Thanks... old lady." Freya rolled her eyes. "I'm gonna miss you, too. I'm glad we got to work together, even if it didn't turn out the way we hoped—well, for me, at least. Hey, at least I got a girlfriend out of it, right?"

Freya chuckled, nodding in agreement. "That's true. I'm glad I could help with that, at least. Listen, before I go, let's have some tofu fish stew at Mami Wata's, my treat. A little goodbye gift from me to you."

"That sounds great," TJ replied, his spirits lifting slightly at the thought of sharing one last meal with his friend.

"And let's keep in touch, aye? I want to hear all about your adventures. We can swap tales of the Orisha Planes and the Otherworld. And... maybe we can visit each other sometime..."

"Definitely," TJ agreed, finally tearing his gaze away from his staff to meet Freya's eyes.

With a final hug and a promise to meet at Mami Wata's that weekend, Freya left the clearing, leaving TJ alone with his thoughts. He sank onto a nearby log, his staff resting across his knees. The sadness crept back in, disappointment settling on his shoulders like sandbags.

He was so lost in thought that he didn't hear Ayo approach until his friend was standing right in front of him. TJ looked up, a frown sunk into his face.

Ayo's eyes were bright with excitement under his designer glasses, his hands moving rapidly as he signed, "I hear what happen, bruh. But I know what make it better, make you happy!"

"What is it, man?" TJ groaned.

"I-I-I did it!" he said out loud. "I-I-I don't know how, man, but I-I-I did it! I got access from J-J-Jimoh! This weekend, we're suh-suh-suh-sneaking into the Veiled Caravan!"

# 38

# UNEXPECTED MENTOR

Ayo's elevated spirits stood in stark contrast to TJ's dour feelings. As Ayo explained how he finessed Jimoh, he practically skipped all the way from the staffcrafting forest clearing to the mess hall.

"You not believe how I make Jimoh tell about caravan," Ayo signed, his hands moving animatedly as he spoke. "I think it take month, but only take one week!"

"How'd you manage it?" TJ asked, genuinely curious.

Ayo grinned. "Well, I maybe insult you a little. Tell him how you struggle with staff. Guess he think it make him look better, feel better. He always arrogant."

"Gee, it's a wonder you two were ever friends."

"Right!?" Ayo replied, missing TJ's sarcasm.

TJ frowned, not particularly thrilled about being the butt of Ayo's manipulations. But he couldn't deny the results. Plus, he deserved it for stuttering in Ayo's face. "That's great, Ayo. Really. I'm glad you got access. Definitely needed that good news."

As they emerged from the wooded trail, the mess hall's thatched roof and open-wall shelter came into view. Amber crystal light dotted the edges of the space, giving the teenagers hungrily scrounging for food a gentle radiance. Most of them seemed happy, cracking jokes, laughing. Umar was in one corner, engaged in an intense match of *Major League Crossover* with Coach Ali. Titi was bunched with a few girls who giggled over a baby kongamato that they were tasked to take care of that week. The girls kept feeding it puff puffs, which TJ was *pretty sure* was not part of the pterodactyl-looking creature's diet. Tunde, still popular as ever, was surrounded by what seemed like all the juniors in the academy as he performed a freestyle rap. One of his friends—who wore a huge headwrap—served as his beat box.

Ifa Academy was in full swing now, yet TJ couldn't help continuing to sulk. It didn't help that, when he and Ayo grabbed plates of pounded yam and *egusi* soup, Ayo signed, "No talk about my big win. What happen with your staff?" He eyed the wooden shaft hanging out of TJ's backpack. "It look good but I hear it no good?"

TJ sighed, recounting his experience with Staffmaster Bamidele. "He didn't approve of my mixing ancestral magicks. Said it could lead to 'unpredictable results.'"

Ayo scoffed as they found a table to sit down at. "Sound like Baba with 'pure' talk. Don't let it get to you, man. Just… use it."

They ate in silence for a moment until Manny found them in the bustling dinnertime crowd. "Freya let me know what happened." She kissed TJ on the cheek. "Sorry, boo." Ayo made gagging noises behind her. "What are you going to do with your staff now?"

TJ set a hand over the moon crescent, careful not to poke himself at the pointed edges. "I guess I gotta break it down and start over."

"Nah, don't do that," Manny said. "You should still attune with it and put your hat in for the final trial. Prove Bamidele wrong."

"That's what I say too," Ayo agreed, signing with his fork between his fingers. "Trial test magic anyway. And get three teachers for pass—no, um, license—not just Bamidele. I hear Elder Akande from Camp Olosa is one. She likes you, right?"

TJ and Manny gave each other a look. "Uh…" Manny said. "We might have lied to her back at camp, back when we were trying to figure out why Dayo's old staff kept changing colors. I mean, she probably don't hate us or nothin' but I don't think we gave the best first impression…"

"Ah, don't trip." Ayo waved it away. "Her remember no good, right? She forget."

"Who's the third judge?" TJ asked.

Ayo shrugged. "No idea."

TJ nodded, considering their words. It was comforting to have his friends' support, even if he still harbored doubts.

"Hey," Ayo signed, a sudden idea lighting up his eyes, "bring staff with us to Veiled Caravan? Good small test before full trial."

Manny swallowed down her latest spoonful of soup. "That ain't a bad idea."

"Yeah..." TJ said softly at first, then more loudly, almost deviantly, "Yeah! That'll at least prove to *me* my staff isn't worthless. I'll start looking into the basic moveset of the staff tonight. I think I read something in my sister's journal about a specific Ogun activation."

Manny gave him a gentle squeeze around his thigh. "That's our TJ. Prove that old fool wrong."

Feeling better, TJ watched Ayo as he signed the details of their upcoming infiltration of the Caravan. "Sneak in before full moon, after hours, before window closes. It be a small squeeze." He paused. "Tight squeeze, but we can slip in and no one sees."

Manny raised an eyebrow, a hint of skepticism in her voice. "I'm surprised Jimoh didn't put up more of a fight giving you his family's password. How'd you get that done?"

Ayo leaned back, a cocky grin spreading across his face. "What me say? Me just have way with people."

TJ rolled his eyes at Ayo's bravado, but he couldn't deny the effectiveness of his friend's persuasion skills.

"Do you think we should tell the UCMP about this now that we got an in? Elder Adeyemi?" Manny murmured as a group of SS2 students rushed behind them with plates that still needed to be cleaned of their vegetables.

When they passed along, TJ quickly shook his head. "No, I don't trust Bolawe. The fewer people who know, the better. It's not that serious. We're just taking a look at a cabinet or two. We're not crossing realms or anything like that."

"Plus," Ayo signed, "If word get back to Baba, he go mad. He no want me messing with Ogun."

"Yeah, but Jimoh's family is associated with Keepers, right?" Manny asked. "What if they catch us creepin' around?"

Manny's tone gave TJ a slight pause but he still said, "We'll be fine. We can do this alone. We've got each other's backs."

As they continued their discussion, the mess hall continued to ramp up with activity as students returned from their final classes and extracurriculars. Students bustled about, their laughter and chatter filling the air, the kind of energy that only came about before a weekend. For once, TJ didn't feel envious of the carefree lives they led. Instead, he found himself filled with a newfound determination. He was ready to face the challenges ahead, to make it all work.

With positive thoughts swirling in his mind, TJ dug into his steaming bowl of egusi soup, savoring the rich ground melon seeds, spinach, and goat. He knew the path ahead wouldn't be easy, but with his friends by his side, he felt capable of taking on anything.

LATER, AFTER THE SUN WENT DOWN, TJ SAT CROSS-LEGGED ON the forest floor, his newly crafted staff resting across his lap. The night air was cool and crisp, filled with the gentle chirping of crickets and the soft glow of fireflies dancing through the trees. He had come out here—away from the raucous Friday night dormitories—to practice some movesets. He would need to master them for the upcoming staff trial—and to prepare for his infiltration of the Veiled Caravan.

Beside him, propped open on a rock, lay his sister's journal. The pages were filled with her chicken-scratch handwriting and rough illustrations, guiding him through the intricacies of Orunmila's light magicks. TJ focused on the first note, studying the figure-eight motion, which was the basis for the moveset associated with Orunmila's manifestations. Dayo's note read:

*Double helix wood design should help with this.*

TJ stood up, gripping his own staff tightly, and began to trace the pattern in the air, his movements slow and deliberate at first, then gradually gaining speed and confidence. Despite his best efforts, TJ struggled to illuminate Orunmila's Glow with his staff. He tried again and again, frustration mounting, but the emerald crystal remained stubbornly dark. Just as he was about to give up, a voice startled him.

*Practicing late, I see.*

TJ yelped, whirling around to find Ninki Nanka watching him, her reptilian eyes glinting in the moonlight. "You got a way of sneaking up on me, Headmistress," he said, trying to calm his racing heart.

Ninki Nanka smiled, a hint of mischief in her expression. *Well, my bestial origins are aligned with the Hunter Spirit,* she thought-spoke, her voice smooth and almost playful. *Speaking of which, how is Oshosi doing these days? I've not heard or seen of him in some time.*

TJ swallowed hard, avoiding her gaze. "I... I have no idea. I haven't spoken with Oshosi since the day I came back from the Court of All."

The Headmistress studied him for a moment, her reptilian features making it difficult for TJ to gauge her reaction. An awkward silence stretched between them before Ninki Nanka finally thought-spoke again. *That's too bad. I would have liked to have a conversation with my old friend. You're keeping both your feet in the Mortal Realm, yes?*

TJ shifted uncomfortably under her scrutiny, the sickly yellow venom of her eyes in the shadows of the night only adding to his unease. Still, he resolved to answer, once again lying that he was staying put in the Mortal Realm, just as she had wanted him to.

*That's good to hear,* Ninki Nanka said, nodding slowly. *Your education is of the utmost importance, after all.*

The forest was quiet, save for the gentle rustling of leaves in the night breeze. TJ stood there, his staff in hand, as Ninki Nanka continued to study him intently. *Staffmaster Bamidele was quite displeased with your work today, from what I've heard.*

TJ bristled at her words, his grip tightening on his staff. "You here to ridicule me too?"

*No, not at all,* Ninki Nanka replied, her tone surprisingly gentle. *In fact, I think it's a novel idea, mixing magical elements together. Diviners can be a bit too dogmatic at times, forgetting that the practice of Ifa has always been one of the more malleable disciplines, unlike those of the Abra-*

*hamic faiths or otherwise.* She paused, her gaze drifting upward to the starry sky. *It's why the Orishas have survived so well in the New World as opposed to their Motherland here in old Yorubaland.*

The Headmistress' response took TJ aback, a wave of shame washing over him. He had never really given Ninki Nanka the time of day, dismissing her entirely because she had always felt like a pestering force against him as he tried to figure out how to save Shango and the others. He had never taken the time to listen to her wisdom.

Crickets chirped softly in the background, fireflies continuing their ethereal dance through the trees. Ninki Nanka stretched her long giraffe neck down to Dayo's notebook propped up on the rock. She read a few lines, a smirk playing at the corners of her sharp mouth.

*Your sister had a keen mind,* she thought-spoke, *but most of all, an* open *mind. She came to visit me once while I was waking—it takes me a few years to rouse from my slumber.*

*Talk about snoozing*, TJ thought.

*She had questions she thought I could help with, but I was quite grumpy with her. Since then I've heard nothing but good things about Ifedayo.* She turned her gaze from the night sky and back to TJ. *What basic moveset are you practicing right now?*

TJ shuffled his feet, clutching his staff uncomfortably. "I was practicing my figure eights. Or um… the Orunmila activation. The um… Luminary Figure Eight, I think it's called."

*I wouldn't get too worked up if you can't get it,* Ninka Nanka said. *Many students this year are having trouble with channeling the Ashe of Orunmila. His Stars are more faint these days. Even so… show me your form. You may have more luck than they.*

TJ hesitated for a moment before squatting down and starting his moveset. He traced the pattern in the air, his movements more confident than before.

*Good,* Ninki Nanka said, *but your rotations need to be sharper.*

TJ heeded her words, focusing on the precision of his movements. Suddenly, the glow he had been seeking all night filled the entire forest around them, bathing the space in a vibrant green light.

TJ couldn't believe his eyes, the result of his newly mastered moveset. A sense of pride swelled in his chest, a feeling he had been chasing for *hours*. But more than that… he had a sneaking suspicion the demonstration of his skill shouldn't have been so powerful. Not with Oracle Ruby constantly fatigued and everyone else barely being able to connect to Orunmila. What did that mean for him? Was he simply above the disintegration of the Orishas? Because he himself was one of them… sort of? It was consistently frustrating how no one could tell him who he was. But it proved useful in situations like these.

Ninki Nanka's beady eyes sparkled with approval. *Well done, Mr. Young. You've made great progress tonight. Keep at it, and master the other activations as well. I look forward to overseeing your trial when the time comes.*

TJ's heart soared at her words, a grin spreading across his face. "Thank you, Headmistress. I won't let you down."

Ninki Nanka bowed her long head, her reptilian features softening. *I have little doubt of that, young mortal. You have a bright future ahead of you if you keep to the straight and narrow. A void is approaching. We'll need everyone at their best when that time comes.*

TJ's insides curled at those last words. How much did the Headmistress know about what was going on in the other realms? He would have liked her to explain further but she had already turned away, her crocodile body skulking into the dark forest once more.

"W-wait, Headmistress!" he called after her. "What do you mean you'll be 'overseeing' my trial?"

But Ninki Nanka was gone, swallowed by the shadows as quickly as she had appeared. TJ stood there, puzzled, until her voice echoed in his mind again. *I might have forgotten to mention,* her tone was coy, *that I will be the third judge at your trial.*

# 39

# THE ROAD TO NOWHERE

"Shango's Axe! Head Teacher going to be our third judge!?" Ayo asked the following week as they gathered offerings for Ogun in Teacher Payne's classroom. "Man, she gives me the creeps."

Manny pulled a handful of kola nuts from a shelf and stuffed them into her backpack. "I don't know. Once you get used to her talking in your head, she ain't so bad."

"That's 'cause you ain't seen her at night," TJ said, deciding between taking an iron hammer or iron chains for Ogun—he couldn't remember from class which one Ogun preferred. "When you see her yellow eyes coming out of the shadows, you'll be changing your tune *real* quick."

TJ marveled at the classroom's ethereal beauty for a moment, easily making it one of his favorites at Ifa Academy. The room, reminiscent of an elven sanctuary, was crafted from polished wood and crystalline glass, with tree bark sprouting this way and that throughout the space. Expansive windows gave way to views of the enchanted forest housing the academy.

As they gathered their offerings for Ogun, TJ couldn't help but smirk at how easily they had convinced Teacher Payne of their intentions. The unsuspecting instructor had readily believed their tale of an Ogun-focused project, blissfully unaware of their true plan to communicate with the Orisha under the cover of night.

That, or the instructor thought whatever they were doing was on the orders of Elder Adeyemi.

Manny reached for another offering of kola nuts, her hand inadvertently grazing TJ's staff, which was propped up just next to her. The staff teetered precariously, and TJ's heart skipped as it fell to the floor. Fortunately, Manny's quick reflexes saved the day, and she steadied the staff with an outstretched foot with an apologetic smile. "My bad, Teej. How's the staff feeling, by the way?"

TJ grabbed the staff and ran his fingers along the wood, a sense of pride swelling within him. "It doesn't feel unbalanced or wrong at all. In fact, I mastered the basics of Orunmila's Glow last Friday. Even spent some time developing Ogun's Grounding Pulse technique with Freya over the weekend."

Ayo's eyebrows hiked, then he signed, "Really? Can we see a look... a... um..." He spoke out loud. "D-d-demonstration."

TJ grinned, eager to showcase his newly acquired skill, and there was a loose piece of floorboard that needed mending. Grasping his staff firmly, he took a deep breath and focused his Ashe. With a series of deliberate, stomping movements, he tapped the staff against the floor, culminating in a powerful, centered push. He had gotten the motion so quickly since it was similar to what that shaman was doing when he and Mom went to Thornriver.

The wooden floorboards beneath them cracked, and a gnarled tree root burst forth, its twisted form reaching toward the ceiling. TJ's face fell. He was only supposed to strengthen the board, not uplift a whole new root!

"Oh, man," he said. "Of course that would happen to me. Even if I tried to do something that powerful, I couldn't if I tried." He cringed at the damage done, and his mind rushed back to Staffmaster Bamidele's warning. "Do you think Teacher Payne will notice?"

Manny chuckled. "Nah, I mean... there are roots sprouting everywhere in this place. Shoot, what you did even looks... intentional."

Ayo snorted, barely containing his laughter. "Yeah, and if he no believe that, we blame it on eloko that got free in Teacher Ikenna's class week before. I hear they make big big trouble."

THE NEXT COUPLE OF WEEKS FLEW BY AS TJ TRAINED WITH HIS staff under the well-intentioned but slightly misguided tutelage of Manny and Ayo. Despite their lack of expertise in stafflore, they encouraged TJ to keep practicing Ogun's Grounding Pulse, hoping it might impress the Orisha if he asked for a demonstration.

As the sun set on the Big Sunday of their mini-operation, TJ's nervousness grew. The plan was to sneak into the Veiled Caravan just after it closed for the night, but a minute before the hidden path's window shut during the turn of the new moon. That meant working under *very* tight margins. A specialty of TJ and his friends, sure, but this was cutting it close—even for them.

As the sun completely dipped under the horizon of Ifa Academy's Oracle Rock, TJ, Manny, and Ayo gathered their offerings for Ogun, stuffing them into backpacks and satchels. TJ gripped his staff tightly as they prepared to leave the campus.

To avoid suspicion, they used the excuse of visiting and staying the night at TJ's grandma's as they passed through the Summoning Statues. It wasn't entirely a lie, of course. They just deliberately failed to mention how much later they would actually get to the Abimbola family compound.

There were no issues as they were checked out: TJ going through the Eshu statue, Manny through the Oya statue, and Ayo through the Shango statue without a hitch. But there was a bump in the road when they set foot onto New Ile-Ife proper, where Titi stood waiting in the courtyard near Oduduwa's giant head and Dayo's mural. She waved over to them with glee, her long skirt and crop top catching TJ's eye even from a distance. As she walked, her denim jacket and the white sneakers added a cool edge to her look, and he couldn't help but notice how effortlessly stylish she appeared, her crossbody bag swinging with her every step.

If TJ were a betting guy, he would say…

"Looks like Titi is ready for a date," Manny murmured, speaking TJ's mind.

Ayo cursed under his breath and pulled his friends close to him, signing, "I forget I have thing with Titi tonight. Just play with what I say!"

TJ and Manny exchanged a glance, suppressing their laughter at Ayo's expense. "You owe us for this," TJ teased, and they both agreed to follow Ayo's lead.

Laughing, TJ turned his attention to the rest of the village center. It was a lively night, with the drum circle hosting Ghanaian dancers doing a sponsorship for Anansi's Arcade. A pair of UCMP officials tried and failed to merge with the shadows. TJ had gotten better at pulling them out. Today, one of them was especially tall with a crooked back, and their eyes never left Ayo, who turned on the charm with Titi, his hands moving with practiced ease as he signed. Despite the smoothness of his movements, Titi corrected one of his signs with a giggle, her eyes sparkling with amusement. The sight brought a bittersweet memory to TJ's mind—Emeka was the reason she was so fluent in Yoruba Sign Language to begin with.

Ayo played it off, his smile never faltering. "You know I love it when you fix me," he signed, his expression playful. "It means I get to have more time learning from you."

Titi's gaze turned skeptical as she looked Ayo up and down, taking in his casual attire and the overweight backpack he carried. "You're not dressed like you usually are for our dates," she pointed out, her hands moving with a questioning flourish. "And what's with the backpack?"

"Babe, you can speak to me. I no deaf; I just got stutter."

"Sorry, sorry, I keep forgetting. Just a habit." A shadow of a frown crossed her lips. "But don't go trying to change the subject. What's with all this, eh?" She went rummaging through his backpack, pulling out kola nuts and iron weights. "The hell is all of this?" TJ and Manny waved awkwardly as Titi's attention shifted to them, her eyes narrowing in suspicion. "What are y'all up to now?"

TJ angled away from Titi, trying to hide his staff, which had been poking out from his backpack.

Ayo floundered, his hands moving in fits and starts as he tried to come up with an excuse. "W-well, y-you see, I-I thought—"

"He wanted to surprise you with a double date!" Manny interjected, stepping forward with a bright smile.

"Yeah, that's right," TJ chimed in, nodding enthusiastically. "A double date."

Titi's expression remained unconvinced, her gaze shifting

between the three friends. Ayo's smile was strained, and TJ could practically hear his friend's heartbeat from where he stood. But then, slowly, Titi's face lit up with delight. "A double date? For real? I *beeeeen* saying that all term. That's so sweet! I was thinking about that after I saw you two sucking face." She pointed to TJ and Manny cheekily. Heat rushed through TJ's ears, and when he looked at Manny, she appeared no different.

"So," Titi asked, "what do you have planned?"

Ayo threw his arm over Titi's shoulder like it was his arm's natural home. With his free hand, he signed, "Babe, I no want ruin surprise. But got us big big invite."

Titi rocked her shoulders with excitement. "Oooh, is it John's thing? He said he finally got some palm wine from some clouded market! Wait, no, it's Fatima's watch party for the new Blood Moon movie, right? No! Don't tell me! I can wait!"

The group collectively relaxed, the tension dissipating like a held breath. TJ couldn't help but remember a similar situation from the previous year when Ayo had claimed the Nigerian Independence Day party he threw was "actually" for TJ's birthday—which Ayo had forgotten.

TJ and Manny fell back a few steps behind Ayo and Titi, whispering to each other as they walked through the night village. The UCMP official with the crooked back and their partner fell in step with them.

"How are we going to bring Titi along without her realizing what we're *actually* up to?" TJ asked.

Manny shrugged, her thick eyebrow scrunching. "I don't know. I wish we could sign to Ayo like we usually do in classes around people who don't."

"I guess we'll just have to go along with it for now."

"We'll figure something out," Manny reassured him, though her tone betrayed her own uncertainty. "Maybe we can distract her with a factoid about statistics. Something about the dangers of teen fornication or... nah, that ain't finna work..."

They continued to brainstorm as they walked through the night village. The streets bustled with activity despite the late hour. They passed The Walking Stick staff store, where a crowd had gathered around a display of glittering crystals, each promising to enhance a different magical affinity. A potion shop next door advertised a two-for-one deal on love elixirs, the pink bottles frothing in the moonlight. The sound of raucous laughter drew TJ's attention to an open bar, where patrons crowded around a screen showing an MCA—Mystical Combat Arena—match. The duel was between a wizard with a wand thrashing a shapeshifting boar with spells that bounced off the animal hide like nothing. Some of the customers had clearly had too much to drink, their cheers and shouts growing louder with each traded blow. TJ even thought he saw some of the "elder" students from Ifa Academy who suffered from CDS among the group. A few of them turned and TJ saw the distinct recognition filling their eyes when their laggard gazes caught his. Before they could talk to him about Eko Atlantic, he covered his face and speed-walked away.

As they reached the outskirts of the village, TJ turned to Ayo. "Hey, Ayo," TJ called out, keeping his voice casual. "Hey, buddy-ol-pal. How are we going to get to this 'special place' for the date, anyway?"

Ayo grinned, his hands moving in a flurry of signs. "Good thing you ask." He gestured to a sleek, yellow-gold Tesla Model X waiting for them just outside the village gates.

TJ did a double-take, his eyes widening as he took in the luxury car. The tinted windows gleamed, and the custom headlights cast a soft baby blue glow on the bushes along the dirt road. But it was the license plate that caught TJ's attention:

OSN-515

"OSN" for Oshun; "5" and "15" for Oshun's sacred numbers.

There was only one person the car could belong to.

Eniola. Eni.

TJ's ex-girlfriend.

As if on cue, the driver's side falcon wing door opened up, and Eni stepped out, flipping her long braids, looking like a model straight out of an Afrobeat music video. Her outfit was chic and fashionable, dominated by shades of yellow and gold that perfectly complemented her dark skin. TJ's gaze was drawn to her long, unblemished neck, a feature he remembered all too well from their... extracurricular time together.

Eni was an SS3 student, two years ahead of him, which meant

he rarely saw her outside of SS Ere Idaraya training. He made a point to avoid her, given their history, more so now because of his current relationship with Manny.

Lost in thought, TJ didn't realize he had been staring until Manny's hand slipped into his, her fingers intertwining with his own. He glanced down at their joined hands, wondering if Manny had noticed his lingering gaze on Eni.

Eni, for her part, didn't seem to miss the gesture. Her eyes flicked down to their interlocked fingers, lingering just a moment too long before she looked Manny up and down, her expression unreadable.

A perfect model's blank stare.

Ayo stepped between the group, his hands held up in a placating gesture as he seemingly sensed the tension brewing. He clapped his hands together, drawing everyone's attention to him. "Okay, okay, I know I no explain everything to everyone. But I promise, all make sense when we in car. Trust me. Trust me." He turned to Titi, his expression sheepish. "I sorry for no telling the plan, babe. I just want surprise."

"Um, so what did he say?" Eni asked the group.

Titi was the one to answer, still staring lovingly at Ayo. "Oh, nothing. He just said this will be the start of a very lovely evening." She squealed and did a little jump. "It's going to be amazing!"

Ayo, looking a bit embarrassed with a hesitant giggle, ushered Titi toward the car, opening the fly-up door for her with an exaggerated butler's flourish. As she climbed in, chattering excitedly about the possibilities of their destination, TJ's unease grew.

The Veiled Caravan, which had been his primary focus just moments ago, now seemed to drop lower on his list of concerns. Between his current girlfriend and his *very* recent ex, TJ found himself in an uncomfortable predicament.

As they approached the car, TJ couldn't help but dread the impending journey. It was going to be awkward, dreadful, or both.

*Likely both*, he thought to himself, stomach twisting inside out.

Manny squeezed his hand, drawing his attention back to her. She leaned in close to say, "You okay? You look a li'l purple."

TJ forced a smile, not wanting to worry her as he ducked under the fly-up door, making sure his staff didn't scuff any surface of the luxury car.

"Me?" TJ muttered back. "Purple? Nah... I mean... Y-yeah, I'm fine. Just... a lot on my mind, you know? Veiled Caravan. Ogun's Cabinet."

Manny nodded, her expression understanding. "We'll be all right. Now let's get out of here."

TJ SAT IN THE BACK OF THE SLEEK TESLA MODEL X, HIS HAND still firmly grasped by Manny, who seemed to refuse to let it go in the vicinity of Eni. The car ride was quiet, save for the low-level vaporwave tunes playing through the speakers. TJ couldn't help but notice Eni's unique taste in music, something he hadn't picked up on during their time together.

Eni and Ayo sat in the front, while TJ, Manny, and Titi occupied the back. The silence was palpable, broken only by the occasional excited whisper from Titi, who seemed oblivious to the tension.

Eventually, Eni spoke up. "Sorry I couldn't portal transfer you guys this time. After what happened to John, I decided to cool it on that until I *fully* master it. Plus, where we're going is only an hour away, so it ain't no thang for me to drive."

"Oh, poor John..." Titi murmured. "You know, Chrono Displacement Syndrome only affects ten-percent of the diviner community when overusing portal travel at 150% capacity. You'd probably be okay, Eni. The reason John aged up like he did is because of the pressure. But I understand the fear. To lose all those years of your life. It must be terrible, oh?" Ayo's hands moved in a flurry of signs, the tattoo below his eye twitching with the smirk on his face. Titi translated, "Ayo says you're just trying to show off your new license now that you're eighteen and old enough to drive."

Eni sucked her teeth long and hard, reaching over to smack Ayo on the shoulder, making the car jerk. "Stop making me look conceited, or I'll rethink driving you and your friends. Damn, I hate when I owe you favors."

Ayo laughed, throwing up the one sign Eni seemed to understand.

"Hah. Hah," Eni said. "I love you too, I guess."

Under her breath, Manny said, "Watch the road, prima donna."

"What's that?" Eni asked, looking through the rearview mirror.

"Oh nothing," Manny said, "Just a little comment about the painted lines on the road, and how it's so nice how they're there to keep everyone's cars in order."

Another awkward silence settled over the car. TJ squeezed Manny's hand and murmured, "Play nice. We need the ride tonight."

Manny cleared her throat, putting on a friendlier tone. "So, um... Eni, you're eighteen, then? How does it feel? You goin' to university next year?"

"I'm thinking of taking a year off to travel before sorting that out," Eni replied as a huge cargo truck passed by them, briefly filling the car with light. "But I'm eyeing the Institute of All Magicks in the UK after that. We'll see." She chuckled. "Guess you'll have TJ all to yourself then, Manuela."

Manny squeezed TJ's hand again, cringing at the use of her full name. Her hard Brooklyn tone came out sharp, almost all of that previous friendliness gone. "What's that supposed to mean?"

Eni threw up a hand in apology. "Sorry, sorry. My bad. Terrible joke."

Eni's other hand tightened around her steering wheel. TJ remembered how she often made bad jokes when nervous—not unlike him. Before she could tell another to save face, he cleared his throat, turning to Ayo. "So, where exactly in *Ogun* State are we going?"

Ayo signed his response, which Titi translated for Eni's benefit. "Ayo says the secret surprise is just outside a small village named Lumogo."

Polite small talk filled the rest of the journey, punctuated by several arguments between Ayo and Eni, and occasional bursts of excitement from Titi when she saw a landmark. TJ tried to focus his mind on the mission, on Ogun, and on the Veiled Caravan, but he couldn't help noticing the frequent looks traded between Eni and Manny in the rearview mirror.

# 40

# THE VEILED CARAVAN

After an hour of driving across shadowy highways, TJ stepped out of Eni's car, his feet crunching on the gravel of a desolate village that appeared almost forgotten. TJ wasn't even sure the place was occupied since none of the homes had lights on. Then he remembered the Nigerian government sometimes had light curfews, leaving its citizens in darkness unless they had generators. Still, the night air was thick with an eerie stillness, broken only by the distant hoot of an owl.

Manny and Ayo joined him, their faces illuminated by the pale moonlight filtering through the wispy clouds. Eni and Titi sat silently in the car, brows furrowed and lips parted slightly as they leaned forward, straining to decipher Ayo's flurry of signs.

"We just need to check something real quick," Ayo signed. Titi translated Ayo's gestures for Eni. "Won't be more than few minutes. You two stay here and keep the car running, eh?"

Eni sucked her teeth. "Boy, you better not be telling me you had me come *way the hell out here* to be a getaway driver."

Ayo ignored her, saying out loud, "J-J-Just a few m-m-minutes."

Tension coiled in TJ's core as Titi's gaze flickered sharply between them, her gaze darting between him, Manny, and Ayo. He could almost see the gears turning in her head, piecing together their secretive behavior and hushed conversations.

"Wait. A. Minute," Titi said "You're not just 'checking something,' are you? This is some kind of mission. Like that time y'all used me and Emeka for that golden chain!"

Ayo's shoulders caved in. "Fine. We look for something. It's important."

"We couldn't tell you even if we wanted to," Manny added.

"Tongue-tied trance?" Eni asked.

They all nodded. It wasn't true for TJ, who could still speak freely, but he wasn't about to confess that.

Titi rolled her eyes. "And you didn't think to have *actual* backup? Not even look outs? Child of Shango, ugh." She sucked her teeth, shaking her head in disbelief.

A flush of embarrassment rang in TJ's ears. They hadn't considered lookouts, too focused on just getting there undetected.

"We can be back up." Titi gestured to herself and Eni, seeming eager to contribute and be useful. "Happy to do it. You didn't see us with TJ and Manny against that wave. We got skills."

"Whatever you're doing," Eni said, "it's probably meant to be secret. But I need to know something." She fixed TJ with an intense stare. "On a scale where Eko Atlantic is an eleven, how bad is what you're doing tonight?"

TJ went dry, trying not to let that nightmare seep into his mind right now. He didn't need an anxiety attack when they were headed into potential Keeper territory. Before he could formulate a response, Ayo answered.

"No more than a two," he signed, and Titi translated. "Maybe three. It's an in and out thing. For real, for real."

TJ nodded in agreement, hoping his face didn't betray the nervousness gnawing at his insides. This was all Ayo's fault; they shouldn't have brought the two along to begin with.

Eni rolled her eyes, paired with another sucking of her teeth. Titi fidgeted in her seat before saying, "This place is hella sus."

"Hella?" TJ laughed. "You been hangin' around me *too much*."

Ayo flashed her a charming smile. "No wahala, beautiful. Night still young. We back quick quick. Then I take you out somewhere real nice. Trust me."

It wasn't lost on TJ that Ayo's signing was a lot more fluent with his sweet talking, and TJ didn't have to wonder why when Titi faux-pouted and gave Ayo a kiss on the cheek.

With that, TJ, Manny, and Ayo turned toward the dense forest that loomed ahead—just outside the village, an unsettling fog creeping out from between the trees. TJ gripped the staff hanging from his backpack, pulling it out. It was time to put it to the test. Already the channeling of his Ashe was made easier by simply holding the wood in his palms. The connection was even sharper than when he had used his sister's old staff at camp.

They walked for another few minutes before Ayo held them back with a hand, hiding behind one of the village buildings as several groups of shady-looking diviners came out of the fog. Ayo checked his watch, then signed, "Almost 11:59 p.m., that's our time to get in."

"How do we know if everyone actually leaves the caravan?" TJ asked.

"We hope Jimoh's info is right. He say everyone leave before midnight."

After a while, Ayo's phone beeped, signaling that it was time. For the past few minutes, no other diviners had left the fog; they could only hope the coast was clear.

As they approached the treeline, whispers, sibilant and eerie, wormed into TJ's ears. He blinked and Ashe revealed itself to him. A huge barrier hiding itself in the fog. He glanced at Ayo, who seemed to hear the whispers as well, his eyes darting nervously around the forest.

"You hear that?" TJ asked, his voice low.

Ayo nodded, signing sharply. "Yeah."

"Hear what?" Manny asked, failing to hide the nervousness in her voice.

"Must be because me have password," Ayo signed. "TJ Ashe pick up on it too."

Manny shivered as she adjusted the strap of her overweight backpack, her free hand reaching for her phone. "Yo, this is mad creepy. Maybe we should call Elder Adeyemi for backup? I mean, we're already here and everything."

"No, we can't risk it." TJ shook his head, placing a comforting hand on Manny's shoulder. "They'll come stop us, and we'll lose our chance to get at the cabinet."

"TJ's right," Ayo agreed. "We do this. Only us. Only way."

Manny took a deep breath, steeling herself. "A'ight then... lead the way, Mr. Password."

With that, the trio ventured forward. The fog enveloped them, thick and clinging like a damp shroud. The air grew cooler, the murky silence punctuated by a chorus of whispers that seemed to seep from the very mist around them. With each step deeper into the shadowy heart of the forest, the whispers swelled, morphing into a cacophony of indistinct murmurs that seemed to come from nowhere and everywhere at once. The ground beneath their feet became increasingly spongy, absorbing their footfalls, as if the earth itself was attempting to silence their passage. Overhead, the branches twisted together in gnarled arches, blotting out the feeble moonlight. Were there unseen watchers lurking in the gloom?

Ayo stepped ahead of them, his hands moving in a series of intricate signs, attempting to convey the password phrase through YSL. But the fog remained thick, and the whispers only grew louder, their breathy voices weaving together into a chorus that set TJ's teeth on edge.

Ayo's face contorted as he signed to his friends, his movements becoming more frantic with each passing second. "I no understand why it no work!"

"Maybe the password chant needs to be spoken out loud?" Manny suggested feebly, her voice cutting through the eerie whispers.

Ayo's eyes widened, and he said back nervously, "I c-c-can't say that m-m-many words w-w-w—" He scowled but finished, "without st-st-stuttering."

"Come on, bruh," TJ said. "I believe in you. This ain't nothin'. Here, I don't know if it'll work but I'll try to boost you. Maybe jog your voice a little."

Despite his hesitation, Ayo took a deep breath and began to speak in Old Yoruba, his words coming out in a halting, stuttered cadence. But the fog remained unmoved, and the whispers only grew louder, their voices now a deafening roar in TJ's ears.

"We can't say the password for him?" Manny asked.

"Nah, Ayo told me it don't work like that." TJ lifted his voice. "Jimoh gave the password to him, so he has to do it. Ayo, try to focus on the words! Don't let the whispers distract you." But the relentless mutterings drowned out his own voice, and he could barely even hear himself.

Manny, seemingly unaffected by the whispers, called out to Ayo, "Maybe use your telepathy to say the spell phrase!?"

Ayo visibly gulped. TJ knew what his friend was thinking—he wasn't ready for telepathy. He had barely mastered communicating with animals and was still a long way from human communication. But perhaps speaking to the whispers would be easier?

TJ lifted his staff, the head crystal already pulsating with the cadence of his breath. He focused his Ashe-boosting on Ayo, trying to help his friend form the words in his mind. TJ still didn't think it would work, but it was worth the try. Ayo was struggling, the weight of the task bearing down on him like a physical force, and now on TJ too. It didn't help that the whispers grew louder still. TJ gritted his teeth, pouring all of his spirit into helping his friend. Ayo seemed to struggle to form the words in his mind, his face scrunched tight with the effort.

The sounds became too much, and TJ thought he might actually go deaf as he dropped to his knees. He clutched his ears in pain as he dropped his staff.

And then, everything went quiet.

TJ looked up. Ayo was performing a concise ritual, his chants resonating through the mist and echoing in TJ's mind. *Ìṣúra àṣírí, ẹnu ìṣúra, ṣí fún mi, ẹnu àṣírí, ṣí fún mi, ẹnu òkùnkùn, ṣí fún mi.*

As Ayo's final thought-spoken words dissipated into the chill air, the dense fog mysteriously parted like a curtain, ushering them into the clearing of the Veiled Caravan. Bathed in an eerie moonlight, the clearing revealed itself to be a spectral tableau: Ghostly caravans, seemingly abandoned, huddled together in a tight circle as if conspiring in silence. Each cart, draped in tattered and ethereal coverings, appeared to quiver slightly, as though breathing in the cold night air.

It looked like everyone had closed up shop for the day, just as Ayo had said would be the case. So that was good. There were no other patrons or shop owners, though there were pieces of trash here and there.

It almost felt too easy.

Turning to check on his friends, TJ found Ayo hunched over, rubbing his temple vigorously. A pool of blood glistened on the dirt in front of him. Worry gripped TJ's heart. Had one of the whispers attacked Ayo? Or had Jimoh given him a false password, causing the Veiled Caravan's security to curse him?

TJ rushed to his friend's side, pulling him up. Thankfully, it was only Ayo's nose that was bleeding, though heavily. Very heavily. That successful use of telepathy had taken a lot out of him. Manny quickly pulled out a bubbling green potion from her backpack and forced it up Ayo's nose. She and Freya had brewed it together. It was supposed to be some special druid recipe. The potion worked its magic quickly, the bubbles fizzing and popping as they made contact with Ayo's skin. A faint green glow emanated from his nostrils, and then the bleeding stopped.

Manny kissed the empty vial in her hand. "Thank you, Freya!"

"Good freaking work, Ayo," TJ said, patting him on the back lightly. "Good shit, my guy. I'm proud of you."

"T-T-Thanks, Teej," Ayo breathed out heavily. "I a-a-appreciate you."

"That'll only work for a few hours," Manny told Ayo, bottling the potion and stuffing it into her backpack again. "We'll need to visit the Hospital Tree to get one of the healers to *really* fix it up."

Ayo signed his thanks to his friends, apologizing for the struggle they had just endured with the fog.

"Don't trip about it, man," TJ said. "You did more than good. We're just glad you're okay."

TJ and Manny helped Ayo to his feet, gathering the Ogun offerings that had fallen out of his backpack. Ayo strapped the backpack on again and surveyed their surroundings as TJ went to retrieve his staff from the ground.

"Damn," Ayo signed, wiping his nose clean of blood. "This place got c-c-corrupt. Sure, it was always about b-b-black market stuff, but it was c-c-chill, you know? Now it's different. D-d-dominated by Keepers."

Long, twisted shadows danced across the ground under the pale light of the moon. A whispering wind carried faint, dissonant melodies, as if the caravans themselves murmured forgotten tales. Thick with an unspoken warning. Whatever lay within wasn't just abandoned—it was left to be forgotten, and perhaps for good reason.

"You sure you good to go, Ayo?" Manny asked.

Ayo's expression sharpened. "Y-y-eah, I'm good. I gotta c-c-carve that ancestral path to S-S-Shango one way or another, and t-t-this is our best shot. We good though. That was h-h-half the battle. The rest s-s-should be easier."

"A'ight, then, big shot," Manny said. "Don't jinx it. Watch, now it's gonna be ten times harder."

TJ, Manny, and Ayo crept stealthily toward Jimoh's family caravan, their footsteps muffled by the soft earth beneath their feet. As they approached the cart, TJ couldn't help but notice the bone-white wood that made up its exterior, reminding him of the eerie jungle outside of Thornriver Correctional. The sign etched into the entrance read:

*Oladipo's Oddities*

THE LETTERS WERE SEEMINGLY CARVED BY A SHAKY HAND, spelled out with rough and wavy lines. Small steps led up to the entrance, and TJ held his breath when he grabbed the door handle and pushed.

There was no resistance. No lock. Was that normal?

Ayo, seeming to know what was on TJ's mind, signed, "Our lucky day?"

Once inside, the group marveled at the impossibly vast scale that defied the caravan's modest exterior. The shop extended deep and wide, stretching seemingly endlessly, lined with ancient artifacts of Sub-Saharan African origin. Each shelf and table was cluttered with an array of mystical items: carved Nkisi figures with mirrored eyes, potent for protection; intricately beaded Yoruba divination chains used in Ifa which TJ was already familiar with; and Zulu lust potions contained in delicate gourds.

"Yo, this place is *mad* sketchy," Manny whispered, her eyes wide as she took in the chaotic array of relics.

Ayo nodded, signing, "Finding cabinet in this mess going to be challenge. And who knows what traps they set here?"

TJ frowned, his gaze sweeping over the maze of a shop. "We'll have to be extra careful. Stay alert and watch your step."

As if on cue, Manny's foot caught on a nearly invisible tripwire, and she stumbled forward. TJ's heart leaped into his throat as a glowing *adinkra* symbol flared to life on the floor beneath her. Acting on instinct, TJ lunged forward and yanked Manny back just as a shimmering net of energy sprang up from the sigil, narrowly missing her.

"Phew, that was close," Manny breathed, her face pale. "Thanks, Teej."

TJ nodded curtly, nervous heat still coursing through him. "What are boyfriends for?" Ayo gagged but TJ ignored him. "Let's just be more careful from here on out."

Taking the lead, TJ focused his Ashe-sensing abilities, intertwining them with the power of Oshosi's Psychometry. He moved slowly through a maze of wooden statues that look similar to the sentries from Camp Olosa. His senses attuned to the subtle energies that permeated the space. At one point, a tingle of warning prickled on his neck, and he stopped short, holding up a hand to halt his friends. A pressure plate lay hidden beneath a tattered rug, waiting to trigger some unseen trap. When TJ sensed it, he saw a man with long dreadlocks and a thick beard he recognized. The man who set the trap. The same man who had helped kidnap him last year.

Being careful of their steps, they slowly skirted around the trigger, holding their breath until they were safely past.

Twice more, TJ's heightened perception allowed them to avoid traps—a hidden switch that would have sent a cascade of cursed skulls tumbling down upon them, and a nearly invisible glyph that pulsed with dark energy. Finally, as they neared the back of the shop, TJ's senses locked onto a cabinet that seemed to call out to him.

The cabinet was intricately designed, with patterns of leaves and vines carved into its dark wood. It was sandwiched between a sinister-looking mirror that seemed to absorb light rather than reflect it and a twisted sculpture of a kishi taxidermy. Yet despite its unassuming position, TJ knew without a doubt that this was Ogun's Sacred Cabinet.

He knew it *for sure* when he touched it.

Like when he touched the doll at Emeka's memorial, or when he brushed against Grandma's picture on her desk, he was flung into a sharp vision. Shadow enveloped his view, clearing slowly to reveal three female figures. One was a younger Adeola, now with braided hair on one side and the other side shaved. The second was a still-alive Jessica with her long hair pulled back in a bun. Last was Dayo with her free-form Afro bringing up the rear.

*"What if Oladipo finds us?"* Jessica said, voice shaky.

Adeola sucked her teeth. *"Dayo, I told you we should have left her behind. She's always complainin' about something."*

*"Enough, you two,"* Dayo silenced them. *"The Keepers are getting too close to crossing over. We need to store the cabinet here. Keep everyone safe from the void."*

*"What void?"* Adeola said bitterly. *"What does that even mean?"*

*"I told you already, I don't know. But when has my gut ever led us astray?"*

Jessica whipped her head around, peering into the shadows. *"What was that? Is someone here?"*

*"Deola, Jessie, go,"* Dayo said as more commotion rose behind them in the darkness. *"I'll hide the cabinet. Go now!"*

Adeola was reluctant, but she stepped away, grabbing Jessie by the shoulder and heaving her back into the shadows. Dayo stared straight out, straight toward TJ, as she lifted her staff. Was TJ's point of view from the cabinet? It had to be. Suddenly, Dayo stopped for a moment, staring straight at the assumed cabinet. But when TJ examined her gaze further, he realized she was looking directly at him.

*"I remember this..."* a voice said. Dayo? Or someone else? He couldn't tell.

Everything in TJ hit pause. His brain, his heart, the blood flowing through his very veins. He did *not* imagine that. This wasn't like the other times, not like the mirror in the hospital or Dayo's face in the tablet screen. This was a true connection. But when TJ tried to call back, he had no voice to speak with. In fact, he had no mouth at all. He tried moving it but only felt wood. He was right. He *was* the cabinet.

Then, suddenly, a slap came across his face.

The shadows disappeared, Dayo's perplexed face drifted away, and the Oladipo shop manifested before him again. Back to reality. Just ahead of him was Manny, with her hand held back, ready for another slap.

"Wait, wait, wait!" TJ shouted.

Manny stopped herself, looking relieved. "Sorry, sorry! You was mumblin' that you were remembering something, and we thought you was possessed."

"D-d-damn, Manny!" Ayo said from behind her. "L-l-look what you did to his f-f-face!"

The soreness on TJ's left cheek flared, and he rubbed it to soothe the pain. "Ouch."

"Sorry, sorry, sorry," Manny said, kissing his cheek, which only made it worse. "Is the cabinet cursed? What did you see?"

TJ took a moment to catch his breath. "I saw Dayo, and… and I *think* she saw me."

# 41

# THE LORD OF IRON

THE DIM LIGHT OF THE DUSTY SHOP CAST LONG SHADOWS OVER the cluttered book cases. Each shelf was filled with ancient artifacts, some tattered, others broken… all of them hella creepy. TJ, Manny, and Ayo stood among the stacked relics, their faces illuminated by the flickering light of a single crystal lamp overhead.

"Guys, this was different," TJ whispered, his voice echoing slightly off the walls as Ayo handed him his staff—he must have dropped it when he touched the cabinet. "When I saw Dayo this time, it wasn't like before. She... she saw me, too. It felt like she was right there with me."

Manny's face went flush. "What did she say?"

"It was just three words, but it was like she was right there, not just an echo. She said, 'I remember this.' Or maybe I said that. I don't know. My visions of her have all been weird lately. But she never told me about that… about a cabinet or anything… she never…" TJ turned back to the cabinet, half expecting to see Dayo there or to sense her. But there was nothing. Just the flush wood and the carved designs of iron links and cauldrons. "She was afraid of this cabinet. Afraid of the void it would bring." TJ's hands trembled as he recounted the vision. His hands moved despite him *not* willing them with Oya's Wind.

Ayo, who had been quietly listening, rubbed his chin thoughtfully. Then he signed, "A nothing space? That sound like the…" He couldn't find the word so he said out loud, "G-G-God Eaters we been w-w-warned about." He went back to signing. "Maybe Dayo sense the danger of them, not danger of cabinet."

Manny paced a few steps, chewing on her lip. "But what if it's more than that? What if the cabinet itself is a risk? We can't just ignore a warning from Dayo, even if she was speaking from the past."

"I don't think she was warning us," TJ said. "But you're right. What if this is a direct path to the End Realm or the Court of All instead of a path we can use for Ayo through Ogun?" No, that didn't feel correct. "We gotta remember that Dayo didn't know everything. Not what we know now. She might have sensed the threat without understanding it fully. Remember, we're not crossing over, just communing. If we try to leap realms, the Court of All would be right on top of us, never mind the God Eaters."

Each of them dropped their heads, working through their thoughts. At least, that's what TJ was doing.

"Hey, TJ?" Manny asked.

"Yeah?"

"Um... in your vision... was anyone with Dayo? Anyone like..."

"Yeah... Jessie was there." How could she not ask about her late cousin? "But it was only for a minute. She was really scared trying to hide the cabinet. Deola was there too. She wasn't being too nice."

"Got it..." Manny trailed off.

After another long pause, Ayo finally signed again, his gestures firm yet cautious. "I think we try it. We strong now, more knowing than Dayo. We know about the," he switched to speech, "G-G-God Eaters," then back to signing. "And we learn how to be safe."

"TJ," Manny said, "you got the clearest connection to all this. It's your call."

TJ met her gaze, then glanced toward the cabinet, its weaving symbols seeming to pulse faintly in the lamplight. "Let's do it. We'll be careful, use everything we've learned. We can't let fear stop us. This," TJ pointed to the cabinet, "this is it right here. No doubt. So now what?"

He turned to Ayo, who signed, "Now we create ritual space for Ogun."

TJ, Manny, and Ayo began to set up the area in worship of Ogun, carefully arranging the offerings they had brought. Manny placed a beautifully crafted iron hammer and a set of intricate metalworking tools on one side of the space, while Ayo contributed a bundle of medicinal herbs and a small clay pot filled with palm oil. TJ reached into his own backpack, pulling out a bottle of gin he got thanks to John. Then he drew out a plate of roasted yams they had wrapped up. He placed them alongside the other items, forming a semicircle around the central point where they would place the Ọpọn Ifá. Manny tossed a collection of kola nuts into it. As they worked, the trio fell into a focused silence, and, after a few minutes, they had their entire setup complete.

TJ couldn't help but chuckle as he surveyed their handiwork, trying to break up the tension. "All we're missing is a ouija board."

The eerie atmosphere of the shop seemed to swallow his attempt at humor. Despite the unease, the group was satisfied with their work. They exchanged a few words, double-checking that everything was in place before they began.

TJ focused his Ashe boosting, lifting his staff overhead, pouring his energy into a chant, hoping to elevate it beyond an ordinary prayer and catch Ogun's attention.

*Oh, Mighty Ogun, Orisha of Iron and the Forge,*
*Protector of the path, warrior fierce and bold,*
*Your strength unmatched, your resolve unyielding,*
*We call upon you with respect and reverence.*

As the final words of the prayer faded, TJ actively felt a pull toward the Orisha, and it linked perfectly with the cabinet. To finish off the chant with a flourish, he twisted his staff and employed Ogun's Ground Pulse technique. This time when he finished, the ground didn't crack and sprout a tree root. Instead, an earthly rumble rang out and shook the artifacts around them.

*Ogun, we thank you for your protection and guidance,*
*May our actions reflect the strength and fairness you embody,*
*As we move forward, keep us safe, keep us strong,*
*Oh, Ogun, we honor you today and always.*

*Ashe.*

There was a brief beat before Manny spoke up, "Was that enough? Did that do it?"

"I think so," TJ said, still enveloped by the Ashe they had stirred up.

"Only one way to find out," Ayo signed, then pulled the doors to the cabinet open.

It creaked, a stale odor wafting from its interior. Manny stepped in first, followed by TJ. Ayo was last, closing the door behind them. They waited in the dark, their breaths the only sound in the confined space.

Seconds turned into minutes. The Ashe roiling in TJ's belly did not cease, yet nothing changed in the dark space. None of them dared to speak, not wanting to ruin whatever spirit they'd built up before. But after five *long* minutes, TJ wondered if it was all for nothing. After all, Ogun was one of the most reclusive Orishas—according to his studies. He wasn't as lively as an Oya or Shango, keeping mostly to himself.

When another five minutes passed, TJ's phone buzzed in his pocket, making him jump and hit his head on the top of the cabinet.

"Ow!" he grunted.

"You all right?" Manny asked.

"Yeah, yeah, fine," TJ said, lifting his phone to his ear. "Hello?"

"*Y'all okay in there?*" It was Eniola. "*It's been a minute.*"

"Yeah, yeah. Just keep your eyes peeled for anything. We'll call you right back."

"*All right. Be careful.*"

TJ hung up the phone as Manny said, "Well, if the ritual wasn't already ruined, that's definitely gonna do it."

TJ's shoulders slumped. He guessed it didn't work after all. TJ was near to calling the whole thing off, but something in the air changed. A small leaf sprouted between TJ's legs.

"S-S-Shango's Axe!" Ayo stuttered. "Y'all s-s-see this?"

The single leaf quickly expanded, replicating over and over in a green hue that lit the dark space.

"What is that?" Manny asked. "Where's it coming from?"

Leaf after leaf manifested at their feet until they collectively made an entire forest floor. The cabinet's interior brightened into a mystical landscape with the features of the Terra Realm, complete with a distant cave. Its far-off interior flickered with an inviting orange light from within.

A flicker of memory surfaced. This was Orun—he, TJ, had seen it before, with Oshosi. Then… panic gripped his heart, and he turned to his friends, his voice urgent. "This is the Terra Realm! Themis and the Court of All will know I've crossed over into an Orisha Plane! We have to go back! We have to go back now!"

But Ayo, ever the voice of reason, signed calmly, explaining that they should be safe. He walked forward, demonstrating by hitting an invisible edge, his movements precise and controlled, almost like a professional mime. "Nah, we good, Teej. See? We still inside cabinet. Sort of. No crossover, just normal talk with Orisha."

TJ's nerves settled slightly, though his heart still thumped lightly in his chest. When he pulled his collar to see his birthmark, his heart stopped its drumline entirely. There was no glow there. So Ayo was right about them not really being in Orun or any other ethereal space.

Manny's sudden gasp drew his attention, and she pointed toward the cave entrance ahead. "Look!"

From within the cave, a giant figure emerged, riding upon a spotted hyena just as large. It was Ogun himself. His dark skin glistened like polished iron, and he wore simple, durable clothing of green, black, and red. His outfit was adorned with a utility belt bearing an array of high and low-tech tools that blended his domains of iron and technology. A power drill hung next to a shotel; a hefty strapping tool next to a rough machete. Ogun's hair was styled in dreadlocks on top, with shaved sides.

"*Who summoned me?*" Ogun said, his voice quieter than what TJ had expected it to be. But not weak. It was stable and strong, though it was slightly distorted by the realm barrier between them. "*I've not heard a call that strong in many ages.*"

TJ raised his hand. "That'd be me, oh Great Orisha, Lord of Iron, Father of Technology." He prostrated himself, his elbows hitting the sides of the invisible cabinet walls. Ayo and Manny mirrored TJ's gesture, though it was awkward with the lack of space.

"Y'all can hear him too, right?" TJ murmured to his friends. "This isn't just a 'me' thing?"

"This isn't just a 'you' thing," Manny said back, her head so low that her hair brushed along the ground. "The cabinet and your boosting must be helping with that."

*"Ah,"* Ogun intoned. *"You must be that mortal boy I've heard whispers about. Tomori Jomiloju, yes?"*

"Y-Yes, Great One."

*"It's been quite some time since I've given a mortal the time of day. Be brief. I've work to get back to. What is it you seek?"*

Ayo stepped forward but forgot a wall blocked him, his hands raised to begin signing. However, he hesitated, uncertainty clouding his features as he glanced between his hands and Ogun.

*"Fear not, young mortal. I was once close with Oshosi, who loved his hand gestures. I am happy to see that the Hunter's exercise bore fruit for the mortals beyond a silent means to stalk gazelle. I* can *understand you."*

Relief washed over Ayo's face, and he signed with renewed confidence. "Great Ogun, Oshosi is reason we here today. The Court of All charge Shango and Oya with The Channeling, and blame Shango for the death of Thor. My friend here," he nodded to Manny who still hadn't picked her jaw up from off the floor, "already creates her ancestral path to reach Oya with Yemoja. Now, we need your help to create path to Shango. Since, you know, I have halfway aligning with you, and this only work through our… um birth line… um… no… line of elders. Dead elders."

With a determined look in his eyes, Ayo pulled off his copper ring etched with the lightning rune. "Thor give me this ring. I believe meant for this—to connect again with Shango and free him from Court, to use ring to travel me into Shango."

Ogun considered Ayo's words, his gaze fixed on the ring. He had an odd way of moving, and he hardly made eye contact with them as he spoke. Finally, after what felt like an eternity, Ogun leaned down and whispered something to his hyena companion. The beast responded with a cooing howl, its eyes gleaming with an otherworldly intelligence.

Ogun looked upon the ring pensively. *"Copper. I usually prefer working with iron or steel. Copper is too malleable for my hands."*

TJ, Manny, and Ayo exchanged worried glances.

*"That tattoo by your eye,"* he said to Ayo, his eyeline just away from a proper stare. *"It is intriguing. Asgardian?"*

Ayo's hand instinctively went to his eye, tracing the simple design of the archway. Ogun hummed under his lips, deep and low. TJ recalled from his classes that Ogun did indeed favor tattoos as a quality in his divine children. It seemed Ayo's unique marking had caught the Orisha's attention in a favorable way. Good, they needed every advantage they could get here.

*"I will infuse the ring on one condition,"* Ogun said. *"You must pledge to me, as I sense you have not done so since childhood."* He sniffed the air. *"Yes, I smell much of Shango on you."*

Ayo rubbed at the edge of his glasses. "That my Baba's fault. He calls us 'truebloods...'"

*"I see, and I take it that... he would not be happy with you bowing to my offered power?"*

Ayo dropped his head, still signing. "No. He not like that. But..." He lifted his head. "I promise I make pledge to you, Ogun, so we make path of elders that goes to Shango. To save Shango."

Ogun nodded, his locs falling over his shoulders. *"Before we continue, I must be candid, mortal. If you do this, your ties with Shango will diminish. Your use of fire and lightning will weaken, and you may never achieve the true heights of mastery with those elements. Do you understand this, what you're agreeing to?"*

Ayo dropped his head low again, fidgeting with the ring in his hand. What could he be thinking?

"And..." Ayo began to sign. "And... what I gain if I submit?"

*"Access to my insights and power of iron, craftsmanship, how to toil the earth to your uses, and most importantly, technological advancement and ingenuity. A jack-of-all-trades instead of a specialist. You may become more reclusive as I, but you will enjoy new breakthroughs with your Ashe."*

Ayo swallowed, still playing with the ring, rotating it around his finger so hard, TJ wouldn't be surprised if he was rubbing it red. That was a big ask. Ayo—perhaps at the behest of his father—was extremely proud of his ties to Shango. Not just that, but at being the best at what he did. And now Ogun was saying that his friend would essentially have to diminish his shine. It was a big ask for the kid.

*"Do not worry yourself too much. Shango and I align in more ways than one. Your aptitude for war, for resilience, for justice… those will multiply."*

A few more rotations of the ring and Ayo finally stopped, face depleted, a deep frown carved in his forehead. Then, slowly, he pulled the ring off, saying out loud, "I'm sure, Great One. I p-p-pledge myself to you. I will h-h-honor the Way of Iron from t-t-this day until I become one with the a-a-ancestors."

Ogun grunted low, satisfied with Ayo's promise. "*Push the ring through to my side,*" he ordered, gesturing to the invisible barrier between the realms.

Ayo looked to TJ for help, and TJ focused his boosting abilities, lending his strength. He was careful to ensure Ayo's skin didn't cross over, knowing the consequences that could bring. Still, a flicker of worry crossed TJ's mind, wondering if even this act would attract the attention of the Court.

Ogun took the ring and began a short ritual, his movements precise and powerful. He struck the ring with a hammer from his belt, sending sparks flying. The ring glowed with a mystical energy, absorbing Ogun's essence. When he was done, Ogun lifted the ring to the sun on his side, and TJ, through his Ashe Vision, saw another bridge forged between the ring and somewhere in the distance—another path to the Court of All, to Shango, he assumed.

Ogun sent the ring back, and TJ's nerves were on edge again, half-expecting Themis or Yamaraja on his giant bull to appear at any moment. Would Ogun's giant hyena be able to stand up to them?

But nothing happened. All seemed well.

Ayo took the ring in his hand and turned to TJ. "D-D-Did that work?"

"I-I think so." TJ poked at the ring. "Your path seems even easier than Manny's. Looks like you can transport straight through the ring. No need for a Frost Realm. But if you use it, I bet the Court of All will pick up on it faster. Who knows? We'll ask Elder Adeyemi."

Manny put up prayer hands. "Thank Thor for that."

Ayo dropped his head humbly and signed, "No, thank Ogun."

Ogun inclined his head gently.

"Of course!" TJ said, then turned his voice toward Ogun.

"Thank you, Great One. This is going to help a lot. Hey! Why don't you help us? Yemoja and Eshu are already working to get Shango back. We definitely could use you as well."

Ogun shook his head slowly. *"No, the Lost Monarch has tasked me with a great work. I have been toiling with it since The Great Separation. I must heed Their order above all else and may not assist in other labors until this one is complete. That much was made clear."*

"But you came to speak to us just now," Manny pointed out.

A low grunt left the Orisha's lips. *"Yes, well, it has been* many *ages since I've had a direct communion. And as I said, a call from this Tomori Jomiloju made me curious. Eshu speaks earnestly about your abilities, young one. I was intrigued to see you for myself. And that curiosity has been satiated."* He turned away before Ayo could sign a thanks. Manny was waving awkwardly as well.

"Well, that ending was a bit awkward," TJ said.

Manny watched as Ogun returned to his cave atop his hyena. "Definitely could use some work."

Ayo signed, "So the stories about Ogun really are true. He is a… um… social… inside social." He couldn't find the sign. "I-I-Introvert."

"Well…" TJ said. "That was way easier than the Frost Realm. Almost seemed too easy."

"Don't jinx it!" Manny bit out, halfway to smacking TJ. "We need a break at this point."

"C'mon, let's head out." TJ dove back into himself, seeking the Ashe that would turn the window into the Terra Realm back into the darkness of the cabinet. Quickly, the imagery around them dissolved into black, and they stepped out of the cabinet and back into the dingy shop.

Before TJ's eyes adjusted to the dark, Ayo said. "D-D-Dammit, TJ. You had to j-j-jinx it."

A group of Keepers in white robes and masks were gathered ahead of them. They stood, staggered between the tight confines of an Egyptian statue of Anubis and an Akan totem of Anansi. TJ's heart dropped, not just because they were cornered… but because the Keepers had Titi and Eni within their grasp, holding them as hostages.

"Hand over the ring," one of the masked Keepers demanded, her voice cold and threatening, "and no one gets hurt."

# 42

# THROUGH NOOKS AND CRANNIES

TJ'S BREATH CAME FAST, HIS CHEST TIGHT. HE GRIPPED HIS STAFF so hard he would've sworn the new wood was cracking. The spooky shop and all its ancient relics felt downright terrifying now that they were surrounded, outnumbered by the Keepers.

The men and women, clad in their stark white robes and eerie masks, encircled them like a poisonous mist. Eni and Titi winced. A Keeper each held their hands behind their backs as another pair leveled staff crystals to their necks. Their eyes shone bright with fear against the shadows. A sick feeling curled in TJ's stomach. How was he supposed to get them out of this?

He was stupid for not realizing it sooner. It had been too easy—getting into the caravan, finding the cabinet. The Keepers *wanted* them there. They had been waiting. But why?

"What did Ogun say?" the tallest of the Keepers with a crooked back asked curiously with that misty tone all of them seemed to get when talking about the Orishas.

"Like we'd tell you!" Manny threw back, wind spiraling around her arms already. Her eyes ping-ponged between the female Keeper before them and Titi, who she held onto tightly at the collar now.

A thinly-framed Keeper TJ didn't know spoke up next. "My son didn't know what you were up to. But considering you've activated Ogun's dead cabinet. We are most intrigued." That must've been Mr. Oladipo of Oladipo's Oddities. Jimoh's father.

TJ glanced at Ayo, who met his eyes. The same dawning realization—along with a heavy dose of frustration—was written all over his face.

The female Keeper in the middle, the one holding Eni hostage, said, "Our terms are simple. Give up the ring, or we'll see how bad I can ruin this precious model's face."

TJ recognized that voice. It belonged to Sister Bisi. The wretched woman that had killed Emeka. She didn't make threats lightly. TJ knew that firsthand. The old scar near his shoulder was a sharp reminder—the place where she had grazed him with a lightning bolt last year. The memory forced a reaction from him, and he lifted his staff in warning, the green light from the crystal head filling the space around them.

The large male near the front spoke next, his tone soft and smooth. "Put that away, boy, unless you intend to use it."

"Oh, I *intend* to use it," TJ said defiantly. With his staff in hand, he felt like he could take on the world, and he could already feel the Ashe stirring in his friends. If they could muster the same force as they did against Mirror Bolawe, he'd love to see these Keepers hold up against that.

"Be reasonable, and don't hurt yourself," the man said. "Lower that staff. And while you're at it, why don't you tell us where Bolawe has been hiding these past few months?"

TJ's insides tingled uneasily at that voice as he finally recognized it. That was Brother David. The man who had pretended to be a UCMP officer when he flew from New York to Nigeria last year. The one who kidnapped him for the Keepers' blood ritual. Dreadlocks fell from under his white mask.

Adeola had been telling the truth. Bolawe was no longer a Keeper.

Now it seemed like he was their enemy.

Sister Bisi sneered, showing her fanged teeth, seeming to welcome the challenge. "If that's how you want to play it, then so be it, boy." She turned to her cohorts. "We'll force them to tell us what we want and do away with them. Send them back to Bolawe in a box. See how that traitor likes it."

TJ, Manny, and Ayo exchanged worried glances. TJ knew their minds were doing barrel rolls and somersaults. The value of the ring was immense, but so were their own lives, the lives of their friends. They needed to stall for time, to find a way out.

"Tsk, tsk." Mr. Oladipo removed his mask, revealing a brown eye on one side and a cloudy one on the other. "You were always so sharp when we've broken bread together, Ayodeji. I was surprised you didn't sniff out Jimoh's ruse. Now I owe him a gift. Perhaps associating with this pretender," he angled his staff at TJ, "has removed a few brain cells from your precious head."

Ayo scowled deeply.

"Settle down," Manny murmured. "Don't listen to him."

Sister Bisi pressed her staff against Eni's neck. The staff crackled with lightning, causing a small wound on Eni's skin. Eni's eyes scrunched up, shoulders bunched even tighter. TJ jittered with anger. He would never forgive himself if Eni or Titi got hurt. He couldn't have another Emeka on his head. Manny and Ayo came voluntarily. The others were just dropped into all this mess.

Screams and cries forced their way into TJ's mind. Creaking metal. Tidal waves. People calling his name for help.

"I won't ask again," Sister Bisi warned, her voice as sharp as the bolts that danced along her staff.

Then, Ayo did something TJ didn't expect. He didn't lift his hands with balls of flame. He did not turn to run. Instead, he stepped forward, casually pulling out the ring. It gleamed faintly in the dim light as Ayo's lips twisted into a cocky grin. "Y-y-yeah, we saw Ogun. W-W-Who wants the power of an Orisha and an Asgardian?"

TJ blinked. *What are you doing, Ayo?*

Sister Bisi looked at the ring hungrily. "It's imbued with the magic of *two* deities?"

"T-t-that's right."

"What's wrong with his voice?" the tallest of the Keepers with the crooked back said. "Was he cursed by Ogun?"

"No, no," Brother Oladipo cut in. "My son told me he's got a stutter now."

Another Keeper near the back seemed less convinced. Before Ayo could respond, another woman with dark braided hair and an air of forced calm raised a hand. "Sister Bisi, we should be careful. That ring might not be what it seems."

"Olugbala, not Sister Bisi," Oladipo corrected, "don't forget yourself. She is our leader now, and you will address her as such."

"Forgive me." The Keeper receded back into the final line of the group. So Bisi had taken the moniker from Bolawe. The Keepers were already bad before. With her at the helm… he didn't want to know what violence they had gotten up to.

A faint tickle flicked in TJ's mind. It was Ayo, trying to send a telepathic message. The words came in fragments, like a choppy radio transmission. When TJ edged his eyes toward his friend, there was already a trail of blood leaking from Ayo's nose.

*TJ, boost,* Ayo managed to send. *Manny wind, Ayo throw.*

Sister Bisi gestured her hand harshly. "All right then, boy. Give it here."

"Wait!" Brother David halted. "Olugbala, look at his nose."

"He's bleeding!" another back-row Keeper said.

"The ring is cursed!" said another.

More commotion and debates rippled through the group. Lines were being drawn between the Keepers, and TJ saw it all through his Ashe Vision, his mind's eye splitting into its familiar prism. They were already splintering—falling apart without Bolawe to lead them.

Bisi's hand hovered dangerously close to Eni's throat, lightning sparking along the length of her staff.

Brother David, his voice steady but cold, said, "We need to handle this carefully. That ring—"

"Enough!" Bisi barked, her eyes locked on Ayo. "Give me the ring, boy."

Ayo's grin widened. "C-c-ome and get it."

With a quick flick of his wrist, he tossed the ring high into the air. TJ allowed Manny to use his Ashe to boost an airblast that sent it even farther. The copper band sailed over the heads of the Keepers, landing somewhere in the cluttered mess of the shop.

Pandemonium ensued. Bisi's group lunged for it, knocking over priceless relics in their frenzy to retrieve the ring. Egyptian spears clattered to the ground, followed by the crash of an Eshu sculpture shattering against the floor. In the chaos, TJ registered the meekest of the Keepers; those toward the back were less willing to go near the ring, while the more aggressive of the group wanted to grab it up first. The two groups crashed into each other like opposing waves. Between Keepers shouldering into each other and artifacts falling on top of their heads, their grips loosened on Titi and Eni.

Ayo exploded into action, creating a small combustion in the air. The sudden burst startled their captors further. Amid the confusion, TJ and Manny grabbed for Titi and Eni, dragging them away from the in-fighting of the Keepers.

"Are you okay?" TJ asked them, breath hitched. "Can y'all run?"

Eni was shaking too much to answer; Titi nodded curtly.

"A'ight then, let's book it."

TJ darted through the narrow aisles, ducking under hanging relics and weaving through tight passageways. Behind them, the pounding footsteps of the Keepers who did not go for the ring echoed, their voices rising as they gave chase. Spells crackled through the air, narrowly missing the group as they ran. A burst of lightning shattered a wooden Ashanti figure, sending splinters flying past TJ's face.

As they rounded a corner, TJ's eyes landed on a narrow staircase leading up. "There!" he shouted, pointing. They scrambled up the stairs, but when they reached the top, they found themselves on a dead-end balcony overlooking the chaos below. It was like a fireworks show was let off in the shop. TJ swore he heard Sister Bisi's cackling amidst it all.

"Well, that's g-g-great," Ayo muttered, eyes scanning for an exit. "What now?"

TJ's eyes darted around the space, landing on a series of old hanging ropes and beams near the ceiling. His stomach dropped, but they had no other choice. "We swing."

Manny's eyebrows shot up. "Swing? Like… Tarzan swing?"

"Exactly like that," TJ said, grabbing one of the ropes and testing its weight. "No time to argue. Just grab a rope and go."

The pursuing Keepers were already climbing the stairs.

One by one, TJ, Manny, Ayo, Titi, and Eni leaped from the balcony, grabbing onto the ropes and swinging across the shop floor. TJ landed awkwardly, nearly losing his grip, but managed to keep hold. Manny wasn't so lucky—her feet tangled in the ropes mid-swing, but Ayo grabbed her arm, steadying her.

Just as Titi and Eni jumped, what looked like Brother David's group reached the top of the stairs. They evaded the outstretched hands, windblasts, and rock balls of the Keepers. But when they landed, Eni's designer shirt was soaked with blood on one side. She looked completely miserable, but there was no time to check in.

"Move, move, move!" TJ bellowed as air blasts whistled past, narrowly missing them as they darted into another stretch of the impossibly large shop.

"Hurry!" TJ shouted, leading them through a maze of cauldrons.

Manny glanced over her shoulder, her face pale. "How did you know they'd split like that?"

"I d-d-didn't," Ayo said with a grin. "But the Keepers are p-p–predictable. They'll fight over p-p-power every time."

TJ shook his head, impressed despite himself. "And while they fight, we escape."

TJ's pulse thundered in his ears as they darted through the winding aisles of the shop, the squeaking of their hurried footsteps bouncing off the dark walls. Each corner turn revealed another stretch of the dim, cluttered maze stacked with too many artifacts to count. Occasionally, a fire plume in the distance would light the way as Keepers fought over Ayo's ring.

Who would win? TJ had his cowries on Bisi.

Just when a sliver of hope flickered in TJ's mind that they might make it out, two figures materialized from the gloom ahead. The tall Keeper with the crooked back and a large Keeper, whose broad shoulders filled the narrow passage, stood firm, effectively sealing off any chance of escape. The flickering overhead crystals deepened the shadows around them and snuffed out TJ's fleeting sense of relief.

But there was no time to sulk.

TJ reached out to Manny with his Ashe, melding with the wind magic that was already building in her palms mid-run. Like a held spear, TJ raced over fallen books with his staff cast forward. Together, he and Manny created a vortex that whipped around the pair blocking their way, disorienting them. As they stumbled, Eni manifested her own golden rod of a staff to her hand, holding it at the ready with shaking hands.

"*Iná, wá sí mi,*" Ayo signed, and his palms heated with fireballs.

"*Omí, wá sí mi,*" Eni said weakly at his side, and jets of water shot from the end of her staff.

Ayo's fire and Eni's water came as one, creating a dense steam cloud that blinded their foes. In the confusion, Titi's eyes darted around the shop's clutter. She cupped her hands and made a weird warrior call from her mouth. A tower of drums and symbols thumped and crashed, somehow made louder by Titi's sound magic. The raucous noise should have been ear-splitting, but Titi seemed to redirect it toward the Keepers instead. With a path open, they all bull-rushed through as TJ caught sight of the Keepers' bleeding ears.

Titi cried out with glee as they ran past. "I've never done that before! I could never control the Ibeji twin Ashe like that."

"Get used to it, girl," Manny said through haggard breaths, her voice carrying over the chaos as artifacts still tumbled. "That's what it's like rollin' with TJ!"

It was true. TJ felt more alive than ever with his staff in hand. Everything went through him so easily, like a perfect conduit. Is that why Manny and Ayo's Ashe wasn't as diminished as the others with wind and fire?

Titi grinned. "I should hang out with you guys more often!"

Eni didn't seem to agree. All color had gone from her face.

Before TJ could give her words of encouragement, the sounds of battle behind them fell eerily silent. TJ's heart clenched.

"Why did it go quiet?" Eni whispered, gripping her staff tightly as they all stopped. Even in the dark, TJ could see her shake.

A piercing scream cut through the silence. Sister Bisi's voice, sharp with rage. "Fools! It's a fake! Get those children. Don't let them leave!"

TJ spun on Ayo. "A fake? What? How? But…"

Ayo pulled out the real ring from his pocket with a wink. TJ wasn't sure how he didn't see it before. The ring that was in front of him was glowing brightly with Ashe. And now that TJ thought on it, the one Ayo threw was completely dull.

TJ threw his hands in the air. "Ayo! I could kiss you!"

Ayo made a face, throwing up awkward signs. "Don't let Manny see you."

"Okay, okay, my cousin's a genius," Eni said. "B-but how do we get out of here?"

Manny pointed down a narrow space between a pair of bookshelves and a mirror with an ornate frame of giraffes. "I remember this when we came in. The exit's just through here." But she could only take a single step before Sister Bisi appeared before them, rounding a corner. They all turned to run, only to find Brother David blocking their path from behind with his group. TJ's breath caught in his throat, the ancient masks around them seeming to leer menacingly from the walls.

Eni clutched her golden staff more like a blanket than a weapon.

TJ leaned close to her ear. "Eni, you've got to make us a portal out of here. I know you're afraid of aging up like John, but we need a miracle right now."

Eni closed her eyes, focusing her energy, but nothing happened. TJ could see her Ashe wisps in the air bloom, then fizzle, bloom, then fizzle.

"The hell?" Eni gasped.

The Keepers' laughter rang out, cruel and mocking. Jimoh's father, Mr. Oladipo, appeared from behind a disproportionate statue of an aziza warrior, just at Sister Bisi's shoulder. "Foolish, girl," he sneered. "No one can portal into or out of my shop."

TJ's chest tightened as the truth struck him. They were cornered, completely at the Keepers' mercy, with no exit in sight, and no more tricks. His pulse quickened as the full impact of their predicament took hold. Escape was off the table. They had to stand their ground and fight.

TJ reached deep to find the bit of courage that was already becoming paper thin, like an adrenaline rush that had nearly run its course. Where mindless bravery had taken hold before, crippling fear was starting to rear its nasty head.

Eni stepped forward, her eyes blazing under the dim light. "I might not be able to throw up a portal, but I can still do this!" She raised her staff, and a modest torrent of water surged from its crystal head, flooding the area in a thin layer of liquid.

"Manny, ice it!" TJ commanded, leaving his Ashe well open. He hoped her time with Yemoja in the Frost Realm might crossover to the magic here, even if Manny's memory of it was gone.

Brother David was quick to counter. With a stomp of his foot, stones from a set of crates rose, forming a barrier that diverted the water away from the Keepers. But when he retaliated, he didn't seem to attack the group with the same ferocity as the others, especially Sister Bisi, who fought like a wild kishi.

The fight was chaos—fire, wind, and raw sound colliding in a deadly storm. TJ's breath hitched as he pulled Ashe from his core, sweat dripping into his eyes. He didn't dare wipe it away. Any misstep, even an inch, meant the worst. Ayo's lightning forked, his runic tattoo glowing with each expulsion. TJ shoved energy into him, reigniting the bolts just as Ayo's sharp uppercut sent a Keeper sprawling.

On his left, Manny whipped a gale toward a brute, her strength wavering. TJ surged Ashe into her, sharpening the wind's edge. It howled into the brute, slamming them against a pillar with bone-cracking force.

Titi's sound wave ripped through the room but lacked punch. TJ siphoned a trickle from Eni, who crouched behind cover, and funneled it to Titi, sharpening her next attack. The wave split, knocking out a pair.

Ashe burned in TJ's veins, an unrelenting tide. Ayo's flames roared, Manny's wind howled, Titi kept blasting—and they all kept standing because TJ didn't stop. He couldn't. He was the only thing keeping them alive.

But the Keepers wised up.

TJ attempted to sap from the Keepers as his own energy fell, but most of them were using their Ashe in staccato beats, just as Bolawe had instructed them last year, making it harder for TJ to source from them.

The seasoned staffwork of the Keepers countered with sharp bolts of lightning that cracked the air, stones that struck with the force of hammers, and ice that bit into flesh. TJ's grip tightened on his staff, his jaw clenched. Fear started to win out against the courage within him. Their efforts, fierce but frantic, seemed absolutely inadequate against the Keepers' relentless assault.

They were pros. Adults. Seasoned duelists. And at the end of the day, TJ and his friends were just teenagers.

TJ had hoped the Keepers would be more diminished, especially Sister Bisi's use of lightning when she should've been drained of Shango and Oya's Ashe. But the Keepers had held onto most of their strength, somehow. But how?

Despite their best efforts, the teens were outmatched. A bolt of lightning struck Manny's arm, leaving a searing wound. She cried out, her steady wind magic faltering. Titi, distracted, didn't see the stone hurtling toward her until it was too late. It struck her head, and she crumpled to the ground, bleeding.

The crack of the impact brought TJ down low, the last remnants of his resolve withering to nothing. He felt terrible and his body shook uncontrollably. The hit to Titi seemed bad. Really bad. It was Emeka all over again.

Emeka.

The thought of his friend sparked something deep in the void of his heart. An ember he held onto, to force his legs to shuffle protectively around Manny and Titi.

Brother David stepped forward, his voice dripping with false sympathy. "It didn't have to be this way."

Sister Bisi sneered, "But we're more than okay with taking the ring over your corpses. Just like that boy on the beach."

A newborn rage surged through TJ, but ultimately, what could he do with it? It was the worst kind of feeling. To be so helpless, *feel* so helpless. It reminded TJ of being in that room when the Keepers forced blood from him. But that sickening feeling was quickly replaced with a guilt that consumed him. It was his fault they were here. He couldn't imagine how Ayo must've been feeling to see his girl in such pain.

Suddenly, a familiar voice came from behind TJ. Turning, he found Bolawe reaching out from within the mirror bordered by giraffes, his figure shimmering with a mystical light.

*"TJ, use your abilities to merge with my Ashe,"* Bolawe called out from within the reflection.

TJ hesitated, unsure whether to trust him.

Sister Bisi approached with a raised staff but stopped abruptly when she saw Bolawe, too. She pointed a finger, a vein splitting between her rough brows. "Bolawe! There you are, you filthy ọlọ́ṣì! You cower in the Mirror Realm!"

*"Quickly, TJ,"* Bolawe urged. *"Grab your friends. Make a chain. And merge with me."*

TJ threw himself at his friends, linking to them like a human chain. Fire licked at the back of his neck; a rock caught him in the gut. But he couldn't falter. Without a moment's hesitation, Bolawe extended his protection. TJ could feel it, feel the man's Ashe enveloping his own like a boa around its prey. Could Bolawe truly be trusted? What choice did TJ have?

Just as the Keepers' spells flew through the space they had occupied, the group vanished, whisked away to the confines of the Mirror Realm.

Alone, with Bolawe.

# 43

# THE REFLECTION'S DOMAIN

DESPITE NOT USING OYA'S WIND, DESPITE BEING COMPLETELY drained of Ashe, TJ's hands wouldn't stop shaking. He pressed them to his sides, but it didn't help. All he could see was Titi falling, blood streaking her face, her body crumpling like a broken doll. It was Emeka all over again. The nasty feelings bubbling inside clung to him like wet, heavy clothes, impossible to pull away.

And now, this place. The Mirror Realm.

It was like stepping into a dream, or maybe a nightmare. Reflections were everywhere, stretching in every direction—some clear, some foggy, others shattered into strange, jagged shapes. Light bounced off the glass, turning into rainbows that flickered across the ground, if you could even call it that. The floor shifted under his feet, part glass, part empty air, like it might vanish if he stood still too long.

For a moment, he caught his reflection—a dozen of him, hunched, pale, wide-eyed. He turned away, swallowing hard. But his face showed itself again and again. He couldn't avoid the shame written all over it.

So he turned back to his original reflection. On the other side of the mirror that TJ and his friends had been transported through, Sister Bisi pounded on the glass surface soundlessly, madness in her eyes. She lifted her staff and blasted the reflection with a lightning bolt, fracturing it and severing the connection.

Bolawe touched the reflection and said, "Oh, Bisi, how misguided all that power of yours is. Such a waste."

TJ threw an eyebrow up at those words, then centered himself, gathering his bearings in the new space. Manny's wincing captured his attention as she tended to the lightning burn across her arm. TJ tried to soothe her, but Manny played it off, joking, "It's not so bad." She nodded to the scars on his arm hidden under his gloves. "Now we can be twinsies."

"I'm so sorry, Manny." TJ held her arm gingerly. "Do you have more of Freya's potion? We should have never been there. We should've known it was too easy, we shoulda—"

"We opened Ayo's path." She placed a hand on his cheek. "It's worth it, TJ. Shango and Oya are worth the danger. It will always—"

Ayo's whimpering over Titi's body stopped her. Titi was not moving, her wound grievous and still bleeding freely.

"Mr. Oyelowo, let me see her," Bolawe said. Ayo held her closer to him, blocking Bolawe's way and shaking his head. The former Keeper sighed, genuine lines of concern carving his pockmarked forehead. "I can heal the girl. If I don't now, she will likely die... just like her twin."

Eni gulped, clenching a pale grip around her staff. Ayo ground his jaw, but he gave Bolawe the space to do his work. The former Keeper hurried his approach with deferential hands at his side. He stared at Titi for a while, whispering, his eyes closed. Eventually, he kneeled, hovering his hands over Titi's bleeding head. Through his Ashe Vision, TJ could see the churning of the healing magic working between Bolawe's palms and Titi's wound.

Manny and Eni embraced Ayo, who was teary-eyed, while TJ, too angry to go over to his friend right away, scowled at Bolawe—the man he had nothing but hate for. The man he had tried to kill only a few months ago if Bolawe hadn't been in his Mirror Realm form.

Now he was nothing but flesh and bone.

His back turned to TJ.

Vulnerable.

TJ swore he would avenge Emeka's death, the anger simmering in his belly now nearly boiling over. He peeked to his right, seeing his staff at his side, the rainbow prism of the floor haloing it beautifully. It was a sign. Oya's Wind called to him. He was exhausted, but he had just enough strength to nudge the wood toward him. The staff vibrated at the touch of his Ashe. All he had to do was lift it, point it at Bolawe, and...

"You shouldn't do it, TJ," Bolawe said, as though reading TJ's thoughts. "At least not until after I save Miss Yemisi-Ojo." He did not look up when he spoke, his eyes still half closed. "Plus, I would hope that you would allow me to explain myself before you pick up that staff to do harm."

TJ blinked, finding himself again. He hadn't realized his hand had already found the double-helix of his new staff. But he wasn't about to show his shock to Bolawe, so he steadied his voice before saying, "I already know what you 'bout to say. I know the Keepers ain't your homies no more."

Eni looked up from her embrace with Ayo, asking, "Huh? Why?"

Bolawe waited before responding, ending his chant and placing a final hand over Titi's forehead. "Ashe," he said gently, and the magic cemented. The bleeding had finally stopped, and it even looked like Titi was getting her color back.

"Part of the reason I am no longer," Bolawe cleared his throat, "working with my previous followers is because of Titilayo's twin, in fact."

"What do you mean?" TJ asked—small defiance in his voice.

Bolawe stood up slowly, his hands still at his sides. He looked directly at TJ, a weariness in his eyes that TJ hadn't seen in a while. "The boy's death was senseless. I left the Keepers because of a disagreement about the killing of yet *another* diviner. And a *young one* at that. It was something I wanted to avoid above all else after what happened to your..." He couldn't go on but TJ knew who he was referring to.

TJ bit the inside of his lip. He couldn't believe what he was hearing. Bolawe, the man who had orchestrated so much death and destruction at Eko Atlantic, was claiming to have a moral compass?

"I almost left the Keepers after what happened to your sister, too," Bolawe continued. "I felt responsible for it, as I almost confessed to you in that cafe. It was a decision that haunted me, but

I stayed because I believed in the cause. But this... this was the last straw in a long line of disagreements." Bolawe paused, seeming to gather his thoughts. Ayo, Manny, and Eni listened intently, their jaws slightly agape. "And regardless of whether I wanted to leave. Sister Bisi and some of the others thought I was growing too soft, that my resolve was not strong enough."

Another surge of anger rushed through TJ. "So you let them kill Emeka because you didn't want to seem weak? You said it before, you would let it happen again if—"

"If it meant bringing back the power of the Orishas, yes. But what happened that night was avoidable. It was needless. The followers I had amassed, however, did not believe diviners should be off limits—namely you, Mr. Young. I tried to stop it, but I was overruled. And when I saw the lengths they were willing to go to, the lives they were willing to sacrifice... I knew I couldn't be a part of it anymore. Part of being a man—a leader—is knowing your lines, knowing your principles, and holding true to them. So when I discovered how to access this place," he gestured to the endless mirrors around them, "I kept it to myself. And I did not return. So yes, I am a free agent now, I suppose."

TJ didn't know what to think. On one hand, he couldn't forgive Bolawe for his past actions. But on the other, he could see the genuine regret in the man's eyes.

"I don't expect you to forgive me," Bolawe said. "But I want you to know that I am *truly* sorry for the pain I've caused." He looked between the others and Titi, who finally stirred, eyes fluttering open. "All of it. I'm here now because I want to make things right, to make sure the Orishas are protected."

TJ eyed Bolawe, suspicion heating behind his expression, though a sliver of reluctant respect hung there too. He shot a quick glance at his friends to see how they were taking things. Manny looked like she was battling against a scowl by sheer willpower, her face a mashup of emotions she couldn't quite hide. Ayo, on the other hand, was locked onto Titi's limp body, his eyes glossy with unshed tears, as if even crying would mean admitting something he wasn't ready for.

The silence stretched, dense with their shared history, until Bolawe spoke again. "We need to get you all back. I have a mirror threshold set up to lead us back to headquarters. Elder Adeyemi and your families are waiting for a debrief. And, as you might suspect, they are quite miffed."

"They know!?" Manny said.

TJ was ready to get angry again, but the mention of his family had distracted him from his ire. After everything they had been through, the thought of seeing them again stirred a longing deep within him, one he hadn't realized was there. He definitely wanted to give Mom a long hug.

"Only just now," Bolawe said. "Only after I discovered you all had gotten yourselves into Oladipo's shop. Naturally, I've been keeping tabs on the Keepers. I may not be their leader, but I'm still responsible for at least half of whatever they go on to do."

"Just like you were keeping tabs on Manny before..." TJ said, irritation entering his voice once more.

"Yes." Bolawe's gaze shifted to Eni and Titi, where the Mirror Realm radiated angelically about them. "Eniola and Titilayo will be taken to Babalu-Aye Medical. What's important now is making sure Titilayo makes a *full* recovery."

TJ said nothing but tilted his head slightly in a nod. They needed to focus on getting her the help she needed. Make sure she didn't have any permanent damage.

As if on cue, Ayo rose to his feet, cradling Titi in his arms. His arms shook, but he seemed determined to keep her lifted, to do it himself. TJ moved to his side, placing a reassuring hand on Ayo's shoulder with the help of the little of Oya's Wind he still had.

Together, they followed Bolawe as he led them through the labyrinth of mirrors. It was like walking through one of those carnival fun houses, except the mirrors here reflected every color of the rainbow in an ethereal gleam.

TJ's mind raced with questions and doubts, but he pushed them aside. There would be time for answers later. For now, all that mattered was getting his friends to safety and ensuring Titi's recovery. The path ahead was uncertain, but as they walked, TJ caught a pulsing energy casting from Ayo's ring. A reminder that they had opened the last ancestral path. So TJ allowed himself to indulge in the small victory. It was that or allow the crippling guilt to sink in and completely darken his mood.

# 44

# SOME EXPLAINING TO DO

TJ STOOD IN THE COMMAND CENTER OF OPERATION Stormbreak, the buzz of adrenaline a distant memory, all of it discarded at the Veiled Caravan. The gently falling waterfall at the back of the cave room helped settle his nerves, though. Around him, the faces of his companions reflected a mix of relief from Mom and Ayo's dad, exhaustion from Ayo, and apprehension from Manny, who was held close by her aunt. Tia Teresa hadn't said much since she had gotten there, but at least she was there for her niece in this circumstance.

Elder Adeyemi's gaze swept over the group, her expression tight. "I cannot begin to express my disappointment in your actions today," she began, her voice almost as sharp as the cut of her uniform. "Going off on your own, without informing any of us, was reckless and dangerous. The Veiled Caravan is not a place to be taken lightly."

TJ had already felt guilty. Adeyemi was just adding salt to the wound. He glanced at Ayo and Manny, seeing the same in their eyes.

"I understand you were trying to help," Elder Adeyemi continued, her tone softening slightly. "And I am grateful you were able to commune with Ogun and empower Ayo's ring. That is no small feat. But I should stop being surprised where you three are concerned."

Mr. Oyelowo shook his head, his eyes narrowing as if the name

Ogun carried a bitter aftertaste. The faint creak of the chair under him filled the pause. TJ wouldn't be surprised if he had a clenched fist hidden under the table.

"But you must understand the severity of what you've done," Elder Adeyemi pressed on. "The Keepers are not to be underestimated. You put not only yourselves but also Eniola and Titilayo in danger."

Mom reached out, placing a comforting hand over TJ's gloved one. He leaned into her touch, finding solace in her presence, and then he wondered if she wasn't as angry as he had expected because she was so proud of what they achieved.

That'd be on brand for Mom.

"I know we messed up," TJ said, his voice quiet but steady. "We thought we could handle it on our own, but we were wrong. I'm sorry."

Manny and Ayo echoed his apology, their heads bowed in contrition.

"I appreciate your honesty, Mr. Young," Elder Adeyemi said. "But this cannot happen again. We are a team, and we *must* work together. The stakes are too high for solo ventures. Not just for your well-being but the well-being of our Orishas of the Storms as well."

Bolawe, who had been silent until now, tucked into a corner in his Mirror Realm form, spoke up. *"I agree with Elder Adeyemi. The Keepers are a formidable force. I should know. They would go to any lengths to reach their ends. We cannot afford to be divided."*

Ayo started to sign and TJ translated for him, saying, "What did they want with Ayo's ring, anyway? If they want to save the Orishas, bring them back to full power, wouldn't they want us to do what we did?"

Bolawe sighed. *"They do not trust leaving this mission to teenagers."*

"They trusted Dayo—"

*"Ifedayo was different—"*

"Dayo never spoke to the Orishas. *I* have."

Bolawe huffed through his nose deeply. *"You're right, TJ. I'm agreeing with you. You and Ifedayo are and were anomalies. Another reason I was cast out when I said this whole plan would only work through you, Miss Martinez, and Mr. Oyelowo. But as we discussed months ago, our best bet is to funnel transport via you young ones because you have all crossed over success-*

*fully before. And as has been demonstrated, your Ashe has waned less than other diviners."*

He took a beat. "*Sister Bisi is aligned with Shango* and *Oya both, and she believes she could make the trip herself—despite the risks. And as you all saw tonight, she too has held onto her Ashe particularly well. We were initially looking for ways to save the Orishas on our own by way of,*" he gestured around him, "*the realm that I stand in now. When I put my foot down and said we'd have to work through you, Mr. Young, well... you saw what Bisi did to that mirror. And you already know I'm not the most accomplished duelist.*"

He pulled down the collar of his dashiki and showed red scarring in the shape of tree branches. Manny rubbed at her own very similar scar on her arm, wincing.

TJ nodded, the seriousness of their mission settling in, like the chill before a hard rain—unavoidable and creeping closer by the second. They'd made it this far, but the hardest part was still ahead. "We understand," he said, speaking for the group. "It won't happen again. We're in this together."

Elder Adeyemi regarded them for a long moment, her eyes searching their faces. Finally, she nodded. "Very well. Let this be a lesson to all of you. We have much work ahead of us, and we must be united in our purpose."

"Wait, what about LaVont and Jimoh?" TJ said.

Elder Adeyemi canted her head. "What about them?"

"They're the ones who tipped off that shop owner. Oladipo. Will they get kicked out of the academy now?"

"I'm afraid we can do nothing about LaVont and Jimoh right now. My hands are tied without direct evidence or proof of a crime."

A quiet storm rumbled in TJ. Just the idea of running into those two at the academy again—after everything—made him feel sick.

Mom's voice sliced through his thoughts, though. "I would hope these boys will be far away from my son during their lessons together, eh?"

"I understand your concern," Adeyemi said. "I'll have my people on the grounds keep a close watch on LaVont and Jimoh. We'll also keep tabs on Aisha—Sister Bisi's niece—just to be safe."

TJ gave a slight nod. It wasn't much, but it was better than nothing. Still, the unease gnawed at him.

Mr. Oyelowo cleared his throat, pulling all eyes toward him. "I still have contacts in circles that overlap with Oladipo. I'll see what I can do to keep the boys in line. Though… knowing how the Keepers operate, they'll want to lay low."

"How did this happen to begin with?" Mom asked. "I thought the kids were being watched when in the village. I want to know who was supposed to be monitoring their movements tonight."

TJ stood straight. He thought he knew the answer to that… the woman with the crooked back.

"Fair point," Adeyemi said as she moved to a water bowl at her desk. She sprinkled some water within, then spoke to it. "Omo, who was charged with Mr. Young's care tonight?"

There was no face, but Omo of Fon's voice spoke back. *"Agent Bisola."*

"Has she checked in tonight?"

*"No, she has not."*

"Send out a search party. The Keepers might've gotten to her."

*"Right away."*

Elder Adeyemi sighed before speaking again. "There's one thing I need clarification on, Mr. Young. You mentioned Brother David seemed less inclined to harm you, that he appeared reluctant during the encounter. Could you explain what you meant by that?"

TJ gave a small nod, his mind drifting back to those tight, uneasy moments at the Veiled Caravan. "Yeah… it was strange. He didn't act like the others. It was like he was holding something back —like he didn't really want to be there. Same with… well, there was this woman with a crooked back. I think… I think she might have something to do with this Agent Bisola. I don't think your agent should be hurt though! At least… not after the way that lady was acting in the shop."

Before TJ could say more, Manny jumped in. "And there was a girl too—young, dark braids, maybe a little older than us. She didn't cast to kill either."

TJ glanced at her, surprised she'd picked up on the same thing. Bolawe's face shifted as if a thought had clicked into place, a faint smile pulling at the edges of his mouth. *"Sister Efe and Sister Tolani."* Then, as quickly as the smile appeared, his expression hardened. He turned to Elder Adeyemi, his mirror form crunching. *"If we need more support for prayers on the Hero's Equinox, Brother David and these two young women are probably our best shot. David has always been… more reasonable than the others. Easier to talk to, if you know how. And they have influence in several communities. Here and in the diaspora."*

Elder Adeyemi tilted her head, deep in thought. "Agreed. What we need is a way in—something to sway them. I'll make it my priority to figure that out over the next fortnight or so. You are dismissed for the night," Elder Adeyemi concluded. "Please stay safe for the next few hours of your weekend."

With slumped shoulders and downcast heads, the group made their way out of the command center and into the adjoining room, which was now filled with mostly empty desks. It was the weekend and late at night, so most of the UCMP officers had the time off. There were only a couple still working in a quiet corner of the room, an aziza and a robed human by the looks of them.

"Son," TJ heard Mr. Oyelowo's voice behind him. "Let me see that ring."

TJ turned alongside Mom to watch the exchange. Manny and her aunt did the same. Ayo hesitated, his eyes darting to TJ and Manny for support. But not wanting to upset his father further, he reluctantly slipped the ring off his finger and handed it over.

Mr. Oyelowo examined the ring, turning it over in his smooth hands. His brow wrinkled as he lifted it closer to his face. Suddenly, he sent a jolt of lightning into the ring. It crackled and sparked, sending a shock back at him. He yelped, nearly dropping the ring.

"Utter blasphemy!" he shouted. The two UCMP officers lifted their heads. "You will never use an artifact empowered by Ogun to reach Shango. It would sully our bloodline and Shango's power both. This," he lifted the ring, "will damn you."

"B-b-but, Baba—"

"I told you Adeyemi and I were working on a direct line to Shango. Something pure. And then you go off and defer to Ogun…" An idea seemed to pop into his mind as he looked Ayo up and down. "You didn't… pledge anything to him, did you?"

Ayo dropped his head with a frown. He couldn't look his father in the eye as he signed, "Y-y-yes, Baba."

Mr. Oyelowo looked near to throwing up. "You see, this is why you stutter like that. It's a curse from Shango, for what you've done with—"

"That's not it at all," TJ cut in. "I met Shango. I spoke with him. He asked about Ayo with, like, concern. He didn't curse him, he wouldn't—"

"I wasn't talking to you, mutt."

Mom stepped between them quickly at that. "Excuse you, Mobalaji?"

With the raised voices, the UCMP officers started taking steps toward the group, the robed human pulling out his staff.

"I said what I said, Yejide," Mr. Oyelowo bit back. "Unlike my son, I did not stutter. You nearly ruined the purity of your family line by breeding with that clouded American."

"*Wa si mi,*" Mom snarled, manifesting her staff into her hand and holding its tip inches from Mr. Oyelowo's face. TJ swallowed hard. Both Mom and Ayo's dad were hotheads. Seeing them collide would cause some serious damage. "Choose your next words very wisely, òlọ̀ṣì."

Now the UCMP officers had stepped fully into their space, the robed human held his staff at the ready, activating a Yemoja's Ripple Flow TJ recognized from his studies. The aziza stood with two ice balls in her hands, saying, "Let's everyone cool down, shall we?"

Mom and Mr. Oyelowo stared each other down, murder in both their eyes. Ayo's dad glanced at the ring in his palm again, smoothing his finger over the runic symbol carved into its surface. "A disgrace," he muttered. "No son of my mine will ever use a ring like this."

Ayo flinched, but when he caught his dad's fiery gaze, his nostrils flared. *I am not a disgrace!* His lips didn't move, but his voice slammed into their minds like a cannon blast. Everyone jerked back as if hit by a shockwave. TJ winced, clutching his temples. Manny staggered, her hands pressed to her forehead. Even the UCMP officers stumbled, exchanging confused looks as they rubbed their heads.

The flood of thoughts came fast and wild, spilling from Ayo's mind like a dam breaking. *I tried, Baba! I tried so hard to be the son you wanted, and it's never enough!* Years of hurt and disappointment surged through the telepathic link, battering everyone in the room with emotions so raw they stung. *You think I'm broken because of this stutter? You think I'm a failure?* You're *the one who's never seen me!* Blood streamed from Ayo's nose again, his ears too, but he didn't stop, even as his entire body literally shook. *You always told me to be strong —but the second I am, you call me a disgrace? You don't get to decide who I am!*

Ayo's breathing came fast and shallow, and the blood dripped steadily from his nose, staining his shirt. For a moment, Mr. Oyelowo just stood there, stunned. Ayo probably had never spoken to him like that—verbally or otherwise. And maybe that's what made his expression shift. The anger faded from his face, replaced by something else.

"You're right," he said quietly, like the admission pained him. "You are not a disgrace."

Ayo blinked, the sudden gentleness seeming to throw him off balance.

"But strength alone is not enough." Mr. Oyelowo's voice softened further, laced with sorrow. "Your mother… she was strong, too. And it wasn't enough to save her…"

Ayo stumbled, not from exhaustion but from what must've been sheer confusion. "W-w-what are you talking about?" he stuttered. "Y-y-you said Mom died because of a d-d-disease."

TJ squinted at the pair. Hadn't Ayo said he had a father *and* a mother?

Mr. Oyelowo sighed, as if the truth had been sitting on his chest for years. "She died… because we defied Shango's Will."

The room seemed to hold its breath. TJ shifted uncomfortably while Manny's mouth parted slightly in shock.

"When she fell sick," Mr. Oyelowo continued, "it wasn't a sickness that could be cured. It was a punishment. No medicine, no magic, no prayer could undo it. Your mother and I thought we could outrun the will of Shango—thought love or shame would be enough. But it wasn't. The Hero demands obedience, not defiance."

"Y-y-you lied to me."

"I lied because I didn't want you carrying that burden," Mr. Oyelowo said bitterly. "I wanted to protect you. I've had my own challenges worshipping Shango after what happened. I don't want that burden on you as well, son." He glanced down at the ring in his hand, turning it slowly. "But now that you've pledged to Ogun, regaining Shango's favor will be near impossible. I should have been more forthright."

All of Ayo's energy seemed to leak out of him. His knees quivered, and he looked like he'd aged himself well past his teenage years. "How do I k-k-know you're not just trying to c-c-control me again?"

Mr. Oyelowo stepped closer, his expression softer than TJ had ever seen. "Because I've already lost your mother. I can't lose you too."

The words hung between them, heavy and raw. For a second, it looked like Mr. Oyelowo might hand the ring back. His hand wavered. But in the end, he slipped the ring into his coat pocket.

"We'll do this the right way," he said quietly, as if convincing himself. "I'll get you to Shango, my son. But it has to be safe. It has to be the right way. Come on, let's get you cleaned up." He lifted a hand to Ayo, but his son shook him away. "I understand. When you're ready, then." With that, he patted the ring in his pocket and turned to leave, his footsteps echoing in the quiet office.

Everyone let out a long and sustained breath. The robed officer relaxed his grip on his staff, and the aziza quietly dispelled the ice balls she'd conjured.

Ayo wiped the blood from his face with the sleeve of his shirt, his shoulders slacking with exhaustion. But something in Ayo had changed. He stood taller now, even without the ring.

"We'll get the boy to Babalu-Aye," the aziza said. "Just for a quick check-up."

The human pulled a potion bottle from his robes and dabbed its contents on Ayo's nose and ears. "You were using the methods of Olowokandi, weren't you, boy? *Clairvoyance for Cretins,* I believe? It will get you quick results but at a danger to yourself… and others." The man eyed TJ and the rest of the group. Mom and Manny were still rubbing at their ears, and TJ felt a migraine coming on.

After regaining some stability, TJ rested a hand on Ayo's shoulder. "We'll figure this out, Ayo. Ring or no ring."

TJ's heart sank. All their work, all the risks they had taken, and now Ayo's dad had taken it all away in a moment of anger. The hope that had been building inside him deflated like a punctured balloon.

Manny placed a comforting hand on Ayo's shoulder, her face a mirror of TJ's own disappointment. Mom, trading the warrior face of Yemoja for the nurturing one, pulled Ayo into a hug, whispering words of reassurance.

But TJ couldn't find the words. He stood there, feeling helpless and lost. How were they supposed to save Shango and Oya now? How could they complete their mission without Ayo's ring?

45

# THE QUINCEAÑERA

THE BURDEN OF RECENT EVENTS PRESSED DOWN ON TJ AS HE walked through the dirt paths of Ifa Academy the following week. Ayo's dad had taken the ring, dashing their hopes of using it to save Shango; Titi was still recovering in the hospital; and Manny's aunt went back to giving Operation Stormbreak the cold shoulder. On top of it all, TJ's anxiety about his upcoming staff trial nagged at him. Would Staffmaster Bamidele let him pass after hearing about his exploits at the Veiled Caravan? It didn't help TJ's nerves that Jimoh and LaVont hadn't returned to Ifa Academy. Were they laying low or something else?

Between classes, TJ referenced his list:

1. ~~Gotta figure out how to reverse this channeling thing by dreamwalking with Obatala and Oshosi.~~

2. ~~Open up the ancestral path from Yemoja to Oya through the Frost Realm for Manny.~~

3. ~~Unlock ancestral path from Ogun to Shango's using Ayo's Norse ring. (And find Ogun's Sacred Cabinet)~~

3b. *Figure out how to get ring back from Ayo's dad (with his consent)*

*4. Complete my staff to sustain the ancestral path ritual to the Court of All jail cell.*

*5. Save Shango and Oya on The Hero's Equinox.*

*6. Don't die*

As the winter holiday break approached, TJ found solace in the fact that he'd be spending most of it in New York, preparing for Manny's quinceañera. The change of scenery and the festive occasion provided another much-needed respite from the challenges they had faced so far.

The journey from Nigeria to New York was a stark contrast. TJ, Mom, and Tunde left behind the dry December heat of Nigeria and stepped into the biting cold of New York. They settled into a family friend's house the night before Manny's quince where Dad waited for them, the warmth of the home a welcome refuge from the chill outside.

TJ's mind had finally emptied of all his responsibilities back in Nigeria, but Tunde seemed to shove him back there. At least twice a day he would share a message board from Evo about this theory or that about the waning magic of Shango and Oya's diviners.

"Come on, Teej," Tunde would say. "Just make an account and tell these idiots they're wrong." He raised his phone in front of TJ's face.

THUNDERCLAP99

I thought it was just me messing up, but this makes me think it's bigger than that. Could the Orisha be...angry with us?

TEMPESTXTRME

Angry? Doubt it. Oya doesn't get weak when she's mad; she gets stronger. Maybe there's something interfering with their connection to us? Like some kind of outside force blocking the flow of ashe?

NO11AJ

Y'all don't know the half of it.

The last user was Tunde's user name, TJ knew. "Don't you dare say a thing, Tunde," he said. "I know you know more than you should, but *please* keep it on the low."

TJ wished Ayo could come along with him to New York, but he was stuck in Lagos in his father's skyscraper. "House arrest" he called it. Grounded for the rest of the year. Maybe he could've settled Tunde down with theory talk.

TJ still texted Ayo often, though.

TJ

how's titi and eni doing?

AYO

full recovery. both. eni needs an anxiety potion tho. titi was shaken up too but not as bad.

TJ

good. my mom sent stuff to them from me

AYO

yea they got it. chocolate is their favorite. good call.

TJ

hyd man?

AYO

ah… u kno… nothing retail therapy can't fix. my baba feels bad fr. got me a rolex and all that

On the day of Manny's birthday, Mom helped TJ get ready in a deep purple suit and black bowtie. As she adjusted his tie, she waved her hand, and a shimmer of Ashe danced around the fabric, Oya's Wind straightening it perfectly—though it took Mom a few times to find the right air current to make the magic work. Despite sad thoughts entering his mind, TJ smiled, appreciating the magical touch.

*Don't think about it,* he told himself. *Just think about Manny's quince. That's it. Not the Court of All. Not Shango or Oya or Oshosi. Not anything else.*

"Now, remember," Dad said, looking him over, "this is a formal event, and you're Manny's man. I was reading up on those quince parties. You're the *chambelán,* right?" Dad totally butchered the pronunciation.

"Yes, that's what she said. I have to do this dance and *everything,*" TJ groaned, dreading when that moment would have to come.

"Well, then," Mom chimed in, making sure the bottom of his purple pants weren't flooding. "Treat her like a lady, honey bunny. Open doors for her, pull out her chair, and make sure she always has a drink in her hand. She'll be doing *a lot* of talking."

TJ nodded, taking mental notes of his parents' advice. "I will. I want to make this night special for her."

Dad smiled, his eyes softening as he patted down a crease on TJ's black vest. "I know you do, li'l man. Just be yourself and let her know how much you care about her. That's what matters most." TJ hugged his parents, feeling grateful for their guidance and support.

"And don't forget to have fun," Dad added. "Forget about everything that's going on right now at that academy. Mom says they're working you hard this year. Tonight, all that don't exist. The only thing that should exist for you is that young woman. That's an order from your old man, you hear?"

"Yes, Dad."

Was he reading his mind?

"I'm serious, TJ. This is a huge coming-of-age event for Manuela, for her culture. You need to make sure to take *all* the stresses away."

"I got it, Dad. For real."

"And make sure your phone is *charged,*" Mom jumped in. "I expect a call from you no later than ten o'clock on the—"

"Of course, Mom. Can I go now?"

Mom peeked at her watch. "So sorry, honey bunny—Oh, yes, you should be off. Your train leaves in five minutes. Your dad, brother, and I will get in earlier than you. We got a matinee for *The Lion King*."

"Mooom," Tunde complained from the other room he and TJ were sharing. "You said we could go see *Hamilton*!"

"But your dad's work got discount tickets. Next time, baby!"

TJ gave Mom a swift kiss on the cheek and Dad a quick hug before

Tunde started his rebuttal for all the reasons they should have watched one musical over the other. Taking one last look at himself in the living room mirror, TJ took a deep breath, ready to face the evening ahead.

Two trains and a jog later, and TJ finally stumbled into the venue, gasping for air. There were a few times he wanted to air-step to make up time but thought better of it. He had to pull on his gloves a few times to make sure his glowing tell wasn't showing, glad for the cold weather, which made his look make sense. If it was summer, he wasn't sure how he'd play it off. But when TJ crossed the threshold of the venue, the sight inside stopped him cold. The transformation was unreal.

The rec room he'd seen during yesterday's dance rehearsal—empty and smelling vaguely like wet socks—had undergone a complete transformation. But tonight, it was like stepping into another world—like Oya herself had swept through and painted the space with storm clouds and sunsets. Rich purples, deep reds, and burgundies draped every surface, from the walls to the tables, like they were dressing the room for royalty. Sheer fabrics spiraled down from the ceiling, wrapping the chandeliers, which glittered like stars about to burst.

Lively samba beats mingled with the rhythm of reggaeton, and the scent of flowers—bold hibiscus and sweet orchids—hung in the air. At the center of it all was a wide dance floor, gleaming under the soft glow of the lights, waiting for something big to happen.

TJ wiped the sweat from his brow, only half from the jog. Even though the room swirled with color and chatter, he couldn't shake the nerves twisting in his gut. His clothes—formal shoes and a too-tight borrowed jacket—felt like they were strangling him. TJ took a picture and sent it to Ayo.

TJ

dude this place is amazing, but i cant breath in this jacket u gave me

AYO

shango's axe! you forgot the enlargement charm i taught you eh?

TJ

u kno i did! This is torture!

AYO

u say that now. wait until u have to dance in front of everyone. And damn... i didnt kno manny's family had it like that.

TJ

most of it is donated, remember? everyone seems to know Manny's family around here. they volunteer a lot.

AYO

nah, no way you get all that just with donations...

Before TJ could respond, the music shifted, and Manny's mom came jogging over to him in a green-and-yellow dress. "There you are! Get over here to the lobby. The grand entrance is about to start."

TJ allowed himself to be corralled as a ripple of excitement spread through the crowd. Conversations quieted, and all eyes turned toward the entrance as the procession began.

The Court of Honor entered first, *damas* gliding in pairs with the chambelánes beside them. The damas' dresses swished as they walked, each in vibrant tones that echoed the deep hues of the night. TJ shuffled forward awkwardly with the other chambelánes, his limbs stiff and uncooperative. They'd practiced this march a dozen times, but the real thing was way more intimidating.

The court lined up neatly at the edge of the dance floor, their positions flawless—or at least passable. TJ's heart pounded as he stole a glance at his phone, which read:

AYO

u got this. dont trip and die and ur golden.

Then came the part everyone had been waiting for. The music swelled, the entrance doors swung open, and there she was.

Manny stepped into the room, arm in arm with her father, and the crowd drew a collective breath. No one else would have noticed, but TJ noted the makeup covering up her lightning scar from the fight at the caravan. He swallowed back the fresh surge of guilt and focused back on her smiling face. Manny glided forward, her gown trailing behind her like water pulled by the tide. The colors shimmered with every step—stormy purples, silver streaks, and deep crimson that gleamed under the lights.

TJ couldn't move. For a second, he forgot how to breathe.

Manny carried herself differently tonight—not like the no-nonsense, trash-talking Manny he'd come to know from Camp or Anansi's Arcade. This Manny was poised, graceful, and entirely in her element. A queen. And TJ? He suddenly felt very small and very sweaty.

Her father escorted her to the center of the dance floor, gave her a proud smile, and stepped aside. Manny stood tall, her gown swirling gently around her feet as the Court of Honor gathered in formation.

The music softened, and Manny's dad kneeled before her, a velvet pillow in his hands. TJ tried to keep his mouth closed as Manny's dad removed her simple flats and replaced them with silver heels, a quiet but powerful gesture—like handing her the key to something new. Manny gave him a quick hug, her eyes shining.

Next came her aunt, Tia Teresa, who stepped forward carrying a tiara. She placed it gently on Manny's head, brushing a hand over her hair with a look of pride. The tiara caught the glow of the chandeliers, making Manny look like she was wearing a crown of stars. TJ was happy to see Teresa looking a lot more healthy, more jovial. Or at least the quince was having that effect on her. Manny gave her aunt a quick smile, but there was something in her expression that TJ couldn't quite place—like she was proud but also holding something back, something private.

Then Manny's father handed her a doll—a beautiful porcelain figure dressed in a tiny version of Manny's gown. For a moment, Manny held it close, her face unreadable. Then she kneeled down and passed it to one of her younger cousins, who beamed as she clutched it in her arms.

It wasn't just a doll. It was Manny quietly and gracefully letting go of the last piece of childhood. Dad and TJ had gone over that the night before.

The band struck up a waltz, and Manny's father extended his hand, his white hair and beard stark against his dark skin and darker zoot suit. Manny took his hand, her dimples caving, and the two glided across the dance floor, their movements smooth and practiced. TJ shifted nervously, knowing his moment was coming. He specifically didn't take Mom's lunch that day for the very reason of not having to battle keeping it down.

After a few elegant turns, Manny's father gave her one last twirl, sending her spinning toward the line of chambelánes.

TJ swallowed hard. *Here we go.*

He stepped forward, holding out his hand. Manny took it, her fingers steady against his shaking glove.

"You ready for this?" She smiled, eyes twinkling.

"Nope," TJ muttered, trying to look braver than he felt.

She laughed that perfect laugh of hers, and they began to waltz. For the first few steps, TJ was sure he was going to trip over his own feet. But Manny—of course—had everything under control. She gave him small nudges, guiding him effortlessly through the routine.

"See? Not so bad," she whispered as they spun together.

"You're only saying that because I haven't fallen yet," TJ whispered back. He was only half joking.

The song ended, and the crowd burst into applause as Manny gave TJ a playful bump with her shoulder. "Not bad for someone who said he couldn't dance," she teased.

"You're impossible," TJ muttered, though he couldn't help but smile.

"And you love it," she shot back with a wink.

Before TJ could respond, the music shifted to something faster, and Manny's grin widened.

"Surprise dance," she said, grabbing his hand before he could bolt. "C'mon, just like we practiced."

"Oh no..." TJ groaned, but it was already too late. "I forgot we weren't done yet!"

The court launched into their choreographed routine—an energetic mix of salsa, reggaeton, and hip-hop. TJ stumbled through the first few steps, but Manny pulled him along, laughing the whole way. By the time the routine ended, TJ was out of breath and drenched in sweat, but the crowd was cheering, and Manny looked like she'd never been happier.

As the music shifted back to lively samba, Manny twirled away into the crowd, greeting guests with hugs and easy smiles. TJ stood there, catching his breath, watching her move through the room like she belonged to it.

*She couldn't be any more perfect if she tried,* TJ thought.

TJ watched her, a smile on his face, as he did his best to be the perfect boyfriend. He held doors open for her, pulled out her chair, and made sure she always had a drink in her hand, just as his parents had advised. The presentation, the large crowd, all made it clear how important this day was to Manny and her family, a celebration of her transition into womanhood.

The week leading up to the event, TJ had visited Manny's apartment a few times, and her family was packed in tight. They even stored their dishes in the oven. If he hadn't seen her place and only saw the ballroom, though, he would have thought she came from money like Ayo said. But apparently, everyone in the neighborhood had pitched in, including some old guy who had owned a video store to a local vet Manny volunteered at before. Everyone seemed to have a story about how Manny had helped them here or defended them there.

"I'm so happy she chose you," Manny's mom said somewhere between one of her daughter's outfit changes. Besides her lighter skin, she looked how Manny might in a couple of decades. "You are such a wonderful young man, you know that? We wondered when she'd have her first boyfriend."

"First?" TJ asked, taken aback. He knew for a fact that wasn't true. Perhaps he was the first boyfriend Manny told her parents about. He distinctly remembered her having "someone in New York" last year.

"And you're doing such a great job," Manny's father added through a sip of piña colada. "Keep up the good work. Maybe one day I'll call you son."

"Oh, stop it, Zé." Manny's mom smacked him across the shoulder in a way that was very familiar to TJ. It even brought phantom pain to the shoulder Manny always smacked him on. But at least he was on his girlfriend's parents good side.

⚚

IT HADN'T EVEN BEEN AN HOUR, AND TJ WAS STARTING TO regret the whole idea of being Manny's escort. He did his best to be the perfect boyfriend, but it seemed like the universe had other plans—or Eshu was playing a cruel joke on him all the way from the Frost Realm. As he navigated the crowded ballroom, he found himself constantly dodging Manny's countless cousins and little brothers. They ran around, knocking over decorations and bumping into guests, causing TJ to wonder if they had indeed been secretly granted divine powers of chaos. But Manny was the only one in her direct family to be a diviner.

Just when TJ thought he had a moment to catch his breath, he noticed Manny's dress had a small tear at the seam. He quickly pulled her aside and, with a subtle wave of his hand, used a bit of Ashe to mend the fabric. Manny flashed him a grateful smile, giving him a swift kiss on the cheek before being whisked away by her tias for photos.

As the night wore on, technical difficulties plagued the event. The sound system crackled and popped, causing the music to cut out intermittently. TJ rushed to the DJ booth to see if he could help. After a few minutes of tinkering—all the fool had to do was turn his laptop off and on—TJ managed to get the music back on track, much to the relief of the guests who were eager to keep dancing.

But the challenges didn't stop there. The catering staff informed TJ they were running low on plantains, and there had been a mix-up with the schedule, causing some of the planned events to overlap. TJ felt like he was playing a game of whack-a-mole, trying to address each issue as it popped up. But he made sure every mole was whacked before they came within sniffing distance of Manny.

No one was working harder than TJ that night.

"Don't kill yourself, young blood," one of the cooks had told him in a thick Brooklyn accent. "Shouldn't the family be doin' most of this?"

TJ pointed to a group of Manny's family who'd had too much to drink, wobbling from side to side. "Do they look like they are capable of keeping everything straight?"

The cook shrugged. "Looks like they're yankin' your chain 'cause you're the new guy tryna impress. Hah, I'd pull that same shit too if it was my daughter's sweet sixteen."

"I'll take the hazing," TJ said as he chased after another of Manny's little cousins.

# 46

# TURNT AND TURBULENT

Exhausted from putting out fires, TJ made his way to the bar. He ordered a Jamaica for himself, and when he sipped it, it reminded him a lot of the zobo hibiscus tea he drank in Nigeria. They had a similar reddish-purple color as well. And they were both absolutely refreshing. As he took his second sip, a familiar chorus of voices called his name from behind. He turned to see Andressa and Antonia, the albino Brazilian-American twins from Camp Olosa, waving at him. Lorenzo, with his green eyes, stood beside them as well, his hand intertwined with another guy TJ had never seen before.

"TJ!" Andressa exclaimed, pulling him into a hug. "It's so good to see you!"

"You too! Did you just get here?" TJ grinned, returning the embrace warmly.

"Ah, you know, Brown people time." Antonia waved his words away. "*Aye caramba,* TJ! How tall can you get?" She hugged him next, barely coming around his middle.

"How have you been, Antonia? Where are you going to school now?"

"We're at the Escola de Magia in São Paulo. It's been amazing! We're learning so much about our Afro-Brazilian magic roots. Did you know capoeira was created by diviners to channel the Orishas before it became a martial art? You should try the exchange program and visit us. *Como está o seu português?*"

"Eh... *mas o menos*."

"*Mais ou menos, sim*," Lorenzo corrected TJ, who had spoken Spanish instead of Portuguese, an old joke with this group. "Aye, Manuela is doing a terrible job teaching you, I see. I'll get on her later about that. Don't want to go messin' with her quince."

A sudden spike shot through TJ. "Yes, please don't."

"Oh!" Lorenzo slapped his forehead, making his curly hair bounce. "This is my boyfriend, Carlos, by the way. He don't talk much but he's cool. Speaks Spanish and everything. So y'all can be the best of friends, hah!"

Andressa stepped in with a chuckle. "He's our adopted introvert. Every group needs one, right?"

"Hey..." Carlos, who wore a Call of Duty shirt and Diamondbacks beanie, said tentatively.

"How about you, TJ?" Lorenzo went on, his smile as big as TJ remembered it from camp. "How's Nigeria? How's Ifa Academy treating you?"

TJ hesitated, unsure of how much he could share. "It's been... challenging, but I'm learning a lot. Staffcrafting has been a big focus lately."

He held back on the details of his missions, the encounters with deities, and the looming threat of the God Eaters. As he listened to his friends chat about their classes, their crushes, and the latest magical gossip, a familiar envy filtered through TJ. They were dealing with normal teenage problems while he was wrapped up in celestial conflicts and life-or-death situations. What he would have given to have that experience right now.

But as he glanced over at Manny, her face alight with joy as she danced with her little brothers, TJ pushed those thoughts aside. Tonight was about celebrating her, and he was determined to make it a night she'd never forget.

Tia Teresa entered the ballroom again, her presence casting a subtle shadow over the festivities. Despite her participation in the dancing and socializing, there was a noticeable weight on her shoulders now, a distant look in her eyes that hinted at the burdens she still carried. Much different from during the grand entrance. At first, TJ just thought she'd had too much to drink—she certainly seemed it with how she wobbled—but it seemed deeper than that.

She was about to make some trouble, and TJ wouldn't have it.

Dismissing himself from his old friends, TJ made his way through the crowd, but got intercepted by one of Manny's family friends. The guy was insanely handsome, with a rugged five o'clock shadow and a towering height that made even TJ feel unusually small in comparison.

"I ain't know who you was before the night started, my guy," he said, speaking loudly over the music. "You ain't told me you was Manny's new boo. What up, player. Name's Andre. Me and Manny used to have a thing a few months back. Been knowin' her since elementary."

That stopped TJ cold. This was *that* guy? Manny had only been texting him, but still, TJ never would've thought... this guy didn't seem her type at all. Well, TJ didn't know what her type was, exactly, but it definitely wasn't *this* guy. Andre was built like a football player or something. And he gave off that conceited vibe, sort of like Ayo, but... worse. He was totally giving where-my-hug-at energy.

"Cool." TJ deadpanned. "That's what's up. Well... nice to meet you."

"The pleasure's all mine," he said, looking TJ up and down. TJ was considering squaring up on this fool until he remembered what he was doing in the middle of the dance floor to begin with. As he took his awkward steps away, he could've sworn he heard Andre suck his teeth and murmur, "Lame-ass goofy-ass lookin'—" But he didn't have the time to verify or confront that mess. Andre didn't want to see what TJ could do with a sharp gust of wind.

Searching the party for Manny again, TJ realized she was no longer in the main room. He weaved through the crowd, his eyes scanning for her familiar dimples, the fuchsia dress she had changed into a half hour ago. As he approached a dark corner, he heard voices—Manny and her aunt—engaged in a heated discussion.

"I stored my memories before leaving the Frost Realm," Tia Teresa was saying, her voice tinged with frustration. "They're all fuzzy like a dream, but I still feel them. I didn't want to forget what the Orishas did, or rather, what they *didn't* do for Jessie."

TJ stood frozen, pulse quickening as he listened to the heated exchange between Manny and her aunt. Tia Teresa's voice trembled with raw emotion as she spoke. "I prayed, Manuela. Every night, I prayed to the Orishas for Jessie's safety, for her protection. And what did I get in return? Silence. Nothing but deafening silence. Do you understand how much I've lost?" A choked sob punctuated her words. "But the Saints, they answered me. They showed me the truth. This mission, this... Operation Stormbreak, it's doomed to fail. That's what they told me in my dreams. This whole thing will bring damnation. We shouldn't go through with it. And I can't lose you too, *sobrinha*. Not like Jessie. Not after you barely made it out of that caravan place." Teresa grabbed drunkenly at Manny's arm, wiping part of the makeup away to show she knew what was hidden underneath.

Manny shooed her away before saying, "Tia, I understand your pain, your doubts. For real. But this mission, it's not just about us. It's about somethin' bigger, somethin' that affects all of us. We have to try, for the sake of everyone, for the future." Manny's voice was laced with conflict, the struggle between her loyalty to her aunt and her own beliefs. "The Orishas," Manny went on, "they haven't abandoned us. They're still here, guiding us, even if you can't always see it. But I have seen them, Tia. I've walked among them. Oya mounted me last summer. We have to have faith. Faith in ourselves, in each other, and in the path we've chosen."

Tia Teresa's voice softened. "I want to believe, Manuela. I really do. But after everything that's happened, after losing Jessie, it's hard to trust in anything anymore. You must come and listen to the Saints. If not, at least listen to your Tia."

"No! You listen to *me*!"

As the argument escalated, it attracted the attention of the other guests. The mood shifted from celebration to concern, and a surge of protectiveness for Manny filled TJ. This is exactly what he was trying to keep away from her.

"Don't you dare use that tone with your Tia."

"I'll use that tone if you keep up with all this bull—"

TJ turned the corner to butt in. As he did, he overheard one of the family members mutter, "There she go again, talking about her witchcraft. *Bruxa louca*. That side of the family has always been weird."

When TJ turned the corner, he was surprised to see how close Manny and Tia Teresa were. Nearly nose to nose. Without hesitation, he sliced between them while saying "that's enough, that's enough" over and over again. He gently took Manny's hand and whisked her away through the backroom, even as she fumed.

TJ led Manny up a narrow stairwell, their footsteps echoing off the concrete walls. The music from the party faded as they climbed higher, replaced by the distant sounds of the city. When they reached the rooftop, Manny tried to push past TJ, but he blocked the door, his body a solid wall between her and the way back.

Manny pounded on his chest, her strong fists striking against his bird chest. It hurt, but TJ didn't move, absorbing the pain for her, his eyes filled with understanding and concern. She needed to cool off. When Manny realized she couldn't get past, she stomped to the edge of the roof and screamed, a primal cry that sent a small wind blast rippling through the air.

TJ let a long silence pass, taking in the night air. The New York City skyline stretched out before them, a glittering tapestry of lights against the inky black sky. The distant sounds of traffic and the muted thump of music from the party below created a strange, yet comforting symphony. Up here, away from the prying eyes and ears of the guests, TJ and Manny could finally breathe, it seemed.

"I just want my family whole again," Manny said, her voice cracking. "Like before, when Jessie was still alive."

TJ stepped closer. "Manny, you are so special to your family, to me. They love you more than anything." He turned her around, forcing her to look at him. "We're all here for you, no matter what. You're not alone in this."

"But my Tia—"

"Will come around," TJ said. "Because she'll see the fight in you. The fire." Manny's eyes searched his, a flicker of doubt still lingering. TJ took a deep breath, his heart pounding. He didn't allow his own doubt to enter his mind. He didn't even think when he said, "Your family loves you, dude. Your friends love you. And..." He gulped, but only for a moment. "I lo—"

"Don't say it. Not yet. Not right now."

TJ's broken confession hung in the air, his stomach twisting, regretting his impulsiveness. He nervously shifted on the gravel, eyes darting around, avoiding her gaze. Caught between hope and dread, he braced himself, his pulse pounding in his ears as he said, "Sorry, sorry, sorry! I didn't mean—I mean—I do like you—but I—"

"Stop. Doing. That." Manny threw a fist into his chest with each word. "What did I tell you about that? Even at camp. You have to be confident in the things you say, TJ. You gotta say your words with strength. If you, you know, 'l-word' me then..." She paused. Just a beat. "Then say it with your whole chest. Because when you do those things, when you're fighting off Keepers without fear and realm-hopping without really complaining about it... that's when I 'l-word' you, too."

TJ's head was in a whirlwind. What was he supposed to do? Tell her or not tell her? Girls were so confusing! "So um... what?"

"Ugh, what I'm trying to say is that when you do do it, say it strong. But... don't you dare say it right now. But also... don't lose your confidence."

Manny's words hung in the crisp night air, and TJ felt a sudden surge of warmth that dispelled the chill of the rooftop. "Right, confidence..." he trailed off.

"But not too much..."

"In between." TJ nodded. "According to a few deities out there, I'm pretty good at that."

Manny sunk her head into TJ's chest. He got a whiff of her lilac perfume. "Yeah, you are," she said. "And you should believe it, not just 'cause I told you to. You feel me?"

"I feel you," TJ said, lightly stroking the lightning scar on her arm. The makeup was still holding up, covering it, but he knew it was there.

They both stared out into the night, watching the traffic pass by peacefully. TJ wouldn't mind if he could just put his life on pause right then and there. He didn't need anything else. Just him and his girl holding each other. Forever.

"You know something?" he said. "You really are a child of Oya and Yemoja, dude. That little speech you just gave me had elements of both. And don't think I missed that you said you basically 'l-word' my goofy-ass too."

"I do." Manny looked up at him now. "I've... never felt this with anyone. I always thought..." She bit her lip, something on her mind. TJ lifted her chin with his fingers. "I just didn't think I could get this close to someone like you..."

"What? An extremely tall, mildly handsome geek from Cali?"

Manny giggled. "Yeah, something like that. I like you, TJ. A lot. I knew it from the moment we met. Goofy as that shit sounds. I just... knew. I can't explain it—the feelings I feel, but... I know it runs deep, as deep as the Ashe that runs through me."

"Ah, I see what this is. I guess the jig is up."

Manny threw up an eyebrow.

"The Ashe running through you," TJ said. "I've been using my magic to influence your heart, boosting this burning infatuation you have for me."

Manny sucked her teeth. "Oh, shut up, you knucklehead."

TJ rocked back with Manny, doing his best not to step on her long dress. "It's the only way this," he squeezed her closer, "makes sense. I mean, dude, you're way out of my league."

"Not as much as you think. I mean, you're a way better kisser than I expected. Nice. Gentle. Never rushed."

"I had plenty of time with this." TJ patted the inside of his arm, even though the real answer was the time he spent with Eni last year. "This arm taught me everything I know."

Manny rolled her eyes. "Okay, whatever... shut up and kiss me."

They leaned in, their lips meeting in a tender, sweet kiss. As they pulled apart, TJ smiled softly. "We'll all make it work, some way. All of it. Because we have each other. Even if we have to take on the world. Even if we have to take on the universe."

Manny giggled.

"What?" TJ said.

"I told you already. I'm lactose intolerant." TJ rolled his eyes, but Manny went on. "But I don't think I could have asked for a better boyfriend, TJ. I don't ever want to lose you."

"And you won't."

# 47

# IT TAKES A VILLAGE

THE HOLIDAYS PASSED IN A WHIRLWIND OF NEW YORK CITY nights. As the crisp chill of December wrapped itself around the city, TJ found himself stepping into a world vastly different from the Christmases he knew back home.

Growing up, Christmas was church services and carols on Dad's side of the family, followed by a hearty meal that brought cousins, aunties, and family friends together around tables laden with ham, macaroni and cheese, collard greens, and sweet potato pie. In contrast, Manny's Latin American household was a flurry of customs TJ had never experienced. Their celebration kicked off with the lively *Posadas*, reenacting Mary and Joseph's search for shelter, leading up to *Nochebuena*, where midnight mass gave way to a feast of tamales, roast pork, rich flan, and aromatic *ponche*. And, strangest of all, they opened Christmas gifts on the *eve* instead of the *morning*. Despite stark differences, family, faith, and the shared joy of the season filled both homes.

On the following day, TJ woke to the warm, sugary scent of his mom's cinnamon rolls drifting up the stairs of their home away from home. It pulled him out of sleep slowly, like his brain needed a second to connect the smell with *Christmas morning*. A soft, colorful glow crept under his door—must've been the Christmas tree lights downstairs, flickering against the walls in little shifting patches.

TJ swung his legs over the side of the bed, instantly regretting it as his toes met the freezing hardwood—yep, Christmas in New York was *much* different than Los Angeles. He hissed through his teeth, grabbed his robe off the chair, and threw it over his shoulders.

Downstairs, the tree looked like something out of a snow globe, every branch heavy with ornaments—though it was missing some of his homemade disasters from when he was five. Most were sleek glass orbs Mom had bought in bulk from Costco. Presents fanned out across the floor, overflowing from the tree's skirt in a haphazard jumble of reds, greens, and shiny silver paper.

His parents were already on the couch, nursing their coffee mugs like they hadn't been waiting for him to wake up for the last hour. Tunde was already playing with the edges of his first gift, revving to get started with the rip and tear. TJ had already opened a few of his presents at Manny's but had saved the rest for his own family. Mom beamed at him over the rim of her mug. Dad set his cup down with a soft clink.

"Merry Christmas, li'l man."

"Merry Christmas," TJ mumbled, rubbing the sleep from his eyes.

Mom patted the spot next to her, and TJ plopped down, his big feet tucked under him to escape the cold floor. They took turns tearing through gifts—Mom's classic system. One at a time, no rushing.

TJ got a fresh pair of sneakers from Mom, exactly the ones he'd been hinting at for months. There were books, too—the *Tristan Strong* series TJ kept eyeing every time they walked by the bookstore. Then came a soft, thick sweater that he put on immediately in place of his robes. In an instant, the living room went from a frigid icebox to a mild one.

"Love it," TJ said quietly, offering Mom a quick smile. "Thanks."

Tunde even got TJ some new gloves made out of kishi hide.

"Just don't wear it around Teacher Ikenna," Tunde said with a candy cane sticking out of his mouth. "He might get offended, even though it's only made of hyena hide."

"Sure thing." TJ said, but stuffed the gift away to be forgotten later. "And thanks. My gloves are getting old."

At the end of it all, Dad reached behind the tree and pulled out one last package, small and carefully wrapped. He turned it over a few times in his hands, studying it like it held some sort of secret.

"This one's from me," Dad said, eyes steady on TJ. "I found it when I was cleaning the garage a few weeks back. Thought it might come in handy."

TJ peeled the paper away and blinked at the sight of the tarnished bronze medallion inside. The surface had grown a little dull over the years, but the waves etched into the metal were still sharp. It took TJ half a second to recognize it: his *Most Improved Swimmer* award from that summer at camp—normal camp—the one where he'd finally worked through his fear of the deep end at the pool.

TJ's throat went dry as a desert.

"I remember how proud you were," Dad said softly, leaning forward with his elbows on his knees. "You worked your li'l ass off, even though I know you were scared to death." He paused, tapping a finger against his mug. "I figured after…" He seemed to change his words. "Well… maybe it could help with this whole staffmaking thing you've got going on. Or… you know…" He rubbed the back of his bald head. "That stuff you're going through with water and all that. It ain't got no magic or Ashe in it but it's sentimental… that has to account for something, right?" He frowned. "Sorry, it's the best I could do."

TJ turned the medal over in his palm, the cool metal grounding him. "Dad, this is—" His voice croaked, and he swallowed hard, trying to rein it back in. "This is perfect."

Dad smiled—small, but real. "I can't wrap my head around all this stuff. The Orishas, the crafting… It's way over my head. But I want you to know, TJ—I'm still here for you, even if I don't have all the answers."

With the assistance of Oya's Wind, TJ clutched the medallion tight, letting the edges dig into his pale and ruined hands. "You're doing great, Dad. Really. Just… being here. Texting me. Believing in me. That's enough."

For a second, neither of them spoke. Then Dad reached out and pulled TJ into a hug, firm and steady, the kind that made TJ feel like everything might just be okay. The medallion pressed between them, solid and reassuring—like a promise neither of them needed to say out loud.

Ɏ

ALMOST THE MOMENT AFTER THE HOLIDAYS ENDED, TJ, MANNY, Mom, and Tunde got a special transport portal from the UCMP straight from the New York embassy—which apparently was connected to the subway system—to the one in New Ile-Ife.

TJ's security detail had doubled as he was escorted through the village and toward the entrance of Ifa Academy. TJ kept pulling down his beanie so as not to be seen, but Tunde kept jumping up and down, wanting everyone to know how his family rolled. He even shouted to one of his friends when they passed Anansi's Arcade.

"Yeah, yeah!" Tunde shouted. "That's right, my family got it like that."

"Must be nice..." his friend replied, stepping away from the *Djambe* Drums he was playing.

Aisha, who was alone instead of being flanked by LaVont or Jimoh, scowled. Manny made sure to walk between her and TJ, saying, "Don't look at her. Just keeping walking forward."

TJ, tall as he was, was still short enough to hide behind their escorts. At the very least, not too many reporters came at him. And it wasn't long before he was back on academy grounds.

The familiar scents of sage and rainwood greeted TJ as he pushed open the door to his dorm room back at Ifa Academy. Just a half hour ago, he'd been in the middle of New York's biting air, lugging his bags past holiday travelers with Manny, Tunde, and Mom at his side. Now? He was halfway across the world, standing inside his dormitory carved into the roots of an ancient tree, where the air smelled like earth after rain, and the magic in the walls hummed quietly, like it had been waiting for him to come back.

TJ let his duffel bag slump onto the bed with a heavy thud, barely getting his bearings, when Ayo materialized at his side, cradling a fishbowl in both hands, a broad grin already plastered across his face.

*So...* The goldfish inside the bowl twisted in a lazy circle, its mouth moving in perfect sync with what seemed to be Ayo's thoughts. *You really went and dropped the 'L' word on Manny, huh?*

"Wait, wait wait," TJ said. "First, what's with the fish? And... What? Already? How did you know?"

Ayo smirked, clearly having way too much fun. *News travels fast, my guy. And say hello to Goldy. He'll be my voice for the time being. Real chill guy. And hey, don't change the subject. What's this about you and Manny and the 'L' word.*

Heat crept up TJ's neck, settling just under his ears. "And what about you?" TJ shoved one of his hoodies into the narrow dresser. "You really finna tell me you never told Titi you love her?"

The fish darted in a small loop, as if scoffing. *Me and Titi are different.*

"Sure. Different. Got it. And... Okay, that's just weird, dude. Can you stop making Goldy's lips move like that? Can't you just speak directly through his mind instead."

Ayo waved the notion away. *That's just a side effect. Don't trip off that.* Goldy swam more erratically, reflecting Ayo's growing irritation.

"Ayo, Manny and I told you to stay away from the book. That's really jacked up. I really don't think Goldy's mouth should be moving like that."

*Stop changing the subject, bruh! You and Manny have been together what —a few weeks? A month? You can't just* say *the 'L' word like that! You're teenagers! You've barely even been through—*

"Again," TJ cut in, slamming another drawer shut. "*You and Titi*?"

*That's* different, Ayo thought-spoke as Goldy snapped.

TJ shook his head, trying not to roll his eyes. But the doubt wormed its way into his thoughts. Maybe Ayo was right. He and Manny weren't together that long, and yeah, things had been *intense* lately. But it wasn't like the words nearly slipped out by accident—he meant it. He knew it when he was about to say it. He knew it for a while. Even before they were official.

"I don't know," TJ muttered, folding a shirt before opting to use Oya's Wind directly. "Saying it felt right in the moment."

Goldy floated near the surface, staring at him with his wide, unblinking eyes. *That's called* trauma bonding, *my friend.*

TJ glared at the fish. "Wow. Thanks for that." Then he shook his head and glared at Ayo instead. Talking to Ayo-Goldy was going to take some getting used to. "Who gave you Goldy, anyway?"

*Ninki Nanka! She's in tight with all kinds of animals and wildlife. I should have taken private lessons with her months ago. When I told her how I can speak to you through animals, she told me to pursue that path. She thinks if I get good enough, it'll help my telepathic communication with humans.*

A sharp creak from the door saved TJ from responding further. He turned just as LaVont and Jimoh strolled in, their trunks trailing behind them, grins plastered across their faces like they were already on the lookout for trouble. TJ seized up, then tapped Ayo to look.

"I didn't think we'd see them again," TJ murmured. "I saw Aisha near the arcade earlier."

Goldy practically scowled as Ayo thought-spoke, *Me too. Surprised they'd show their faces again.*

"Well, well, well," LaVont said with a slow, smug drawl. "Look who's back. The lovebirds."

Jimoh chuckled, dumping his bag at the foot of his bed at the far end of the room. "Bet y'all spent the whole break practicing your kissing."

TJ's hands clenched at his sides, the muscles in his jaw tightening. The air shifted—just slightly—and the residual Ashe in the room grew sharper, buzzing at the edge of his senses like a restless spark. TJ allowed it to fill him up. Welcomed it. His staff wasn't far away if he needed it, just under his bed.

TJ took a confident step forward, and Ayo matched it instantly, his stance firm, his eyes narrowing behind those designer glasses.

"What the hell are you doing back?" TJ's voice came out low, steady as a drumbeat.

LaVont grinned wider. "Relax, man. We just playing."

"Yeah," Jimoh added, his grin a little too sharp. "Just having a little fun."

"Yeah, bet your asshole of a father had fun chasing a bunch of kids around his shop."

The hum in the walls vibrated harder now. With his breath, TJ took it in. His magic itched, coiling beneath his skin, ready to explode if he let it. He could see it—one flick of his wrist, and

Jimoh would be flat on his ass, right where he belonged. Ayo was ready too, the fish swimming wildly in its bowl, reflecting every ounce of his friend's agitation.

"I think it's time to put Goldy down," TJ said out the side of his mouth. Ayo agreed, and put the fish safely on his end table.

Ayo's voice turned cold as he said, "Say one more t-t-thing. Go ahead."

For half a second, Jimoh's expression altered, like he was weighing whether it was worth pushing them any further. But then LaVont nudged him with a laugh, and whatever hesitation he'd had vanished.

"Aw, what's the matter?" LaVont sneered. "Gonna go cry to Manny about it?"

TJ took another step, ready to blow the whole situation wide open, but before he could act—

"Hey!" Umar's voice snapped through the room, cutting through the tension like a whip. They all turned to him walking through the door and dropping his bags to get in the middle. The sight was somewhat comical, what with Umar's short arms outstretched from his long body. "We just got back," he said, his tone flat. "Can we not do this right now?"

For a moment, no one moved. The Ashe in the room sizzled in the air, buzzing like the last spark before a fire caught. TJ could feel Jimoh and LaVont's magic building, and he was ready to use it against them, to feed Ayo, who was also revving up silently. But would they know how to counter TJ the same way the Keepers did? The thought forced a slow exhale from TJ's lips, and his fists loosened at his sides. Ashe drifted back, reluctant, but it went. And good thing it did, because Oroma stepped into the room.

The caretaker only stood half the length of the door but somehow her shadow loomed long across the room. Like always, her hair was immaculate, hair braided down in an intricate design with no fly aways. "You two," she said, pointing to LaVont and Jimoh. "Pick up your things. You're bunking with the juniors for the rest of the term."

"What!?" Jimoh exclaimed.

LaVont joined in. "You can't be serious."

"Serious as a perfect plait, and you know I don't mess those up."

She snapped her fingers. "Now. This is on the Headmistress' orders. Take it up with her if you're so miffed about it."

Jimoh and LaVont looked at each other like the other would have answers, but they reluctantly grabbed their things and started heading their way out.

"Enjoy the j-j-juniors, fellas," Ayo stuttered. "Be careful who you b-b-bunk with. They might be b-b-bed-wetters."

TJ didn't have any words for the pair of them. Just a flared nose and slitted eyes.

"My father will hear about this," Jimoh said as he passed. Then under his breath he said. "Can't believe they're having us with the juniors. What kind of nonsense is that."

When they finally were out of view in the forest thicket outside, Oroma at their heels, TJ finally said, "Well. Welcome back to us, I guess."

*The new year's already startin' off great,* Ayo thought-spoke sarcastically, lifting his fishbowl again.

TJ sighed, dropping onto his bed with a heavy thud. "Yeah. I can already tell."

# 48

# READY OR NOT

THE DAY BEFORE HIS NEXT STAFFCRAFTING SESSION, TJ FOUND himself alone at lunch. Ayo was engrossed in a telepathy session at the Hospital Tree, and Manny was sweating it out at crossover practice before their next big game. Usually, TJ avoided Eni, but that day, he decided to approach her, especially as she was sitting next to Titi.

"Hey, uh… mind if I sit?"

Both girls snapped their attention to him, their faces a synchronized wall of disapproval. TJ's breath hitched. Yeah, he wasn't walking away from this unscathed.

"You better sit," Titi said, her Nigerian accent sharp. "Got a lot of explaining to do."

Eni leaned back, arms crossed, her elegant brow arched. "Took you long enough, TJ. Thought you were going to avoid us forever."

"C'mon, it's not even been a full day yet." TJ slid onto the bench, feeling like a mouse trying to explain itself to two very large, very annoyed cats. "I'm sorry, okay? I messed up. Big time."

Titi snorted, adjusting her glasses. "That's one way to put it. How you go'n drag us into that mess without telling us how dangerous it was? And now I've spent most of my vacation at Babalu-Aye because of you!—Those chocolates were nice though, not gonna lie."

"We trusted you, TJ," Eni said. "I thought you were just

hopping realms or something. Didn't know we'd be on the lookout for Keepers like that. Not cool, my guy."

"You're right. I should've told y'all everything from the start. I thought I could handle it on my own, but... I didn't think it through. And because of that, you guys got hurt."

"*That's* an understatement," Titi muttered, dragging her spoon through her goat stew. "If I had known what we were walking into, I wouldn't have gone. I lost my brother already, TJ. What would my family have done if I..." Her voice wavered just slightly at the end, but she caught herself, folding her arms and straightening her back.

Eni leaned forward, her expression softer but still firm. "You think you have to protect everyone. But you can't just make those choices for us. We deserve to know what we're getting into."

TJ let out a long breath, hands gripping his knees. "I'm sorry. I mean it." Aisha, LaVont, and Jimoh walked by, so he lowered his voice further. "I didn't want anyone else to get hurt. I thought if I could just get through the mission, everything would be fine."

"But it wasn't fine!" Titi snapped. "And now we're left picking up the pieces."

"I know. I'll make it right. I promise. Whatever you need—whether it's being your personal errand boy, or... I don't know, making sure Ayo doesn't get on your nerves for a week—I'm in. Whatever it takes."

Titi gave him a flat look. "Ayo annoys me no matter what. But I do like the idea of having a personal assistant. I'm terrible at communal magic studies and that essay is due in..."

"I got it! I'll write it. Guaranteed A."

Eni smirked, though there was no warmth in it. "And I've got a live test coming up near the willows. If you can make an excuse for being there, I sure could use a bit of a boost."

TJ raised both hands, palms out in surrender. "Deal. Just... please, don't stay mad at me forever."

Eni looked him over once or twice before her stern face cracked. "Okay, don't pout so much like that. I'll figure out something to get us even again. You already see what happens when Ayo owes me, or I him."

TJ dropped his head on the table, extinguishing all the air from his entire lungs in relief. The force of his breath was so powerful, and he used Oya's Wind so much, that he knocked over Eni's staff, which sat next to her on her bench.

"My bad, my bad!" TJ got up to retrieve the staff. "I'm not off to a good start, am I?"

"Don't trip," Eni laughed. "How's it going with your crafting this year?"

TJ groaned. "So much stress. Hey, actually, I had a question about your staff."

Eni craned her long neck, her eyes curious. "What's up?"

"Last year, when you got that piece from Egypt, how did you pass your trial?" TJ nodded to Eni's staff, which lay next to her on her bench.

Eni gave him a short laugh. "That's part of the reason I did my test in Egypt and not at Ifa. The Egyptian council was more open to unconventional staff designs. Sort of makes sense when you consider how many times Ancient Egypt was conquered over the years. Their culture was ever-changing back when their magic was most powerful."

TJ sighed, running a hand through his Afro. "Oh great, I should have just gone with Freya and gotten tested in the UK."

Eni shook her head. "Nah, it's better this way. I didn't have the heart to stand up to Bamidele. You, on the other hand, have the chance to show him he's wrong." She reached across the table, placing her hand on TJ's. A familiar warmth shot through him. Eni's touch always had that effect. "And we're *rightfully* giving you a hard time but… thank you for saving us. Your voice, your spirit… it never faltered in that caravan. Just like at Eko Atlantic." Perhaps sensing the tension in TJ's hand, she pulled hers away, remembering herself. "I feel sort of bad. I'm the only one who got out of that without getting seriously hurt. I think that's because I kept holding back. I wasn't being useful… when you and your friends… Manny… you just stood your ground like you didn't care. How do you do it? How aren't you ever scared?"

TJ's expression softened. "I'm always scared, Eni. But I can't let that stop me from protecting my friends."

"You're a good one," Eni said. "Friend… that is."

"Not always. I can do better." TJ rubbed the side of his fade.

"And I can start right now. Let me get those plates for you." He grabbed up the leftovers of their food and took them back to the counter for them. When he returned, he did his best to small talk but he was never good at that, so he decided to stay quiet and make sure Eni and Titi's cups were filled.

Eventually, TJ thanked them both, took a deep breath, stood, and made his way to the staffcrafting clearing. There, he placed his staff in the middle, a silent declaration of his readiness for the trial. As he stepped back, he glimpsed Bamidele watching from the shadows of the trees, his bald head and wild beard camouflaging him in the thick forest.

"Mr. Young," Bamidele said sadly, "you are making a grievous mistake."

TJ turned to face him, tapping at his side. "I know you don't agree with how I built this, but these tests are supposed to show if there is any danger, right? Let me go through the trials, at least."

Bamidele ran his hand down a nearby tree with sprawling branches, as though sensing its spirit. "Are you familiar with the albizia tree? Do you know why it's so special?"

TJ shrugged, not expecting the question. "Uh... it's... tall?"

Bamidele's lips twitched, almost but not quite a smile. "True enough. But it's not just tall, Mr. Young. I learned about this tree when I vacationed to Kauai—erm, Hawaii. It's considered an invasive species in that place, as so many plant life there are. Do you know why?"

TJ shook his head.

"In fertile lands," the Staffmaster went on, "like the rich soils of Hawaii, the albizia grows faster than almost anything else around it. Fifteen feet in a single year. Twenty, even, if the conditions are just right."

"Twenty feet!?" TJ echoed, eyebrows shooting up as tall as the tree. "That's... ridiculous."

"It is. Ridiculously fast. But do you know what happens when the wind picks up? When storms come?"

TJ swallowed, knowing a lesson was coming. "No idea."

"The branches snap." Bamidele pinched the thin tree at its base and it came crashing down. "Sometimes the whole tree falls.

Because, despite all that growth, albizia wood is weak. Brittle. It doesn't have the strength to support itself."

TJ shifted uncomfortably. He wasn't sure where this was going, but Bamidele's words pressed down on him all the same.

"Your magic," Bamidele continued, "your Ashe, is like the albizia, Mr. Young. You have grown faster than anyone I've trained —faster than Ifedayo, even."

TJ blinked. He wasn't used to being compared to his older sister so favorably. Pride flared, but Bamidele's next words smothered it.

"But speed isn't everything," the Staffmaster said, his voice firm. "Your Ashe is powerful, yes. Raw, like the rich soil under the albizia's roots. It's why your staffwork is so impressive already. But fast growth can lead to a weak foundation. A few strong winds, and..." He snapped his fingers around another of the branches. "You break."

TJ looked away, his hands flexing around his staff. He caught sight of the faint scars on his arms and quickly tugged his gloves higher, as if covering them could hide the truth.

"I won't break," he said, his voice tighter than he wanted it to be. "I'm ready for the trial."

Bamidele's gaze softened, but only slightly. "I know you *think* you are. But readiness isn't just about strength. It's about being able to bend without breaking. To hold steady when everything around you is in chaos."

"I hear you; I'm not gonna snap."

For a long moment, Bamidele studied him. Then he nodded, just once. "Good. Because I don't want to lose one of the most promising students I've ever had to his own ambition." He moved forward, leaving the clearing.

"Best student?" TJ asked. "It didn't seem like that to me."

Bamidele chuckled through his nose. "I don't tell my students when they are my favorites. Not since your sister. Tends to go to one's head."

"Huh?"

"Rest well, young diviner. I'll be seeing you tomorrow morning."

# 49

# OF THE BODY

TJ TOSSED AND TURNED ALL NIGHT, HIS MIND SWIRLING AS THE night stretched on. The trial loomed large, a daunting challenge that consumed his every sleeping moment.

Would Staffmaster Bamidele pass TJ if he knew what was at stake?

Did TJ even want to pass if he wasn't actually ready?

As the first rays of sunlight crept through the bark windows of his dorm, TJ realized he had barely slept. His stomach churned with a potent mixture of nerves, a restless ocean that threatened to overwhelm him. He took a deep breath, trying to steady himself as he prepared for the day ahead.

Manny was there when he walked out of his dormitory. Outside of "good morning" they didn't say much to each other. They didn't need to say anything at all as they walked hand in hand to the dense forest. And that's exactly what TJ needed. Just a quiet moment. When they got to the treeline leading to the staffcrafting area, Manny stopped them, kissed TJ on the cheek, and said, "You're going to do great. Because you're TJ Young. And don't you forget that."

"Thanks, Manny."

"Go get 'em, Lucky Charm."

As TJ crossed into the staffcrating clearing, the supportive glances from his classmates and the silent nods from the small council of elders both uplifted and unnerved him. Ayo and Titi sat near the front, shoulder to shoulder. Each of them gave TJ a fist of solidarity. TJ nodded back to them in kind.

Morning sun filtered through the branches, casting streaks of gold and green across his staff, which still stood upright at the center. Ready. Waiting. TJ moved to it, wrapped it in his gloved hand. The runes at the bottom pulsed faintly; the double helix of Dayo's old design buzzed with untapped Ashe, and the crystal at the head winked with a gentle light. Then TJ's gaze fell upon the muted Celtic charm, the cauldron piece associated with Cailleach. Would it work despite what Freya told him about the dead god linked to it?

TJ's eyes automatically shifted to where Freya usually sat during their sessions, and he frowned when he did not find her there. Hopefully she was off with the druids in Scotland, passing her own trial. Despite the sunlight, the air felt cold, like the clearing didn't quite belong in the same season as the forest that bordered it.

At the far end, Ninki Nanka curled lazily around a pedestal, her shimmering green scales catching every flicker of light. *Good morning, Mr. Young,* she thought-spoke, and TJ gave her a curt nod.

Nearby, a woman TJ didn't recognize sat cross-legged on a low stone seat. She looked to be in her late thirties, early-forties, her thick jawline and square face giving her a sharp, angular appearance. Her hair was dark as midnight, straight, long, and going down her back and shoulders. Dressed in navy, practical clothing, she gave off the impression of someone you wouldn't notice until she *wanted* you to. A faint wisp of smoke drifted from a golden earring hooked in her left ear, curling upward in slow, deliberate spirals. A strange prickling sensation crawled at the back of his neck as she watched him—calm, patient, like she was measuring something he couldn't quite grasp.

"You're not Elder Akande," TJ said with a canted head.

The woman's mouth curved slightly, a polite acknowledgment more than a smile. "I am not. My name is Karminder Khatri of the UCMP. Elder Akande is—otherwise occupied, and I offered to stand in for her for your trials today." Her voice was soft yet deep, resonant, like a struck bell. "I understand the two of you are acquainted. She mentioned Camp Olosa, changing crystal colors, and something about being kidnapped..."

TJ sighed heavily. "Long story…"

Bamidele stood beside her, arms crossed, his stern gaze locked on TJ. Today, he wore full traditional àṣọ òkè robes that actually looked clean, unlike his usual forest-man getup.

*Well,* Ninki Nanka rumbled, drawing TJ's attention. *Shall we?*

TJ's fingers tightened around his staff, the smooth wood warming under his grip as Bamidele stepped forward, his robes brushing softly against the dew-covered grass. "The trial is divided into three parts. "The physical, the mental, and the spiritual—the three pillars that have guided diviners and staffmakers for centuries."

TJ's thoughts flickered back to the endless days at Camp Olosa, those brutal training sessions that left him drenched, aching, and barely standing by nightfall. His gaze drifted across the clearing and landed on Ayo, who caught his eye and gave a small, confident nod. TJ straightened, the familiar gesture grounding him—until a snicker from the back row sliced through the quiet.

He glanced over to catch LaVont and Jimoh whispering behind cupped hands, smug grins stretched across their faces. Great. Nothing like knowing a couple of assholes were betting on you to fail.

Bamidele continued, unfazed. "Headmistress Ninki Nanka will oversee the physical trial first." He gestured to her large form, her giraffe neck lifting high. "You'll be tested on how well you channel Ashe through movement and quick-witted scenarios." Bamidele nodded toward the Khatri woman. "Miss Khatri will judge the mental aspect. She'll be testing your fortitude and give a general assessment on your maturity and ability to wield such great power."

The scent of her earring smoke drifted through the air—sugary, like burnt honey. What was it? TJ could have sworn she was almost listening to the trinket like a whisper.

"And finally," Bamidele said, "I will test your spiritual connection—the bond between you and your staff. How much stress it can endure. No diviner can succeed without understanding the soul of their instrument, and the limits of its power."

TJ froze as Bamidele's eyes landed on his staff, and a familiar knot tightened in his stomach. His staff wasn't like the others—a blend of many cultures, Nigerian and otherwise. TJ pinched the medallion Dad gave him for Christmas, and it settled his nerves. He forced himself to square his shoulders, standing tall so that the morning light danced along both the worldly charms and Yoruba craftsmanship wound into the wood.

Bamidele's gaze lingered a moment longer before he gave a slight nod. "Are you prepared to begin, Mr. Young?"

TJ's throat was dry, and he swallowed, hoping no one noticed. Every part of him screamed to bolt, to find an excuse—any excuse. But running wasn't an option. Not now. Not with Ayo and his fellow students watching, and definitely not with LaVont and Jimoh waiting to pounce on the first sign of weakness. Plus, it wasn't just TJ's staff license riding on this. It was the Orishas he needed to save too.

He exhaled slowly, grounding himself, and forced his voice to stay steady. "Yes, sir. I'm ready."

Ninka Nanka's voice slithered into his mind. *So it begins.*

Without warning or fanfare, the ground beneath TJ softened, mud creeping through cracks in the stone and spreading like it had been waiting centuries to reclaim the space. The heavy scent of wet earth clung to the cool air. Roots coiled upward, winding between ancient stones, as if the forest was tugging at the seams of the trial grounds.

TJ shifted his stance, but the mud sucked at his Jordans, dragging at him like it intended to pull him under. And that pull brought him back to Eko Atlantic, to Olokun. His Ashe, which had thrummed through him like a second heartbeat just moments ago, now trickled slow and unsteady. The swamp's magic pressed in on him. Siphoned his energy. Left his limbs heavy and reluctant to obey.

*You've got this, man!* Ayo's voice rang out in his head. *Ogun's Grounded Pulse, man! Show 'em how the Orishas really move.*

Despite everything, a small breath of laughter escaped TJ, loosening the tight knot in his chest.

Titi called out, too, "Don't think—just move! Trust your staff."

TJ tightened his grip on the smooth wood, shifting his weight as the mud thickened around his ankles, creeping higher, as if testing how far it could climb. His Jordans dragged with every step, Ashe leaking from him like water through a crack. Drowning screams peppered his ears, crashing skyscrapers flared in his mind.

A quiet snicker drifted over the mist. "Three minutes, tops," Jimoh muttered, just loud enough for TJ to hear through Umar's encouraging yelps.

LaVont leaned lazily against a low stone pillar, a smirk playing on his lips. "Think he faceplants? Or just sinks?"

*Ignore them. Just focus.* But the murmur of their voices pressed into him, poking at the edges of his concentration.

From her corner, Ninki Nanka stirred, her green scales shifting against the grass. Her slitted pupils narrowed, and her massive head turned toward the boys, her tongue flicking once, tasting the air.

*Be silent,* Ninki Nanka hissed, her voice low and cold. *Let him concentrate.*

Jimoh mimed zipping his lips, though the mischievous gleam in his eyes remained. LaVont gave a lazy shrug, throwing TJ a smug glance. They clearly weren't done causing trouble—but for now, they kept quiet.

Ninki Nanka's gaze lingered on them a second longer before sliding back to TJ.

He forced himself to breathe. The mud tugged at his feet, thicker and heavier with every moment. His Ashe felt weaker now, draining away too fast. He had to act before it slipped out of his grasp entirely.

He stepped forward—and the mud sucked harder, pulling him off balance.

A sudden gust of wind whipped through the clearing, scattering leaves and kicking up the mist. Had that come from the swamp? It hit TJ just as he shifted his weight, and his sneakers slid out from under him.

He wobbled dangerously, his heart lurching as he fought to stay upright. The "ooo's" and "aaah's" from the crowd mingled with the wailing from his past trauma at Eko Atlantic.

From the corner of his eye, TJ caught the flicker of magic fading from Jimoh's hand. The boy's snicker followed a beat later, soft but unmistakable.

TJ clenched his jaw so tight his teeth ached. They were cheating. It wasn't the swamp. TJ could see the Ashe at play from the boys. He couldn't let them get to him—not now.

"Focus, TJ!" Titi's voice cut through the fog. "You know what to do!"

With a grunt of effort, TJ planted his staff in the ground and called on Ogun. It was so much harder using magic on his own.

Wait, he didn't have to use his own Ashe. LaVont and Jimoh were supplying him with what he needed without their realizing it. They weren't screwing him over; they were throwing him a rope!

Using another blast of wind, TJ latched onto it and turned it to his favor. The air responded in a swirling rush, lifting him just high enough to pull his sneakers free from the mud. He stumbled forward onto solid stone, shoes skidding awkwardly—but he stayed upright.

TJ breathed out a sigh of relief. *Easy. Nothing to it.*

The mist shifted, revealing the next challenge: a massive serpent of ebony, its scales gleaming like polished obsidian, gliding through the haze with a deliberate grace. The serpent's tongue flicked the air, tasting TJ's presence. Its eyes gleamed with quiet menace, the slow, cold patience of a predator that saw no reason to hurry.

TJ planted his staff, heart pounding against his ribs. The serpent wasn't real—at least, not entirely. But the way it moved, the scrape of scales against stone, felt all too real. If he hesitated for even a moment, it would unravel everything he'd worked for.

"Bet he freezes," LaVont whispered, low but smug. "Any second now."

TJ ground his teeth. He wasn't giving them the satisfaction.

"Enough!" TJ muttered as he eyed the medallion his father had given him. Shoving away his trauma, the jeers from the bullies, his own self doubt, he slammed his staff into the ground.

Vines erupted from the earth, twisting upward in thick coils. They wrapped tight around the serpent's gleaming body, squeezing until the creature hissed—and then unraveled into mist, dissolving into the air like smoke.

The swamp vanished with it. Mud slithered back into the cracks between the stones, and the mist thinned, leaving behind only the faint scent of damp leaves.

TJ stood there, breathing hard, his hands trembling around his staff. It hadn't been perfect. The stumble, the distractions—it had all thrown him off. And Ninki Nanka had *seen* it. Every hesitation, every mistake.

Her yellow eyes blinked slowly as she uncoiled from her resting place, her body shifting with a sound like silk sliding over stone. She skulked forward slightly. Her head tilted as she studied TJ. Then her tongue flicked once, tasting the air between them, as if measuring the weight of his effort.

TJ kept his face steady, though his heart hammered painfully in his chest. He wanted to believe he'd done enough.

Ninki Nanka hummed, a deep, resonant sound that seemed to vibrate through the ground beneath his feet. It wasn't approval—at least not entirely. But it wasn't rejection either.

TJ swallowed hard, adjusting his grip on his staff. He'd made it through the trial. Barely. But whether it had been enough... only time would tell.

The Headmistress' gaze slid away from him, turning back toward LaVont and Jimoh. Her eyes narrowed, her tongue flicking once, sharply. *You. And you.* The boys stiffened under her stare. *I warned you, and you ignored me.*

Jimoh shifted nervously, but LaVont crossed his arms, forcing a lazy grin, saying, "We didn't mean anything by it."

Ninki Nanka's pupils narrowed to slits. *Detention. Leave this space at once.*

Jimoh's mouth snapped shut. LaVont glared at TJ one last time, but even he wasn't foolish enough to argue. They slunk away toward the edge of the clearing, muttering under their breath.

*The trial continues,* Ninki Nanka said low and soft.

TJ spun his staff once and rested it against his shoulder. Khatri's trial was next. The woman lifted her hand and waved TJ to follow, and he did, straight into a separate grove just a few dozen yards from the main clearing. The rest of the students stayed behind. It seemed this was to be a more private trial than the last.

The grove felt like it had been pulled from another world, too perfect to be real. Sunlight dappled the ground through the thick canopy, and the air was warm, almost too warm, like it was pressing down on him. The scent of flowers TJ didn't recognize mixed with the faint, sweet smoke curling from Khatri's earring. It wasn't unpleasant, but it made him feel unsteady, like he was trying to stand on a boat in calm but shifting waters.

At the far end of the clearing, Ninki Nanka lay coiled in her shimmering scales, her golden body catching flickers of light with every subtle breath. The creature's massive head rested on her fore-claws, eyes half-closed as though she was merely pretending to ignore what was happening.

Staffmaster Bamidele stood off to the side, silent and unreadable. He didn't need to say a word to remind TJ of how much pressure was riding on this moment. The way his arms were crossed and his gaze fixed on TJ like a hammer waiting to drop was enough.

But none of it compared to Khatri. She sat perfectly upright on her stone bench, legs crossed, a porcelain teacup resting on the stone beside her. That endless swirl of incense-like smoke spiraled up and around her head, twisting in intricate patterns TJ swore were almost letters. She was calm, collected, and patient. Too patient.

TJ shifted uncomfortably on his own bench. He gripped his staff like it might keep him anchored, but the polished wood was slick with sweat from his palms.

Instead, her almond-shaped eyes locked on him like she was reading a book she didn't much care for but couldn't put down. "Let's talk about Eko Atlantic," Khatri said.

*Damn, we startin' there straight out the gate?*

# 50

# OF THE MIND

"Do you believe you could have saved more people?"

The question hit harder than TJ expected. He blinked, trying to push away the memories—water crashing through streets, faces lost in the flood. He thought of Emeka, everyone. What did this have to do with his staff?

"I stayed," TJ said quietly. "I tried."

Khatri tilted her head slightly, watching him without judgment. "But was it enough?"

TJ's gaze dropped to the ground. "It had to be."

She didn't respond right away, just watched him with that same patient calm, as though she was letting the silence do the work for her. "I've heard," she said finally, "that you sometimes put your friends at risk as well. Is that true?"

He shifted uncomfortably in his seat, trying not to let his eyes shift to where the students waited outside the private grove. "I… I don't mean to."

"That is not what I asked."

TJ pressed his lips together. The memories rushed in again—Titi bleeding on the floor of the caravan, Ayo struggling with his stutter, Manny's lightning wound along her arm, Emeka getting blasted through his chest, that elder at Eko Atlantic with her sunhat…. Not to mention the three Orishas wasting away in the Court of All. Every moment where things could've gone terribly wrong because of his decisions, because he hadn't been quick enough or smart enough to stop it.

"Yes," he said quietly. "I have. But I don't have a choice. I can't do anything on my own, and even if I could, I'm just one kid!"

Khatri's expression didn't change, but something in her gaze softened—just a fraction. "There is always a choice. And you are selling yourself short, young man. But for what it's worth, you are right to stand with your friends. The world is not yours alone to save."

She produced another teapot and cup from nothing and offered to pour TJ some tea. He nodded, figuring it was best to be polite, and accepted the cup with thanks. He sipped, wincing at its bitter taste while he waited for her to continue her questions.

Khatri poured her own cup and sipped carefully herself, clearly in no rush to continue the interview. The waiting was making TJ even more nervous than he had been before. He took another drink of tea out of habit, forgetting he didn't like it.

Finally, Khatri spoke up again, "Which is more important, your friends or your magic?"

TJ didn't even have to think. "My friends. That's not even a question."

"And which is more important, your friends, or your gods?"

"Why is it even a choice?"

"Because *I* am asking." Khatri took another sip of her tea.

"Well, my friends still. And to save us some time, it's always gonna be my friends. Well, them and my family."

"Very well. That established, why is it then, do you think, that you risk both in your struggles to protect your pantheon?"

TJ didn't understand the point of these questions, or what the woman was supposed to be getting at. What was he supposed to do? Just let the world burn?

"Because we want the world to be better, not worse. The Orishas are part of that."

Her eyes flickered up from her cup to lock straight on TJ's stare. "Do you suppose the victims of Eko Atlantic would agree?"

A flash of flooding water. The crash of shattering window glass. TJ shook his head. "What?"

"Would Emeka?" She was staring at him hard now, that wisp of honeyed smoke spiralling more intensely up into the air.

"Who—who the hell are you, lady? What even is this?" TJ angled around her to look to Ninki Nanka and Bamidele for answers. But both observed like all of this was perfectly normal. What was this? An interview for therapy?

"Why, Mr. Young," Khatri continued, resting her sharp chin atop her long hand and fingers, "why do you wish to save the very beings who slaughtered your own people?"

Heat rose though TJ now. "That wasn't—you don't know what you're talking about!"

Khatri was remaining calm, and that just angered TJ even more. She set down her cup with a soft *clack* against the stone. "Explain it to me, then. Why do you risk the lives of your family and friends? Those you claim are more important to you than anything? I would assume this includes your gods."

"Deities, not gods," TJ retorted, but it was a hollow response. To him, the difference between the terms was semantics, but he had to fight back with something.

TJ's throat went dry. He looked at Khatri, then at the ground, then back at her again. Why did she have to make it sound so... accusing? His voice cracked when he finally spoke again. "Because if I don't fight for something bigger than all of us, then what's the point?" He paused, gripping his staff tighter. "Yeah, I want to keep my friends and family safe—I need to—but if I don't stand up, the world we're living in won't be safe for any of us. The Orishas, the other pantheons, they're not perfect, okay? I know that. But they're still part of the balance. If we lose them, it all falls apart."

Khatri tilted her head, her eyes narrowing slightly as if weighing his words. The smoke drifted closer to her ear, curling tightly, and she gave a barely perceptible nod before taking a slow sip of tea. "I understand. Taking a step back from Orishas and world-saving for a moment, then, tell me about your sister, Ifedayo Young."

The mention of Dayo hit him like a sucker punch. TJ's shoulders stiffened. Why was she bringing her up?

"What about her?"

"I never had the pleasure of meeting her myself, though some of my colleagues did. They spoke highly of her. It must have been difficult, losing such a sister."

The edges of TJ's vision blurred with unwelcome memories—Dayo's laugh, the way she used to flick his ear to get his attention, and then the silence after she was gone.

"What do you want me to say?" His voice wavered, and he hated it. "That it broke me? That it still does every day? Because it does. But talking about it doesn't bring her back. Everyone keeps talking about her like it'll bring her back."

Khatri didn't flinch, but the smoke curled again, briefly forming what looked like a question mark before vanishing. "If I pressed you, what would you like to say? I should like to hear about her from one who knew her best."

TJ swallowed hard. He didn't want to talk about this. Not with her. Not with anyone. But the words came anyway. "Dayo was... she was everything I wanted to be. She was strong, smart, always, like, two steps ahead of everyone. But she had this way of making people feel like they actually mattered, like they could do more than just get by. She made me believe I could be more, even when I didn't see it myself."

Khatri said nothing, her teacup set down on the stone table between them.

The silence dragged. TJ squirmed, his voice rising defensively. "What? Why aren't you saying anything?"

The smoke swirled tighter, almost like an exclamation point, and Khatri's lips curved into a faint smile. "I suppose I just have the feeling you have more to say. You must have felt conflicted, learning your sister was a member of the Keepers, for instance."

TJ froze. His hands tightened on his staff until his knuckles ached. How did she know that? How could she have known? TJ wasn't going to let her see any shock on his face though, he said, "Yeah... she was a Keeper. She wasn't perfect, okay? None of us are. But she turned her back on them. She didn't want any part of it anymore, and that's what matters."

For the first time, Ninki Nanka lifted her head with curiosity. Had she not known about Dayo?

"I'm glad to hear you knew that." Khatri's tone didn't change, but something about it felt sharper. "Out of curiosity, did she ever mention why she decided to turn on them? What specifically pulled her from their path?"

TJ scrambled for a response. "She um... she um... didn't really talk about it with me, but her best friend, um... Adeola... she said Dayo couldn't stick with the Keepers after seeing how far they'd fallen. It wasn't about balance anymore—it was just payback for the Orishas, for the Keepers. You know... stuff like Eko Atlantic."

"I see. And her friend Adeola, she's not the biggest fan of the Keepers now herself, I believe."

Again, TJ had to do his best to let shock not take over his face. This woman was a UCMP official, after all. She would have all this information. Hell, Elder Adeyemi might have been the one to send her. Maybe TJ shouldn't have been so defensive.

"She's not a fan at all," he answered. "The Keepers left her to rot in—" TJ stopped. Khatri might have known all about Adeola, but Ninki Nanka and Staffmaster Bamidele did not. "Let's just say they didn't treat her any better than Dayo." Then something dawned on him. Why wasn't she asking him about his techniques or his spell-work? "Wait! What is this? What does any of this have to do with my staff?"

"Everything and nothing," Khatri replied evenly. "We pour a great deal of ourselves and our inspirations into our artifacts, young man. Wands, rods, staffs, they all share that secret piece of who we are in common. And your staff there shares much in common with your sister's." TJ eyed the double helix at his staff's center. "It's important to understand the why behind that if you are to truly master its power. Do you think you have your why?"

That question held TJ a little longer than the rest. What was his core reason for doing all of this? Sometimes it felt like he was just being pulled along by circumstance. But what drove him, really? "Honestly? I don't know. I thought it was to protect the people I care about, to make sure what happened to Dayo and Eko Atlantic doesn't happen again. But sometimes it feels like I'm just trying to prove I can. Is that enough of a why?"

Khatri's eyes didn't waver. "It's certainly the start of one. To whom are you trying to prove yourself, do you think?"

"Everyone who said I couldn't. Everyone who's counting on me. The Orishas, my family, myself. Take your pick."

"And your parents? Your father is of non-magical origin, I believe. What does he think of all you've accomplished?"

"He's... supportive," TJ muttered, his voice quieter now. "But he doesn't really get it. Magic's not his world, so it's like we're speaking two different languages sometimes."

"That can be difficult. What about your mother? How does she feel about it all?"

"My mom? She's... complicated. She's proud when I do magic stuff, I guess. But when I wasn't... it's like I didn't even exist to her. I don't really get what any of this has to do with my staff, though."

Khatri took a long sip of her tea, the cup held elegantly in her strong hands. "As I said, we put a great deal of ourselves into our artifacts, young man. Our passions, our hopes, our fears. Identifying the source of your pressure is perhaps the most important piece of your puzzle here today."

TJ rose from the bench, the frustration boiling over. "Look, if you're looking for some big, deep answer, here it is: everything I've been through is in that staff. Pressure? You already know everything about me, don't you? So you know I've dealt with the Keepers, like, three times. Faced off with deities, giant monsters, and everything else this world and all the other worlds have thrown at me. That's what's in my staff—every bit of it. All the jacked-up mess, all the fights, all the bullshit no one should have to deal with at my *goddamn age*. It's not perfect, and neither am I, but how many people my age have been through half the crap I've handled? What else do you want from me? I've given enough." He paused, realizing how harsh he sounded. "My bad… about the language."

Khatri rose gracefully, her tea dish vanishing into the air. She brushed her hands over her navy and gold-trimmed coat as if dusting off invisible dirt. Again, she seemed to whisper at the smoke in her earring before turning to TJ. "Worry not, young man. I ask only to get at the heart of things. You have a great deal of potential, Mr. Young. Keep working at your why, and I am confident you shall grow into it quite nicely."

TJ blinked. "Wait, what? That's it? Did I pass?"

She didn't answer, only nodding to Staffmaster Bamidele and turning to rejoin Ninki Nanka.

TJ slumped back onto the bench, his heart pounding. "Great. Just great."

This was *not* going well. And he hadn't even started with his biggest critic: Staffmaster Bamidele.

# 51

# OF THE SPIRIT

STAFFMASTER BAMIDELE WAVED TJ TO FOLLOW HIM OUT OF THE private grove and back to the clearing where the other students waited. No words of encouragement. No advice. Just TJ, his staff, and Bamidele watching him like he already knew how this would end.

What were the other students thinking? They must've been gone a while. TJ tried to make his face as neutral as possible, not wanting to give away how awkward his time with that Khatri woman had been. But he wasn't fooling anyone. Even Ayo gave him a sheepish grin that TJ didn't have the heart to return. Things weren't going well.

Bamidele flicked his wrist, and with a low rumble, a slab of stone rose from the ground. It settled with a dull *thud*, thick enough that cracking it with magic—let alone carving through it—felt impossible.

"This is your task." Bamidele folded his arms, his expression unreadable. "You will hit the stone with water magic. And you will keep hitting it until it breaks, or you do… You need only create a concave in the stone to showcase the sustained power of your staff and your spirit." He pointed to one of the deeper valleys in the stone. "This one was made by your sister. The deepest valley made by any of my students."

TJ stared at the slab. It didn't budge, didn't shift. It just *sat there*, immovable and unyielding.

"Cast," Bamidele said flatly, the word hanging in the air like a dare.

TJ activated Yemoja's Ripple Flow, accepting the challenge. He held the staff out in front of him, gripping it firmly, hands spaced evenly along the wood. He took a deep breath. His hands spun. The staff flowed in his hands like a ripple in a pond, smooth and steady. The movement rolled down the length of the staff from one end to the other, almost like he was coaxing water to slide along it.

With each twist, he tried to keep the motion fluid, as a wave drifting lazily across the ocean—right up to the point where he snapped it upward in a quick flick, bringing the whole thing to a sharp, focused crest. Manifested water impacted against the stone, drilling like a power driver. The carvings along the wood hummed faintly with power, though TJ could already feel something strained and wrong. He ignored it. He didn't have a choice.

"Again," Bamidele said, unmoving.

TJ exhaled, steadied his grip, and pointed the staff toward the slab, summoning another jet of water. The magic spluttered, dribbled. Weak spurts cast off before dying altogether. The runes along his staff flickered like a dying lightbulb. Was the Staffmaster right? Had he defiled his staff with the runes?

Bamidele didn't so much as blink. "Again."

TJ's jaw clenched, and he pushed harder, forcing more Ashe into the spell. This time, the water hit the stone in a thin stream, stronger than before, but still wrong—unstable and uneven. The staff wailed with resistance, the foreign charms seeming to clash against one another like mismatched gears.

TJ pressed a thumb to his swimming medallion, centering himself once more. Sweat trickled down his hairline. His shoulder throbbed. His grip faltered for a second, and he quickly adjusted, fighting off the ache creeping down his arm.

"Harder," Bamidele ordered, voice cool and unfeeling.

TJ planted his feet, eyes narrowed, and poured everything into the next spell. Water shot from the crystal head, striking the stone harder—but it was still off, wobbling as if the magic itself were protesting.

"Again." Bamidele's command was calm, relentless. He looked less like a judge and more like someone waiting for TJ to shatter.

TJ's pulse pounded in his ears as he braced himself for another spell. Lead poured into his body, his strength draining faster than it should. What the hell was this slab made of? The staff trembled in his grip, every cast demanding more of him than the last. His shoulder was on fire, the ache spreading down his arm with each attempt.

"C'mon," TJ muttered to himself. "Come. On."

"Again."

TJ wanted to scream, to throw the staff on the ground and walk away—but he couldn't. Not with Bamidele standing there, the unspoken accusation clear in his eyes. Not with everyone else watching.

With a final surge of desperation, he raised the staff again, biting the inside of his mouth as he forced the magic to respond. He pushed harder, pulling from every corner of his energy. It was impossible to create a concave in the stone. But the pockets left from other students forced TJ to press on. For a moment, the magic swelled, obeying him—and then, with a deafening *crack,* his staff splintered down the middle.

Pain exploded through his arm, sharp and icy. The shock raced from his shoulder to his fingertips, his whole arm going numb as if his veins had filled with ice. He stumbled, nearly dropping the staff, and the fractured wood scraped his skin. But when he looked up, a hole the size of a basketball shot through the slab. He had done it, but at what cost to his staff? It was like what happened with Dayo's—only less severe, a mere fracture.

Bamidele's eyes stayed on him, unreadable. "This is exactly what I warned you about."

TJ cradled the broken staff close, his hands shaking with the weight of failure. He could barely feel the staff in his grip, but the jagged crack running down the center was like a mark branding him. *You tried and failed...*

Bamidele's voice rose for the others to hear. "This staff will destroy you! And anyone foolish enough to stand near you!"

The words hit like a slap, but there was no point in arguing. Bamidele was right—whether TJ wanted to admit it or not.

As Bamidele moved to address the other students, TJ tugged his collar aside, glancing down at the scar on his shoulder. Pale and raw, it stretched from his collarbone to his upper arm, a reminder of every warning he'd ignored. He covered it quickly before anyone noticed.

*Damn...*

At the edge of the clearing, Ayo wandered over. He dropped down beside TJ, his fingers drumming quietly against his thigh. No pity in his expression, just a raised eyebrow. "You a-a-all right?"

TJ exhaled shakily, pressing the fractured staff closer to his chest. "Not even close."

Ayo nudged him with his shoulder, a faint grin tugging at his mouth. "It's still standing. You'll f-f-fix it."

TJ gave a slight nod, though he wasn't sure if Ayo meant the staff or him. Either way, the thought of fixing things felt like a challenge he wasn't ready to face yet.

Khatri walked up to TJ as well. "Chin up, kid." She tapped the Celtic charm on his staff. Before it looked dull, without an ounce of luster. Now it radiated with a slight hue of blue. "That should not be possible for you. The druidic arts do not answer just anyone's call. Take pride in that much, at least." She turned to join her fellow judges, her enchanted earring trailing a thin ribbon of smoke behind her as she went.

But before TJ could even try to feel hope, the final judgments began.

Bamidele led the other judges to the center of the clearing, each with their scrolls and notes floating near their heads. Ninki Nanka slithered forward, her scales shimmering as she regarded the students in silence. Her unblinking gaze swept over TJ, pausing just long enough to make his stomach twist.

Khatri stepped forward first, her voice clear. "The mental trial... For what you have been through, TJ Young, you have shown resilience. You know when to stand your ground and when to reconsider. Both will serve you well in the trials to come. So for your mental evaluation, I would say... pass."

The word rang out in the silence, simple but heavy. TJ held his breath, relief flooding him even as he caught Bamidele's sharp frown. How did he pass that trial? It felt like Khatri wouldn't favor him at all.

Bamidele's gaze hardened. He stepped forward, his voice carrying a hint of finality. "The trial of the spirit." He didn't look at TJ directly, only at the fractured staff. "Fail."

The word was brutal, but it was a blow he expected. TJ's grip on his broken staff slackened. The heavy crack biting into his glove. He forced himself to look up, though the disappointment in Bamidele's eyes was almost worse than the pain in his shoulder.

That left Ninki Nanka, her large yellow leveling on TJ, her tongue flicking thoughtfully. The clearing grew colder under her scrutiny. She'd made no secret of her disapproval throughout the year—her wariness of him, her disapproval of Elder Adeyemi and the UCMP. Every moment with her had felt like a test he'd barely passed.

And now she would decide if he'd failed for good today.

The silence stretched as she studied him, her eyes unblinking. TJ swallowed hard, steeling himself. He tried to keep his expression steady, but the tightness in his chest made his breathing shallow, uneven. After what felt like forever, she leaned forward, her massive head dipping just slightly, and closed her eyes. *You truly are a unique diviner, Mr. Young. Besides those who are exchange students here, I've not seen such an attempt at mixing so many different magical disciplines into one instrument. Before I make my final decision, I've a question to ask. What prompted you to go against the advice of your Staffmaster?*

TJ held her gaze, though he felt Bamidele's scowl fully. He couldn't be fully honest with the Headmistress but there was a truth he could divulge. "My second great-great-grandfather," he confessed. "My… family. Well, my grandma said there was a curse. A curse I broke. And well… I had trouble finding materials that spoke to me. That was… until I…" His breath caught and his pulse lifted when he realized what his next words would be. "Well… until I followed my ancestors." He turned his gaze to Bamidele now. "You say I will fail because I didn't follow my ancestral magic. But you're wrong. I did. I followed what my grandfather would have done. It might not be perfect. But perfect is the enemy of the good."

*Well said, young man,* Ninki Nanka. *I've heard all I needed. My final decision is*… TJ held his breath. Ayo held his. Hell, he was pretty sure no one was breathing at that moment. *Pass*.

TJ blinked, the word barely registering, but a pure lightness filled his soul. Relief washed through him, but he fought to keep his face impassive, to keep from letting it show. He glanced up at Ninki Nanka, her gaze still fixed on him as if daring him to make something of the chance she'd given him.

A soft grumble escaped Bamidele, barely audible but loaded with disapproval. But he said nothing more, stepping back as the decision was finalized.

At his side, Ayo jabbed him with his elbow, then gave a grin and a thumbs-up, mouthing, "Told you."

"Thank you." He bowed his head to Khatri. "Thank you." This time to Ninki Nanka. "And thank you too, Staffmaster. I know you don't agree but I'll do my best to keep a cap on the limits of my staff." TJ's fingers trembled around the cracked wood of his staff. The trials were over. He was through. And, most of all, he was proud of what he achieved. No matter how messy he might have been getting there.

## 52

# A FEELING MOST FAMILIAR

NEWS OF TJ'S SUCCESS REACHED ELDER ADEYEMI'S EARS quickly. Before TJ could even get his own message out to her, he was already being summoned by Oracle Ruby for another meeting that weekend at the command center. Manny and Ayo had already gone off for an early breakfast, leaving TJ to sleep in after his grueling trial, so TJ walked alone on the dirt path to the Summoning Statues, list in hand:

*1. ~~Gotta figure out how to reverse this channeling thing by dreamwalking with Obatala and Oshosi.~~*

*2. ~~Open up the ancestral path from Yemoja to Oya through the Frost Realm for Manny.~~*

*3. ~~Unlock ancestral path from Ogun to Shango's using Ayo's Norse ring. (And find Ogun's Sacred Cabinet).~~*

*3b. Figure out how to get ring back from Ayo's dad (with his consent)*

*4. ~~Complete my staff to sustain the ancestral path ritual to the Court of All jail cell.~~*

*5. Save Shango and Oya on The Hero's Equinox.*

*6. Don't die*

TJ grinned, surprised by how much they'd pulled off in just a few months. The plan actually looked possible, and they still had time—a couple months until the equinox. Energized, he made a quick detour before heading to the Summoning Statues.

He ducked into the Baobab Grove, skipping as he pulled off the Cailleach charm from his staff—which was still cool from the Ashe he'd used to bring it back to life during his trial. Last night, he had decided to send it to Freya to show off. He couldn't just mail it to her through the regular post in the village, however—magical items were illegal to send by mundane services. But here, in the grove, enchanted messengers made sure magical packages got to the right hands.

With a quick scrawl, TJ folded up his note, read it over, and chuckled, already imagining Freya's reaction. He tucked it and the charm into a small, hollowed-out gourd that hung from the nearest tree, then hung it on a low branch of the oldest baobab.

He waited a moment before an *àwòrin* bird—a small, sleek creature with black feathers tipped in luminous blue—fluttered down from the branches, eyeing TJ as if sizing him up.

"Think you can get this to Freya's druids in Scotland?" TJ murmured, holding up the gourd. "Um… Freya Innes is her full and true name. She's got big hair and—"

The bird tilted its head and squeaked as though to say it knew who Freya was. Then it took the gourd in its claws. It soared skyward, disappearing through a brief shimmer that flickered in the morning light.

TJ stuffed his hands in his pockets, still beaming as he strolled out of the grove toward the Summoning Statues, eager to tackle the rest of his day. Sure, his staff was busted but he could get Grandma to help him fix it like she did with Dayo's staff.

As he approached the stone slabs, his mind raced with the details of the upcoming meeting. Would they test his staff with the final ritual? Had Elder Adeyemi finally convinced the diviner hubs in the Caribbean to join up? He couldn't wait to find out now that he had almost everything done with.

TJ stepped forward, expecting the familiar tingle of magic as he passed through, but instead, he found himself blocked—as if an invisible wall had sprung up before him. Confused, he tried again, first with the Eshu statue again, then with Yemoja, and then with Shango, but the statues remained unresponsive, their stone faces impassive.

A rustling sound behind him caught his attention, and he turned to find an unusual trio: a blackhawk, an orange cat, and a red-eyed owl, all staring at him with uncanny intensity. They all looked familiar to TJ. Had he not seen that bird and cat near his family's compound? And he was pretty sure he had seen that owl during his night sessions, when he was practicing with his staff. But it was the figure behind them that made his heart sink—Ninki Nanka, her hodgepodge form towering over the animals.

*You will* not *be joining Simisola today, young man,* she said, her voice carrying an undercurrent of authority that brooked no argument. *I have been observing your actions closely, Mr. Young. Did you think your dealings with the UCMP would go unnoticed?*

"What?" TJ said. "No, it's not what you think. I mean—it's not like that. I mean—you have to let me pass. You can't do this."

*This isn't a question of authority; it's a question of how much risk you're willing to carry on your shoulders, and so quickly. I passed you during your trial because I see your potential. But you will only squander it rushing headfirst into all of this.*

TJ braced himself, forcing his thoughts to settle as he absorbed her words. This was no small warning—it felt like a line drawn in the sand. "I... I didn't mean to disrespect you, Headmistress. And I thank you so much for passing me—believing in me. I just want to help. I thought I could make a difference."

Ninki Nanka regarded him with an inscrutable expression, her serpentine eyes seeming to pierce right through him. *Your intentions may be noble, but your actions have consequences. You've barely had the time to understand your own powers. You're rushing toward danger without fully seeing what's at stake—for yourself and for everyone relying on you. Look at your staff.* TJ stared down at the crack that was still there. *Bamidele was wrong not to pass you, but he was right that you could cause yourself serious harm. I can't even imagine the amount of Ashe you'd have to use for your mission. And you cracked your staff by merely puncturing stone. To do it with the Ethereal Realms... you'd destroy the staff you have now, as you did with your sister's. To say nothing of what's left of your arms, or, more importantly, your spirit...*

She bobbed her head in the direction of TJ's marked arms, and he pulled at his gloves self-consciously.His grip tightened on his newly crafted staff, the smooth wood warm to his fingers even with his gloves on. He had worked so hard to get to this point, had poured his heart and soul into every step of the staffcrafting process. The thought of losing it all now was almost too much to bear.

"I get why you're worried, Headmistress," he said, trying to keep his voice steady. "But I gotta do this thing. Shango and Oya are counting on us. On *me.* Oshosi too. I can't just sit back when I'm the only one who can actually help."

Ninki Nanka's tail twitched, the movement sending ripples through the air. *No matter what choice you make, I do not wish to see you sacrifice all you've worked for. Sometimes rushing forward only costs us what we're fighting for. And you still have time. The Hero's Equinox is not for a few months yet. I'm sorry, but you will be remaining on school grounds for the time being.*

Before TJ could respond, a force clamped around him, binding his wrists and ankles as though invisible ropes had lashed him to the spot. He fought back, summoning Ashe to his hands, but it was no use. Ninki Nanka's magic wasn't like anything he'd felt before—it felt older, deeper, almost woven into the roots of the world itself. His Ashe fizzled in his grip, snuffed out.

"Hey—wait!" he protested, but his vision blurred as the world twisted around him. His legs moved forward, though he didn't will them to, the pull of her magic guiding him along the main paths of the academy grounds. Trees and students whipped past him, and soon he was heading up the slope toward the dark mouth of the Headmistress's cavern.

With a sickening lurch, TJ hit cold stone, knees buckling. He steadied himself, blinking at the dim blue light of the cavern office. Once, this place had been a refuge, where Elder Adeyemi showed him spells and charms she'd sworn "weren't in the usual curriculum." Now, it closed around him like a prison.

The underground lake stretched out before him, dark and still, lit only by the eerie glow of blue crystals. A stone desk sat on an island in the center, and at the far end, a waterfall cascaded down in shimmering sheets, echoing softly through the cavern.

But where there'd once been shelves full of books and artifacts, the ledges along the walls were now crowded with animals, watching him in silence. A black hawk perched high above, eyes fixed on him like twin lasers. An orange cat sat below, tail twitching, and in a dark corner, a red-eyed owl stared unblinking. Ninki Nanka's spies—her silent audience, set to report his every move.

TJ took a steadying breath, the weight of their stares pressing in from all sides. Whatever refuge he'd once found here was gone, replaced by something cold, something that saw him as prey.

*Stay here, Mr. Young,* Ninka Nanka said. *Simisola will be hearing about this from me. No one can hold you indefinitely, and I know I can't decide for you, but if I could keep you safe here, I will try. That's what I want you to understand.*

"Wait! Headmistress, you can't just leave me here!" TJ shouted, but Ninki Nanka disappeared into the shadows without a word. He ran toward the entrance, but a blast of cold air slammed into him, throwing him back.

"Fine," he muttered. "Guess I'll find my own way out."

He surveyed the underground lake and summoned Ashe. Stones rose across the water, forming a path to the far side. TJ stepped across, reaching the waterfall—but the closer he got, the harder the spray hit, drenching him until he was forced back, sputtering and soaked.

Dripping, he glanced around and caught the unblinking eyes of Ninki Nanka's spies. The hawk tilted its head, the orange cat's tail twitched, and the red-eyed owl sat in silence.

"Any chance one of you could help me out? Or are you just here for the entertainment?"

Nothing. Just stares. TJ sighed, his gaze shifting to the dark walls of the cavern. No other exit, only stone and the cold weight of their eyes, as if they, too, were in on keeping him trapped right where he was.

The only real light in the cavern came from the faint glow of the spiritual pool, casting strange, shifting patterns across the walls. TJ paced back and forth, his footsteps echoing off the stone floor as the minutes crawled by. His frustration grew with each tick of the clock, bubbling up like a pot about to boil over. The longer he waited, the smaller the cavern seemed to get, and the more his thoughts raced, spinning with every possible thing he could do.

Just then, a familiar figure rose from the depths of the pool—Eshu. A rush of relief ran through TJ and he darted to the edge of the water, barely keeping his balance.

"Eshu, you're a lifesaver," he exclaimed. "I need to get out of here and go to the meeting."

Eshu's smile was enigmatic as he extended a hand. *"No worries, young TJ. Elder Adeyemi sent for me. Something about a Ninki Nanka?"*

"Yeah, yeah, she's holding me here on campus. Feels more like kidnapping if you ask me."

*"The Gatekeeper will take you where you need to go."*

TJ clasped Eshu's hand, bracing for the familiar lurch.

Teleporting wasn't exactly smooth—it felt like being yanked through a pinhole and spit out the other side. The Mortal Realm vanished in a flash of heat and pressure, leaving TJ weightless for what could have been seconds or hours. Time always bent weird between realms.

The in-between was worse than usual this time. A thousand streaks of light flared and twisted around him, like stars caught in a whirlpool. His stomach churned. Air felt heavy, metallic, like it had weight. Somewhere in the void, distant echoes hummed—a song he didn't know, pulsing through his bones.

Then, with a jolt that rattled his teeth, his feet hit solid ground. He staggered, blinking to clear the static in his vision. But something was off. Way off. This wasn't the command center.

Golden light shimmered around him, bouncing off polished bars—bars that caged him in like a trophy. A jail cell.

The Court of All.

Well, this wasn't good.

"Bah, I was hoping you wouldn't get caught," a familiar voice drawled from the prism cell next to him. TJ turned to see Oshosi, large, wide, and slumped over, lounging against the wall, with Shango and Oya huddled in their egg-shaped cocoons of a prison. Like before, the Orishas were hanging in mid air, still being channeled, looking more dead than alive. "But from the little I knew of you," Oshosi said, "I almost expected it."

TJ's heart sank as the realization hit him. Eshu had betrayed him once again, leaving him trapped and powerless, with Operation Stormbreak hanging in the balance. TJ stared at Eshu through the strange glass of his cell, grinding his teeth as disbelief churned in his gut. The Trickster stood outside, his usual mischievous grin replaced by a look of genuine remorse.

"Was it the God Eaters?" TJ bit out in question. "Please tell me something is fogging up your brain. Why would you sell me out like this?"

"I'm sorry, TJ," Eshu said sadly. "Forseti broke through my illusions. I had no choice but to give you up."

"You could have fought him!"

"I would have lost. My Ashe was far too diminished holding that illusion wall up for as long as I did."

TJ scoffed, the sound harsh in the eerie silence of the Court of All jail room. "Fool me once, shame on you. Fool me twice, shame on me. But fool me three times? Ugh—I should have known better than to trust you again."

Eshu flinched at the accusation, his shoulders slumping. "I never meant for this to happen, TJ. I was trying to help you, to get you to the meeting. But Forseti... he's too powerful for me right now..."

TJ shook his head, his grip pressed up against the prism. "You played in my face every chance you got: Camp Olosa, the Sky Realm—now this? Why should I believe anything you say.?"

"I know I have let you down," Eshu admitted, his gaze dropping to the refracting floor. "But I truly did want to help you."

TJ sighed, the anger draining out of him, replaced by a bone-deep weariness. "Sorry doesn't change the fact that I'm stuck here, Eshu. It doesn't change the fact that the mission is in jeopardy." He threw a glance to the jailed Orishas. They looked even worse than they had before when he had visited them in Forseti's mind. How much time did they have left? A couple more months? Weeks? Days?

Eshu opened his mouth to respond, but the sound of footsteps echoing down the hallway cut him off. A chill crept up TJ's spine as he recognized the figure approaching—Lord Vishvakarman, the Architect. He walked with a measured grace. His four hands carried a measuring tape, two books, and a pot. His curly, snow-white beard framed his wizened face, and his loose robes flowed elegantly with each step he took. His eyes, sharp and calculating, scanned the corridor ahead of him, while the subtle smile playing on his lips suggested a mind always at work, crafting and plotting.

"Well, well, well," Vishvakarman said, his voice dripping with malicious glee. "If it isn't the young diviner who thinks he can meddle in the affairs of spirits, deities, and gods."

TJ swallowed hard, a sense of foreboding settling over him like a heavy cloak. He knew what Vishvakarman wanted—his magic, the unique ability to create portals between realms. And with Eshu's betrayal and his own foolishness landing him in this cell, TJ feared that the Architect might just get what he desired.

"Themis will be here shortly," Vishvakarman said. "She will be so very pleased to begin *your* Channeling, young mortal. Yes... most pleased."

# 53

# INTO OBLIVION

TJ BLINKED, TAKING IN HIS NEW SURROUNDINGS: A PRISM-shaped cell with glassy walls that shimmered like oil on water. His own reflection looked stretched and warped, blending with those of Shango, Oya, and Oshosi in nearby cells. His heart pounded, his hands clenched tight as he tried to keep his breathing steady. So these were the jail cells of the Court of All. In the flesh. Or—in the spirit? TJ wasn't sure.

Footsteps reverberated through the eerie space, sharp and unhurried, each one a reminder of just how trapped he was. TJ looked up as three figures came into view: Themis, Yamaraja, and Forseti. Themis stopped in front of his cell, her blindfold casting shadows over her face.

"Well, well," she said, her voice smooth and sharp as glass. "Look what we've caught." TJ scowled as she continued. "It is clear to me now what your purpose is, young mortal. What the Fates wanted us to do with you." She knelt to get her giant form on level with TJ. "I did warn Oshosi that I would channel you myself, and I apologize for the threat. It was beneath me. Something said out of frustration" Oshosi crossed his arms. "There is a greater purpose at play here. Not just frustration." Now that TJ took a closer look, her blindfold did look like it sagged a bit, and her tight bun was a bit wild. "This... this is what Anansi wanted. It wasn't clear before what it meant when he said you were the key to seal the End Realm for another thousand years, but look." She angled her hand to direct his eyes to all around them, to the endless window that looked out into the gas clouds of the End Realm. Within the starfield was a large gash across the space, which was poorly stitched up. "Without Thor, without Zeus and all those that we've lost, look at the state of this place. If the End Realm falls, the Mortal Realm falls. Can you understand this?"

Lord Vishvakarman, assessing TJ with a calculating gaze, nodded in agreement. "The boy's power is indeed capable of sealing the fissure," he confirmed, his voice cold and clinical.

TJ stared out at the galaxscape again, trying but failing to wrap his mind around the enormity of it all.

"There's gotta be another way," TJ said, gulping.

"I see no other option, mortal. And I do not do this lightly."

"The Norns—the Fates, tell me this is true," Forseti added. Eshu's eyes seemed to shift at all."

"But, please, tell me," Themis said, "what other choices do you think we may have here? I will allow you to speak before we begin this Channeling, out of respect for the power you possess within."

TJ scowled, turning away from Themis and looking straight to Eshu. "You really gonna let them do this to one of your own? A divine child of the Orishas?"

Eshu held his head low.

"You've got it all wrong, young mortal," she said calmly. "This is a happy moment. It may not seem it now, but it truly is. We *know* your purpose now without a doubt." A shadow seemed to leak from her blindfold as she said. "You should be proud of this great honor. Your sacrifice will ensure the safety of countless realms. It is a noble cause. A noble passing."

TJ turned to Eshu, his eyes pleading. "Eshu, please, you can't let them do this!"

Eshu's expression was somber, his eyes filled with sadness as he said, "TJ, I understand your fear, but Themis has a point. In our own discipline, many sacrifices are made for the greater good. It is a heavy burden, but one that must be borne to fend off the God Eaters. It's the reason Olodumare agreed to The Great Separation. It's what They would have wanted. You must endure the trial and trust in 'The Way' to restore balance. Embrace The Channeling, and everything will be made right again." Somehow the last of his words sounded odd. Like he was speaking in code.

This was all too much. This was all happening too fast. TJ slammed his fist against his glass prison. There was no way out of this. No Patheon's Parley. No Mirror Realm to slip through. The thought of becoming a sacrifice, of enduring the unknown trial, filled TJ with a terror that chilled him to the bone. He was just a teenager, a boy on the cusp of manhood, not ready to take on the burden of the universe on his shoulders.

"Wait!" TJ said. "A Channelling might not even work on me! I'm not really an Orisha at all—I'm mortal."

Themis's brow furrowed slightly beneath her blindfold. "You possess divine power, young one. Mortal or not, it may be enough."

Yamaraja tilted his head, the bull he sat upon mirroring his movement. "This is untested territory. It could backfire, drain his power completely, or fail entirely."

"Or," Forseti interjected, stroking his long braided beard, "it could work exactly as intended. After all, this boy managed to infiltrate my mind, wrest control from me." Forseti's eyes gleamed coldly. "To do that to a god? It takes more than simple Ashe. Any power that potent should translate, mortal or not."

TJ stewed, rage simmering in his chest. His eyes darted to Eshu. "You told them that too?" His voice dripped with accusation. Eshu avoided TJ's glare, his face set in a look of quiet resignation. "So you just handed them everything, huh?"

"TJ, please," Eshu said sadly. "Listen to my words. Just... follow the ancestors. Accept what must come to pass."

A bright light filled the entire corridor, flashing from the galaxy clouds outside. A great roar followed, something felt deep in TJ's chest. He lifted his eyes to see the poorly stitched reality fissures bursting at the seams. Shadows seemed to pour out of it.

"I'm sorry, young mortal," Themis said. "We truly have no other choice. And we've run out of time. I've defended the End Realm for too long for it to fall now. If there was another way..." She bit back her next words. "Forseti, Yamaraja. We need to start the ritual post haste. Now, before the Sovereign One breaks through."

Before TJ could muster another argument, the Gods began a

ritual chant, their voices rising in an ancient, otherworldly language. He cried out, begging them to stop, his pleas falling on deaf ears.

"Oshosi, do something!"

Themis lifted a hand, and her group stopped her chanting. She narrowed her blindfold on TJ and asked him earnestly, "Look into yourself, young mortal. You know your power better than we do. Tell me, with honesty, if you think this will not work. That you do not possess the power to protect not only this realm but all the realms tied back to the home of your fellow mortals. *My* mortals."

TJ frowned. He knew she was right. He could sense the power. But he would never have thought this was what he was meant for. Sure, his power was used to help others... but... He swallowed as realization dawned. The Channeling was meant to help people too.

Like it or not, it did align.

He stared at Shango and Oya, who were being channeled. Their power was waning in the Mortal Realm, but at least their Ashe would be repurposed for the End Realm, to stave off the God Eaters so they never got to Earth. That was a noble thing, wasn't it?

Themis took his extended silence as an affirmation, it seemed, because she said, "It was nice knowing you Tomori Jomiloju. We'll make sure the Mortal Realm sings your song for generations until the end of time," and then she began the chant again.

"No, no, no!" TJ cried, hot fear winning out. "Shango, Oya, anyone, please help me! Wait! Wait! What if you're wrong about me?"

But the imprisoned deities, near to death themselves, could not answer his cries.

All Eshu offered to TJ was three familiar words, "Follow the ancestors. Please, heed these words."

And the phrase took on a new meaning for TJ. Follow the ancestors meant something he wasn't ready to do... But he knew he had to...

Die.

That simple revelation seemed to unlock something, and as the chanting of the Gods reached a crescendo, a strange sensation filled TJ's chest, as if an invisible force was pulling at his very essence. It was like a vacuum, sucking out his life force through every pore of his body. TJ screamed, his voice raw with terror and desperation, as the world around him began to fade away.

An overwhelming force surged through TJ's body as The Channeling began. It was undeniable. He tried to reach inward, desperately seeking an equilibrium, a way to protect himself from the onslaught as he had done against the Keepers. TJ attempted to extend his magic outward, as he had done before in the Sky Realm, but The Channeling was too powerful, too all-consuming.

It was like being held down under a dogpile, but instead of playful friends, it was the crushing weight of almighty Gods. TJ was helpless, his voice stolen by the ancient ritual. He wanted to scream, to beg for mercy, but no sound escaped his lips. The ritual lit a fire to every muscle in his body, and his consciousness slipped away, his identity being erased by the relentless force.

Amidst the chaos, a familiar voice echoed in TJ's mind. It was Dayo, her presence a fleeting comfort in the storm. *"Hold on, TJ,"* she urged, her words barely audible over the roar of The Channeling. TJ tried to call out to her, to plead for help, but again, he was without a voice. Dayo's message was a whisper in the darkness.

*"Listen to Eshu. Follow the ancestors,"* she said, before her presence faded away.

Suddenly, the scene before TJ shifted, as though Dayo's words had changed it. He was transported to a different realm, found himself soaring over vast African plains, the golden grasses stretching out to the horizon. He dipped into lush jungles, the canopy a vibrant green, alive with the calls of morning birds and the rustling of unseen creatures. As TJ emerged from the jungle, he found himself over an expansive ocean, the waters a deep, mesmerizing blue. In the distance, he spotted a gate rising from the depths, its ancient stone structure weathered by the ages. TJ approached the gate, floating in his dream-like state, a sense of both trepidation and curiosity filling his heart.

Standing before the gate was a figure TJ had only seen in old photographs—his second great-grandfather, Tomori Jomiloju. The man was tall and proud, his dark skin lined with the wisdom of years. He wore traditional Yoruba attire, a flowing àgbàdá robe in vibrant colors. His eyes, a deep brown, seemed to hold the secrets of generations. He smiled at TJ, a warmth emanating from his presence, and beckoned the young man forward.

TJ stood before the ancient gate, his mind reeling from the journey he had just experienced. It was a replay of his ancestry, his family's Yoruba beliefs, a revelation about the concept of reincarnation within the ancestral line, known as "àtúnwáyé." The idea that an ancestor's soul could be reborn into a new body, strengthening familial bonds and ensuring the continuity of heritage.

But TJ did not want this. He had to get back. To his friends. His family. Everyone counting on him.

He was supposed to follow the ancestors but…

He never got to say goodbye.

As TJ gazed upon his great-grandfather, more figures appeared, other ancestors who bore striking resemblances to TJ. A woman who had his height, a man who had his chicken legs, and another with a nose that matched TJ's own. All of them pulled at their collars and revealed the birthmark TJ also had near his collarbone. Only the ones who were farther back in the row had more distinct birthmarks that didn't look like a blob. TJ just wasn't familiar with what the symbol was. It was as if he was looking at different aspects of himself, reflected through the generations.

However, among the joy of this reunion, a pang of sadness entered TJ when he realized that Dayo was not among the ancestral line. If TJ was dying, if he was rejoining the ancestors, couldn't he have at least seen Dayo too?

Suddenly, Eshu appeared at the gate, standing alongside TJ's great-great-grandfather, who wore his funky red glasses. Out in the distance, TJ thought he could also make out the fuschia dress of Yewa peeking through the line of his family line. Or maybe that was his imagination. But all of this seemed like his imagination. A fever dream.

Eshu and the original Tomori Jomiloju both looked at TJ with a mix of solemnity and understanding. This Eshu seemed different from the one TJ knew. Somehow, this one seemed more wise and… serious.

"It is not time," they all said in unison. "The cycle will not continue again. You are the last. You shall not cross over to the Orisha Planes, to Orun. You need to look... to the ancestors."

What was that supposed to even mean? Did they mean his ancestors specifically, or all ancestors? As if reading his thoughts, his great-great-grandfather and Eshu smiled.

At this revelation, a surge of energy coursed through TJ's entire being. His spirit, his omi, began to separate from his physical body. The scene shifted once more, and TJ found himself looking down at his own form, still trapped within the cosmic jail cell, surrounded by foreign gods and their ritual. Did he make it back to his own reality? He tried to move, to break free from the confines of his prison, but something held him back. A tether, an invisible force, kept his spirit bound to the cell, causing an immense strain on his very essence.

As the terror threatened to consume him, a small spark of defiance ignited within TJ's soul. He couldn't accept this fate, not without a fight. The Court may have decided his path, but TJ refused to go quietly into the night. He was a divine child of the Orishas, and he would not let his life be taken so easily. But what could he do? What could a mortal do against the strength of the gods?

The simple truth was a haunting, harrowing: Absolutely nothing.

# 54

# THE SPACE BETWEEN NOTHING

MANNY NEVER LIKED THE COMMAND CENTER OF OPERATION Stormbreak. She couldn't decide why that was, though. Maybe it was the rough edges of the walls or the way the crystal lights threw the crags in harsh shadows. Or maybe it was because every time she and her friends were summoned to the place, it meant putting a pause on what was turning out to be a great term at Ifa.

It meant going through some new trauma.

She hunched her shoulders, trying to shake it off, but Jessie's image hit her hard and fast, making her shrink into herself. If TJ were here, he would've noticed her change of posture in a heartbeat—because TJ noticed everything about her, always. It was both irritating as hell and... well, kind of sweet. But right now, everyone was wrapped up in their own heads. No one paid attention to Manny. Typical.

Elder Adeyemi and Oracle Ruby hovered over the central table, murmuring to each other in voices low enough to sound like buzzing flies. The table's misty projection displayed a map of the Court of All, and judging by the tight lines on Elder Adeyemi's face, it wasn't good news. Oracle Ruby looked worse. She'd aged a decade over a few months; her bloodshot eyes and the deep bags beneath them clashed hard with her green-tipped dreadlocks.

In the corner, Ayo tapped out a nervous rhythm on his thigh. His father—who Manny silently cursed every time his name came up—was nowhere to be seen. Probably still off trying to find a path to Shango "worthy" of their bloodline. Manny's fingers traced the scar along her arm, the one she got from that crazy Keeper during their last mission. They found Ayo's path. Fought like hell for it. Nearly died for it. But of course, for Ayo's father, that still wasn't good enough.

*If that man was my dad...* Manny clenched her jaw. Not that she knew what she'd do, anyway. It'd been two weeks since she spoke to her tia, thanks to both of their stubbornness.

Family. They were exhausting.

Manny exhaled sharply, focusing on the entrance instead, where Omo of Fon stood guard, her feathered wings twitching at every sound. TJ's mom was pacing beside her, worry etched into every line of her face. Bolawe, meanwhile, was sitting cross-legged, barely moving in his mirror form.

*Where the hell are you, TJ?*

Ayo had said TJ was wiped out this morning, knocked flat from everything he'd been through with his trial. She and Ayo had gone to breakfast without him, figuring they'd catch up later. TJ deserved the rest after what he'd been carrying these past few months. At least he'd finally gotten his staff done. She'd seen the weight lift off him a little last night when they met at the three flat bridges, and that alone was worth it.

A sudden flash of red light yanked her out of her thoughts. The table's misty display flared crimson, casting the entire room in a bloody shadow. Manny straightened, eyes narrowing. Whatever this was, it wasn't good.

Elder Adeyemi's head snapped up, the red hue spilling onto her grave face. "There's been a breach at the entrance. Omo of Fon, it's probably just another pigeon triggering it. Entirely my mistake. I cast the shield charm too quickly this morning. But check it out."

The aziza nodded, her wings unfurling as she took flight. She pushed the doors open into the office space where the other UCMP officials were already up and alert. More red lights from crystal fixtures bloomed and receded over and over.

As Omo of Fon flew between the tables outside, a pair of officials followed in her wake. Manny thought it might have been that guy from Norway, Tore Stadheim, and another aziza that hung around.

A pulse thrummed in Manny's neck. This was the first time they'd had a breach. Could it be the Keepers looking for TJ? Maybe it was one of the gods from the Court of All seeking them out? TJ was always talking about how scared he was to see Morpheus.

Manny turned back to the others. Maybe she was being dramatic and it really was just a bird or something. Her eyes met TJ's mom's. Her palm-tree locs didn't jitter like they did when she freaked, so she wasn't overly concerned.

When Manny's face relaxed, though, TJ's mom asked softly, "Who do you think is trying to get in?"

Manny shrugged. "I'm hopin' it's just a mistake, or it could be TJ coming through finally."

"Yes, me too," she said. "We don't need any more roadblocks. How are things going with your aunt?"

Manny sighed, her shoulders dipping. "It's been a hot mess. She's still buggin' out about what happened in the Frost Realm, with losing Jessie all over again. I been tryna talk to her, but she just shuts down. Did TJ tell you what happened at my quince?"

"He did. I was hoping he was just exaggerating. We really do need your aunt in all of this. That path has already been opened. If she doesn't come through, we'd have to do it all over again with another one of your family members."

Manny frowned. "But me and my tia are the only diviners in our family."

*Not sure I'd call my tia a diviner anymore, though...*

TJ's mom cuffed her arms into her long green robes. "It's not easy losing someone you love. Give her a little more time. She'll come around."

"Will do."

Elder Adeyemi turned to Ayo. "What about your father? Why isn't he here?"

Ayo shifted uncomfortably in his seat, then signed, "He took ring. Wants to get to Shango with no Ogun. He thinks it's only way."

Manny translated before Elder Adeyemi replied, knuckling her forehead. "Oh, that man... He wasn't so steadfast when he was my student."

Oracle Ruby raised an eyebrow. "Why don't you just force them to cooperate? Surely you have the power to do that."

*Yeah, like that tongue-tied trance she put on me and Ayo last year.*

Bolawe sat up in his Mirror Realm form, his movements crunching all the while. "It doesn't work like that. For the ancestral path and ancestral magic to work, we need the *full consent* of Teresa and Mobalaji. We can't force them to do anything they don't want to do. If we do, the children and their guardians will be split apart when they attempt to birth from Shango and Oya, respectively."

"You mean m-m-metaphorically, right?" Ayo asked out loud.

"No, I do not," Bolawe said matter-of-factly.

Manny shivered. It almost sounded like what TJ described when he crossed over into the Aqua Realm to stop Olokun. But he was TJ. He could do things the healers said were impossible. Manny still couldn't keep her memories, but TJ remembered everything the Orishas did. So if they crossed over without full consent, she could only imagine how painful and skin-splitting that could be.

*Like John Henry or Banjoko the Bold,* Manny heard TJ's voice in her mind and she couldn't help shaking her head and smirking.

Just then, Omo of Fon returned, floating at the entrance of the meeting room. Perched on each of her shoulders was a black hawk Manny could've sworn she had seen before, along with a red-eyed owl. Both of their feathers gleamed in the dim light. Below the aziza's feet, an orange cat circled lovingly.

"Family drama might be the least of our worries right now," Omo of Fon said, her voice grim. "Ninki Nanka is topside. She says she has TJ locked away in her office until further notice."

Manny tensed. Why did the Headmistress have TJ locked away? Did he get himself in trouble the *same* day they had their most important meeting?

Omo of Fon's gaze shifted to Elder Adeyemi. "Should I let her in?"

The former Headmistress worked her jaw before asking, "And did Ninki Nanka explain *why* she is holding TJ?"

"She said you would know why—that we would all know why."

The Headmistress had been hounding TJ all year. None of them had to guess what this was all about. Elder Adeyemi hesitated. Manny always had a hard time reading the woman's expressions. TJ probably had an easier time recognizing her subtle facial cues, but Manny had only come to know Adeyemi more closely the last few months, and even then, the Elder mostly focused her attention on TJ.

After a long moment, Tore Stadheim leaned close to Elder Adeyemi to whisper in her ear. Then she nodded, saying, "Yes. Let her in, I suppose. She clearly knows what's going on."

After a few moments, Omo of Fon left and returned with the Headmistress. Ninki Nanka descended into the meeting room, her crocodile form just slipping into the cavern space. Like the Healers' Tree, the space expanded to accommodate her large frame—though she had to dip her long giraffe neck low to pass the threshold. When she finally settled into a corner that could barely accommodate her size, the atmosphere in the room shifted, the tension thick.

"We need TJ back," Elder Adeyemi demanded, her voice offering no hesitation. "The UCMP has tasked me with a most important mission. The operation cannot continue without him."

*Not even a hello, Simisola?* Ninki Nanka sighed, closing her yellow eyes. *TJ is not ready. I understand the importance of what's happening, but this is all being rushed. There'll be nothing left of the boy at this rate.*

"You don't understand—this isn't just about TJ. It's about the Orishas. If we don't act now, we risk losing Shango, Oya, and Oshosi forever. That *cannot* happen."

Ninki's golden eyes narrowed, her tone sharpening. *What cannot happen, Simisola, is you sacrificing these children for a fleeting chance. Or have you forgotten the price others have paid for your desperation in the past? Have you forgotten about Biafra?*

Adeyemi stiffened. "Of course I haven't. That's *enough*."

*No, I don't think it is.* Ninki's voice rumbled like distant thunder, her neck snaking closer to meet Adeyemi's gaze head-on. *You've always been reckless. Always pushing for glory—whether it's glory for yourself or the United Council, I can't tell anymore.*

"This isn't about me!" Adeyemi snapped, her composure cracking. Her voice almost sounded like a whining student instead of the dignified woman Manny had come to know. "Do you think I don't see the weight of my decisions? The people we've lost? But doing nothing—giving up—just isn't an option. Not when the fate of Shango and Oya's children are at play."

*And yet,* Ninki hissed, her tail thrashing against the stone, *it is to be these children shouldering the burdens of this mission. Burdens that should never have been theirs. You claim you remember the last time such happened, but I think you forget more than you realize.*

Adeyemi's jaw tightened, guilt flickering in her eyes for a brief moment. "Mistakes were made. I freely admit that. But I won't let fear paralyze me now." She straightened, her voice regaining its edge. "We need TJ. And if you won't release him willingly, he'll come back to us, eventually. The Hero's Equinox is not long away."

*True.* Ninki's massive form went still, her presence as heavy as a storm cloud. *Simisola… Which is why I—*

Ruby let out a strangled cry, collapsing to the ground.

Everyone's head turned to the Oracle, who spasmed on the cool stone floor. For a split second, time froze—then Manny's chest seized, a sudden, clawing ache dropping her to one knee. Across the room, Ayo slammed his hands on the table in pain, then slapped his ears as though they needed to be popped.

"Ow!" Manny strained out. "What's happening?"

"Ugh!" Ayo groaned in confused response.

TJ's mom darted between Manny and Ayo, her hands hovering uselessly as she tried to decide who needed help first. Ruby thrashed on the ground, foam bubbling at her lips. Mom's eyes found Elder Adeyemi's, silently pleading for guidance. Even Ninki Nanka's massive form shifted anxiously, her double horns twisting to attention like dog ears.

Adeyemi's composed mask slipped as she stepped forward, hand half-raised. "Ruby…" Her voice trembled. The Oracle's body twisted violently, each spasm more brutal than the last.

Omo of Fon was reaching for Ruby, wings flaring. "No… no… Don't touch her. She's having a vision."

The pain in Manny's chest receded almost as suddenly as it came. What had come over her? She had no time to wonder as she regained her composure and made her way to Ruby as well. "We can't just watch!" she said desperately, looking to Ayo for support, who's painful episode also seemed to have passed.

TJ's mom stepped closer, torn between Ruby's agony and the stricken looks on Manny and Ayo's faces. "Are you two all right?"

Manny forced out a shaky breath. "We're fine. It was just a quick pain."

"Yeah, I good," Ayo signed, then pointed. "But what about Ruby? Is it Shango?"

TJ's mom turned a sharp tone in Elder Adeyemi's direction. "Simisola, do something! Orunmila's Stars! She's frothing."

Adeyemi's jaw clenched. "Ruby hasn't had a clear vision in months... We have to let it play out..."

*Like hell we do!* Ninki Nanka's voice boomed as she pushed forward. Her massive form shifted with barely contained rage as Adeyemi stepped forward to block her.

*Simisola. Stop this. Help her. Now!*

"Come now," Tore Stadheim said. "What's more important? Keeping the Orishas intact or—"

*Not like this, foreigner.*

Ruby's body arched again, her eyes wide and unseeing. The room held its breath. Manny's heart roared in her ears. She felt helpless, trembling, but it was nothing compared to Ruby's agony.

Ninki Nanka's long tongue fell from her mouth and flung forward like it was going to slap Ruby across the face, but a wind wall generated from Elder Adeyemi stopped her in her tracks.

"We have to let her finish," Adeyemi insisted, though her voice lacked its usual steadiness.

Ninki Nanka loomed closer, her giant body blocking out almost all the crystal light. *This is exactly what I am warning against. How can you allow the suffering of one of your—one of* my*—instructors?* She turned her long giraffe neck on Omo of Fon. *Omo, I expected better of a Warrior of Fon.*

Omo of Fon glanced at Ruby's writhing body, then dipped her head low in an uncharacteristic look of shame. "It's not so simple, Ancient One. We don't have many options. Any options, really."

Ruby sprang up as though an invisible hook curled under her neck. Manny gasped. It looked like she was being hung now. Ninki Nanka growled. Then, with preternatural speed for her size, pushed through Adeyemi's wind wall. The Headmistress' magical giraffe tongue darted out and slapped the Oracle across the face.

Ruby's seizure stopped instantly. Almost like she was made into stone. Manny held her breath, praying that she would breathe again. They couldn't lose Ruby too—no, they hadn't lost TJ to begin with. Then… Ruby coughed, stirring. Manny rubbed at the latent pain in her chest as Ayo massaged his temples. What had made them all feel such pain? Did it have to do with the Orishas? With Oya?

Ruby's eyes fluttered open, her voice weak as she spoke. "S-Something is wrong. TJ—TJ's gone."

"Gone!?" Manny blurted out.

"W-w-what do you mean g-g-gone?" Ayo stuttered.

"Excuse me?" TJ's mom lifted Ruby's head and patted her cheeks as the Oracle's eyes faded from exhaustion. "Ruby? Ruby, what do you mean, gone? Ruby, answer me!"

*Impossible.* Ninki Nanka said. *He's in my office. It's protected. He'd never get past the defenses.*

*Right,* Manny thought, convincing herself everything was okay. *Right, she said he was in her office. Ruby hasn't had an accurate vision in months. This was just another very bad reading.*

"No," Ruby whispered. "He's not."

The room fell deathly silent.

"What did you see?" Adeyemi's voice came sharp and strained.

Ninki's eyes glowed brighter as she tilted her own head back, looking as though she were communing with someone. *The hawks... The cats... They say he left through the lake… with Eshu.*

Elder Adeyemi gave her former mentor a look. "I told you the boy would find his own way; he always does."

"Why would Eshu take him?" TJ's mom whispered, her voice trembling.

Ninki Nanka shook her head, her tail thrashing. *My familiars didn't say. But if Eshu took him…* She didn't finish the thought, but the implication hung heavy in the air.

Manny's stomach dropped. Her mind raced, piecing together fragments of memories, fears, and half-formed ideas. "You think they were captured? By Themis? Or Forseti? Or Morpheus?"

"D-d-damn, TJ," Ayo said. "How many opps you g-g-got?"

The Headmistress didn't answer, but the look on her face was all Manny needed to see.

Adeyemi stepped forward, her voice firm despite the guilt flickering in her eyes. "We'll try to commune with Eshu. He'll know what happened."

They gathered around the waterfall, the sound of rushing water filling the tense silence as Adeyemi led the incantation. But as the spell finished, the water stilled, offering no response.

Ruby, breath coming out harsh, said, "That won't work."

Manny's chest tightened. "Why isn't he answering? I know we can't hear his voice like TJ but we gotta have something… right?"

Adeyemi rubbed at her temples. "I do not know."

Manny turned to Omo of Fon and Ninki Nanka, who could usually hear the spirits. "Right!?"

Neither gave her an answer. Even the Norwegian guy had nothing to say, no theories or goofy speculation about magical theory. And Bolawe remained silent in his corner, pondering.

Manny clenched her fists. "We can't just sit here! TJ's out there, and we're wasting time!"

*And rushing blindly will only make things worse,* Ninki Nanka snapped. *You are all too emotional to see it, but the risks are piling up, and the price may be more than you're willing to pay.*

What if TJ was in trouble? He always found a way out, no matter how dire the situation. He was the one who always came through, who never gave up. But there were plenty of times he needed a helping hand. Too many times.

The dark thought clung to Manny like a heavy blanket. Her heart shattered into a million pieces. There was so much she and TJ hadn't done together yet, so much she hadn't told him about herself. The thought of losing him, of never seeing his goofy smirk or hearing his awkward motor-mouth again was unbearable. "There has to be something we can do. Right now… can we start the operation right now? Can we just take Ayo's ring back without consent? We already made the path to the Frost Realm. I don't need my tia for that, right?"

Around the room, faces fell. TJ's mom looked stricken, her hand covering her mouth as she collapsed to her knees. That was a second child she was going to lose. Manny couldn't imagine what was going through her mind. Ayo's eyes were wide with shock, his hands trembling, chest falling and rising rapidly. Even Ninki Nanka looked somber, her massive head bowed. Bolawe's eyes were unmoving. Like someone had sucked out his soul.

"It's... very unlikely," Elder Adeyemi admitted. "We can't do this without TJ."

"That's not good enough!" TJ's mom snapped, taking the words right out of Manny's mouth. "We've always been told what we *can't* do. But there has to be another way to use the paths. We can find out where he went!"

*Everyone, listen to me,* Ninki Nanka thought-spoke. *You're not ready to attempt this without TJ. The paths require stability. You'd be risking your lives—and likely failing.*

"So what?" TJ's mom gritted out. "We're just giving up on him?"

"That's what this sounds like!" Manny added.

Adeyemi's jaw clenched. "We're not giving up. But we can't throw you into a plan destined to fail. That's one thing I agree on with regards to your headmistress. We need to regroup, come up with a Plan B."

"Plan B? There's no 'Plan B' for this. TJ doesn't have time for us to sit around 'regrouping.' We can't leave him to do whatever he's doing right now alone."

Bolawe spoke up next. *"Manny, none of us want that. But rash action—without TJ's anchoring presence in the paths—risks losing you all. We need to think this through."*

"No one asked you, *murderer.*"

TJ's mom stood shakily, fury blazing in her tear-filled eyes. "So we think it through faster. We find *any* way. We do whatever it takes."

Manny clenched her jaw, swallowing hard. "We *have* to."

Adeyemi's face hardened, but her silence spoke volumes.

# 55

# AMONG THE WALKING DEAD

THE STREETS OF NEW ILE-IFE FELT TIGHT, STICKY, AND ALL wrong to Ayo. Even the wind, which usually carried scents of fresh-cut palm fronds and sizzling plantains, seemed choked by the heat. Stagnant and lifeless. Like the Ashe just wasn't hitting the same way.

Ahead of him, Manny walked with a purpose that matched her posture—stiff, shoulders squared, head high. But he wasn't fooled. That smile she'd been forcing all morning was the kind that cracked under too much pressure.

It had been a week since TJ went missing, and there had been no calls from any Orishas *anywhere*. So Manny got the bright idea the following weekend to visit Madam Lucienne—a necromancer.

Yeah, the girl was *that* desperate.

"Positive thoughts," she said, flashing those too-perfect teeth. "This'll be the same as last time. Madame Lucienne and I will commune with Yewa, and she'll confirm TJ's just… doing his thing on the other side. Nothin' to bug out over." Her tone had a snap to it, like she was daring the universe to disagree.

Ayo didn't dare say what was really on his mind: *Last time doesn't mean this time.* Instead, he kept pace with her, trying to ignore the prickle of unease crawling up his spine.

They turned into a narrow alley tucked between Mami Wata's Eatery and an out-of-business shop that used to specialize in lightning rods. The Necromancer's Nook loomed ahead—a weathered wooden door framed by heavy purple drapes, their edges singed as if they'd brushed against flames too many times.

Manny hesitated for half a second before pulling the door open.

The air inside hit Ayo like a thunderclap. Thick with the scent of burnt herbs and something metallic. Rows of shelves lined the walls, cluttered with jars of cloudy liquids, bone fragments, and crumbling scrolls. Candles burned low on every available surface, their wax pooling in chaotic spirals. *This most def is a fire hazard.*

He shifted his gaze, shivering when he spotted a human skull perched on one shelf, its hollow eye sockets staring down like it was sizing him up.

Madame Lucienne stood at the center of it all, her silhouette stark against the flickering blue glow of her candles. The old woman's face was a maze of wrinkles and tribal tattoos.

"Yuh come back," she said, her voice low and raspy, thick with a Caribbean accent. Her gaze shifted to Manny, then to Ayo. "And yuh bring company dis time, eh? Good. Spirits like when there are more hearts to call to them."

Ayo wasn't so sure about that, but he kept his mouth shut.

"Thanks for seeing us on a short notice," Manny said, her tone teetering between polite and urgent. Then she threw a small hill of enchanted cowries on the table. "I hope this is enough."

"Dat'll do just fine."

"D-d-damn Manny," Ayo stuttered. "Where you get all t-t-that. You know I coulda h-h-hooked you up."

Manny ignored him and gestured toward the rickety wooden table in the center of the room. "Can we start? I just need to know what Yewa sees. If she's seen anything. I'm sure you heard about TJ Young by now. That he's missing again."

"Oh, that one can't catch a break, can he?"

"Tell us about it."

Lucienne nodded slowly, motioning for them to sit. "Place yuh hands on the table," she instructed, her movements deliberate. "Clear yuh minds. Think 'bout the boy you seek. Nothin' else."

Ayo settled into the chair across from Manny, who was already gripping the table's edge like it might run away. He glanced down at the Ọpọ́n Ìfá adorned with cryptic symbols. Madame Lucienne placed it gently on the table, her gnarled hands steady despite her age. She lit three candles, their flames burning fuschia, then she began to chant.

The words were ancient, heavy, rolling off her tongue like a slow drumbeat. The air thickened, pressing against Ayo. He tried to focus, but his thoughts splintered, bouncing between Manny's desperate expression and his own nagging doubts.

*What if we don't get an answer?*

*What if we do, and it's bad?*

Madame Lucienne's voice grew louder, the chant vibrating through the room. The candles flickered violently, their flames twisting upward like claws. A chill ran down Ayo's spine.

Then, just as suddenly as it had begun, the ritual stuttered. The flames sputtered out, plunging the room into semi-darkness. The Ọpọ́n Ìfá, which had been glowing faintly, went dim.

Lucienne sat back, her weathered hands trembling slightly as she folded them in her lap. She looked at Manny, then at Ayo, her eyes soft with regret. "I sorry, chile. There's nothin'. No trace of him. No message from Yewa."

Manny stiffened. "What do you mean, nothing? Yewa always answers. Always." It was like when they called to Eshu before. No answer. "Did you tell her it was me? She met me a couple summers back. Camp Olosa. She'll remember me from then."

"S-S-She don't see a lot of m-m-mortals," Ayo said. "She'll r–r-remember us."

Lucienne shook her head slowly. "Not this time, chile. It's like… like the connection's gone. Severed."

Ayo's heart sank. He wasn't sure what he'd expected, but this hollow silence wasn't it.

Manny shot to her feet, her chair scraping loudly against the stone floor. "Nah. I don't believe it. Try again. Do it again!" She tapped the divination board violently.

Lucienne held up a hand, her expression pained. "I've done all I can, chile. Whatever blockin' the connection, it bigger than me. I go refund yuh—"

"I don't want your money!" Manny snapped. "I want answers! This can't be it. There has to be another way—something else you can try!"

"M-M-Manny..." Ayo said quietly, but she wasn't listening.

"This is your *whole* job, right? You're the one who connects people to the other side. So *do* it!"

"Yo, c-c-chill, my guy," Ayo tried again.

Lucienne's face hardened. "I understand yuh pain, chile, but even the spirits have limits."

Manny stared at her, chest heaving, before turning on her heel and storming out. The hanging beads rattled violently as she shoved through them.

Ayo lingered awkwardly, reaching into his pocket. He pulled out a handful of enchanted cowries and set them on the table. "F-f-for your time," he mumbled. "And your t-t-trouble." He added some more. "Peace and b-b-blessings."

Lucienne nodded, her gaze weary. "I hope yuh find what yuh lookin' for."

Ayo gave a stiff nod and followed Manny out into the humid alley.

---

THE BEADS OF LUCIENNE'S DOORWAY RATTLED AGAIN AS AYO stepped into the alley, the brightness outside like an assault after the dimness of the Necromancer's Nook. He spotted Manny a few feet ahead, pacing like a caged lion. Her fists were clenched, her whole body vibrating.

He signed, careful, deliberate. "Yo, what the *hell* was that? You mad disrespect back there."

Manny spun around, her braids whipping the air. "*I* was disrespectful? You're the one who stood there all quiet. Your best friend is out there, maybe hurting bad, and you act like you don't even care."

Ayo's hands moved fast, his signs jagged and harsh. "No start with me, Manny. You think *I* no care? I do everything I can. I—"

"You're doing everything you can? Really? The same way you've been practicing to fix your speech impediment?" Manny jabbed a finger at him. "Or last year when you took forever to tell your dad about Olokun? TJ's supposed to be your 'boy,' Ayo. Your best friend. And you're just—what? Gonna keep being all 'cool guy' about it while I try to figure out how to fix this?"

Ayo stiffened. "Cool guy? That what you think? You think I no care because I no yell like you? I try to think—be smart—because running wild like you no get us nowhere."

"Oh, right. Big Brain Ayo. Always too good to feel anything real." Manny stepped closer, her words hitting like thunder. "You know what your problem is? You're all about shortcuts. Always looking for the easy way out. That's why you never actually tried to fix your speech. You just waited for some magic to come along and do it for you."

That one landed, and Ayo flinched like he'd been slapped. His chest heaved as he shot back, signing faster now. "You no know what hell you talk about. I work on voice but it no easy! And no act like you saint. Half time, you throw self at stuff, hope something sticks. You think that help TJ? You think yells at dead-speaker fix anything?"

"At least I'm *trying*!" Manny's voice hitched, but she didn't back down. "You're just standing there, acting like this is all gonna work out on its own. TJ would never give up on *you* like this. He jacked up his arms getting to you!"

Ayo's hands froze mid-air, the accusation hitting harder than he wanted to admit. He stared at Manny, his jaw tightening. "I no give up."

Manny's lips parted, but whatever retort she had was swallowed by the sudden buzz of magical energy. It rippled through the alley like invisible static before he saw them—reporters flooding in like a wave, their floating quills and enchanted cameras locking onto him and Manny like predators scenting blood.

"Oh, great," Manny muttered. "Just what we needed."

One journalist had a silver orb hovering near her head, projecting her voice in amplified tones that reverberated through the narrow street. "Manny Martinez! Ayodeji Oyelowo! What's happening with TJ Young?"

"Are the Orishas refusing to communicate with mortals again?"

"Is TJ the cause of this disconnect?"

Ayo tensed as the swarm closed in, reporters pushing forward with glowing microphones and enchanted recorders. One journalist wore glasses that blinked like eyes. Ayo knew them as lie detectors —his aunt's own design. Another tapped a staff against a slate that instantly displayed Manny's image alongside a headline:

**TJ Young's Closest Allies Break Their Silence!**

Manny froze, her hand gripping the doorframe leading into the Necromancer's Nook. For a moment, it looked like she might retreat, but instead, she squared her shoulders and strode into the chaos.

"Manny," Ayo signed, hands moving fast, "No. We just leave."

She didn't even glance back. "I got this," she said, but Ayo didn't believe her for a second.

The reporters pounced like a pack of wolves.

"Miss Martinez, can you confirm that TJ Young is missing?"

"Sources say the Orishas haven't responded to mortal calls since his disappearance. Is that true?"

"Do you believe TJ's actions might have caused this? Has he put us in danger again like he did with Olokun last year?"

Ayo's chest tightened. The questions weren't just intrusive—they were dangerous. Rumors like this could spiral out of control, and the last thing they needed was more attention on TJ.

Manny raised her hands, trying to command the reporters' attention. "We're not answering any questions right now! Y'all need to back off!"

But the reporters didn't back down. If anything, they pressed closer, their enchanted tools buzzing and whirring like insects. Where was Manny and Ayo's protection? Whenever stuff like this happened, TJ always had a few UCMP officials to swoop into the rescue.

"What did Madame Lucienne say during the session?"

"Are you stalking children?" Manny shot back. "Pretty sure that's illegal."

"You were asking if TJ was glimpsed by Yewa again, right?"

Manny found a pocket to get herself away from the bulk of the crowd as she said, "Yewa didn't see him. He's just gone."

"Miss Martinez, is TJ dead?" The chatter among all the

reporters stopped at once. All of them giving silence for Manny's answer, waiting with bated breaths.

Ayo's heart dropped. The word "dead" hung in the air like a curse, and he saw the impact it had on Manny. They hadn't used the word yet. It would make even the thought of it too real. And sure enough, that's exactly what it did. Her tough front cracked, just for a second, but long enough for the reporters to notice.

One of them, a sharp-eyed man with a pen that wrote in gold ink, seized the moment. "You said he's 'gone.' Gone as in dead, correct?"

Manny's mouth opened, but no sound came out.

"Can you clarify, Miss Martinez? Is TJ Young no longer among the living?"

"I—" Manny stumbled over her words, her face pale. "That's not what I meant!"

"But you said he's gone," the man pressed, his pen scribbling furiously in midair.

"I didn't mean it like that!" Manny's voice cracked, her frustration spilling over. "We don't know what's going on with him right now!"

Heat rose in Ayo's chest. He stepped forward, raising his hands to sign a calmer response, but the reporters were too focused on Manny's outburst to notice him.

"You're saying there's no contact with TJ?"

"Is the UCMP covering up his fate?"

"Are the Keepers involved in his disappearance?"

Ayo couldn't take it anymore. He grabbed Manny's wrist and tugged her away, dragging her out of the throng, static-shocking anyone who came near.

"Hey!" she protested, yanking her arm back as they rounded a corner leading to the main street. Ayo didn't stop until they were well out of sight, the reporters' voices fading into the background.

Manny pulled away from him, her face flushed. "What the hell, Ayo?"

His hands flew up, signing sharply. "What you think? You give them something to twist!"

"I didn't give them nothin'!" Manny's voice wavered. "They were… they were gonna twist it no matter *what* I said!"

"So no say anything," he signed back, his movements quick and pointed.

Manny threw her hands in the air, spinning away from him. "You think I don't know that? I'm trying to hold it together, but it feels like everything's falling apart, okay?"

Ayo watched her, his anger softening into something heavier. He wanted to say something—anything—but the words stiffened in his fingers, tangled up with his own frustrations. TJ was good at keeping Manny cool, not him. Without TJ, the bond he thought they shared seemed a touch weaker.

Behind them, the magical cameras clicked one last time before retreating, their lights winking out like fireflies.

"We're screwed, Ayo," Manny said finally, her voice flat.

Ayo nodded slowly, his hands sinking into his pockets. He didn't have the heart to argue. Because she was right.

FEBRUARY AT IFA ACADEMY WAS BRUTAL. ARTICLE AFTER ARTICLE spread faster than a wildfire fueled by enchanted winds, and with it came an avalanche of questions, whispers, and stares. Ayo tried to keep his head down, focusing on the steady rhythm of classes and assignments, but it was impossible to escape the growing tension.

Everywhere he went, people cornered him and Manny. The one thing that seemed to keep them together was their opposition to the rest of the student body. They were almost as bad as the reporters...

"What happened to TJ?" someone asked on Tuesday morning, their voice cautious.

"Are the Orishas really not talking to anyone anymore?" whispered another during lunch on Wednesday.

By Thursday, the speculation had taken a darker turn. "Do you think TJ did something to cause the severance?" a JS1 student muttered to her tablemate in the mess hall, her voice too loud to ignore. Ayo's jaw clenched so hard it hurt. He kept walking, pretending he hadn't heard.

The mess hall wasn't the only place it happened. In the middle of staffcrafting class, Staffmaster Bamidele made a pointed comment during the lecture. "Not every diviner is ready to wield a staff, no matter their ambition. True readiness comes from discipline, from understanding one's place in the balance of Ashe."

Ayo didn't need the man to call his name to know he was the target. He kept his head down, his hands working carefully on the iron shaft before him. The base of the staff was nearly complete—a sleek, polished metal etched with intricate patterns he'd spent weeks perfecting. His goal was to finish it by next month, in time to get TJ back when the Hero's Equinox came.

His new alignment with Ogun had helped, assisting him to see ways to build his staff more efficiently. He had to be ready for when TJ got back. It would be any week now, any day, any minute.

"Looking good, Ayo," whispered Titi, glancing at his work as she filed the edges of her own wooden staff. "You're really going for it, huh?"

"Of course," Ayo signed back, a small surge of pride flickering in his chest.

But the satisfaction was short-lived. As class ended, Staffmaster Bamidele pulled him aside. "You've made progress. But building a staff isn't just about the craft. It's about proving you're ready to use it."

"I'm r-r-ready," Ayo said out loud, his voice firm despite the stutter.

Bamidele raised an eyebrow. "We'll see. Keep working, Oyelowo. Here's hoping you do better than Mr. Young." With that, he turned and left, his loincloth sweeping dramatically behind him.

ᛉ

BY FRIDAY AFTERNOON, THE CONSTANT QUESTIONS AND STARES finally cracked them. Ayo and Manny were leaving for dinner when a group of students caught them near the Library Tree.

"You guys should take it easy," one of them said, their voice dripping with false sympathy. "You've been through a lot. It's okay to let go. Don't be in denial."

"Wouldn't you be too if that was your friend?"

Ayo's temper snapped. The pressure of the week boiled over, and before he could stop himself, he shouted, "Shut up! TJ's not d-d-dead!"

Manny was quick to jump in, her voice sharp and unyielding. "He's alive, okay? We don't need your pity. Just leave us alone!"

The group fell silent, their wide eyes tracking Ayo and Manny as they stomped off.

"They don't believe us," Manny muttered, her fists clenched so tightly her knuckles turned white. "Nobody does."

Ayo didn't respond. The truth was, he wasn't sure he believed himself anymore.

# 56

# UNDER PRISTINE TILES

Ayo's father's luxury apartment within New Ile-Ife sprawled like a magazine cover brought to life. The white marble floors gleamed with a polished shine so bright that it could reflect the pores on your skin. Gold accents framed the walls and doorways, and abstract Nigerian artwork hung along the walls. The open floor plan gave way to a sunken living room filled with furniture so pristine, it felt like sin to even breathe on it.

Ayo lounged on the oversized sectional, legs stretched out, his phone balanced on his chest. He wasn't scrolling anymore, but the last headline on his screen refused to leave his mind.

**Closest Friends Confirm TJ Young Is Gone—Is He Dead?**

He groaned, tossing the phone onto the glass coffee table, where it landed with a sharp *clack*. From her spot by the spiral staircase, Manny jumped slightly, shooting him a glare.

"Y'know," she said, voice tight, "not everybody has a fancy table like that. Back home, if you slammed somethin' on the coffee table, you might end up missin' a leg."

Ayo barely looked at her, signing. "You want me apologize to table?"

"No, but you could be a little more careful. Not all of us grew up in a museum."

Ayo's head snapped up at that. "Museum? What that mean?"

It felt like all they did was bicker lately. They still hung out with each other almost exclusively since anyone else who tried to hang around them always turned the conversation to TJ. But the more time they shared with one another the more they were starting to feel like an old married couple.

Manny gestured around the room, her eyes wide like she couldn't believe he didn't see it. "This! This whole place. Look at it. Everything's shiny and perfect and... untouched. Like nobody actually lives here."

"That no my fault," Ayo signed defensively. "My dad likes things neat. Cleaners come every day."

She snorted. "Must be nice."

"It is," Ayo shot back, sitting up straighter. "What, I supposed to feel bad for having clean place to stay?"

Manny rolled her eyes and started pacing again. She hadn't sat down once since they got there, and it was starting to bug him. Her scuffed sneakers made soft squeaks on the marble, a sound that felt out of place in the otherwise pristine silence of the apartment.

"You can take shoes off," Ayo signed weakly to himself almost.

Manny froze mid-step, glaring at him. "What was that? Sign that again."

He realized too late how it sounded. "I no mean it like that. I just—"

"Yeah, I get it. I'm messin' up your perfect little space with my dirty sneakers, huh?"

"That's not what I said!"

"You didn't have to. I get it, Ayo. Your life's all neat and tidy, and mine's... not. But don't act like I'm the problem just 'cause I don't fit into your fancy world."

"Where this come from? I no try to act better. But maybe—maybe if you chill out for two seconds, we focus on what's important."

"You mean TJ," Manny said, her voice sharp. "Yeah, that's what I'm tryin' to do. But you? You're over here actin' like he's already gone."

Ayo hesitated, the words forming on his hands and fingers before he could stop them. "What if he is?"

Manny stared at him, her face stone. Never a good thing. "What'd you just say?"

"I just say—what if he is?" Ayo lifted from his couch, signing. "We no know what is going on. No one hears from him. Not Yewa, not the Orishas, not us. What if—what if this is it?"

Manny's fists clenched at her sides, her jaw tight. "Don't. Don't you dare start talkin' like that."

"I no try to start something," he signed quickly, holding up his hands. "But we gotta be real about this. What if—"

"What if nothin'!" she snapped. "TJ's not dead, Ayo. He's out there, and he needs us to believe in him. If you're already givin' up, then maybe you don't know him as well as you think you do."

"That no fair," Ayo shot back, his voice rising. "I no give up. I just—think about the possibilities. Try to be real."

"Stop," Manny said, her voice trembling. "Just stop."

For a moment, neither of them spoke. The silence was thick, oppressive, broken only by the faint hum of music coursing through the apartment's walls.

Then Manny grabbed her bag from where she'd dropped it near the door. "I can't do this," she muttered, slinging it over her shoulder.

Ayo's chest tightened. "M-M-Manny—"

"No one believes in him anymore. Not you, not the reporters, not anybody. I need to be alone."

As she turned to leave, Ayo's voice stopped her. "I do b-b-believe in him."

She paused, her hand on the doorknob, but didn't turn around.

"I do," he said again, softer this time. "But I try to k-k-keep my head on straight, too."

Wrong move, the wrong thing to say. Without another word, Manny opened the door and stepped out, letting it swing shut behind her.

Ayo sank back onto the sectional, his head in his hands. His designer ring caught the faint light, glinting like a cruel reminder of everything he couldn't fix.

"Get your head on straight," he muttered to himself, but the words felt hollow.

MANNY WASN'T COMPLETELY WRONG. IT DID FEEL LIKE THEY were the last ones to believe TJ could be reached. And now just Manny. For the first few weeks after the articles dropped, it looked like they might have been able to break through to TJ. Elder Adeyemi even tried to get help from Olosa and Ol' Sally back at camp in the States, but Olosa was quiet like the other Orishas and Ol' Sally hadn't seen Yewa for a while.

Ruby even induced sleep on herself several times to commune with Obatala, but the Dreamweaver never responded, lying low or ignoring mortals like all the rest. Was it because of all that business with Morpheus TJ had mentioned? Darker thoughts creeped in as well. What if it wasn't just TJ who was… dead. What if it was all the Orishas? No, that couldn't be. Ayo could still use fire and lightning. The Orishas' Ashe still filtered through to the world.

But still... It didn't matter who they tried to commune with since none of them had access to the Court of All to begin with. TJ was the key, and that key was… misplaced. *Just* misplaced. Not gone. Ayo had to believe that.

Ayo sat on the edge of his bed a few hours after Manny left, the first weekend of February settling heavily on his shoulders. He had been reading a piece of paper left behind by TJ:

1. ~~Gotta figure out how to reverse this channeling thing by dreamwalking with Obatala and Oshosi.~~

2. ~~Open up the ancestral path from Yemoja to Oya through the Frost Realm for Manny.~~

3. ~~Unlock ancestral path from Ogun to Shango's using Ayo's Norse ring. (And find Ogun's Sacred Cabinet).~~

3b. Figure out how to get ring back from Ayo's dad (with his consent)

4. ~~Complete my staff to sustain the ancestral path ritual to the Court of All jail cell.~~

5. Save Shango and Oya on The Hero's Equinox.

*6. Don't die*

Ayo had been staring at the last line in particular. He had even circled the note to make damn sure TJ wouldn't die. Any time Ayo doubted himself, he went back to the list, trying to recall TJ's goofy voice. He might have been staring at it the moment Manny left, in fact.

The late afternoon sun streamed through the wide windows of his room, casting long shadows on the intricately tiled floor. His phone screen glowed in his hand, displaying headlines from Evo that blurred together like some twisted nightmare:

**Ashe Fading Across the Globe**

**Major Yoruba Diviner Rituals Collapse**

**What's Happening with Magic in the Sub-Saharan Diviner Hubs?**

Each swipe revealed another wave of bad news—rituals in Louisiana failing spectacularly, wards flickering out in Cuba, sacred sites in Brazil that now lay as empty as broken shells. A sick churning settled deep in Ayo's stomach. This all had to be connected to TJ, but none of the forums seemed to have connected the dots yet. Comments littered every conspiracy theorist post.

NO11AJ

The signs are clear. We face weakening magic akin to the Manichaean Sorcerers' fall. It's gradual, but the numbers are pointing in the same direction.

ST0RMRIDER

My sister's a Seer. She said this day would come near the Spring Equinox. A great changing of seasons.

HONEYDRIP515

False! DT reported that all predictions were down 90% late last year. That lines up with Adeyemi's announcement of Orunmila kicking it. So your sister couldn't have made that BS prediction.

ST0RMRIDER

My sister made her prediction before all that! I swear. I can DM you.

Ayo started a new tab on his phone and looked up what that one user meant by "the fall of Manichaean Sorcerers." It sounded familiar. A quick search on Evo got him his answer. Apparently, the Manichaean Sorcerers were legends of a lost magical lineage who had vanished in the 14th century due to fading belief and ritual. Ayo had always thought their story was cautionary, an old tale to keep young diviners' prayers focused on the Orishas. In fact, wasn't it his father who told him that story?

Ayo went back to the forum to add a message of his own.

FLAMETHROWER06

I ain't buying that whole Manichaean sorcerer hype. The mystical pros been saying for a minute that the Mesoamerican Archivists or the Scottish ones would fall off way before any diviners. There's way less of them than us, anyway. For real, diviners don't even crack the top 10 of endangered magic user groups. And seriously, where y'all pulling these numbers on the "gradual decline" from? All the experts been showing is Shango and Oya dipping a bit these past few months.

NO11AJ

Crystal power, man. It's always the first to go. You see it with those clouded crystal girls who claim they are magic. Crystal power is so strong that even they can sense their energies. But over the last month, their social media presence has seen a 10% decline. I have a bunch of charts I can DM you. Something serious is going down.

The words sent a chill down Ayo's spine. Diviners, endangered? This wasn't how it was supposed to go. Panic crawled up his chest, leaving a bitter taste in his mouth. What would he do if he couldn't touch Ashe any more? He rubbed his fingers and cast a lightning bolt between them. It was weaker, for sure, but not gone. Not yet.

He went back to his phone.

FLAMETHROWER06

Yeah, hit me with those charts.

He tossed the phone aside and pressed his hands against his temples. How could this be happening? Worse—how did TJ's disappearance tie into the worldwide decline of Ashe? Ayo had always known TJ as a dope friend and a formidable booster of their collective magic, but a source? The literal lynchpin of their Ashe? That was just nuts.

His phone buzzed and he reached for it to check the new message.

NO11AJ

Change of plans. Meet me at the Oduduwa statue at New Ile-Ife instead.

FLAMETHROWER06

Wait. What? How did you know I was in NIL?

NO11AJ

I sort of looked at your background. I know who you are. I won't out you on here. Just meet me. It's important. It's about TJ Young.

Ayo sprang up on his bed, standing as he read the last message over and over.

FLAMETHROWER06

Pause. Who the hell is this? I'm not meeting until you tell me.

NO11AJ

Sorry, man. No names. And don't try to look me up. I got my shit on lock. Just meet me.

Ayo didn't believe that for a second. He slid over to his laptop and spent the next half hour trying to break this person's account—whoever they were. But their online footprint was on lock, everything covered. Whoever this was must've had some insider information. Maybe a UCMP agent? Maybe that Tore Stadheim guy or one of those officials at those desks?

The walls of his room pressed in too close. Ayo pushed himself to his feet, shrugging on a jacket and tossing on a baseball cap as he moved. He needed air—and answers. He slipped out of the house and into the winding streets that led to the village square.

TJ's sister's mural loomed over the square of New Ile-Ife, her painted eyes watching the gathering crowd below. Ayo found himself staring at it for some reason. Maybe it was the way the artist depicted the eyes. He almost felt like they were alive or somehow... familiar. He shook the thought away. He needed to focus on who had summoned him there. He hadn't realized there was some big event that day. Granted, he hardly left his home during the weekends lately.

A stage stood before Oduduwa's statue head, packed with elders, students, and UCMP officials in their formal fits. The air was tense, charged in a way that made Ayo's stomach knot. It wasn't just the crowd—though there were more people here than he'd expected, their conversations overlapping in a low hum of unease. It was the way their eyes darted, the way some of them whispered to one another, glancing furtively at the stage or at the growing clusters of elders and officials in their ceremonial robes.

Ayo stuck close to the edges of the square, scanning the faces for anything familiar or suspicious. Was the person who messaged him here already? He couldn't tell. Every time he caught someone's gaze, they either looked away too quickly or stared a little too long.

His mind jumped to worst-case scenarios. What if this was a trap? What if whoever had contacted him wasn't some helpful insider but someone looking to make sure he stayed quiet about TJ? He rubbed his fingers together, sparking a tiny crackle of lightning between them to remind himself he wasn't defenseless. Still, the feeling wouldn't go away.

"If Yewa truly saw Tomori Jomiloju Young," an Elder's voice boomed from the podium, "we must accept what that means. The boy is gone. We do him no honor by refusing to mourn him properly."

A funnel of wind whipped through the crowd, carrying Eni's voice. "It's only been a few weeks! He's been gone longer than this before!"

The Elder's expression hardened. "Young lady, in all those times, Yewa never saw him. That makes this different."

"That's a lie! The sources never said anything about Yewa seeing TJ, only that his friends asked about it! Stop the fake news!"

Umar, who had climbed on stage, whispered something to the Elder. The Elder nodded and let him have the podium. "I know it's hard to accept," Umar said. "TJ was a personal friend of mine. We talked crossover all the time. I fought alongside him during the Great Drowning. And if we hold off honoring him in death, he might not have an easy path to the ancestors. We owe him that much. I owe him that much." He paused, looking as though holding back a cough. "To start the mourning… I was thinking we add to Dayo's memorial." He thumbed to the mural behind him. "TJ deserves to be remembered beside his sister."

The square erupted in heated arguments, the sound reverberating like a stormcloud overhead. Half the crowd claiming fake news, the other clamoring for a proper send off to his friend. Eni and Titi were the loudest among the crowd, supported by what looked like TJ's grandparents. It was too loud to tell which side they fell on. But Ayo could guess.

Ayo's pulse thudded as he turned away from the noise. He pulled his baseball cap down, more out of instinct than practicality. No one seemed to notice him, but he couldn't shake the feeling that he was being watched. He glanced around the edges of the square again, his unease growing with every second.

He'd just stepped closer to the mural's shadow when a tug pulled at his sleeve. He spun, his heart leaping to his throat, but stopped short when he saw the kid standing there. At first, Ayo didn't recognize him. The boy was wrapped in a black hoodie two sizes too big, the hem brushing the tops of his worn sneakers. His face was half-hidden, but the familiar sun-baked dreadlocks and sharp, knowing eyes gave him away.

"Tunde?" Ayo signed and said at the same time.

"Yeah, it's me," Tunde said, his voice low but steady. He glanced around, his small frame tense as though he expected someone to jump out at him. "You're early. Thought you'd spend a few more hours trying to break my firewalls."

Ayo's brow furrowed. "You the one who send me mail? Why no say that earlier?"

Tunde canted his head; Ayo forgot he didn't sign. So he pulled out his phone and typed out what he said.

Tunde shrugged, his expression unreadable. "Had to make sure you weren't followed. This place is public enough for a quick meet, but it's not safe to talk here. Let's head back to my grandma's homestead."

Ayo hesitated, his hands flying over his keyboard.

AYO

Why all the sneaking? What you know?

Tunde's gaze sharpened, his voice dropping lower. "I know TJ's not dead. And I can prove it."

The words struck Ayo with a force that left him reeling. His breath hitched, and a cascade of questions surged through his mind, unanswered and urgent. But Tunde was already moving, his steps drawing him toward a quieter path beyond the square. Ayo's fingers curled tightly, the rapid thrum of his pulse driving him forward as he followed.

# 57

# CARVED IN WOOD AND STONE

THE WALK TO THE ABIMBOLA HOMESTEAD FELT LIKE CROSSING realms. Tunde led the way, his hoodie pulled low over his face, and Ayo trailed behind, his hands stuffed in his pockets. The farther they moved from the village square, the quieter it became. Gone were the bustling market stalls and echoing shouts of diviners. The dirt paths gave way to trails flanked by tall oil palms swaying lazily in the humid breeze.

When they reached the compound, Ayo hesitated. The sight of the house struck him. It wasn't the size—there were plenty of larger houses in New Ile-Ife—but the door. The door was alive in a way Ayo appreciated, its carved brass surface glowing faintly in the evening light.

He took a step closer, drawn by the intricate design. Farmers bent low in the fields, their tools raised mid-motion, while hunters with bows and spears crept through forests dense with twisted trees. Women balanced heavy pots of water on their heads, their carved faces etched with serene determination. Ayo's eyes followed the flowing patterns, each small figure contributing to a larger story he couldn't quite piece together. It was a classic Yoruba home. One he was not used to.

"This your grandma's door?" Ayo signed, looking over at Tunde, who had stopped to pull his hood back.

"Yeah," Tunde said quietly, a small smile tugging at his lips.

"Pretty sick, right? Every time I come home, I find something new in the carvings."

Ayo nodded, his fingers lingering near the brass. The metal hummed faintly under his fingertips, almost like it was alive. It made him feel... small, but not in a bad way. Like he was standing on the shoulders of history.

But before he could get lost in the door's story, raised voices from inside the house broke the moment. Ayo's head snapped toward the sound, his body tense. Tunde froze mid-step, his shoulders stiffening as the muffled argument grew louder.

"Tunde—" Ayo started to sign, but Tunde shook his head quickly, putting a finger to his lips.

"Wait," Tunde whispered. "Let's just... stay back for a sec."

Ayo followed him to the side of the house, crouching near the edge of a window, the curtains withdrawn just enough to let sound escape.

"I can't believe you!" It was TJ's father, and his voice boomed. "You let me find out from some damn article that our son is dead? What kind of shit is that, Yejide!?"

"It's not that simple!" TJ's mom shot back, her voice sharp and brittle. "You think I wanted you to find out like that? I was trying to fix it before—"

"Before what!? Before I started asking questions you didn't want to answer? Before I started pointing out how far you've dragged this family into your magical *deathtrap*?"

Ayo winced at the bitterness in Mr. Young's voice. Tunde's jaw clenched as he leaned closer, his hands balled into fists.

"You don't understand," Mrs. Young said. "You're clouded—"

"Clouded? I don't think I'm the clouded one here. You mean normal, right? You mean someone who doesn't buy into all this magical garbage. I'm the one who's seeing clearly here, Yejide. Our son is dead. TJ is *gone*. And I'm stepping in before you let this madness take our last child, too."

"Don't you dare—"

"I'm done! I've stayed quiet for *years*. Let you drag us deeper and deeper into this insanity. And what did it get us, huh? Dayo? Gone. TJ? Gone. You're not taking Tunde down with you, Yejide. No more!"

"TJ isn't gone," Mrs. Young snapped, though her voice trembled. "I—I can still fix this. We can bring him back."

"And how many more children are you planning to lose before you realize you can't fix anything!?" A clatter of keys; the whoosh of a bag being picked up. "You promised me, Yejide. You promised to protect our family. My boy. *TJ was my boy.*"

Ayo's stomach churned. He glanced at Tunde, whose face was pale, his eyes wide and unblinking.

"What's he talking a-a-about?" Ayo whispered.

Tunde swallowed. "Because TJ used to be clouded."

Inside, Mr. Young's voice softened, but it was no less resolute. "You want to keep playing with these people? Fine. But I'm done. Wipe my memory. Do whatever it is you do. I don't want to remember a damn thing about this jacked-up magical world. And you know what? Maybe it's better if Tunde doesn't either."

Tunde shot to his feet at that, his face darkening. "What the hell?" he hissed, storming toward the door.

"Tunde, wait!" Ayo signed, but the younger boy couldn't see his gestures.

Tunde pushed open the intricately carved brass door, and Ayo's first impression of the Abimbola home was how much it felt like stepping into another world. The air inside was warm and rich, carrying the faint scent of cocoa and something floral, like hibiscus.

The door swung shut behind them with a soft click. For a moment, the house seemed like a sanctuary—a cozy refuge where nothing could go wrong. Sunlight streamed through open windows, mingling with the soft, golden glow from the crystals embedded in the walls. The light played off dark wood furniture polished to a mirror shine, making every surface seem alive with a quiet kind of magic.

Ayo's gaze swept over the walls, nearly hidden beneath dozens—no, *hundreds*—of framed photos. Smiling faces stared back at him, their joy frozen in time. The arrangement wasn't orderly like a gallery; it was crowded, chaotic in a way that felt deeply human, like every memory mattered too much to leave out. It was the kind of clutter his father would've hated, but Ayo found it... comforting.

In the corner, a broom moved back and forth, animated by a simple spell. The rhythmic *swish-swish* was oddly soothing, like a heartbeat keeping the house alive. Everything about the space felt lived-in, warm, and unapologetically imperfect.

But the peace didn't last.

Through the archway leading deeper into the house came the sharp rise and fall of voices, shattering the tranquility. The glow from the crystals flickered faintly, as if the argument had reached into the house itself, disturbing its balance. Ayo stiffened, the inviting warmth of the room now feeling like a mockery against the tension ahead.

Tunde had already stopped just a few steps inside, his fists still clenched at his sides. His whole body seemed rigid, his gaze fixed on the source of the voices. His steps quickened, leading Ayo toward the archway and into the storm.

"Woah, woah, woah!" Tunde called out. "Why are we talking about wiping memories? What—what even is this?"

Mrs. Young's face softened in panic. "Tunde, this isn't—"

"Don't lie to me," Tunde cut her off. "First TJ's gone, and now you're trying to take me out of the picture, too? What is wrong with you people?"

Mr. Young stepped forward, placing a firm hand on Tunde's shoulder. "We're leaving. Now."

"No!" Tunde shrugged off the hand. "You don't get it! I've been looking into this—TJ's not dead. I have proof. There's something happening to Ashe, and I think it's connected to him—"

"Tunde. Enough," Mr. Young said with finality.

"But—"

"No." Mr. Young's grip tightened. "You're a kid. You don't know what's best for you, but I do. And I'm not letting you get dragged into this madness like TJ was."

"What?" Tunde said. "No... Mom, tell Dad to stop."

Mrs. Young opened her mouth to argue, but Mr. Young silenced her with a look. Tunde's shoulders sagged, his resolve crumbling.

"This is done, Yejide. We're leaving. You can find us in L.A. where we should've stayed."

As Mr. Young led Tunde toward the door, the boy turned back to Ayo, his eyes desperate. Without speaking, he slipped a small, glowing external drive into Ayo's hand.

"Don't lose that," Tunde whispered before his father pulled him away. "You can crack it. Just look into the charts."

Ayo stared at the device, its faint light flickering in his palm like a fragile flame. He looked up as the door shut behind them, leaving him alone with Mrs. Young and the secrets of what the glowing external drive held within.

# 58

# BEHIND AN AWKWARD KISS

MANNY GRUNTED AS SHE SPRINTED ACROSS THE NEW ILE-IFE crossover field, her feet pounding the earth with each step. She focused on the air currents around her, manipulating them to create resistance, making each stride a battle against an invisible force. Sweat drenched her tanktop dashiki, the fabric clinging to her skin as she pushed herself to the limit.

But her wind was weakening.

Where before she could manifest resistance for minutes at a time, simulating the pressure she'd get from her opponents, now she could only maintain her Ashe for seconds.

So she transitioned into a series of burpees, using her earth magic to make the ground beneath her hands and feet shift and undulate, forcing her to maintain balance and control. Each rep became a test of strength and focus, her muscles burning with the effort.

But her earth magic was even weaker.

That didn't make sense. Sure Oya's Wind had been hard to manifest since last summer but earth was connected to Oshosi, to Osain, Aganju. The simulated pressure of crossover earthballs swallowing her feet was nothing more than a gentle caress. That wouldn't do. That wouldn't do at all.

So, finally, she relented and dropped into a plank position, holding her body rigid and parallel to the ground. She held the pose, her arms and core trembling as she counted the seconds in her head. The mundane exercise, devoid of any magical enhancement, forced her to dig deep.

After what felt like an eternity, Manny collapsed onto the grass, her chest heaving as she gulped in air. Her stomach churned, and she rolled to the side, retching until there was nothing left in her system. She lay there, her muscles on fire, as she tried to listen to the wind and the birds, seeking a moment of peace.

But peace eluded her.

TJ's screams from the Court of All echoed in her mind, mingling with his descriptions of the agony Shango and Oya had endured. She pressed her hands to her ears, trying to block out the dark thoughts, but they persisted, tormenting her. Unable to contain the anguish any longer, Manny let out a wind-scream, a primal release of her pain and frustration.

"Whoa!" a shout rang out, followed by the sound of someone falling. Manny turned to see Ayo using weak and clumsy air-steps to break his fall, his hands moving rapidly as he signed, "Watch it!"

Manny grimaced, pushing herself up to kneel on one knee. "Sorry. I didn't see you there."

Ayo dusted himself off, his eyes widening as he signed. "Damn, Manny. You okay? That's a lot of throw up."

Manny waved her hand, using wind and water magic to clean the mess and wash out her mouth. "I'm fine. Happens all the time after a tough workout. Just pushed myself a li'l too hard."

Ayo raised an eyebrow. "I mean… real talk… You jacked, girl." Manny could almost hear his tone of voice perfectly through his YSL now. "Biggest and strongest I seen you. You must be big mad."

Manny scowled. "Whatchoo want, Ayo? Just get to the point."

Ayo frowned and looked around the field to the empty stands, the gaping totem poles on either side of the field. Manny had come here because she got too many questions at the academy, at the crossover field there. No one was playing pickup because they were all at the village center talking about how they'd "honor" TJ. She didn't need that, didn't want it.

"My bad, Ayo," she finally said. "I'm just heated. What is it?"

Ayo stuck his hand in his pocket and pulled out his phone. His screen glowed between them, displaying message boards filled with reports and schematics she had no clue about.

"What..." Manny's eyes scanned the text. "What does all this mean? In regular-people terms, please."

"Even I no understand all of it. But basically TJ could still be alive. Like, we can *prove* he is. I just need help to break this code. I no smart enough to crack code of Tunde alone. So I was thinking..."

Manny's eyes lit up. "Oracle Ruby?"

Ayo smiled, then signed. "Glad we on same page again."

ᛉ

THAT FOLLOWING MONDAY, WHEN THEY RETURNED TO THE academy, more and more parents were pulling their children from school. As they watched a half dozen JS1 students being carted away, Manny and Ayo set off to meet with Oracle Ruby.

The path to Oracle Rock felt longer than Manny remembered. She and Ayo walked side by side, their footsteps crunching on the slopes that wound through the back of Ifa Academy's sprawling campus. The morning sun was a weak thing, half-hidden behind a thin veil of clouds. The huge rock structure loomed ahead, gray and weathered, its jagged edges almost blending into the overcast sky.

Manny hadn't been here in a minute, not since Orunmila's Ashe —the divine wisdom that once filled the rock—had disappeared. Most students and even teachers avoided the place now. What was the point? Without the Ashe, Oracle Rock was just an empty monument.

But now, something stirred inside her, a spark she hadn't dared to acknowledge for the past couple days—maybe weeks. Ayo's proof—that sliver of possibility—was like pouring oil onto a dying ember. It hadn't been enough to erase the ache of loss, but it was enough to make her believe. Hope didn't just return; it flared, stubborn and wild.

She glanced at Ayo. He was unusually quiet, his lips pressed tight as he clutched his phone. The screen's glow reflected in his glasses, the coded messages still shining on it. Manny knew he felt it too, the fragile weight of what they might uncover.

The once-bustling Oracle Rock was empty now, save for a single lion-skin tent pitched at its center. Oracle Ruby's tent. She was the last of the Oracles to remain, not because of faith, but because of her technology. Ruby's blend of hardware and old magic kept her work relevant, even when everything else had dimmed.

"You ready?" Ayo asked, his fingers tapping nervously against his phone case.

Manny squared her shoulders. "Let's do this."

Oracle Ruby's tent smelled like burnt sage and faint motor oil. Strings of LEDs flickered across the canvas ceiling, their glow a mix of traditional and futuristic. Monitors hummed quietly, arranged on a weathered wooden table. One screen displayed streams of code; another showed a swirling mass of Ashe readings.

Ruby sat cross-legged on a stool, her bright green-tipped locs coiled like a crown today. She glanced up, her sharp eyes narrowing as Manny and Ayo stepped inside.

"This better be good, loves," she said, pulling her headphones down around her neck. "I'm halfway through a slog of a recalibration."

"It's g-g-good," Ayo stuttered, holding up his phone. "I got something n-n-new about TJ. A code given to me by his b-b-brother, Tunde. But we can't crack it."

Ruby raised a skeptical brow. "Tunde? As in, the tech genius who doesn't know how to say hello without stammering? That Tunde?"

Manny folded her arms. "That Tunde. And trust me, he's better at apps than stringing words together when he's around you."

"Didn't he just get pulled by his clouded father? Come to think of it, there were no roses outside my tent this morning..."

"Yeah..." Manny ran her fingers through her curls uncomfortably.

"So you can h-h-help?" Ayo asked, holding up his phone again.

Ruby snorted, taking the phone from Ayo. Her fingers flew across her keyboard as she connected the phone to her system. The screens lit up, one by one, displaying fragmented text and graphs. Ruby muttered to herself, her focus unbreakable.

"This code's impressive," she said after a while. "Tunde's good. Like, *scarily* good. Remind me to tell him that—he deserves it. Anyway, give me a second."

Minutes passed as she worked, the tent filled with the soft clatter of keys and the faint buzz of monitors. Then Ruby leaned back, pushing her glasses up the bridge of her nose.

"Okay," she said. "There's definitely channeling happening here. Ashe is being siphoned, almost like it's being rerouted. And looking at this..." She pointed to a graph on the screen. "The rate of the diminishing Ashe matches The Channeling..." She pressed a tablet stylus between her teeth. "Yeah, looks like whoever developed this code is tracking the recent decline along with the decline we know about about with Shango and Oya. And he's using the zero-sum of Orunmila. Yeah... yeah! He reckons this new energy spike being channeled along with them is..."

Ayo's eyes lit up. "Tunde was s-s-saying he had proof TJ is a-a-alive. He thinks TJ's the one b-b-being channeled!"

Manny leaned in. "So if there's channeling, that means there's *something* to channel."

Ayo's eyes lit up. "Which means T-T-TJ—"

"—could still be alive!" Manny finished, spinning to face him.

"Maybe he's s-s-stuck on the other side—"

"Or holding out until someone finds him—"

"Maybe he's channeling Ashe to s-s-stay alive—"

Ruby raised a hand, cutting through their excitement. "Hey! Let's keep the hopes tamped, loves. We don't know if it's not just another Orisha. Oshosi was captured too, yeah?"

"But, correct me if I'm wrong 'cause I don't understand none of this," Manny said. "But that would only read as Oshosi's specific Ashe being affected, no? I bet TJ's general connection to Ashe is what's affecting it all at once."

Ruby frowned. "Okay, sure, maybe. That still leaves us with a channeled TJ. That's not great news, loves."

But Manny and Ayo were already grinning, jumping up and down like kids who'd just cracked open the best secret ever.

The tent lights exploded into chaos. LEDs overhead flickered like a bad rave, and Ruby's monitors spasmed—graphs flatlining, Ashe readings twisting into jagged shapes, code stuttering across the screens. Then, out of nowhere, lo-fi beats drifted through the tent.

"What the—" Manny spun around, her arms crossed tight. "Ruby, what's happening?"

Ruby was already moving, yanking cables and hammering keys. "Not me. Something's feeding back into the system—external interference! It's overriding everything!"

Ayo edged closer to Manny, clutching his phone like it might save him. The whole tent felt alive, the air charged with static. A monitor flared so bright he flinched, its glow catching in Manny's eyes. She looked sharp, focused—like the chaos didn't faze her.

And then it hit him.

At first, it was small, easy to ignore, like a ripple in his chest. But then it grew—bigger, heavier, until it was impossible to shake. Ayo found himself staring at her. *Really staring*. The way her Afro curls framed her face, catching the light. The way her jaw tightened. The fire in her eyes, the one that refused to dim no matter what was thrown at her.

He'd seen Manny a million times before, but not like this. Not with his heart pounding, not with this sudden, overwhelming urge to just… move closer. Hug her. Or maybe more.

Ruby slammed a palm on her keyboard. "I'm trying to reset, but it's reacting! This isn't random—it's deliberate!"

"Reacting to what?" Manny demanded.

"I don't know!" Ruby said, pulling another cable free. "It's like the Ashe in the room took over!"

Ayo's stomach flipped. He glanced at Manny again, and it was like everything else in the tent blurred—just her standing there, the gentle light hitting her like one of those old Hollywood movies. His hands itched to move, to grab hers, to steady himself in the storm of feelings crashing over him.

The air shifted, a soft pulse rolling through the tent. The monitors glowed faintly, the chaos quieting into something calmer—but not less intense.

"Whatever's happening," Ruby murmured, staring at the screens, "it's not over."

Ayo's breath hitched as Manny's fingers brushed the table. She leaned in, her voice steady. "Then we figure it out. This can't be a coincidence."

Before Manny could say anything further, Ayo stepped forward and kissed her.

It wasn't long, just a quick brush of lips, but it stopped Manny cold. She froze, blinking at him like he'd grown a second head. Then, before she could even process, her hands shot out and shoved him away. "Ayo! What the *hell* was that?"

Ayo stumbled back, eyes wide and hands up like he was surrendering. "I—I don't know! I swear, I don't know. That was weird."

"Weird?" Manny's voice climbed. "Weird!? What—what is wrong with you? You know I'm TJ's girl. Always have been. Don't get it twisted."

Ayo scratched the back of his head, his face burning red. "I know, Manny! I *know*. I didn't m-m-mean to. I don't even know what c-c-came over me. It's like—I wasn't thinking. It just h-h-happened."

Manny glared at him for a second longer, her chest rising and falling with deep breaths. Then, finally, she huffed and turned away. "Yeah, well. Don't let it happen again."

"I w-w-won't," Ayo muttered. "For real. I-I-I'm sorry."

As if on cue, Ruby's monitors flickered, their lights dimming before restarting with a loud *beep*.

Ruby sighed, pinching the bridge of her nose. "Fantastic. That's three hours of recalibration down the drain."

Manny scowled, rubbing her temples. "Never mind that, keep figuring this out, Ruby. Let us know the second you have more."

Ruby waved them off. "Yeah, yeah. Go before you break something else. I'll reach out when I have news, loves."

As they stepped out of the tent, the sky above Oracle Rock seemed a little brighter. Manny wasn't sure if it was the sun breaking through the clouds or the fragile, beautiful spark blooming in her chest.

Hope.

Manny practically danced her way down the rocky path, arms pumping in victory. "Did you hear her, Ayo? Did you *hear* her? Tunde was right. TJ's alive!"

Ayo grinned, jogging to keep up as he signed, "I hear. I got ears, Manny."

"Ears, but no chill!" Manny spun around mid-step, throwing her hands in the air like she'd just won a championship. "My boy's out there, holding on. Probably waiting for us to come drag his sorry self back."

The awkward silence hung between them for a beat. Manny kicked a rock out of her path. Was she trying to get her mind back on track?

"Okay," she said, her voice steady now. "What's next? If we're doing this—if we're bringing TJ back—we need a plan. What do we need?"

Ayo sighed in relief, grateful for the pivot. "My ring. But my dad still has it, and you know how he be."

"Yeah, I know." Manny rubbed her temples. "And I need Frost Realm access, but that's locked down tighter than a bank vault. Which means what we both need is..."

"Bolawe," they said in unison, glancing at each other.

Manny groaned. "Yeah... I still got that mirror I didn't enchant to let him through. It's in my dorm, buried under some books. You think we can use it?"

Ayo shrugged, his grin returning as he signed. "Worth shot. If anyone know how to deal with this, it's Bolawe. I no trust others. They no let us do this before spring time. But he will..."

They bumped fists, the tension from earlier fading under the light of their new mission. As they parted ways, Manny felt her hope solidify into something stronger—something unstoppable. TJ was out there. And they were going to bring him home.

# 59

# WITHIN BRUSHING WINDS

THE WHISPERING WILLOWS WEREN'T MUCH TO LOOK AT DURING the day—just thick, gnarled old trees tucked behind the academy dorms. But at night, they transformed. Their willowy branches swayed, though no breeze touched them, and the moonlight made the leaves reflect like shards of glass. Manny had always found comfort there, a spot where the world seemed lighter.

Not tonight.

The branches swayed like accusing fingers, whispering every doubt and fear she refused to voice. Her grip on the mirror tightened as she stepped into the clearing. Her dashiki uniform offered little warmth against the bite of the night breeze. She had hope for TJ but apprehension about relying on Bolawe.

Ayo was already there, pacing. His round frame cut soft shadows against the delicate glow of the academy lights in the distance.

"You got it?" he asked, signing, stopping mid-step.

Manny held up the mirror. The silver frame was tarnished, its surface dim but pulsing faintly with Ashe. "Yeah, I got it. You sure about this?"

Ayo's mouth twitched. "No choice."

Manny sighed and knelt on the grass. "All right. Let's do it."

The mirror's weight felt heavier than it should as she placed it down. Ayo crouched beside her. What would Bolawe say? Would he stop them before they started?

Before Manny could call out Bolawe's name, the mirror rippled, its surface glowing faintly before cracking into a sharp hum. For a moment, nothing. Then, a face appeared. Bolawe's. The former Keeper's pockmarked features came into view. Manny's stomach clenched, but she didn't flinch.

*"Did you call to me?"* Bolawe asked.

"No…" Manny looked to Ayo with a questioning stare. "I mean… I was about to. How did you know I was trying to call you?"

Bolawe looked misty-eyed, or perhaps confused. *"I thought I heard something… a voice. Are you sure it wasn't you?"*

Manny turned to Ayo again, and he shrugged.

"Whatever," she said. "We, like, you know, need your help."

*"What could you possibly need from me?"*

*And why aren't we talking to Elder Adeyemi?* Manny could guess he was thinking.

She squared her shoulders, the words not coming easy as she said, "We need your help."

Bolawe smirked. *"Be specific, child."*

Ayo leaned in, his hands moving fast as he signed, "It's about TJ. He's alive. We need Frost Realm access to reach him. And I need my ring back. My dad still has it."

After Manny translated for him, Bolawe's smirk faded. His eyes narrowed, and his voice took on an edge. *"How can you know this?"*

Ayo withdrew his phone and did his best to explain the code he and Ruby had started to decipher. Manny hoped she was translating well enough but Ayo was using terms she wasn't familiar with at all. Eventually, it seemed like Bolawe got the gist, rubbing his chin as he said, *"So, you want me to steal from your father and give up the frost shard? You really don't ask for much, do you?"*

Manny straightened, bristling at his tone. "We have to. It's for saving someone we love. Even you love TJ in your… jacked up way."

*"And the ring?"* Bolawe's gaze shifted to Ayo. *"Consent isn't a trivial matter. We're talking your very life. You may rip apart like TJ should have last year. Using a tool like that without permission—"*

"Isn't the i-i-issue," Ayo interrupted, stuttering. "It's m-m-my ring. My consent. That's all that m-m-matters."

Bolawe tilted his head, studying them both in silence. Then, he chuckled, a low, unsettling sound. *"I'll give you credit—you've got fire. The pair of you. You'd have made excellent Keepers."*

Manny's fist went white around the hand mirror. "Don't. Even."

Bolawe's smirk returned. *"Touchy, aren't we? Fine. I'll help. But don't think for a second this will be simple. Be ready."*

The mirror's glow dimmed, and Bolawe's face vanished, leaving the two of them in heavy silence under the swaying branches.

NOT EVEN THREE DAYS LATER, BOLAWE CALLED TO MANNY'S mirror. Manny snuck out of her dorm room to find Ayo and they headed back to the whispering willows. In the Mirror Realm, Bolawe held up the ring and frost shard in each hand, casually shrugging as if he hadn't just committed to the impossible.

"What!?" Ayo signed. "How you get past baba's security? He has at least a dozen guards in the lobby, not to mention—"

Bolawe didn't need the translation this time, replying, *"I told you and the group before. I am resourceful. And you're not even asking the best question. I got this too."* He dipped low and out of sight to lift up and display TJ's staff.

Manny scrunched up her face. It was true the man was practically a career criminal. But she wanted to make sure he didn't take those objects in nefarious ways. "Who did you kill to get it?"

Bolawe looked taken aback, and if he wasn't holding three items between his hands, Manny would have sworn he would have exaggerated putting a hand to his chest. *"I told you, girl, I don't kill diviners. That's why I left the Keepers, remember?"*

"My name is Manny," she spat back. "And I know what you said, but it ain't always what you do." A second thought occurred to her then. "Did you… did you kill any clouded to get that ring?" Ayo's dad might have employed a few.

Bolawe's expression shifted for a moment. *"No… no killing for this endeavor. I swear it on the Orishas. Now… shall we continue?"*

Manny swallowed long and hard, trying her best to uncover

what had changed in the man's expression. Maybe he was just surprised at how astute Manny's questioning was. Or maybe he *had* killed someone. But he had sworn on the Orishas, something no Keeper would do lightly.

"Yeah, we good," Manny said, nodding for Ayo to come forward.

Bolawe handed Ayo's ring to them through the mirror surface. The moment the ring slipped onto Ayo's finger, something shifted. The air around him seemed to thrum, charged with an invisible force that made Manny's skin prickle. A faint blue glow pulsed beneath Ayo's eye, spreading warmth across his face. His shoulders straightened, his chest rising as if he could finally breathe again. Power poured into him—not loud or flashy, but steady, like the return of a long-lost piece of himself. Manny swore she could feel it too, radiating outward, making her heartbeat quicken. Ayo blinked, his lips parting in surprise, and for the first time in weeks, he didn't look tired—he looked *whole*.

"How does it feel?" Manny asked, her voice soft.

"L-l-like I'm a new man," Ayo answered.

"Good. Now… how about that ice shard." Manny waved a waiting hand.

Bolawe closed his fingers around the shard. "*Same deal applies. I won't be handing this over until we've begun the ritual. I'm sure you can understand why those are agreeable terms.*"

Manny huffed through her nose. The Frost Realm was Bolawe's only leverage. She didn't like it, but she couldn't think of a better counter. "I'm guessing the same goes for TJ's staff?"

Bolawe smiled wickedly. "*You catch on fast.*" He brushed dust off his robes. "*Very well. You've got your tools. Now, what's your link to TJ? That little formula you showed me a few days ago said that might be a missing link. I personally would suggest his staff. Powerful. Saturated in his latent Ashe.*"

Manny frowned. "Even if you did give us his staff now…"

"It's broken." Ayo finished, signing.

Manny glared, pacing as her mind raced. "We need someone who can revive it. Someone who knows his staff well..."

"Teacher Bamidele?" Ayo signed in question.

"Nah… he didn't believe in TJ. He tried to fail him. That

wouldn't work. We need something or someone who believed in him."

Ayo hesitated, then looked at her, shrugging.

Bolawe's expression shifted in the Mirror Realm, a flicker of curiosity flashing across his face. *"Is it not obvious? The girl made her staff side by side with TJ all year. She's bold, too—just like you... Manuela."*

Manny ignored the jab, and the fact that Bolawe knew about Freya to begin with. But she turned to Ayo, her fists tightening. "He's right... I think she's our best play."

Ayo balled his hand into a fist, Ashe crackling faintly around his ring. "You got her number?"

# 60

# BY BLOOMING LAVENDERS

FREYA STOOD AMONG A LAVENDER GARDEN, AWED BY THE SEA OF purple blooms that swayed gently in the early spring breeze. It had become a favorite spot of hers, partly because of the flowers, mostly because it was her girlfriend's family home. The vibrant hues were a stark contrast to the dying winter's monochrome, and bees buzzed softly, busy at work among the flowers. The soothing scent of lavender filled the air, promising the arrival of warmer days.

It was only a few weeks until the start of spring and the Druid Festival of Vernal Gathering. Each druid of the land was charged with planting a tree, shrub, or flower that would contribute to the reforestation of the local area of Balloch. And of course, Freya chose one of the more difficult plants to grow in the chilly Scottish climate. If it weren't for her new staff, she wasn't sure she'd actually be able to do it.

With a smile, she admired its wood finish, the way it spiraled and fit in her hand as she pointed it at a patch of slightly wilted lavender that needed some tender loving care.

*"Blàth, beò agus anail,"* she said, her words like a cycle of sunlight, nurturing soil, water, and fertilization all packaged in one. The drooping lavender slowly but surely spread up and outward. Standing perfectly at attention.

From the other side of the garden, another young woman with muscular arms and fiery red hair stomped her way toward Freya.

Her name was Eilean and she had at least forty pounds of fertilizer on each shoulder. She wasn't even breaking a sweat. To top it off, she carried two mugs of hot chocolate steaming from her hands. Freya smiled, grabbing for the mugs with a grateful kiss on Eilean's cheek. "You're such a show off, you know that?"

Eilean dropped the fertilizer like the sacks were were made of feathers. "And I told you you'd pass your staff trials," she said, her green eyes sparkling, red hair tied back in braids. "Did I not tell you you could do it?"

Freya rolled her eyes as she smoothed a blanket beneath them. "You told me I could do it." She placed the staff on the blanket next to them and took a sip from the mug, delicious hot chocolate filling her throat. "But what you failed to mention was how hard it would be."

Eilean shrugged and, with only a brief pause, rested her hand on Freya's thigh. It didn't matter how long they'd been together, Eilean still questioned if Freya was okay with her touch. "Eh, what do I know about staffs? I'm a sword girl, remember?" She rubbed the back of her braids, but Freya knew she was doing it to show off her biceps. "And who needs staffs when I've got these?"

"Yeah, yeah. But I almost failed the water challenge." Freya shook her head. "But I managed to summon a mist from the moisture in the air at the last second. Thankfully, the test was in the early morning or I would have mucked that up."

Eilean laughed, the sound as delightful as the garden around them. "And the earth trial? I heard you nearly got tangled in thorn bushes."

"Don't remind me," Freya groaned, rubbing at the barely healed wounds on her arms.

They clinked their mugs together, enjoying the rich cocoa under the open sky. Suddenly, Eilean's brow furrowed. "Hey, isn't that the charm that TJ kid sent you?" She pointed to the cauldron charm of Cailleach on Freya's staff.

Freya's eyes widened as the charm started to frost over, odd among the blossoming garden. She set her mug aside and pushed herself up to sit with her legs underneath her. Her fingers found the twisted curve of her staff, and she held it tight in her grasp. With a tongue sticking out, she pulled the wooden shaft closer so she could examine it in more detail. Indeed, the charm was coated in frost. That had never happened before.

Sure, Cailleach was associated with the winter, but like she told TJ… Cailleach was gone. Dead. The charm should have been just as barren, just as bare as her prayers to her.

But then she remembered something TJ had written to her when he sent the charm over in the mail.

"Eilean, can you grab me my sack?"

"Sure." Eilean leaned over and grabbed Freya's bag, passing it over. Freya fished inside it, holding her staff with her free hand. When she felt the paper she was looking for, she unraveled it with her mouth and read:

> *Guess who's Nigeria's latest licensed staff user? I'll give you a guess. His name rhymes with Parlay (oh, by the way, remind me to tell you about the story of when I had to use a Pantheon Parlay, it's a good one).*
>
> *Anyway, you owe me one of those Scottish shortbreads!*
>
> *I told you even the dead can manifest Ashe.*
>
> *Maybe this little trinket can get you a passing grade for your trial. Fat chance, considering I did all the heavy lifting getting you your new staff! JK! ;P*
>
> *But for real, hopefully the charm of "the old hag" can help my favorite old lady. Don't worry, I warmed it up for you. Or actually… I guess… I cooled it down. You know what I mean.*
>
> *See you around, Freya!*
>
> *– TJ*
>
> *P.S. Oh! And don't forget to take out your dentures before bed, old lady.*

Freya chuckled at the last line. She'd forgotten he'd written that. She was so stressed about her trial she had barely skimmed it. Still, the letter was puzzling, and the frost on the charm was even more head scratching. What was TJ trying to tell her?

Freya called TJ through Discord, and the line just kept ringing. Odd. He was on the app all the time. But it said his last login was near the start of the year. She frowned, lowering her phone and staring at the frosted charm on her staff. What in the world was going on?

Before she could puzzle it out, her phone buzzed in her hand. Manny's name lit up the screen. "Manny? Hey, I was just trying to—"

"*Freya, thank Oya!*" Manny cut her off, her voice shaky and uneven, like she'd just finished running a marathon. "*We need your help.*"

"What's going on? Is TJ okay?"

"*No, he's not okay!*" Manny's voice cracked. "*You get* Divination Today *over there, right? You need to see something...*"

Freya blinked. "What are you talking about? What's in *Divination Today*?"

"*Just look!*" Manny snapped.

Freya muted the call and motioned wildly at Eilean, pointing at her phone. "Can you check *Divination Today*? Manny says there's something we need to see."

Eilean's brow furrowed, but she pulled out her phone and started typing. A moment later, her face paled as she held the phone up for Freya to see. The headline read:

**TJ Young—Dead?**

"Well, that's not good," Eilean said. "I should probably subscribe to *Divination Today*."

Freya's stomach plummeted. "What the...?" Her voice cracked, and she unmuted the call, her heart pounding. "Manny, is this some kind of sick joke? Am I reading this right? *Dead*? He can't be—"

"*He's not dead! That's what I'm trying to tell you. People think he's gone-gone because he's been missing for a while now, but he's not dead. We're working to get to him. To bring him back. Long story.*"

Freya's grip tightened on her staff, the frosted charm biting into her palm. She barely knew TJ, but he'd been one of the few people who made her feel seen back in Nigeria, like she wasn't just another oddball in their magical world. The charm in her hand thrummed faintly, like a heartbeat, and she couldn't shake the feeling that he was still out there.

"Manny," Freya said, her voice shaking, "what's goin' on? Why do people think he's dead?"

*"It's complicated,"* Manny admitted. *"He's been missing for a while. A lot to explain. There's a Court of All. Greek gods. It's a whole thing. You already know what sort of things TJ got into. He told me you did. But his brother—his brother came up with this formula. It's hard to explain over the phone, but it might mean TJ's still alive. And we may be the only ones to bring him back, to reach him."*

"Reach him?" Freya echoed, her mind racing.

*"At the Court of All,"* Manny said quickly. *"It's where his Ashe is tied up. Ayo has this ring from Thor, and we're using it to open a connection. But we can't complete the process without TJ's staff."*

Freya's eyes fell to her staff and the frosted charm of Cailleach. "What does that have to do with me?"

*"You're the only one who can wake up his staff, we think,"* Manny said. *"You helped him build it. You believed in him. That connection—Freya, it's our best chance."*

Freya closed her eyes. This was all too much. She didn't want to be in this spot. But she couldn't turn away from it either. "Okay," Freya said finally, her voice steady despite the storm inside her. "Where are you?"

*"Nigeria still. New Ile-Ife,"* Manny said. *"But we don't have time for flights. We need you here, like, now."*

Freya turned to Eilean, gripping her staff tight. "Do you think your government-secret-cell-agent-or-whatever friends can get me to Nigeria on short notice?"

Eilean crinkled her brow, then reached over to mute Freya's phone. "Easy. Especially for the TJ kid. That's why I told you to keep an eye on him when you went over. He's on their list."

Freya nodded, still unsure about all that, but her resolve hardened. She unmuted the phone. "Hang tight, Manny. I'll get there. Meet you at the embassy?"

*"You better,"* Manny said, her voice quieter now but no less desperate. *"He doesn't have much time, Freya. Please, hurry."*

# 61

# WHERE FIRE MEETS EARTH

Freya stepped into the New Ile-Ife Embassy not three hours after her call with Manny. The grand hall glittered in the sharp morning light, all polished stone and smooth glass, with long shadows cast by the towering masks and carvings along the outer walls. Freya shifted her weight. Her stomach hadn't quite recovered from the teleportation—sorry, "interdimensional travel via magical gateway"—and she swore she could still feel the way her molecules had been yanked through a portal like laundry in a high-spin cycle.

"'Quick and painless,' was it?" Freya muttered, scowling as she trailed after the agent.

Her escort glanced over her shoulder, one perfectly arched brow raised. Her long navy coat swayed as she walked, the gold trim glinting faintly in the sunlight. Her polished boots clicked softly against the stone as she turned back around, utterly unbothered by the accusation. "I said *quick,* Miss Innes. I made no promises about painless."

Khatri Karminder was the name of the agent or officer or whoever was serving as her escort. She was clearly very used to portal travel, and possibly the most infuriatingly composed person Freya had ever met. The woman barely broke a sweat, even here, in the humid, sticky warmth of late February Nigeria, where Freya could feel her curls frizzing up by the second. Khatri, meanwhile, looked like she'd just stepped out of some high-fashion spy thriller —her tailored coat catching the morning breeze and her dark hair tucked into a neat braid that didn't dare misbehave. Smoke drifted lazily from the gold earring in her left ear, curling around her sharp features like it had a mind of its own.

Freya didn't know what to make of her, but one thing was clear: Khatri missed nothing. Those dark, unblinking eyes swept over everything like she was cataloging the entire world, and Freya had the uneasy feeling she was being assessed, too—like a specimen under a very posh microscope.

Turning from her escort, she surveyed more of the embassy halls. The building stretched upward, its walls adorned with elaborate masks and tapestries depicting ancient Nigerian legends. If this had been a few months ago, she wouldn't have recognized most of them. Now she could point out Eshu-Elegba figurines that rested on the welcome table, the iron staffs that represented Ogun strung up from the walls, or the glass case housing Oshun's river gourds.

Her fingers curled instinctively around the icy Cailleach charm hidden in her pocket, letting its sharp, cold pulses ground her. "So, how d'you know Eilean?" she asked, trying to sound casual. "She's not exactly the government-agency type."

Khatri's lips twitched faintly, though her face remained calm and unreadable. "Classified," she said.

Freya frowned. "Right. Sure. Okay. What is she getting up to with you lot then? Eilean doesn't talk about it, and she tells me everything. Maybe not right away, but she gets there. What do you actually *do*—besides… y'know…" She waved a hand vaguely in the air. "Escort random teenagers halfway across the planet?"

Khatri's brow quirked again, and this time the corner of her mouth lifted in a subtle, fleeting smile. "You are far from 'random', Miss Innes. And for the rest, I'm afraid you don't hear about it for a reason. And you'll have to suffer me once more because… it's classified."

Freya let out a groan. "You can't just say that for *everything!* At some point, you're gonna have to give me a straight answer."

"Am I?" Khatri seemed to study her for a moment longer, then turned sharply and resumed walking, her coat swirling behind her.

"All I can tell you is you're here because you are believed to be the right woman for the job. Whether you will prove that belief well-founded remains to be seen. Eilean certainly thinks so."

Freya frowned, her frustration at the secrets bubbling to the surface again. "Right… And if I do a good job, you'll let me in on all the cloak and dagger rubbish?"

"Who knows? For now, let us both simply do a good job and find out."

Outside, the village streets stretched nearly empty before them. The sun died on the horizon. Metal gates covered shop windows, their protective charms dulled and lifeless. The silence felt wrong.

"The shops…" Freya started.

"Yes. It's all very grim. We suspect that Ashe as a whole is now dying, not just that of Shango or Oya."

"Because of TJ?"

"Perhaps. The magic that powers these businesses, their protections… it's all fading. Which is why helping TJ is crucial." She paused, smoke from her earring coiling around her face. "He is trapped in the Court of All, being drained. Your connection to his staff might be our only chance to reach him."

Freya followed Khatri past more shuttered shops, her heart sinking at each darkened window. A group of young diviners huddled near a fountain, their staffs raised in concentration. One girl's face screwed up with effort as she tried to summon water—nothing happened. Another boy's staff sparked weakly as he attempted to create light, the glow dying before it could properly form.

The final alley they turned into seemed to stretch endlessly, its walls pressing closer with each step, the weathered stone scraping against Freya's shoulders. When it finally opened up, Freya's breath caught in her throat like a trapped bird.

The fighting pit spread before them, vast and haunting in the fast approaching twilight, its stone walls scarred by countless lightning strikes that had left deep, jagged grooves in the ancient rock. Copper braziers, now cold and empty, lined the edges where fire must've once danced and flickered during countless battles. Wind chimes hung silent and still from towering posts decorated with

Oya's machete and Shango's double-headed axes, their metalwork dulled by time and neglect. The whole space felt frozen, as if waiting for the return of its warriors and the crackle of their magic.

Manny and Ayo waited beside a small table, a mirror propped between them. Manny's posture stiffened at the sight of Khatri.

"Why is she here?" Manny stepped in front of Ayo. "Who are you?"

"Eilean connected us," Freya explained. "She trusted her to help get me here safely. No one else knows..." She turned to her companion. "Right?"

"Right. I am only here to protect Freya and give whatever guidance I can. Nothing more." She bowed her head slightly to Manny. "You must be Manuela. I am Khatri Karminder."

Manny looked her up and down. "You UCMP?"

"After a fashion."

Ayo started signing, but Freya couldn't understand him. When he got done, she turned to Manny for a translation.

"He says this Khatri was there for TJ's trials; that she made sure he passed." Manny took a step to Khatri, stretching out her hand. "If you're a friend of TJ's, you're a friend of ours. Thank you for getting Freya here so quickly."

Khatri took Manny's hand and shook. "Of course."

The propped mirror surface rippled, catching Freya's attention. She hadn't realized it before, but there was a man's face in there. A man with bad acne and a head of hair that seemed to never know the stroke of a comb.

*"Hello there, Miss Innes,"* the man said, voice distorted through the mirror. *"I'm Olufemi Bolawe. A former mentor to TJ, and a close friend of his late sister."* Freya caught Manny rolling her eyes. Was the man lying? *"What we're attempting is incredibly dangerous. I'm sure Khatri caught you up on the gist? You understand what's at stake?"*

Freya and Khatri nodded simultaneously.

The man—this Mr. Bolawe—turned to Manny and Ayo. *"The strain of channeling this much power could kill you both. You do understand this, yes? Your bodies are not as strong as TJ's. You could be ripped apart from the exertion. Not that I'm seeing any other options..."*

Ayo started signing. Freya didn't need a translation to know he was saying he was down for anything. Manny, too, sounded it off with resolve. Freya had only known Ayo and Manny in passing, mostly through stories shared with her from TJ. She had expected them to be strong friends, but she couldn't say she expected *this*. They didn't even blink. But... did that mean Freya would be subjected to the same danger?

"Wait... what are we talking about here?" Freya asked.

Ayo lifted his finger, a copper ring glinting against the brazier lights that fired up as the sun dipped below the horizon. "Long story s-s-short," he stuttered. "We have items that can g-g-get us to TJ, to help him. But without the consent of our p-p-parents, well..."

"There's a risk," Manny finished for him. "But a risk we're willing to take."

Freya's stomach twisted. "This is mad, but..." She touched the Cailleach charm in her palm, thinking of those she would be there for, her granda, Eilean. Those she loved and held dear. "I understand why you'd risk it for him. Maybe I can help keep you safe, though." She lifted the charm. "I think TJ's trying to communicate through this. Maybe it's his way of protecting you guys through the transition."

Manny's dimples caved at that. "Yeah... I'd love to think that, too."

But what Freya didn't say out loud is that she had her own theory. Yes, perhaps it was TJ communicating to her. Though from where? Not all communication was from the living. And just like his letter said...

"So, what do you need from me?" Freya asked.

Manny withdrew from the group and grabbed something from behind the table where the mirror sat. It was TJ's staff. The wooden shaft looked the same as it did when she saw it last. The Egyptian headpiece of the sun and moon still encircled the Orunmila crystal. The unique dark center with its double helix, the same. And the Nordic runes at the bottom to round it out, not to mention a few charms, one of which was missing. The one in her hand. Yes, the staff looked the same, save for one deep gash down the center.

Manny lifted it toward Freya and asked, "You fixed a staff before, so... do you think you can fix another one?"

Freya swallowed hard, staring down at the charm again, which, at that moment, pulsed cold and steady once more. She looked back up to the group, to Manny, who bit her lips, to Ayo, who rubbed his hands, to Khatri looking stoic as ever, and to the mirror man Bolawe, who stroked at his pockmarked skin.

"Well…" Freya said. "For TJ… I'm willing to try."

And so they got to work, letting stars and fire braziers light the way. Freya knelt beside TJ's staff in the fighting pit, her fingers tracing the deep gash that split the wood. Moonlight caught the Egyptian hieroglyphs, making them shimmer like liquid silver. She closed her eyes, remembering TJ's excited chatter during their crafting sessions, how his hands had moved with such certainty despite his constant self-doubt.

"The base needs reinforcement first," she muttered. "Ayo, could you—"

He was already there, copper ring glowing as he steadied the staff's Norse foundation with his half-Norse ring. Manny worked opposite him, her wind magic wrapping around the fracture like invisible bandages.

"Wait," Freya said, sensing the magic Ayo was pressing into the staff. "That sensation… are you using a silent prayer to Ogun? TJ said you were Shango's divine child."

"Yeah…" Manny answered for Ayo. "That was a whole thing. Ayo actually pledged to Ogun. Directly. And it's helped a lot for stuff like this, actually." She turned to her friend, smacking him across the shoulder. "Should have done it years ago!"

"What do you mean by… directly?" Freya asked. "Like… you and TJ did another realm hop?"

"Kinda sorta," Manny said. "Except we actually remember that one. It's a whole thing."

They continued to work, Manny and Ayo sharing more stories about TJ; even Bolawe chimed in a few times. But every time he opened his mouth, Manny had a scowl for him, or Ayo would pretend not to listen. Halfway through the night, Freya had to ask.

"So, um…" she murmured. "What is it with this Bolawe guy? I'm getting bad vibes between you all."

"Another long story," Manny answered. "But he used to be the leader of the Keepers. You know them?"

Freya shook her head.

It was Khatri this time who knelt down to explain, her voice low as well. "They're a radical group among the diviner community here in West Africa. Responsible for much destruction and many deaths. Including that of TJ Young's sister."

"And my cousin," Manny added sadly.

"And we're working with this guy... why?" Freya eyed the mirror a few yards away from them. Bolawe had a book propped up before him. Some tome of spells about staff repairs.

"'Cause we have t-t-to," Ayo stuttered quietly. "That's how we g-g-got TJ's staff, my ring, and Manny's access to the F-F-Frost Realm."

Freya folded her arms, glancing between the others and the mirror where Bolawe's face lingered like a shadow. "I still don't get it. If he's the reason for so much destruction, how can you all just... trust him? How does that make sense?"

Manny sighed, brushing a stray curl from her face. "It doesn't make sense. But if it's between saving TJ and holding a grudge, we know what he'd choose. And we need to think like TJ right now to get him back."

Freya hesitated, the anger bubbling in her chest dimming slightly. She could still feel the cold pulse of the Cailleach charm in her palm, as if TJ himself were telling her to let it go—for now.

"Fine," Freya muttered. "But we don't forget who we're dealing with. Once TJ's safe, I want him out of the picture."

"Oh trust," Manny said. "Once that moment happens, we're taking it."

Freya turned her focus back to the staff and ran her fingers over the fractured wood. "The crystal," she directed. "It needs realignment."

Khatri appeared with fresh crystals and placed them before Freya. The raw power thrumming through the gems made Freya's fingers tingle.

"Great, now we just need to do a short prayer to Orunmila," Freya said. "That's what TJ did. These other crystals should start spiraling around it to basically, like, recharge it." The spiraling crystals caught her eye again, moving in that same rhythmic pattern. Freya had noticed it before—the way TJ's crafting blended traditions so effortlessly. The spiral wasn't just Yoruba; it mirrored the ones her Celtic teachers had taught her, too. Of course, he'd teased her for knowing that, called her a "granny druid" like it was some big joke. But seeing it now, she couldn't help but admire how he'd tied everything together—Celtic and Yoruba magic, his and hers. Brilliant, really.

Still. Next time she saw him, he was getting an earful about that old lady crack.

"*Such potential in this staff,*" Bolawe's voice rippled from the mirror. Freya nearly jumped, wondering when his attention had turned to them. Did he hear what they were saying before? "*Such potential and TJ wielded it like it was nothing.*"

Freya's throat tightened as she fitted the original crystal back into place. "I don't understand how he managed it. There's so much raw energy here—it's like trying to contain a storm."

"*That's because TJ* is *extraordinary,*" Bolawe said, pride evident in his voice. For such a dangerous man, he spoke of TJ rather highly. "*What that young man is capable of... he's barely touched the surface of his true potential.*"

Freya's hands faltered over the Nordic runes. Everyone spoke of TJ in the present tense, as if he'd just stepped out for a moment. But the cold pulse of the charm against her chest whispered other possibilities—ones she couldn't bear to voice.

She shook her head, focusing instead on weaving the magical threads back together. The torches around the fighting pit cast dancing shadows across the ancient half walls as she worked, their light reflecting off the copper braziers. Each careful repair brought back memories of TJ's laugh, his patient explanations during their practice sessions, the way his eyes lit up when something finally clicked.

"Ayo, I need help with the pommel base here," Freya said, pointing to the Nordic runes. "There's only so much I can do here, but your ring might do the trick."

Ayo got up, rubbing his hands eagerly. He stuttered another prayer to Ogun, and, oddly, a second prayer in what sounded like some Scandinavian language. Freya thought she could make out the name of Thor. Before long, Ayo's ring pulsed with lightning bolts that licked at the base of TJ's staff.

"Hold it steady," she instructed as she began the final binding. The staff hummed with power, almost singing as the magic flowed through it. Manny's and Ayo's combined energy merged with hers, watched over by Khatri's steady presence.

The repair took shape under their hands, magic and memory intertwining in the cool night air. Freya pushed away the gnawing doubt, the fear that they were working to save someone already lost. She couldn't let those thoughts taint the healing. TJ had taught her that much—intention mattered in magic, perhaps more than anything else.

When everything was done, Freya took the charm and latched it near the head of the staff, right next to the dull metal coin with a swimming boy next to it. Nothing happened, though. They all stared at each other and back at the staff, waiting for something to change. Some sort of sign. Maybe they had done something wrong?

Then Freya remembered something, whispering to herself, "Even the dead can manifest Ashe."

Then, suddenly, a blazing light flashed in the pit. The green crystal exploded with its emerald hue, its beam vaulting up directly to the stars. The staff floated on its own, enveloped by all the elements, wind tumbling around rocks, fire intertwining with lightning, all in the pattern of the spiral. A tear crested over her cheek at the sight.

Khatri put a hand over her shoulder, saying, "I think you did it, Miss Innes. Well done."

Manny and Ayo jumped up and down, hugging each other. And Bolawe gave them all a cold smile before clearing his throat. "*Well then. No time to waste. Let's go save our boy. Hold on one moment and I'll retrieve the Frost Shard.*"

Bolawe turned from his mirror for a moment. "*One thing before we start,*" he said. "*I know all of this was meant to be low key, but I took the liberty of inviting another.*"

Freya's stomach bottomed out. This is what Manny and Ayo had been warning them about. And here this Mr. Bolawe guy went... betraying them.

"Hello there, children." They all turned to find an elder female wearing robes that seemed spun from midnight itself, with glimmers of stars cascading down its folds. Along the sleeves, glowing runes appeared and faded in rhythmic pulses, like a whispered spell trapped in the fabric. Freya looked to the others, who were totally shell shocked. The old woman merely smiled and pointed to the stars. "*That* looks promising."

Freya leaned into Manny to ask, "Who's that?"

Manny gulped and answered. "That… is Elder Adeyemi."

# 62

# BY THE FLAME OF PETITION

MANNY'S FISTS CLENCHED AT HER SIDES. THE RISING SUN painted the fighting pit's stone half-walls in shades of amber, but the warmth did nothing to thaw the ice in her veins. Elder Adeyemi's silhouette stretched long across the packed earth, her robes billowing in the dawn breeze.

Manny hadn't even realized they had worked all the way through the night. When was the last time she even slept? This was supposed to be their moment. Their chance to save TJ without all the red tape and rules that had failed them before. But Bolawe just had to open his big mouth.

"You snitch," she muttered under her breath, glaring at Bolawe's stupid, smug face in the mirror. Her hands trembled with rage. All those weeks of planning, the careful preparation, getting Freya here from Scotland—and this fool just had to run telling tales to her former Headmistress.

The braziers around the pit still flickered, their flames competing with the growing daylight. TJ's staff floated between them, its green crystal pulsing like a heartbeat. Like *his* heartbeat. He was out there somewhere, counting on them, and now Elder Adeyemi was going to shut this whole thing down.

Manny stepped closer to the staff, positioning herself between it and the Elder. No way was she letting anyone take this from them. Not when they were so close. The morning light caught Elder

Adeyemi's starlit robes, making the odd symbols dance across the fabric like living things.

"With all due respect," Manny started, but her voice cracked with frustration. She cleared her throat and tried again. "We don't need supervision. We got this far on our own."

Ayo shifted nervously beside her while Freya looked between them all with wide eyes. The fighting pit felt smaller now, the ancient walls closing in as Elder Adeyemi took another step forward, her shadow stretching across the ground between them like a bridge—or a barrier.

Oddly, the Elder... smiled. "What do you think I'm here to do, Miss Martinez?" Manny gulped; Elder Adeyemi narrowed her eyes to Bolawe. "What did you tell them, Olufemi?"

*"Nothing,"* he said from the Mirror Realm. *"And perhaps that's the issue."* He turned his voice on Manny, Ayo, and Freya. *"I know you didn't want to involve too many others, but you all forgot one very important thing. The prayers that were going to empower The Hero's Equinox to begin with. The ones Adeyemi has been building up tirelessly this past year. She will be vital in making any of this work."*

Manny's skin heated with embarrassment.

"Thank you for watching over them, Khatri," Elder Adeyemi said. "You are always such an asset."

Khatri bowed her head. "Of course, Director."

Manny's heart pounded as Elder Adeyemi's next words sank in. "In half an hour, hundreds of diviners will surround this pit. Perhaps thousands, Orishas willing. They think they're coming to say goodbye to TJ. But we know better." She smiled proudly. "The combined prayer force should power both the staff and create a pathway to the Court. And prayers won't be coming just from those with us today. If the coordination is right, I'm hoping for thousands upon thousands of voices to cry out at once across West Africa and the diaspora. However, that means that—"

"We might die. Yeah, Bolawe covered that part." Manny's voice came out harder than intended. She didn't care about the risk. She'd walk through fire if it meant seeing TJ again. She couldn't come through for Jessie, but she still had a shadow of a hope for TJ.

"I'm pleased you made this choice on your own." Elder Adeyemi's eyes softened. "The magic requires *willing* sacrifice and *consent.*"

She pulled Manny and Ayo into a tight embrace. Sweet sandalwood filled Manny's nose as tears threatened to spill from the Elder. "Your courage honors your ancestors, children."

Manny bit her lip. Children. That's all they were to these adults. But they didn't understand. They hadn't seen TJ's smile fade when he thought no one was looking. Hadn't felt their heart skip when he laughed. Hadn't laid awake at night wondering if they'd ever get the chance to tell him that she… No, she wasn't being fair. Adeyemi was putting her neck out on the line, as well.

"Okay then…" Manny said tentatively. "Let's make this happen, then. How do you want us to start this?"

SHANGO'S FIGHTING PIT HADN'T BEEN USED IN MONTHS. WELL, really it hadn't been used properly in many ages, not since Shango would have called himself mortal. During a time when diviners dueled in a world that did not know The Great Separation.

Manny wondered if, at its height, it was filled with as many people as were there that morning. Just as Elder Adeyemi had said, hundreds upon hundreds of people filed in. Several with photos of TJ, others with signs in English, Yoruba, even Igbo. Almost all were dressed in traditional West African clothing.

As what seemed like all of West Africa filed in, Manny got dressed. Bolawe had picked out an outfit that would invoke Oya's strength, her burgundy and orange robes billowing like storm clouds. A crown of bright feathers framed her determined face, lightning-shaped charms jingling with each step. Gold-beaded necklaces caught the morning light, while bronze arm cuffs gleamed. She was Oya's tempest, ready to unleash chaos upon the Court of All.

Ayo strode into the fighting pit, his crimson and black tunic flaring with each step. A bronze chest plate etched with lightning bolts gleamed under the torchlight, while a belt of hammered iron links clinked softly. His iron-tipped boots struck the ground like thunder, embodying Shango's fire and Ogun's strength. Manny gave him a short nod, and he gave her one back. She knew he had no doubts.

There was no room for it.

Manny turned her attention back to her surroundings as she recognized more faces coming in, fellow students, even some folks from Camp Olosa. All their faces were sad, many were crying. It felt wrong not being honest, but now she sort of understood where TJ was coming from when they invoked Eshu last year during crossover practice. Only that time, she was on the wrong side of the deception. Maybe that's why Elder Adeyemi threw herself into the mix, thinking that the fake memorial would manifest some great Ashe from Eshu.

The fighting pit was nothing like Manny had imagined it would be when Ayo showed it to her. It was known as a cursed place now, one of the few sacred sites around the village that the Elders deemed off limits. Shango's old stomping grounds in New Ile-Ife were carved into the earth like the crater of a dead volcano. The walls sloped steeply downward, jagged and blackened from centuries of battles fought with flame and fury.

The former Keeper had told her and Ayo that it was their best launch point to springboard to Shango and Oya in the Court of All, since it was here where the couple had sparred and experimented with the combination of wind, fire, and the nature of storms. Manny was not convinced this was such an "optimal" location when it looked so jacked up under the afternoon sun. That was until a hymn sung by Elder Adeyemi and the others properly activated the pit.

The air smelled of ash and history. Fires licked the edges of the pit now, plumes of orange and gold that glowed brighter with every passing minute, throwing long, flickering shadows over the crowd gathered above. Manny caught sight of their little team: Oracle Ruby, Omo of Fon, Tore Stadheim. But where was TJ's mom? Ayo's dad? Surely they would have sniffed out what was going on here. Then again… Elder Adeyemi was pretty damn crafty at keeping things from others.

They had taken the time to make calls to close family and friends without disclosing what they were getting up to. Ayo's calls took less than fifteen minutes. Manny's calls took nearly an hour as she cycled through all her brothers, cousins, her parents, and even Niko, her favorite video store owner back home. There were so many people who would have missed Manny if this ritual went to shit. And for Ayo…

She tried not to think of his lame-ass father.

Or her aunt... who didn't pick up her phone.

Elder Adeyemi and Oracle Ruby approached, their faces heavy with the kind of quiet sadness Manny couldn't put words to.

"You've done more than anyone could've asked, loves," Oracle Ruby said. "If this works, the magical world will know your names. And if it doesn't..." Her words trailed off, leaving the rest unspoken. They didn't need to say it. Manny already knew.

Elder Adeyemi offered a quick, fleeting smile as she leaned in to squeeze Manny's shoulder. "Don't let the fire scare you. You've got this."

Oracle Ruby lifted Manny's hand mirror where Bolawe was. The man said, "*Thank you both. For your service.*"

Service. Like they were soldiers marching into war. Maybe they were.

"And you're not going anywhere without me!" a voice called from within the small crowd. The voice of TJ's mom. Her makeup was ruined and for once her palm-tree locs fell over her shoulders instead, making her look a bit unhinged. She must've lost the fight with her husband. "I might not have my son's Ashe, but I can give as much as I can."

Oracle Ruby stepped up. "You can't, you'll die, Yejide. There's some precedent for the kids making it through, because of their links to Shango and Oya, but you don't share in that. You'll almost certainly burn up as you cross."

"It would help these two get through to the other side, at least, right?"

Ruby swallowed long and slow. "In theory, but—"

"Then I will join them. Someone has to wield TJ's staff to make this right, eh? It's what my son would have done. And, as his mother, it is my duty to give him the best shot possible."

"I thought you might have said something like that." TJ's grandmother shouldered through the masses, looking over TJ's staff. "I see you did well with the mending. I was hoping to do the same. Have it ready for when TJ made it back to us. How did you fill the gash so well?"

Manny nodded up to the stands where Freya and Khatri stood. "Thanks to our friend from Scotland, to be honest."

"Ah, that's the one TJ was talking about," TJ's grandma said, and her eyes traveled to a different part of the crowd. "I'm happy to see Bamidele swallowed his pride and showed up as well. You make sure to give the staff back to Tomori Jomiloju when you see him on the other side, you hear?"

Mrs. Young nodded earnestly. "In the flesh or in spirit."

"In the flesh or in the spirit," TJ's grandma repeated, hugging her daughter deep and long.

When they broke, Mrs. Young took the staff made by TJ lovingly, then outstretched her other hand where her own iron staff manifested from thin air and smacked into her palm. She turned to Ayo and Manny and said, "You ready?"

"Not really," Manny answered, biting her lip. "But for TJ, we have to be."

After a group prayer and last goodbyes, Ayo, Manny, and Mrs. Young descended into the pit together, the heat from the fire brushing against their skin. Above them, the gathered UCMP officials, elders, and allies stood silent, their faces lit by the flickering flames. According to Elder Adeyemi, no one would be able to pass the fire bordering the pit until the ritual was over.

The three of them stood in a rough triangle at the center of the pit. The fire at the edges roared louder now, as if sensing their intent. The ritual had to be perfect. No hesitation. No mistakes.

Manny's voice broke the silence first, her words steady and commanding. "For TJ."

Ayo nodded and replied without stuttering, "For TJ."

"For TJ," Mrs. Young finished.

Manny's pulse thundered in her ears. Ayo slipped on the ring given to him by Thor, the copper seeming to ground him like Ogun. He could do this. They all could do this. They would get to TJ, free him, and bring him back. Because they had to.

Mrs. Young started the chant, saying:

*Olodumare, Great Creator, source of all that is,*
*Bless us with your infinite wisdom and light.*
*May your will guide us through paths unknown,*
*And your grace shield us from harm.*

Then Ayo joined in, and again, surprisingly, he did not stutter:

*Shango, King of Thunder and Fire,*
*Grant us the courage to stand in our truth,*
*The strength to face life's battles with honor,*
*And the power to overcome injustice and fear.*

Manny was last with her own hymn:

*Oya, Mistress of Winds and Change,*
*Sweep away obstacles with your fierce breath,*
*Transform our struggles into opportunities,*
*And open the gates to new possibilities.*

They repeated it all together this time. Again and again until their sung hymn was one, the words ancient and rhythmic, calling to Ashe itself, reaching across realms to find the one they'd lost. And then, on the fourth, fifth, or sixth go around—Manny couldn't be sure—the link between them solidified, strong and steady in her chest.

*Together, may your forces unite within us—*
*Wisdom, strength, and transformation—*
*So we may walk boldly in our purpose,*
*And honor the divine in all that we do.*
*Ashe.*

The rest of the group watching on the outskirts said "Ashe" in unison, and the fire rose higher, swirling like a living thing, and for a moment, Ayo thought he could feel it—a flicker of something, a presence just beyond reach. The familiar pull of TJ when he uplifted them all in so many different uses of rituals and spells.

But then a roar split the air. A shadow moved above them, massive and serpentine: Ninki Nanka descended, her scales gleaming like molten gold, and on her back—Ayo's dad and Manny's aunt.

# 63

# WHISPERS THROUGH THE FIRE

"No!" Ayo's dad bellowed, his voice frantic as the fire swirled up, barring him from entering the pit. "Stop this! You don't understand what you're doing!"

Ayo didn't flinch, his eyes locked on the fire. "We're b-b-bringing him back!"

"This isn't the way!" Manny's aunt shouted, leaning forward on Ninki Nanka's back. "You don't know what this will cost!"

*How dare you, Simisola,* Ninki Nanka spoke. *How dare you risk these children and this innocent woman? You're acting less like an Elder and more like a Keeper.*

Ayo's dad slammed his fists against the invisible barrier of heat, shaking his hands as they burned. "Ayodeji! Listen to me! Don't do this, son. This is how we lost your mother."

The words hit Ayo like a punch to the gut. He froze, the chant faltering on his lips. "W-W-What?"

"It was a ritual like this," his father said, voice cracking. "We tried to save someone. Your mother thought she could handle it, thought she could bear the cost, but it killed her. It destroyed her, Ayodeji. Don't do this. Don't let it take you too. This is what I've been trying to avoid!"

Ayo's knees wobbled, the enormity of the truth crashing down around him. His mother. Her death. The connection he never knew.

"You lied..." he whispered, his voice shaking. "You never told me..."

Above them, Manny's aunt called out. "Manny, stop! We can do this together. Please. I can't lose you too. Not like Jessie."

Manny's gaze flicked to her aunt, her resolve wavering. She turned to Ayo, her eyes full of conflict. "What do we do?"

Ayo's throat tightened, his father's words echoing in his head. He looked to Manny, to the fire, to the weight of everything they were trying to save. "Do you believe them?"

She nodded. "I think so."

"No, we can't stop!" Mrs. Young said. "TJ's so close. You can feel him, I know you can. We have to keep going. He's dying. My baby is dying. And I need to make this right."

Ayo stood on the edge of the pit, the heat clawing at his skin, the flames twisting in frantic, dangerous patterns. His chest heaved, every breath sharp, as his dad's words pounded in his ears.

"You're going to get yourself killed!" his dad barked. "This isn't some game, Ayodeji! You think TJ would want you risking your life for this?"

Ayo's fists clenched, his nails biting into his palms. "And w-w-what do you want me to do, huh? Just l-l-leave him? Pretend like he's gone forever? I can't d-d-do that, Dad!"

Beside him, Manny's lips tightened into a thin line, her shoulders squared. "We *have* to do this. If we don't try—if we just stand here—we'll lose him for good. You don't get to tell us to stop."

Her aunt, standing just behind her, threw her hands up, exasperated. "Manny, you've got no idea what you're messing with! Think about Jessie! She'd never want you to risk yourself like this."

Manny whipped around, her eyes flashing. "Don't you dare bring Jessie into this. She'd fight for him just like we're doing now, just like she fought with Dayo."

Up on the ridge, Elder Adeyemi stood like a stone monument, her voice booming over the crackling fire. "This is what has to be done. All Ashe is at risk."

"*What these three are doing is honorable!*" Bolawe agreed at her side, flashing from his Mirror Realm form.

Ninki Nanka shook her head. *Siding with Keepers, Simisola? I cannot believe it has come to this.*

"I'm not siding with anyone," Elder Adeyemi threw back in a shaky voice uncommon for her. "I'm siding with the right thing to do. Or do you believe the extinction of divinerkind is preferable?"

Ayo's dad moved closer, his face tight. "Your mother wouldn't have wanted this either, Ayodeji."

"Stop it!" Ayo snapped. "Don't b-b-bring her into this. Don't you d-d-dare." His voice shook, but his anger burned steady beneath it. "This isn't about you or M-M-Mom. It's about s-s-saving *him*."

"Saving him means losing yourself!"

"Then it's worth it!"

Behind them, the ground trembled as Ninki Nanka, her scales gleaming like molten bronze in the firelight, stretched her long neck toward the pit. Her voice rumbled low, disappointment laced in every word. *Elder Adeyemi, your rashness blinds you. We are supposed to protect them, not shove them into oblivion.* She shifted closer, ignoring the burn of the flames licking at her skin as she leaned into the pit. *If you won't stop this madness, I will.*

"Headmistress!" Ayo's heart jolted as he saw her glowing scales blacken, the acrid smell of burning flesh filling the air. "Stop! You're h-h-hurting yourself!"

Manny grabbed his arm, her voice urgent. "She's going to kill herself trying to stop this!"

Above them, Elder Adeyemi's voice roared again. "Headmistress, don't be a fool! This has to be done. You'll ruin everything. You have to learn—"

*Learn what?* she shot back, her voice hotter than the flames. *That we failed them? That they're alone in this?*

Ayo's heart thudded against his ribs as he watched her weaken, the glow of her body dimming. "We can't let her d-d-die," he muttered. "She didn't a-a-ask for this."

Manny hesitated, her jaw working as she warred with herself. Then, finally, she nodded. "Fine. Fine! We'll stop. But not because you're right—because we don't want more blood on our hands." Manny stepped up beside him. "We'll find another way. We *will*. But if we keep going now, Ninki Nanka dies. And that's not what TJ would've wanted."

The flames crackled louder, as though echoing the weight of

their words. Ayo's dad stepped back, silent for once. Elder Adeyemi folded her arms, her expression unreadable. And Ninki Nanka, her head now singed and blackened, pulled back from the pit, her breathing labored.

"Is it over?" someone asked.

"Did it work?" another whispered.

Ayo stared at the pit, his fists trembling. Manny stood beside him, her jaw tight, her breaths shallow. Neither of them answered. Then a voice rose above the quiet.

"No," Ayo's dad said, stepping forward, his voice cutting through the tension. "He's not dead. Not yet."

The murmurs stopped. All eyes turned to him.

"What are you saying?" Elder Adeyemi asked.

"I'm saying this isn't over," he replied. "TJ's spirit—it's stuck, caught in the in-between. I've seen this before. With my late wife. We can bring him back, but we'll need everyone's help. Every ounce of Ashe, every bit of focus. No fear, no hesitation."

"How do you know this will work?" Manny's aunt challenged.

"I don't," he admitted. "But I know we can't stop now. If we don't act, we lose him forever."

Manny's shoulders squared. "Then we act. What do we need to do?"

Ayo's dad turned to the crowd. "We'll need all of you—diviners and anyone with even a *drop* of Ashe. This time, we do it together. And *no one* dies."

The crowd hesitated, the weight of his words hanging heavy. Then, slowly, people began stepping forward. A murmur of agreement rippled through them, faint but growing.

Manny grabbed Ayo's hand. "We'll get him back. We have to."

Ayo looked at the pit. *Hold on, TJ. We're coming for you.*

# 64

# REUNION

Ethereal strands of limbo curled around the young man like mist. He stood upon an endless ocean, a dreamscape that shifted and morphed. Sky and water bled into each other beyond mere reflection. As the young man stood, however, he was also untethered, floating just an inch above the water, never actually touching it. On the other side, deep below the gentle waves, he could just make out a figure that was once very familiar to him: A boy… tall, awkwardly lanky, and with an Afro curling atop his head.

The boy below was suspended in air, trapped between prismatic walls refracting every color of the rainbow. Something inside the young man told him the boy needed help, but he could not provide aid because he was foggy, elsewhere.

Prayers from familiar voices filled his ears, their words echoing through the still air like whispers. He needed to heed them, needed to guide them, assist them. That's what he did. That's what he was good at. What he was always good at. Nothing else mattered. Not even his own existence. At the edges of his consciousness, he reckoned it wasn't a bad idea to answer the whispers' pleas.

Why not?

They were asking so nicely, and so sadly.

And, after all, he had nothing better to do atop this vast ocean.

But the young man stood at the crossroads between the whispers in the sky and the boy trapped in the ocean. Again, the voices from above called to him, urging him to heed their pleas and guide them. Yet, the sight of the boy suspended in the prismatic prison beneath the waves tugged at his heart. The boy needed his help as well.

Somewhere in the recesses of his mind, someone called Eshu smirked at the dichotomy of choice presented before him.

As the young man contemplated his path, a figure slowly emerged from the ocean horizon. As it drew closer, something like recognition reverberated in his chest and at the back of his neck. The silhouette went from an amorphous mass to the shape of a young woman, a young woman who had a name. She held a special place in his heart, but try as he might, he couldn't find her name in his mind.

She was tall and elegant, with a long, graceful neck. Nearly as tall as him. She had a pair of pointed ears that made her look slightly like an elf. And her almond-shaped eyes gleamed in the bright daylight. Her messy Afro danced in the ethereal breeze, and she wore beautiful green and yellow àsọ̀ òkè robes that flowed around her like liquid sunshine. When she smiled, it was like the heavens themselves beckoning him.

Warm. Radiant. Perfect.

"Brother," she spoke, her voice a melodic lilt. The young man wasn't sure why he was being called a "brother," but somehow, the title felt appropriate. "Look how you've grown. I couldn't be more proud of you. Your spirit and Ashe are so pure. So few could reach the in-between that you find yourself in now. Though you do have some help from the others, I suppose."

She stared up into the sky, where the whispers reverberated. The young woman's smile faltered, replaced by a frown that dimmed the light around them. Did she control the light? Was she some sort of deity?

"Sadly, you will not remember this. You may not even know who you are. It took me a long while—too long—to remember in this strange ocean. We both denied The Gate. Or perhaps," her frown deepened, "The Gate denied us..."

Sadness etched itself into the lines of her face, her eyes glistening with unshed tears. She reached out a hand, her fingers trembling slightly. "Brother, may I hug you? It's been so long. Too long."

The young man shrugged. It was an odd request to ask of a stranger, but the young woman looked so sad, and he wanted to see her smile again. He remembered loving her smile.

The embrace was gentle at first, then deeper, and deeper, her hands gripping his back, and he would have sworn wet tears soaked his neck where her head lay. Then, without realizing it, there were tears in his own eyes.

A shockwave spiked through his arms, making his skin prickle with goosebumps from an energy he couldn't describe—yet, it felt familiar somehow.

He had felt this before.

Felt this very exact sensation before. But from where?

This wasn't the first time this young woman had hugged him. This was the way he felt when she'd hugged him countless times before, the way he felt when she laughed at his bad jokes…

"Ifedayo…" he whispered.

Flashes of colors ran across his eyes, and his body spasmed. As he did, the young woman held him even tighter. No, not the young woman. Ifedayo Young. His sister. His… Dayo.

The space around them had changed. The ocean remained, but the sky was now a galaxy of gas clouds. Did Dayo control the stars? Three colossal shapes watched over him. He had seen this before, too. Had experienced this very moment.

At the funeral. When he had touched Dayo.

A hand pulled his chin from the large shapes, forced him to look at almond-shaped eyes and a wide smile over perfect brown skin. "There's nothing we can do for them anymore," she said quietly. "They got you here, where you always needed to be. I don't know what happens next. You followed the ancestors as far as you can. You've broken the family curse. Now you must shepherd your friends." She kissed him on the cheek, savoring it like it would be her last. "It's so nice to see you again, TJ."

The young man's body jerked violently, his muscles contorting in an agonized twist; Dayo held him firm again, as though making sure he would stay put.

TJ.

Tomori Jomiloju.

That was *his* name.

It was the name of the boy beneath their feet in that prison, too. And with that revelation, it was as though a lifetime of memories rushed back into him. Flooding him. It was almost too much, seeing so many images flash before his eyes. His body spasmed, and, again, Dayo kept his back straight.

"Dayo!" he exclaimed, throwing his head into her shoulder. "Dayo! I missed you so much. I wanted this for so long. I never thought—"

"You can't stay, TJ." Her words stopped him cold, and for the first time, she pulled away, though she still held onto his arms. The warmth of her presence, the comfort of reunion—it all shifted under her words. He frowned, searching her face, trying to understand.

Then he saw it. Understood it.

Below them, deep beneath the ocean's surface, the prismatic prison shimmered. Inside, a boy with an Afro—*his Afro*—floated, motionless. Suspended. Trapped. His stomach lurched; his mind scrambled.

*No. No, no, no.*

"I—I don't understand." But he did. He just didn't want to.

"Don't you see..." Dayo said, "*you* are the promised child. The one who will rise with the light of a dying, falling star. I am that star; Orunmila is that star. You have to stay so the Lost Monarch can return once more."

"No." TJ shook his head. "No, *you* were the promised child."

"And I died. As I was supposed to. So that you," she jabbed a finger at TJ's chest, "and your Ashe could manifest. So that the family curse could break. You know it's true. Remember that note you found from that reporter... my last words. I realized it too late: 'I am the falling star. The falling star is me.'"

TJ stared at Dayo, his mind reeling from her words. The promised child? Him? He couldn't be. Dayo had always been the special one, the prodigy, the one destined for greatness. He was just TJ, the awkward middle child, the one who struggled to find his place in the world.

Dayo's grip on his arms tightened, her eyes fierce with conviction. "TJ, listen to me. You have always been special, even if you couldn't see it. Your Ashe, your spirit, it's unlike anything I've ever seen. You have the power to change the world, to bring the Lost Monarch back."

The Lost Monarch? Yes… he remembered that, too. Remembered the story from Camp Olosa. But he had never gotten a whiff of the deity. TJ's mind raced, trying to make sense of it all. He hadn't even thought of the Lost Monarch, of Olodumare, in a long while. Hadn't Yemoja said she was looking for Them?

TJ thought back to all the times he had felt out of place, like he didn't belong. But then he remembered the moments when his Ashe had surged through him, when he had felt a connection to something greater than himself.

Maybe he was the one to find Olodumare after all.

But where?

"But... but what about you?" he asked, his voice unsteady. "You're the one who sacrificed everything. You're the one who died."

Dayo smiled sadly. "That was my destiny, TJ. To be the falling star that would light the way. Now I know it was for you. So that you could become who you were meant to be."

Tears stung TJ's eyes. He didn't want to believe it, didn't want to accept that his sister's death made him who he was today. But deep down, he knew she was right. The truth of her words resonated in his soul. His Ashe.

Dayo hummed, as though reading his thoughts. "You're ready now, TJ. It was nice while it lasted." She placed her hands on his chest. "Now… let go of the ancestors, and think of home."

She pushed, and he jerked back as though yanked by the force of a thousand waves. Falling back and back and back, finally breaking the barrier of the ocean below.

"No—Dayo!" His hand shot out, flailing for her, grasping at nothing but air. He reached, desperate, unwilling to let go, unwilling to leave her again. His chest clenched as his vision blurred with unshed tears.

But Dayo only smiled—a soft, knowing smile, warm like the

sun. The kind of smile that had always made him feel safe, like everything would be okay.

His breath hitched; hand wavered. And slowly, reluctantly… he let it fall. TJ swallowed hard and did as she told him.

He let go of the ancestors.

He thought of home.

# 65

# THE SCAR ACROSS THE STARS

The reunion with Dayo slipped from TJ's mind, like water through his fingers. He tried to hold on to it—onto her—but the more he grasped, the faster it faded. As TJ drifted through the watery dreamscape, his mind filled with thoughts of home.

There were vibrant family celebrations, chaotic quinceañeras with Manny, and surprise dinners courtesy of Ayo's rich family. At home, the wind, a whisper of Oya's spirit, caused the tall trees to bow, a motion that reminded him of Manny. There were subtle echoes—the nurturing depth of Yemoja's waters that he traveled through. Within him, fierce ironclad fire kindled—Shango and Ogun's call driving him onward.

Then falling snowflakes entered his head, dusting the landscape in his mind's eye with purity, reminding him of rebirth, of the Frost Realm, of Cailleach, of all the other Great Energies that rested outside and within the Orishas.

All the while, the calls, the prayers of his friends, resounded. The gentle Brooklyn husk of Manny. The clear and unstuttered voice of Ayo. Even Freya's Scottish tones were in there as well, backed by hymns sung by Mom, Grandma, Tia Teresa, Mr. Oyelowo, Elder Adeyemi, Omo of Fon, Oracle Ruby, Bolawe, and more. *Much, much more*. Hundreds of voices, no thousands, perhaps millions. Each voice gave him the strength to push forward.

With a newfound sense of direction, TJ hoped for a chance to return home, to the love and affection he craved. He wished he could convince time to slow down, to grasp it and bend it to his will, like the Fates seemed to do, like Orunmila seemed to do.

*Yes, TJ, yes,* he heard Dayo's voice in his head and he knew he was on the right path.

TJ focused his Ashe, his ability to make change, willing it to manifest. His world had transformed, but he remained steadfast in his purpose. Despite the disorientation of his mind being spun around in space, he maintained his lucidity throughout the experience.

His ancestors, his family, his friends, an anchor.

And for the first time, TJ reached beyond the familiar Orishas —Eshu, Shango, Oya, Olokun, and Yemoja—and sought the Lost Monarch. He delved deeper than ever before, tapping into a truly awesome power. So much Ashe usually made him feel "full" or near to bursting. But now, the more that poured in, the more alive he became. Hyperaware. With fervent prayers of his own, he funneled what was given and pushed it back out.

He called out to Olodumare.

*Please, don't hide what's right in front of me, Great One,* TJ thought-spoke. *Help me figure this out—should I run, stay put, or just go with whatever the big plan is?*

As TJ descended, an ethereal pull tugged at him, guiding him back to his physical form. His top-down view revealed the prismatic prison in the Court of All, where his body lay suspended, a tiny figure amidst the vast cosmic expanse outside its walls.

TJ re-entered his body, his consciousness settling back into the familiar confines of his physical form, like pulling on an old glove. Proper senses returned, and the weight of his muscles pressed in, the rhythm of his breath re-emerging, and the steady beat of his heart echoing from his chest. But the magical suppression within the prison sapped his strength, and the suspension in the air left him disoriented, his limbs heavy and unresponsive.

He grasped onto the power he held before, the power he had in that in-between. And, with a single thought—like it was no sweat at all—TJ severed The Channeling, using all those prayers that had built up in his spirit from before.

The connection snapped like a taut rope. His physical body

dropped to the ground with a thud, his knees and hands impacting the hard surface with a jolt that reverberated through his bones.

He had done it; he was back! But how? Was his Ashe too much for the Court's Channeling? Why couldn't Shango and Oya do the same with all the prayers they got over the past few months?

TJ looked up through the prismatic glass walls, back up to that ugly scar cutting through the galaxy clouds outside. The tear looked nearly stitched. Had his Ashe done that? Was he near to being depleted completely?

Turning to either side, heart racing, he took in the sight of Oya and Shango, suspended in the air. Through the prismatic glass, they looked half-dead, their forms drained of the deep energy that once pulsed through their spirits. Still contained in those egg-shaped containers. Their once-vibrant ebony forms were now withered and drained, nearly pale like the skin of Obatala. A pang of sorrow and anger at the injustice rushed through TJ.

As Oshosi said, it was time for that payback he had promised. It was time to finally free them.

Suddenly, Oya and Shango began to shake and spasm, their bodies convulsing in syncing motions, a violent dance that sent ripples of Ashe through the air.

*"What?"* a familiar voice called from the side. *"What's going on?"* From across the hall, Oshosi stood in his own fractured cell, his giant headdress of green-and-white brushing against the ceiling. His voice came out muffled through the glass. *"TJ, is that you? What did you do to them? I thought you were gone, child."*

TJ shrugged—then his entire body seized.

A violent tremor ripped through him. His muscles locked, Ashe surging through his veins like lightning. Something was wrong. The rift outside—he could *feel* it. A shift. A fluctuation. Like reality itself had taken a deep, shuddering breath. The half-healed scar in the galaxy pulsed, glowing with a sickly, unstable light. And then—

Shango jerked, his body convulsing within his egg-shaped contraption. Oya followed, her form snapping back like she'd been yanked by an unseen force. The walls of the prison trembled, the prismatic glass humming with raw energy.

TJ's vision swam. What was happening? Did he take in too much Ashe, or not enough?

A low, guttural groan rumbled from Shango's chest. Then, without warning, his torso erupted in a brilliant, blinding red light.

TJ flinched, his heart lurching in his chest. His entire body ached with the sheer force of it. His instincts screamed that something *huge* was happening, but before he could move, before he could even think—

Two figures *burst* from Shango's chest, crashing onto the ground of his cell with heavy, unceremonious thuds. TJ gasped.

Mr. Oyelowo and Ayo lay sprawled across the floor, unmoving. They breathed heavily, their faces contorted. Mr. Oyelowo held an ebony wood staff topped by a quartz crystal that appeared to be struck by lightning. Ayo lifted his ring, which sparked with bolts of purple. A mix of Shango's red and Thor's blue lightning? When had he gotten his ring back? How long was TJ out?

Gales of wind stole TJ's attention from Shango's cell. He turned, eyes bulging, as Oya's egg-shaped chamber erupted into a storm. A cyclone churned within the prismatic walls, crackling with bright blue and gray energy.

Then—something moved inside it. A hand. TJ stiffened. His pulse hammered as fingers curled through the spiraling light, grasping blindly, as if clawing through layers of reality. A forearm followed, then a shoulder.

*Manny?*

Her head emerged next, curls whipping wildly in the storm, her face contorted in effort as she dragged herself forward. A mirror flashed in her grip, its silver surface catching the stormlight.

Beside her, another figure took shape. First a hand, then the curve of a face, then the full form of an older woman pulling herself free from Oya's chest. Her auntie. A thick, leather-bound book tumbled from her grasp, its gold edges glinting as she collapsed onto solid ground.

TJ barely had time to process it—Manny and Tia Teresa had just *crawled out of Oya*. Both women gasped for air, chests heaving with the effort of their transition.

Before TJ could call out to his friends, a tingling sensation entered his own heart, an odd feeling, like his chest cavity was opening up, a yawning void that threatened to consume him. TJ wanted to claw at his chest, to stop the pain, but he knew he had to stay his hand. Keep it at his side. Like with Ayo and Manny, someone was traveling through him as well. But the strain was too much.

Until TJ heard the laughter.

Like a guffawing hyena, Eshu's chuckling entered his ears, easing the discomfort in TJ's chest. Through gritted teeth, TJ let out one long breath as Eshu *squeezed* through a light between TJ's torso. It was a bizarre sight as TJ looked down to find Eshu's jovial face sitting mere inches from his own. The pressure compressed Eshu's neck like a pinched balloon as he smiled and said, "TJ, you amazing human, you. Never a dull moment! I knew you could do it."

In an exaggerated show of sucking in air, Eshu's entire body spilled out into TJ's cell, where the Orisha nearly filled out the space of the entire room. Then the Orisha stuffed his hand into TJ's chest to pull out... Mom? She, like the others, dropped to the ground with violent coughs.

Power surged through TJ, not just saturating the air but coursing through his very bones. His skin burned—not from pain, but from sheer, uncontainable energy, like fire and lightning had fused beneath his flesh. Every nerve hummed, every muscle tensed, his entire being vibrating on the edge of something vast, something limitless.

It was Ashe in its purest form—wild, electric, alive. It roared through him, pushing at the limits of his body, daring him to break past them. His breath came sharp, uneven, the force of it rattling his ribs.

The chamber pulsed with it. The ground beneath him cracked. Light bled from his fingertips, golden and searing, illuminating the air with flickering embers.

Something inside him had shifted—no, something inside him had awakened.

Oya and Shango coughed as their divine children tended to them. TJ was struggling to breathe as well, the power so great it was overwhelming his senses.

Looking down at his ungloved hands, TJ noticed they had a constant, faint glow now, not radiating and then going away like when he used Ashe before. He pulled at his collar, and the birthmark near his collarbone was glowing steady as well.

"Oh, my honey bunny!" Mom exclaimed. Suddenly, TJ was wrapped in a hug, kisses peppering his cheek. "I'm so happy to see you alive and well. You're a worthy diviner, don't you see? Not like any other bird. I knew you could do it! I'm so proud of you!"

TJ blushed, a bashful smile on his face. "Thanks, Mom," he said, returning her embrace. "But I don't know what I did. I just..." A faint memory of Dayo entered his head. Some landscape of an endless ocean. "I think... I've been... dreaming this whole time?"

"Nearly three months of dreaming," Eshu dusted himself off, his floppy hat perched atop his head and his wooden staff clutched in his hand. "That was one hell of a ride, TJ! I wasn't sure if I'd ever fit in that small bird chest of yours!"

"I lost that much time again!?" TJ's entire body seized. Everyone must've been so worried.

Then—like a dam breaking—his memory surged back. He had been channeled. Held in place like a puppet, his spirit stretched thin, siphoned. The Court. The glass prison. And before that...

Eshu.

TJ felt sick. Eshu had brought him here. Betrayed him. His fists curled, fingernails digging into his palms that still glowed. Heat rose in his face, but beneath the anger, something colder lurked. He should have seen it coming. He should have known.

"Wait, wait. This is your fault." He pointed at Eshu. "Why did you bring me to the Court to begin with!?"

A muffled voice suddenly shrieked from Eshu's waist.

"*Because*," the voice sneered, "*your dear* friend *is a meddling little pest, that's why.*"

TJ blinked. Hanging from Eshu's belt was a large, dark palm wine gourd. And inside—something was moving. The gourd wobbled erratically as the voice growled in frustration.

"Oh," Eshu sighed, rolling his eyes. "Right. Forgot to mention my passenger." He patted the gourd fondly. "Say hello to Lord Vishvakarman. He tried stopping us when we were sneaking in. So, naturally, I captured him."

"You *caged* a god!?" TJ blurted.

"More like *borrowed*. I *was* going to let him go, but then he started shouting all kinds of ridiculous things about how he was 'protecting the integrity of The Channeling' and 'safeguarding the cosmic balance' and blah, blah, blah."

"*That's because,* you ignorant fool," Vishvakarman hissed, the gourd shaking again, "*you have no idea the* catastrophic *consequences of what you've done! You think you saved him, but you've* unleashed *something far worse!*"

Eshu sighed and flicked the gourd, making it rattle. "I told you, Vishy, you have a real problem with dramatics. Now hush, the grown-ups are talking." He ran a hand over the gourd. A layer of Ashe settled over it, muffling Vishvakarman's outraged yells.

Ayo ran up to the glass surface next to TJ, his eyes wide with disbelief. "*TJ, is that really you?*" he exclaimed, his voice clear and steady, without a hint of a stutter. The Ethereal Realm had returned him to full form.

TJ, still scowling at Eshu, changed it halfway to a smile. "Yeah, it's still me, Ayo. Good to see you." Judging by Ayo's wild face, TJ's response was underwhelming. But it didn't feel like he was gone that long.

Manny pressed up against the other side of the glass, standing next to Oya's giant suspended form. Her voice trembled as she spoke. "*We thought we lost you. It felt like we really did this time.*"

"Even Yewa said as much," Eshu added. And with the name, TJ recalled a faint memory of the Orisha in her eerie fuchsia dress.

The gourd jostled again. "*Because he was supposed to be lost! You—*"

Eshu groaned and flicked the gourd again. "That's enough out of you." He set another layer of Ashe over it. "Gee, it's so hard keeping Gods contained."

TJ's smile softened, and he quipped to Manny, "Well, it got pretty close there for a second, but I made it through. Which, again," he turned to Eshu, "explain yourself. I was brought here, Channeled, and now… what… I beat it?"

Eshu cracked his knuckles. "Well, I'd love to get into all the juicy details, but we need to move before somebody notices we—"

"*Idiooots!*" Vishvakarman screeched from within the gourd. "*You think they haven't noticed!? You stopped The Channeling! Themis and the others will come any moment now, and when they do—*"

Eshu silence him again.

"He's right though," TJ said. "Why haven't any alarms gone off yet? Shouldn't Themis and the others be coming at us right now? Hell, shouldn't they be in an active ritual Channeling me?"

"They're too busy, it seems." Eshu lifted his chin to the ugly scar in the starfield above. "They had you on auto-loop, I would presume. Plus... we haven't broken any barriers yet. The cells are still closed. All we did was put ourselves in prison with you lot. That's what Obatala told me. He said you can unlock these things. But when you do, we'll need to have our guards up." Eshu stepped forward, a mischievous glint in his eye. "Now, after all this craziness, it's not up for debate anymore—at least not for me. TJ, you *are* an Orisha—a new one made from flesh for reasons only the Great Monarch would know."

"The falling star is me..." TJ murmured to himself, and something at the edge of memory tugged at him. "A promised child will rise with the light of a dying, falling star." The words somehow made sense to him then, but he did not understand why. Still, for the first time, TJ agreed. The power inside him was palpable.

He *was* an Orisha made new.

But why him? Why not Dayo? Could it be because of everything he had just endured, or—as Ol' Sally once told him in the Aqua Realm—his abilities were always boosted within the Ethereal Realms?

Before TJ could dwell on the thought, Bolawe's voice cut through the murmurings around them. The reflection in Manny's mirror shimmered as the ex-Keeper's face appeared. "*We need to get a move on. We've broken no barriers since everyone is in their cells. But they'll sense the Channeling has stopped.*"

TJ nodded and stood up straighter, an extraordinary sense of ease washing over him. His breath came effortlessly, his movements fluid and unburdened. With a mere thought, the chains binding Shango, Oya, and Oshosi trembled. He focused on the chains, feeling his Ashe slither through them like a living entity. It wasn't about breaking them by force; it was about *suggesting* to them that they needed to be open. It was the same process he'd surmised with Obatala and Oshosi in Forseti's dreams. All TJ was doing was reversing the ritual in his mind.

And it worked.

The chains shattered with an echoing symphony, freeing the

bound Orishas. TJ focused his mind on the door and forced those open as well.

TJ stared at his glowing hands, checked his birthmark again. This new power felt easy, but his body seemed to disagree. His scarring had reached to his shoulders and spidered toward his chest..

Alarms wailed through the Court of All, piercing the air with their shrill warning. They'd have company soon. Probably Themis herself would show up.

A flash of color caught TJ's eyes. Through the prismatic walls, the galaxy clouds that surrounded the Court of All began to split. The fissure he had seen when he was first brought here was still long and ugly, a red-orange blight across the cosmos. But now it was ripping to shreds. Despite its distance, TJ felt it, felt it deep. And he knew it was he who had caused its split.

From that yawning chasm came darkness that seeped into the realm. They all stared up through the prism walls, upward to the menacing shadows spilling through, an uninvited chaos descending upon them.

The God Eaters.

The alarms weren't for them. They had blared *because* of TJ, but no one was coming to put them back in chains when reality had suddenly been cut through the starfield above.

*"Fools! I tooold you!"* Vishvakarman managed to get his head out the tip of the gourd, his olive-skinned forehead painted in red lines. "It's the God Eaters! They've broken through. The Sovereign One approaches!"

# 66

# THE HERO'S EQUINOX

OUTSIDE THE COURT OF ALL, CHAOS REIGNED SUPREME. FROM where he was in his cell, TJ could barely see the shadows spilling out from the reality tear, but he could feel the God Eaters as though their void was already seeping into him. If he truly was an Orisha, he would be one of their top targets.

That notion did not sit well with his human stomach.

Shadows darkened the stars as the hordes descended. Though TJ had never encountered them before, an inexplicable dread consumed him, as if these beings were ancient adversaries from a past life.

The air buzzed with urgency as the alarms continued to blare throughout the Court of All.

TJ swallowed. What was the Sovereign One? Who gets a name like that? Better yet, what God names an entity like that? It didn't sound good, whatever it was.

A telepathic announcement from Themis echoed in TJ's mind: *All prisoners. Evacuate through the Golden Fountain immediately. No deity, spirit, or god will allow themselves to be taken by the Eaters. Again, this is not a drill. Evacuate through the Golden Fountain immediately. The way will be sealed to all once the Eaters breach the walls.*

Themis, allowing prisoners to flee? Damn, shit just got *real* real.

The glass surface beneath TJ's feet shook and every cellblock and jail cell opened simultaneously, releasing their occupants. Vishvakarman wiggled his way out of Eshu's gourd, struggling to escape.

TJ turned his head back out toward the tear, where the God Eaters spilled into space like a dark cloud of gnats. But they were being headed off by something far and unseen. Fiery orange combustions erupted in the air.

A titanic battle was being waged.

A battle between Gods and shadows.

TJ's attention was drawn back to the cellblock as creatures from every pantheon flooded the corridors, running, flying, and crashing over the prismatic ground in a desperate scramble for escape. Vishvakarman finally was able to get all four of his arms free, then he sped off with the rest, saving his own butt.

A half-spider half-woman wearing a kimono scurried down the hall. Nearby, Hades' Cerberus bounded forward, its three heads snapping at anyone who got too close. Above them all flew Garuda, the majestic bird from Hindu mythology, his wings beating powerfully as he soared toward freedom. How many had Themis put in cells? Wouldn't they have been better placed fighting the God Eaters to begin with?

Turning to Eshu, TJ asked, "Was this part of your plan?"

Eshu scoffed and shook his head, his floppy hat wagging with him. "You mean did I plan for you to tear the fabric of reality open and bring the God Eaters here, resulting in Themis letting everyone out? No. Not part of it at all. I just thought we'd get Shango, Oya, and Oshosi out and make a mad dash for it. But when life gives you lemons..."

TJ glanced at Shango and Oya as they stirred from The Channeling. He could sense the lingering burn from the sapping ritual's heat, as if a laser had recently seared their skin.

TJ walked out of his cell as a dog-like creature with a hand for a tail dashed by. Then he ducked his head into Shango and Oya's chambers. "How do you feel?"

Shango flexed weakly while Oya let out a low grunt.

Oshosi stepped out of his own cell, saying, "In Warrior Speak, that means they're doing pretty bad. They'll need a boost if we're going to get them out of here."

Taking Oshosi's words to heart, TJ placed his hands on

Shango's and Oya's giant ankles. As he funneled his Ashe through them, an electric sensation coursed back in return—an invigorating blend of strength and energy that surged between their bodies.

"This should help," Mom said, handing TJ his staff. He peered over it for a moment, took in the various charms, the double-helix center, and the seemingly mended scar. The moment the wood touched TJ's palm, he knew he could do this.

"Everyone, help me!" TJ urged his companions—Mom, Manny, Tia Teresa, Ayo, and Mr. Oyelowo. Even Oshosi and Eshu joined in.

From Manny's mirror, Bolawe said, *"I'll tell the others to generate a fresh prayer. Adeyemi will have everyone working on it again. The Equinox is at its peak now."*

So it was the Hero's Equinox on the other side. No wonder so much energy raced through TJ. Attuning his senses, TJ could feel prayers from the Mortal Realm filtering through him like an ethereal river of power.

"There *are* so many voices," TJ said as he continued recharging Shango and Oya. "I've never heard prayers directly like this before. It's... it's a lot. But... it feels good."

"Welcome to the Orisha clan, brother," Oshosi said with a curt nod.

"Elder Adeyemi did a good job gathering crowds all around West Africa and the diaspora for this," Eshu said as he swirled his staff in the air. "And it seems like it's working. We're being empowered by prayers from millions of Yoruba practitioners and at least half a million diviners."

Eshu was right. As he put a number to the prayers, TJ felt each individual voice within that collective surge—the songs of children and elders alike; diviners and non-magical folk united in purpose. Campers from Camp Olosa, students from Ifa Academy, courtyards all across Nigeria, Benin, the Caribbean, Brazil, and more. He could sense his friends, distant family, even Tunde, *even Dad*. The sheer volume of prayers enveloped him in warmth and light as if sacred power infused every breath taken.

Ashe vibrated through his staff, but TJ held it steady, infusing his own magic into it like he did when he boosted others. When the

Ashe cycled back, it doubled in power. Tripled. Quadrupled. Folds upon folds.

Shango and Oya stirred, their immense forms gradually coming to life. Shango's body, though still weakened, emanated sparks of fire and lightning that swirled around him in an angry dance. The air crackled with energy, each bolt illuminating the giant Orisha's war-battered face.

Oya, too, rose higher. Her eyes flickered open as gales of wind and flashes of electricity swirled warlike around her. The gusts whipped at TJ's clothes, a chaotic yet invigorating reminder of her strength. She breathed in deeply, drawing the very essence of the storm into her lungs. With a mighty exhale, she released wind so powerful that TJ and the others had to brace themselves to avoid being sent flying. A passing group of kitsune fox spirits scurried along the walls to avoid the blast. A few of them cried and barked in Oya's direction, but kept going after looking up at the shadows in the stars.

"Feeling all right?" TJ asked, his voice steady despite the turmoil.

Oya let out another torrent of wind before answering, "Better."

Shango flexed his hands again, and his flexing muscles looked depleted—still formidable, but lacking their usual strength. "We'll be needing our weapons if we cross paths with the Eaters."

TJ glanced around the cellblock, now almost empty as mythical creatures fled. He turned back to Shango and Oya with a furrowed brow. "How will we get your weapons back? Where are they? That was never part of the plan."

Shango and Oya exchanged glances before turning to Oshosi. The Hunter Orisha smiled knowingly and leaned down to TJ's mortal height. "This is where you give me a bit of a boost to find the weapons cache, fellow Orisha."

---

The Court of All's Weapon Room stood apart from the rest of the celestial chambers TJ had seen. Its architecture was almost ordinary. Stones, instead of prismatic glass, filled the walls. Weapons of all sorts—glowing swords, bone-white wands, crooked staffs, and ruby-infused shields—lined each surface. Runes and symbols, ancient and powerful, adorned every surface, radiating a palpable aura that thrummed beneath TJ's skin.

But TJ and his companions weren't the only ones who had the bright idea of ransacking the place.

Several other entities were searching for their weapons before making their way out. A six-armed titan wearing red robes over armor snatched up anything his hands could get to; another god with a lion's head and a human body withdrew a golden scepter before scurrying away, and an ice giant that looked very similar to the one TJ had faced before pulled out a long ice shard before stomping off. Ayo and his dad had to duck behind a spear as tall as a redwood. Another creature had bumped into a crate of them, making them fall. Tia Teresa kept casting protection circles from her leather book to avoid getting smushed several times.

It was a discomforting feeling, seeing giants in a panic—eyes darting every which way as they mustered for battle or retreat. TJ had not yet seen a God Eater, but if they were already eliciting such reactions as these, he didn't plan on meeting one anytime soon.

"Well, we definitely found the right place," Eshu said, holding up his staff to light the way down a dark corner.

The room was impossibly large, sinking deeper and deeper into a darkness far beyond. Shango and Oya's diminished strength was painfully evident in the way their shoulders still slumped. But they played it off by getting their heads up, their eyes fierce.

"TJ, we're up," Oshosi said. "I'd do it myself, but we need to work fast. Touch my ankle. Let's find these weapons and follow everyone else out of this doomed place."

"Why not just pick up any ol' weapon like the others?" Manny's aunt asked from the rear. It sounded like she was forcing her voice not to break, her stance tight, her grip tighter on what TJ now understood to be a Holy Bible.

Oshosi turned back to her as though she had cut the wrong wire on a bomb. Even Shango and Oya had looks for her. It was Eshu who answered, though. "Not just any ol' weapon will work when they've been wasting away. Oshosi included. If we're to stand a chance, we'll need the divine weapons tied to our own."

Manny stepped in front of Tia Teresa, waving her away as

though she were talking nonsense. "Sorry, she wasn't part of the plan as much as she should've been." She lowered her voice. "Tia... remember, the whole reason we're here is to boost their weapons."

Manny's auntie winced. Heck, even TJ wasn't aware of that part of the plan. That must've all happened when he got taken from them, or when Eshu caught them up in the transition.

TJ nodded, placing his hand on Oshosi's rough skin. Immediately, light flared behind his eyes. His Ashe Vision alighted and several paths revealed themselves to him. The rest of the objects in the room desaturated, fading to the sides. There were only a handful of items in the grand room that aligned with the Orishas and his Ashe.

And of course they were near the back.

"There!" TJ pointed ahead. "I think I see Shango's axes and Oya's machete."

"And my quiver and bow seem to be there as well," Oshosi added.

Manny stood beside Bolawe's mirror projection, her face set in a determined expression as she communicated silently with their former mentor. The mirror flickered with each exchange, casting a soft glow over her features. "Bolawe's saying we need to bounce! He's spying through some other reflections and he says a group of God Eaters broke the line and are headed straight here!"

"Right." TJ swallowed hard, wondering how close the Eaters were. "Oshosi, let me climb on your shoulder and we'll lead everyone else."

"Let us be off, brother." Oshosi scooped him up, and they made their way through the congested room. They stepped over overturned javelins laced in glittering gold, cut through more spirits in search of their own weapons, and pivoted around crates full of bubbling potions. When they were close to their target, a pair of gruff voices caught TJ's attention.

"Lift it harder, you fool," one of the voices said.

"What do you think I'm doing?" the other snapped back.

In the dim light, TJ could make out a familiar pair of heads, one blond, the other red. Magni and Modi. The sons of Thor. They were surrounded by several phantoms—or maybe they were ghosts—

who glowed different colors. It was like they were part corpse and spirit in one.

"Wait, wait, stop here," TJ said to Oshosi. "There's another glow. Do you see it?"

Oshosi followed TJ's gaze. "Glow? No. Two bickering brothers? Yes."

Through TJ's eyes, something bright was being held between them—whatever they were fighting over. Something in the shape of a "T."

"Hey!" TJ called to them. "What's that you got there?"

As though caught in the act, Magni jumped back, his golden hair slapping across his face. "You have no business here, mortal. Begone with you."

Modi's eyes narrowed as the rest of the group funneled behind TJ and Oshosi. "You'll not take Mjölnir this time."

"This time?" TJ questioned as Modi tried to hide the hammer.

"He's talking about me," Shango said, shuffling slowly to TJ and Oshosi's side.

"How did *you* get out?" Magni grunted and spat. "And what curse did you put on our father's weapon?"

"Curse?" Shango said darkly. "And what kind of curse would I have been able to cast on it, you fool?"

"Perhaps it's not a curse at all," Oya added, her voice strong but her body weak. "Perhaps the hammer is meant for Shango. Let him try to lift it. Unless you fear the weapon's true allegiance. We've been through this dance before."

There was clearly a battle warring in the brothers' mind as they looked between each other with the hammer and TJ and his group. Hadn't TJ seen this in his vision before? Hadn't Forseti claimed that the weapon no longer answered to them?

Shango stepped forward, grunting through the effort. "The Eaters will not wait for us to debate. We need our weapons for the trials ahead. *Every* weapon that will heed us."

A tap came at TJ's elbow as the back and forth continued between the Asgardians and Orishas. It was Ayo.

"Do you hear that?" Ayo asked in a murmur. "Ogun's speaking to me."

"Nah, I don't," TJ said. "Touch my elbow again." Ayo did as he was told, but there was still nothing. "Actually, wait. No. Touch me with your ring. Right on my skin." Again, Ayo did as directed and this time a loud voice sounded in his head.

*Hello again, Tomori Jomiloju.* It was Ogun's voice.

*Um... hey,* TJ thought-spoke back.

*Eshu mentioned you might need me.*

TJ gave a fleeting look to Eshu, who looked back and winked. Magni and Modi were still arguing, and they didn't seem like they were looking to fight. Shango and Oya did a good job putting on a face. Plus, it helped that they were backed by another pair of Orishas.

Did the brothers *fear* the Orishas? They were outnumbered... though those weird glowing spirits flanked them. Dad always said it was easy to tell when someone wasn't *really* ready to fight. You could see it with any of those boxers who faced Mike Tyson in his prime, or whenever Michael Jordan gave his opponent the mean eye. Magni and Modi, instead of puffing out their chests, seemed to curl into themselves. Their eyes were constantly darting as though looking for help, or an escape.

They figured they had already lost. They hadn't realized how wounded half of TJ's team was. That gave TJ the time to take his call with Oshosi.

*What's going on?* TJ thought-spoke into Ayo's ring. *What's the plan?*

*You're in the Weapon Room, yes?*

*We are.*

*Good, make sure that divine child of mine gets to Shango's and Oya's weapons. I can infuse them with some of my iron magic, help them in the fight. The Equinox is unusually strong this cycle.*

*Yeah,* TJ thought-spoke. *We have a few million worshippers helping us with that.*

*Very good. Shango and Oya must be greatly weakened at present, eh?*

TJ eyed them. *They've definitely had better days. But yeah... their weapons. Let's make it happen. Ayo, are getting all this?*

*Loud and clear. I'll wait for your signal. My baba, Manny and her aunt, and me will go for the weapons, bring them back, and mess up these* òlóṣì.

TJ looked up again. Eshu held a fist behind his back. TJ took that to mean they needed to wait. "This argument is silly, friends,"

Eshu said to the others. "Magni. Modi. We know how this will end. Just make it easy on all of us and hand over the hammer."

"Over our dead bodies," Magni spat.

Modi flexed his hands around his long battle axe. "For Thor!"

"Well, we figured as much," Eshu said. He uncurled his fist behind his back and waved everyone away. Ayo and his group peeled off and rushed for the weapons.

Magni and Modi followed the action, their scowls chasing after the screeching feet of the mortals. "Honorable Dead! After them."

It was the distraction Shango needed.

In a split second, TJ saw the weak wisp of Ashe building in Shango's gut, filtering up his arm, through his bicep, and out of his hand, which manifested in crackling lightning. TJ, activating the Ember Spiral form, threw his spiritual weight into the Ashe the moment Shango's fist connected with Magni's blond beard. In the next breath, Oya flung her own uppercut, which billowed with wind.

The moment the first blows landed, the air around TJ shuddered with intensity. Shango and Oya moved with a grace and ferocity that belied their exhaustion. Shango's fists sparked with residual lightning as he swung at Magni, while Oya's swift strikes with her wind kept Modi at bay.

To the Asgardians, it probably felt like an equal match. They didn't realize it was TJ doing the heavy lifting. Not to mention the help provided by Eshu's illusions. Every time Shango faltered or mis-stepped—leaving himself open to a counter—Eshu cast a doubled image of the Orisha, disrupting Magni's and Modi's axe strikes. Every time Oya overextended or tripped, Eshu manifested fake storms that crashed against the Asgardians harmlessly.

In truth, Magni and Modi fought well. If they had known how much of an act Shango and Oya were putting on, the burly gods may have pushed through and over-matched them.

TJ stood at the periphery, his heart pounding. His eyes darted to Ayo and Mr. Oyelowo, deeper within the shelves of weapons. He hadn't noticed that Oshosi had joined them. Good, they needed an Orisha supporting them. And those spirits the Asgardians called "the Honorable Dead" were just on their heels. Now that TJ had a better look, the figures looked like they were once human. Some wielding katanas; others, old musket rifles.

"Get in here!" Tia Teresa shouted, pulling Mom, who was last to make it. "Into the protection of my circle." TJ's Ashe Vision couldn't pick up anything, but his eyes did. Blood came down Teresa's hand, and there was an unbroken smudge of a circle around her as she read scriptures from her Bible. "'Contend, Lord, with those who contend with me!'" she repeated over and over.

The Honorable Dead flew from the protective circle where Oshosi cleaned them up. Only using his hands, elbows, knees, and feet, the Hunter did most of the damage, destroying the strange spirits that couldn't get to Ayo's group. The ones who got through leaped at the mortals, smashing against an invisible force TJ couldn't quite see with his Ashe Vision.

Were they in their communion with Ogun already? From where Teresa had placed her circle and how the rest were gathered near one of the shelves, it certainly looked that way—

A flash of movement. A roar.

TJ barely had time to register it before Magni's axe came hurtling toward his head.

He ducked. The blade whistled past, close enough that he could feel the wind from it. Magni overextended, and Shango capitalized, planting a bare foot into the Asgardian's chest and sending him skidding backward. Modi howled and swung for Oya, but she weaved around him like mist, her counterstrike snapping his head to the side.

TJ exhaled sharply. *Focus.*

He turned back just in time to see Ayo press his ring to the nearest shelf, a pulse of deep, iron-gray Ashe rippling outward. The weapons hummed in response, their divine energy flaring to life.

*Okay, good. They've got that handled.*

But the Honorable Dead weren't letting up. They clawed at the barrier around Teresa's circle, their hollow eyes burning with battle lust.

And there were still more coming.

A heavy *whoosh* passed over his head, and TJ ducked. Magni had nearly missed taking Oya's head off. He needed to focus back on their fight; he had to trust that Ayo had it covered.

Glancing back once more, TJ noticed that Teresa's circle seemed to protect the weapons as Ayo did something with his ring. Even his dad seemed to be chanting over the collection of Shango's axes, Oya's machete, and Oshosi's bow.

But their Ashe was faltering…

The Honorable Dead kept coming and coming. What they lacked in power against Oshosi, they made up for in sheer numbers. The Orisha hadn't been Channeled, but his powers had clearly atrophied with the rest from TJ's own Channeling. More and more of those spirits were getting past him. But Mom, with her short iron staff, flung sheets of water to bat them back, but none of her spells seemed to do any actual damage.

TJ turned back to his group. They weren't doing much better either.

Eshu's illusions wove through the battlefield like mists given life, drawing Magni's and Modi's attention away from the vulnerable ritual. Then TJ realized the nasty trick at play. He was manifesting fake God Eaters. Or… was Eshu slipping again?

TJ reset his boost, changing his staff form from the Ember Spiral to Ogun's Ground Pulse, pulling his energy away from Shango and Oya and recasting it to his mom and friends. Sure enough, as his spiritual energies interlocked with their own, he found their ritual fell a little short of what they needed. So TJ lifted his staff and placed it between his feet, stomping the ground. The vibrations waved from TJ's position and rolled toward his friends in waves. His energy merged with Teresa's Holy Circle, which bloomed with the green light of Ogun.

Which was a bad thing.

Magni's keen eyes caught sight of Ayo and the others' celestial glow, realizing the true focus of their efforts. With a roar, he redirected his fury toward them. And there was nothing TJ could do.

# 67

# BEYOND THE BREAKING POINT

"No!" TJ shouted, thrusting his staff forward.

Magni had seen the celestial glow around Ayo's group and must've seen what they were doing with the weapons. The Asgardian pivoted, muscles tensing, legs bracing to charge straight for them.

TJ barely had time to think. Flowing and multiplying Ashe back and forth through Shango and Oya had been one thing—forcing a burst out against the might of an angry god by himself was quite another. The moment he wrenched the Ashe from Oya, his bones screamed in protest, like his very essence was cracking under the pressure, his scarring growing larger up his arm.

But he did it anyway.

Wind howled to life at his command, slamming into Magni and forcing him to veer off course. TJ's knees nearly buckled. He gritted his teeth, digging deep into his reserves to keep the barrier standing.

Oya capitalized on the diversion. In a flash of motion, she intercepted Modi's axe before it could split TJ's head open. Their eyes met for the briefest moment—hers fierce, determined. A silent exchange. *I've got your back. Keep going.*

Close calls became all too frequent. A deflected hammer strike from Magni sent shards of stone flying toward Manny and her aunt. TJ barely managed to help Shango summon bolts strong enough to divert the deadly projectiles. The consequences if he failed—he couldn't afford to think about it.

Blond hair flaring behind him, almost like a cape, Magni lunged toward Mr. Oyelowo, who was deep in a trance. Oshosi slammed a shoulder into Modi, forcing him into a set of chariots meant for flying pegasi. But that meant he left Teresa's failing circle to defend against the horde of Honorable Dead.

Modi lunged, red hair wild, axe raised high.

TJ saw him coming, saw the fury in his eyes, the raw power behind his swing. Time stretched, slowed to a heartbeat-by-heartbeat crawl.

He could dodge. Break his connection, pull back the Ashe, save himself.

But then what?

"*Help them!*" Bolawe shouted from Manny's mirror.

His friends needed him. Ayo, his dad, Manny—they were inches from restoring the Orishas' strength. If TJ wavered now, if he flinched, the ritual might fail. They might lose the battle.

His fingers tightened around his staff. He stayed rooted, bracing for the impact he knew was coming.

At the last moment, just before the axe could cleave him in two, a body crashed into its path.

Shango.

The Orisha took the full force of the blow, muscles straining, jaw clenched tight. Lightning sparked at his knuckles as he pushed back against Modi's strength. TJ's pulse slammed against his ribs, his focus wavering for half a second before he forced it back in line. No room for hesitation now. The impact sent Shango staggering, and the game changed, again…

Modi's eyes shined with new recognition. Was that the first time he landed a blow in the fight? Had he fought Shango before? Did he recognize when the Orisha was wounded and on his back foot? It seemed so, because Modi turned his attention from the ritual circle to Shango with murderous intent. Like a red-haired wolf sensing the kill.

Where were Oshosi and Magni? Still tussling in another corner?

TJ needed more help.

Modi's battle axe carved through the air, every swing meant to kill. He wasn't just attacking anymore—he was pressing forward, forcing them back, herding them toward a breaking point.

Eshu darted between strikes, his illusions flickering, unraveling at the edges. The strain showed in his tight jaw, the sweat glistening on his forehead. Oya's wind bursts still knocked some of Modi's blows off course, but each one came a second too slow, a fraction weaker than before.

And Shango—Shango was bleeding.

The wound Modi had left on his side darkened his tunic, and though he fought on, the fire in his eyes dimmed with every labored breath. His swings lacked their usual force, his steps just a little too heavy.

They were losing ground. Fast.

In that critical moment, TJ realized their mistake: turning away from the ritual circle. He glanced over his shoulder. He couldn't see his friends or Mom or Mr. Oyelowo. Had the Honorable Dead got to them? Were they gone?

TJ's body quivered, and he couldn't make it stop. He reached out with his Ashe and what he felt was blinding…

A storm of lightning and fire filled the chamber. The Honorable Dead crumbled back from the heat and electrical charge. When the glow cleared, a figure held an infused form of Shango's giant battle axe aloft: Mr. Oyelowo. He gritted his teeth, the power of the weapon clearly too much for him.

"Dad! Let go!" Ayo was shouting. "Dad! Look at your skin!"

The skin on Mr. Oyelowo's hands and arms blackened, heat searing up his limbs like burning charcoal. His grip trembled, but he held firm, swinging the axe in a wide arc. The first strike sent a shockwave of fire crashing through the ranks of the Honorable Dead, scattering them like ash on the wind.

He roared through the pain, lifting the axe again. The second blow cracked the ground beneath him, forcing the spirits to retreat even farther.

But the third—

The third was too much.

"I love you, son!" Ayo's dad shouted. "I'll tell your mother you say hello."

Ayo couldn't stop him before he swung.

Lightning and fire erupted from the axe, a final explosion of power too massive for the room to contain. The storm ripped outward, rolling over the rows of divine weapons, setting them ablaze with energy. Shelves toppled like dominos, metal clashing, the entire chamber shaking beneath the force.

The weapon hit the ground. The stone split.

A shockwave engulfed the space, tearing through the Honorable Dead. Spirits shrieked, their forms scorched out of existence, vanishing in dying embers. The pressure was so intense that even the air itself seemed to warp and bend, the walls groaning under the weight of the unleashed divine energy.

Then—silence.

The Honorable Dead were gone.

The last of the shelves buckled, weapons spilling across the ruined floor. Oya's machete and whip manifested anew, then Oshosi's bow—each one restored.

Shango's infused axe slipped from Mr. Oyelowo's grasp; but Ayo's dad never hit the floor.

He was already fading, his form peeling away in glowing embers. By the time Ayo reached for him, all that remained were the scattered traces of his essence, visible only through TJ's Ashe Vision, drifting like dying stars.

Ayo's father… was gone.

But there was no time to mourn. Not yet.

"Noooo!" Ayo cried.

*"Get them their weapons!"* TJ shouted, funneling Ashe into his voice. He did his best to ignore Ayo's grief. It would only cripple him, too. But it made him sick.

As if guided by invisible hands, the weapons floated across the room, and they landed softly in the hands of their rightful owners.

Shango's eyes lit up with renewed vigor as he grasped his fused battle axe, which started as two and was now merged as one, thanks to Mr. Oyelowo. The air smoked with electricity as he swung it, releasing arcs of lightning that illuminated the room. Oya's machete and whip glowed with a fierce light as she spun both through the air, creating whirlwinds that knocked Magni off balance. Oshosi notched an arrow on his bow; it shimmered before flying true into Magni's axe, causing it to splinter.

The tide had turned.

Shango stepped up to where Mjölnir rested on its pedestal. Before lifting it, TJ thought he heard him murmur, "I feel you, brother. I'll make it right."

Who was he talking to? Talking about?

Then, with no effort at all, Shango wrapped his fingers around the hammer's handle and lifted.

Magni and Modi froze.

"Impossible," Magni whispered.

"It can't be..." Modi said, aghast.

A crack of thunder split the air, deep and resonant, as if the skies themselves had witnessed the act and passed judgment. The chamber trembled. Modi flinched, glancing upward as if expecting to see his father's wrath descend upon them.

Shango turned slowly, facing the Asgardians. His eyes burned bright and red, his expression unreadable. Then, with both Mjölnir and his own battle axe crackling with divine power, he charged.

Magni barely had time to react before the first strike sent him sprawling across the floor. The impact shook the chamber, electricity arcing wildly across the stone.

Modi snarled, lifting his axe, but Oya's windstorms knocked him off his feet. Before he could recover, Oshosi's arrows pinned him in place. He swung wildly from the ground, but his attacks landed on nothing but air.

And Shango didn't stop advancing.

With Mjölnir raised high, he loomed over them, eyes alight, power surging through his veins. One final blow, and it would be over.

Magni and Modi knew it.

Their rage spluttered out. Magni's chest heaved.

"We yield!" they shouted in unison, throwing down their weapons, which were cracked at the pommel.

Shango paused for a moment before lowering his weapons. His eyes still blazed with crimson power as he stepped back. "Only because Thor wouldn't want me to." He pointed a sharp finger at them both. "The *only* reason."

With their weapons finally in hand, the Orishas stood taller, their presence steadier—but the toll of the battle still weighed on them. Shango rolled his shoulders, testing his grip on Mjölnir, but his breaths came heavy. Oya leaned against her machete for a beat longer than she should have, masking fatigue with sharp eyes. Even Oshosi, with his bow now slung across his back, stood with the rigid stillness of someone forcing themselves to stay upright.

They were stronger, yes—but far from fresh. And there was still so much more fighting ahead.

Manny came running, scurrying past the same kitsune they had seen before, who were now rummaging through a collection of naginatas.

"TJ, are you okay?" she said, smothering him in a hug.

He hugged her back. "I'm okay... I'm okay. But..." They both looked to each knowingly, and, at the same time, glanced over to Ayo.

TJ's heart ached as Ayo sank to his knees, hands trembling as he tried to gather the scattered remnants of his father—his singed clothing, at least. The weapons chamber felt colder now, shadows creeping along the walls like fingers of grief reaching out to embrace them all. The scattered weapons and battle debris only emphasized the emptiness where Mr. Oyelowo had stood moments before.

Manny squeezed TJ's hand before they both moved to Ayo's side. TJ's throat tightened as he remembered seeing Dayo's body—at least they'd had something to bury, something to say goodbye to. Ayo had nothing but ash and scattered energy that dissipated with each passing second.

Mom kneeled beside Ayo, wrapping her arms around his shaking shoulders as he sobbed. Even Manny's aunt Teresa tried to comfort him, murmuring prayers in Portuguese, but Ayo remained inconsolable. His cries echoed off the chamber walls, a sound that made TJ's chest constrict.

*"He was a good man..."* Bolawe said from Manny's mirror.

He didn't think he'd ever see it happen, see what happened to Banjoko the Bold and John Henry happen right in front of him. Staring down at his own hands wrapped around his staff, he wondered if that's what should have happened to him time and time again.

Heavy footsteps approached, and TJ looked up to see Shango standing over them. The Orisha's presence seemed to still the very air around them. Oya, Eshu, and Oshosi came to his flanks.

"Your father's sacrifice made this possible," Shango said, his voice deep with respect as he held up his axe and hammer. "Without him, we might never have reached our weapons. And the power I sense in this axe now..." He paused, studying the weapon's gleaming surface. "I suspect Ogun's hand was at work here as well."

TJ's gaze dropped to Ayo's copper ring. Ogun had indeed been preparing for this moment, empowering them all through Ayo's father.

"It was him," Ayo sniffled. "Baba actually gave deference to Ogun. The ritual was failing. It would not have worked if it wasn't for my dad throwing worship to Ogun to give us a fighting chance. Or at least..."

*That's what Ayo wanted to believe,* TJ thought.

"Your baba died a true warrior," Shango continued, kneeling to meet Ayo's tear-stained face. "For one of my divine children to fall in such a manner—protecting others, turning the tide of battle—it is the highest honor possible. You should be proud, Ayodeji." He turned to the group. "All of you should be proud."

Divine beings and humans alike exchanged respectful nods, acknowledging each other's contributions. But then—the air changed.

A slow, creeping dread slithered into the room, pressing against their skin like a warning. The lingering Ashe in the chamber recoiled. The walls, once humming with divine resonance, stilled—as if the very space around them was holding its breath.

Oya stiffened first, her hand flying to her whip. Shango's grip tightened around his new axe and hammer. Even Eshu, who always had a quip at the ready, stood unnaturally still.

TJ felt it before he saw it. A weight, not physical but spiritual—a void in the world, drinking in everything around it. His throat became a desert; his hands stiffened around his staff.

Then—movement.

Between the towering aisles of weapons, shadows twisted where no shadows should be. A blur of something wrong, shifting, writhing, peeling away from the fabric of reality itself.

The first God Eater stepped forward.

It had no face, no true form—just a silhouette barely holding together, its edges flickering between existence and something deeper than a void. Limbs folded and unfolded in unnatural patterns, its body warping with every step, like it couldn't decide what it wanted to be. Others quickly joined it. *Many others.* Then came the sound.

Not a growl, not a voice, but a distortion. A deep, resonant hum, vibrating through the chamber, making TJ's skull ache. Like the universe itself was protesting their presence. His pulse thundered. His feet refused to move.

These were not Gods, not spirits, not demons, or anything else.

These were something that devoured them all.

# 68

# LAST JUDGEMENT OF THE BEARD AND THE BLUE

THE GOD EATERS EMERGED FROM THE SHADOWS, THEIR FORMS A nightmarish amalgamation of writhing tentacles, iridescent scales, and misshapen wings that seemed to blot out any light in the weapon room. The chamber, once filled with the gleam of enchanted armaments and the residual glow of divine power, now fell into an oppressive darkness. Every flicker of crystal light and sparkle of magic dimmed as if the God Eaters devoured even the essence of illumination.

TJ's breath caught in his throat. He had thought himself past *true* fear—after everything he'd faced. But as the God Eaters advanced, their cold, malevolent eyes piercing through the shadows, a primal terror surged through him. Whispers invaded his mind. They sounded like a thousand tormented souls, each cry clawing at his sanity.

He glanced at Shango, who held Mjölnir and his new axe with hands that trembled ever so slightly.

Oya's eyes, usually ablaze, went wide and doe-like as she tried to hold her machete steady.

Oshosi's practiced aim faltered for a fraction of a second as he notched another arrow.

Eshu clutched at his head. "No, not again, not again."

TJ's heart hammered in his chest, his skin prickling with cold sweat. The fear was a tangible thing—an icy grip around his throat that squeezed tighter with every inch the God Eaters approached.

But then TJ noticed something peculiar: Manny and her aunt, Ayo and Mom—they didn't seem affected by the same terror. Manny stood tall beside him; Mom clutched Ayo's hand firmly but didn't falter; Tia Teresa looked on with calm resolve.

No, not calm. It was something else.

They thought they were fighting ordinary shadows.

They couldn't know what was in TJ's heart, what he knew was in the Orishas' heart as well. They didn't *feel* the terror. Was it something only deities, gods, and spirits could sense?

Magni and Modi, who moments ago had been formidable opponents, now cowered in a way that made their previous deference seem insignificant. Magni's broad shoulders hunched protectively over his brother as they took tentative steps backward. They had fought the Eaters before, hadn't they?

TJ swallowed hard. *Push through it. Push through it.*

Shango cursed under his breath. "This... this isn't normal."

Oya shook her head, eyes darting wildly between the creatures. "We've killed these things before," she whispered. But it didn't sound like she believed it.

"They're not the same." Oshosi's voice was raw. "They've changed."

The largest of the God Eaters stepped forward—if something that shifted between forms could be said to "step." Its shape twisted with each movement, its body warping in ways that hurt to look at, like reality itself didn't know what to do with it.

Magni took a stumbling step back, his face pale beneath his blond beard. "This... this is impossible."

Modi let out a shaking breath. "No, it's not." His voice was hollow beneath his red mustache. "We merely fought their spawn before. This is them. The First Ones."

The words landed like lead in TJ's gut.

The First Ones.

The deities—the gods—hadn't fought the *real* God Eaters before. Just their offspring. Their leftovers.

The realization came a second too late.

The lead God Eater flicked what might have been a hand—or a

tentacle, or a claw, or something that was somehow all three at once —and the entire room shook with pure malice.

"Magni, Modi!" Shango commanded curtly. "Buck up and defend yourselves. We're not done here."

Magni's jaw tightened, and he grabbed a claymore sword nearby. Modi followed suit, clutching a jewel-covered mace with a white-knuckled grip.

Oshosi turned to TJ, his expression grave. "TJ, build up your Ashe. Everyone here is about to need a boost. A *gargantuan* boost."

TJ nodded, focusing inward, the familiar hum of Ashe coursing through him. But his fear threatened to choke off that power—especially as several kitsune leaped from an aisle of weapons to confront the God Eaters.

The fox spirits shimmered and split into dozens of illusionary forms, darting around the monstrous entities with fluid grace. They shifted shape mid-air—one moment foxes, the next ferocious warriors wielding ethereal blades.

The God Eaters struck back with horrifying speed. A tentacle ensnared one kitsune, its essence visibly drained as it let out a harrowing scream. Another kitsune's illusion faltered as an appendage impaled it, its spirit dissipating into nothingness. One by one, they fell—their cries joining the cacophony already ringing in TJ's head.

The God Eaters absorbed their essence, their power visibly swelling with each vanquished fox spirit.

TJ could almost feel that power growing within the God Eaters —the very air seemed to vibrate with it. Had these abominations already absorbed the Gods fighting at the front lines?

TJ eyed the kitsune charm on his staff; it was fading.

The God Eaters did not stop. They surged forward, crossing the space where the kitsune had just stood, pushing straight for them.

Shango slammed Mjölnir into the nearest one with enough force to shatter mountains. The creature's body bent around the impact, absorbing the blow like liquid shadow before reforming, its eyes locking onto him with a hunger that had only grown.

"They're adapting," Oshosi hissed, shooting an arrow that should have gone straight through an eye. The Eater caught it and twisted the projectile into nothing.

Oya slashed through one with her machete, only to find another already sliding toward her from the side. "We need a new plan."

"We need a way out," Eshu snapped. His hand was glowing with barely contained divine magic, but even he hesitated before throwing it. Like he knew it wouldn't be enough.

They backed up, step by step, but there was nowhere left to go. The vault was massive, lined with weapons that once held the power to kill gods, but even those artifacts felt dimmer now, useless. The farther they retreated, the less space they had to maneuver.

TJ's breath came sharp and shallow. Fear clawed at him, an instinctive part of his brain screaming that this was it. No way out. No more tricks. Just a slow, inevitable end.

"We need to cut through them and make a run for it," Oya suggested, her voice barely concealing her urgency.

"Don't let them touch you," Magni roared, his blond beard whipping in Oya's Wind. "If they do! They'll drain your soul."

Modi shook his head, his red braids flailing. "We'll never be able to fight them all."

Oshosi kneeled and touched the ground, his eyes lighting up as he sensed their surroundings. "He's right. There are too many. No route of escape."

*"I don't see a way out,"* Bolawe cried from Manny's mirror. *"These shadows are obscuring almost every reflection in this place. I have no line of sight."*

Shango bellowed, "Stand your ground! Don't let them flank!"

TJ mirrored Oshosi's move and saw an endless sea of God Eaters throughout the Court of All. It seemed like an impossible task.

He stepped in front of Mom, Manny, Ayo, and Teresa. "Stand behind us," he commanded firmly. "The God Eaters will be too much for you."

They were definitely all feeling the fear now. They might not have felt it in the same way TJ did, deep down where he had to stamp it out, but they saw how overworked the titans who fought to protect them were.

Shango exhaled. Then his voice rumbled through the chamber. "I have faced titans. I have crushed demons. I have fought Gods—

and *won.*" His red eyes burned like embers in the dim light. "I have felt fear, but fear has never felt *me.*"

Oya raised her chin. "I am the First Storm. The Mother of Hurricanes. I have shattered mountains with the wind of my voice. Do you truly think I will fall to shadows?" She gripped her machete. "We are warriors. We are Orishas. We do not fear death—death fears us."

Shango slammed Mjölnir into his palm, and electricity coiled around his knuckles like leashed dragons. "You call yourselves devourers of gods?" He scoffed. "Then *choke on me.*"

Oya moved first. She flew forward, wind howling, cutting through the fear with every step. Mjölnir followed an instant later, Shango swinging with enough force to puncture asteroids.

The weapon room echoed with the clash of divine power against the God Eaters' malevolent presence. TJ's heart was a frantic drumbeat in his chest as Shango swung Mjölnir with unabated fury.

Shango landed a thunderous blow, splitting several God Eaters in two. The creatures' essences dispersed like dark mist, but their shadows reformed almost instantly, more ferocious than before. Their horde slithered in where their partners failed. As if the line had never been broken. A surge of guilt cut through TJ; he should have boosted Shango before the Eaters reformed, but TJ's power was failing him under terror. It was like his willpower was being overworked.

Oshosi notched an arrow, his eyes glowing with a hunter's cold fury. He released it with pinpoint accuracy, and the arrow split into dozens mid-flight, each finding its mark in the writhing masses. For a fleeting moment, the God Eaters recoiled, their advance halted. TJ poured Ashe into Oshosi. The Hunter Orisha grunted in gratitude before launching another volley.

Oya summoned gusts of wind that sliced through the dark shapes like blades. She danced among them with her machete, each movement graceful and deadly. Her winds formed a protective barrier around them, holding back the encroaching horror for just long enough to regroup. TJ funneled Ashe into her too, feeling the storm within her grow fiercer.

Eshu weaved through the chaos, his staff moving in sharp, fluid motions as he conjured illusion after illusion. Normally, his tricks bent reality itself—shadows turning into warriors, false paths leading enemies into traps. But now?

Now his illusions flickered, unraveling the moment they formed.

The God Eaters didn't just see through them—they broke them. Twisted them. Warped them into writhing mockeries of his own magic. One illusion turned against him entirely, shifting into a monstrous reflection of himself that lunged at his throat. He barely dispelled it in time.

The hesitation cost him.

A God Eater lashed out, seizing the opening.

Eshu stumbled back, shaking his head as if trying to clear something from his mind. The whispers—the ones that had been digging into him since the moment they arrived—grew louder.

***No way out. No trick will save you this time.*** It was the God Eater's voice, like a thousand voices spoke at once. Could everyone hear?

Eshu cursed under his breath, but his movements had lost their usual ease. The Trickster was off-balance. And the Eaters knew it.

Magni and Modi fought side by side, their claymore and mace cleaving through the monstrous forms with raw power. Magni hurled his claymore into a particularly large God Eater, pinning it to a wall of spears before it burst into harmless smoke. Modi followed up with a whirlwind attack that shredded another foe.

But it wasn't enough.

They were driven back step by step until they found themselves cornered against the far wall of the weapon room, Oya's wind bubble protecting them. The mortals stood huddled behind them, quivering lips and hiked brows dominating their faces.

TJ's hands shook around his staff as he tried to muster more Ashe from within to boost his companions further. The oppressive aura of dread weighed on him like leaden chains, sapping his strength and resolve.

And then, suddenly, the blue-skinned Yamaraja, astride his colossal bull, burst through the horde of God Eaters. Forseti followed close behind, wielding a golden staff and sword in each hand. The whip of his long beard punctuated each spin on his heel. Yamaraja's bull charged, its hooves striking the ground with ground-shattering force, scattering the smokey forms of the God

Eaters like blackened leaves in a storm. Coming up behind their rear were the golden statues that guarded the Court.

Yamaraja's eyes burned with a fierce intensity as he wielded a peculiar rod. With each strike, Yamaraja slowed the God Eaters in *literal time,* allowing Forseti to cleave them with his sword and obliterate them with a spell from his staff.

Relief washed over TJ as the Gods fought. Their abilities were awe-inspiring—each movement exact, each strike lethal. Perfectly in sync. Like they had been doing this for years. For a millennia. The sheer force of their calculated assault created a breach in the horde of God Eaters. The statue guards were more distraction than effective combatants, throwing themselves into the hordes like sacrificial pawns.

"Oya!" TJ shouted, his voice barely audible over the din of God Eaters.

Oya didn't need further prompting. She raised her machete and whip, summoning a powerful wind tunnel that held back the encroaching darkness.

TJ planted his feet, gripping his staff so tightly his knuckles ached. The storm of Ashe inside him was too small, too dim against the crushing presence of the God Eaters. They needed more.

"Everyone—through me!" TJ shouted, voice raw. TJ commanded everyone to channel their Ashe through him. One by one, they did so—mortals and Orishas alike—infusing TJ with an overwhelming surge of power.

As he worked his magic to boost Oya's wind tunnel, Yamaraja bellowed above the chaos. "Themis ordered us to save you."

TJ quirked an eyebrow. "But I thought she was angry with me."

"Oh! She is. Very much so."

Waist-length beard whipping through the air, Forseti sliced through another three God Eaters trying to get through the tunnel before saying, "If you could break The Channeling, you have a power you need to nurture and develop. It may one day rival The Sovereign One. The Fates have plans for you—plans even we may not fully know. A few God Eater sentries shouldn't be what takes you down. You've more work to do, young one."

"The Sovereign One?" TJ asked. Themis had mentioned that

name before. Dayo, too, when she spoke in his head. Was that the leader of the God Eaters or something?

Oya's eyes blazed as she channeled more magic into the wind tunnel. "Cut the chatter and keep up your efforts!"

"Everyone funnel through the wind corridor!" Yamaraja commanded, waving them along with his blue-skinned arms. "We'll hold off any that get through."

Forseti nodded firmly. "Upon departing the weapon chamber, take two leftward turns, then a right, and you shall reach the Room of Frost. Beyond it, Themis awaits."

Magni and Modi stepped forward, weapons ready. "We'll stay back to defend Forseti," Magni said.

Shango exchanged nods with them. "May your cleaves strike true."

"Take care of Mjölnir," Modi said, smashing a God Eater that slipped through the tunnel. "If we can't have it, the God Eaters can't either."

"I wouldn't have it any other way," Shango said.

With Oya at the rear maintaining the wind tunnel, everyone rushed through. The howling wind wall clashed with the cries of the God Eaters behind them.

TJ poured every ounce of Ashe into keeping the wall intact as they raced down corridors—two lefts and then a right—until they reached the safety of the Room of Frost without daring to look back. The large doors closed behind them, and they entered utter stillness.

"How—" Mom started to say to TJ. "How did you do all that?"

TJ shrugged, catching his breath. "Things are different for me in the Ethereal Realms."

"I always forget how powerful TJ is in these places." Ayo hunched over. "You never mention it when we forget on the other side."

Manny placed a hand on TJ's back. "That's because he's too humble to big himself up like that."

*"The story hasn't been written for you yet, Mr. Young,"* Bolawe added proudly from Manny's mirror.

A huge slam rocked the door behind them, making them all jump.

And that's when they heard the cries of Forseti and Yamaraja.

# 69

# THE SOVEREIGN ONE

"We need to move," Oshosi said urgently, pulling TJ back from Forseti and Yamaraja's deathrattles.

There was no time to waste. Manny and her aunt scrambled onto Oya's broad shoulders. Ayo and Mom climbed onto Shango's powerful frame, while Eshu shot ahead.

The Room of Frost looked oddly familiar as they raced across stones that cast off a smoky cold. The impossibly tall and wide chamber appeared as if carved directly from the Frost Realm, stretching a mile. It looked just like a ravine, like the valley TJ and the others had ventured through.

Then the rune bloomed in TJ's Ashe Vision. One specific rune: Isa.

Had this been what his visions were truly about? The dreams he spied in Forseti's mind when the Asgardian had tried to commune with the Fates?

Another deafening slam against the grand doors echoed through the chamber.

"We need to go faster, everyone!" Oshosi urged, racing across the icy floor with TJ perched on his shoulders.

"What do you think we're trying to do, Hunter?" Oya bit back as she air-stepped from boulders covered in frost.

The group ran, air-stepped, and slid as fast as they could. But they were haggard. Oya and Shango in particular were running on fumes. Manny, her brow furrowed, balanced precariously on Oya's shoulders. The Orisha's wild mane of hair flowed behind her like a banner, and with each jump, they left trails of swirling wind and electrical energy. Tia Teresa clung tightly to the Windweaver, her skin flushed as she screamed.

Ahead of them, Shango moved like a wounded lion, proud but unstable. Lightning stuttered around him, bolts thinning out to almost nothing. Ayo hung by the Orisha's neck, eyes pinched beneath his designer glasses. TJ glanced at Mom. Despite the dire circumstances, there was a calm determination in her eyes that TJ found reassuring. It wasn't the first time he'd seen that face on her. It was the same one she'd had at Dayo's funeral when they were attacked, the same face she had when she nearly got arrested at the UCMP Council. Ayo was a zombie, though. TJ could only hope that he'd forget most of the pain on the other side.

As they neared the center of the room, another thunderous crash sounded behind them. TJ risked a peek over his shoulder just in time to see the grand doors burst open.

The God Eaters poured into the room like an inky tide, their slithery forms blotting out the ambient blue that filtered through the chamber. The air vibrated with a low hum that sent shivers down TJ's spine. The oppressive darkness seemed to absorb all hope and warmth, leaving only an icy void in its wake.

"Go! Faster!" Oshosi urged the group, his voice cutting through the growing cries of the Eaters.

TJ tapped Oshosi on the shoulder. "Wait, stop. We're not going to outrun them in time. Look at Shango. Look at Oya." They were absolutely hobbling now. Oya had even forgone using air-steps, now jogging like an antelope with a gimpy leg.

TJ sniffed the air, sniffed the magic of the room, sniffed the residual energy from the deities who had passed through since they were set free or escaping on Themis' orders. It was all just there, under the surface of the ice, where the "Isa" rune pulsated in his vision. Ready for TJ to use.

TJ knew what he had to do.

"C'mon, what are you doing?" Manny asked from Oya's shoulder. "Let's get out of here."

TJ shook his head. "I've gotta stay. I gotta slow the Eaters down."

"What the hell are you talking about?"

"Don't forget. I'm a lucky charm. Just let me cook."

"But..."

"You're not going to lose me again. But you might get iced after what I'm about to do. Go! Get to the next room!"

Oya adjusted Manny on her shoulder, securing her. "Come, child. Let the boy do what he must."

Manny struggled against the Orisha's grip, her voice rising in protest. "No! We can't leave him here! We just got him back. I'm not leaving him again!"

Oya's expression remained resolute as she tightened her hold on Manny, securing her firmly on her shoulder. The Orisha's eyes, though fierce, held a glint of sorrow.

"TJ knows what he's doing," Oya said, her voice carrying the weight of ancient wisdom. "We must trust him."

"You can do this, son!" Mom said from Shango's shoulder. "Stay strong! Keep your chin up!"

Oya raised her hand, and a gust of wind swirled around Manny, forming an impenetrable barrier of air. The wind wall lifted Manny slightly off Oya's shoulder, creating a buffer that prevented any further struggle.

"May Ashe guide you," Shango shouted over his shoulder. "Hold fast! Hold the line!"

"Oshosi, let me down," TJ said. "I got it from here."

"What are you going to do?" Oshosi asked as he sat TJ down on the icy ground.

"Do the impossible. Defend the Mortal Realm." TJ shrugged, pointing to the walls. "You weren't around for the Frost Realm, but I know a good trick." He lifted his staff, readying Yemoja's Ripple Flow. "Go on. Make sure they get across safe. If this works, I'll be right behind you."

"No. *When* this works, brother."

Oshosi gave TJ a final, resolute nod before sprinting across the rest of the room, joining the others. The chamber seemed to darken around TJ as he focused inward, feeling the pulse of latent magic thrumming beneath the surface. It was almost like the echoes of the

Frost Realm when he froze that raven, but this was different. This time, he had an entire chamber's worth of magic to draw from. And from more than just the Norse.

The God Eaters would get to him in mere moments. He closed his eyes, extending his senses into the depths of the room. Dormant energy hummed just below the frost, a powerful reservoir waiting to be tapped. Taking a deep breath, he reached out with his Ashe, drawing in the magic like a sponge soaking up water.

The God Eaters bolted forward, their wicked forms scrambling over the smoking boulders of ice and along the walls with preternatural speed. TJ paid them no mind, holding his staff horizontally in front of him, then moving it in a fluid, undulating motion, mimicking the gentle flow of water. Ashe poured into one end of the staff and out the other like the cascades of a wave rolling across the surface of an ocean. He kept doing this, even when the Eaters were one-hundred yards away, fifty. He had to muster as much as he could. There was only one chance at this.

Fear sliced through TJ like a blade, but he forced himself to focus. At the last moment, he raised his staff overhead, the power building within him. His form was so deliberate and effortless it would have made Staffmaster Bamidele proud.

The cold erupted outward, sprinkling the rune of "Isa" a thousand times through the frosty air.

It wasn't just ice. It wasn't just frost. It was absence. A wave of pure, devouring chill spread in an instant, gripping the God Eaters mid-step. Their clawed limbs slowed, their blackened, smoke-like forms turning sluggish—like time itself had been dragged to a crawl.

The frost spread fast. Too fast.

It clawed up his own arm, threading through his skin like white paint bleeding over brown skin. His already ashen patches expanded, the loss of pigmentation spreading over his shoulder, creeping up his neck.

He tried to move faster, but—no. His limbs were heavier now. Slower.

The field was draining him.

TJ gritted his teeth, pouring everything into the field, watching as the God Eaters struggled—some locked mid-lunge, others halfway through an attack that would never land. For the first time, they weren't advancing.

He forced himself forward, dragging his feet as he neared the final chamber. His shoulder ached, burned, froze—every movement another reminder that he was stretching his power too far.

Then—he was through.

TJ didn't wait to watch them break through. He turned on his heel and air-stepped across the ice toward safety. The frost trembled beneath his feet, cracking with each powerful air-step he took, their delicate balance disrupted by the magic he had unleashed.

TJ burst through the grand doors into the gilded courtroom, his footsteps echoing against the gleaming marble floors. Ahead, Themis stood at the Golden Fountain, ushering the remaining deities through the portal to safety. Her fingers twirled in a graceful arc, and when, through her blindfold, she seemed to catch sight of TJ; she waved her hand, sealing the door behind him. TJ caught a glimpse of the first Eaters punching through his ice wall before the doors closed.

Shango, Oya, Oshosi, and Eshu all made it through the Golden Fountain. Tia Teresa grabbed Manny by the arm and propelled her toward the portal. "Okay, you see he's still alive. Now, go!" she commanded, her voice leaving no room for argument. Manny glanced back at TJ before disappearing into the shimmering light.

Mom clutched Ayo tightly. "You too," she urged, pushing Ayo forward.

Mom reached for TJ to pull him in as well, but Themis intercepted her with a giant hand, saying, "Not him."

The moment Themis' blindfold locked onto TJ, her brow caved. Themis raised her hand, casting a spell that had previously rendered him powerless, motionless. But this time, TJ felt different. The prayers of the Equinox still coursed through him like a river of light, and with a forceful shove, he flung off her magic.

Themis' brows lifted in surprise. "Oh, how I've underestimated you, mortal."

TJ straightened his posture. "Orisha."

"Hmm," Themis conceded. "It appears so. And you are somehow more powerful than even them in this place. So I was right all along—you *can* fix this. You *do* have the power. You *can* stop these God Eaters."

"No," Mom interjected fiercely. "He will not be doing that. He's coming home with me—with his people."

TJ glanced at Mom and then back at Themis. "This realm is done for, and there's another that will need our help. It won't help if I'm gone. I'm… I'm supposed to search for the Monarch of my pantheon. That's my path."

The doors at the end of the room slammed for the first time. The God Eaters were near.

Themis' expression tightened as she spoke again. "This realm has defended all others for countless ages."

"And now it's time to do something new." TJ stood tall. "Why are you so against me?"

Themis softened slightly as she answered. "I've been against what you've been doing; I have never been against *you*."

The God Eaters burst into the courtroom, their erratic forms dimming the golden glow of the pillars that had once stood as beacons of divine power. The golden glow of the courtroom dwindled. Not like a flickering candle, but like a sun being snuffed out. The opulence of the marble, the gleam of the gilded pillars—all bled pale, drained into a lifeless gray.

Then it arrived.

It was giant, massive, oppressive. It didn't move through the horde—it devoured space as it passed. Its body, an endless sprawl of writhing limbs and shifting mass, twisted with a wrongness that made TJ's stomach lurch. The air grew thick, too thick, like the courtroom itself was suffocating under its presence.

TJ's breath caught. His lungs fought for air, but the atmosphere clung to him, stolen away by the thing's gravity. His body swayed forward, drawn toward the giant entity by a pull that wasn't physical—but fundamental.

His stomach curdled. Bile burned the back of his throat. Every nerve in his body screamed to run.

But his feet wouldn't move.

This was the creature Dayo had warned him about.

The Sovereign One.

It was a master of masters, a monster of monsters. There was no language with this being, just an immediate and terrifying understanding. No translation was needed; its essence communicated directly with TJ's soul. The moment their eyes locked, TJ comprehended it all.

***Ah, that's where you've been hiding this whole time. Now I've found you. And now I will devour you.***

Terror surged within TJ, gripping him like a vise. He turned. "Ma, you gotta go."

"I won't leave you," she replied firmly.

"I'm really, really sorry. Don't ground me but—" TJ shoved her through the Golden Fountain. She screamed his name as she vanished, the waters swallowing her whole.

A shadow draped over him, cold as the space between stars. He turned. The Sovereign One loomed. Even frozen, even slowed, the thing was still coming.

TJ could see it now—his Isa-rune was still working. Ice cracked along the God Eaters shifting limbs, slowing the way its form warped and bled through reality. It was trapped in time, but only barely. The frost would hold for seconds, maybe less.

Seconds weren't enough.

Themis stepped forward, her robes tattered, her face set like carved stone. "You go after her too, young one. The Sovereign One cannot take your power. And I must go down with the ship."

TJ turned to her, his breath ragged. "No. We fight him together. No Channeling. Look, I slowed him with the ice magic."

Themis gave a rare, wry smile. "Oh, to be a divine power made new. Be careful with that brazenness, young one. It can spell your doom. The Court of All failed," she continued, voice steady. "We have fallen. If I cannot save it, I will ensure it is sealed forever. That is the only victory left."

She lifted her hand. Golden pillars buckled, tearing free from their foundations with a sound like the breaking of worlds. A temple built by Gods, meant to last for an eternity—now collapsing in on itself, its own creator unmaking it. The chamber shook. Debris rained down, burying the lesser God Eaters under the weight of divinity undone.

But the Sovereign One kept coming.

"Go!" Themis commanded, striding forward with the certainty

of someone who had already accepted their fate. "Do not waste the power you have. I might not agree, but you are the Mortal Realm's best path forward."

"No," TJ whispered, shaking his head. "You can't do this alone. You have to seal the Court, right? You can't do that while fighting. Let me help you!"

"There is no time!"

A shadow stretched across the ruin. The Sovereign One slithered forward, ice breaking from its limbs.

Themis raised her hand, manifested a double-edged sword, magic sparking—

But before she could strike, the waters from the Golden Fountain behind them churned. A dark hand rose from the wide basin. Olokun. His obsidian skin was paler now, tinged with sickness. His long, straight hair hung loose, his breathing slow. Still recovering. Still not whole.

And yet—he was here.

"This will be my last stand, mortal," Olokun said, voice impossibly smooth, impossibly calm. "Do not let it be in vain." He stepped forward, lifting a hand toward Themis. "You focus on sealing the Court. I will buy you the time you need."

Themis hesitated. "You are not strong enough."

"Then let that be my burden. Not the boy's."

Before TJ could argue, Olokun flicked his wrist. A wave slammed into TJ with the force of a crashing tide. He was back to the Great Drowning. To Eko Atlantic. He had felt that force before. But this time… somehow… felt different. Fear didn't come like it usually did. The water that wrapped around him was nurturing, protective.

The last thing TJ saw was Themis spinning her blade, Olokun stepping into the Sovereign One's path—

And then the world dissolved.

# 70

# PUTTING THE PIECES BACK TOGETHER

When TJ got back to the Mortal Realm, he expected to end up back at the command center for Operation Stormbreak. What he did not suspect—and it was something he probably should have—was to wake up in a hospital bed staring up at floating crystals in a dark room.

The images made little sense at first, nor did the sounds that filtered through his ears. He saw everything doubled, and he couldn't keep his sight straight. Colors were inverted as his body thrashed against a soft bed.

"Leave him," a youthful and familiar voice said. One TJ hadn't heard in a long while. Josh? Eshu? "He's going through a metamorphosis. Let him ride it out."

Ride it out? His chest was twisting into itself. Someone needed to make it stop. Hadn't he been through enough?

"Nah, you better do something about that," another familiar voice said. "Make him right. Make him right, right now or I'll—"

"Healer Zakari, remove the father, please."

"I wish you would. Don't you dare point that shit at me. I'll break that thing in half."

Through blurry sight, TJ thought he could make out a wooden shaft capped by a crystal being waved in the air. It was hard to tell. Everything was coming in like a kaleidoscope.

"Jalen, stop, stop! Let them work on TJ."

"Nah, you people haven't done a damn thing but watch him and chant. Why is he glowing like that? Why won't he stop? I want my son with *real* doctors."

"Jalen, listen to yourself. You know that won't work. How would we ever explain the glow to the clouded? Just please, calm down."

"I'm done being calm! First Dayo, now my boy. What's it going to take, Yejide? Tunde, too? Is he next on your people's list? I'm over this. I'm over all of this."

TJ fought against the spasm his body had flown into. Through the pain, he seized control of his arm and latched onto the spirit that was most hot in that room. Thin fingers wrapped around a broad forearm.

Dad stopped shouting.

"TJ?" A large hand engulfed TJ's own. "Thank God, TJ. Can you hear me?"

Smaller spasms rocked TJ's body now. He had no control of his mouth.

"That shouldn't be possible," one of the healers said. "Zakari, what's your assessment?"

"The tissue is dead, but... but his Ashe blooms strong. He's making a turnaround."

"That's more than what I'd expect after a fortnight."

Two weeks!? Was TJ really out that long? How much more of his life would he have to lose? The thought overloaded all his efforts, and his hand slumped to his side again, his vision darkening quickly.

"Mr. Young, like we told you before, your son is fine. He's alive and as well as he can be. He's just going through changes. Yes, they may seem violent, but he's fighting through."

A long beat passed. TJ tried desperately to cling to his consciousness. His tether to the physical world was weak, but he managed—barely managed—to grab Dad's wrist, squeezing twice.

"TJ?" TJ could feel Dad rushing to his side. "TJ. Can you hear me?"

TJ couldn't squeeze again. There was nothing left. He just had to hope his outreach was enough.

"As soon as he's cleared," Dad finally said with quiet anger, "he's never coming back to this place. You hear me? Never." Stomping feet against marble sounded, then the slamming of a door. There were more voices, more murmuring, but TJ couldn't hold on any longer.

ᛉ

"MR. YOUNG, IF YOU CAN HEAR ME, PLEASE MOVE YOUR HAND."

TJ strained to move, but his hand stayed still. His breath quickened, and his heart raced when he found himself immobile, unable to command his limbs. Even with Oya's Wind. His mind screamed as he tried to move, but nothing responded.

His vision blurred, making the room swim in and out of focus. Indistinct shapes—people or figments of his imagination—flitted across his eyes. His hearing was muffled, as if underwater.

How long had he been like this? Days? Another two weeks? The fear of losing more time gnawed at him. He dreaded waking to find life had moved on without him. Again.

"Mr. Young, I'll ask again. If you can hear me, please move your hand."

Were his parents still there? Who was asking him these questions? His mind scrambled through foggy memories—Dad's angry voice demanding proper care. Was that recent or from another time?

TJ focused on the present, trying to ground himself. He needed to move, to break free from the paralyzing fear. Forcing himself to feel the soft blankets against the back of his legs—the only thing he could feel—he attempted again to move his hand, concentrating all his energy.

Nothing happened.

Did he have Ashe at all anymore?

The room remained a distorted blur, sounds drifting in and out like distant waves.

"Mr. Young, if you can't move your hand, can you please move one of your fingers?"

It was like last year all over again, but worse. Last year, he only had trouble moving his hands and fingers after his confrontation with Olokun. But now, he couldn't feel anything above his waist. Not even the rise and fall of his chest as he breathed. Was he breathing at all? He must've been. He could move his toes freely. And that meant he was alive, that air still ran through his lungs.

"No, Mr. Young. Your toes and everything below your waist are fine. We need you to move your fingers."

Another voice joined the first, but TJ was already slipping again. The second voice brought up terms he was not familiar with, muscles and body parts that connected to this tendon and that. It was one of the healers trying to guide him, to get him to get his body moving again. It was the same physical therapy talk he'd had all last year. Only this was more complicated. Far more. The next voice brought focus, however.

"Mr. Young, your scarring has spread from your forearms, up your biceps, through your shoulders, and down near your belly button."

*Orunmila's Stars,* TJ thought. *How am I ever going to move again?*

"But the scarring stops at the neck and it hasn't covered an odd birthmark you have near your collarbone. If that means anything to you, use it."

Odd birthmark? Oh yes, TJ remembered. The same one that everyone in his ancestral line had. The ones who had been cursed. He couldn't begin to understand what that meant, though.

"We've done it before, Mr. Young. It'll take time, but we can get you moving again. Just be patient and get your rest. Your Ashe will take time to rebuild. And you've used far too much of it all at once."

It was the basic tenets of Ashe. One of the very first lessons TJ learned back at Camp Olosa. For something to be given, something else had to be taken away. He had just freed Oya and Shango—burst a tear into the fabric of reality, halted the God Eaters.... all on the back of his Ashe... it would take time to get back. He just had to trust the process. He just had to submit himself back to his slumber.

Moving his fingers could wait until later.

"Hey, TJ, it's Manny. I don't know if you can hear me, but the healers say you can. So... I decided to talk to you. Oh, Ayo is here too. He's saying 'hi' as well." There was a pause. "Oh, wait, sorry, he's signing that he says he 'hopes you're feeling better.' We hope you're doing okay. The Elders are saying you're an Orisha. Like, for real, for real. I know we always guessed at it, but I suppose it's official now, I guess." There was another pause. "Ayo is saying you should see the shrines they have built for you. Every time anyone comes to visit, they prostrate to you and everything. It's kind of weird. Wait, Ayo is telling me to add it's *very* weird. You can't even beat him in Major League Crossover." Manny sucked her teeth. "Ayo..."

TJ wanted to laugh, but lay motionless—his new normal. His insides roiled, giving him a migraine he really didn't need. The notion of being deified ate at him, an itch he couldn't scratch. People bowing to him? Prostrating like he was Obatala or Eshu? It didn't sit right. He wasn't wise or clever like them. Half the time, he didn't even know what he was doing. He was just good at boosting Ashe, using that divine energy to help others. Beyond that? He was still TJ, the lanky teenager fumbling through life, trying to figure out his place.

Lying there, TJ's mind drifted back to simpler times. Before all this madness, when his biggest worry was finishing homework or avoiding embarrassment in front of Manny or Ayo. Now, people were building shrines, seeing him as a beacon of hope. It was absurd.

He wasn't ready for that kind of responsibility. He didn't want it. All he wanted was to get back on his feet, to help his friends and family without being put on a divine pedestal.

"Well, we just wanted to come around and say we missed you. The new Blood Moon movie came out and left the theaters already. I wanted to wait and watch it with you when you woke up, but..." Manny's soft hand covered TJ's own, and he squeezed back. "Oya's Wind!" she gasped. "Ayo! Ayo! Go get Healer Zakari! He squeezed my hand! TJ squeezed my hand!"

But when the squeak-squeak of Ayo's sneakers receded from the room and came back, TJ had already fallen back into another episode of rest.

THE NEXT TIME TJ WOKE, HE DID SO WITH CLARITY. BUT HE could not make sense of where he was. Gone were the floating crystals above his head, replaced by a stucco ceiling. His eyes weighed heavy, and he tried to edge his gaze down to his feet. It took great effort, but he adjusted his sightline to the foot of a bed backdropped by a familiar wall. The room was dark, but the wall shone bright with a starfield, a constellation painting the image of divine beings.

It was Dayo's room. His room now.

Those divine beings were the Orishas. Obatala up above, Oko surrounding the Earth, Olokun wading in a sea of stars. All looking like giants made of golden fireflies.

But why was TJ in his room?

A gentle breeze wafted through the lone window, a breeze TJ could actually *feel* across one of his arms. He tried to roll over but only managed a small shoulder that made his blankets fall a little. A bright light forced a squint from him. It took him a moment to realize it was his own body that made his eyes squint. Dad was right. He was glowing. From his middle to as far as he could see down his chest. The only part of his torso that wasn't was the space around his blotchy birthmark.

He tried lifting his hand to switch on his lamp for a better look, but it was nothing but dead weight. The blanket underneath his arm felt cold and smooth, yet he could do nothing to move it. So he decided to use Oya's Wind.

Would his voice work though?

TJ swallowed, wetting the dry that clung to his throat. He needed the spell phrase for a boost. His first breath came out huskily, but it was there as he said, "*Afẹ́fẹ́, wá sí mi.*"

Ashe bloomed in his vision. A subtle wind wrapped around his hand and fingers, forcing it to move to the bedside lamp. As it was willed to move, TJ realized he had a tube going through his arm. It wasn't until he flipped on the light that an IV stand revealed itself next to him. In fact, that wasn't the only new thing about his room. He was completely surrounded by mountains of flowers, cards, and other gifts that almost filled the entire space. The first he saw was a card from Titi that read:

*Energy is never destroyed, only transferred.*

Then there was another from Staffmaster Bamidele he found in the collection.

*Thank you for reminding me that perfection is the enemy of the good.*

Nearest to him was a copy of *Divination Today,* dated for June. Its title read:

**Waning Ashe Restored, But Where Is TJ Young?**

*June!?* TJ thought. When had he first been taken to the Court of All? January? And when had he gotten back? He couldn't be sure. His friends had come to him during the Hero's Equinox. That had to be March. So he hadn't just lost two months like last summer. He had lost half a year!

Horror and curiosity piqued, TJ read the rest of the article:

*Just a few months ago, magic was waning among divinerkind. Spells weakened, charms faltered, and an eerie silence filled places once brimming with enchantment.*

*Then, as if by miracle, TJ Young returned.*

*His reappearance was a beacon of hope. Almost immediately, magical activity surged. Yoruba schools of magic, thought to be fading, flourished once more. Charms sparkled with renewed vigor, potions brewed perfectly, and complex transfigurations succeeded effortlessly. The community buzzed with excitement, relief palpable in every corner of New Ile-Ife and beyond.*

*Yet, Divination remains shrouded in uncertainty. Seers and oracles report cloudy visions and fragmented dreams. This mystery seems tied to TJ Young.*

*But shortly after his heralded return, TJ vanished. Ashe remains intact as ever, but the boy himself seems to be missing. Reports confirmed that on the 19th of March, his body was transported to Babalu-Aye Medical, a facility renowned for treating magical ailments. Since then, no further information has surfaced. TJ Young has not been seen, and his whereabouts remain a tantalizing enigma.*

*Speculations abound. Some whisper of a rare affliction, others of a secret mission. Though Ashe seems to be restored, that which is associated with Orunmila is still a void. And there are some reports that the divine children of Olokun have turned to Yemoja for water magic rituals. Some believe TJ holds the key to restoring Divination and until his full recovery, our prophetic powers will remain impaired.*

*Babalu-Aye Medical remains tight-lipped, citing patient confidentiality. Despite numerous inquiries, they have released no statements, leaving the community in anxious anticipation.*

*Where is TJ Young? The mystery persists, and so does our hope. We at Divination Today will keep you informed, guided by the flickering light of foresight and the enduring spirit of inquiry.*

*Stay vigilant, dear readers, for the story of TJ Young is far from over.*

Below the article, there were a few pictures of crowds outside the medical facility. Then TJ gasped. Manny and Ayo weren't exaggerating. There were shrines propped up all around New Ile-Ife with his face plastered right in the middle like a funeral procession. After flipping through a few more pages—using Oya's Wind directly—he found another large picture of a giant TJ statue head that had been erected right in the middle of the courtyard where Dayo's mural was. With a rush of wind, he blew the newspaper shut. He couldn't take any more. It's like he had woken up and landed in a bad dream. He wanted to go back to sleep and wake up in a world he understood.

More cards from around his room caught his eyes. Well wishes from Andressa and Antonia from Brazil, Elder Akande from Camp

Olosa, Mrs. Afolabi from Jollof & Jubilee. When he was about to summon cards from the Caribbean, a set of squeaking floorboards caught his attention.

"Tunde!" Mom's voice called out. "I told you, I don't mind you visiting TJ at night but you gotta remember to turn off the light!" She pushed the door open and they stared at each other like deer in headlights.

Mom dropped to the floor and prostrated to him fully, reciting the Yoruba proverb she had apparently fashioned for him as some sort of defied prayer. *"Adé orí ọ̀kín kò lè ṣe déédé orí ẹyẹkẹ́,"* she repeated over and over. *"The crest on the head of the peacock simply won't fit any other bird. The crest on the head of the peacock simply won't fit any other bird."*

"Okay, Mom. No offense. But I would really appreciate it if you *never* did that again."

Mom didn't listen, of course. Instead, rushing over to TJ and smothering him in a warm embrace. "Jalen! Tunde! Come in here! TJ's awake! He's finally awake!"

"Yeah, who would have thought... saving a few Orishas from a cosmic realm takes a few months' recharge." Before Mom could scold him for his poorly-timed humor, a pounding of feet echoed off the hall outside. Dad was the first one to get to the door. There was sleep in his eyes and what looked like a recent stain on his shirt, but it didn't diminish his goatee-framed smile.

"Son!" He rushed up to TJ, hugging him as well. "I can't tell you how good it is to see you. Way to fight through!"

Tunde came in last, along with Simba, the latter of which tackled TJ's chest and licked him in the face.

"Hey, Simba, no fair!" He tried to avoid the lick attack but his arms were still a bit sluggish at the call of Oya's Wind, and he didn't have a good handle on how to move his torso with magic yet. "Anyone going to tell me what I'm doing here? Last time I woke up, I was in a hospital bed. And," he nodded to the article from *Divination Today*, "apparently I'm supposed to be in Babalu-Aye?"

That brought a heavy silence to the room. Smiles were traded for frowns; warm embraces for uncomfortable distances.

Tunde lifted his dreadlocked bangs from his face. "Uh... so...

Mom, you should get on a bowl with Adeyemi and let her know about TJ, right? And, Dad, maybe you call Grandma and let her know the news as well? I'll catch TJ up."

"Good idea, son," Dad said, making his way out of the room with a near skip.

"You stay right where you are, honey bunny." Mom kissed TJ on the forehead.

"Can't really go anywhere until I figure out how to lift my spine," TJ joked.

As soon as Mom closed the door, TJ turned on Tunde with knitted brows. "That was hella weird. What's going on?"

"Yeah... um... Mom and Dad have been fighting. Like, a lot, a lot. And I don't mean their usual fighting. Ever since your body came back from the other side, Dad's been pissed off. That's the reason you're in your bedroom. After you were stable, he said he didn't want you anywhere near Nigeria. He put his foot down and everything, and I've never seen Mom back down to him before. It feels... wrong. Glad you're back. It's been awkward as hell."

The idea of Mom and Dad fighting about TJ made his chest tighten. He'd always seen them as a united front, even in their disagreements. Now, it seemed he had become the source of division.

Tunde shifted uncomfortably, glancing at the door to make sure their parents were out of earshot. "It's more than just them fighting. Mom's... well, she's kind of gone overboard."

TJ raised an eyebrow. "What do you mean?"

Tunde sighed, running his hand through his messy locs. "Mom's become almost embarrassingly proud of you being an Orisha. She's practically the head of this... group that worships you..."

"Worships me!?" TJ echoed, eyebrows hiking up his forehead. The image of his mom prostrating on the floor flashed through his mind, her fervent recitation of a prayer she'd made up for him. He shuddered.

"Yeah..." Tunde continued. "She's been really protective too, like she wants to make all the decisions for you. Loads of reporters and UCMP requests have come through, and she's been stepping in and making sure everything goes through her first."

"That's... weird and uncomfortable," TJ said.

"Tell me about it. But that's not all." Tunde leaned in close and lowered his voice. "I've been getting messages that I've kept from Mom and Dad."

"What kind of messages?" TJ asked, a knot forming in his stomach.

Tunde reached into his pocket and pulled out TJ's phone, handing it over carefully. "I've been safeguarding your phone this whole time. Mostly to block a bunch of trolls tryin' to get at you."

Tunde lifted TJ's phone to see. The screen lit up with a barrage of missed calls and messages.

"There was one weird message from this... Sister Bisi a few days after you got into Babalu-Aye," Tunde said cautiously. "You know who that is, right?"

"She's a hard one to forget," TJ said as the woman's fanged grimace came to mind. "She's the new Olugbala of the Keepers."

TJ's eyes widened as he read the message.

CRAZY KEEPER LADY / (SISTER BISI MAYBE?):

I never believed you could do it—save Shango and Oya—but I can admit when I'm wrong. When you're ready to learn your full potential, you come to us. Just like Ifedayo came to us. Just like that traitor Bolawe wanted. We'll be watching you. As always.

TJ groaned inwardly. The Keepers were the least of his worries these days, but they would still be a problem. TJ nodded slowly to his brother, absorbing the information. The world outside his room felt even more complicated and dangerous than he'd realized. And now, with all these new burdens on his shoulders, he couldn't afford to falter again.

Tunde placed a reassuring hand on TJ's arm. "How are you feeling though, bro? Do you feel different now that you're an Orisha and all that?"

"Yeah, very." TJ lifted his arm with Oya's Wind. He could usually control his hand and fingers, but he only lifted his forearm, making it look like dead weight to prove a point. "In the Mortal Realm, with this mortal body, things are totally awesome."

"Yeah... being the hero sucks, doesn't it?"

"It really does. Can't believe I ever wanted what Dayo had. Trust me, you got it good just being a regular diviner kid."

"Yeah, maybe…" Tunde brought his legs up on the bed, crossing them. "The next few days are gonna be *crazy*. You ready for that?"

TJ settled his head back into his pillow and groaned. "Bro, I'm never ready for any of this. Ever."

## 71

# OLD FACES, NEW STORIES

TJ WAS GLAD HE HAD A CHOICE IN WHO HE WANTED TO VISIT HIM the next day. And it wasn't a hard decision. Besides his family, he wanted to see Manny and Ayo in the flesh. It had been nearly half a year since he saw them properly. Not in the middle of a battle with shadows or racing across rooms of ice. But in the real physical world where they could actually retain their memories.

His friends arrived at the same time, helped along by a fire portal from Manny's New York apartment to TJ's living room. Manny gave TJ a huge kiss on the cheek; Ayo messed up TJ's hair after attempting a hug that was too painful for TJ. They both looked a bit different. Manny's face was a little longer, a little older, the baby fat in her cheeks nearly all gone. And her arms—which were already big to begin with—rivaled Miss Gravés' tree trunk arms. Ayo had grown an inch or two as well. Still shorter than TJ and Manny, but more height than he'd had before.

TJ wondered what he looked like. Had he finally grown a mustache? Were his eyes still the same? He had been stuck to his bed until he figured out how to get his body working again, and he hadn't gotten around to asking for a mirror. But those brief thoughts were soon forgotten as Ayo signed, "God damn, what has your family been doing with your hair, man!?" He snapped his fingers, then signed, "*Wa ṣi mi,*" and some clippers manifested in the middle of the room.

The friends fell right into their regular rhythm of conversation as Ayo cut TJ's hair. Manny and Ayo hadn't lost their memories this time around. Something about the Court of All working different from the Orisha Planes. Still, their memories weren't perfect, and TJ restating what had occurred had helped them solidify what was there just at the edge.

"So, they really think I'm some kind of god now?" TJ said, scratching his head. "I mean, shrines and prostrations?"

Manny snorted. "Yep, people are losing their minds. I saw a dude on Evo claim you're the second coming of Olodumare."

"That's all I need—more pressure."

The clippers buzzed as Ayo continued trimming TJ's hair. Manny sprawled out on TJ's bed, flipping through one of the books on Yoruba cosmology someone had sent him.

Ayo dropped his clippers to sign to TJ. "A lot of folks think you'll bring Orunmila back too. Now that we know for sure that..."

*That Orunmila is gone.*

"And... your dad..." TJ said cautiously. "His body... did it... did he..."

Ayo frowned, which prompted Manny to move over and rub his back. "Nah... he didn't come back when we got back."

TJ's throat went dry. "Sorry, man... I really am. He saved our lives though..."

"Yeah," Ayo signed sadly. "He did. Don't trip, I'm getting through it."

A long silence followed, punctured only by Ayo turning his clippers back on, and the sound of Manny flipping through more books given to TJ.

"What about the God Eaters?" TJ asked after a while. "Are they coming or what?"

Manny's smile faded too. "They're still in the End Realm looking for cracks. But they are slithering into some of the planes, the ones that directly border the Mortal Realm. The clouded don't know anything at all though. Everyone's speculating when they'll show up again. There's been a bunch of stories coming out all over the place. Other people like us from other magic groups. Like Freya and her girlfriend."

TJ peered over to the letter Freya sent, which brought a small smile from him. Once he got back on his feet, he'd make sure to get on a bowl with her. See if he could guilt someone from the UCMP to get her a portal here.

"Some shit went down in Mexico with these two teenage disciples over there," Ayo added. "And remember I told you I knew some people at Greystone Academy? They interviewed me about Thor, and apparently they had some *wild* stuff going on over there with a few of their students."

"It's happening everywhere." Manny closed another book, rested it on her lap, and grabbed TJ's hand. "All the pantheons across the world are coming together. Reporting to one another. Putting up defenses. But..."

TJ waited for her response but it didn't come, so he said, "But what...?"

"Since the Court of All is gone," Ayo signed in place of Manny's silence. "It basically reduced the amount of time we have to get ready. According to Oshosi, we had centuries before. Now, at the most, we have decades."

"Less than that, depending on which pantheon you ask," Manny said. "There's this one Jewish guy named Simon doing all these interviews. He says we only have a few *years* left."

"And what happens after that?" TJ asked.

"War," Manny answered.

A familiar phantom brush came at the back of TJ's neck. Deep within, a whisper stirred. He could almost recall the presence of the Sovereign One. TJ wasn't sure a war with the God Eaters could even be called that. It would more likely be annihilation. Would he be ready for that in a few years? Would he ever be able to go to a university? Have a family? Grow old? Would anyone?

Ayo nodded and signed, "The Elders are saying we need to be ready for anything. They've been training us harder than ever. You should see Greystone. It was already unorthodox. Brutal. But they basically a whole-ass military academy now."

TJ looked out the window at the clear blue sky, a pang of guilt hitting for not being able to help more. He wondered if Ifa Academy's curriculum would be changed as well. "And what about the Court of All? Any fallout from that?"

"There's been a lot of backlash," Manny said. "Some gods are pissed at how things went down. Others are just confused."

"And divinerkind?" TJ asked.

Ayo paused his haircutting to sign, "Mixed feelings. Some think you did great; others think you stirred up more trouble."

TJ sighed lightly, careful not to disrupt Ayo's work. If there was one good thing about having a stiff body, it was that he was the perfect subject for a haircut. "It's not like I planned any of it." Ayo finished up TJ's hair and stepped back to admire his work. "I guess it's just… a lot," TJ finished quietly.

Manny put down her book and sat up on the bed. "We're here for you, no matter what happens next."

The sun rose higher in the sky as they talked about their future plans and reminisced about their time at Ifa Academy and what Manny and Ayo had been up to for the last few months of term. Hours seemed to pass in what felt like minutes.

"So, how did you guys get to me to begin with…" TJ ended up asking.

"Eshu sort of explained it like this…" Manny began. "Everybody had to get their stuff together and vibe with each other before they could even *think* about reaching you. Eshu set it up, trapping you in that cell so we'd have a straight shot to connect."

Another plan of Eshu's? TJ's forehead wrinkled.

"Pulling you straight into the Court of All would get the jailbreak done without tipping off the Courts," Manny explained. "After Oshosi got locked up, and it felt like the ancestral paths were breaking down 'cause of all the drama between me, my aunt, Ayo, and his dad, we didn't have many moves left. Eshu had to come up with a way to sneak you in without the Courts catching on. Plus, with them being the ones moving you there, Eshu could play it like he was helping them out." She gestured to his wall of constellations as though it were a map of the End Realm. "He knew they would bring you straight into the prison where we needed you."

TJ sighed through his nose. "I still don't get it. If I wasn't on the other side to empower you all. How was everyone there? How did y'all fall from Oya's and Shango's chest like that? How did Eshu and my mom squeeze through *my* chest?"

Ayo took over then, signing. "So, after you broke it down for

Shango and Oya—that they were basically stuck in a never-ending war to keep their power—Eshu figured out what was going on. When we did that big prayer, it broke through to him. He said your power to help and lift people up would be the key. Like, it could open a way to sneak everyone into the Court of All without getting caught." Ayo paced around the bed frame, going to the window to let some air in. "But for Eshu's plan to work, you had to think you got played. Kinda like what we pulled at those crossover tryouts with Manny last year."

TJ and Manny exchanged awkward glances. Heat rose in TJ's ears at the memory.

"If you were in on it," Ayo explained through his signs, "the magic wouldn't have even hit right. Plus… Eshu said you ain't got the best poker face. Themis would've seen straight through his plan. And her and the other judges didn't—or couldn't—figure out how your power really works. But Eshu? He knew. He knew it'd all come together."

"Really?" TJ gave him a look, incredulous. "He knew? 100%?"

Manny laughed lightly. "Well, at least 80% sure, he likes to remind us. Those are very good odds where cosmic matters are concerned, according to him."

"'A-A-Anyone would tell you the same,'" Ayo mocked Eshu with a near-perfect imitation—were it not for the stutter.

"Freya was wondering, by the way," Manny said. "The charm… the Celtic charm she had that you used on your staff. Was that you… like… was that you calling to us?"

TJ frowned. His thoughts flickered back to that hazy, in-between place—the endless ocean, the dim gateway, the shifting faces of his ancestors. All those other Tomori Jomilojus. Then a memory of cold rushed over him. A biting frost that wasn't from the End Realm or the Court of All. No—he had *felt* it before, pressing into his thoughts, searching.

"The charm…" he murmured. His fingers twitched, phantom cold spreading over them. He *had* reached for something. Not Orisha magic. Something else.

Then, the memories *hit* him, stacking like dominos: The charm frosting over. TJ calling out to Bolawe when Manny was about to call to him with her mirror. The Oracle Rock tent—the way Ruby's systems went haywire… because…

"It was me," TJ whispered.

Manny and Ayo exchanged glances, saying, "What was you?"

"The mirror. When you tried to call Bolawe, he answered before you even said his name, right?"

Manny frowned. "Yeah, but that was just weird mirror stuff—"

"No. It wasn't. That was *me* too."

Silence.

Ayo was the first to break it, signing slowly. "You're saying… you were reaching out the whole time? Watching us?"

TJ swallowed. "I don't know if 'watching' is the right way to describe it. It was more like just… 'being,' if that makes sense."

Manny shook her head, her Afro curls slapping her cheeks. "There's still a whole lot to learn about what you got going on, Teej."

TJ watched Manny closely, her expression shifting as if she were piecing together a puzzle. Her eyes widened slightly, and her lips parted as if to speak but hesitated. Manny turned to Ayo, saying, "Oh, Ayo, so that's why you tried to… uh… you know. In Ruby's tent…"

Ayo's cheeks purpled, touching his lips. "Oh, yeah… uh… that makes sense."

A jolt of recognition shot through TJ.

"That was me…" TJ breathed out. He ran a hand over his face and sighed. "Um… can we all pretend that never happened? And… I'm sorry. I really didn't mean to make y'all go through that awkwardness."

Ayo and Manny groaned in unison, and just like that, the tension broke into laughter.

"Deal," Manny and Ayo said at the same time.

Birdsong filtered through the open window. The air felt fresh on TJ's skin. It must've been a perfect summer's day outside.

"Oh, I almost forgot," Ayo signed, pulling out a crumpled piece of paper. "You left this behind."

TJ took it and read it:

1. ~~Gotta figure out how to reverse this channeling thing by dreamwalking with Obatala and Oshosi.~~

2. ~~Open up the ancestral path from Yemoja to Oya through the Frost Realm for Manny.~~

3. ~~Unlock ancestral path from Ogun to Shango using Ayo's Norse ring.~~

~~3b. Figure out how to get ring back from Ayo's dad~~ (with his consent)

4. ~~Complete my staff to sustain the ancestral path ritual to the Court of All jail cell.~~

5. ~~Save Shango and Oya on The Hero's Equinox.~~

6. Don't die.

"I crossed out that fifth line for you," Ayo signed. "But I wasn't sure about that last one. The way the Orishas are telling it you did sorta…"

TJ stared at the last line. He was on the edge, but he was still here, right? Using Oya's Wind, he floated a pen from one of the cards near his end table. Then he struck a line through the last line, jagged and cruel.

~~6. Don't die.~~

TJ let out a deep breath. That felt right, even with his body half-dead. "Let's just run away together," TJ said suddenly. "All three of us. Let's just pack up and road trip across the country or something."

Manny and Ayo looked at each other, then at TJ with questioning eyes. It was a sudden thought. A genuine one. But it was one that TJ's friends didn't seem to know how to respond to. So TJ added a quick, "Just kidding." But it was too late. His friends knew the truth of it. He could tell how Manny swallowed hard and Ayo scratched the side of his braids.

"Yeah…" Manny said, placing her hand on TJ's shoulder.

"Yeah, why not? You can get your license now. It's just…" She did her best not to let her eyes fall on TJ's lifeless arms and chest, but the damage was already done in her pause. "Yeah… that's a good idea, Teej." Her words were too somber for TJ's liking.

There was a knock on the door. Mom entered, her face lighting up when she saw them all together.

"Tomori," she said warmly, "you have new visitors."

"Who?" TJ asked, glad for the awkwardness to pass on between his friends.

"Shango and Oya."

# 72

# ASHE

TJ WOULD HAVE DUG IN HIS EARS IF IT DIDN'T TAKE SO MUCH effort. Perhaps he hadn't heard Mom correctly. But the image of Shango and Oya waiting in his living room stirred in his mind.

"We're gonna talk to them through a portal or something?" he asked.

"No," Manny said as she stood up from the bed. "That's another thing we forgot to tell you."

"Oh, yeah," Ayo signed. "You're in for a surprise."

"When you get done with everything, hit us up!" Manny said. "We convinced our families to let us stay in Los Angeles this summer. We're staying at Ayo's vacation condo. Me and my family. And we'll talk more about that road trip, a'ight?"

As Manny and Ayo left, Mom gave TJ a look. "What did she mean by 'road trip', eh?"

TJ took in a deep breath. "It's nothin', Mom. We was just talkin'."

Mom didn't look wholly convinced as two unfamiliar people walked into TJ's bedroom—a middle-aged man and a woman he didn't recognize but felt he should know.

The man had a familiar bald head and a thick beard that was trimmed and shaped to a point. He wore a red dress shirt with black rolled-up cuffs that barely contained his muscled physique.

The woman next to him had a severe expression. The sides of her head were shaved and four rows of braids lined the center of her dome. Like her partner, she wore a purple shirt that had a hard time containing her muscles.

"Shango? Oya?"

"Hello there, brother." Shango nodded.

Oya gave him a small bow. "Good to see you well."

TJ sat up straighter, a strange mix of awe and disbelief rising as he looked at Shango and Oya standing in his bedroom.

"We're going to be teachers at Ifa Academy next year," Shango said, crossing his large arms. "Like many other Orishas who have come over."

"How?" TJ asked. "How do you have mortal bodies?"

"Obatala fashioned them for us," Oya explained, her severe expression softening slightly. "He's quite the craftsman."

TJ's mind flashed back to Camp Olosa. He remembered Eshu—or Joshua, as he was known then—taking on a mortal form. The Trickster had kept everyone on their toes with his pranks and jokes, but TJ had always felt a strange kinship with the boy he once knew. Missed him even.

"Tomori Jomiloju." Shango's voice broke through TJ's memory. "We're not just here to talk about Ifa Academy. We know you'll be meeting a lot of people today."

TJ groaned internally at that. He hoped he could have some breaks between visitors.

Oya stepped forward, holding out a piece of cloth. It was deep burgundy, almost shimmering with an ethereal glow. Yoruba text was etched in gold throughout its fabric. TJ almost rolled his eyes when he realized it was the peacock proverb from Mom. But the sheer beauty of the enchanted clothing took his breath away. Ashe saturated the thing like it was soaked in magic.

"This is for you," Oya said, her eyes intense but kind.

TJ reached out to touch it, feeling the Ashe practically radiate off the fabric. The cloth seemed alive, casting off sparks of energy that danced like fireflies around his fingers.

"It's enchanted with our magic," Shango said. "It will help you recover the strength in your upper body. You've just got to wrap it under your clothes before your day starts."

"We understand that you've been using my wind all year to move your arms. It'll be more difficult controlling your torso as well. So this should help quell the burden. It took us longer than we would have liked. But we managed it. Our own power still needs time to restore."

"You deserve it, brother. Heroes get remembered, but," Shango jabbed his large finger into TJ's chest lightly, "legends like you? Legends never die."

"Has my dad got you watching *The Sandlot*?" TJ asked, recognizing the quote.

Shango shrugged. "There is a lot of human art I need to catch up on. It's a good movie. A lot of those sports movies are, and your baba has good taste."

"Thank you," TJ said, his voice choked as he clutched the cloth to his chest. Already he could feel chest muscles he'd forgotten how to move properly.

Shango waved off his thanks with a dismissive hand. "No need to thank us. We should be thanking *you* for what you did."

After a moment, trying to steady his voice, TJ asked, "How's Oshosi?"

"Keeping an eye on the Terra Realm."

Oya smirked. "Trying to convince Ogun to cross over to the Mortal Realm, more like. But that Orisha is too stubborn to leave his work for the Great Monarch."

"And Eshu?" TJ questioned, just as the door creaked open.

A teenage boy walked into the room. He was noticeably overweight but carried himself with a confidence that made it clear he was comfortable in his skin. His face beamed with a jovial expression that was unmistakable. TJ never thought he'd see the familiar face again.

"It's not an exact copy of our old friend Josh," Eshu said with the youthful voice of the boy TJ never thought he'd hear again, "but it's pretty close, don't you think?"

A rush of warmth flooded through TJ as he took in Eshu's familiar presence, now in this old yet new form. Eshu swaggered into the room, filling the space with a mischievous energy only he could command so nonchalantly. He looked down at TJ with a grin, then rubbed his stomach theatrically. "Obatala got the face right, and the shape right, but he screwed up on one very important thing. Turns out, this body has a gluten allergy. Can you believe that? I can't eat *anything*! I don't know how you humans do it."

TJ chuckled despite himself, shaking his head. "Yeah, that's rough. No bread, no pizza..."

"No pizza!?" Eshu exclaimed, feigning a dramatic swoon. "It's a tragedy."

Shango and Oya shared an amused glance but remained silent, letting Eshu continue. The Trickster settled into a chair beside TJ's bed, his expression turning more serious. "I don't know what these two told you, but a lot of Orishas are back in the Mortal Realm."

"But I thought Olodumare told you to maintain the separation until They get back?"

"True. But the Orishas still can't come back in their full forms. That's why they have to pass through human bodies for the time being. Until the Great Monarch returns to us."

TJ's mind raced with the implications. The world was changing faster than he could keep up with. "Themis? Any sign of her?"

Eshu shook his head. "No."

Then TJ remembered something else. "And Olokun? Before I got out of there, he showed up. He was fighting that big God Eater."

The Orishas looked to each other knowingly. They didn't have to answer. He must've been gone too. For a moment, the room seemed to shrink under the weight of everything unsaid. TJ clenched the cloth in his hands, grounding himself as the reality of their losses sank in. It felt like every time he grasped one answer, ten more questions rose to take its place.

"I know you have many questions, but we have a question for you, brother," Josh said. "It may seem odd, but there is a point. What is Ashe?"

TJ blinked, caught off guard by the sudden shift in topic. He took a deep breath and gave the textbook answer that had been drilled into him at Ifa Academy. "Ashe is the divine energy or life force that pervades all things in the universe. It's what gives everything its power to exist and change."

Eshu nodded thoughtfully. "As far as we can see," he said

slowly, choosing his words carefully, "you are a manifestation of Ashe itself. Perhaps a new intermediary between the Lost Monarch and diviners. Or perhaps between the Lost Monarch and the Orishas."

TJ frowned. "Isn't that *your* job? Aren't you the space between the divine and the Earth?"

"Yes," Eshu replied, his gaze steady and serious. "But I do not have direct control over Ashe as you do. That's a power not seen since The Great Monarch went away." He leaned forward, eyes locking onto TJ's with an intensity that made TJ's heart pound faster. "When you get healthy again, your next task will be to find Them. Fulfill that prophecy you diviners keep going on about. Speaking of which..." Eshu threw up five fingers and then started counting down. When his hand became a fist, there was another knock on the door.

"TJ, is it okay to come in?"

"Oracle Ruby?"

She pushed the door in to reveal her green-tipped dreadlocks and smiling face. "Just Ruby these days, I'm afraid." She opened the door fully and walked in with a water bowl. Behind her was Elder Adeyemi, who practically glided into the room. Like Mom the night before, she prostrated fully to TJ, her elaborate gown shimmering under the afternoon light. This robe depicted an ocean with catfish actively jumping in and out of the water.

Ruby and Elder Adeyemi stepped forward, their faces alight with genuine joy at seeing TJ up and about.

"It's so good to see you doing well, love," Ruby said warmly, her British accent softening her words. "We've all been mad with worry."

Elder Adeyemi nodded, her eyes filled with pride. "You've done more than we could have ever hoped for, TJ. We're incredibly proud of, and grateful for, your courage and strength."

A warmth spread through TJ's chest at their words. "Thank you."

Shango clapped TJ on the shoulder, nearly knocking him off balance. "Well, we'll leave you to your business now, brother."

Oya gave TJ a reassuring nod. "We'll see you soon enough."

Eshu grinned mischievously. "And I'll be on the lookout for a gluten-free pizza joint on the way."

As the Orishas left, their presence seemed to linger in the room like an echo of thunder after a storm. The room felt both emptier and heavier without them. The atmosphere shifted as the conversation turned serious.

A question dawned on TJ. "Wait… what about Bolawe? What happened with him?"

A smile wrinkled in Adeyemi's cheek. "I told you I had plans for him, didn't I?" She withdrew a mirror from her robes. The same mirror Manny had all year. Only it was different now. Frosted. When she flipped the front to TJ, Bolawe was there, frozen in place.

"Is he…" TJ started to say. "Dead?"

"No," the Elder explained. "He's just confined to the portion of the Mirror Realm he was in at the time of Operation Stormbreak. Thanks to you, I had the idea of locking him in place there… with the help of Tore Stadheim."

"Good," TJ said. Happy to know Bolawe was imprisoned like he should be.

Elder Adeyemi placed the mirror back into her robes as the conversation changed.

"There have been numerous memorials," Ruby said softly. "For Orunmila, Thor, Yamaraja… All of them low key. Private. The Ritual of Remembrance for Orunmila was particularly moving." She paused. "I… and many others who called Orunmila our primary head can't read the future anymore. Not through Ifa divination."

A heavy silence filled the room before Elder Adeyemi spoke up. "Ruby, tell us about the prophecy again. Maybe TJ can help with that."

Ruby took a deep breath. "As you know, TJ, Orunmila gave us one final message—a divination of the Unseen Monarch's return. Though debated extensively, one thing is clear: A Promised Child will uncover the Unseen Monarch. Now with the God Eaters being so near… we were wondering… while you were out. Were you able to find anything?" She took a beat. "Anything about a promised child rising with the light of a dying, falling star, and the Lost Monarch returning? I figured the falling star might have been the Court of All itself."

"A falling star..." Elder Adeyemi murmured thoughtfully.

Something stirred within TJ. A faint memory tried to surface but remained elusive. He could only mumble out loud, "I'm the falling star... The falling star is me..."

Elder Adeyemi's eyes widened in recognition. "Those were the last words Dayo said before she died."

TJ struggled to grasp why those words were so significant but found himself unable to recall any further details. All he knew was that it felt important—crucially so.

"I don't remember why it matters," he admitted quietly, frustration evident in his tone. "But I know it does."

Elder Adeyemi straightened. "It's time to put our plans into motion, Mr. Young. We need to help you remember everything so that you can guide us in our next endeavors."

TJ frowned. "What do you mean by that? What plans?"

Adeyemi sighed softly, her gaze steady. "We need to consider revealing the existence of the magical world. If we can recruit more prayers, it will boost your strength immensely. Just like on the Hero's Equinox. Once we realize how much it can enhance your power, we knew what must be done. We need to extend the same support to the other pantheons before the Eaters come."

"But why didn't we do that before?" TJ asked, his brow furrowing. "Why didn't humanity always boost the Orishas with prayer?"

"The Great Separation is designed to keep humanity hidden from the God Eaters. Now that they know about us, that will likely have to change."

Ruby chimed in. "There will be a significant debate about whether to reveal the magical world. A major vote for the UCMP is needed. This would change everything. But are we ready for that? The mundanes might attack diviners and all other magic users outright. Out of fear. And then the prayers would never work at all. It would leave both magical and mundane in jeopardy."

TJ turned to Elder Adeyemi, his eyes searching hers for answers. "Will you vote 'yes' when the time comes?"

Adeyemi gave a small nod. "I'm the one proposing the amendment to the law in the first place. It's a very long process, but now is the time to start those steps."

Ruby sighed. "These things are issues for the future versions of ourselves. For now, I suggest we place our greatest efforts on finding the Lost Monarch. Are you ready for that, TJ?"

# EPILOGUE
## A CONFESSION LONG OVERDUE

LATER THAT NIGHT, AFTER A SERIES OF EXHAUSTING MEETINGS with UCMP officials, TJ felt like a battery being drained. He was naturally an introvert, so talking to so many people at once was a burden. First came Director Bakari, a stern-faced man with a penchant for detail. He questioned TJ about his experiences with the Court of All, scribbling notes with swift precision. "We need every detail, Mr. Young," he emphasized, leaning in closer. TJ did his best to answer, but when he stumbled over an explanation of his newfound powers, Mom stepped in.

"TJ needs his rest," she declared firmly, ushering Bakari out before he could protest.

Next was a young woman from the Magical Creatures Department. She bombarded TJ with questions about the God Eaters and their effect on magical fauna. Her wide eyes and rapid-fire inquiries left TJ's head spinning. Just as he was about to answer her query about kitsunes, Mom intervened again.

"That's enough for tonight," she said, steering the woman out gently but decisively.

Lastly, a reporter from *Divination Today* showed up, microphone in hand. He barely had time to ask questions for five minutes. Once he changed the subject about TJ's transformation into an Orisha, Mom cut him off.

"No more interviews tonight," she insisted. "My son needs sleep."

When the house finally settled into silence and darkness enveloped TJ's room, he lay in bed, eyes fluttering shut. Then he remembered something, a favor he asked of Elder Adeyemi. He wanted to speak to Bolawe one last time before his mirror got stored in Thornriver or wherever. The Elder had shown him how to unfreeze the mirror enough to talk to Bolawe but not allow him to escape. Intrigued, TJ used Oya's Wind to lift his hand and grasp the mirror.

The glass shimmered before him, solidifying into Bolawe's pore-ridden face. Patient eyes and a neutral expression stared back at TJ.

*"Hello, TJ,"* Bolawe greeted calmly. TJ did not respond. Instead scowling. *"You know, you could have told me you and Simisola were trying to pull a fast one."*

TJ didn't know how to feel upon seeing Bolawe. He'd gone from mentor to head Keeper and enemy number one to… whatever he was now. TJ blinked in surprise but composed himself quickly. "I'm glad she finally got you, glad you're paying for what you did."

*"Oh, I'm sure you are. And I'll live with my choices. How do you feel about being an Orisha?"*

TJ sighed heavily, glancing at the wall painting of Orishas glowing faintly in the dark room. "It's overwhelming. I still feel very much like a mortal on this side."

Bolawe's eyes softened slightly. *"I was the first to suggest you might be one, you'll recall. Back in the cafe during that summer. Remember? Everyone seems to agree now—even other Orishas."*

A mix of pride and anxiety churned within TJ as he gazed at the starfield mural on his wall depicting the Orishas in their celestial glory. The thought of being one of them was both surreal and burdensome.

*"What do you feel, TJ?"* Bolawe asked.

TJ winced at the lingering aches from his recent endeavors. "*Very* much like a mortal on this side," he repeated quietly.

Every strain and hurt from his ordeal weighed heavily on him—a stark contrast to the invulnerability he sometimes felt in the Ethereal Realms. He broke the silence with a question that had been gnawing at him. "So... you got yourself a life sentence in this thing?"

Bolawe shook his head slowly. *"That's what they say, but that won't hold. There is work that still needs to be done—on both our ends."* His gaze sharpened slightly. *"You still have your sister's journal, yes?"*

TJ looked around his cluttered room through the dim light but then snapped his fingers to summon Shango's Fire. A small flame lit up the space, revealing Dayo's journal beside the mirror.

"Yes..." TJ answered hesitantly as he picked it up.

*"Have you ever written anything in it before?"*

"No..." TJ admitted. "It feels wrong—it's my *sister's* journal."

*"Write in it now,"* Bolawe urged gently. *"Whatever comes to mind naturally—especially about the Promised Child."*

Skepticism clouded TJ's mind as he held onto the journal tightly. "Why?"

Bolawe's eyes glinted with something akin to knowing confidence. *"I've known your sister for a long while... Let's just say I have a hunch about something. Something that might explain the power within you."*

Doubt lingered within TJ as he pondered what might happen if he followed Bolawe's directions. But then—a whisper echoed softly in his ear, calling him to the journal.

Reluctantly, TJ pulled out a pen and began writing, unsure of what would come forth from within him. His hand moved seemingly on its own accord across the page. It wrote:

*I am the falling star; the falling star is me.*

He repeated it over and over until an entire page was filled with those words alone. Simba barked outside TJ's bedroom door, pawing at the door until it pushed in. He was old with weak knees, yet he leaped onto the bed, turning around in circles like he wanted a treat. Simba kept licking the mirror, and an unsettling realization dawned on TJ.

He no longer saw Bolawe staring back at him—but someone else entirely, someone who should not have been looking back at him...

It was Dayo's face. Not his own face. But her's.

Okay... not Dayo's face.

*My* face.

There's something I need to confess to you here. I've only been telling you half the story so far.

Let me introduce myself properly for the first time. I am Ifedayo Oluwamakinwa Young, and this has been the story I've been telling you. I thought I could go this whole time without revealing that, that my part in this was done already. Sorry, I've been a bit coy. I'm also a little frazzled.

Because right now I'm about to reveal to my brother, my sweet, perfect baby brother that we have finally reconnected.

But how in the world am I supposed to do that?

*What happens when a deity must forge an unbreakable seal?*
*They seek an unshakable bond, of course.*

Discover the story of how Ogun and Oshun failed the Mountain Dwellers and the River People in a time when the Orishas walked among mortals, a journey that directly affect the events of TJ Young Book 4, *The Lovers' Curse*.

visit this link and read the story:
antoinebandele.com/book-page-a-love-cast-in-iron

**What does it take to break an unbreakable curse?**
**You start with love, and hope it's enough.**

TJ Young thought his biggest battles were behind him—stopping a god-devouring force from reaching the mortal realm, uncovering the mystery behind his sister's death, and proving he belonged at Ifa Academy, the most prestigious magic school in West Africa. But when an ancient curse tied to the Orishas of Love and War threatens to unravel the academy's very foundation, TJ and his girlfriend, Manny, are thrown into a trial neither of them saw coming.

The catch? The only way to break the curse is through a true act of love.

With the clock ticking, TJ throws himself into finding answers. But

Manny is hiding a secret—one that could shatter everything they thought they knew about their relationship. And while TJ wrestles with his growing connection to his sister's restless spirit, the Keepers—a rogue faction of diviners—are closing in, leaving a trail of bodies in their wake.

To save Ifa Academy, TJ and Manny must uncover the truth behind the curse before it's too late. But love—real love—isn't as simple as they once believed. And the price of breaking the curse may be letting go of each other for good.

**Dive into this next installment of young adult fantasy based on the mythology of West Africa, where TJ will face fractured relationships, brutal revenge, and the ancient secrets of the Orishas.**

## ALSO BY ANTOINE BANDELE

**TJ YOUNG & THE ORISHAS**

The Gatekeeper's Staff

The Windweaver's Storm

The Hero's Equinox

The Lovers' Curse

**ORISHAS AMONG MORTALS**

Will of the Mischief Maker

When the Wind Speaks

An Axe for a Hammer

A Love Cast in Iron

Where the River Breaks

**TALES FROM ESOWON**

The Kishi

**THE SKY PIRATE CHRONICLES**

By Sea & Sky

Of Ruin & Silk

**LOST TALES FROM ESOWON**

Last of My Kind

Stoneskin

**CHILDREN'S BOOKS**

Mythology & Me

**COLLECTIONS**

TJ Young & The Orishas - Collection 1

Orishas Among Mortals - Collection 1

**ANTHOLOGIES**

Demons, Monks, & Lovers

The Chronicles of Underrealm

Tales from the Otherworlds

Spacefunk

## ABOUT THE AUTHOR

Antoine lives in Los Angeles, CA
with his partner and cat. He is a YouTuber,
producing work for his channel "Antoine Bandele".

He is also an audiobook engineer and publisher.

Whenever he has the time, he's writing books inspired by African folklore, mythology, and history.

antoinebandele.com

*To my beta readers:*

*Andrea M, Brian Letang, Chantis Riddle, Chu Xue Ying, Jewel Scott, Mary R. Lanni, Jordan Fortuin, Matthew Fortuin, Roe R. Adams III, and Tatianna Kaha-Samonte*

*To my proof readers:*
*Sherry Willis Burch, Sequoia L.D., and Ken Pham*

*Thank you for your time and dedication to this project.*
*The story wouldn't be what it is without you delightful diviners.*

# GLOSSARY

- **Adinkra:** visual symbols originating from the Akan people of Ghana, each carrying specific meanings related to proverbs, concepts, or historical events, often used in textiles, pottery, and artwork to convey messages of wisdom, cultural values, and philosophical reflections.
- **Aganju:** a warrior spirit or a figure connected to natural elements like forests and mountains, playing a role in the spiritual and cultural traditions of the Yoruba people.
- **Àgbádà:** a Yoruba tunic.
- **Agege:** a district in Lagos, Nigeria, known for its vibrant markets, cultural diversity, and historic significance, as well as for being the origin of the popular **Agege bread**, a soft, fluffy loaf that is a staple in Nigerian cuisine.
- **Akara:** also known as black-eyed peas fritters, beans fritters, or Acaraje. A very delicious, deep-fried bean cake made from black-eyed pea paste.
- **Algaita:** a double reed wind instrument from West Africa, especially among the Hausa and Kanuri peoples.
- **Anansi:** a legendary trickster figure from the folklore of the Akan people of Ghana, often depicted as a spider, renowned for his cleverness and storytelling, which serve to impart moral lessons and cultural wisdom

- **Ashe:** a Yoruba philosophical concept through which the power to make things happen or produce change is conceived. Within the diviner community, it is known as the source of magic.
- **Asgardian:** the inhabitants of Asgard, the celestial realm of the Aesir gods in Norse mythology, known for their divine power and influence over the cosmos.
- **Àtúnwáyé:** in Yoruba belief, refers to the concept of reincarnation, where a soul returns to the physical world in a new body, often continuing familial or spiritual legacies across generations.
- **Aṣọ òké:** a narrow strip-weaving technique and a variety of Yoruban fabric often incorporated into formal wear.
- **Aziza:** fae creatures who once provided early hunters with magic. They are also known to have given practical and spiritual knowledge to people (including knowledge of the use of fire).
- **Bàbá-àgbà:** in Yoruba culture, refers to a revered elder or patriarch, often seen as a source of wisdom, guidance, and leadership within the family or community.
- **Bàbálàwò:** a priest of Ifa, also known as the Shepard of Mysteries.
- **Babalu-Aye:** the Healer Orisha, characterized as a protector from death, disease, and cemeteries, but also a contributor of those aspects of life.
- **Baldr:** in Norse mythology, is the god of light, purity, and beauty, beloved by the gods and humans alike, whose death, caused by Loki's deception, is a pivotal event leading to the prophesied Ragnarök.
- **Bruxa:** the Portuguese word for "witch."
- **Bùbá:** a Yoruba blouse or top.
- **Cailleach:** a Celtic mythological figure, often depicted as an ancient hag or goddess associated with winter, storms, the changing of seasons, and the shaping of the natural landscape.
- **Cara:** the Portuguese word for "guy."
- **Clouded:** a term used to described those of non-magical lineage within the diviner community.

- **Chambelán:** in Latin American traditions, particularly in quinceañeras, refers to a male escort or attendant who accompanies the quinceañera, symbolizing a supportive and honorable role in the celebration of her transition into womanhood.
- **Damas:** a Spanish word that translates to "ladies" in English, often used to refer to women in a formal or respectful context.
- **Djambe:** a West African goblet-shaped drum played with bare hands, known for its rich tonal range and central role in traditional and contemporary African music.
- **Heka:** the Egyptian deity of Creation, also the rough translation of the word "magic."
- **Ibeji:** the Twin Orishas, characterized as rambunctious, childlike spirits that are full of youthful fun.
- **Ijọba Ipari:** the Yoruba phrase for the "End Realm", an ethereal plane outside of conventional space and time, which houses the Great War against the God Eaters.
- **Ìlẹ̀kẹ:** spiritual beads often worn at the neck by devotees of Ifa.
- **Impundulu:** a mythical bird associated with witchcraft, frequently manifested as the secretary bird, also known as a lightning bird.
- **Iroko:** a large hardwood tree from the west coast of tropical Africa that can live up to 500 years.
- **Irukè:** a traditional Yoruba ceremonial object made from a horse's tail, often decorated with beads or cowrie shells, and used by kings, chiefs, or priests as a symbol of authority, power, and spiritual significance during rituals and ceremonies.
- **Eko Atlantic:** officially Nigeria International Commerce city, also known as Eko Atlantic City, is a planned city of Lagos State, Nigeria, being constructed on land reclaimed from the Atlantic Ocean.
- **Ẹmi:** the Yoruba word for "spirit," also the class title for spiritual guidance at Camp Olosa.
- **Ere Idaraya:** the Yoruba word for "exercise," also the

class title for physical training at Camp Olosa and Ifa Academy.

- **Eshu:** the messenger for all Orishas. The Orisha of trickery, crossroads, misfortune, chaos, and death.
- **Ètùtù:** Yoruba ritual in light of propitiatory performances for the Orishas.
- **Evo:** short for "Evocation." An unlisted search engine used by underground diviners for news not savory enough for most publications.
- **Fìlà:** a Yoruba cap.
- **Forseti:** in Norse mythology, is the god of justice, mediation, and reconciliation, known for his wisdom and fairness in resolving disputes, and is said to preside over a radiant hall called Glitnir, where he arbitrates conflicts among gods and men.
- **Futebol:** the Portuguese word for "soccer."
- **Futhark:** refers to the runic alphabets used by Germanic peoples, named after the first six runes (F, U, Þ, A, R, K), with the Elder Futhark being the oldest and most widely known, consisting of 24 characters used for writing, divination, and symbolic purposes.
- **Garri:** a creamy granular flour obtained by processing the starchy tuberous roots of freshly harvested cassava.
- **Gèlé:** a Yoruba head tie.
- ***Gleipnir:*** the magical, unbreakable chain in Norse mythology that was used to bind the monstrous wolf Fenrir, crafted by dwarves from six impossible materials, including the sound of a cat's footsteps and the roots of a mountain.
- **Greystone:** a magical academy for rune casters who reside in the Scandinavian mountains.
- **Hel:** in Norse mythology, is the goddess of the underworld and ruler of a realm called Helheim, where she oversees the souls of those who did not die gloriously in battle, often depicted as a figure with a dual appearance—half living and half corpse-like.
- **Helheim:** in Norse mythology, is the realm of the dead ruled by the goddess Hel, where those who die of old

age, illness, or other non-heroic means reside, located in the depths of Niflheim and characterized as a cold, desolate place.

- **Ìdẹ:** spiritual beads often worn at the wrist by devotees of Ifa.
- **Ifa:** the name for the system of divination practiced by diviners and devotees. Also the name of the academy for magical students under the guidance of the Orishas.
- **Ile-Ife:** the original city, the homeland of diviners, which in modern times has been moved to New Ile-Ife near Omo Reserve.
- **Inari:** a revered Shinto deity associated with rice, fertility, prosperity, and foxes, often depicted as a androgynous or multi-gendered figure, with kitsune serving as their sacred messengers.
- **Irenku:** in Yoruba funeral tradition, this is the final day of observance, often coupled with a small parade for the dead.
- **Ìrènókú:** in Yoruba funeral tradition, this is a day set for games.
- **Ìró:** a Yoruba wrap-around skirt.
- **Ìtàóku:** in Yoruba funeral tradition, this is the day relegated to feasting and celebration of life.
- **Itis:** African American slang meaning the drowsy sleeping feeling one gets after a significant meal, often after Thanksgiving.
- **Itako:** blind women who train to become spiritual mediums in Japan.
- **Ìyá:** the Yoruba word for "mother."
- **Ìyá Àgbá:** the Yoruba word for "grandmother."
- **Jörmungandr:** also known as the Midgard Serpent in Norse mythology, is a giant sea serpent and one of Loki's children, destined to encircle the world and engage in a cataclysmic battle with Thor during Ragnarök.
- **Jötunn:** Norse giants that are strong, daunting, and often highly misunderstood.
- **Jovem:** the Portuguese word for "young person."

- **Khopesh:** a curved, sickle-shaped sword from ancient Egypt, used both as a weapon in battle and as a symbol of power and authority.
- **Kishi:** a demon creature with an attractive human man's face on the front of its body and a hyena's face on the back. Kishi are said to use their human face as well as smooth talk and other charms to attract young women, who they then eat with the hyena face.
- **Kitsune:** a mythical fox spirit from Japanese folklore, often depicted as an intelligent, shape-shifting being with magical abilities, including illusion and possession, commonly serving as messengers of Inari or mischievous tricksters.
- **Ma'at:** in ancient Egyptian mythology, represents the concept of truth, balance, harmony, justice, and cosmic order, personified as a goddess who regulates the universe and weighs the hearts of the dead against her feather in the afterlife.
- **Macuahuitls:** a Mesoamerican weapon made of wood with sharp obsidian blades embedded along its edges, used by the Aztecs and other cultures for cutting and slashing in battle.
- **Magni:** in Norse mythology, is one of Thor's sons, representing physical strength and might, whose name means "Strength," and who is renowned for his role in rescuing his father during a battle with the giant Hrungnir.
- **Mamãe**: the Portuguese word for "mother."
- **Mami Wata:** a half-human half-snake water spirit venerated in West, Central, and Southern Africa and in the African diaspora in the Americas.
- **Mhamó**: the Scottish word for "grandmother."
- **Midgar:** in Norse mythology, is the realm of humans, situated in the center of the cosmos and connected to other worlds by Yggdrasil, the World Tree, protected from chaos by the gods.
- **Mjölnir:** in Norse mythology, is the mighty hammer wielded by Thor, crafted by the dwarves Sindri and

Brokkr, symbolizing protection, strength, and the power to vanquish giants, and is also used in sacred rituals such as blessings and consecrations.

- **Modi:** in Norse mythology, is one of Thor's sons, embodying the spirit of courage and battle-fury, whose name translates to "Wrath" or "Bravery," symbolizing the raw, unyielding strength inherited from his divine lineage.
- **Naira:** the currency used in Nigeria.
- **Naija:** the term used to refer to "New Nigeria."
- **Ninki Nanka:** a legendary serpent-like creature from West African folklore, particularly in the Gambia, often described as a large dragon or reptile with a giraffe's neck that lives in swamps and rivers, associated with mystery, danger, and omens of death.
- **Nkisi:** sacred objects or spiritual vessels in the traditional belief systems of the Kongo people of Central Africa, often containing spiritually charged substances and used by a **nganga** (ritual specialist) for protection, healing, justice, or communication with ancestors and spirits.
- **No Wahala:** the Yoruba phrase for "no problem."
- **Nochebuena:** the Spanish term for Christmas Eve (December 24th), traditionally celebrated in Latin American, Spanish, and Filipino cultures with a festive late-night feast and family gatherings.
- **Oba:** the Yoruba word for "king."
- **Obatala:** the Architect Orisha, the Healer, or the Shepard of the Imperfect, characterized by his gentle personality and eternal patience.
- **Ode Buruku:** the Yoruba word for "bloody fool."
- **Oduduwa:** the Doted Orisha, the Divine King, characterized by his clear and focused mind.
- **Ogbon:** the Yoruba word for "wisdom," also the class title for Ifa studies at Camp Olosa.
- **Ogiyan:** the Crushed Cassava Orisha, characterized for his ultra specialization of the cassava harvest.
- **Ojo Isinku:** in Yoruba funeral tradition, this is the time relegated to prayer and donation.

- **Oko:** the Agriculture Orishas, the Keeper of the Farm, characterized by his protection of plains, once a hunter turned farmer.
- **Olodumare:** the Almighty Orisha, or the omnipotent, characterized by their great power and all-knowing pools of knowledge. They are all things.
- **Olokun:** the Orishas of the Deep Blue, the Ruler of the Seas. Husband to Yemoja, and parent to most other water Orishas.
- **Olosa:** the Lagoon Orisha, characterized for her abundance, prosperity, and fertility.
- **Òlóṣì:** the Yoruba word for "bastard" or "foolish person."
- **Ọpọn Ìfà:** a divining board of the Ifa divination system, often made of wood and circular in shape.
- **Ori:** sometimes referred to as an Orisha, oftentimes refer to a state of mind relating to spiritual intuition and destiny as it relates to human consciousness.
- **Orun:** in Yoruba cosmology, is the spiritual realm or heaven where deities, ancestors, and other spirits reside, serving as a counterpart to the physical world.
- **Orunmila:** the Divination Orisha, the Miracle Worker, characterized by his separation from other Orisha. Whereas most Orisha do have some interaction with the world, Orunmila spends most of his time in the stars.
- **Osain:** the Orisha of the Wood, characterized by his healing nature and distinguished by his Cyclops-looking appearance.
- **Oshosi:** the Orisha of the Hunt and Justice, characterized by his protective nature and strong sense of duty.
- **Oshun:** the Orisha of Rivers, characterized by her sensuality, love, and purity. One of the wives of Shango.
- **Oya:** the Orisha of Storms, characterized by her tenacity and compassion. One of the wives of Shango.
- **Oyo:** a powerful Yoruba kingdom in present-day southwestern Nigeria, known for its sophisticated political system, military prowess, and thriving trade

networks during its peak between the 17th and 19th centuries.

- **Papai:** the Portuguese word for "father."
- **Patakí:** a scared story, song, or myth in the Ifa faith system.
- **Pẹlẹ̀:** a Yoruba shawl.
- **Ponche:** a traditional hot fruit punch from Latin American cuisine, often enjoyed during the holiday season, made with tropical fruits, spices, and sometimes spiked with rum or brandy.
- **Qi:** the circulating life force whose existence and properties are the basis of much Chinese philosophy and medicine.
- **Quinceañera:** a traditional Latin American celebration marking a girl's 15th birthday, symbolizing her transition from childhood to womanhood, often featuring a religious ceremony, a formal party, and cultural rituals such as the changing of shoes and the first dance.
- **Ragnarök:** in Norse mythology, is the prophesied end of the world, marked by a series of apocalyptic events including a great battle, the death of gods like Odin and Thor, natural disasters, and the eventual rebirth of the world from its ashes.
- **Santería:** also known as **Regla de Ocha**, is an Afro-Cuban religion that blends Yoruba spiritual traditions with Roman Catholicism, centering around the worship of deities called **Orishas**, who are associated with Catholic saints, and practices such as divination, rituals, and offerings to maintain harmony and spiritual balance.
- **Sarawati:** in Hindu mythology, is the goddess of knowledge, wisdom, learning, music, and the arts, often depicted as a serene figure seated on a lotus, holding a veena and sacred scriptures, symbolizing enlightenment and creativity.
- **Shango:** the Thunder Orisha, the Lionhearted, or The Overseer of Masculinity and Masculine Beauty, characterized by his loud personality and substantial presence.

- **Shotel:** a curved sword originating from Ethiopia, characterized by its sickle-like shape designed for slashing and thrusting, historically used by warriors such as the Shotelai to reach around shields and deliver devastating blows in battle.
- **Shuku shuku:** a Nigerian-style coconut macaroon.
- **Sobrinha:** the Portuguese word for "niece," referring to the daughter of one's sibling or sibling-in-law.
- **Ṣòkòtò:** Yoruba trousers.
- **Sūrú, ẹrọ, and ètùtù:** in order, patience, gentleness, and coolness needed in Ifa ritual.
- **Suya:** a popular West African street food consisting of skewered, spicy grilled meat, typically beef or chicken, coated in a flavorful peanut-based spice mix.
- **Tchau:** The Portuguese word for “bye.”
- **Tláloc:** the Aztec rain deity.
- **Truebloods:** a term used in the diviner community for those who claim to have a direct ancestral line to one or more of the Orishas.
- **Uruz:** the second rune in the Elder Futhark runic alphabet, representing strength, vitality, and untamed power, often associated with the wild aurochs, a now-extinct species of large wild cattle, symbolizing raw energy and endurance.
- **Utenheim:** the Norse word for the “End Realm”, an ethereal plane outside of conventional space and time, which houses the Great War against the God Eaters.
- **Uziza:** better known as the West African black pepper.
- **Velho:** the Portuguese word for “old person.”
- **Vishvakarman:** in Hindu mythology, is the divine architect and craftsman of the gods, credited with designing and building their celestial palaces, weapons, and vehicles, as well as shaping the universe itself.
- **Yaji:** a flavorful and aromatic spice blend commonly used in West African cuisine, often made with ground peanuts, chili powder, ginger, and other spices, and popularly used as a seasoning for grilled meats like suya.

- **Yamaraja:** in Hindu mythology, is the god of death and the ruler of the underworld, responsible for judging the deeds of souls and determining their fate in the cycle of reincarnation or liberation.
- **Yemoja:** the mother of all Orishas. The Orishas of creation, water, motherhood, and moonlight.
- **Yewa:** formerly the Orisha of lagoons, now the Orisha of graveyards.
- **Yumboes:** tall fae creatures at a height of two feet all with the hue of white and silver hair. Spirits of the dead.
- **Zobo:** a Nigerian hibiscus drink of deep red made from Roselle plant flowers.
- **Zoot Suit:** a flamboyant, oversized suit popularized in the 1930s and 1940s, characterized by high-waisted, wide-legged trousers and a long, broad-shouldered jacket, often associated with jazz culture and worn predominantly by African American, Latino, and Italian American youth.